D0109722

COOKING *with* MONSTERS
THE BEGINNER'S GUIDE TO
CULINARY COMBAT

WRITTEN BY:
JORDAN ALSAQA

ART BY:
VIVIAN TRUONG

FLATS BY:
DAMALI BEATTY

Note: This is an uncorrected advance galley. Reviewers are requested to check all quotations and page numbers against the published edition. Pagination, price, and publication date are subject to change.

NATIONAL MARKETING & PUBLICITY CAMPAIGN
- In-store and online merchandising co-op
- National print and digital advertising campaign
- Targeted social media and email marketing campaign
- Instagram, TikTok, Twitter, Facebook, and Youtube promotion
- National print and broadcast media publicity campaign
- Book trailer
- Author interviews, excerpts, and review coverage
- Multi-stop book tour (in-person and virtual)
- Podcast tour
- Featured programming and author appearances for local and national events
- Cross-promoted in IDW comic books
- Downloadable teacher's guide and discussion guide

@IDWpublishing
IDWpublishing.com

EDITORS:
**Megan Brown
and Erika Turner**

EDITORIAL ASSISTANT:
Jake Williams

LETTERING AND DESIGN:
**Amauri Osorio
and Nathan Widick**

978-1-68405-983-6

26 25 24 23   1 2 3 4

COOKING WITH MONSTERS (BOOK ONE): THE BEGINNER'S GUIDE TO CULINARY COMBAT. SEPTEMBER 2023. FIRST PRINTING. © VIVIAN TRUONG & JORDAN ALSAQA. IDW Publishing, a division of Idea and Design Works, LLC. Editorial offices: 2355 Northside Drive, Suite 140, San Diego, CA 92108. The IDW logo is registered in the U.S. Patent and Trademark Office. Any similarities to persons living or dead are purely coincidental. With the exception of artwork used for review purposes, none of the contents of this publication may be reprinted without the permission of Idea and Design Works, LLC. IDW Publishing does not read or accept unsolicited submissions of ideas, stories, or artwork. Printed in Canada.

Nachie Marsham, Publisher
Blake Kobashigawa, SVP Sales, Marketing & Strategy
Mark Doyle, VP Editorial & Creative Strategy
Tara McCrillis, VP Publishing Operations
Anna Morrow, VP Marketing & Publicity
Alex Hargett, VP Sales
Jamie S. Rich, Executive Editorial Director
Scott Dunbier, Director, Special Projects
Greg Gustin, Sr. Director, Content Strategy

Kevin Schwoer, Sr. Director of Talent Relations
Lauren LePera, Sr. Managing Editor
Keith Davidsen, Director, Marketing & PR
Topher Alford, Sr. Digital Marketing Manager
Patrick O'Connell, Sr. Manager, Direct Market Sales
Shauna Monteforte, Sr. Director of Manufacturing Operations
Greg Foreman, Director DTC Sales & Operations
Nathan Widick, Director of Design

Neil Uyetake, Sr. Art Director, Design & Production
Shawn Lee, Art Director, Design & Production
Jack Rivera, Art Director, Marketing

Ted Adams and Robbie Robbins, IDW Founders

Special thanks to acquiring editor Erika Turner.
Special thanks to developmental editor Danny Lore.
For international rights, contact licensing@idwpublishing.com

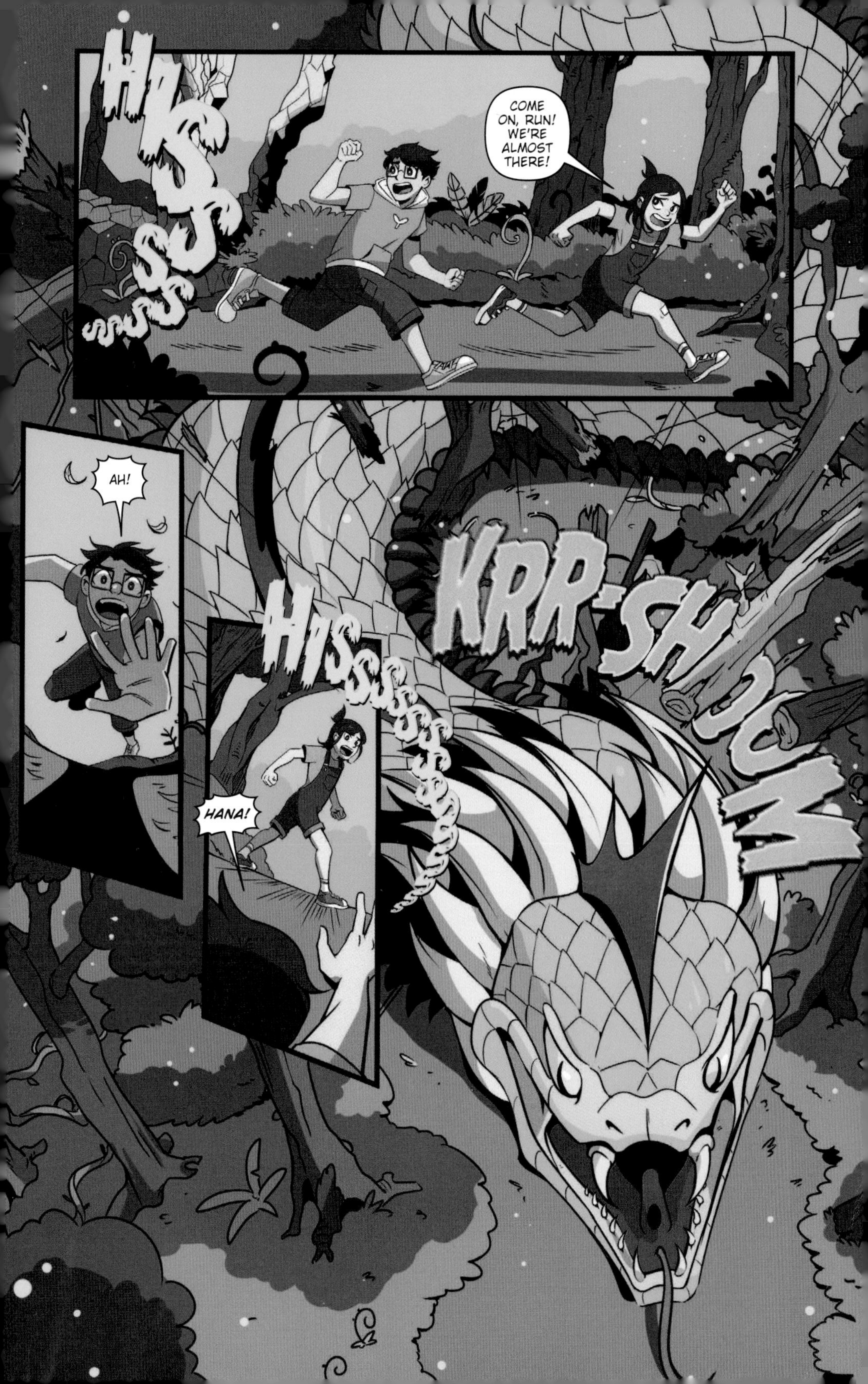
HISSSS
COME ON, RUN! WE'RE ALMOST THERE!
AH!
HISSSSS
HANA!
KRR-SHOOM

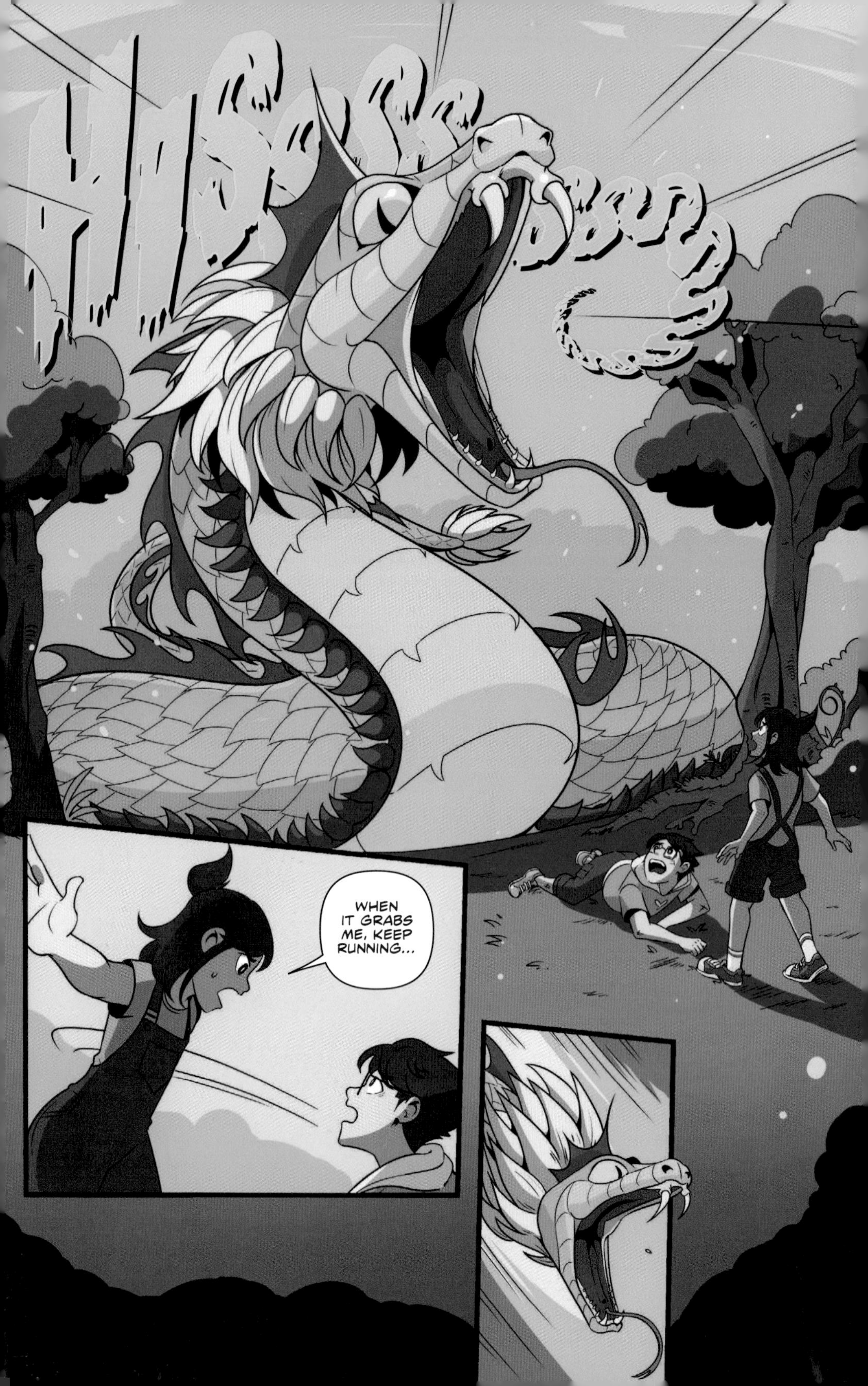
WHEN IT GRABS ME, KEEP RUNNING...

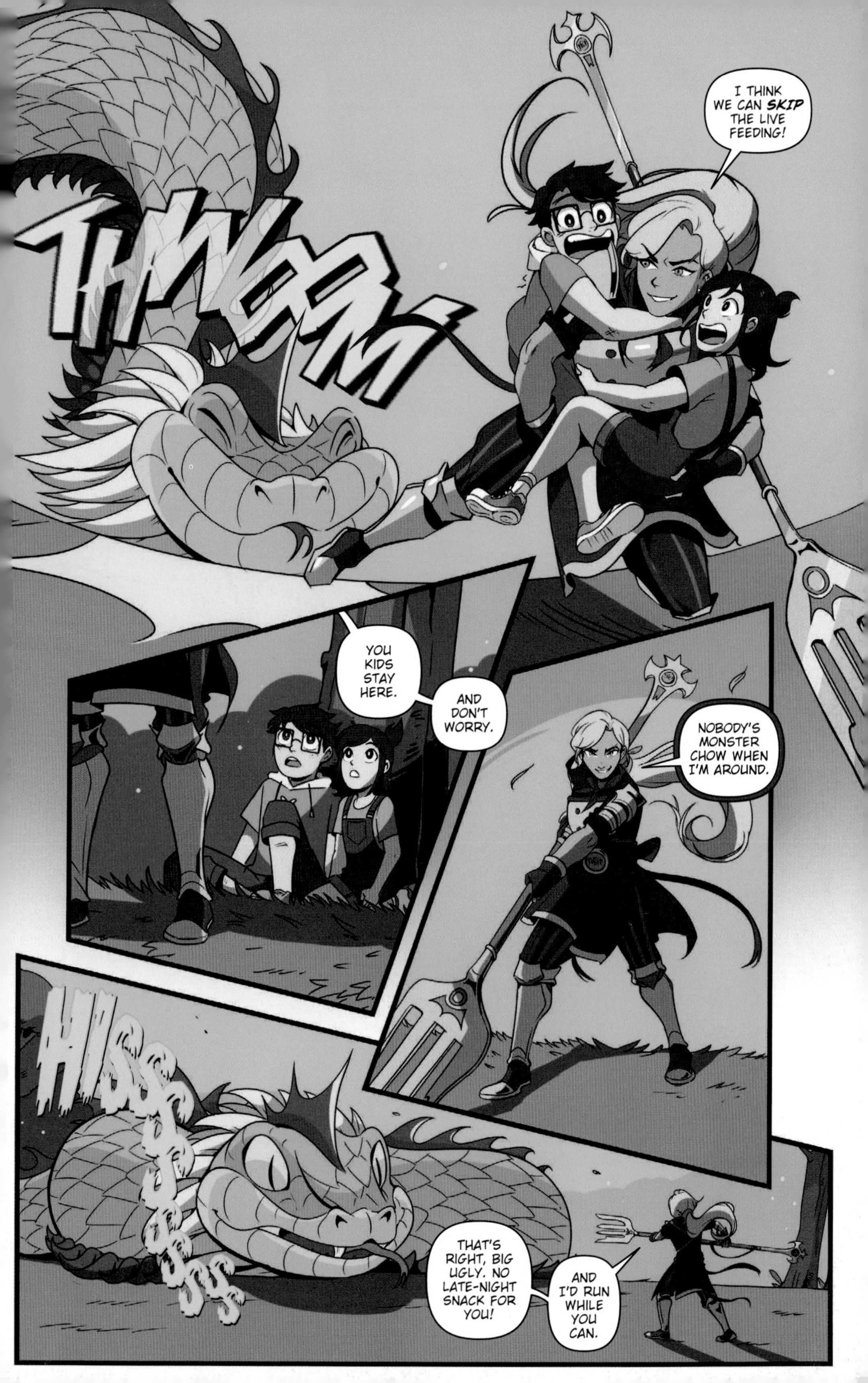
THWOOM
I THINK WE CAN SKIP THE LIVE FEEDING!
YOU KIDS STAY HERE.
AND DON'T WORRY.
NOBODY'S MONSTER CHOW WHEN I'M AROUND.
HISSSSSSS
THAT'S RIGHT, BIG UGLY. NO LATE-NIGHT SNACK FOR YOU!
AND I'D RUN WHILE YOU CAN.

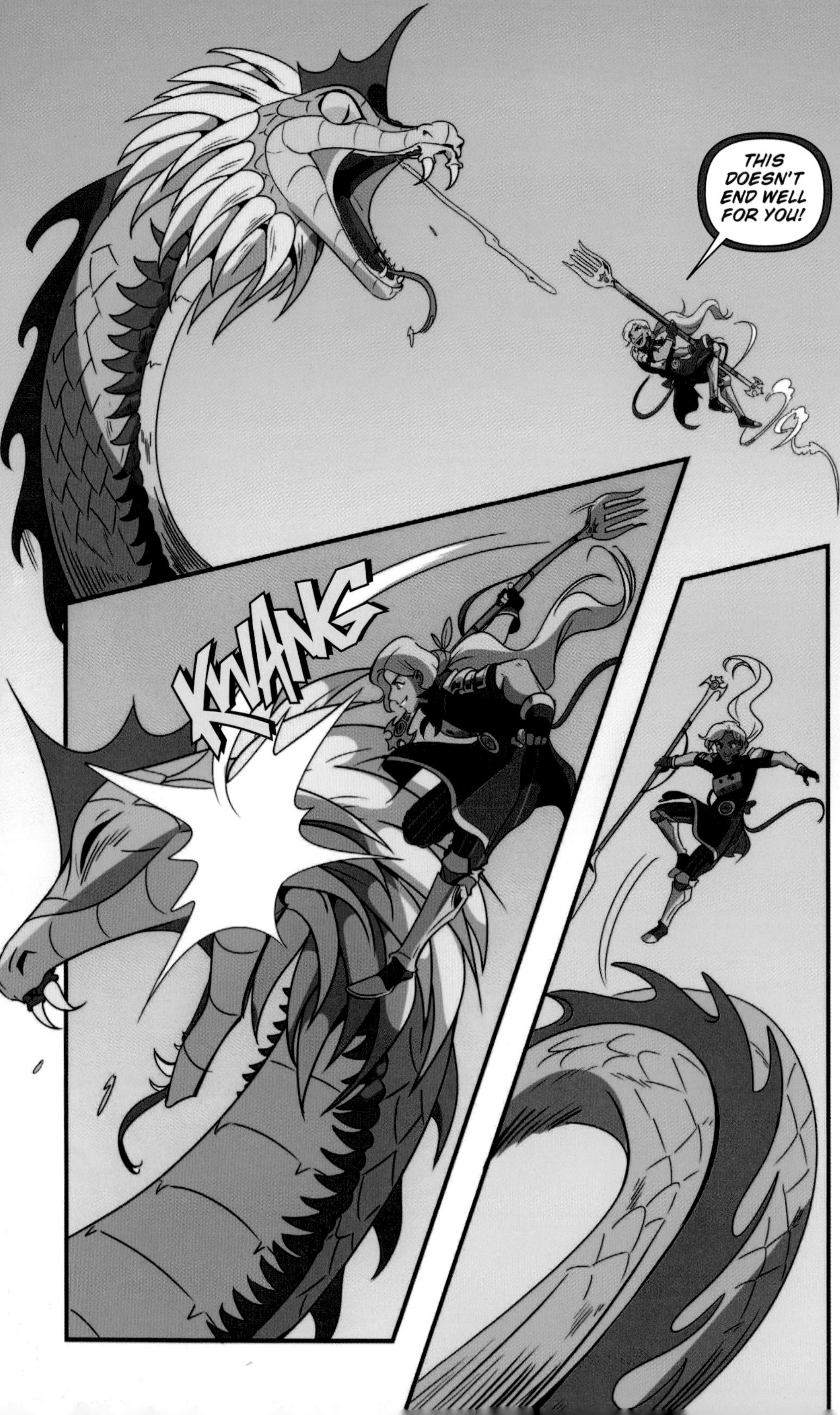
THIS DOESN'T END WELL FOR YOU!
KWANG

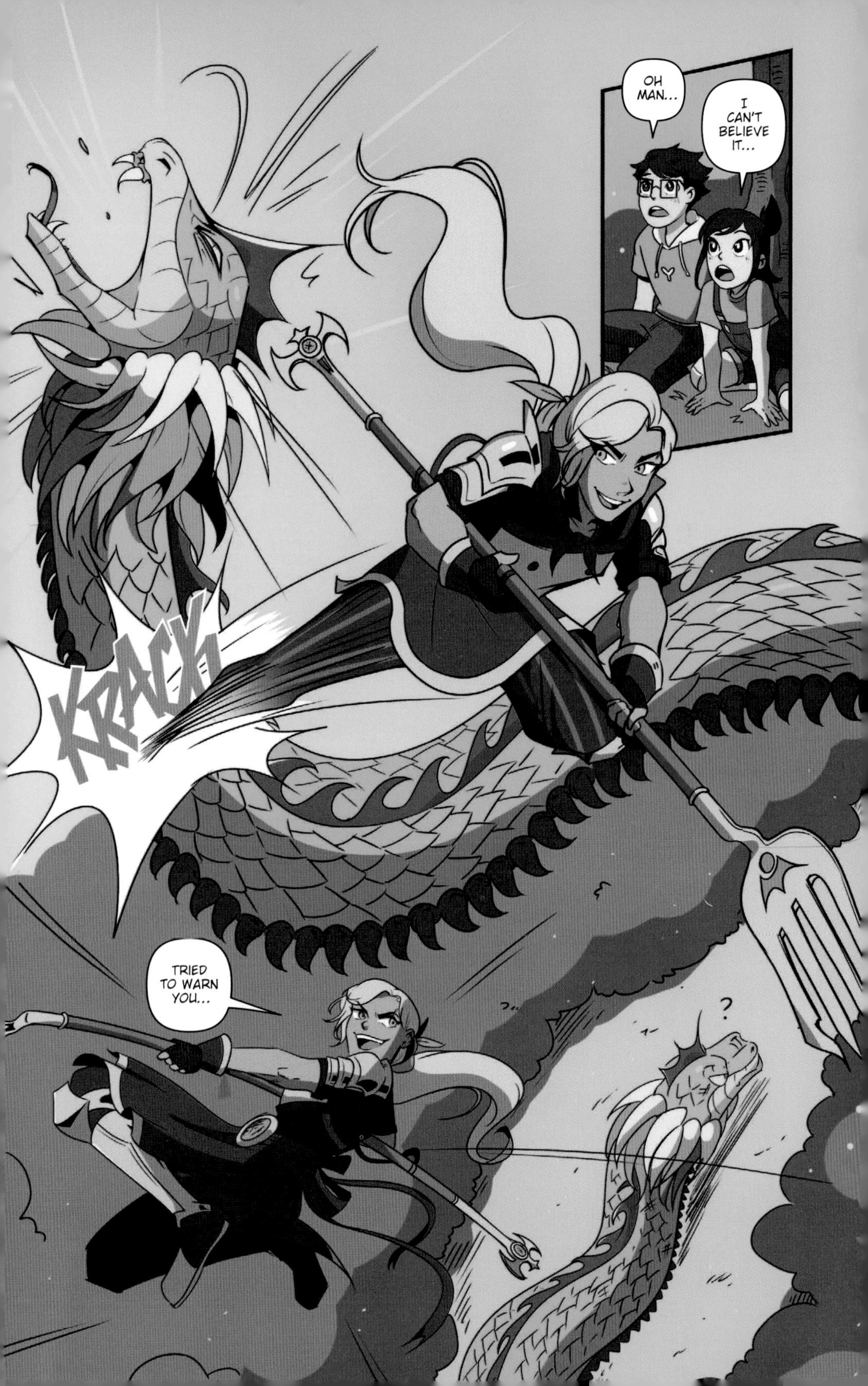
OH MAN...
I CAN'T BELIEVE IT...
KRACK!
TRIED TO WARN YOU...
?

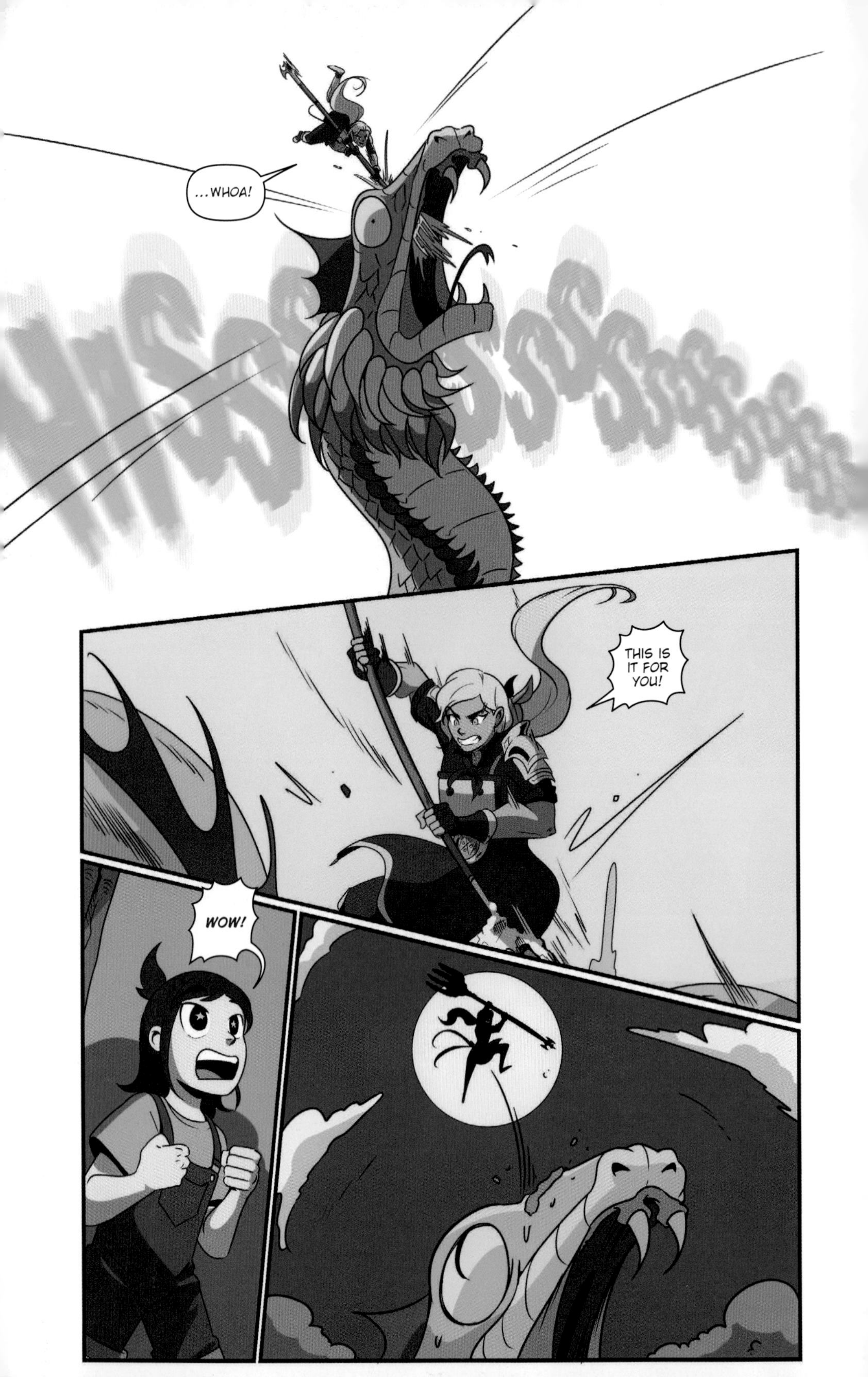
...WHOA!
HISSSSSSSSSSSS
THIS IS IT FOR YOU!
WOW!

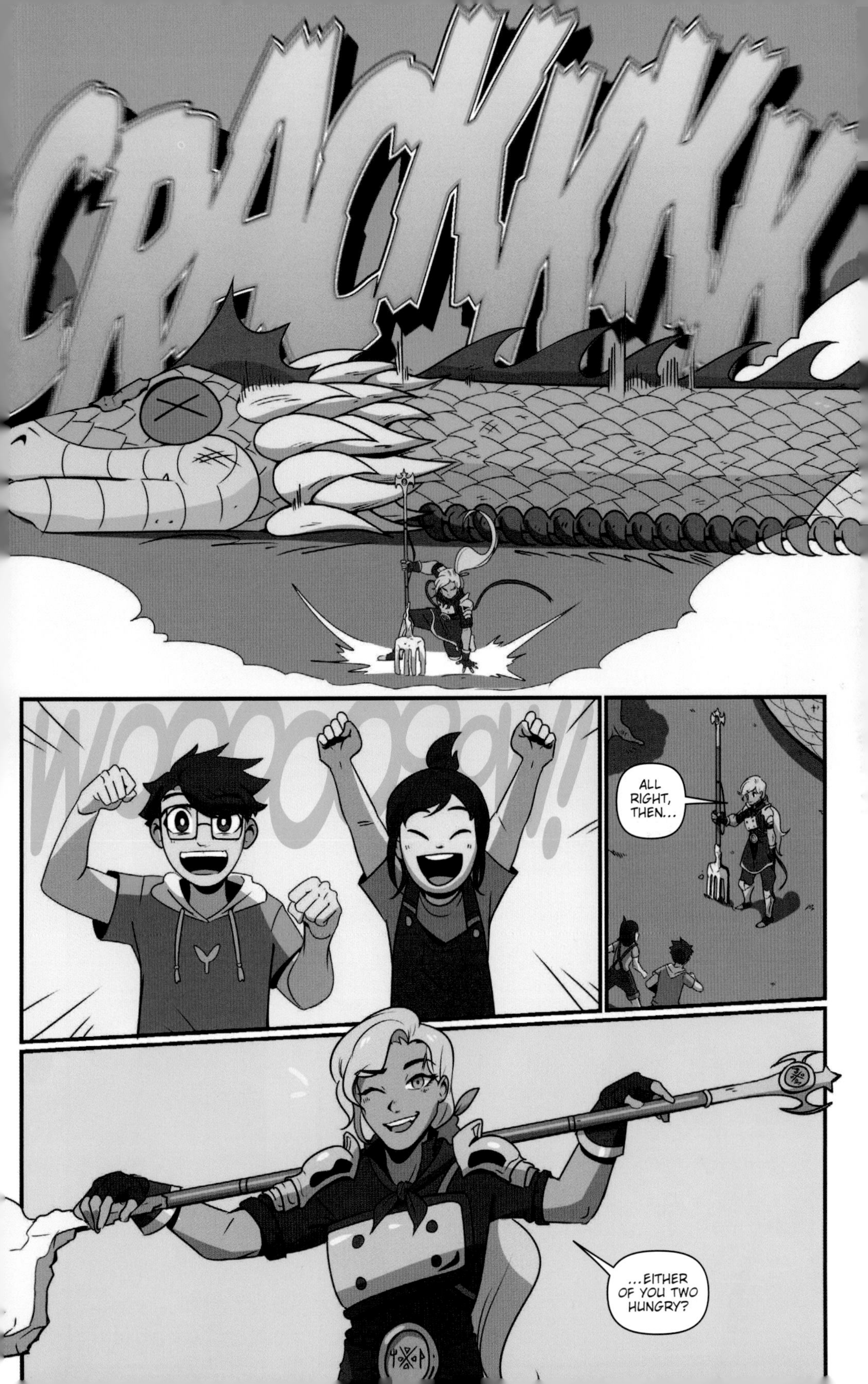
ALL RIGHT, THEN...
...EITHER OF YOU TWO HUNGRY?

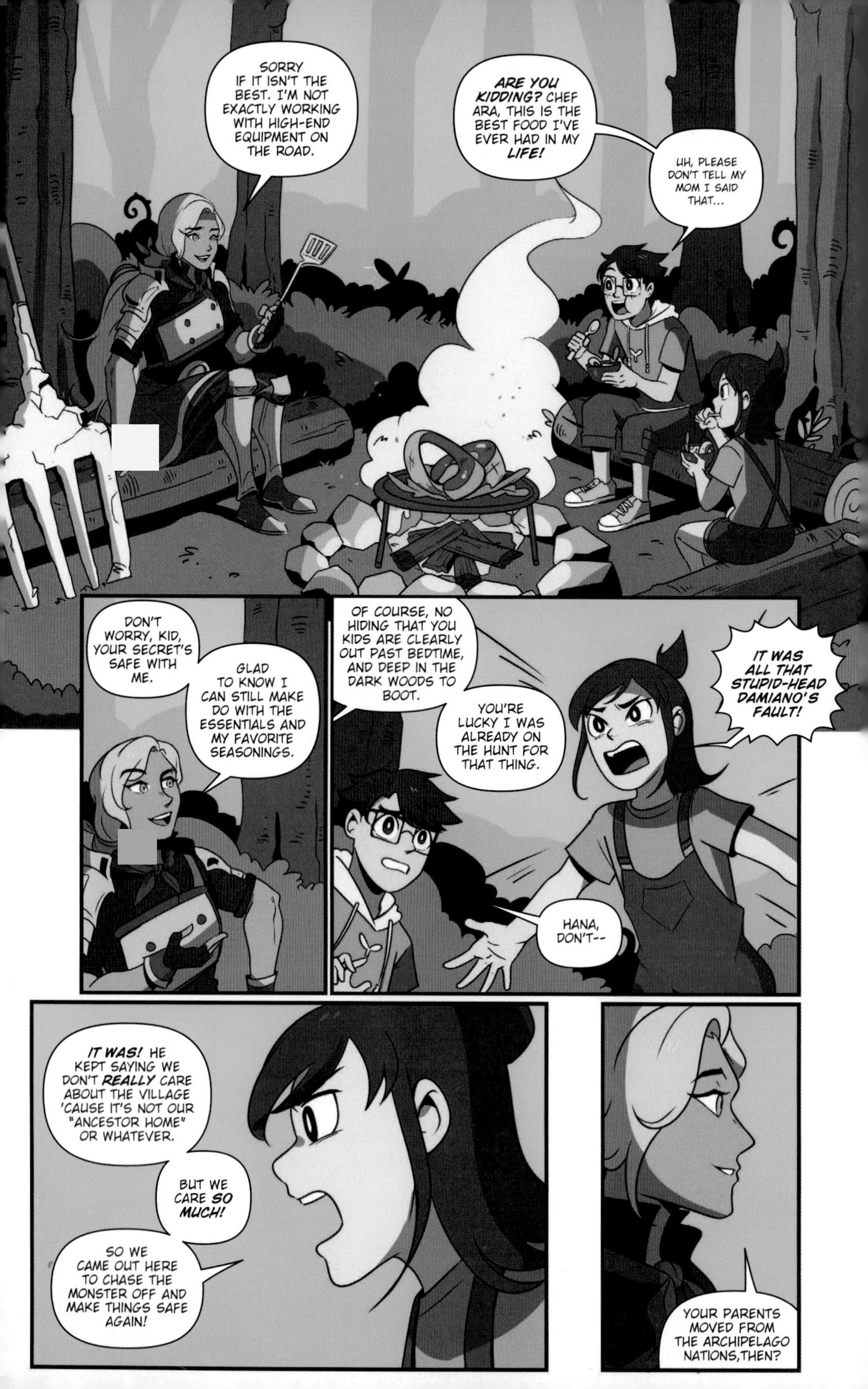
SORRY IF IT ISN'T THE BEST. I'M NOT EXACTLY WORKING WITH HIGH-END EQUIPMENT ON THE ROAD.
ARE YOU KIDDING? CHEF ARA, THIS IS THE BEST FOOD I'VE EVER HAD IN MY LIFE!
UH, PLEASE DON'T TELL MY MOM I SAID THAT...
DON'T WORRY, KID, YOUR SECRET'S SAFE WITH ME.
GLAD TO KNOW I CAN STILL MAKE DO WITH THE ESSENTIALS AND MY FAVORITE SEASONINGS.
OF COURSE, NO HIDING THAT YOU KIDS ARE CLEARLY OUT PAST BEDTIME, AND DEEP IN THE DARK WOODS TO BOOT.
YOU'RE LUCKY I WAS ALREADY ON THE HUNT FOR THAT THING.
IT WAS ALL THAT STUPID-HEAD DAMIANO'S FAULT!
HANA, DON'T--
IT WAS! HE KEPT SAYING WE DON'T REALLY CARE ABOUT THE VILLAGE 'CAUSE IT'S NOT OUR "ANCESTOR HOME" OR WHATEVER.
BUT WE CARE SO MUCH!
SO WE CAME OUT HERE TO CHASE THE MONSTER OFF AND MAKE THINGS SAFE AGAIN!
YOUR PARENTS MOVED FROM THE ARCHIPELAGO NATIONS,THEN?

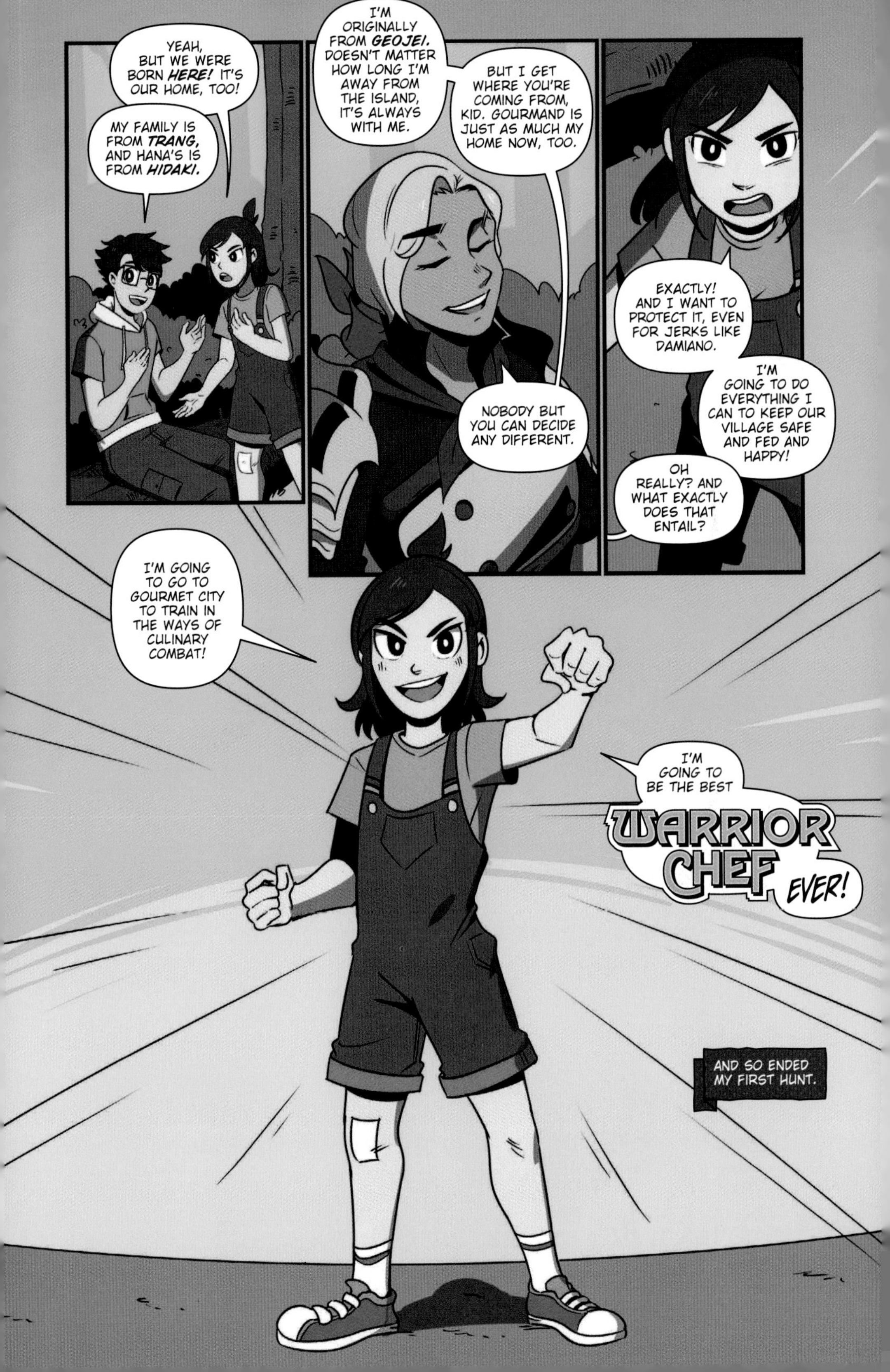
YEAH, BUT WE WERE BORN HERE! IT'S OUR HOME, TOO!
MY FAMILY IS FROM TRANG, AND HANA'S IS FROM HIDAKI.
I'M ORIGINALLY FROM GEOJEI. DOESN'T MATTER HOW LONG I'M AWAY FROM THE ISLAND, IT'S ALWAYS WITH ME.
BUT I GET WHERE YOU'RE COMING FROM, KID. GOURMAND IS JUST AS MUCH MY HOME NOW, TOO.
NOBODY BUT YOU CAN DECIDE ANY DIFFERENT.
EXACTLY! AND I WANT TO PROTECT IT, EVEN FOR JERKS LIKE DAMIANO.
I'M GOING TO DO EVERYTHING I CAN TO KEEP OUR VILLAGE SAFE AND FED AND HAPPY!
OH REALLY? AND WHAT EXACTLY DOES THAT ENTAIL?
I'M GOING TO GO TO GOURMET CITY TO TRAIN IN THE WAYS OF CULINARY COMBAT!
I'M GOING TO BE THE BEST WARRIOR CHEF EVER!
AND SO ENDED MY FIRST HUNT.

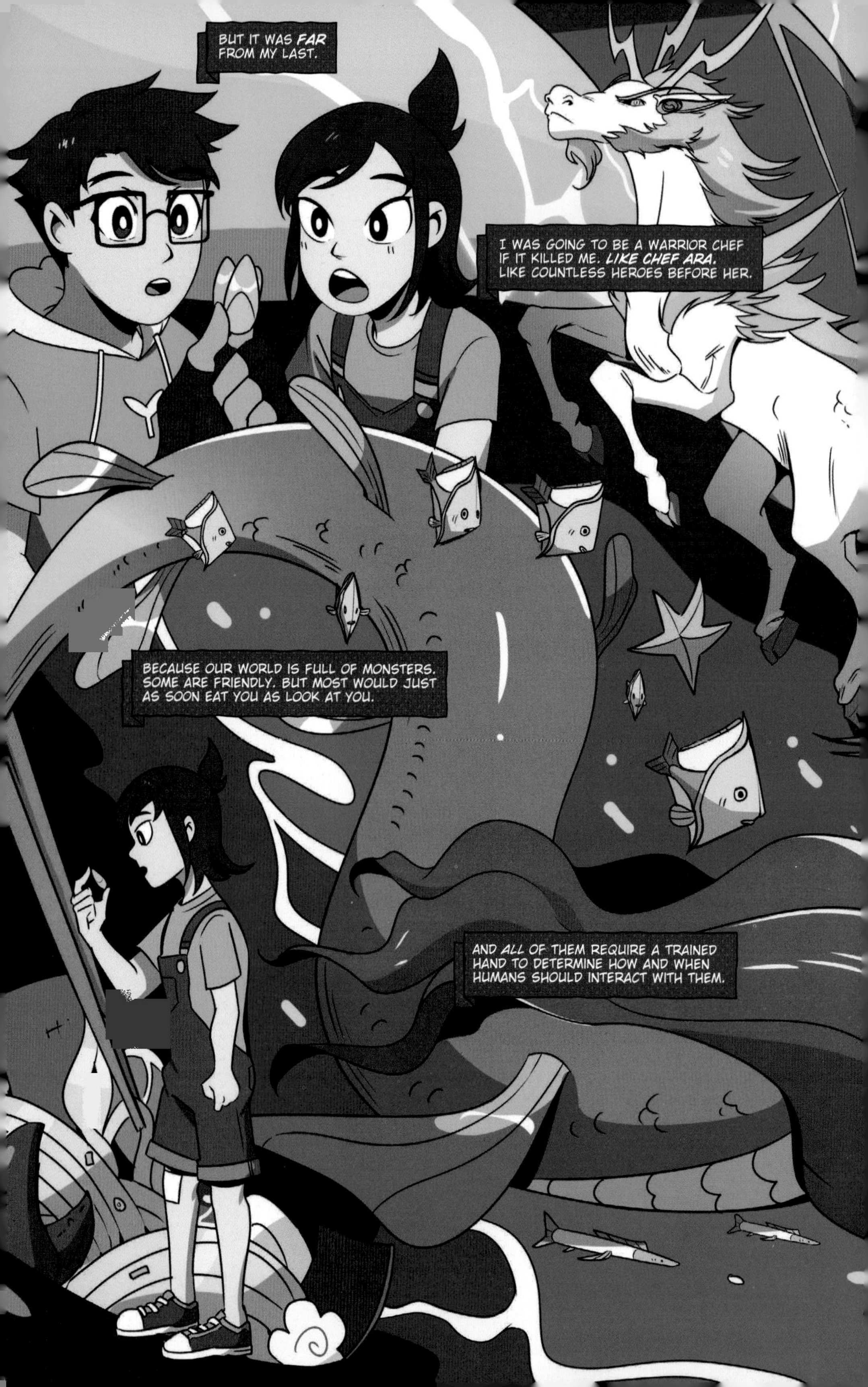
BUT IT WAS *FAR* FROM MY LAST.
I WAS GOING TO BE A WARRIOR CHEF IF IT KILLED ME. *LIKE CHEF ARA.* LIKE COUNTLESS HEROES BEFORE HER.
BECAUSE OUR WORLD IS FULL OF MONSTERS. SOME ARE FRIENDLY. BUT MOST WOULD JUST AS SOON EAT YOU AS LOOK AT YOU.
AND *ALL* OF THEM REQUIRE A TRAINED HAND TO DETERMINE HOW AND WHEN HUMANS SHOULD INTERACT WITH THEM.

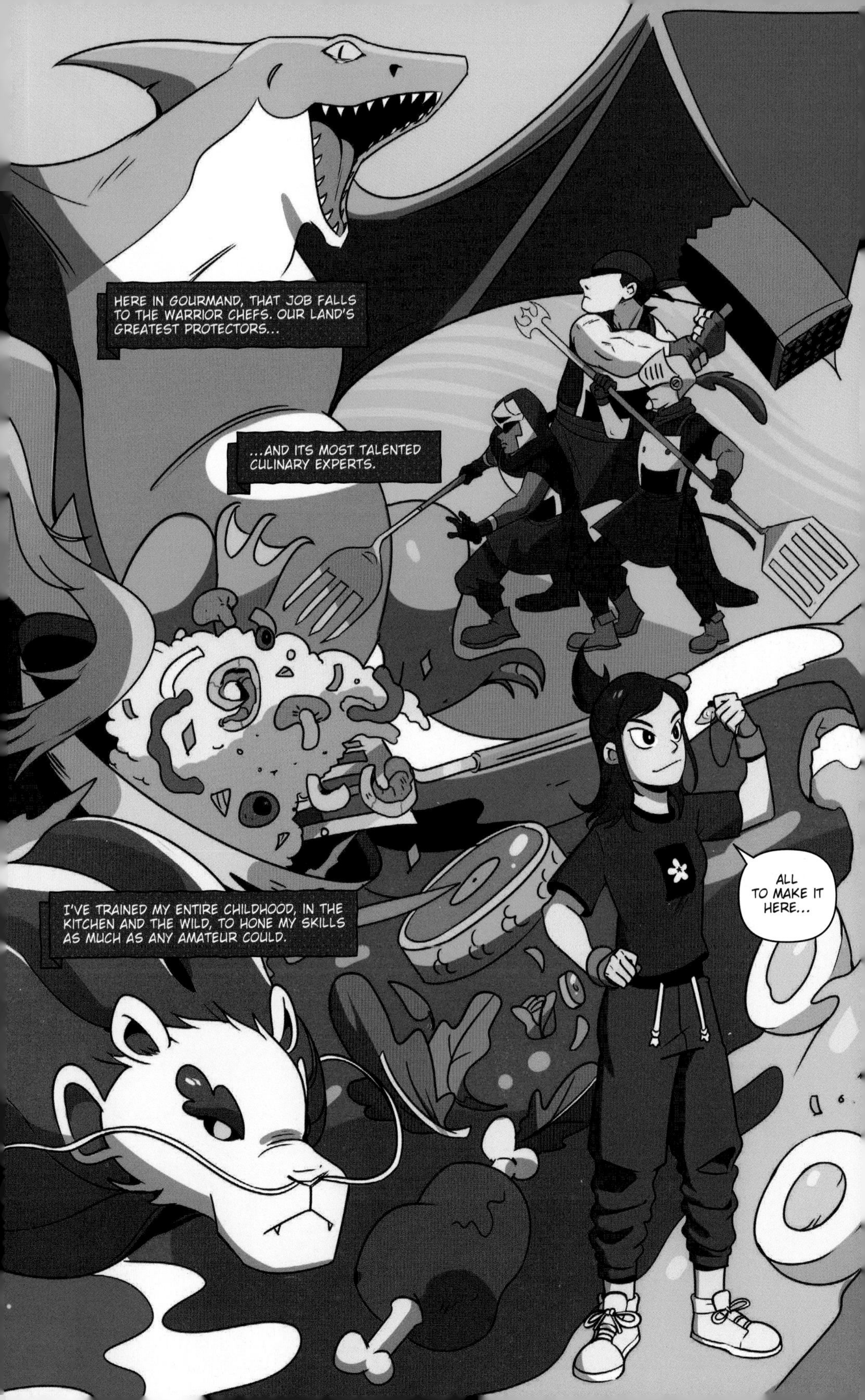
HERE IN GOURMAND, THAT JOB FALLS TO THE WARRIOR CHEFS. OUR LAND'S GREATEST PROTECTORS...
...AND ITS MOST TALENTED CULINARY EXPERTS.
I'VE TRAINED MY ENTIRE CHILDHOOD, IN THE KITCHEN AND THE WILD, TO HONE MY SKILLS AS MUCH AS ANY AMATEUR COULD.
ALL TO MAKE IT HERE...

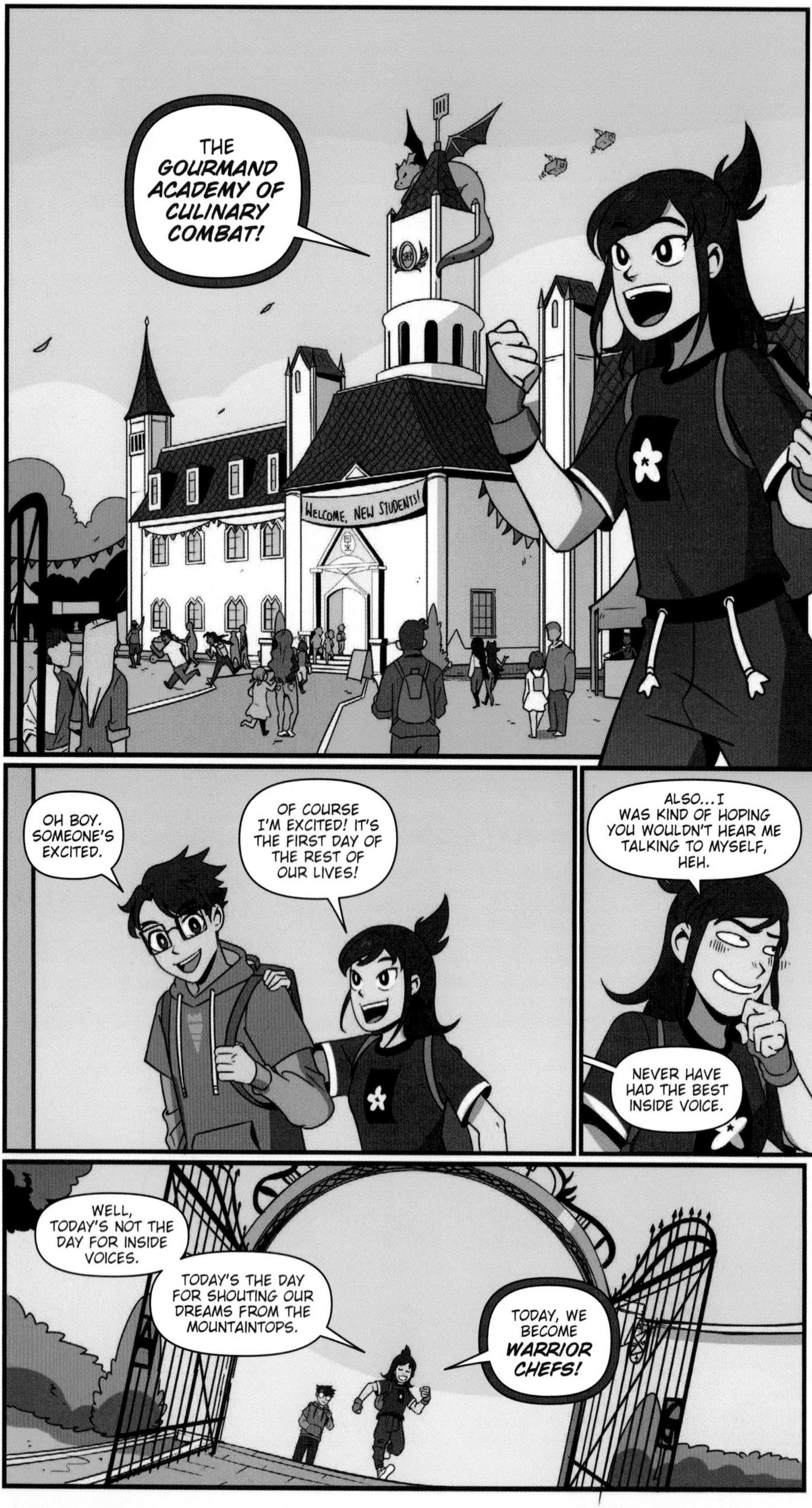
THE GOURMAND ACADEMY OF CULINARY COMBAT!
WELCOME, NEW STUDENTS!
OH BOY. SOMEONE'S EXCITED.
OF COURSE I'M EXCITED! IT'S THE FIRST DAY OF THE REST OF OUR LIVES!
ALSO...I WAS KIND OF HOPING YOU WOULDN'T HEAR ME TALKING TO MYSELF, HEH.
NEVER HAVE HAD THE BEST INSIDE VOICE.
WELL, TODAY'S NOT THE DAY FOR INSIDE VOICES.
TODAY'S THE DAY FOR SHOUTING OUR DREAMS FROM THE MOUNTAINTOPS.
TODAY, WE BECOME WARRIOR CHEFS!

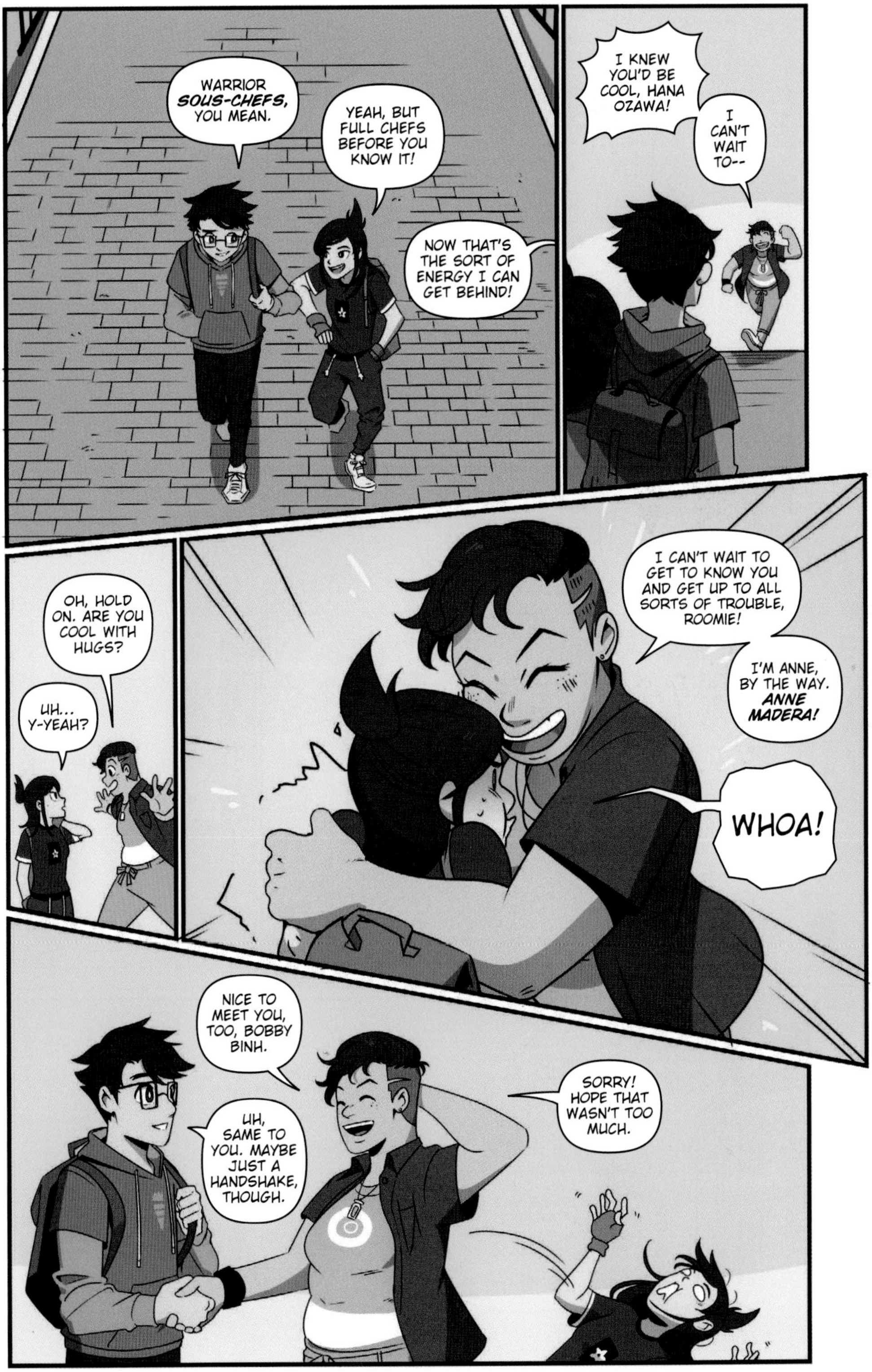
WARRIOR SOUS-CHEFS, YOU MEAN.
YEAH, BUT FULL CHEFS BEFORE YOU KNOW IT!
NOW THAT'S THE SORT OF ENERGY I CAN GET BEHIND!
I KNEW YOU'D BE COOL, HANA OZAWA!
I CAN'T WAIT TO--
OH, HOLD ON. ARE YOU COOL WITH HUGS?
UH... Y-YEAH?
I CAN'T WAIT TO GET TO KNOW YOU AND GET UP TO ALL SORTS OF TROUBLE, ROOMIE!
I'M ANNE, BY THE WAY. ANNE MADERA!
WHOA!
NICE TO MEET YOU, TOO, BOBBY BINH.
UH, SAME TO YOU. MAYBE JUST A HANDSHAKE, THOUGH.
SORRY! HOPE THAT WASN'T TOO MUCH.

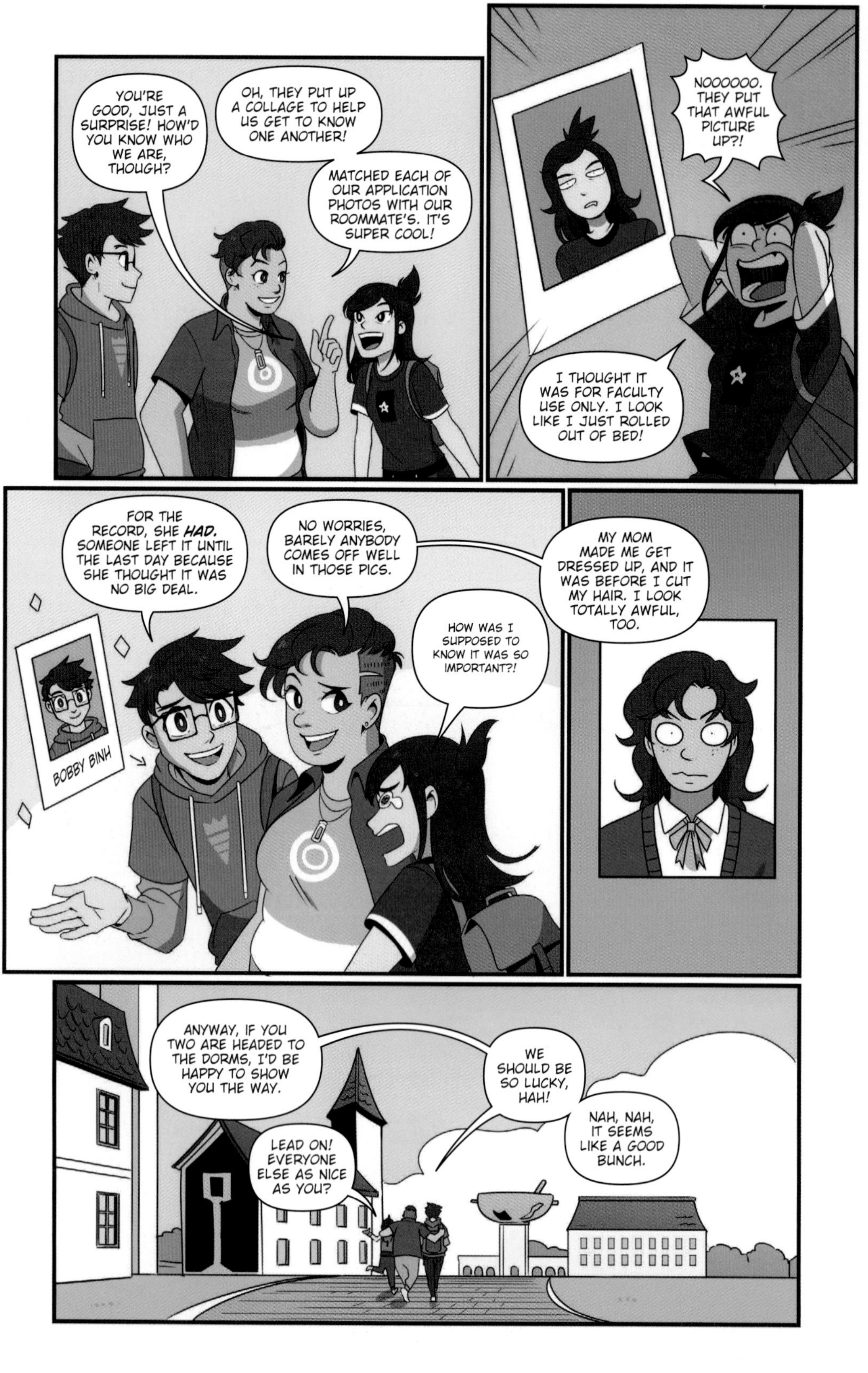
YOU'RE GOOD, JUST A SURPRISE! HOW'D YOU KNOW WHO WE ARE, THOUGH?
OH, THEY PUT UP A COLLAGE TO HELP US GET TO KNOW ONE ANOTHER!
MATCHED EACH OF OUR APPLICATION PHOTOS WITH OUR ROOMMATE'S. IT'S SUPER COOL!
NOOOOOO. THEY PUT THAT AWFUL PICTURE UP?!
I THOUGHT IT WAS FOR FACULTY USE ONLY. I LOOK LIKE I JUST ROLLED OUT OF BED!
FOR THE RECORD, SHE ***HAD.*** SOMEONE LEFT IT UNTIL THE LAST DAY BECAUSE SHE THOUGHT IT WAS NO BIG DEAL.
NO WORRIES, BARELY ANYBODY COMES OFF WELL IN THOSE PICS.
MY MOM MADE ME GET DRESSED UP, AND IT WAS BEFORE I CUT MY HAIR. I LOOK TOTALLY AWFUL, TOO.
HOW WAS I SUPPOSED TO KNOW IT WAS SO IMPORTANT?!
BOBBY BINH
ANYWAY, IF YOU TWO ARE HEADED TO THE DORMS, I'D BE HAPPY TO SHOW YOU THE WAY.
WE SHOULD BE SO LUCKY, HAH!
NAH, NAH, IT SEEMS LIKE A GOOD BUNCH.
LEAD ON! EVERYONE ELSE AS NICE AS YOU?

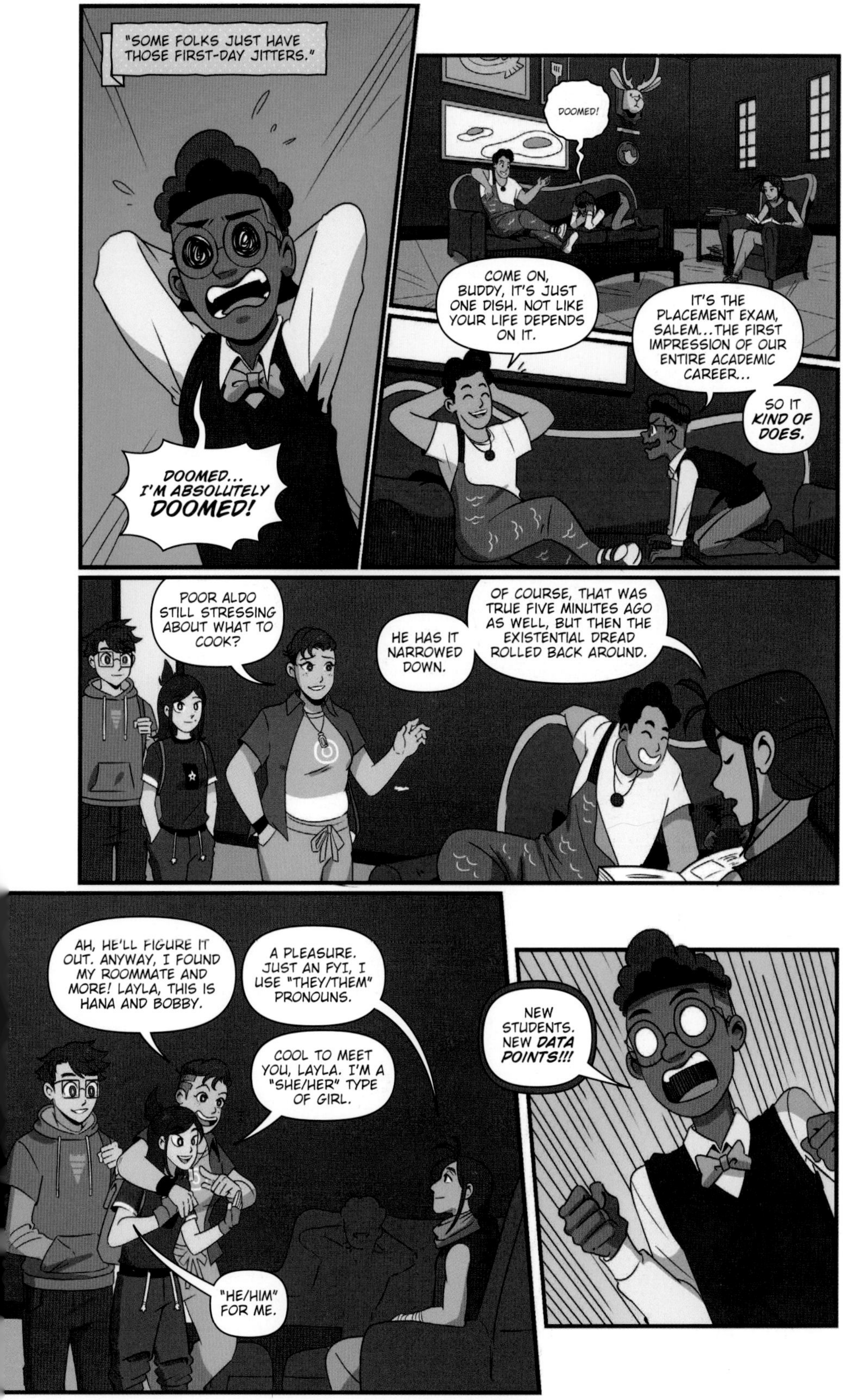
"SOME FOLKS JUST HAVE THOSE FIRST-DAY JITTERS."
DOOMED... I'M ABSOLUTELY DOOMED!
DOOMED!
COME ON, BUDDY, IT'S JUST ONE DISH. NOT LIKE YOUR LIFE DEPENDS ON IT.
IT'S THE PLACEMENT EXAM, SALEM...THE FIRST IMPRESSION OF OUR ENTIRE ACADEMIC CAREER...
SO IT KIND OF DOES.
POOR ALDO STILL STRESSING ABOUT WHAT TO COOK?
HE HAS IT NARROWED DOWN.
OF COURSE, THAT WAS TRUE FIVE MINUTES AGO AS WELL, BUT THEN THE EXISTENTIAL DREAD ROLLED BACK AROUND.
AH, HE'LL FIGURE IT OUT. ANYWAY, I FOUND MY ROOMMATE AND MORE! LAYLA, THIS IS HANA AND BOBBY.
A PLEASURE. JUST AN FYI, I USE "THEY/THEM" PRONOUNS.
COOL TO MEET YOU, LAYLA. I'M A "SHE/HER" TYPE OF GIRL.
"HE/HIM" FOR ME.
NEW STUDENTS. NEW DATA POINTS!!!

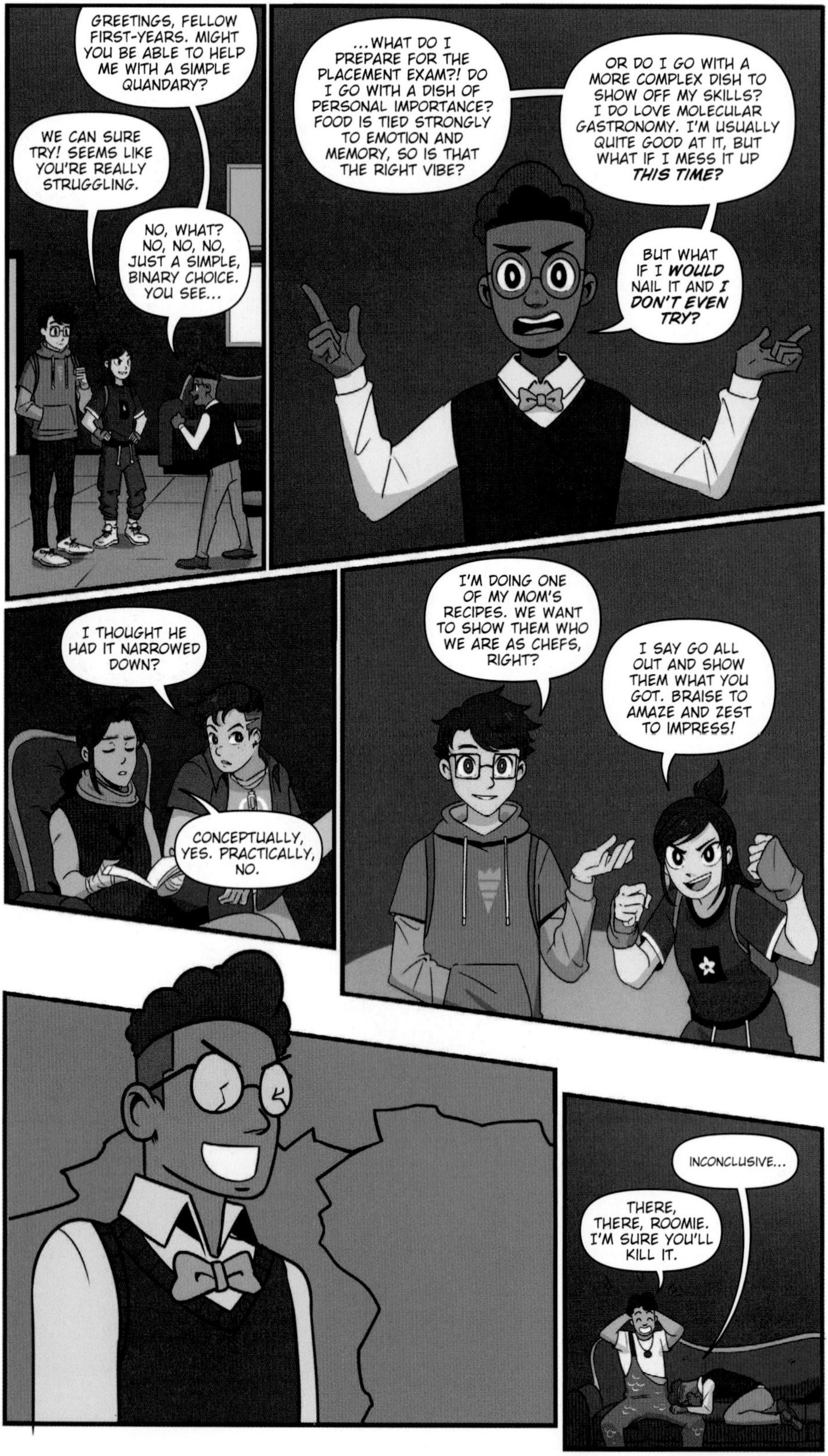
GREETINGS, FELLOW FIRST-YEARS. MIGHT YOU BE ABLE TO HELP ME WITH A SIMPLE QUANDARY?
WE CAN SURE TRY! SEEMS LIKE YOU'RE REALLY STRUGGLING.
NO, WHAT? NO, NO, NO, JUST A SIMPLE, BINARY CHOICE. YOU SEE...
...WHAT DO I PREPARE FOR THE PLACEMENT EXAM?! DO I GO WITH A DISH OF PERSONAL IMPORTANCE? FOOD IS TIED STRONGLY TO EMOTION AND MEMORY, SO IS THAT THE RIGHT VIBE?
OR DO I GO WITH A MORE COMPLEX DISH TO SHOW OFF MY SKILLS? I DO LOVE MOLECULAR GASTRONOMY. I'M USUALLY QUITE GOOD AT IT, BUT WHAT IF I MESS IT UP *THIS TIME?*
BUT WHAT IF I *WOULD* NAIL IT AND *I DON'T EVEN TRY?*
I THOUGHT HE HAD IT NARROWED DOWN?
CONCEPTUALLY, YES. PRACTICALLY, NO.
I'M DOING ONE OF MY MOM'S RECIPES. WE WANT TO SHOW THEM WHO WE ARE AS CHEFS, RIGHT?
I SAY GO ALL OUT AND SHOW THEM WHAT YOU GOT. BRAISE TO AMAZE AND ZEST TO IMPRESS!
INCONCLUSIVE...
THERE, THERE, ROOMIE. I'M SURE YOU'LL KILL IT.

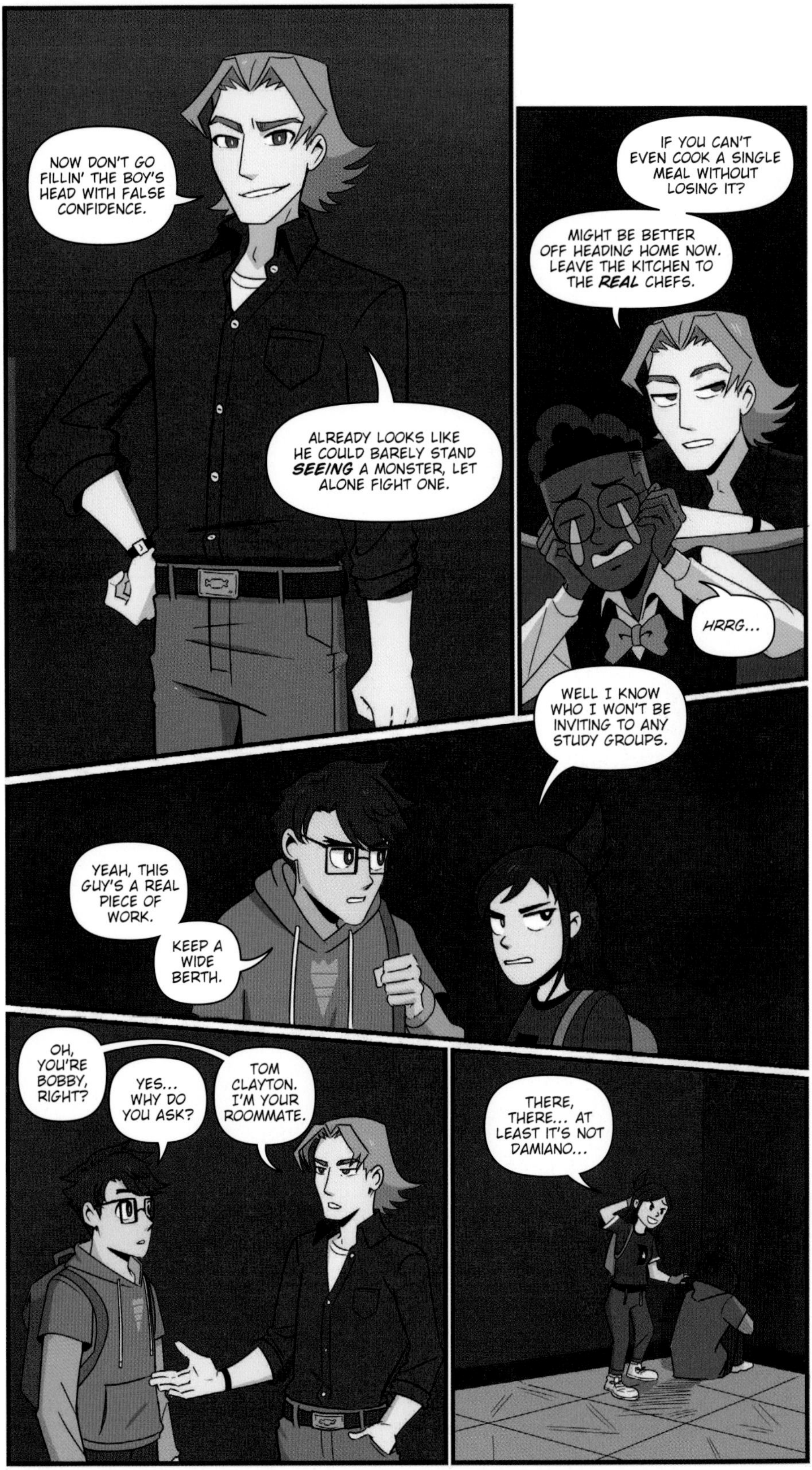
NOW DON'T GO FILLIN' THE BOY'S HEAD WITH FALSE CONFIDENCE.
ALREADY LOOKS LIKE HE COULD BARELY STAND SEEING A MONSTER, LET ALONE FIGHT ONE.
IF YOU CAN'T EVEN COOK A SINGLE MEAL WITHOUT LOSING IT?
MIGHT BE BETTER OFF HEADING HOME NOW. LEAVE THE KITCHEN TO THE REAL CHEFS.
HRRG...
WELL I KNOW WHO I WON'T BE INVITING TO ANY STUDY GROUPS.
YEAH, THIS GUY'S A REAL PIECE OF WORK.
KEEP A WIDE BERTH.
OH, YOU'RE BOBBY, RIGHT?
YES... WHY DO YOU ASK?
TOM CLAYTON. I'M YOUR ROOMMATE.
THERE, THERE... AT LEAST IT'S NOT DAMIANO...

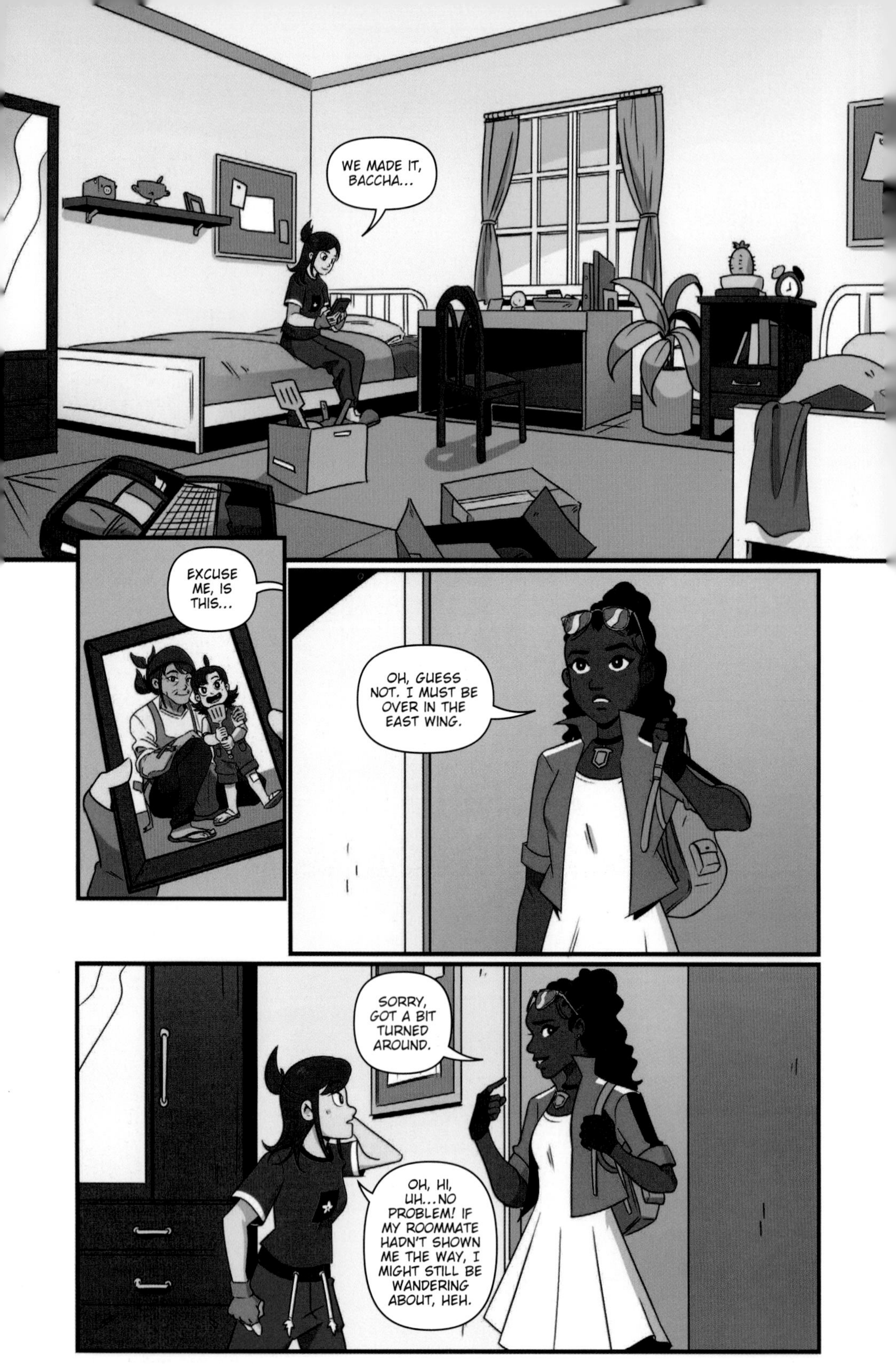
WE MADE IT, BACCHA...
EXCUSE ME, IS THIS...
OH, GUESS NOT. I MUST BE OVER IN THE EAST WING.
SORRY, GOT A BIT TURNED AROUND.
OH, HI, UH...NO PROBLEM! IF MY ROOMMATE HADN'T SHOWN ME THE WAY, I MIGHT STILL BE WANDERING ABOUT, HEH.

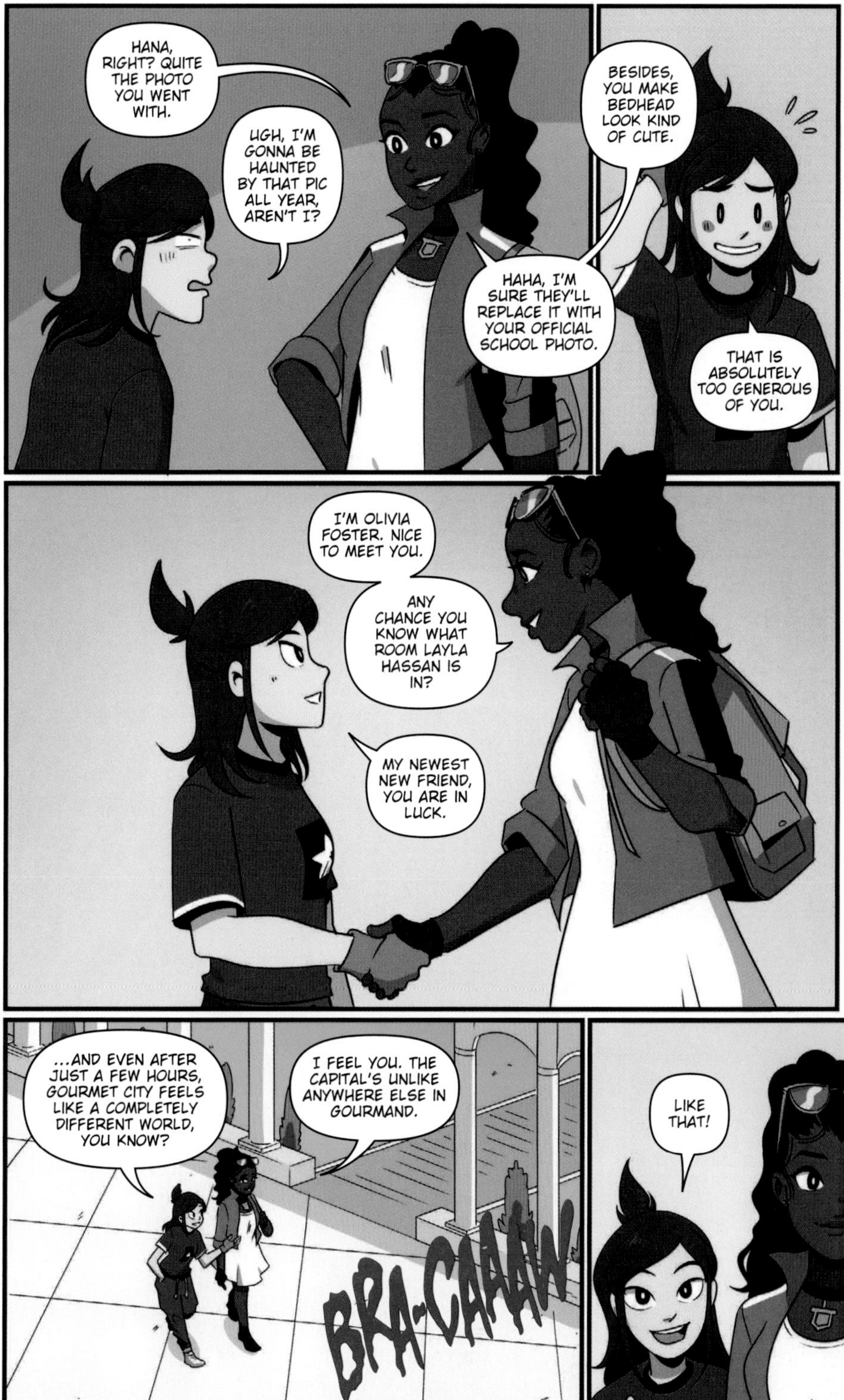
HANA, RIGHT? QUITE THE PHOTO YOU WENT WITH.
UGH, I'M GONNA BE HAUNTED BY THAT PIC ALL YEAR, AREN'T I?
HAHA, I'M SURE THEY'LL REPLACE IT WITH YOUR OFFICIAL SCHOOL PHOTO.
BESIDES, YOU MAKE BEDHEAD LOOK KIND OF CUTE.
THAT IS ABSOLUTELY TOO GENEROUS OF YOU.
I'M OLIVIA FOSTER. NICE TO MEET YOU.
ANY CHANCE YOU KNOW WHAT ROOM LAYLA HASSAN IS IN?
MY NEWEST NEW FRIEND, YOU ARE IN LUCK.
...AND EVEN AFTER JUST A FEW HOURS, GOURMET CITY FEELS LIKE A COMPLETELY DIFFERENT WORLD, YOU KNOW?
I FEEL YOU. THE CAPITAL'S UNLIKE ANYWHERE ELSE IN GOURMAND.
BRA-CAAAW
LIKE THAT!

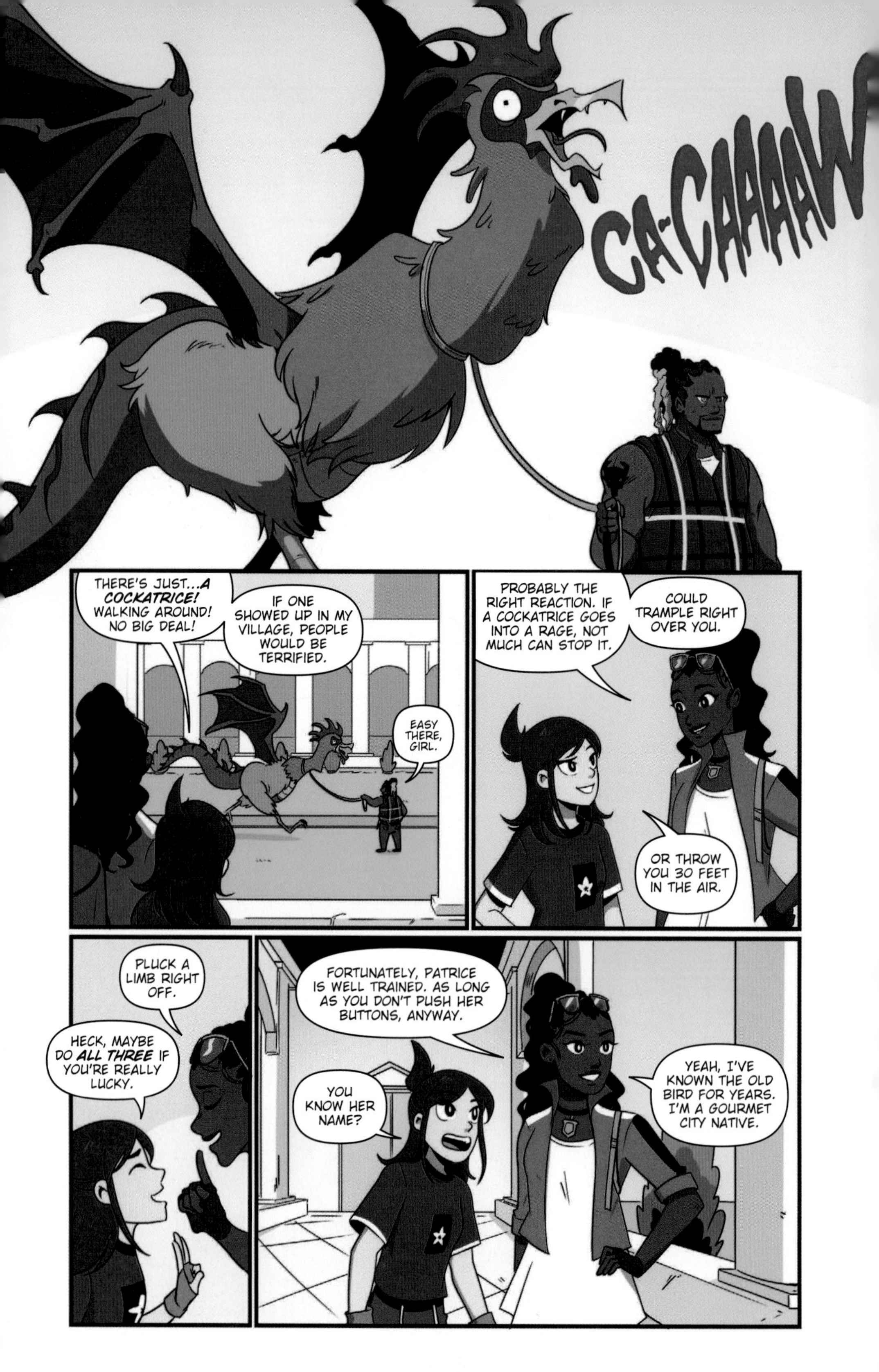
CA-CAAAAW
THERE'S JUST...A COCKATRICE! WALKING AROUND! NO BIG DEAL!
IF ONE SHOWED UP IN MY VILLAGE, PEOPLE WOULD BE TERRIFIED.
EASY THERE, GIRL.
PROBABLY THE RIGHT REACTION. IF A COCKATRICE GOES INTO A RAGE, NOT MUCH CAN STOP IT.
COULD TRAMPLE RIGHT OVER YOU.
OR THROW YOU 30 FEET IN THE AIR.
PLUCK A LIMB RIGHT OFF.
HECK, MAYBE DO ALL THREE IF YOU'RE REALLY LUCKY.
FORTUNATELY, PATRICE IS WELL TRAINED. AS LONG AS YOU DON'T PUSH HER BUTTONS, ANYWAY.
YOU KNOW HER NAME?
YEAH, I'VE KNOWN THE OLD BIRD FOR YEARS. I'M A GOURMET CITY NATIVE.

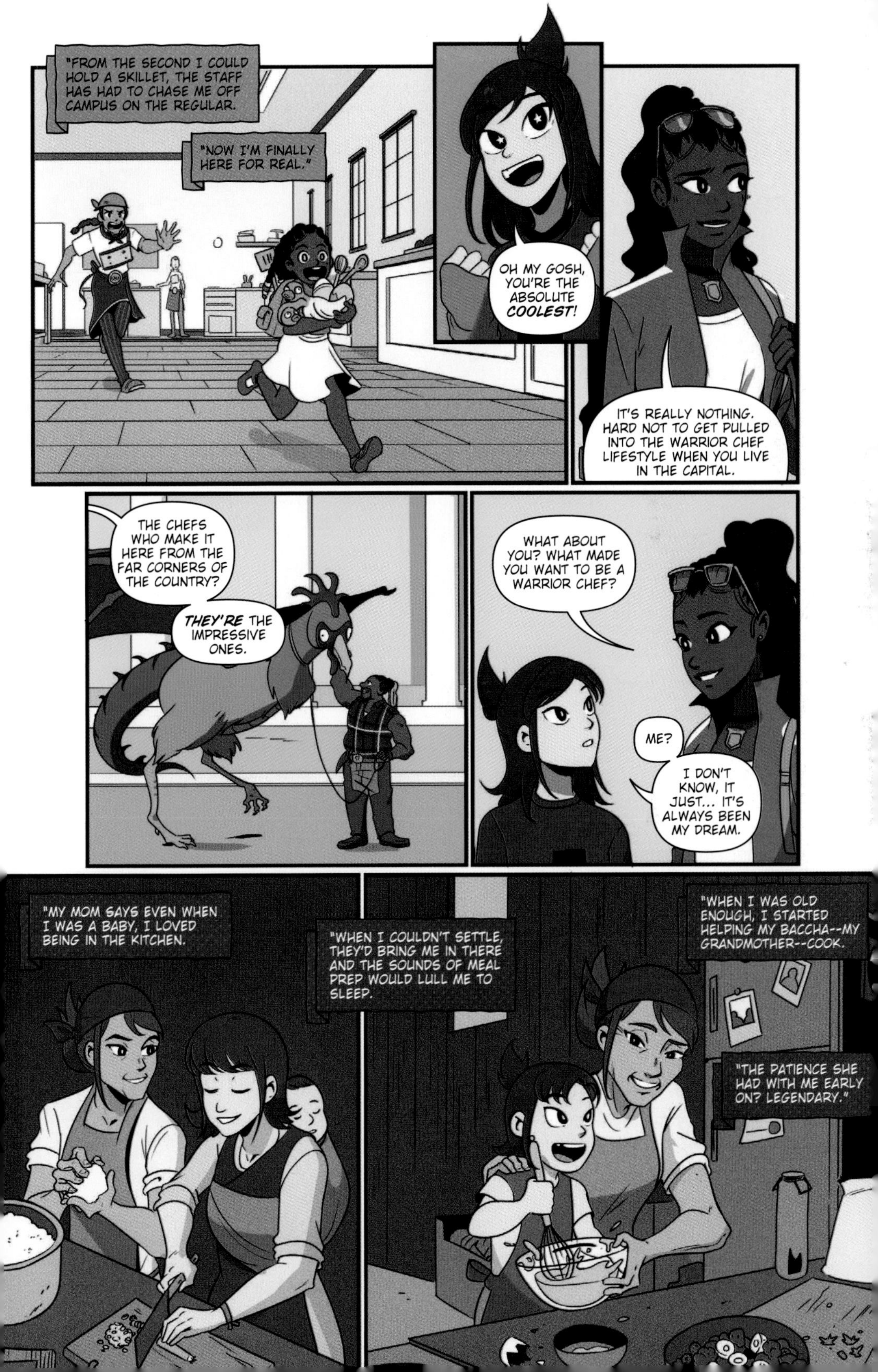
"FROM THE SECOND I COULD HOLD A SKILLET, THE STAFF HAS HAD TO CHASE ME OFF CAMPUS ON THE REGULAR.
"NOW I'M FINALLY HERE FOR REAL."
OH MY GOSH, YOU'RE THE ABSOLUTE COOLEST!
IT'S REALLY NOTHING. HARD NOT TO GET PULLED INTO THE WARRIOR CHEF LIFESTYLE WHEN YOU LIVE IN THE CAPITAL.
THE CHEFS WHO MAKE IT HERE FROM THE FAR CORNERS OF THE COUNTRY?
THEY'RE THE IMPRESSIVE ONES.
WHAT ABOUT YOU? WHAT MADE YOU WANT TO BE A WARRIOR CHEF?
ME?
I DON'T KNOW, IT JUST... IT'S ALWAYS BEEN MY DREAM.
"MY MOM SAYS EVEN WHEN I WAS A BABY, I LOVED BEING IN THE KITCHEN.
"WHEN I COULDN'T SETTLE, THEY'D BRING ME IN THERE AND THE SOUNDS OF MEAL PREP WOULD LULL ME TO SLEEP.
"WHEN I WAS OLD ENOUGH, I STARTED HELPING MY BACCHA--MY GRANDMOTHER--COOK.
"THE PATIENCE SHE HAD WITH ME EARLY ON? LEGENDARY."

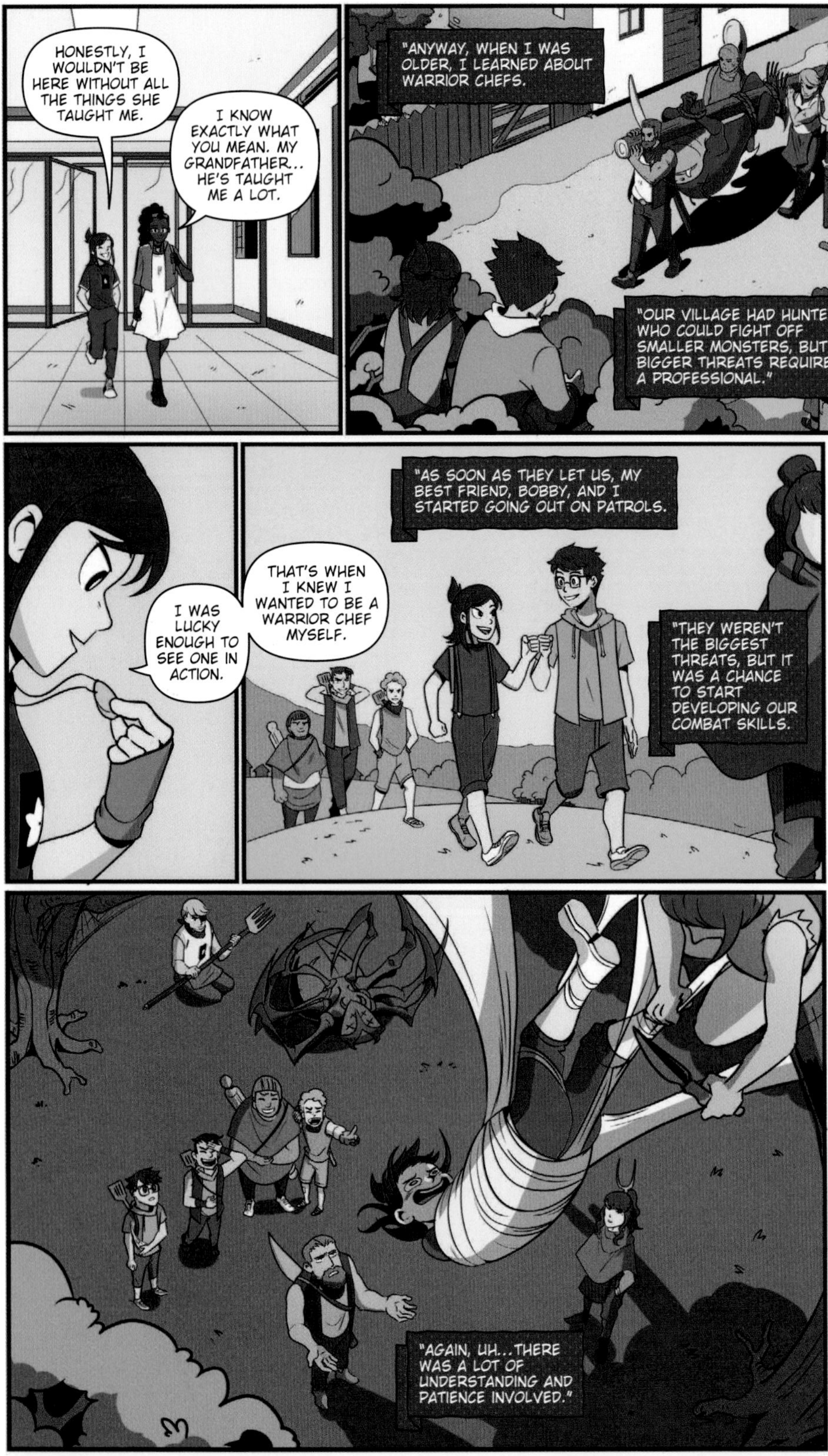
HONESTLY, I WOULDN'T BE HERE WITHOUT ALL THE THINGS SHE TAUGHT ME.
I KNOW EXACTLY WHAT YOU MEAN. MY GRANDFATHER... HE'S TAUGHT ME A LOT.
"ANYWAY, WHEN I WAS OLDER, I LEARNED ABOUT WARRIOR CHEFS.
"OUR VILLAGE HAD HUNTERS WHO COULD FIGHT OFF SMALLER MONSTERS, BUT BIGGER THREATS REQUIRED A PROFESSIONAL."
I WAS LUCKY ENOUGH TO SEE ONE IN ACTION.
THAT'S WHEN I KNEW I WANTED TO BE A WARRIOR CHEF MYSELF.
"AS SOON AS THEY LET US, MY BEST FRIEND, BOBBY, AND I STARTED GOING OUT ON PATROLS.
"THEY WEREN'T THE BIGGEST THREATS, BUT IT WAS A CHANCE TO START DEVELOPING OUR COMBAT SKILLS.
"AGAIN, UH...THERE WAS A LOT OF UNDERSTANDING AND PATIENCE INVOLVED."

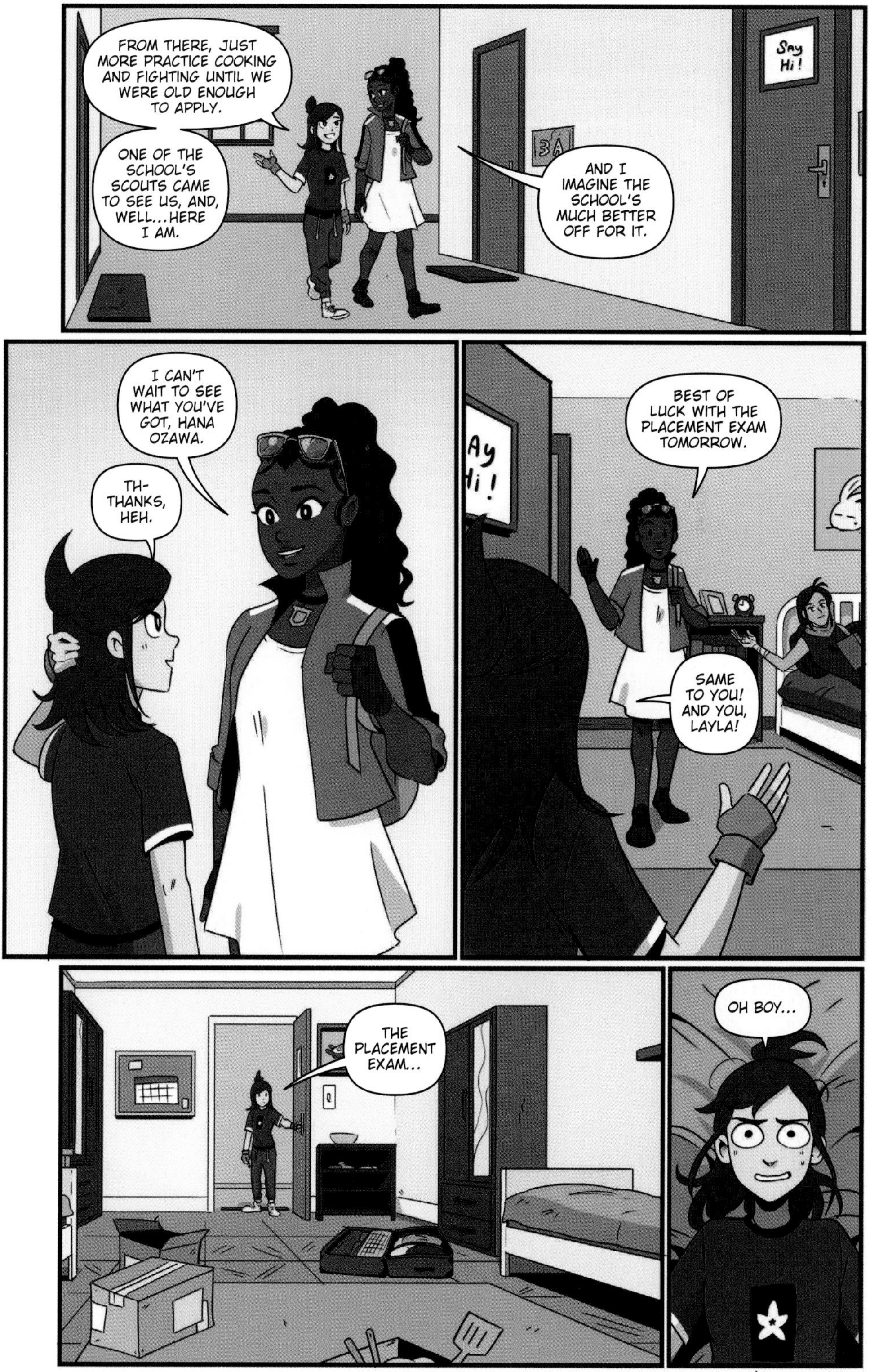
FROM THERE, JUST MORE PRACTICE COOKING AND FIGHTING UNTIL WE WERE OLD ENOUGH TO APPLY.
ONE OF THE SCHOOL'S SCOUTS CAME TO SEE US, AND, WELL...HERE I AM.
Say Hi!
3A
AND I IMAGINE THE SCHOOL'S MUCH BETTER OFF FOR IT.
I CAN'T WAIT TO SEE WHAT YOU'VE GOT, HANA OZAWA.
TH-THANKS, HEH.
BEST OF LUCK WITH THE PLACEMENT EXAM TOMORROW.
SAME TO YOU! AND YOU, LAYLA!
THE PLACEMENT EXAM...
OH BOY...

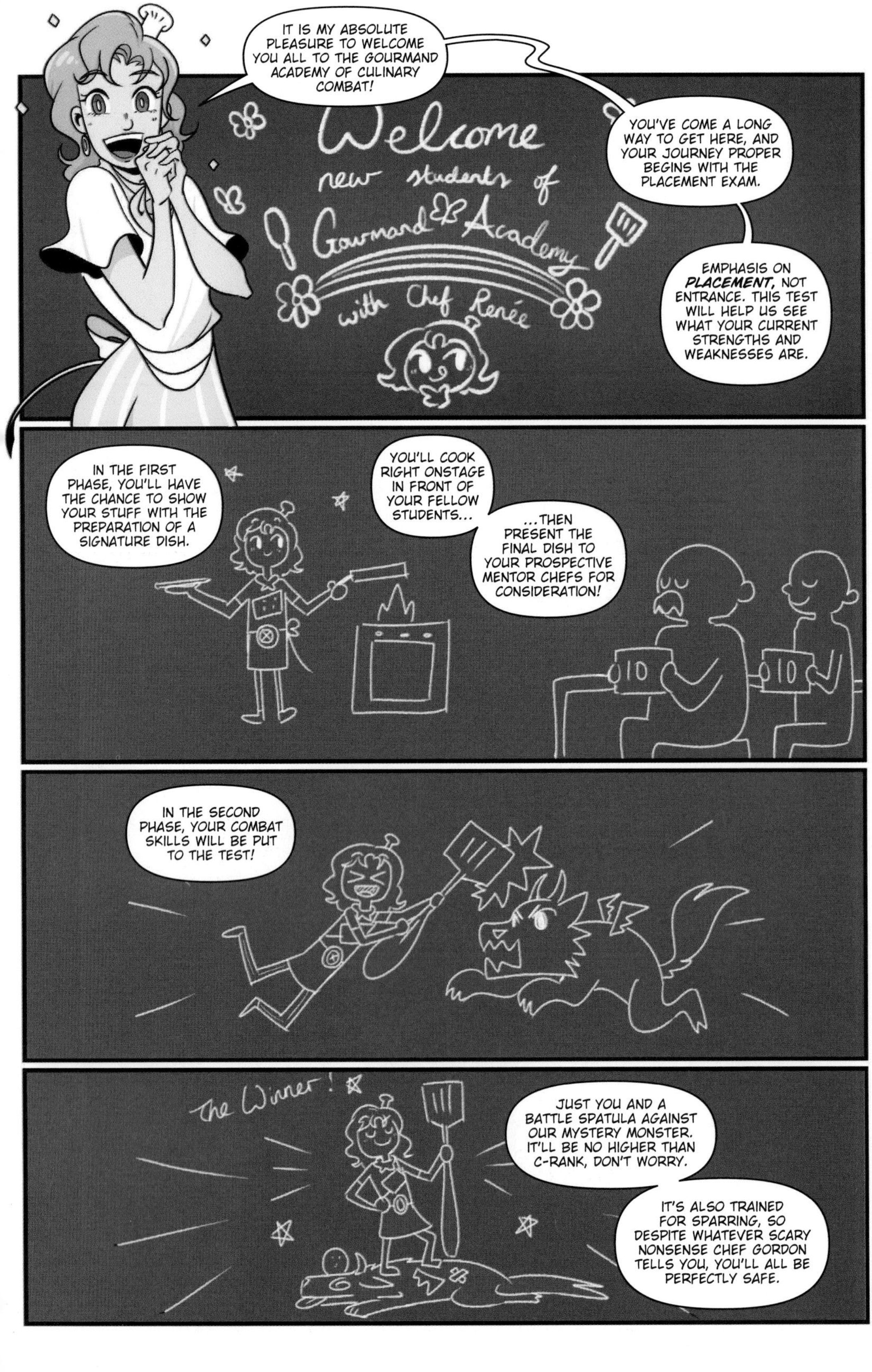
IT IS MY ABSOLUTE PLEASURE TO WELCOME YOU ALL TO THE GOURMAND ACADEMY OF CULINARY COMBAT!
Welcome new students of Gourmand Academy with Chef Renée
YOU'VE COME A LONG WAY TO GET HERE, AND YOUR JOURNEY PROPER BEGINS WITH THE PLACEMENT EXAM.
EMPHASIS ON ***PLACEMENT,*** NOT ENTRANCE. THIS TEST WILL HELP US SEE WHAT YOUR CURRENT STRENGTHS AND WEAKNESSES ARE.
IN THE FIRST PHASE, YOU'LL HAVE THE CHANCE TO SHOW YOUR STUFF WITH THE PREPARATION OF A SIGNATURE DISH.
YOU'LL COOK RIGHT ONSTAGE IN FRONT OF YOUR FELLOW STUDENTS...
...THEN PRESENT THE FINAL DISH TO YOUR PROSPECTIVE MENTOR CHEFS FOR CONSIDERATION!
10
10
IN THE SECOND PHASE, YOUR COMBAT SKILLS WILL BE PUT TO THE TEST!
the Winner!
JUST YOU AND A BATTLE SPATULA AGAINST OUR MYSTERY MONSTER. IT'LL BE NO HIGHER THAN C-RANK, DON'T WORRY.
IT'S ALSO TRAINED FOR SPARRING, SO DESPITE WHATEVER SCARY NONSENSE CHEF GORDON TELLS YOU, YOU'LL ALL BE PERFECTLY SAFE.

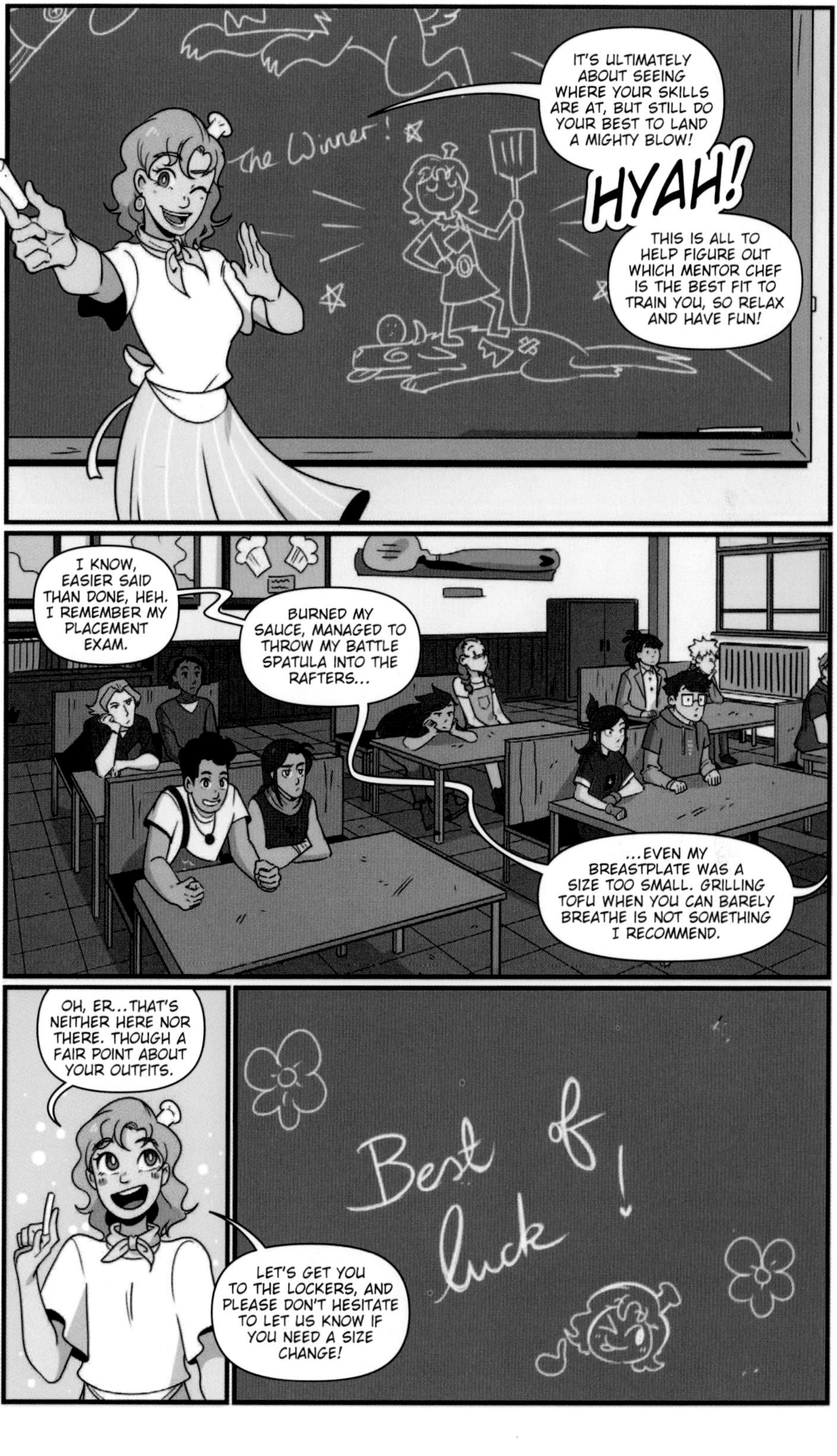
IT'S ULTIMATELY ABOUT SEEING WHERE YOUR SKILLS ARE AT, BUT STILL DO YOUR BEST TO LAND A MIGHTY BLOW!
the Winner!
HYAH!
THIS IS ALL TO HELP FIGURE OUT WHICH MENTOR CHEF IS THE BEST FIT TO TRAIN YOU, SO RELAX AND HAVE FUN!
I KNOW, EASIER SAID THAN DONE, HEH. I REMEMBER MY PLACEMENT EXAM.
BURNED MY SAUCE, MANAGED TO THROW MY BATTLE SPATULA INTO THE RAFTERS...
...EVEN MY BREASTPLATE WAS A SIZE TOO SMALL. GRILLING TOFU WHEN YOU CAN BARELY BREATHE IS NOT SOMETHING I RECOMMEND.
OH, ER...THAT'S NEITHER HERE NOR THERE. THOUGH A FAIR POINT ABOUT YOUR OUTFITS.
LET'S GET YOU TO THE LOCKERS, AND PLEASE DON'T HESITATE TO LET US KNOW IF YOU NEED A SIZE CHANGE!
Best of luck!

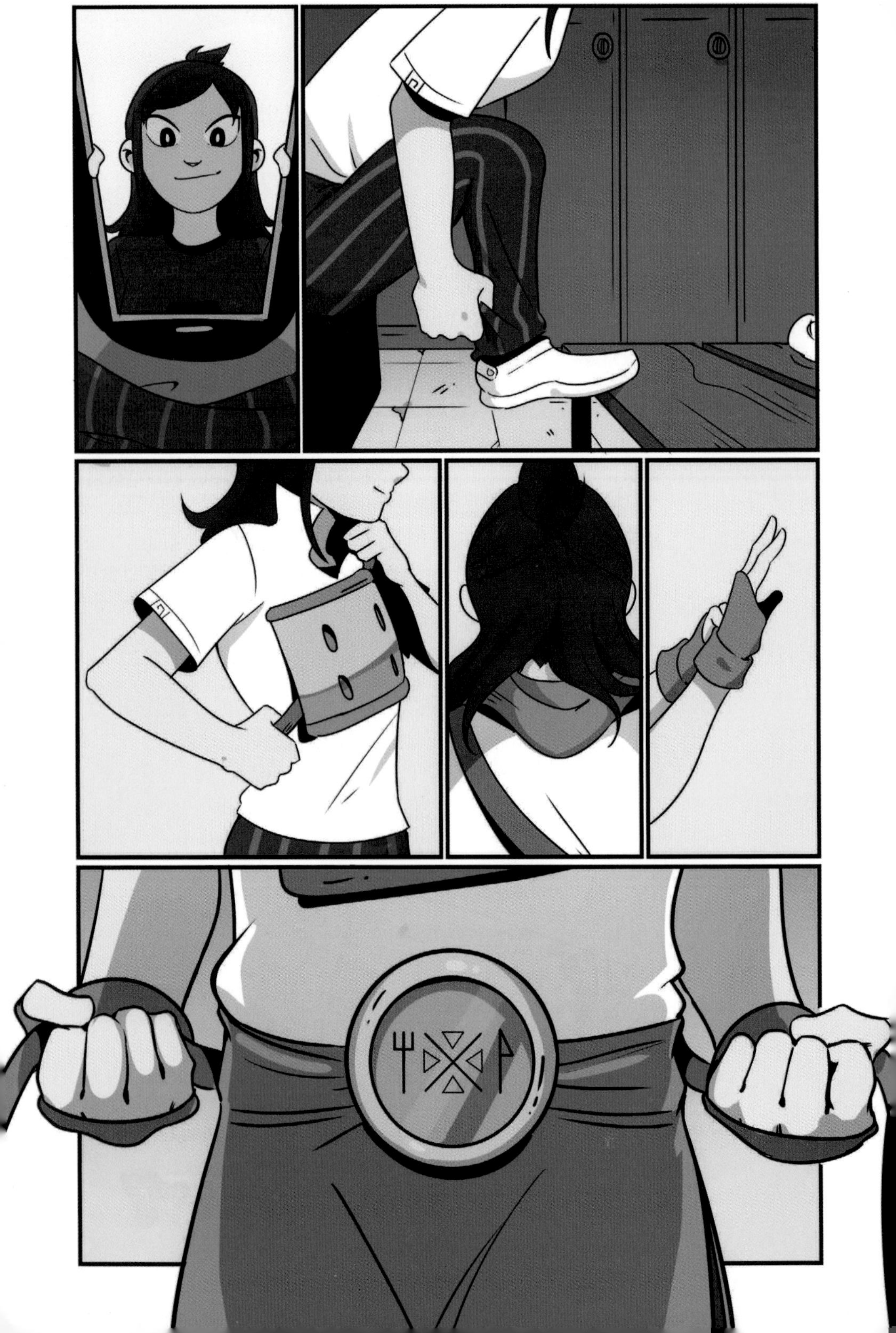

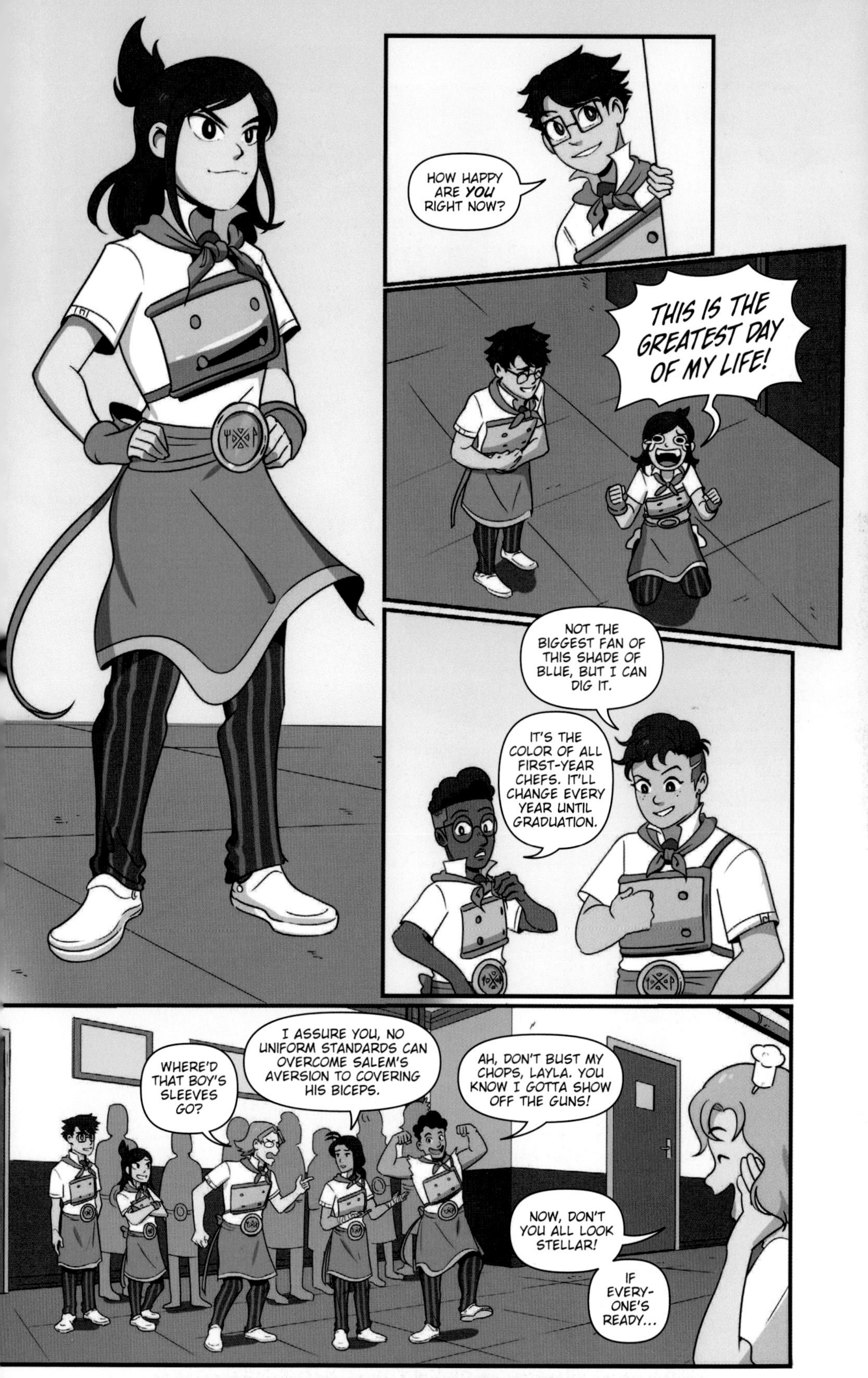
HOW HAPPY ARE *YOU* RIGHT NOW?
THIS IS THE GREATEST DAY OF MY LIFE!
NOT THE BIGGEST FAN OF THIS SHADE OF BLUE, BUT I CAN DIG IT.
IT'S THE COLOR OF ALL FIRST-YEAR CHEFS. IT'LL CHANGE EVERY YEAR UNTIL GRADUATION.
WHERE'D THAT BOY'S SLEEVES GO?
I ASSURE YOU, NO UNIFORM STANDARDS CAN OVERCOME SALEM'S AVERSION TO COVERING HIS BICEPS.
AH, DON'T BUST MY CHOPS, LAYLA. YOU KNOW I GOTTA SHOW OFF THE GUNS!
NOW, DON'T YOU ALL LOOK STELLAR!
IF EVERY-ONE'S READY...

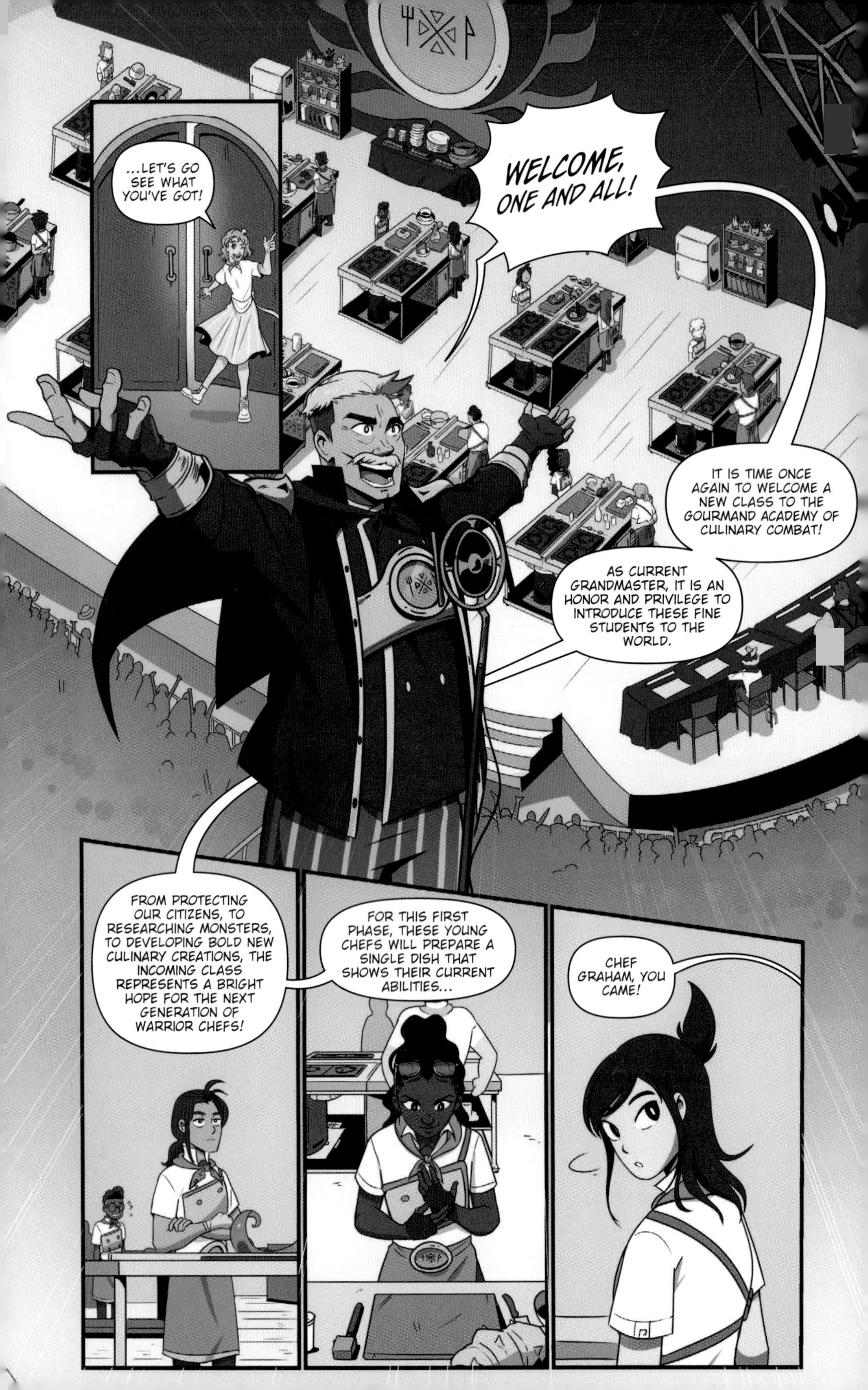
...LET'S GO SEE WHAT YOU'VE GOT!
WELCOME, ONE AND ALL!
IT IS TIME ONCE AGAIN TO WELCOME A NEW CLASS TO THE GOURMAND ACADEMY OF CULINARY COMBAT!
AS CURRENT GRANDMASTER, IT IS AN HONOR AND PRIVILEGE TO INTRODUCE THESE FINE STUDENTS TO THE WORLD.
FROM PROTECTING OUR CITIZENS, TO RESEARCHING MONSTERS, TO DEVELOPING BOLD NEW CULINARY CREATIONS, THE INCOMING CLASS REPRESENTS A BRIGHT HOPE FOR THE NEXT GENERATION OF WARRIOR CHEFS!
FOR THIS FIRST PHASE, THESE YOUNG CHEFS WILL PREPARE A SINGLE DISH THAT SHOWS THEIR CURRENT ABILITIES...
CHEF GRAHAM, YOU CAME!

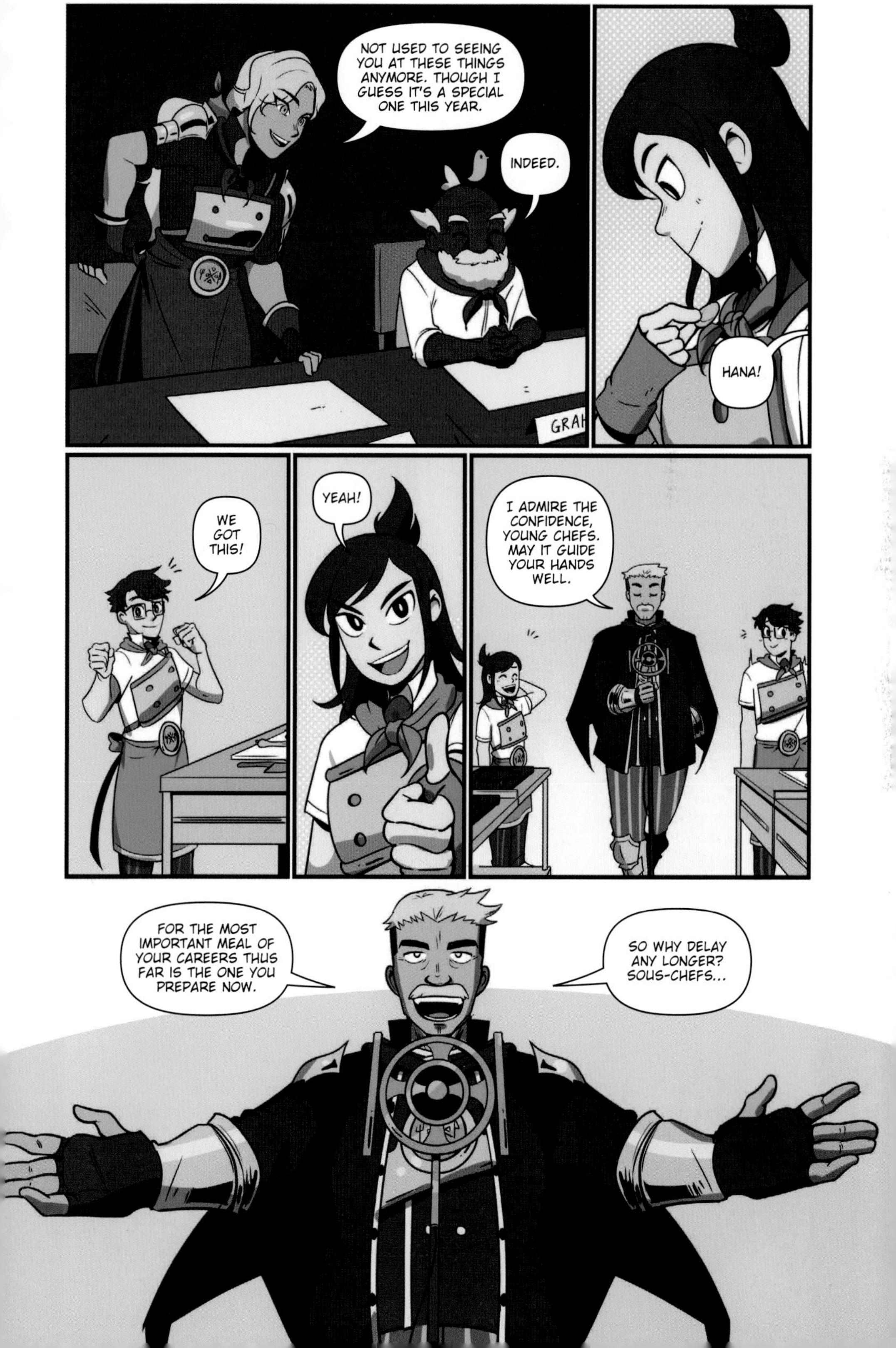
NOT USED TO SEEING YOU AT THESE THINGS ANYMORE. THOUGH I GUESS IT'S A SPECIAL ONE THIS YEAR.
INDEED.
GRAH
HANA!
WE GOT THIS!
YEAH!
I ADMIRE THE CONFIDENCE, YOUNG CHEFS. MAY IT GUIDE YOUR HANDS WELL.
FOR THE MOST IMPORTANT MEAL OF YOUR CAREERS THUS FAR IS THE ONE YOU PREPARE NOW.
SO WHY DELAY ANY LONGER? SOUS-CHEFS...

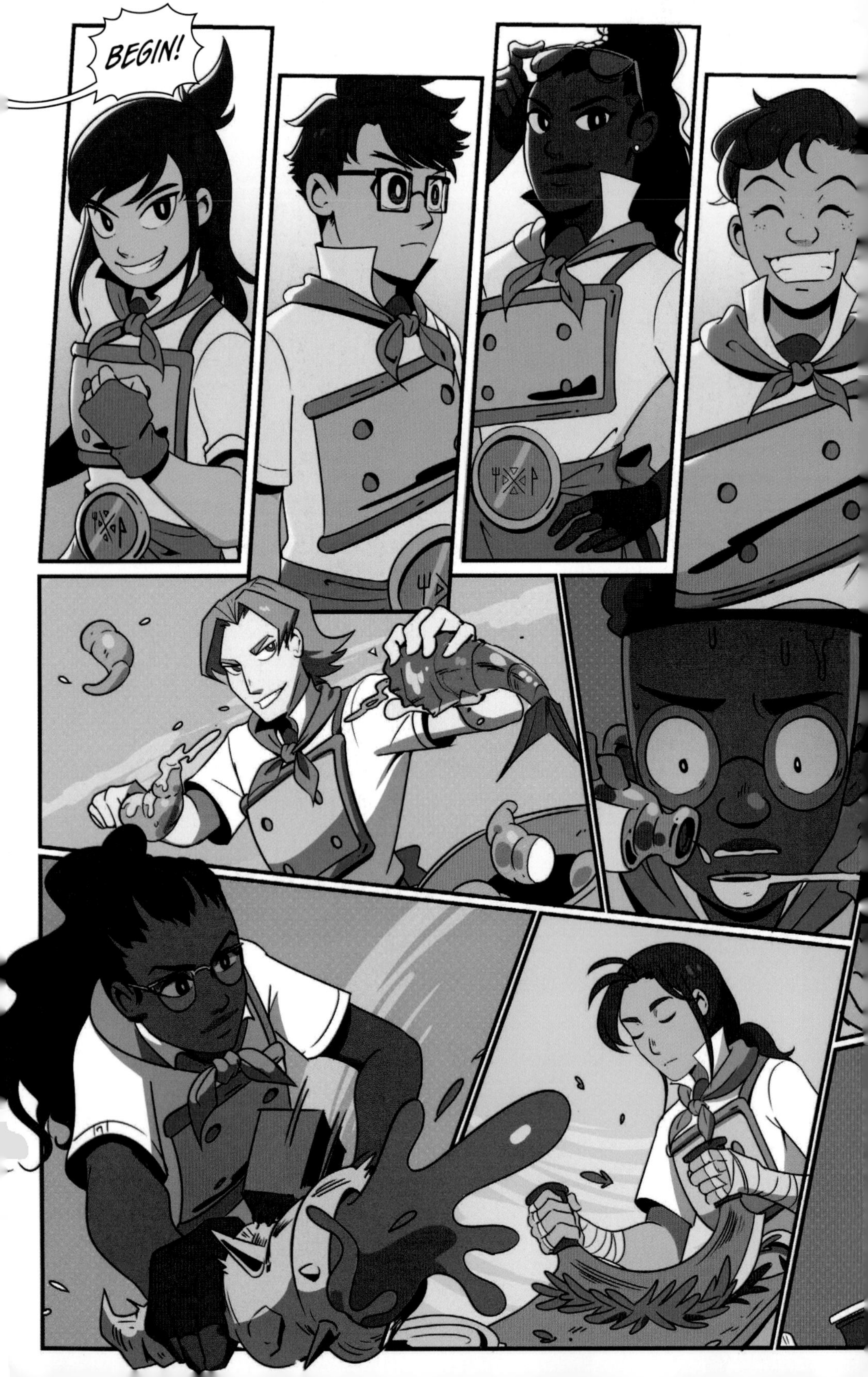
BEGIN!

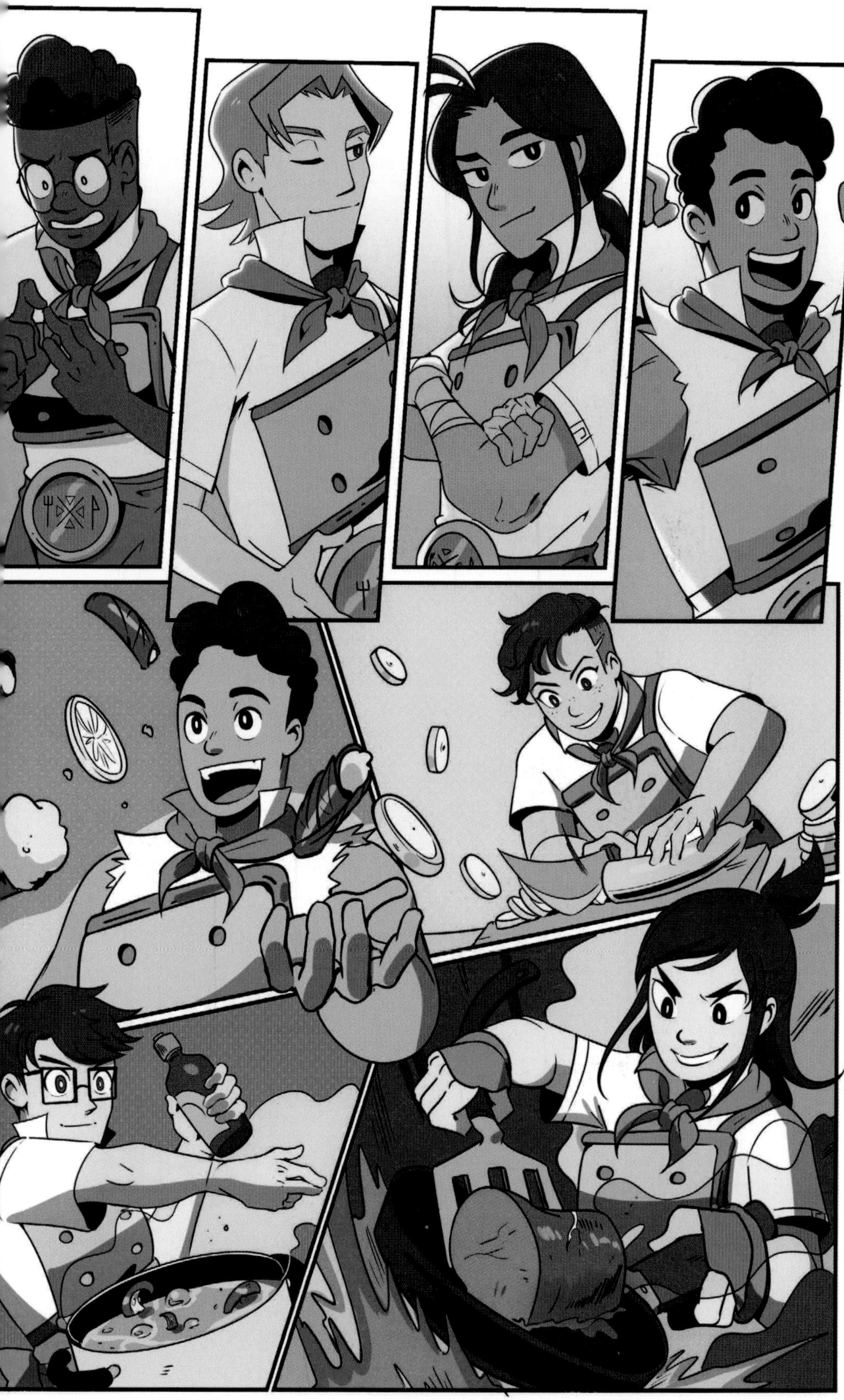

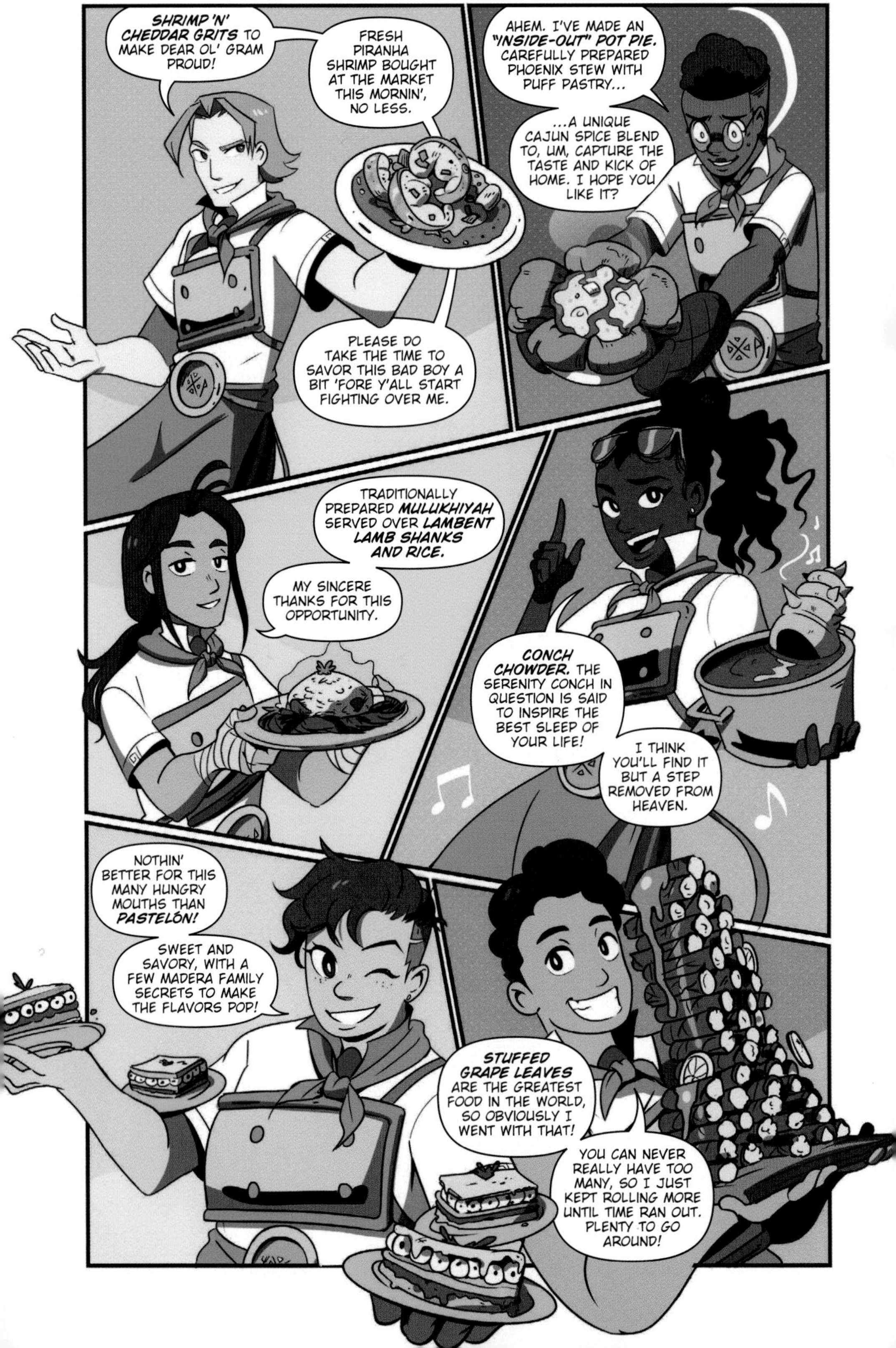
SHRIMP 'N' CHEDDAR GRITS TO MAKE DEAR OL' GRAM PROUD!
FRESH PIRANHA SHRIMP BOUGHT AT THE MARKET THIS MORNIN', NO LESS.
PLEASE DO TAKE THE TIME TO SAVOR THIS BAD BOY A BIT 'FORE Y'ALL START FIGHTING OVER ME.
AHEM. I'VE MADE AN "INSIDE-OUT" POT PIE. CAREFULLY PREPARED PHOENIX STEW WITH PUFF PASTRY...
...A UNIQUE CAJUN SPICE BLEND TO, UM, CAPTURE THE TASTE AND KICK OF HOME. I HOPE YOU LIKE IT?
TRADITIONALLY PREPARED MULUKHIYAH SERVED OVER LAMBENT LAMB SHANKS AND RICE.
MY SINCERE THANKS FOR THIS OPPORTUNITY.
CONCH CHOWDER. THE SERENITY CONCH IN QUESTION IS SAID TO INSPIRE THE BEST SLEEP OF YOUR LIFE!
I THINK YOU'LL FIND IT BUT A STEP REMOVED FROM HEAVEN.
NOTHIN' BETTER FOR THIS MANY HUNGRY MOUTHS THAN PASTELÓN!
SWEET AND SAVORY, WITH A FEW MADERA FAMILY SECRETS TO MAKE THE FLAVORS POP!
STUFFED GRAPE LEAVES ARE THE GREATEST FOOD IN THE WORLD, SO OBVIOUSLY I WENT WITH THAT!
YOU CAN NEVER REALLY HAVE TOO MANY, SO I JUST KEPT ROLLING MORE UNTIL TIME RAN OUT. PLENTY TO GO AROUND!

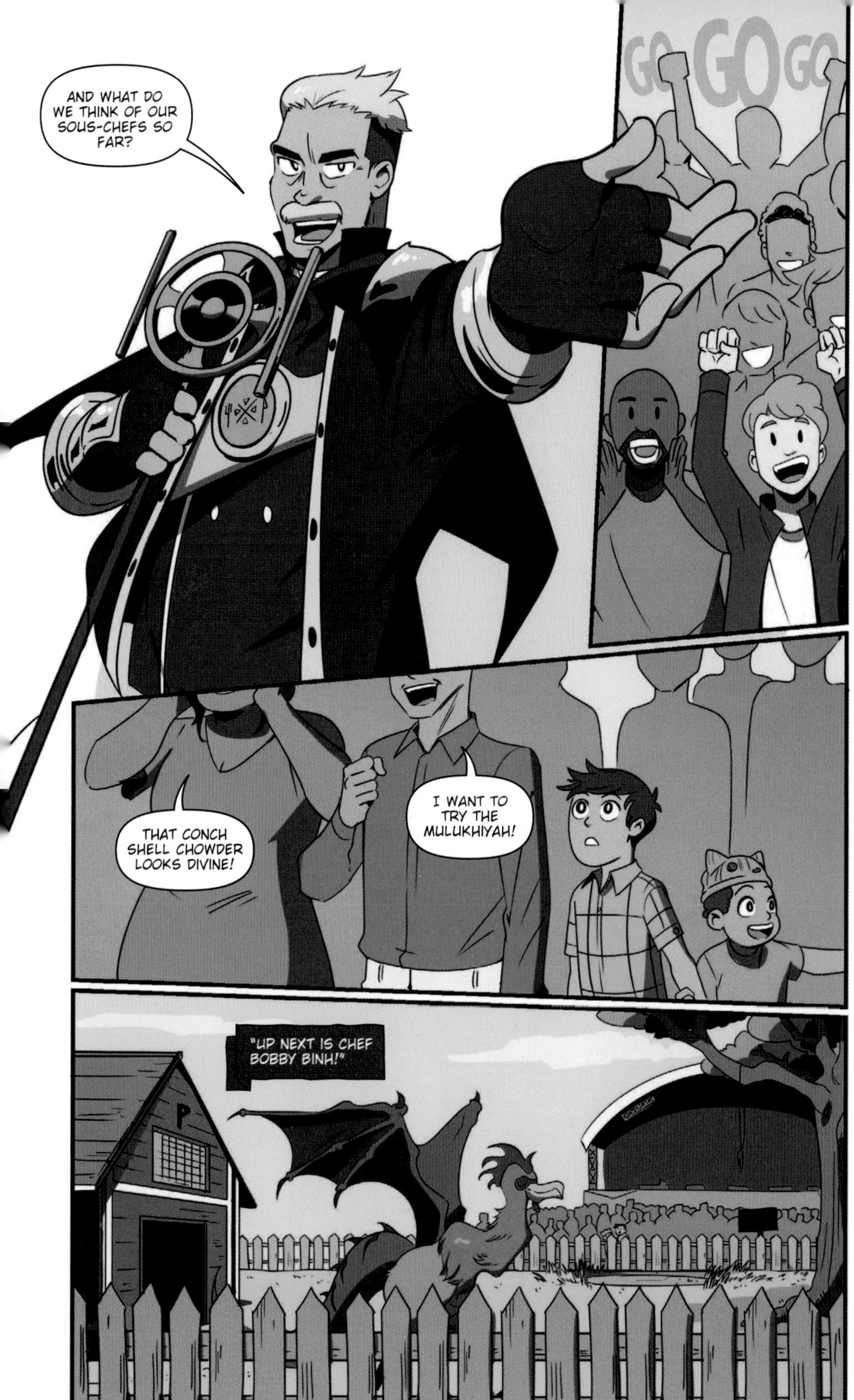

AND WHAT DO WE THINK OF OUR SOUS-CHEFS SO FAR?
GO GO GO
THAT CONCH SHELL CHOWDER LOOKS DIVINE!
I WANT TO TRY THE MULUKHIYAH!
"UP NEXT IS CHEF BOBBY BINH!"

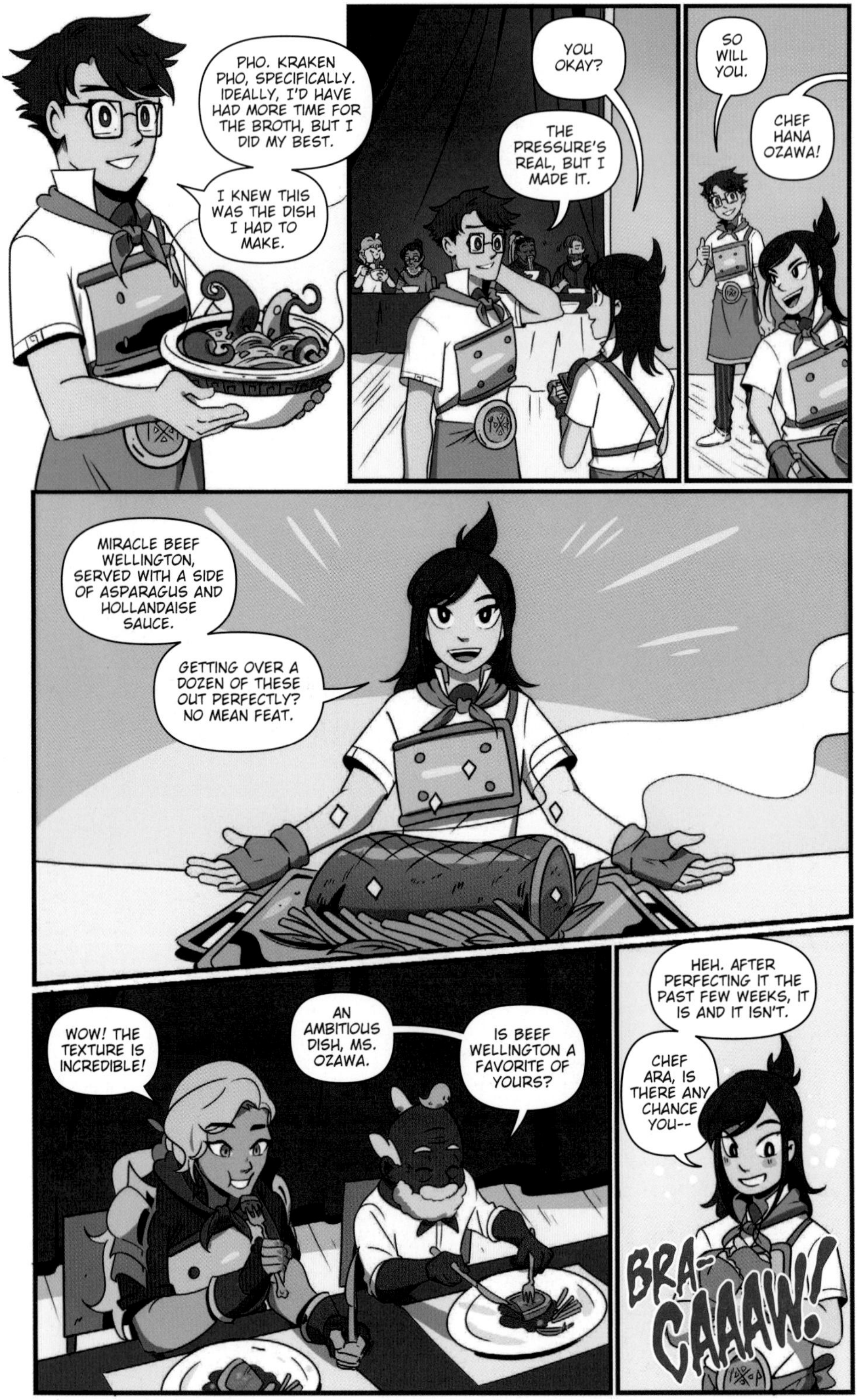
PHO. KRAKEN PHO, SPECIFICALLY. IDEALLY, I'D HAVE HAD MORE TIME FOR THE BROTH, BUT I DID MY BEST.
I KNEW THIS WAS THE DISH I HAD TO MAKE.
YOU OKAY?
THE PRESSURE'S REAL, BUT I MADE IT.
SO WILL YOU.
CHEF HANA OZAWA!
MIRACLE BEEF WELLINGTON, SERVED WITH A SIDE OF ASPARAGUS AND HOLLANDAISE SAUCE.
GETTING OVER A DOZEN OF THESE OUT PERFECTLY? NO MEAN FEAT.
WOW! THE TEXTURE IS INCREDIBLE!
AN AMBITIOUS DISH, MS. OZAWA.
IS BEEF WELLINGTON A FAVORITE OF YOURS?
HEH. AFTER PERFECTING IT THE PAST FEW WEEKS, IT IS AND IT ISN'T.
CHEF ARA, IS THERE ANY CHANCE YOU--
BRA-CAAAW!

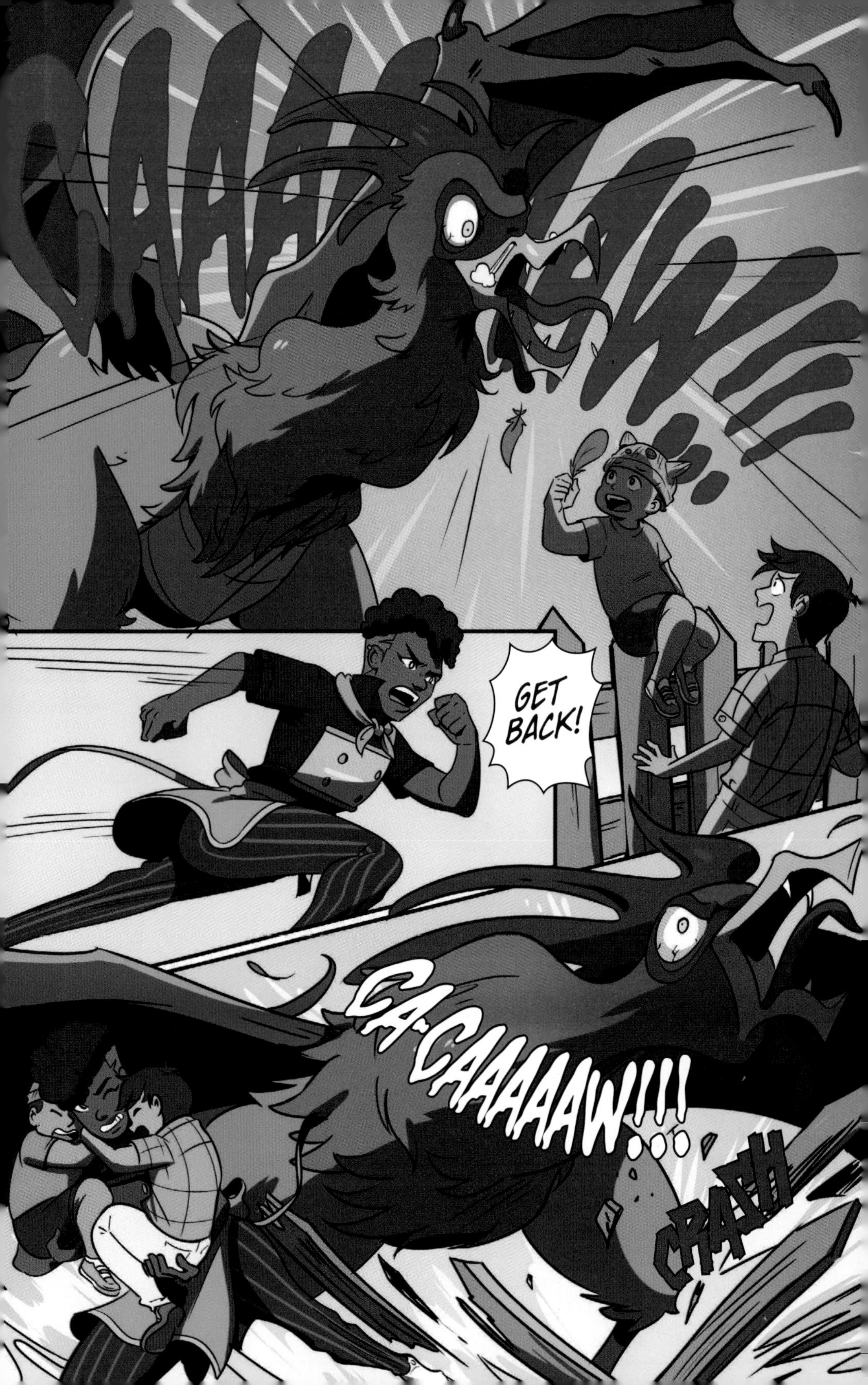
CAAAAAW!!!
GET BACK!
CA-CAAAAAW!!!
CRASH

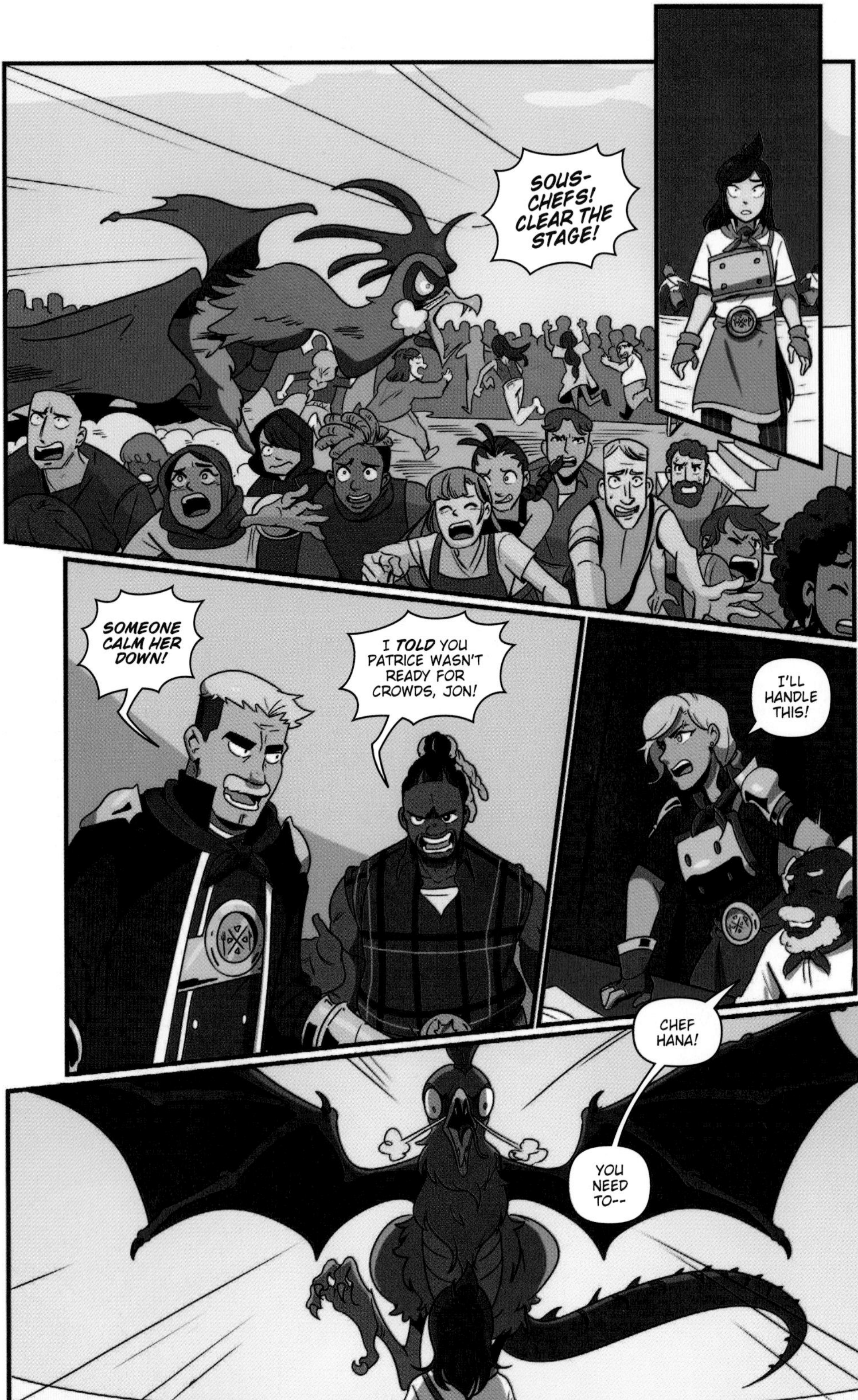
SOUS-CHEFS! CLEAR THE STAGE!
SOMEONE CALM HER DOWN!
I TOLD YOU PATRICE WASN'T READY FOR CROWDS, JON!
I'LL HANDLE THIS!
CHEF HANA!
YOU NEED TO--

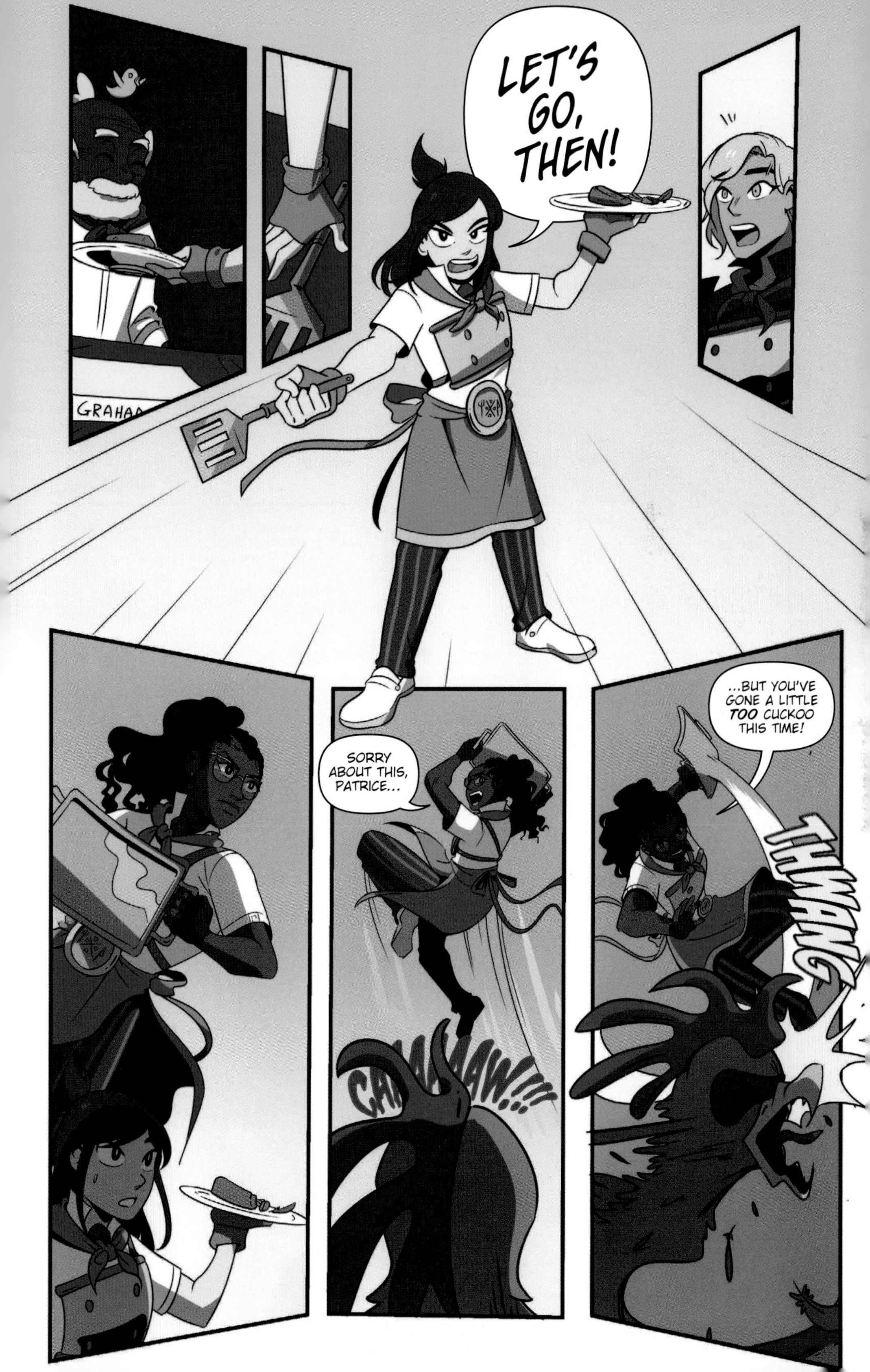
GRAHAM
LET'S GO, THEN!
SORRY ABOUT THIS, PATRICE...
CAAAAAW!!!
...BUT YOU'VE GONE A LITTLE TOO CUCKOO THIS TIME!
THWANG

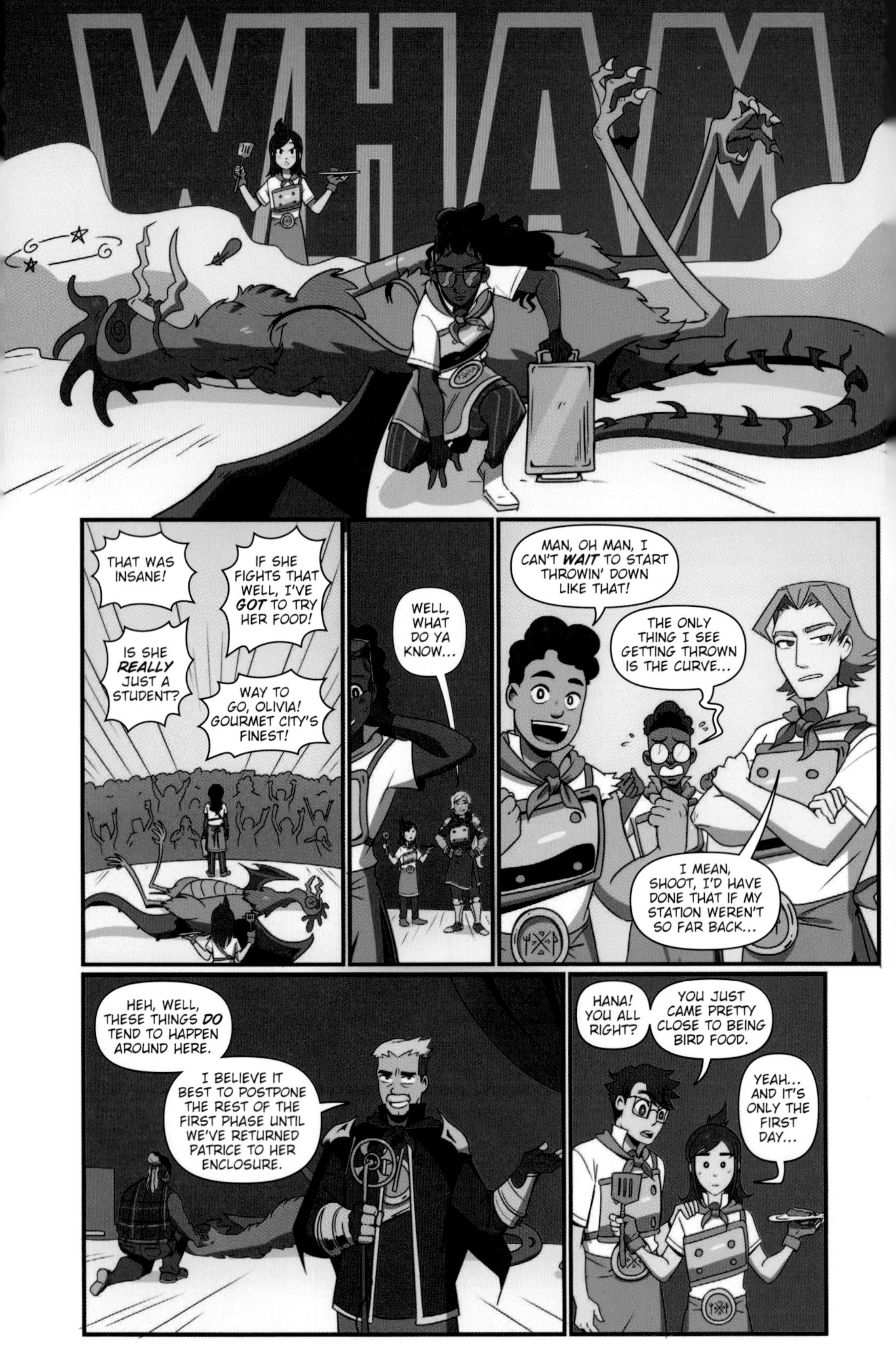
WHAM
THAT WAS INSANE!
IF SHE FIGHTS THAT WELL, I'VE **GOT** TO TRY HER FOOD!
IS SHE **REALLY** JUST A STUDENT?
WAY TO GO, OLIVIA! GOURMET CITY'S FINEST!
WELL, WHAT DO YA KNOW...
MAN, OH MAN, I CAN'T **WAIT** TO START THROWIN' DOWN LIKE THAT!
THE ONLY THING I SEE GETTING THROWN IS THE CURVE...
I MEAN, SHOOT, I'D HAVE DONE THAT IF MY STATION WEREN'T SO FAR BACK...
HEH, WELL, THESE THINGS **DO** TEND TO HAPPEN AROUND HERE.
I BELIEVE IT BEST TO POSTPONE THE REST OF THE FIRST PHASE UNTIL WE'VE RETURNED PATRICE TO HER ENCLOSURE.
HANA! YOU ALL RIGHT?
YOU JUST CAME PRETTY CLOSE TO BEING BIRD FOOD.
YEAH... AND IT'S ONLY THE FIRST DAY...

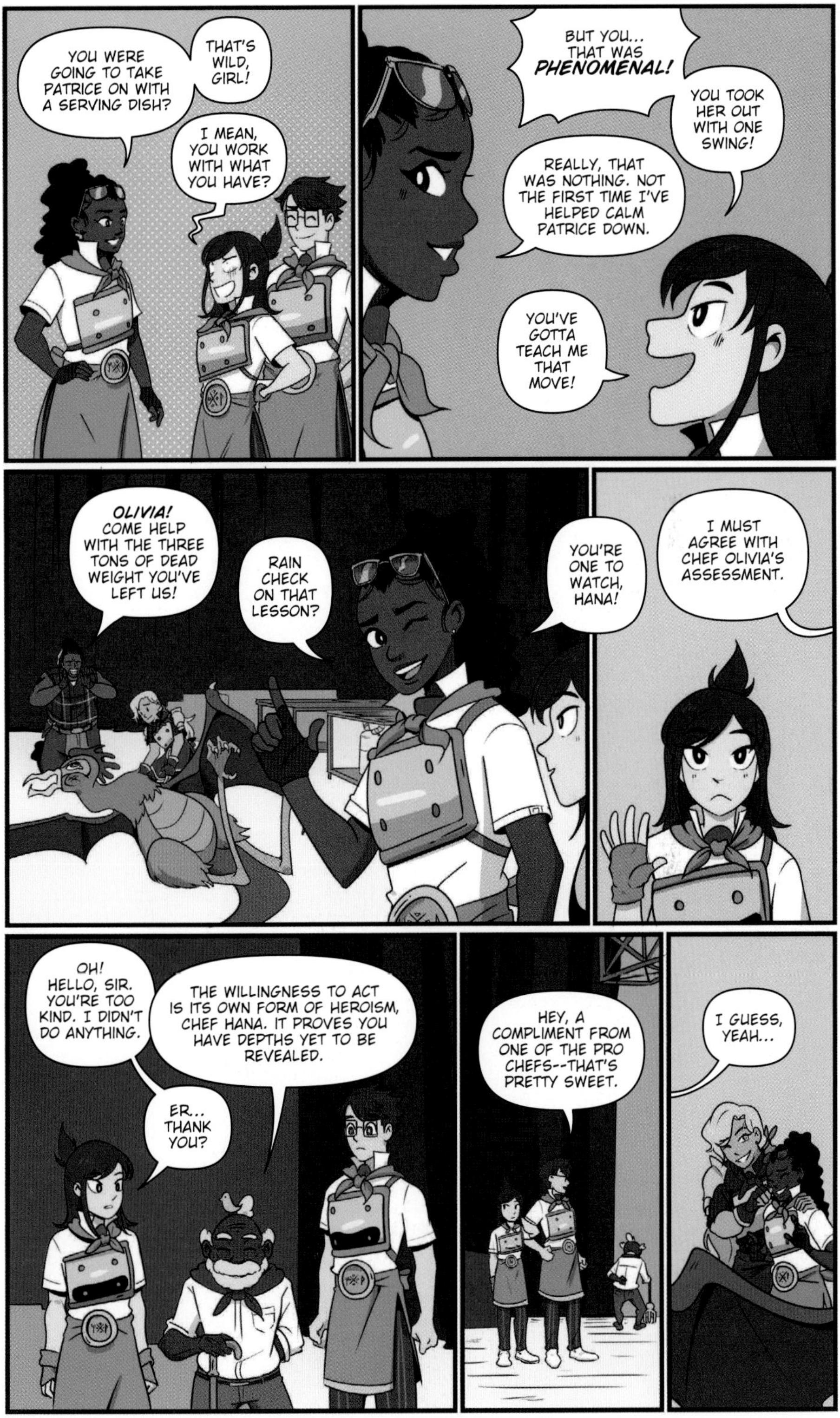
YOU WERE GOING TO TAKE PATRICE ON WITH A SERVING DISH?
THAT'S WILD, GIRL!
I MEAN, YOU WORK WITH WHAT YOU HAVE?
BUT YOU... THAT WAS PHENOMENAL!
YOU TOOK HER OUT WITH ONE SWING!
REALLY, THAT WAS NOTHING. NOT THE FIRST TIME I'VE HELPED CALM PATRICE DOWN.
YOU'VE GOTTA TEACH ME THAT MOVE!
OLIVIA! COME HELP WITH THE THREE TONS OF DEAD WEIGHT YOU'VE LEFT US!
RAIN CHECK ON THAT LESSON?
YOU'RE ONE TO WATCH, HANA!
I MUST AGREE WITH CHEF OLIVIA'S ASSESSMENT.
OH! HELLO, SIR. YOU'RE TOO KIND. I DIDN'T DO ANYTHING.
THE WILLINGNESS TO ACT IS ITS OWN FORM OF HEROISM, CHEF HANA. IT PROVES YOU HAVE DEPTHS YET TO BE REVEALED.
ER... THANK YOU?
HEY, A COMPLIMENT FROM ONE OF THE PRO CHEFS--THAT'S PRETTY SWEET.
I GUESS, YEAH...

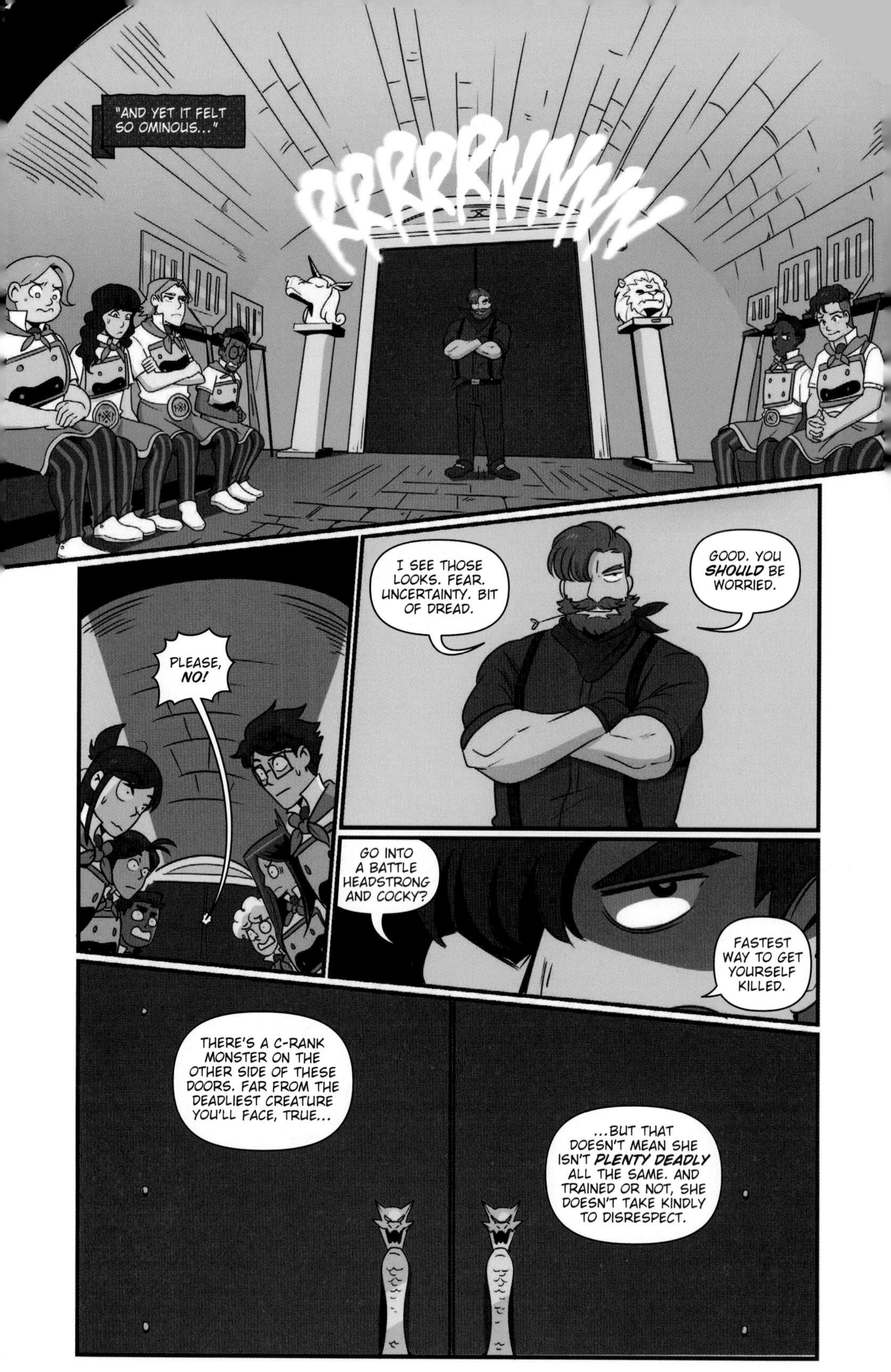

"AND YET IT FELT SO OMINOUS..."
RRRRRNNNN
I SEE THOSE LOOKS. FEAR. UNCERTAINTY. BIT OF DREAD.
GOOD. YOU **SHOULD** BE WORRIED.
PLEASE, **NO!**
GO INTO A BATTLE HEADSTRONG AND COCKY?
FASTEST WAY TO GET YOURSELF KILLED.
THERE'S A C-RANK MONSTER ON THE OTHER SIDE OF THESE DOORS. FAR FROM THE DEADLIEST CREATURE YOU'LL FACE, TRUE...
...BUT THAT DOESN'T MEAN SHE ISN'T ***PLENTY DEADLY*** ALL THE SAME. AND TRAINED OR NOT, SHE DOESN'T TAKE KINDLY TO DISRESPECT.

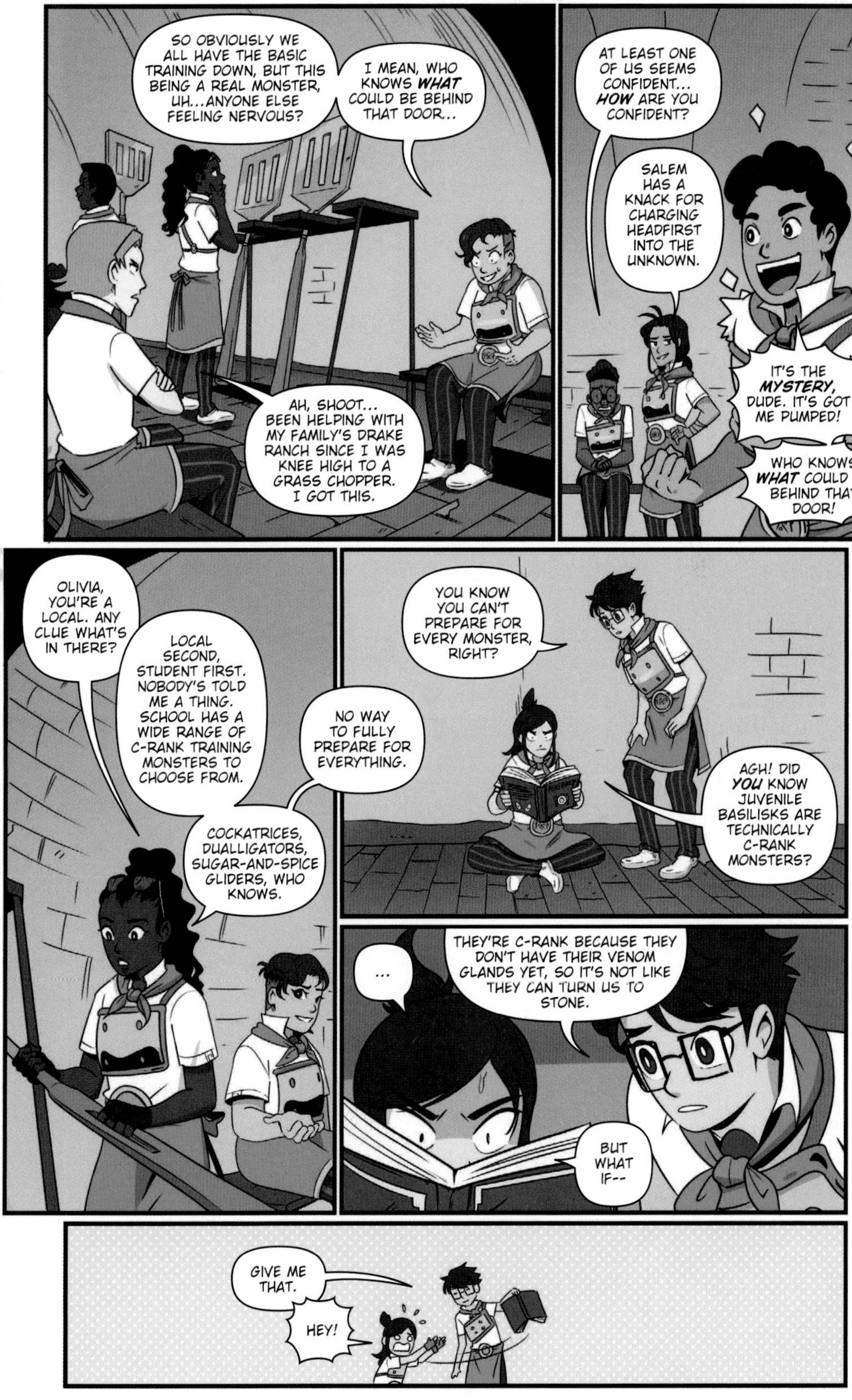
SO OBVIOUSLY WE ALL HAVE THE BASIC TRAINING DOWN, BUT THIS BEING A REAL MONSTER, UH...ANYONE ELSE FEELING NERVOUS?
I MEAN, WHO KNOWS WHAT COULD BE BEHIND THAT DOOR...
AH, SHOOT... BEEN HELPING WITH MY FAMILY'S DRAKE RANCH SINCE I WAS KNEE HIGH TO A GRASS CHOPPER. I GOT THIS.
AT LEAST ONE OF US SEEMS CONFIDENT... HOW ARE YOU CONFIDENT?
SALEM HAS A KNACK FOR CHARGING HEADFIRST INTO THE UNKNOWN.
IT'S THE MYSTERY, DUDE. IT'S GOT ME PUMPED!
WHO KNOWS WHAT COULD BE BEHIND THAT DOOR!
OLIVIA, YOU'RE A LOCAL. ANY CLUE WHAT'S IN THERE?
LOCAL SECOND, STUDENT FIRST. NOBODY'S TOLD ME A THING. SCHOOL HAS A WIDE RANGE OF C-RANK TRAINING MONSTERS TO CHOOSE FROM.
NO WAY TO FULLY PREPARE FOR EVERYTHING.
COCKATRICES, DUALLIGATORS, SUGAR-AND-SPICE GLIDERS, WHO KNOWS.
YOU KNOW YOU CAN'T PREPARE FOR EVERY MONSTER, RIGHT?
AGH! DID YOU KNOW JUVENILE BASILISKS ARE TECHNICALLY C-RANK MONSTERS?
...
THEY'RE C-RANK BECAUSE THEY DON'T HAVE THEIR VENOM GLANDS YET, SO IT'S NOT LIKE THEY CAN TURN US TO STONE.
BUT WHAT IF--
GIVE ME THAT.
HEY!

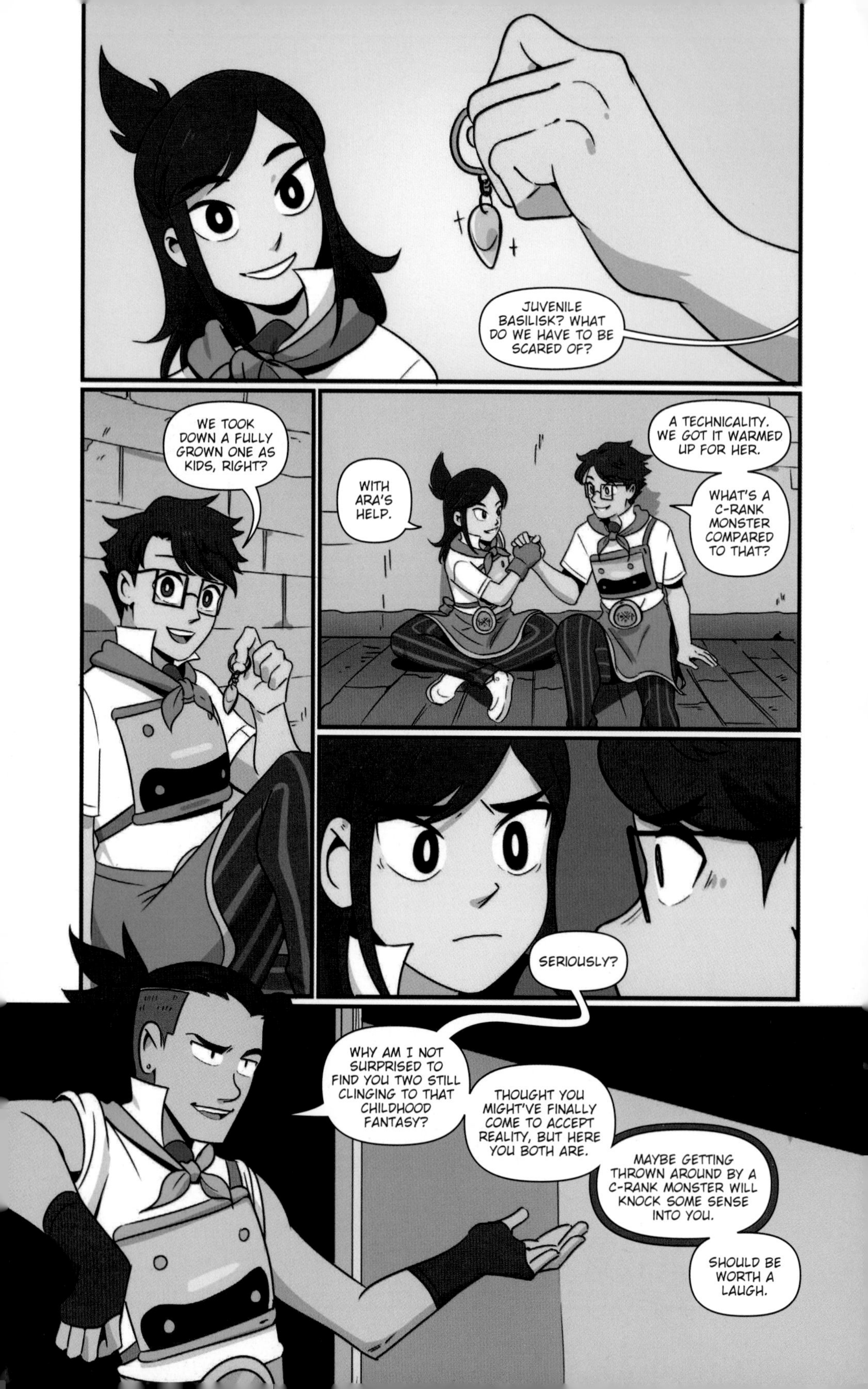
JUVENILE BASILISK? WHAT DO WE HAVE TO BE SCARED OF?
WE TOOK DOWN A FULLY GROWN ONE AS KIDS, RIGHT?
WITH ARA'S HELP.
A TECHNICALITY. WE GOT IT WARMED UP FOR HER.
WHAT'S A C-RANK MONSTER COMPARED TO THAT?
SERIOUSLY?
WHY AM I NOT SURPRISED TO FIND YOU TWO STILL CLINGING TO THAT CHILDHOOD FANTASY?
THOUGHT YOU MIGHT'VE FINALLY COME TO ACCEPT REALITY, BUT HERE YOU BOTH ARE.
MAYBE GETTING THROWN AROUND BY A C-RANK MONSTER WILL KNOCK SOME SENSE INTO YOU.
SHOULD BE WORTH A LAUGH.

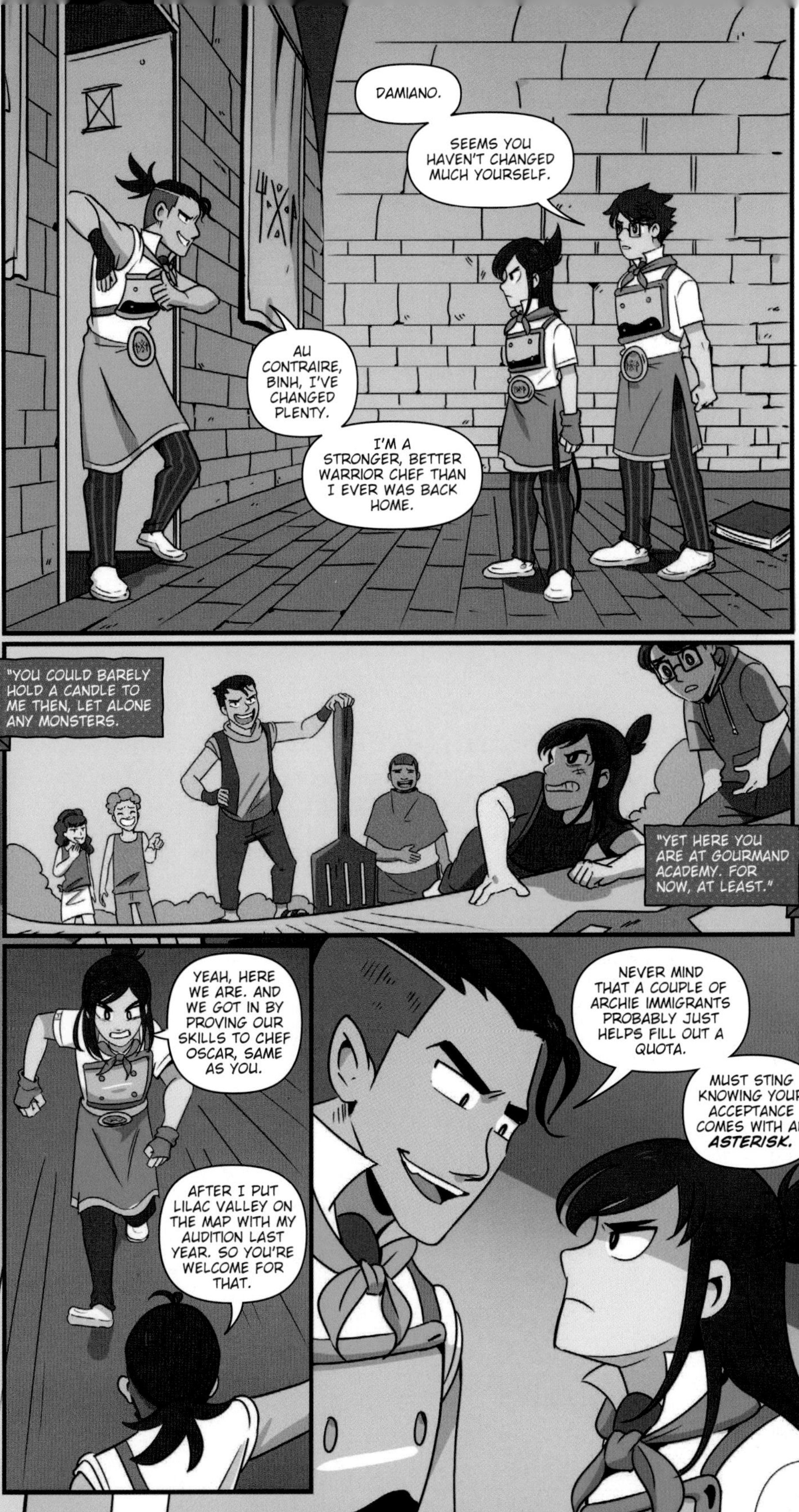
DAMIANO.
SEEMS YOU HAVEN'T CHANGED MUCH YOURSELF.
AU CONTRAIRE, BINH, I'VE CHANGED PLENTY.
I'M A STRONGER, BETTER WARRIOR CHEF THAN I EVER WAS BACK HOME.
"YOU COULD BARELY HOLD A CANDLE TO ME THEN, LET ALONE ANY MONSTERS.
"YET HERE YOU ARE AT GOURMAND ACADEMY. FOR NOW, AT LEAST."
YEAH, HERE WE ARE. AND WE GOT IN BY PROVING OUR SKILLS TO CHEF OSCAR, SAME AS YOU.
AFTER I PUT LILAC VALLEY ON THE MAP WITH MY AUDITION LAST YEAR. SO YOU'RE WELCOME FOR THAT.
NEVER MIND THAT A COUPLE OF ARCHIE IMMIGRANTS PROBABLY JUST HELPS FILL OUT A QUOTA.
MUST STING KNOWING YOUR ACCEPTANCE COMES WITH AN ***ASTERISK.***

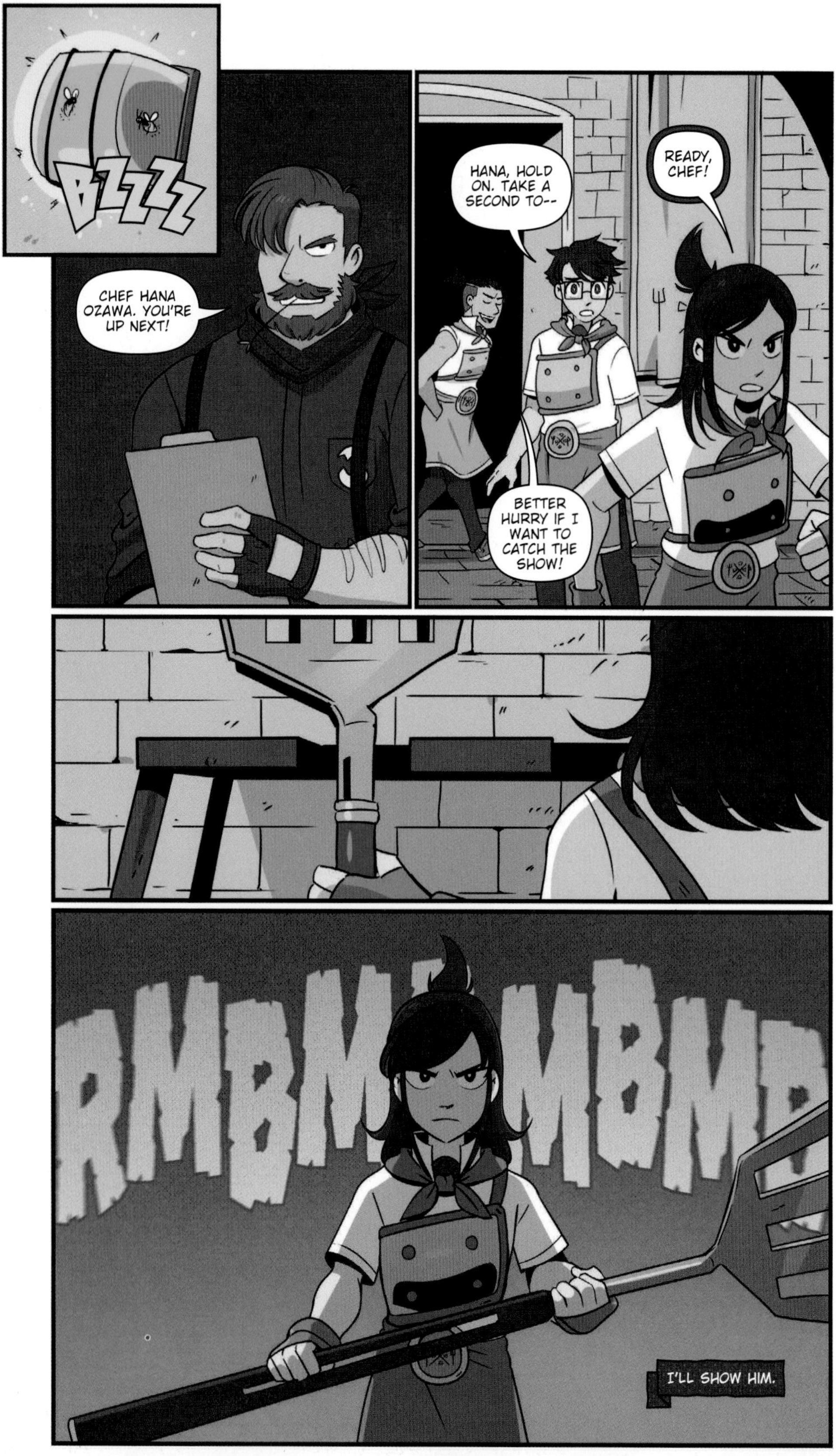
BZZZZ
CHEF HANA OZAWA. YOU'RE UP NEXT!
HANA, HOLD ON. TAKE A SECOND TO--
READY, CHEF!
BETTER HURRY IF I WANT TO CATCH THE SHOW!
RMBM MBM
I'LL SHOW HIM.

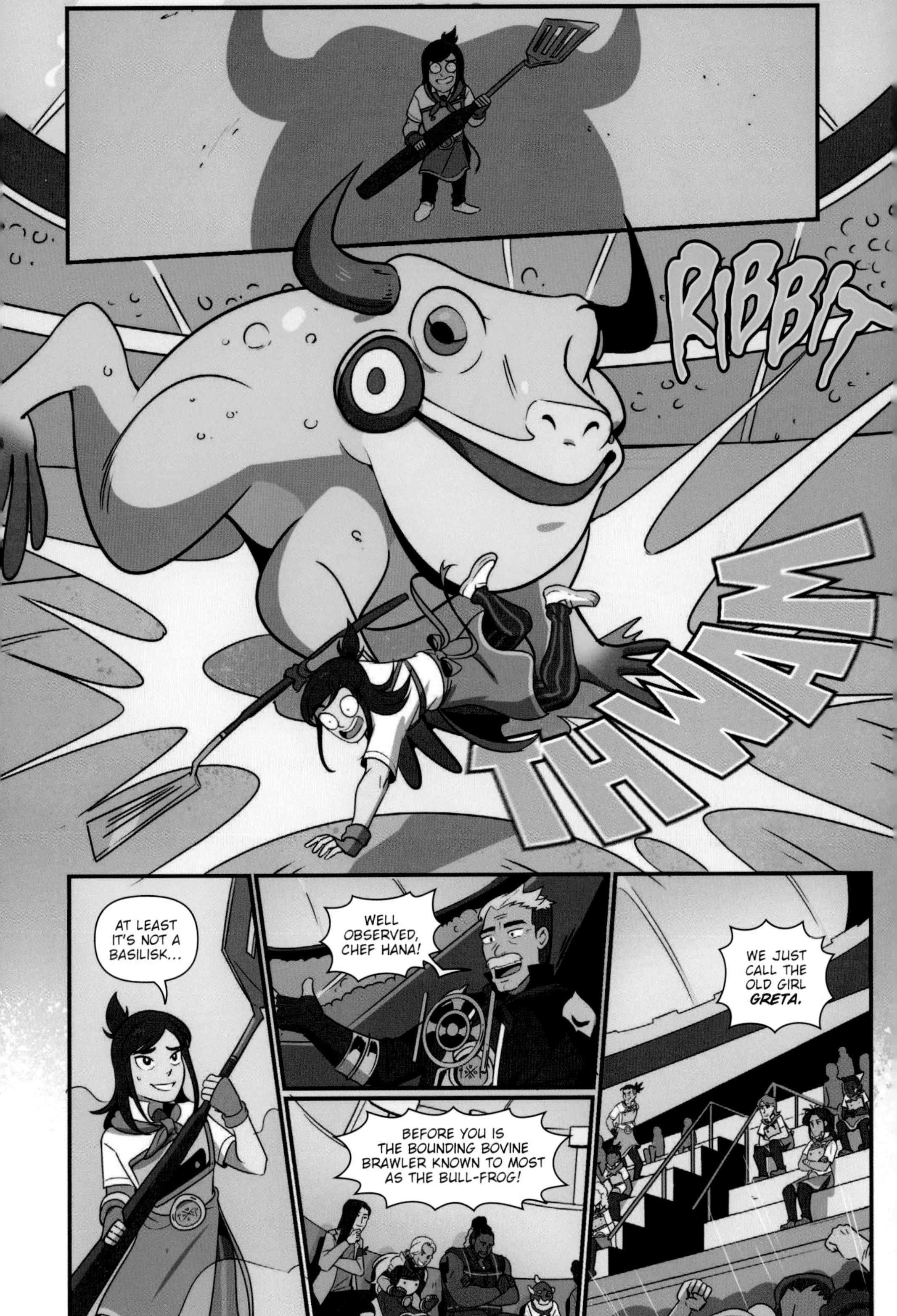
RIBBIT
THWAM
AT LEAST IT'S NOT A BASILISK...
WELL OBSERVED, CHEF HANA!
BEFORE YOU IS THE BOUNDING BOVINE BRAWLER KNOWN TO MOST AS THE BULL-FROG!
WE JUST CALL THE OLD GIRL ***GRETA.***

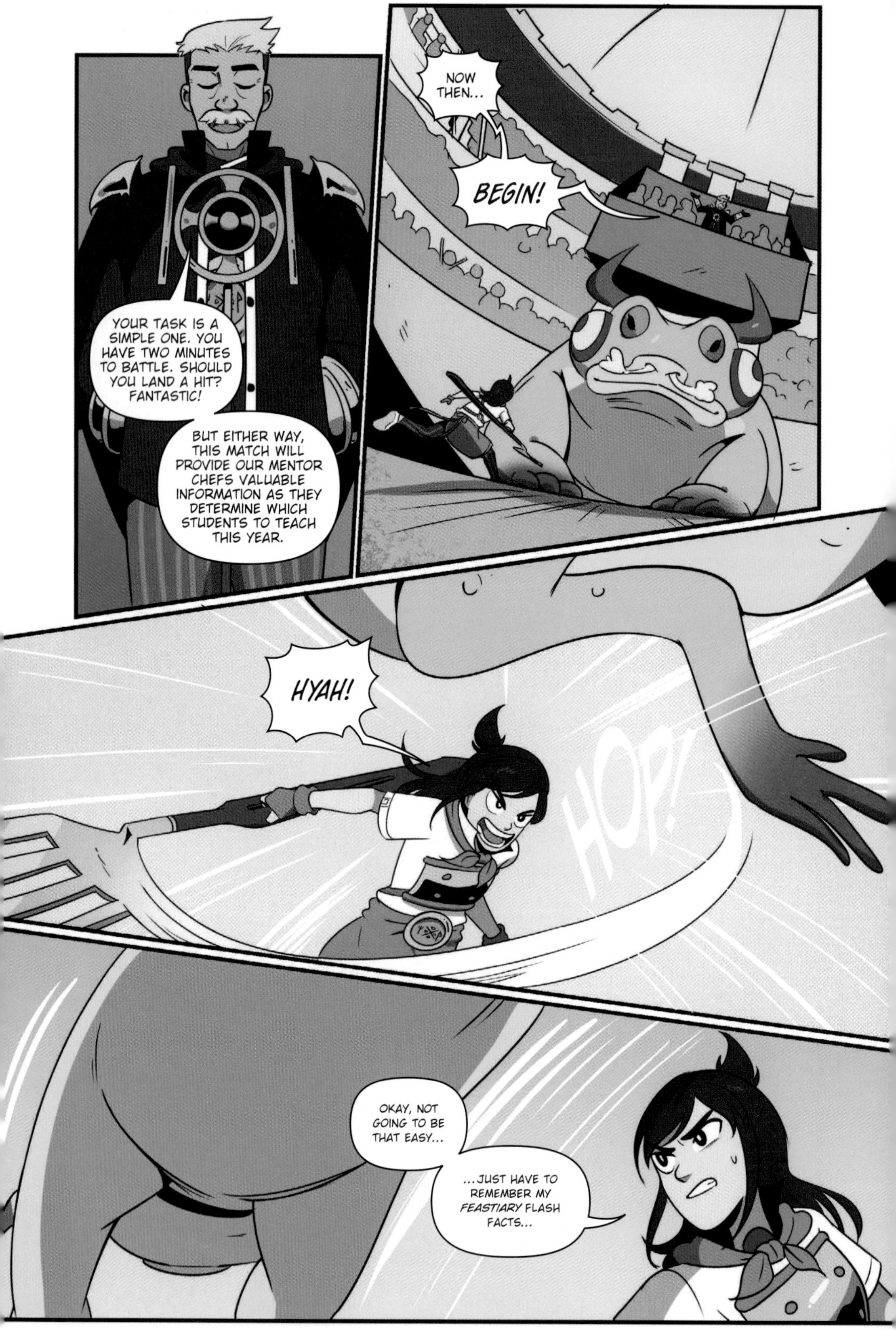
YOUR TASK IS A SIMPLE ONE. YOU HAVE TWO MINUTES TO BATTLE. SHOULD YOU LAND A HIT? FANTASTIC!
BUT EITHER WAY, THIS MATCH WILL PROVIDE OUR MENTOR CHEFS VALUABLE INFORMATION AS THEY DETERMINE WHICH STUDENTS TO TEACH THIS YEAR.
NOW THEN...
BEGIN!
HYAH!
HOP!
OKAY, NOT GOING TO BE THAT EASY...
...JUST HAVE TO REMEMBER MY *FEASTIARY* FLASH FACTS...

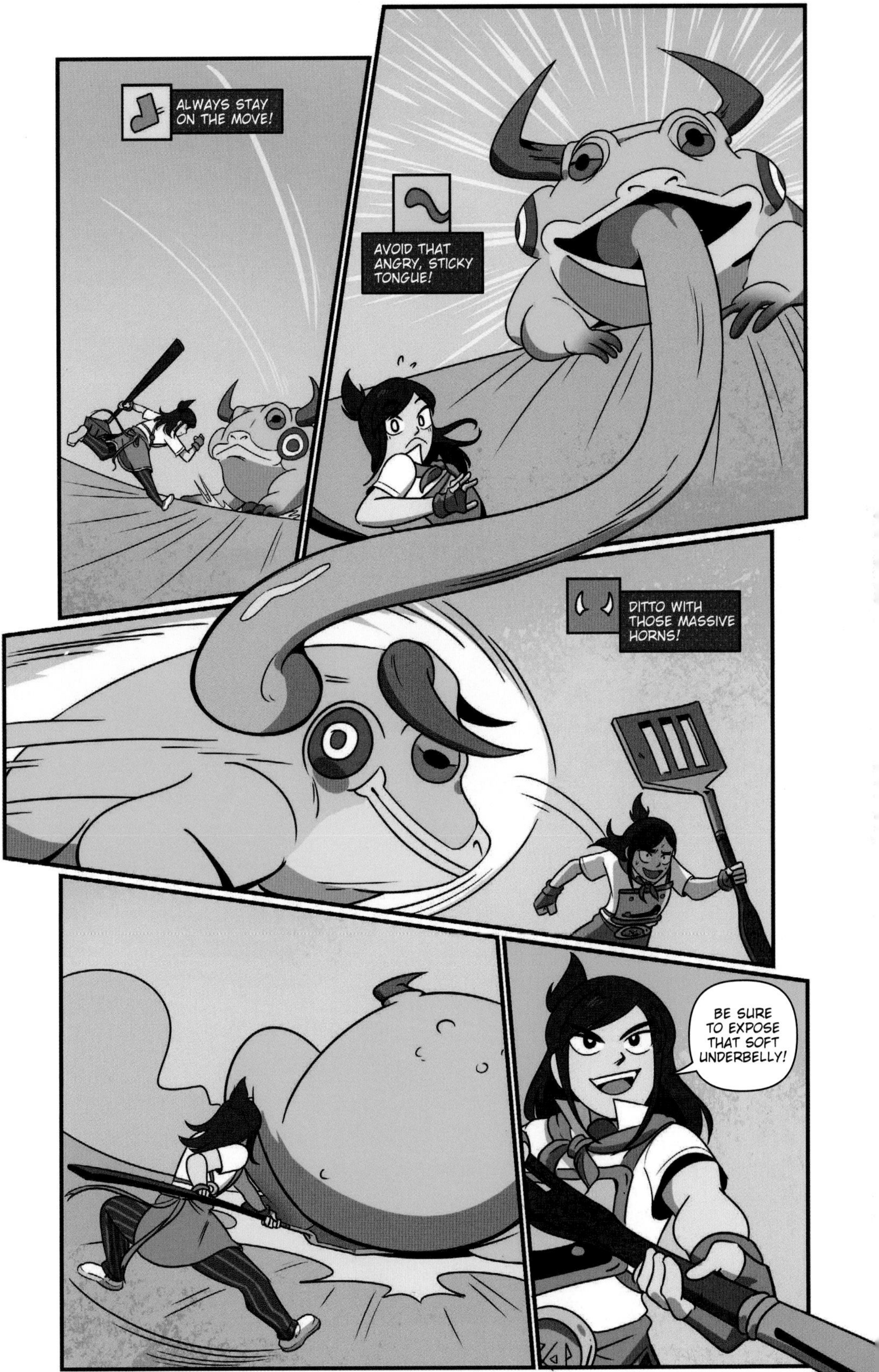
ALWAYS STAY ON THE MOVE!
AVOID THAT ANGRY, STICKY TONGUE!
DITTO WITH THOSE MASSIVE HORNS!
BE SURE TO EXPOSE THAT SOFT UNDERBELLY!

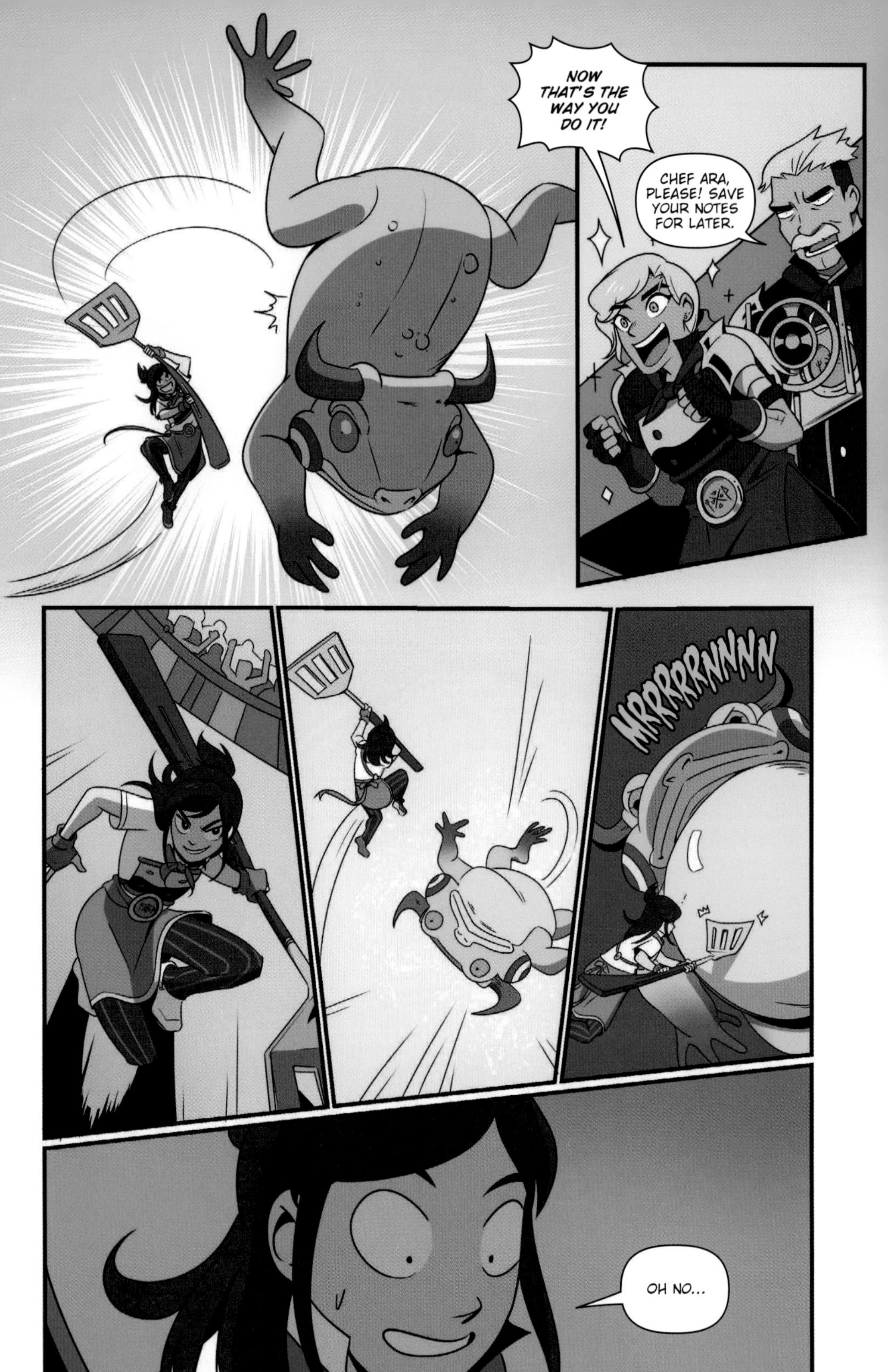
NOW THAT'S THE WAY YOU DO IT!
CHEF ARA, PLEASE! SAVE YOUR NOTES FOR LATER.
MRRRRNNNN
OH NO...

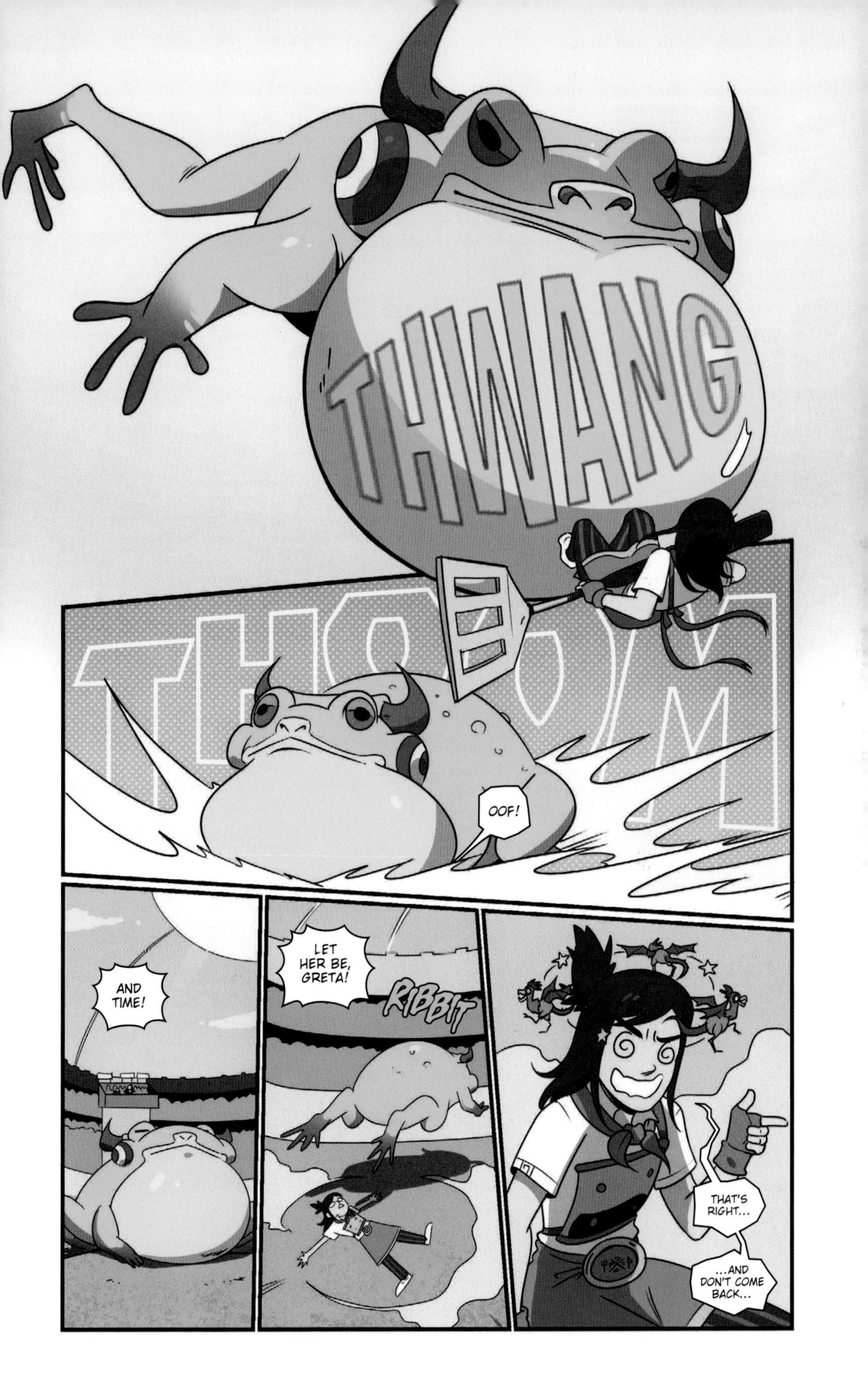
THWANG
THOOM
OOF!
AND TIME!
LET HER BE, GRETA!
RIBBIT
THAT'S RIGHT...
...AND DON'T COME BACK...

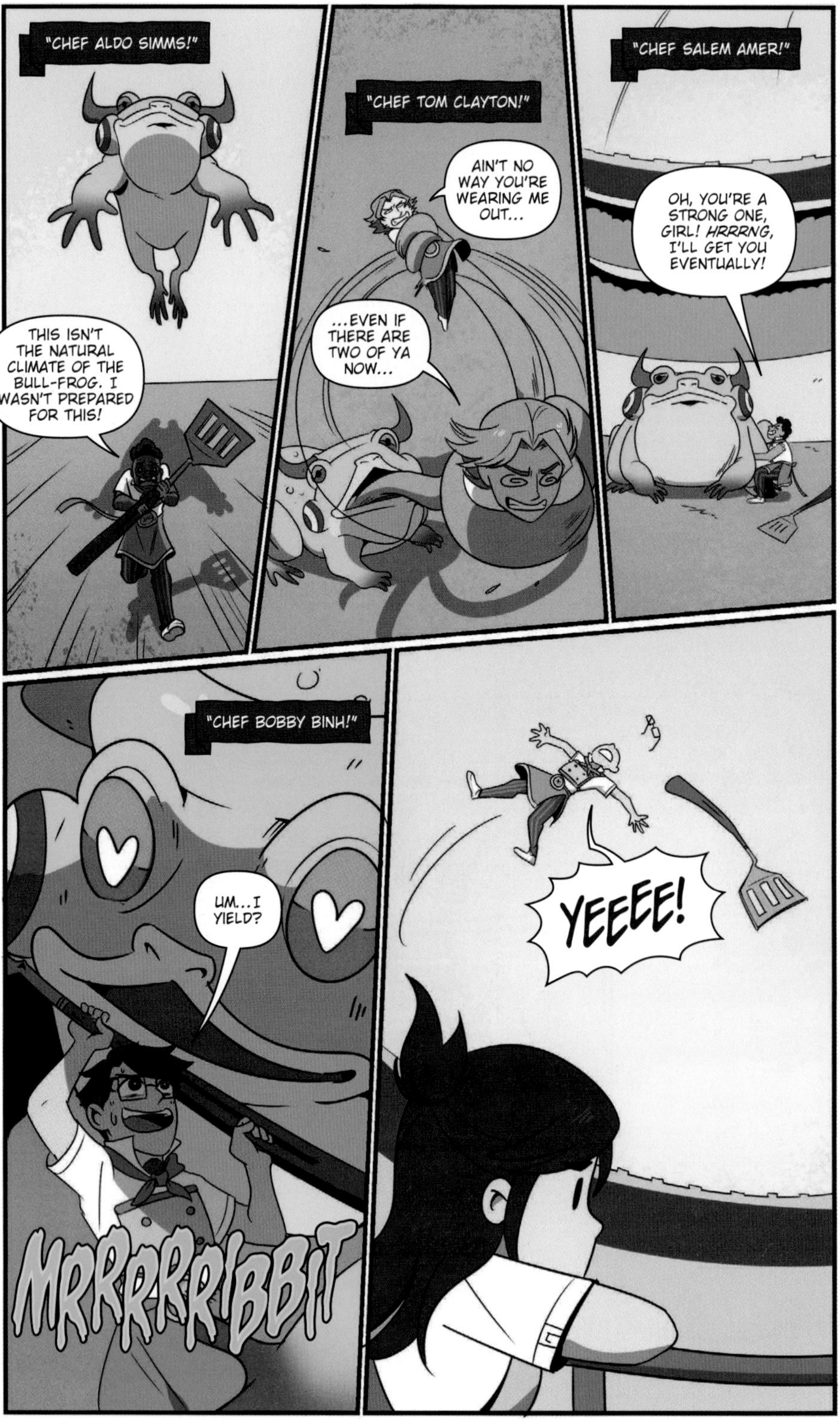
"CHEF ALDO SIMMS!"
THIS ISN'T THE NATURAL CLIMATE OF THE BULL-FROG. I WASN'T PREPARED FOR THIS!
"CHEF TOM CLAYTON!"
AIN'T NO WAY YOU'RE WEARING ME OUT...
...EVEN IF THERE ARE TWO OF YA NOW...
"CHEF SALEM AMER!"
OH, YOU'RE A STRONG ONE, GIRL! *HRRRNG*, I'LL GET YOU EVENTUALLY!
"CHEF BOBBY BINH!"
UM...I YIELD?
MRRRRRIBBIT
YEEEE!

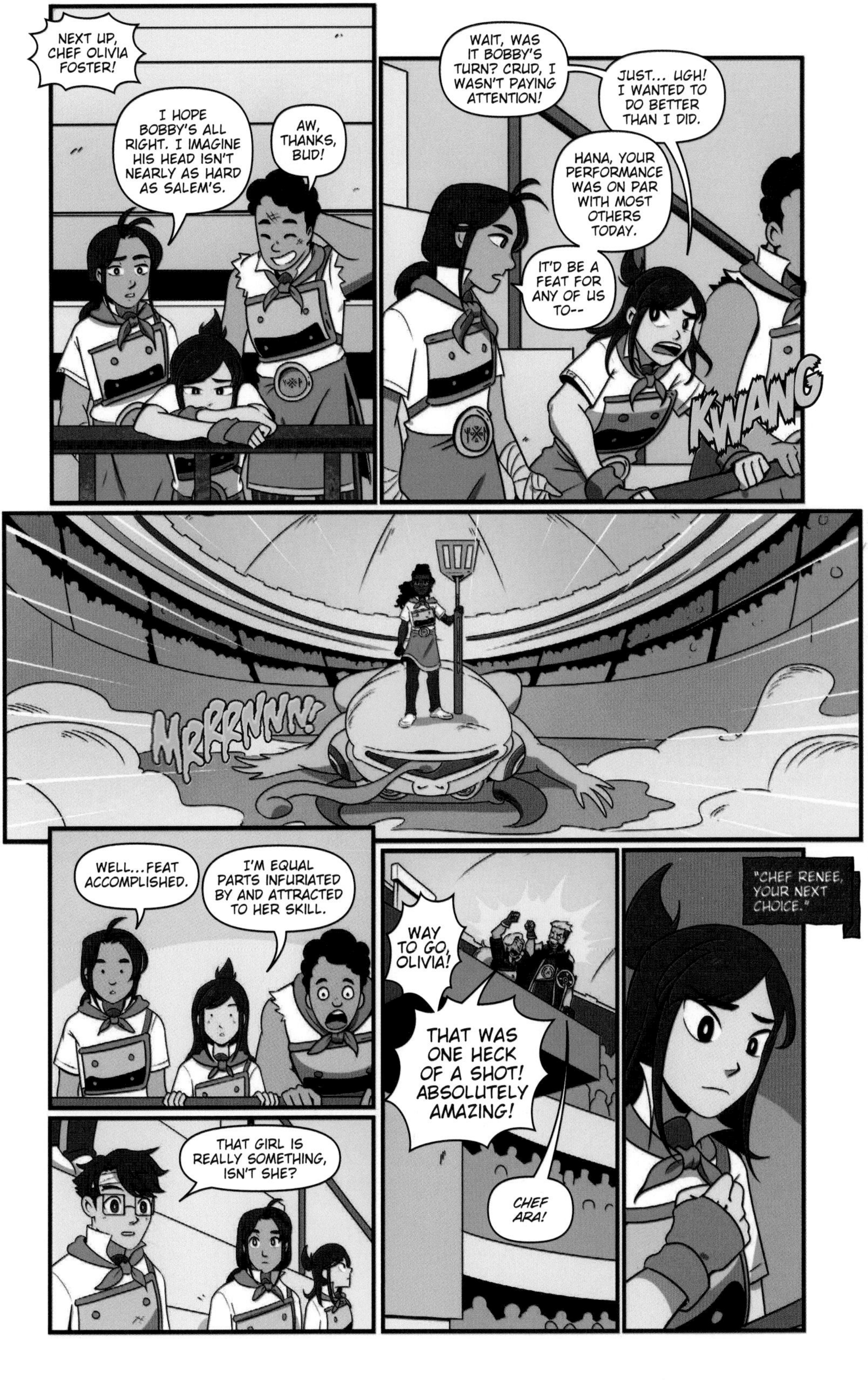
NEXT UP, CHEF OLIVIA FOSTER!
I HOPE BOBBY'S ALL RIGHT. I IMAGINE HIS HEAD ISN'T NEARLY AS HARD AS SALEM'S.
AW, THANKS, BUD!
WAIT, WAS IT BOBBY'S TURN? CRUD, I WASN'T PAYING ATTENTION!
JUST... UGH! I WANTED TO DO BETTER THAN I DID.
HANA, YOUR PERFORMANCE WAS ON PAR WITH MOST OTHERS TODAY.
IT'D BE A FEAT FOR ANY OF US TO--
KWANG
MRRRNNN!
WELL...FEAT ACCOMPLISHED.
I'M EQUAL PARTS INFURIATED BY AND ATTRACTED TO HER SKILL.
THAT GIRL IS REALLY SOMETHING, ISN'T SHE?
WAY TO GO, OLIVIA!
THAT WAS ONE HECK OF A SHOT! ABSOLUTELY AMAZING!
CHEF ARA!
"CHEF RENEE, YOUR NEXT CHOICE."

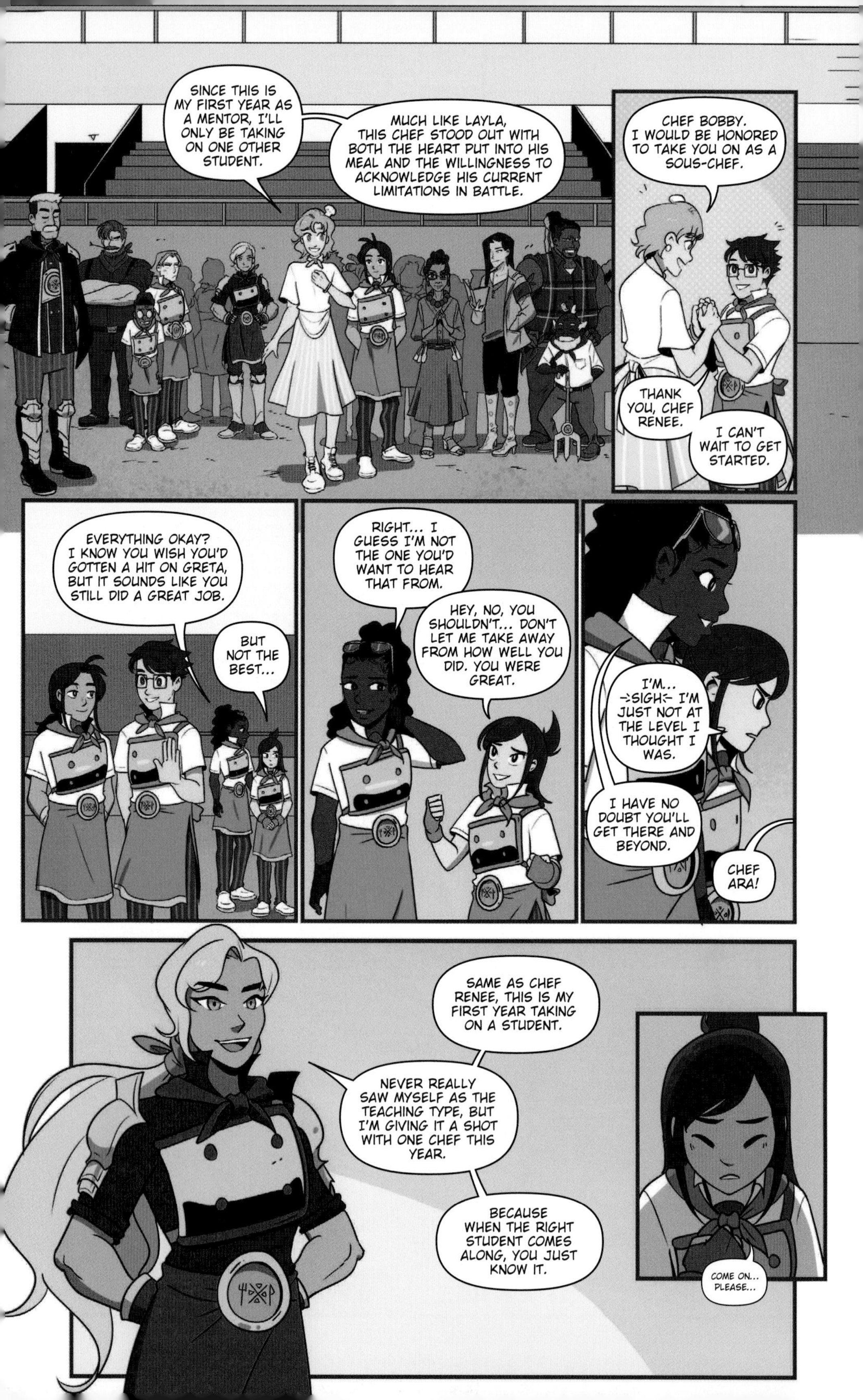
SINCE THIS IS MY FIRST YEAR AS A MENTOR, I'LL ONLY BE TAKING ON ONE OTHER STUDENT.
MUCH LIKE LAYLA, THIS CHEF STOOD OUT WITH BOTH THE HEART PUT INTO HIS MEAL AND THE WILLINGNESS TO ACKNOWLEDGE HIS CURRENT LIMITATIONS IN BATTLE.
CHEF BOBBY. I WOULD BE HONORED TO TAKE YOU ON AS A SOUS-CHEF.
THANK YOU, CHEF RENEE.
I CAN'T WAIT TO GET STARTED.
EVERYTHING OKAY? I KNOW YOU WISH YOU'D GOTTEN A HIT ON GRETA, BUT IT SOUNDS LIKE YOU STILL DID A GREAT JOB.
BUT NOT THE BEST...
RIGHT... I GUESS I'M NOT THE ONE YOU'D WANT TO HEAR THAT FROM.
HEY, NO, YOU SHOULDN'T... DON'T LET ME TAKE AWAY FROM HOW WELL YOU DID. YOU WERE GREAT.
I'M... →SIGH← I'M JUST NOT AT THE LEVEL I THOUGHT I WAS.
I HAVE NO DOUBT YOU'LL GET THERE AND BEYOND.
CHEF ARA!
SAME AS CHEF RENEE, THIS IS MY FIRST YEAR TAKING ON A STUDENT.
NEVER REALLY SAW MYSELF AS THE TEACHING TYPE, BUT I'M GIVING IT A SHOT WITH ONE CHEF THIS YEAR.
BECAUSE WHEN THE RIGHT STUDENT COMES ALONG, YOU JUST KNOW IT.
COME ON... PLEASE...

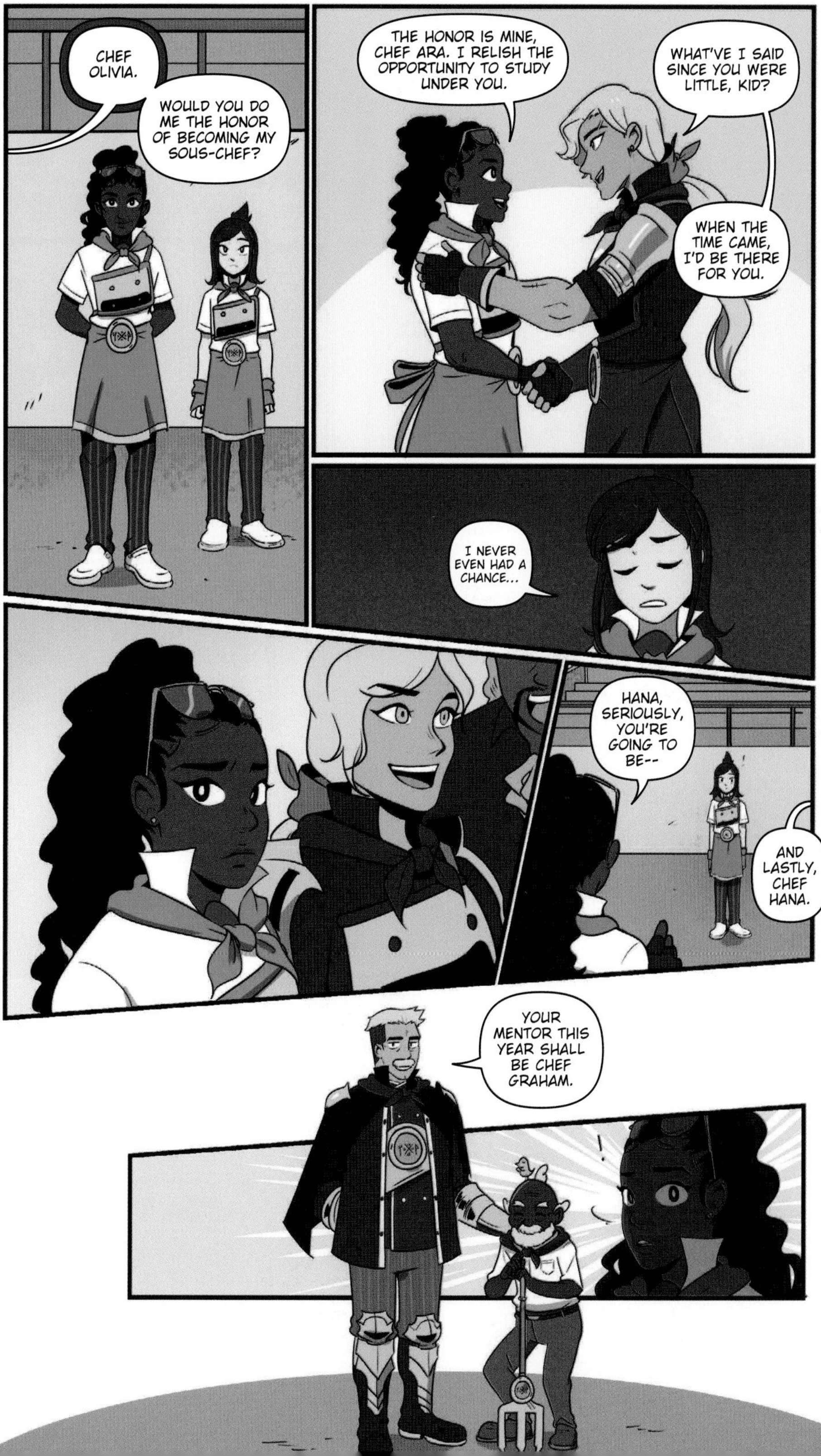
CHEF OLIVIA.
WOULD YOU DO ME THE HONOR OF BECOMING MY SOUS-CHEF?
THE HONOR IS MINE, CHEF ARA. I RELISH THE OPPORTUNITY TO STUDY UNDER YOU.
WHAT'VE I SAID SINCE YOU WERE LITTLE, KID?
WHEN THE TIME CAME, I'D BE THERE FOR YOU.
I NEVER EVEN HAD A CHANCE...
HANA, SERIOUSLY, YOU'RE GOING TO BE--
AND LASTLY, CHEF HANA.
YOUR MENTOR THIS YEAR SHALL BE CHEF GRAHAM.

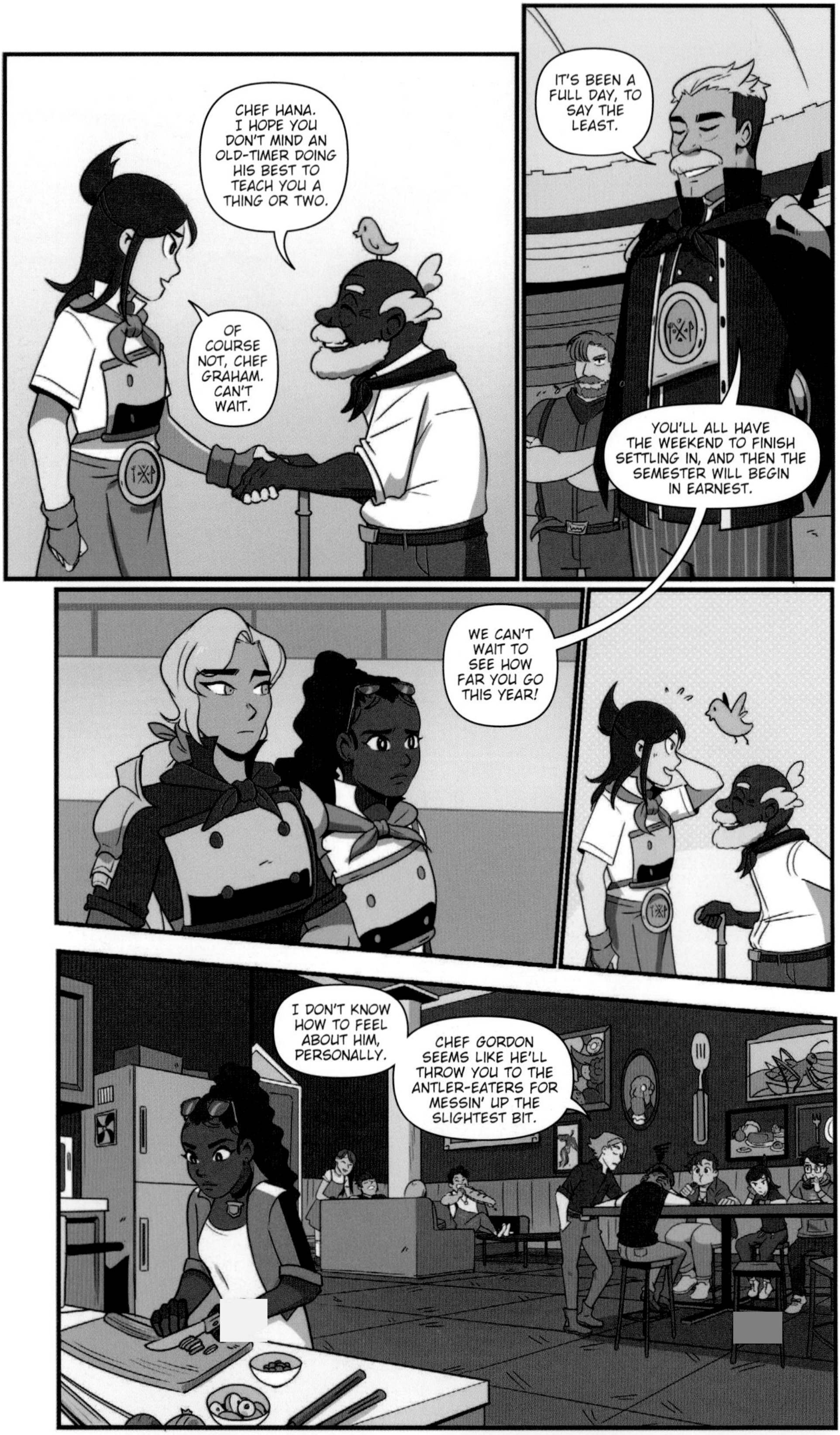
CHEF HANA. I HOPE YOU DON'T MIND AN OLD-TIMER DOING HIS BEST TO TEACH YOU A THING OR TWO.
OF COURSE NOT, CHEF GRAHAM. CAN'T WAIT.
IT'S BEEN A FULL DAY, TO SAY THE LEAST.
YOU'LL ALL HAVE THE WEEKEND TO FINISH SETTLING IN, AND THEN THE SEMESTER WILL BEGIN IN EARNEST.
WE CAN'T WAIT TO SEE HOW FAR YOU GO THIS YEAR!
I DON'T KNOW HOW TO FEEL ABOUT HIM, PERSONALLY.
CHEF GORDON SEEMS LIKE HE'LL THROW YOU TO THE ANTLER-EATERS FOR MESSIN' UP THE SLIGHTEST BIT.

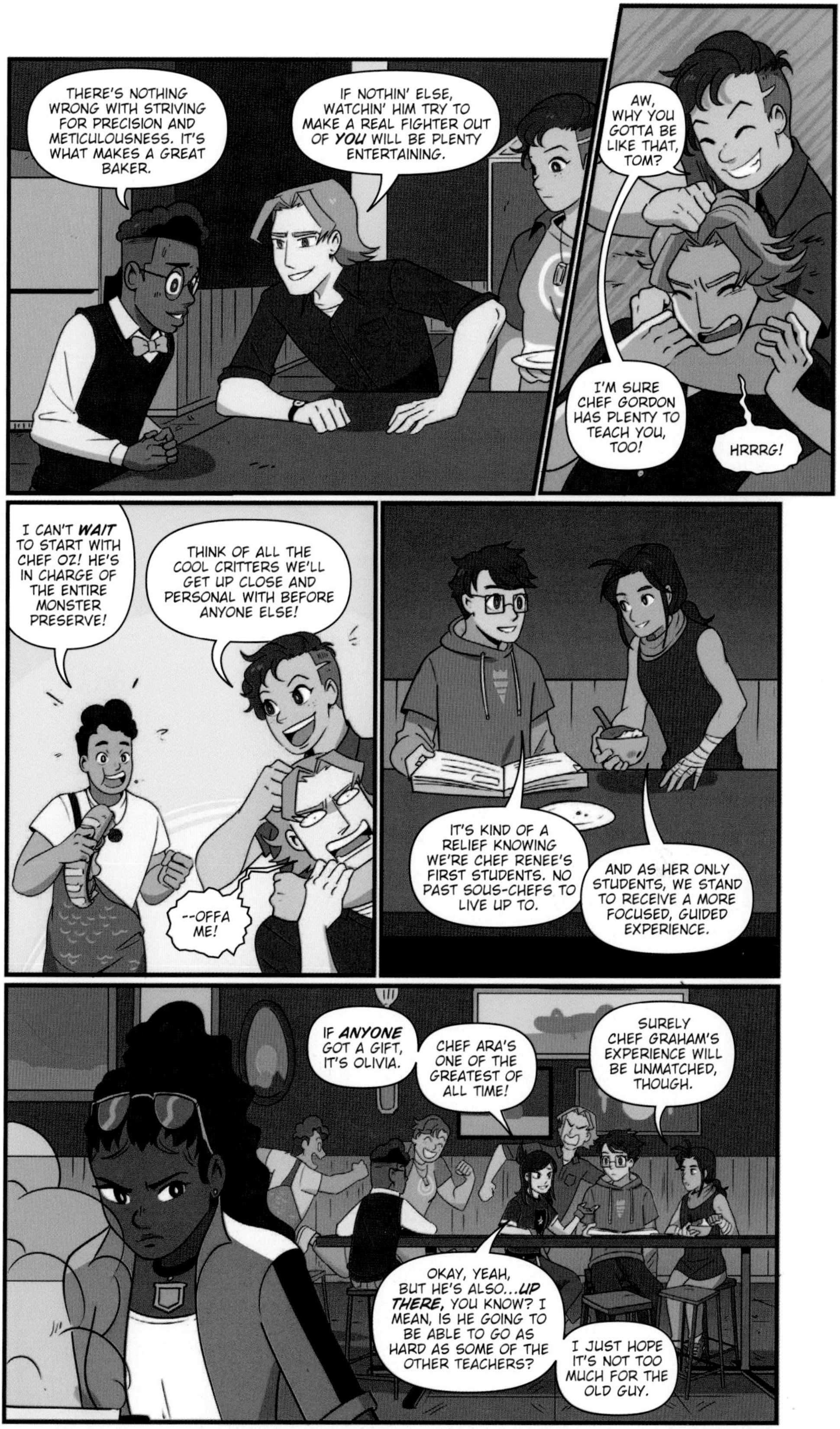
THERE'S NOTHING WRONG WITH STRIVING FOR PRECISION AND METICULOUSNESS. IT'S WHAT MAKES A GREAT BAKER.
IF NOTHIN' ELSE, WATCHIN' HIM TRY TO MAKE A REAL FIGHTER OUT OF *YOU* WILL BE PLENTY ENTERTAINING.
AW, WHY YOU GOTTA BE LIKE THAT, TOM?
I'M SURE CHEF GORDON HAS PLENTY TO TEACH YOU, TOO!
HRRRG!
I CAN'T *WAIT* TO START WITH CHEF OZ! HE'S IN CHARGE OF THE ENTIRE MONSTER PRESERVE!
THINK OF ALL THE COOL CRITTERS WE'LL GET UP CLOSE AND PERSONAL WITH BEFORE ANYONE ELSE!
--OFFA ME!
IT'S KIND OF A RELIEF KNOWING WE'RE CHEF RENEE'S FIRST STUDENTS. NO PAST SOUS-CHEFS TO LIVE UP TO.
AND AS HER ONLY STUDENTS, WE STAND TO RECEIVE A MORE FOCUSED, GUIDED EXPERIENCE.
IF *ANYONE* GOT A GIFT, IT'S OLIVIA.
CHEF ARA'S ONE OF THE GREATEST OF ALL TIME!
SURELY CHEF GRAHAM'S EXPERIENCE WILL BE UNMATCHED, THOUGH.
OKAY, YEAH, BUT HE'S ALSO...*UP THERE*, YOU KNOW? I MEAN, IS HE GOING TO BE ABLE TO GO AS HARD AS SOME OF THE OTHER TEACHERS?
I JUST HOPE IT'S NOT TOO MUCH FOR THE OLD GUY.

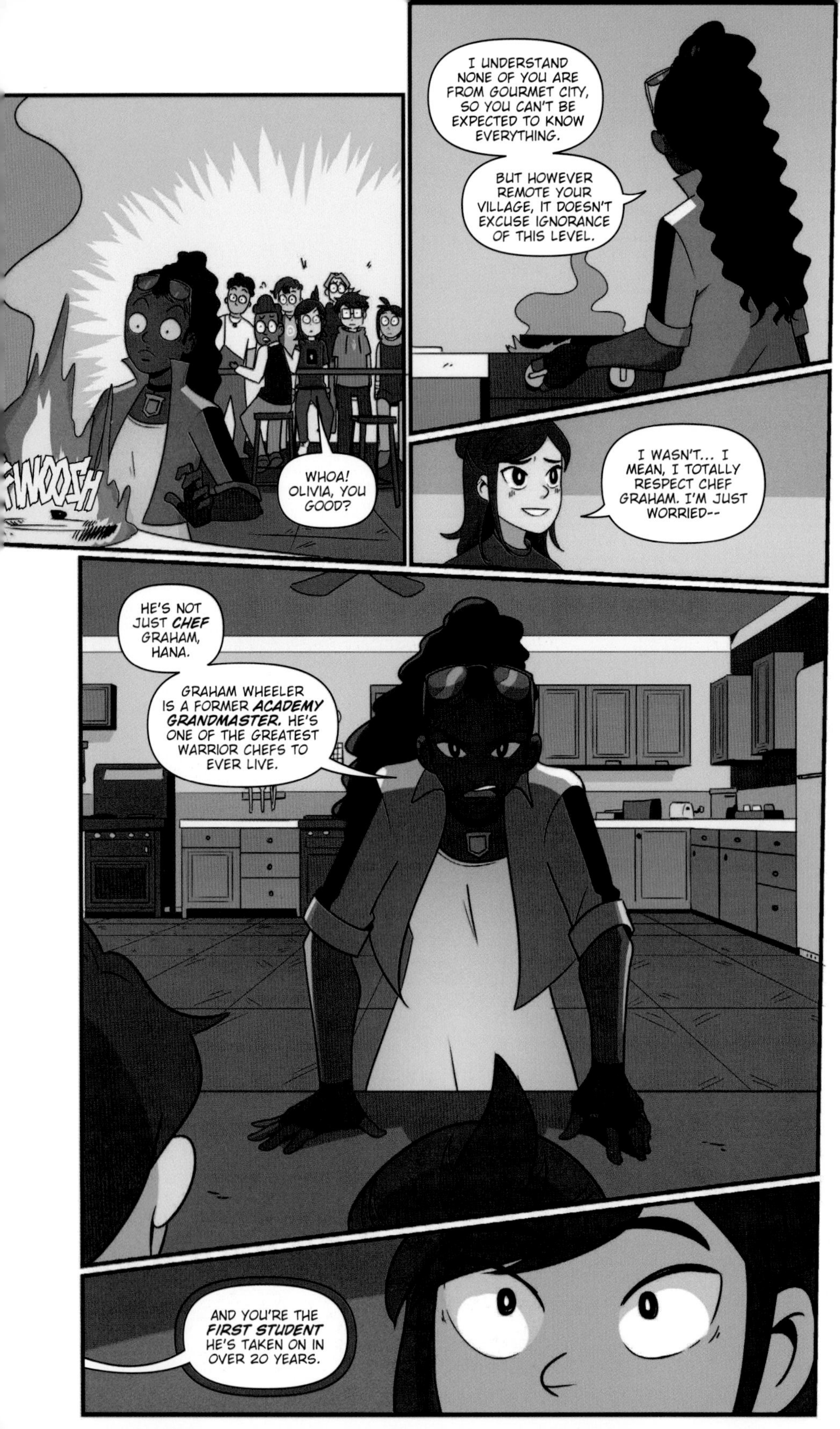
FWOOSH
WHOA! OLIVIA, YOU GOOD?
I UNDERSTAND NONE OF YOU ARE FROM GOURMET CITY, SO YOU CAN'T BE EXPECTED TO KNOW EVERYTHING.
BUT HOWEVER REMOTE YOUR VILLAGE, IT DOESN'T EXCUSE IGNORANCE OF THIS LEVEL.
I WASN'T... I MEAN, I TOTALLY RESPECT CHEF GRAHAM. I'M JUST WORRIED--
HE'S NOT JUST CHEF GRAHAM, HANA.
GRAHAM WHEELER IS A FORMER ACADEMY GRANDMASTER. HE'S ONE OF THE GREATEST WARRIOR CHEFS TO EVER LIVE.
AND YOU'RE THE FIRST STUDENT HE'S TAKEN ON IN OVER 20 YEARS.

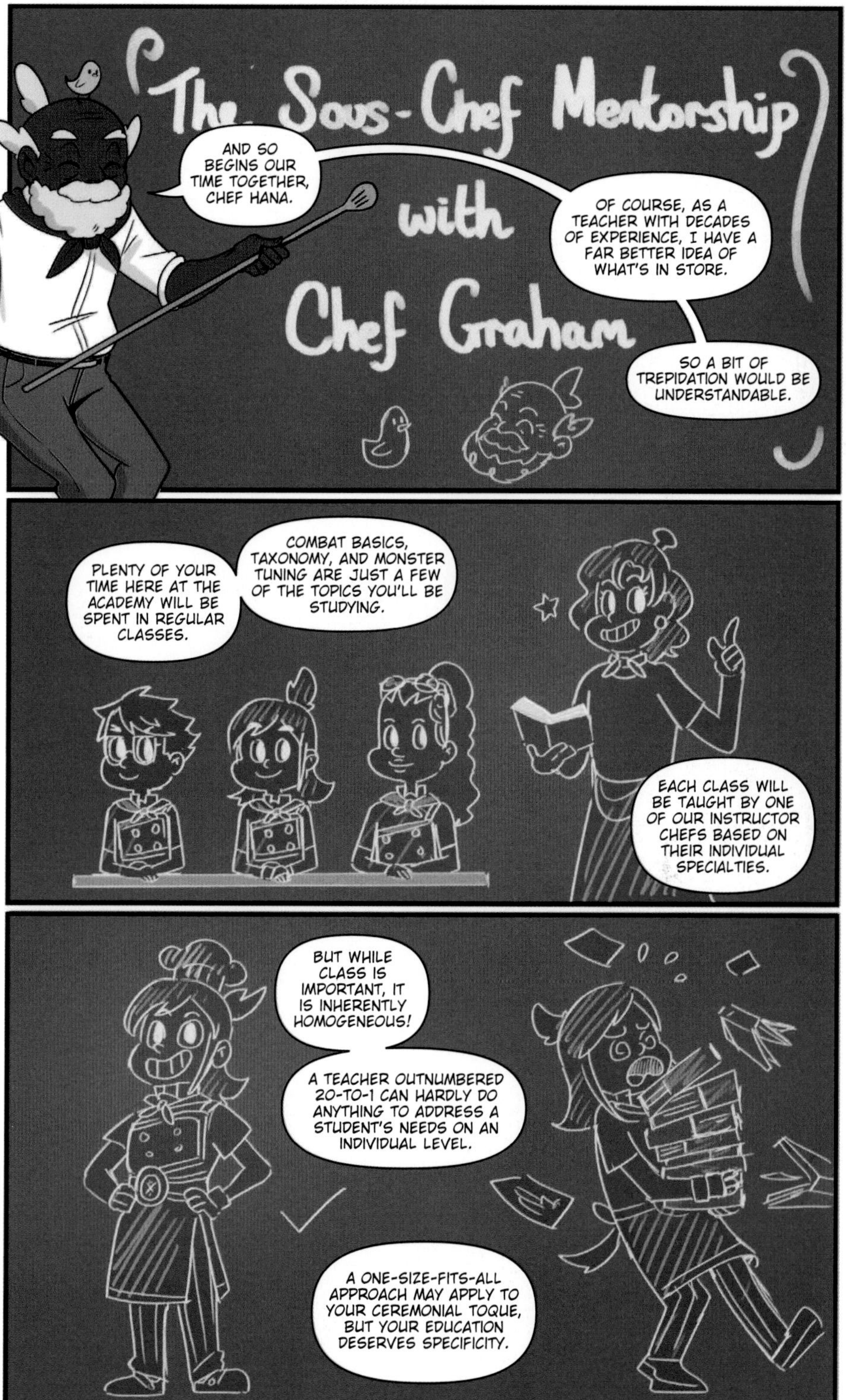
The Sous-Chef Mentorship with Chef Graham
AND SO BEGINS OUR TIME TOGETHER, CHEF HANA.
OF COURSE, AS A TEACHER WITH DECADES OF EXPERIENCE, I HAVE A FAR BETTER IDEA OF WHAT'S IN STORE.
SO A BIT OF TREPIDATION WOULD BE UNDERSTANDABLE.
PLENTY OF YOUR TIME HERE AT THE ACADEMY WILL BE SPENT IN REGULAR CLASSES.
COMBAT BASICS, TAXONOMY, AND MONSTER TUNING ARE JUST A FEW OF THE TOPICS YOU'LL BE STUDYING.
EACH CLASS WILL BE TAUGHT BY ONE OF OUR INSTRUCTOR CHEFS BASED ON THEIR INDIVIDUAL SPECIALTIES.
BUT WHILE CLASS IS IMPORTANT, IT IS INHERENTLY HOMOGENEOUS!
A TEACHER OUTNUMBERED 20-TO-1 CAN HARDLY DO ANYTHING TO ADDRESS A STUDENT'S NEEDS ON AN INDIVIDUAL LEVEL.
A ONE-SIZE-FITS-ALL APPROACH MAY APPLY TO YOUR CEREMONIAL TOQUE, BUT YOUR EDUCATION DESERVES SPECIFICITY.

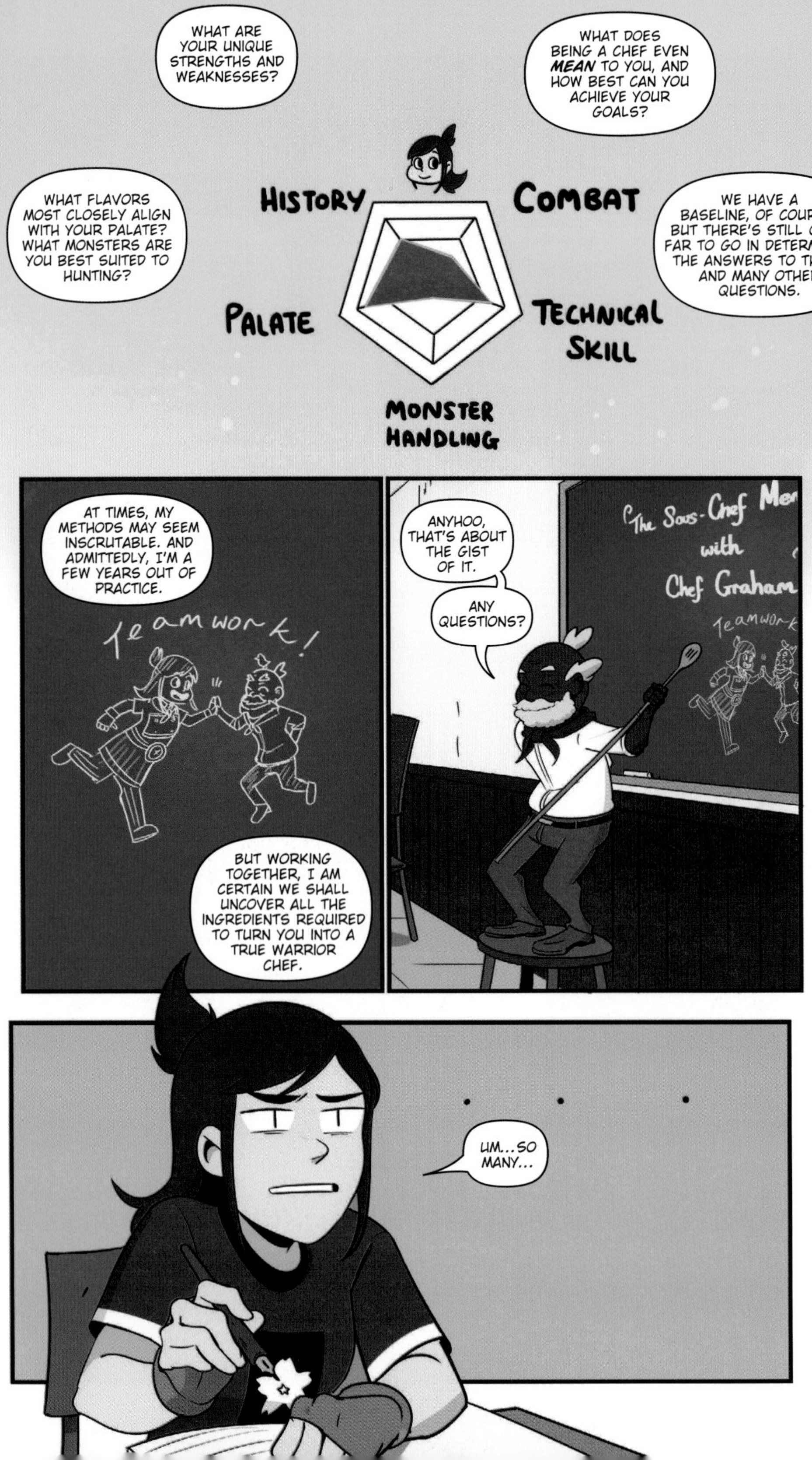
WHAT ARE YOUR UNIQUE STRENGTHS AND WEAKNESSES?
WHAT DOES BEING A CHEF EVEN MEAN TO YOU, AND HOW BEST CAN YOU ACHIEVE YOUR GOALS?
WHAT FLAVORS MOST CLOSELY ALIGN WITH YOUR PALATE? WHAT MONSTERS ARE YOU BEST SUITED TO HUNTING?
HISTORY
COMBAT
PALATE
TECHNICAL SKILL
MONSTER HANDLING
WE HAVE A BASELINE, OF COURSE, BUT THERE'S STILL QUITE FAR TO GO IN DETERMINING THE ANSWERS TO THOSE AND MANY OTHER QUESTIONS.
AT TIMES, MY METHODS MAY SEEM INSCRUTABLE. AND ADMITTEDLY, I'M A FEW YEARS OUT OF PRACTICE.
Teamwork!
BUT WORKING TOGETHER, I AM CERTAIN WE SHALL UNCOVER ALL THE INGREDIENTS REQUIRED TO TURN YOU INTO A TRUE WARRIOR CHEF.
The Sous-Chef
with
Chef Graham
Teamwork
ANYHOO, THAT'S ABOUT THE GIST OF IT.
ANY QUESTIONS?
. . .
UM...SO MANY...

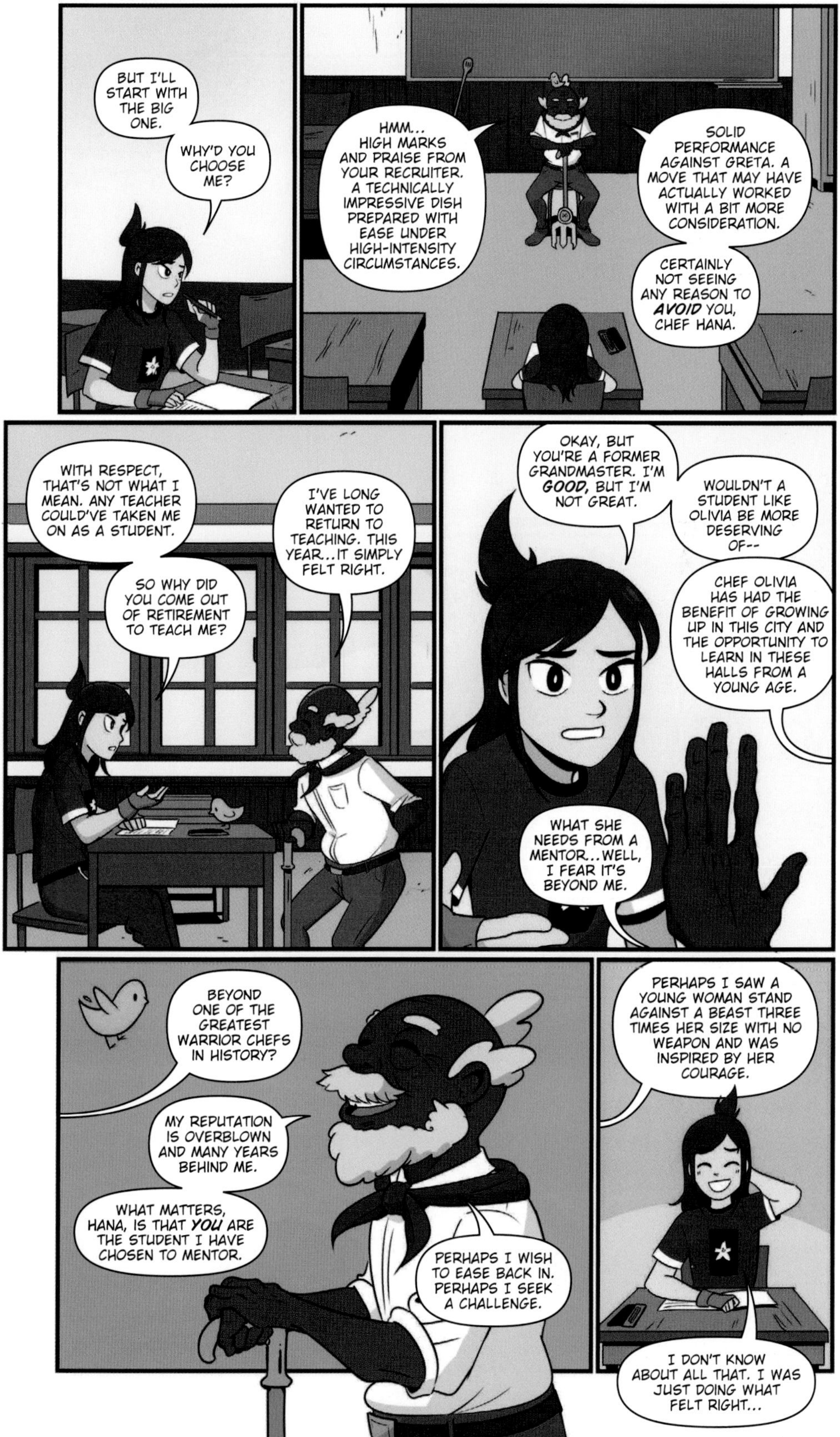
BUT I'LL START WITH THE BIG ONE.
WHY'D YOU CHOOSE ME?
HMM... HIGH MARKS AND PRAISE FROM YOUR RECRUITER. A TECHNICALLY IMPRESSIVE DISH PREPARED WITH EASE UNDER HIGH-INTENSITY CIRCUMSTANCES.
SOLID PERFORMANCE AGAINST GRETA. A MOVE THAT MAY HAVE ACTUALLY WORKED WITH A BIT MORE CONSIDERATION.
CERTAINLY NOT SEEING ANY REASON TO AVOID YOU, CHEF HANA.
WITH RESPECT, THAT'S NOT WHAT I MEAN. ANY TEACHER COULD'VE TAKEN ME ON AS A STUDENT.
SO WHY DID YOU COME OUT OF RETIREMENT TO TEACH ME?
I'VE LONG WANTED TO RETURN TO TEACHING. THIS YEAR...IT SIMPLY FELT RIGHT.
OKAY, BUT YOU'RE A FORMER GRANDMASTER. I'M GOOD, BUT I'M NOT GREAT.
WOULDN'T A STUDENT LIKE OLIVIA BE MORE DESERVING OF--
CHEF OLIVIA HAS HAD THE BENEFIT OF GROWING UP IN THIS CITY AND THE OPPORTUNITY TO LEARN IN THESE HALLS FROM A YOUNG AGE.
WHAT SHE NEEDS FROM A MENTOR...WELL, I FEAR IT'S BEYOND ME.
BEYOND ONE OF THE GREATEST WARRIOR CHEFS IN HISTORY?
MY REPUTATION IS OVERBLOWN AND MANY YEARS BEHIND ME.
WHAT MATTERS, HANA, IS THAT YOU ARE THE STUDENT I HAVE CHOSEN TO MENTOR.
PERHAPS I WISH TO EASE BACK IN. PERHAPS I SEEK A CHALLENGE.
PERHAPS I SAW A YOUNG WOMAN STAND AGAINST A BEAST THREE TIMES HER SIZE WITH NO WEAPON AND WAS INSPIRED BY HER COURAGE.
I DON'T KNOW ABOUT ALL THAT. I WAS JUST DOING WHAT FELT RIGHT...

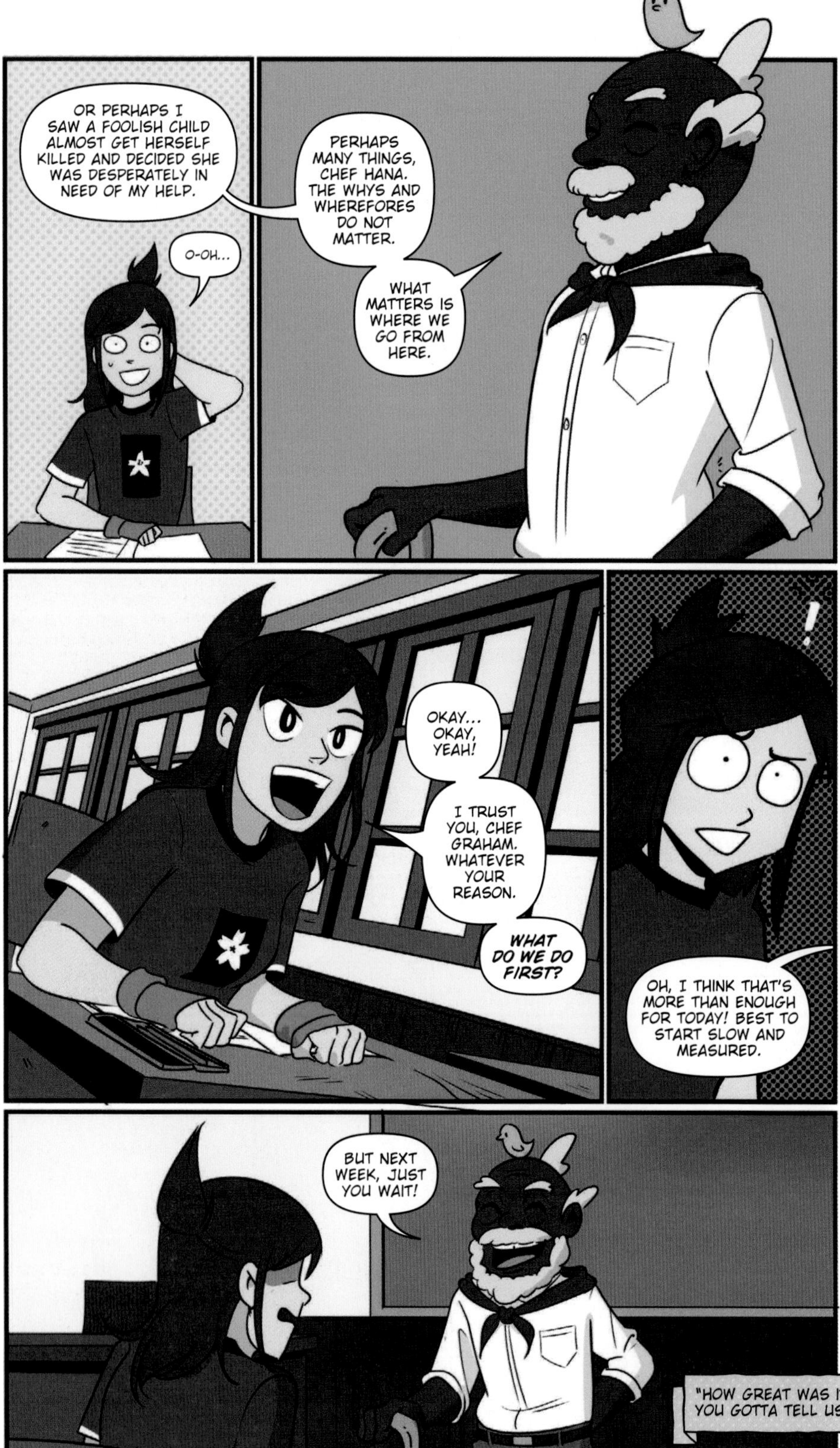
OR PERHAPS I SAW A FOOLISH CHILD ALMOST GET HERSELF KILLED AND DECIDED SHE WAS DESPERATELY IN NEED OF MY HELP.
O-OH...
PERHAPS MANY THINGS, CHEF HANA. THE WHYS AND WHEREFORES DO NOT MATTER.
WHAT MATTERS IS WHERE WE GO FROM HERE.
OKAY... OKAY, YEAH!
I TRUST YOU, CHEF GRAHAM. WHATEVER YOUR REASON.
WHAT DO WE DO FIRST?
!
OH, I THINK THAT'S MORE THAN ENOUGH FOR TODAY! BEST TO START SLOW AND MEASURED.
BUT NEXT WEEK, JUST YOU WAIT!
"HOW GREAT WAS IT? YOU GOTTA TELL US!"

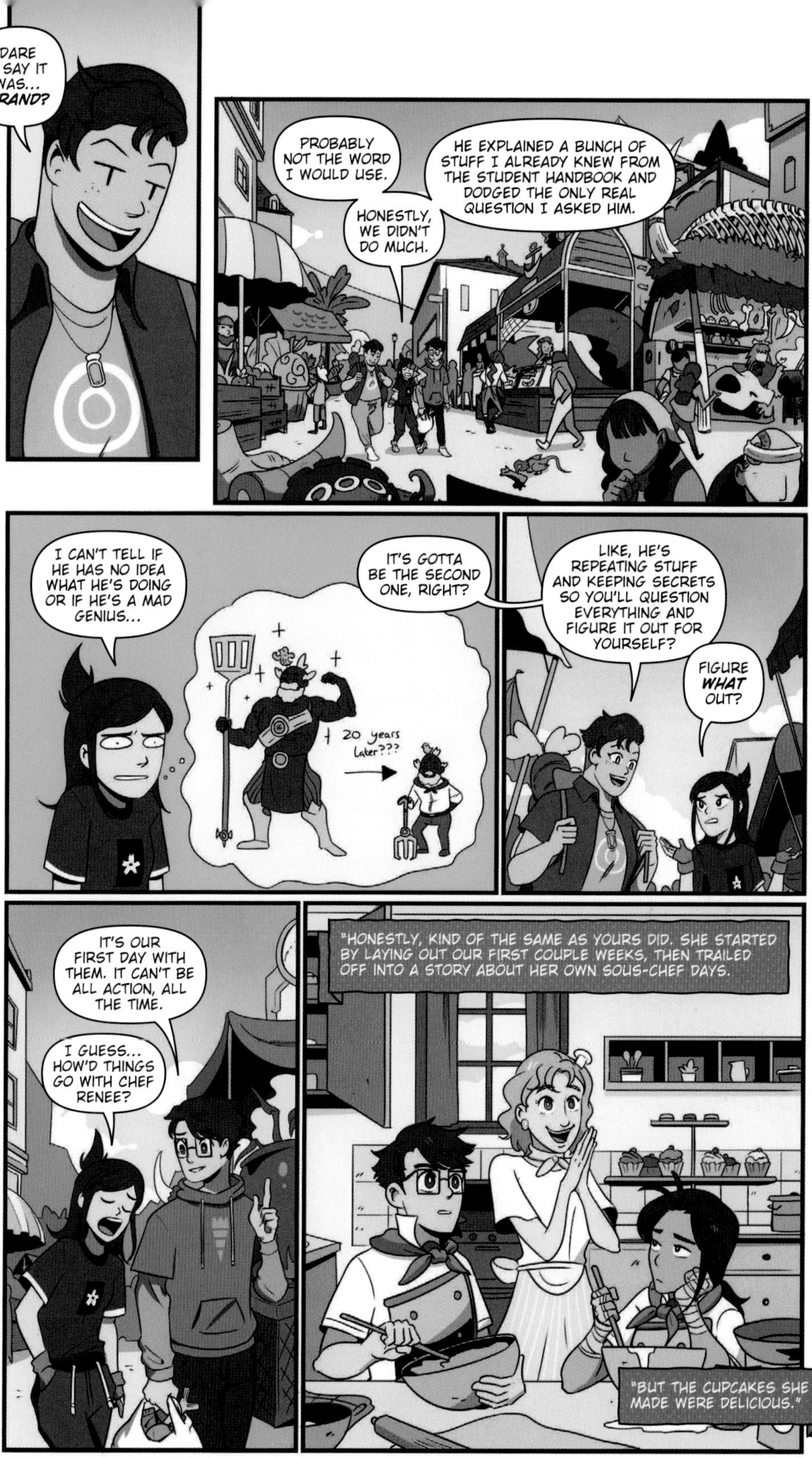

DARE I SAY IT WAS... *GRAND?*
PROBABLY NOT THE WORD I WOULD USE.
HONESTLY, WE DIDN'T DO MUCH.
HE EXPLAINED A BUNCH OF STUFF I ALREADY KNEW FROM THE STUDENT HANDBOOK AND DODGED THE ONLY REAL QUESTION I ASKED HIM.
I CAN'T TELL IF HE HAS NO IDEA WHAT HE'S DOING OR IF HE'S A MAD GENIUS...
20 years later???
IT'S GOTTA BE THE SECOND ONE, RIGHT?
LIKE, HE'S REPEATING STUFF AND KEEPING SECRETS SO YOU'LL QUESTION EVERYTHING AND FIGURE IT OUT FOR YOURSELF?
FIGURE *WHAT* OUT?
IT'S OUR FIRST DAY WITH THEM. IT CAN'T BE ALL ACTION, ALL THE TIME.
I GUESS... HOW'D THINGS GO WITH CHEF RENEE?
"HONESTLY, KIND OF THE SAME AS YOURS DID. SHE STARTED BY LAYING OUT OUR FIRST COUPLE WEEKS, THEN TRAILED OFF INTO A STORY ABOUT HER OWN SOUS-CHEF DAYS.
"BUT THE CUPCAKES SHE MADE WERE DELICIOUS."

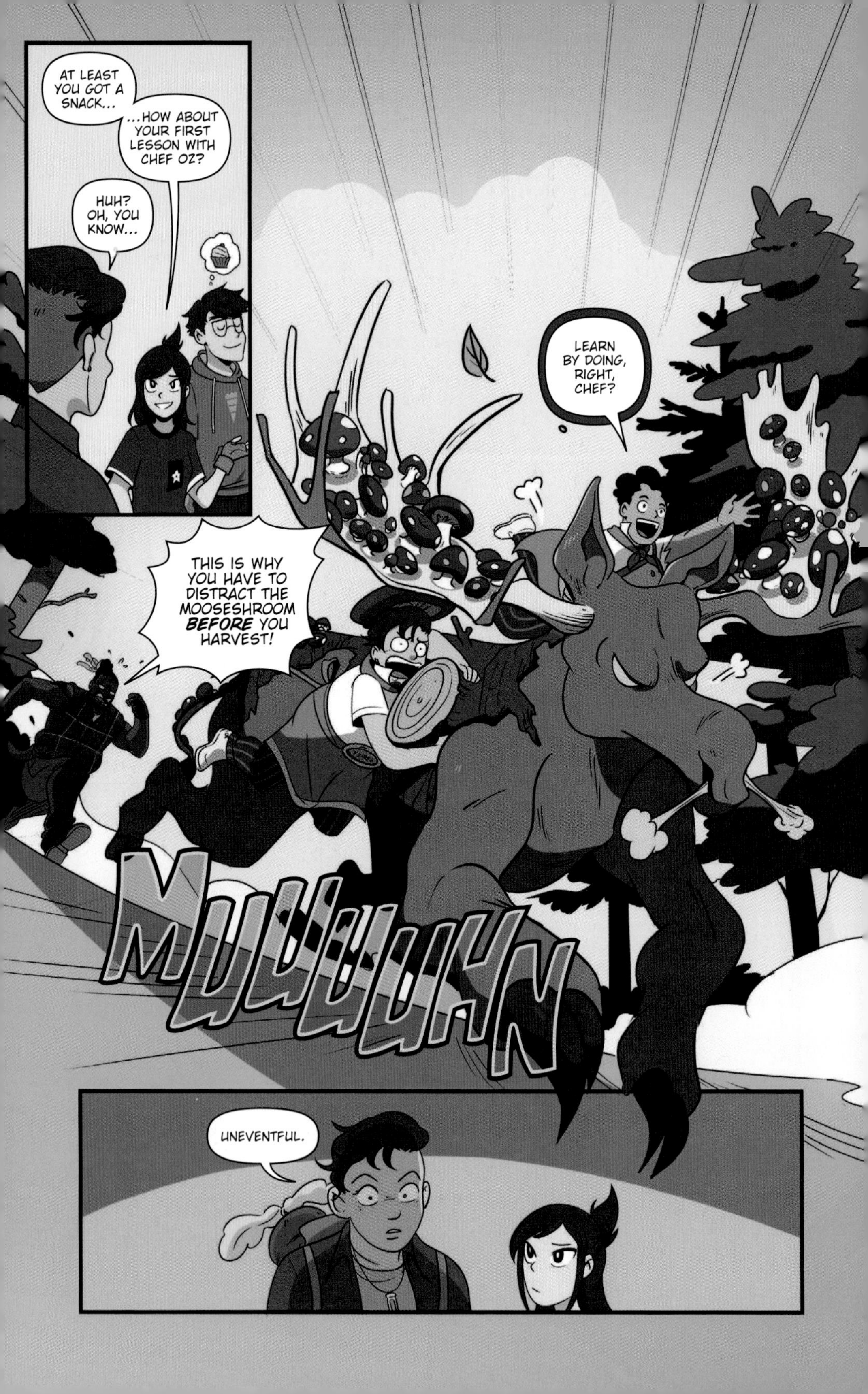
AT LEAST YOU GOT A SNACK...
...HOW ABOUT YOUR FIRST LESSON WITH CHEF OZ?
HUH? OH, YOU KNOW...
LEARN BY DOING, RIGHT, CHEF?
THIS IS WHY YOU HAVE TO DISTRACT THE MOOSESHROOM **BEFORE** YOU HARVEST!
MUUUUUHN
UNEVENTFUL.

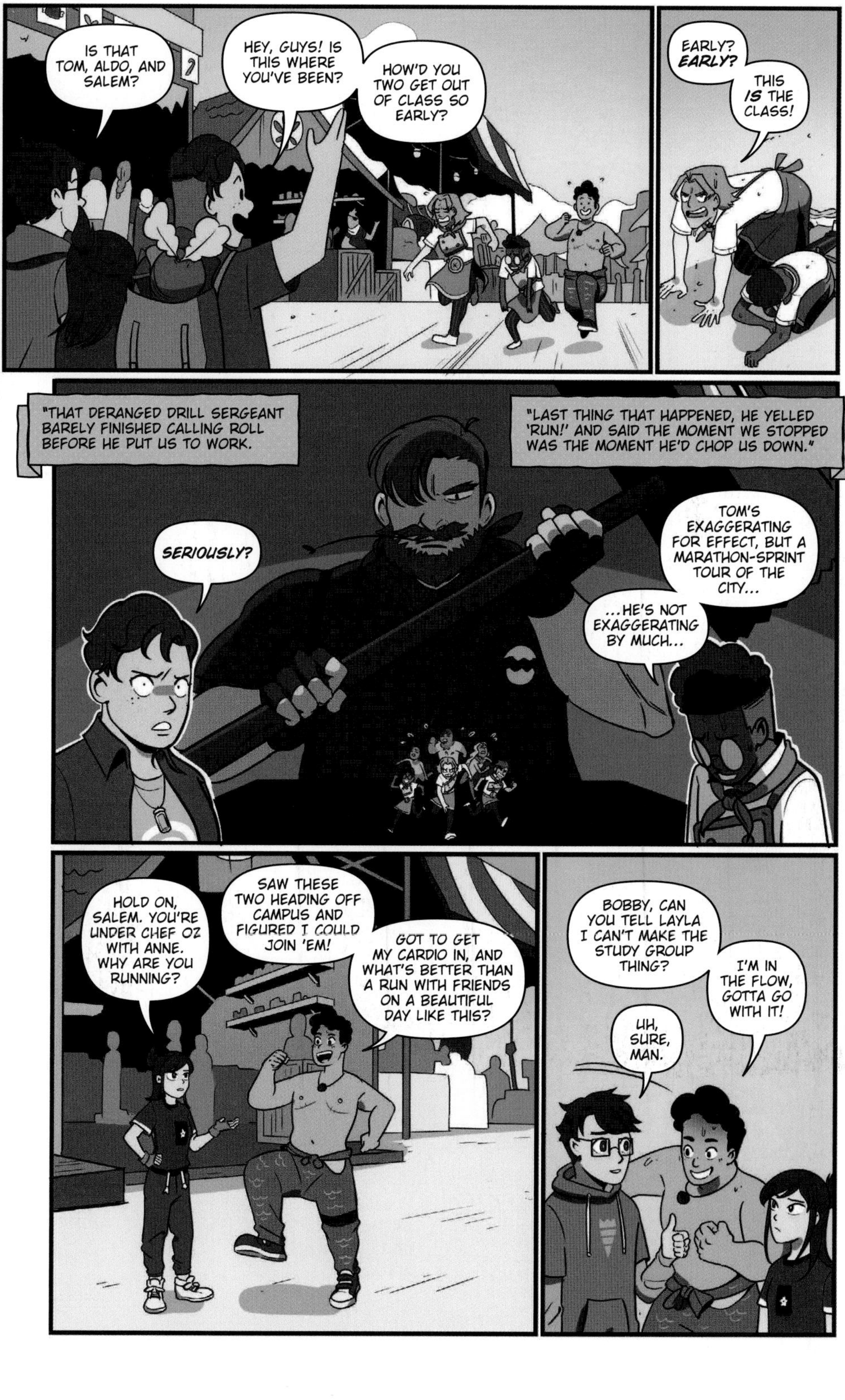
IS THAT TOM, ALDO, AND SALEM?
HEY, GUYS! IS THIS WHERE YOU'VE BEEN?
HOW'D YOU TWO GET OUT OF CLASS SO EARLY?
EARLY? ***EARLY?***
THIS ***IS*** THE CLASS!
"THAT DERANGED DRILL SERGEANT BARELY FINISHED CALLING ROLL BEFORE HE PUT US TO WORK.
"LAST THING THAT HAPPENED, HE YELLED 'RUN!' AND SAID THE MOMENT WE STOPPED WAS THE MOMENT HE'D CHOP US DOWN."
SERIOUSLY?
TOM'S EXAGGERATING FOR EFFECT, BUT A MARATHON-SPRINT TOUR OF THE CITY...
...HE'S NOT EXAGGERATING BY MUCH...
HOLD ON, SALEM. YOU'RE UNDER CHEF OZ WITH ANNE. WHY ARE YOU RUNNING?
SAW THESE TWO HEADING OFF CAMPUS AND FIGURED I COULD JOIN 'EM!
GOT TO GET MY CARDIO IN, AND WHAT'S BETTER THAN A RUN WITH FRIENDS ON A BEAUTIFUL DAY LIKE THIS?
BOBBY, CAN YOU TELL LAYLA I CAN'T MAKE THE STUDY GROUP THING?
I'M IN THE FLOW, GOTTA GO WITH IT!
UH, SURE, MAN.

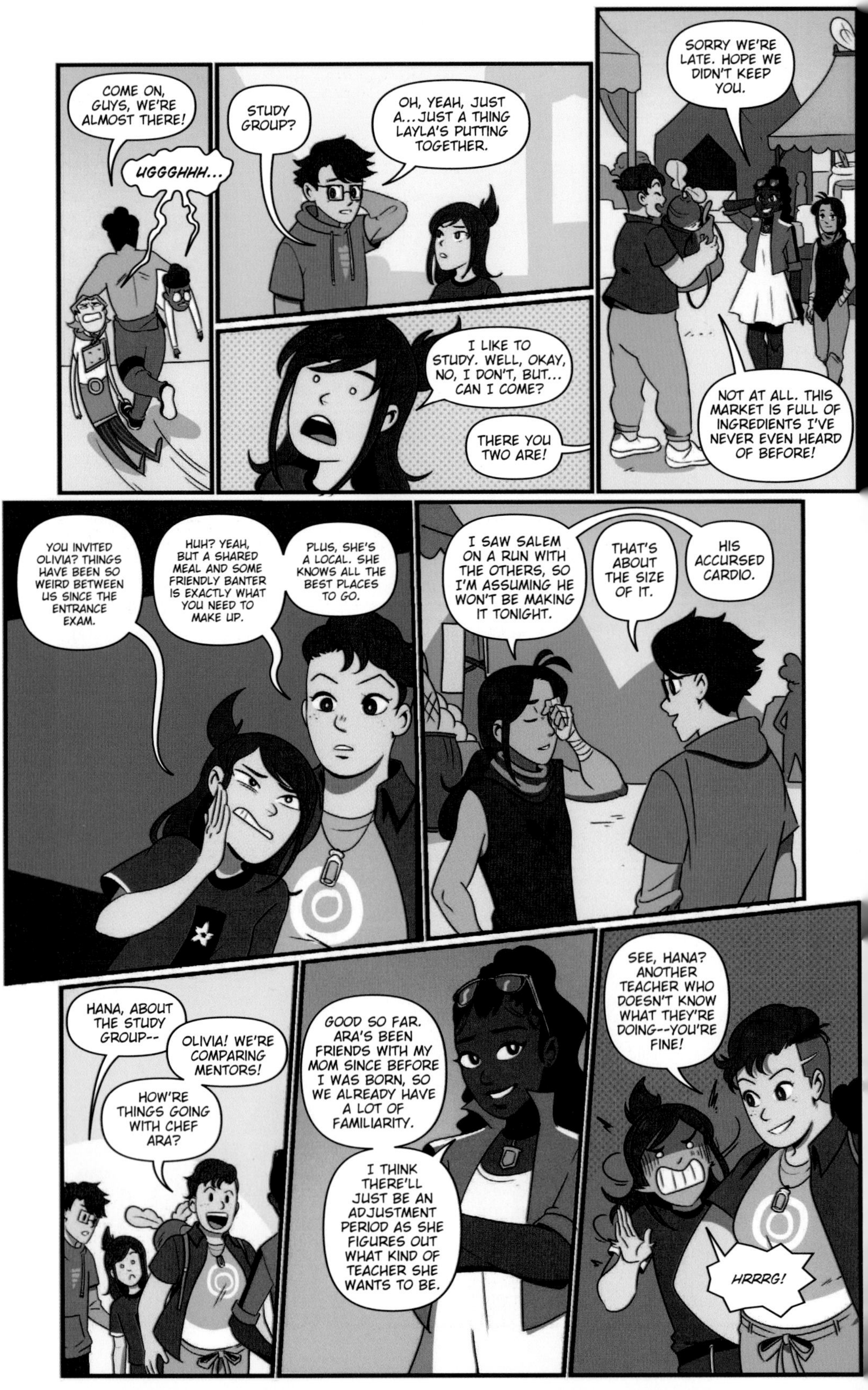
COME ON, GUYS, WE'RE ALMOST THERE!
UGGGHHH...
STUDY GROUP?
OH, YEAH, JUST A...JUST A THING LAYLA'S PUTTING TOGETHER.
I LIKE TO STUDY. WELL, OKAY, NO, I DON'T, BUT... CAN I COME?
THERE YOU TWO ARE!
SORRY WE'RE LATE. HOPE WE DIDN'T KEEP YOU.
NOT AT ALL. THIS MARKET IS FULL OF INGREDIENTS I'VE NEVER EVEN HEARD OF BEFORE!
YOU INVITED OLIVIA? THINGS HAVE BEEN SO WEIRD BETWEEN US SINCE THE ENTRANCE EXAM.
HUH? YEAH, BUT A SHARED MEAL AND SOME FRIENDLY BANTER IS EXACTLY WHAT YOU NEED TO MAKE UP.
PLUS, SHE'S A LOCAL. SHE KNOWS ALL THE BEST PLACES TO GO.
I SAW SALEM ON A RUN WITH THE OTHERS, SO I'M ASSUMING HE WON'T BE MAKING IT TONIGHT.
THAT'S ABOUT THE SIZE OF IT.
HIS ACCURSED CARDIO.
HANA, ABOUT THE STUDY GROUP--
OLIVIA! WE'RE COMPARING MENTORS!
HOW'RE THINGS GOING WITH CHEF ARA?
GOOD SO FAR. ARA'S BEEN FRIENDS WITH MY MOM SINCE BEFORE I WAS BORN, SO WE ALREADY HAVE A LOT OF FAMILIARITY.
I THINK THERE'LL JUST BE AN ADJUSTMENT PERIOD AS SHE FIGURES OUT WHAT KIND OF TEACHER SHE WANTS TO BE.
SEE, HANA? ANOTHER TEACHER WHO DOESN'T KNOW WHAT THEY'RE DOING--YOU'RE FINE!
HRRRG!

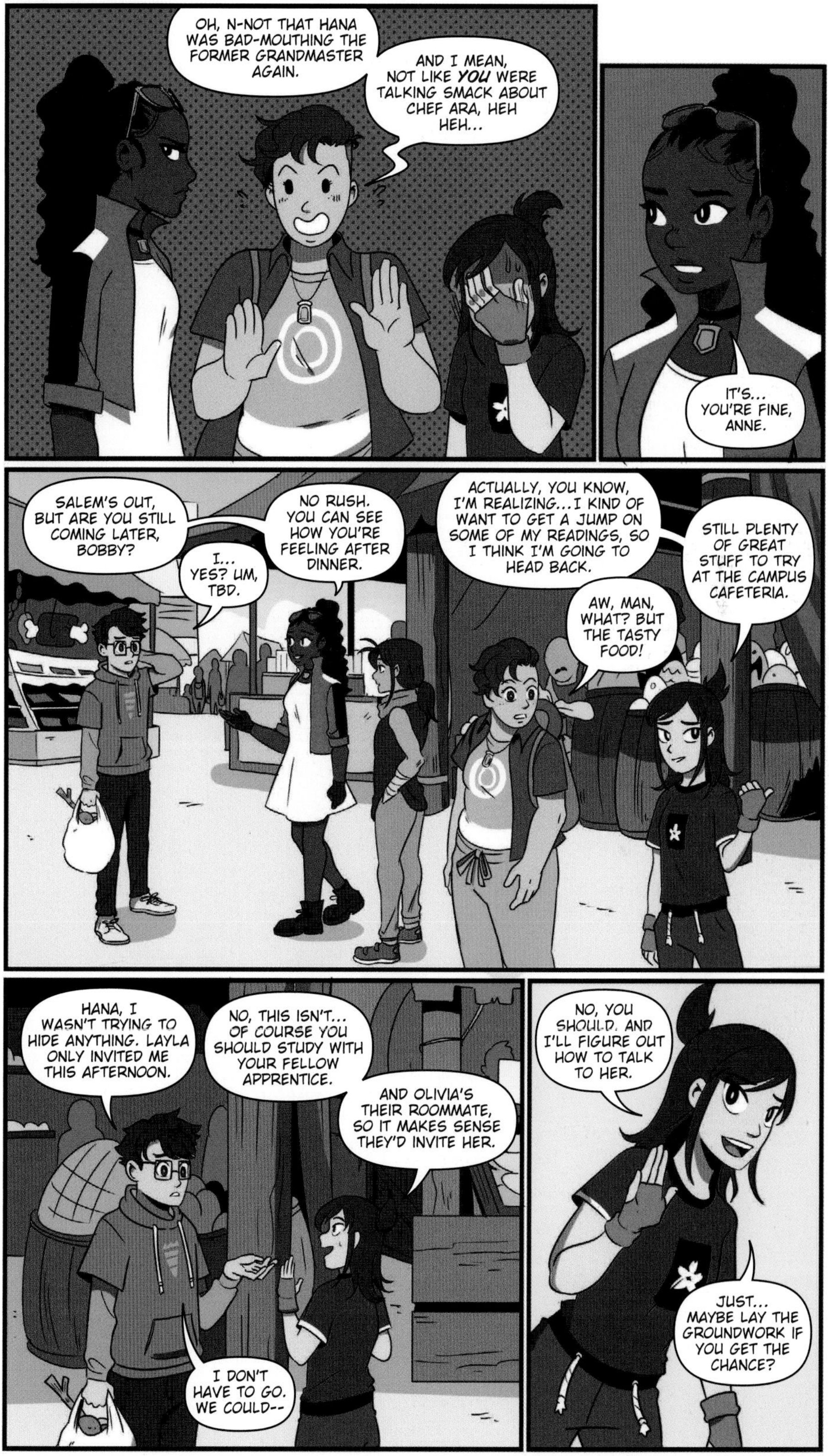
OH, N-NOT THAT HANA WAS BAD-MOUTHING THE FORMER GRANDMASTER AGAIN.
AND I MEAN, NOT LIKE YOU WERE TALKING SMACK ABOUT CHEF ARA, HEH HEH...
IT'S... YOU'RE FINE, ANNE.
SALEM'S OUT, BUT ARE YOU STILL COMING LATER, BOBBY?
I... YES? UM, TBD.
NO RUSH. YOU CAN SEE HOW YOU'RE FEELING AFTER DINNER.
ACTUALLY, YOU KNOW, I'M REALIZING... I KIND OF WANT TO GET A JUMP ON SOME OF MY READINGS, SO I THINK I'M GOING TO HEAD BACK.
STILL PLENTY OF GREAT STUFF TO TRY AT THE CAMPUS CAFETERIA.
AW, MAN, WHAT? BUT THE TASTY FOOD!
HANA, I WASN'T TRYING TO HIDE ANYTHING. LAYLA ONLY INVITED ME THIS AFTERNOON.
NO, THIS ISN'T... OF COURSE YOU SHOULD STUDY WITH YOUR FELLOW APPRENTICE.
AND OLIVIA'S THEIR ROOMMATE, SO IT MAKES SENSE THEY'D INVITE HER.
I DON'T HAVE TO GO. WE COULD--
NO, YOU SHOULD. AND I'LL FIGURE OUT HOW TO TALK TO HER.
JUST... MAYBE LAY THE GROUNDWORK IF YOU GET THE CHANCE?

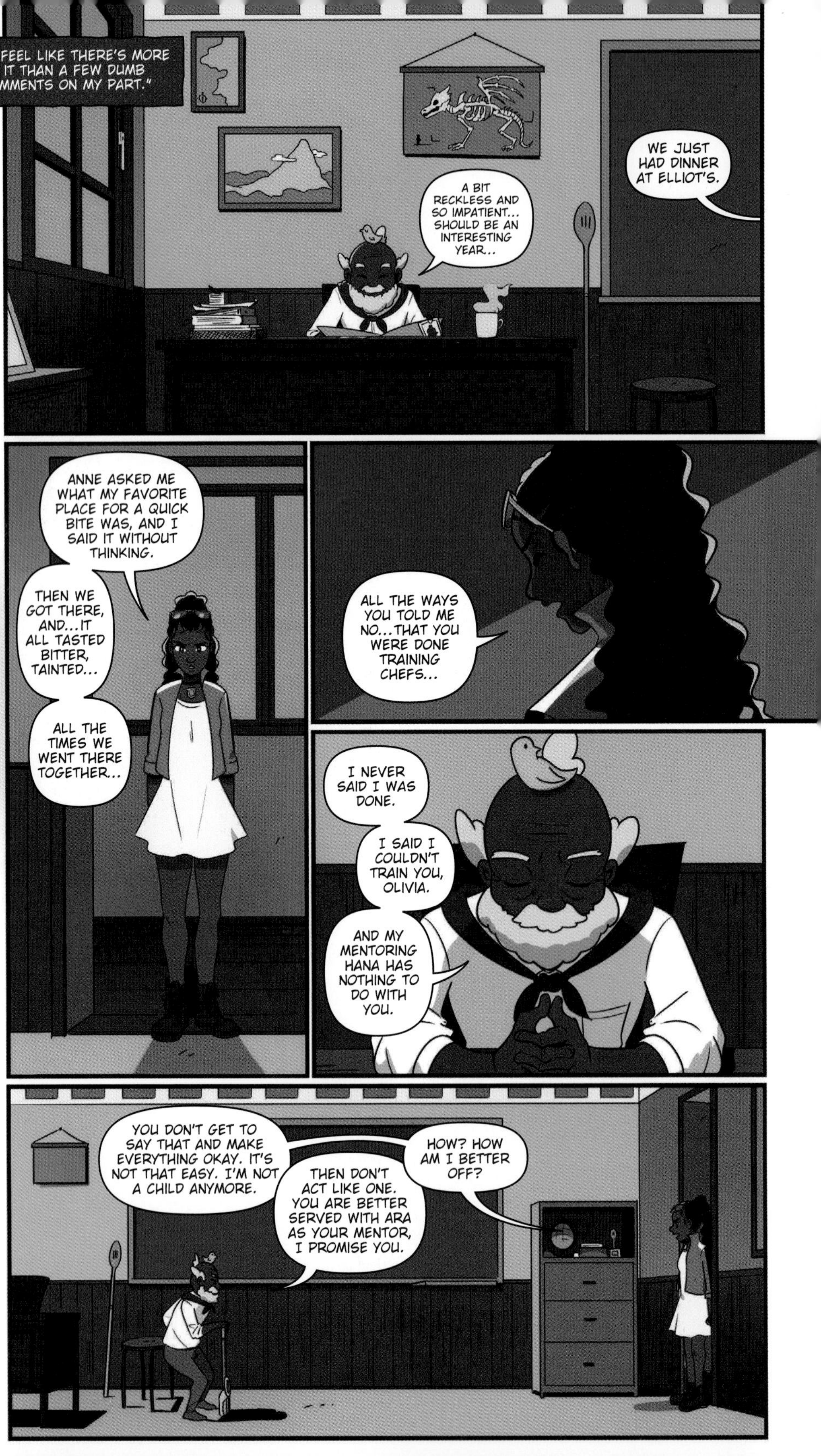
"I FEEL LIKE THERE'S MORE TO IT THAN A FEW DUMB COMMENTS ON MY PART."
A BIT RECKLESS AND SO IMPATIENT... SHOULD BE AN INTERESTING YEAR...
WE JUST HAD DINNER AT ELLIOT'S.
ANNE ASKED ME WHAT MY FAVORITE PLACE FOR A QUICK BITE WAS, AND I SAID IT WITHOUT THINKING.
THEN WE GOT THERE, AND...IT ALL TASTED BITTER, TAINTED...
ALL THE TIMES WE WENT THERE TOGETHER...
ALL THE WAYS YOU TOLD ME NO...THAT YOU WERE DONE TRAINING CHEFS...
I NEVER SAID I WAS DONE.
I SAID I COULDN'T TRAIN YOU, OLIVIA.
AND MY MENTORING HANA HAS NOTHING TO DO WITH YOU.
YOU DON'T GET TO SAY THAT AND MAKE EVERYTHING OKAY. IT'S NOT THAT EASY. I'M NOT A CHILD ANYMORE.
THEN DON'T ACT LIKE ONE. YOU ARE BETTER SERVED WITH ARA AS YOUR MENTOR, I PROMISE YOU.
HOW? HOW AM I BETTER OFF?

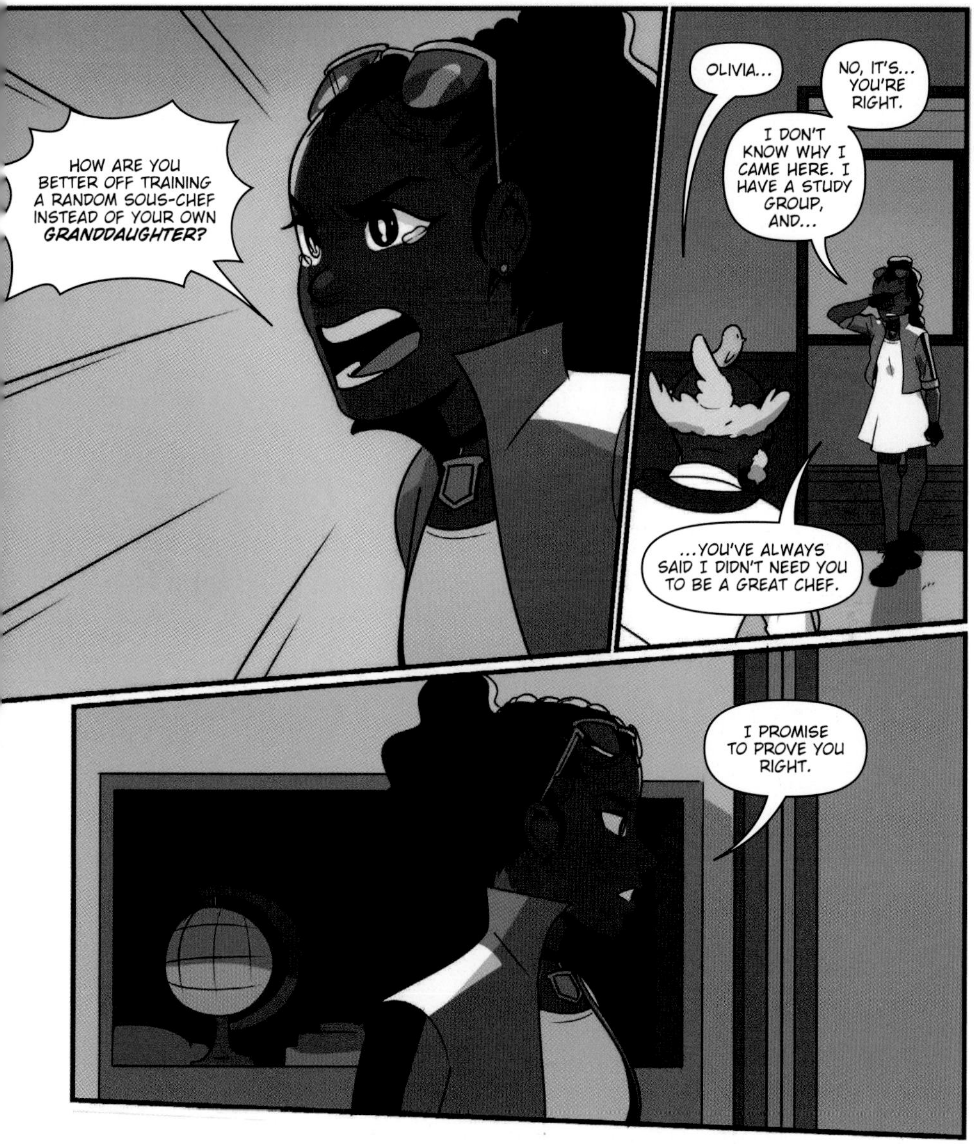
HOW ARE YOU BETTER OFF TRAINING A RANDOM SOUS-CHEF INSTEAD OF YOUR OWN ***GRANDDAUGHTER?***
OLIVIA...
NO, IT'S... YOU'RE RIGHT.
I DON'T KNOW WHY I CAME HERE. I HAVE A STUDY GROUP, AND...
...YOU'VE ALWAYS SAID I DIDN'T NEED YOU TO BE A GREAT CHEF.
I PROMISE TO PROVE YOU RIGHT.

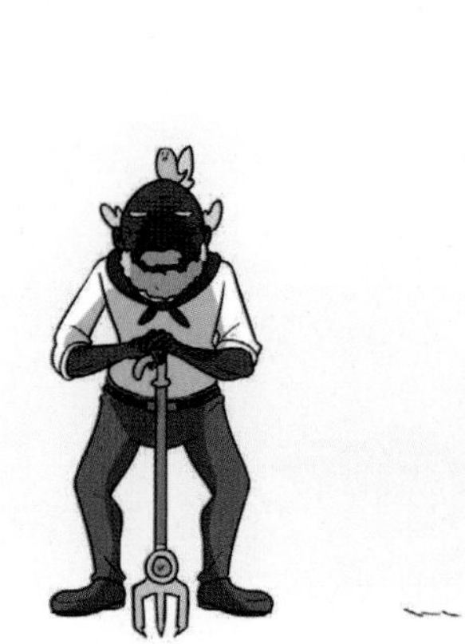

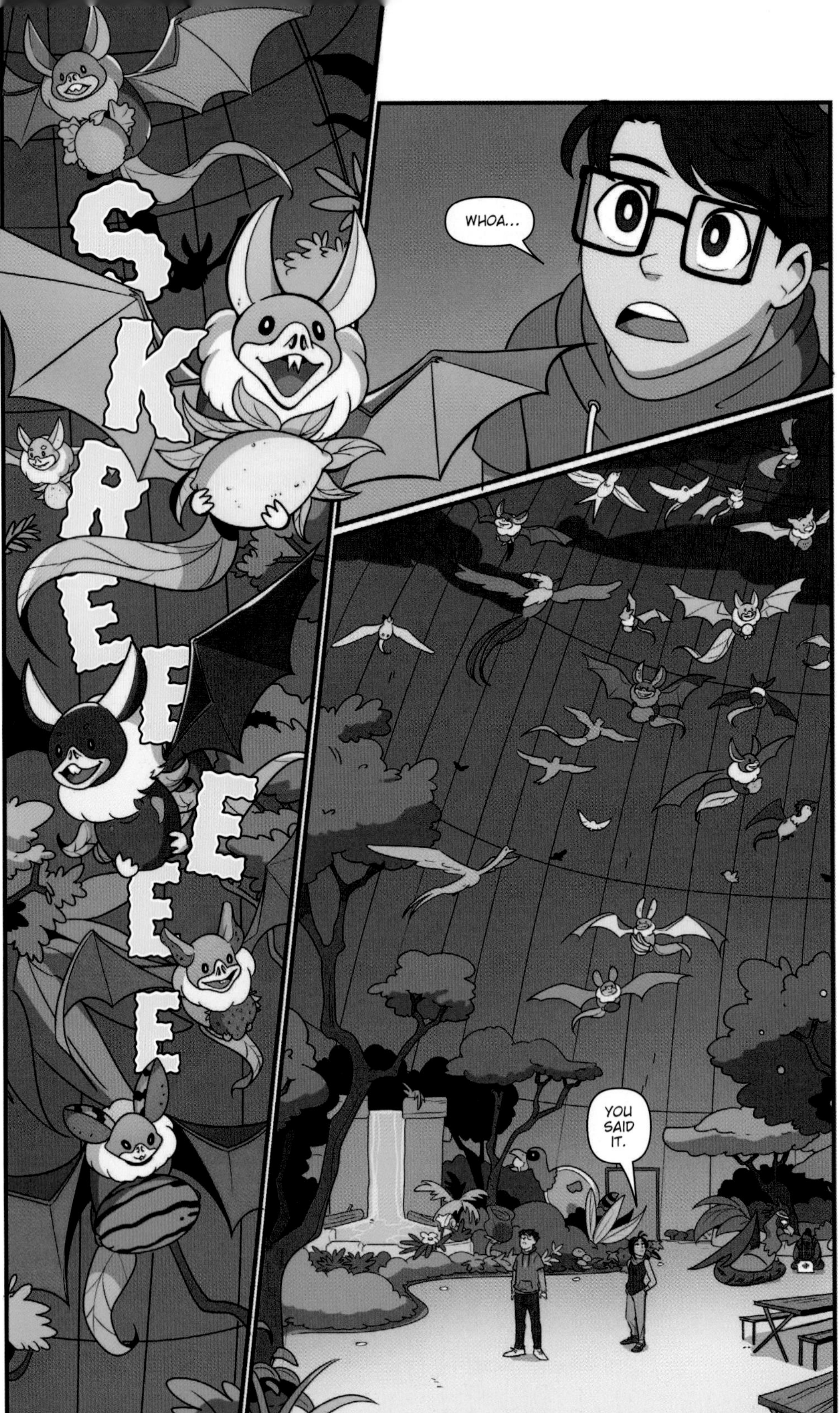
SKREEEEEEE
WHOA...
YOU SAID IT.

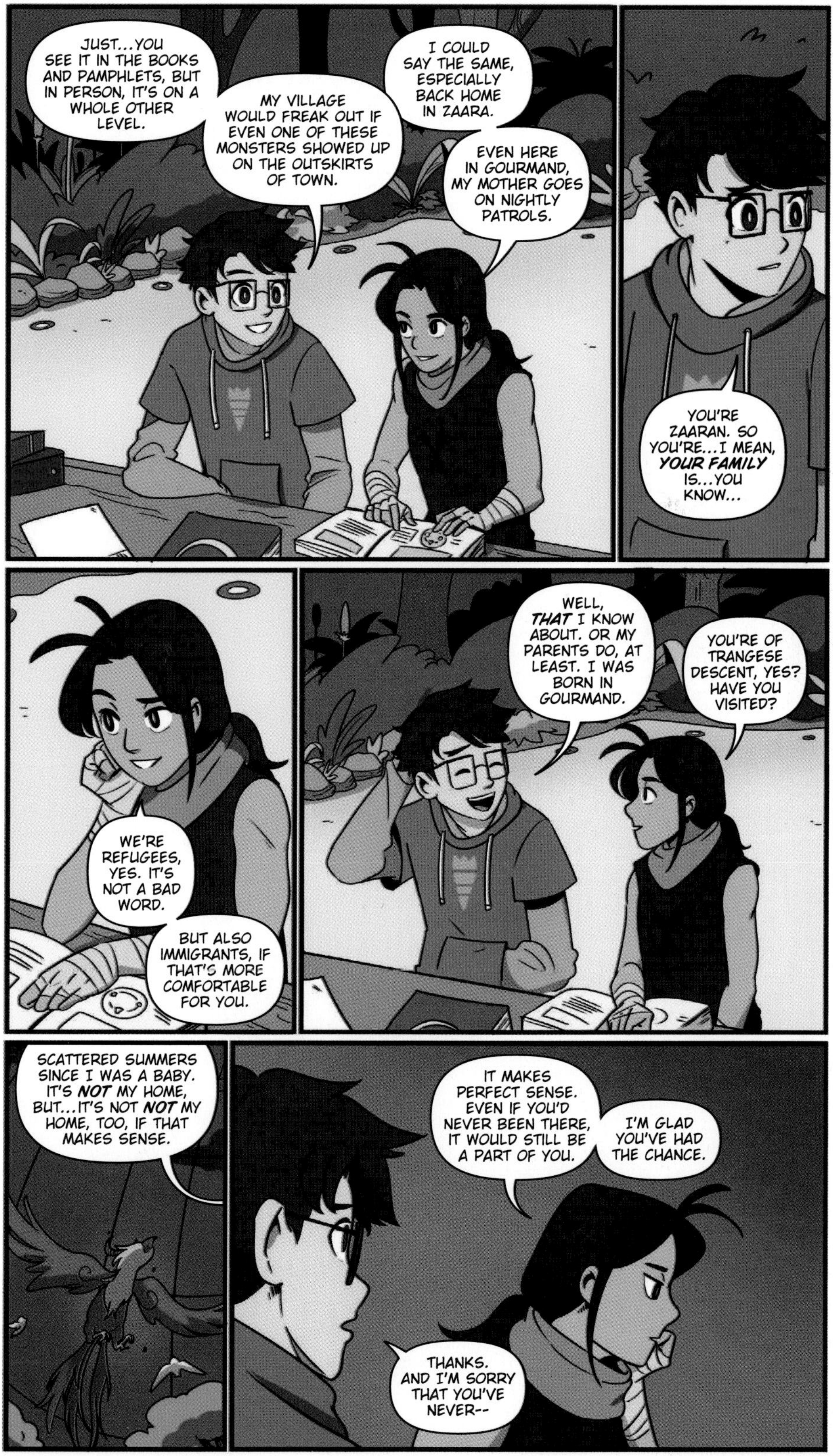
JUST...YOU SEE IT IN THE BOOKS AND PAMPHLETS, BUT IN PERSON, IT'S ON A WHOLE OTHER LEVEL.
MY VILLAGE WOULD FREAK OUT IF EVEN ONE OF THESE MONSTERS SHOWED UP ON THE OUTSKIRTS OF TOWN.
I COULD SAY THE SAME, ESPECIALLY BACK HOME IN ZAARA.
EVEN HERE IN GOURMAND, MY MOTHER GOES ON NIGHTLY PATROLS.
YOU'RE ZAARAN. SO YOU'RE...I MEAN, ***YOUR FAMILY*** IS...YOU KNOW...
WE'RE REFUGEES, YES. IT'S NOT A BAD WORD.
BUT ALSO IMMIGRANTS, IF THAT'S MORE COMFORTABLE FOR YOU.
WELL, ***THAT*** I KNOW ABOUT. OR MY PARENTS DO, AT LEAST. I WAS BORN IN GOURMAND.
YOU'RE OF TRANGESE DESCENT, YES? HAVE YOU VISITED?
SCATTERED SUMMERS SINCE I WAS A BABY. IT'S ***NOT*** MY HOME, BUT...IT'S NOT ***NOT*** MY HOME, TOO, IF THAT MAKES SENSE.
IT MAKES PERFECT SENSE. EVEN IF YOU'D NEVER BEEN THERE, IT WOULD STILL BE A PART OF YOU.
I'M GLAD YOU'VE HAD THE CHANCE.
THANKS. AND I'M SORRY THAT YOU'VE NEVER--

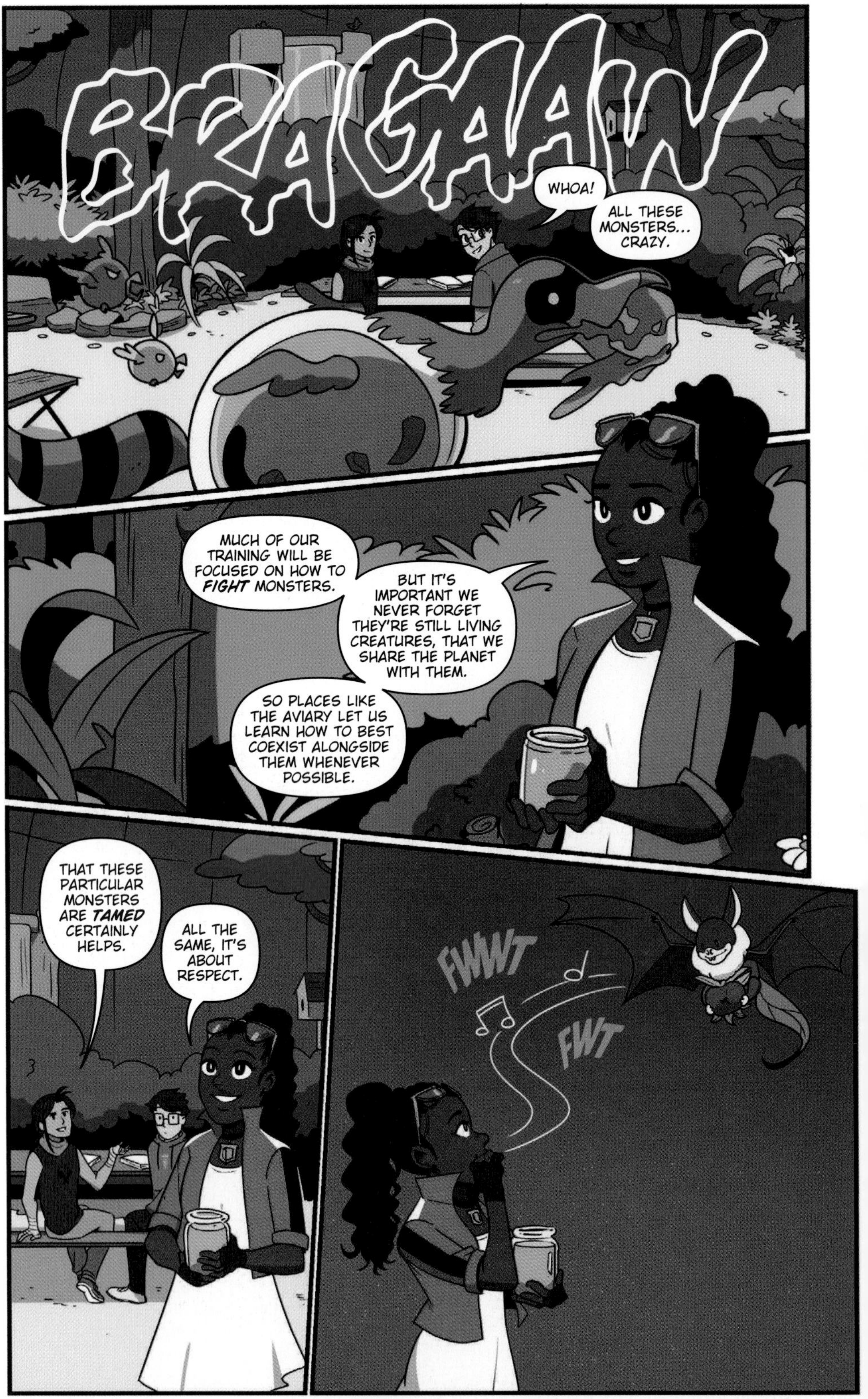
BRAGAAW
WHOA!
ALL THESE MONSTERS... CRAZY.
MUCH OF OUR TRAINING WILL BE FOCUSED ON HOW TO FIGHT MONSTERS.
BUT IT'S IMPORTANT WE NEVER FORGET THEY'RE STILL LIVING CREATURES, THAT WE SHARE THE PLANET WITH THEM.
SO PLACES LIKE THE AVIARY LET US LEARN HOW TO BEST COEXIST ALONGSIDE THEM WHENEVER POSSIBLE.
THAT THESE PARTICULAR MONSTERS ARE TAMED CERTAINLY HELPS.
ALL THE SAME, IT'S ABOUT RESPECT.
FWWT
FWT

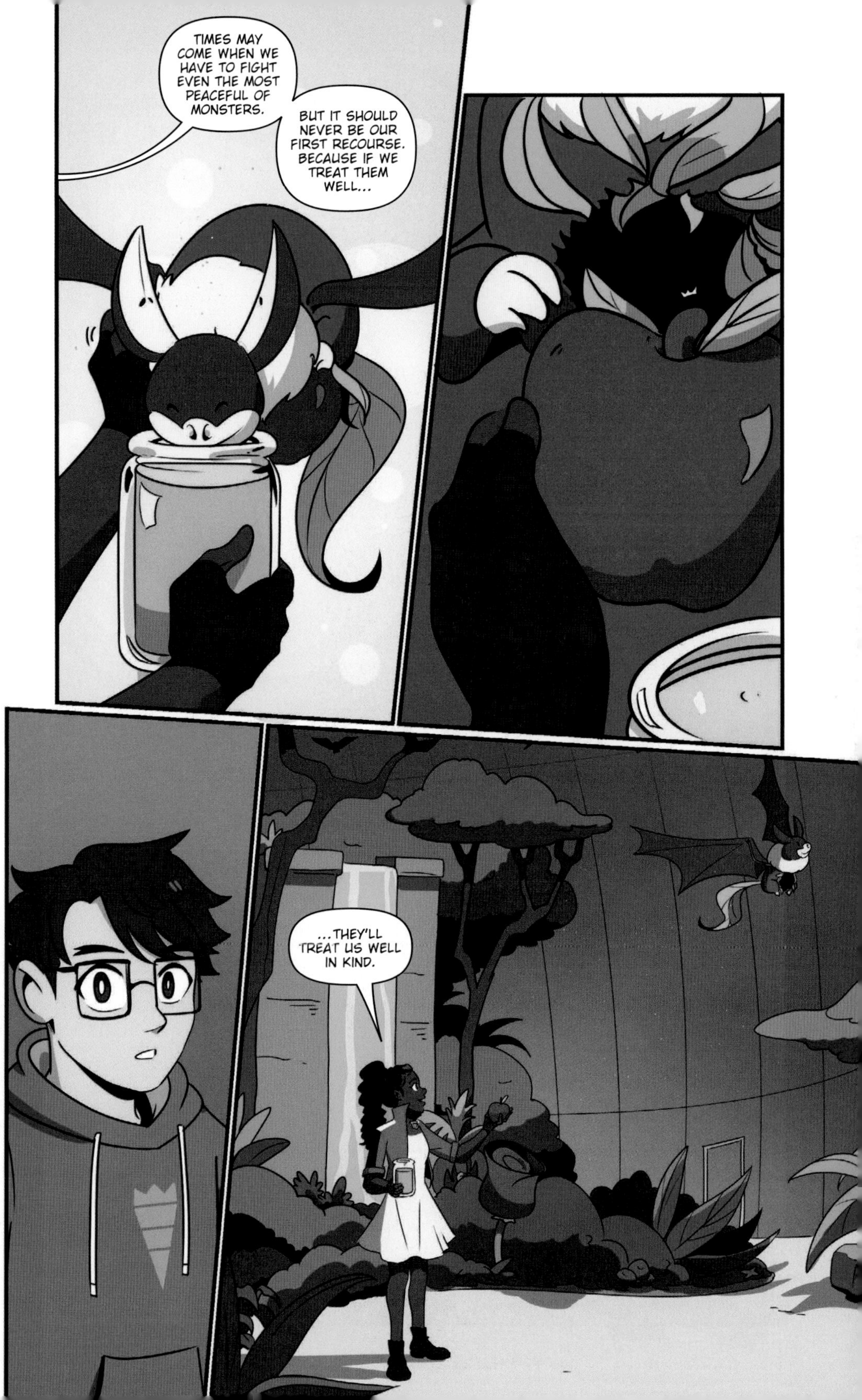
TIMES MAY COME WHEN WE HAVE TO FIGHT EVEN THE MOST PEACEFUL OF MONSTERS.
BUT IT SHOULD NEVER BE OUR FIRST RECOURSE. BECAUSE IF WE TREAT THEM WELL...
...THEY'LL TREAT US WELL IN KIND.

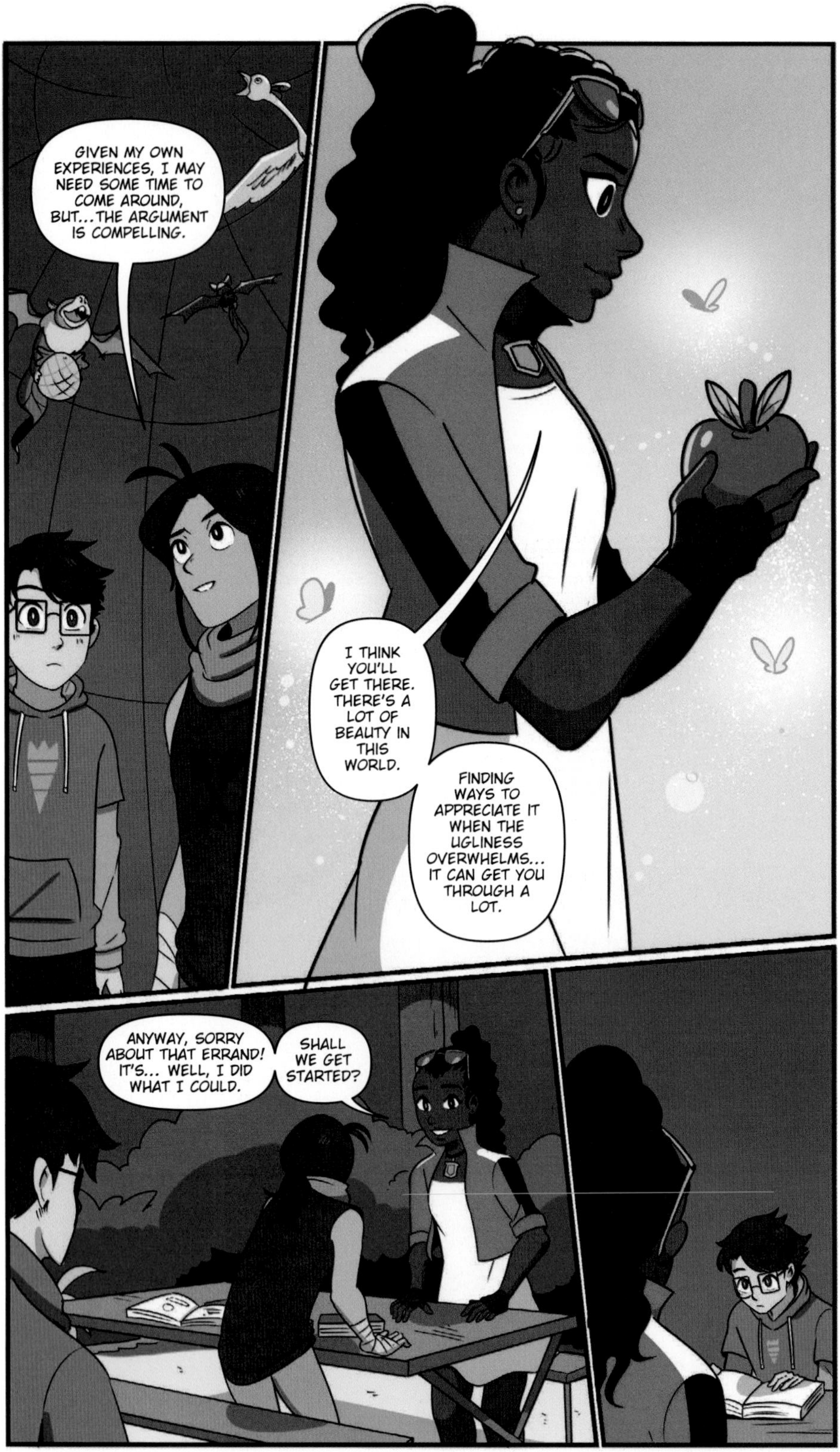
GIVEN MY OWN EXPERIENCES, I MAY NEED SOME TIME TO COME AROUND, BUT...THE ARGUMENT IS COMPELLING.
I THINK YOU'LL GET THERE. THERE'S A LOT OF BEAUTY IN THIS WORLD.
FINDING WAYS TO APPRECIATE IT WHEN THE UGLINESS OVERWHELMS... IT CAN GET YOU THROUGH A LOT.
ANYWAY, SORRY ABOUT THAT ERRAND! IT'S... WELL, I DID WHAT I COULD.
SHALL WE GET STARTED?

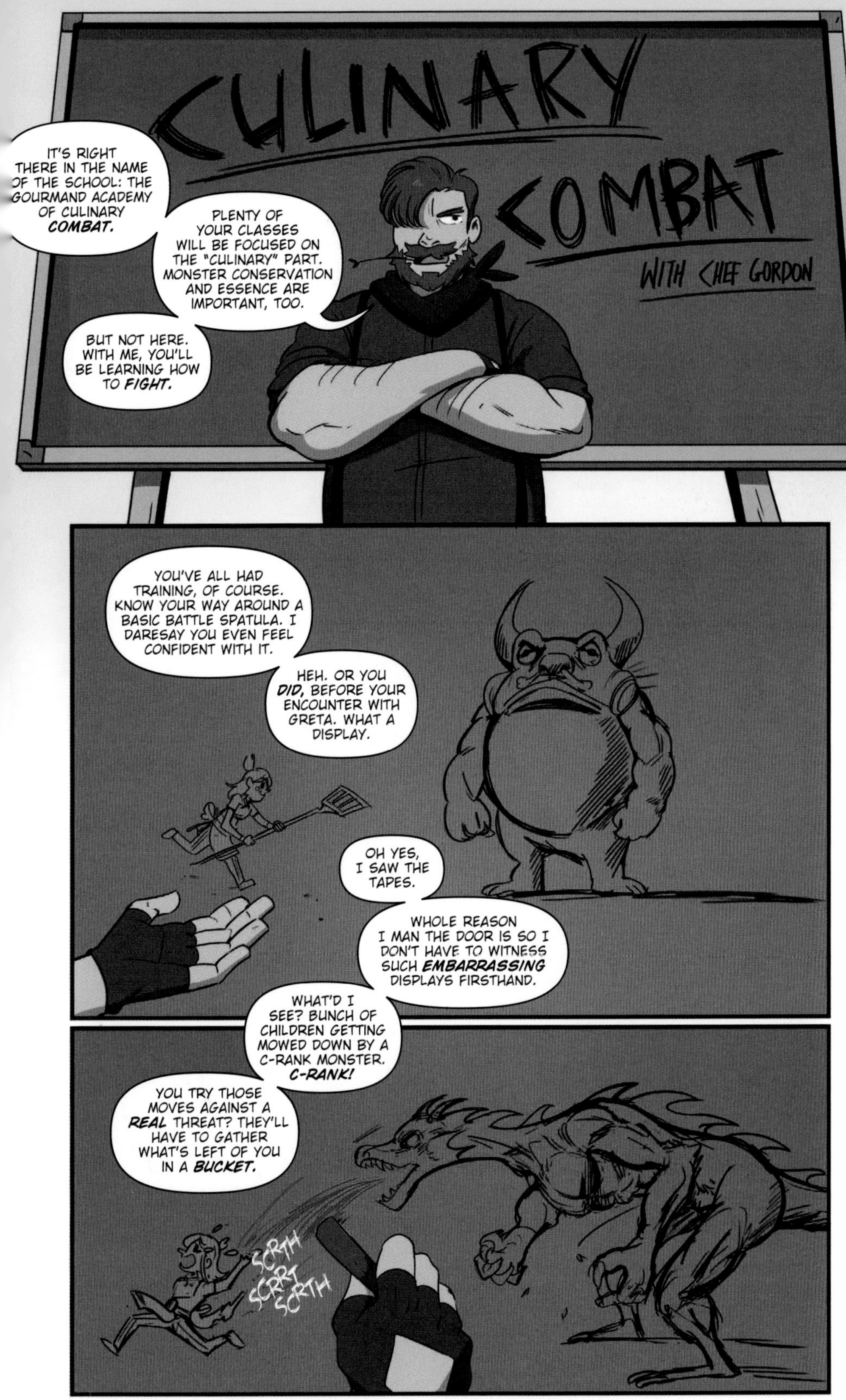
CULINARY COMBAT
WITH CHEF GORDON
IT'S RIGHT THERE IN THE NAME OF THE SCHOOL: THE GOURMAND ACADEMY OF CULINARY COMBAT.
PLENTY OF YOUR CLASSES WILL BE FOCUSED ON THE "CULINARY" PART. MONSTER CONSERVATION AND ESSENCE ARE IMPORTANT, TOO.
BUT NOT HERE. WITH ME, YOU'LL BE LEARNING HOW TO FIGHT.
YOU'VE ALL HAD TRAINING, OF COURSE. KNOW YOUR WAY AROUND A BASIC BATTLE SPATULA. I DARESAY YOU EVEN FEEL CONFIDENT WITH IT.
HEH. OR YOU DID, BEFORE YOUR ENCOUNTER WITH GRETA. WHAT A DISPLAY.
OH YES, I SAW THE TAPES.
WHOLE REASON I MAN THE DOOR IS SO I DON'T HAVE TO WITNESS SUCH EMBARRASSING DISPLAYS FIRSTHAND.
WHAT'D I SEE? BUNCH OF CHILDREN GETTING MOWED DOWN BY A C-RANK MONSTER. C-RANK!
YOU TRY THOSE MOVES AGAINST A REAL THREAT? THEY'LL HAVE TO GATHER WHAT'S LEFT OF YOU IN A BUCKET.
SCRTH SCRT SCRTH

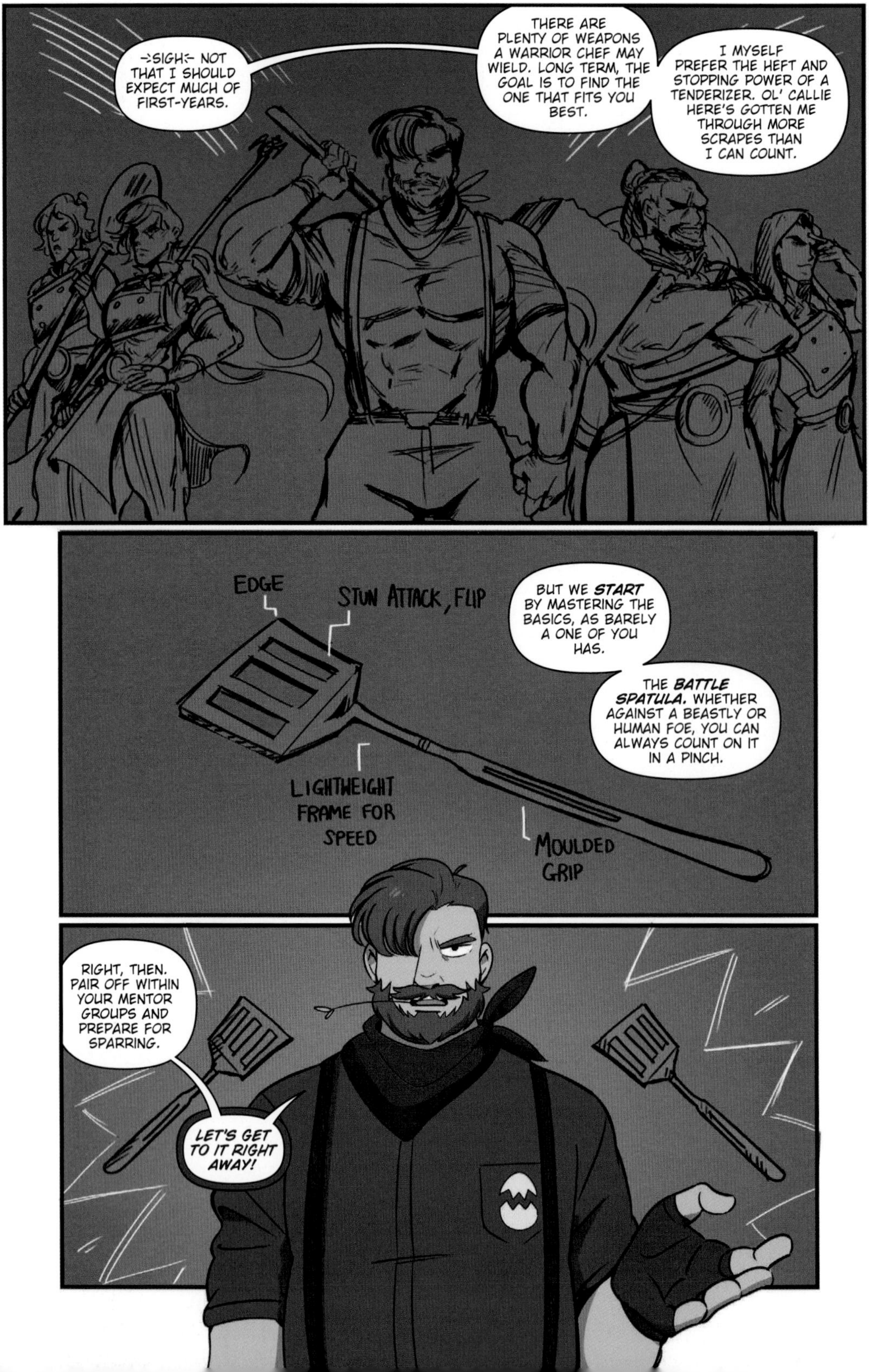

-SIGH- NOT THAT I SHOULD EXPECT MUCH OF FIRST-YEARS.
THERE ARE PLENTY OF WEAPONS A WARRIOR CHEF MAY WIELD. LONG TERM, THE GOAL IS TO FIND THE ONE THAT FITS YOU BEST.
I MYSELF PREFER THE HEFT AND STOPPING POWER OF A TENDERIZER. OL' CALLIE HERE'S GOTTEN ME THROUGH MORE SCRAPES THAN I CAN COUNT.
EDGE
STUN ATTACK, FLIP
LIGHTWEIGHT FRAME FOR SPEED
MOULDED GRIP
BUT WE START BY MASTERING THE BASICS, AS BARELY A ONE OF YOU HAS.
THE BATTLE SPATULA. WHETHER AGAINST A BEASTLY OR HUMAN FOE, YOU CAN ALWAYS COUNT ON IT IN A PINCH.
RIGHT, THEN. PAIR OFF WITHIN YOUR MENTOR GROUPS AND PREPARE FOR SPARRING.
LET'S GET TO IT RIGHT AWAY!

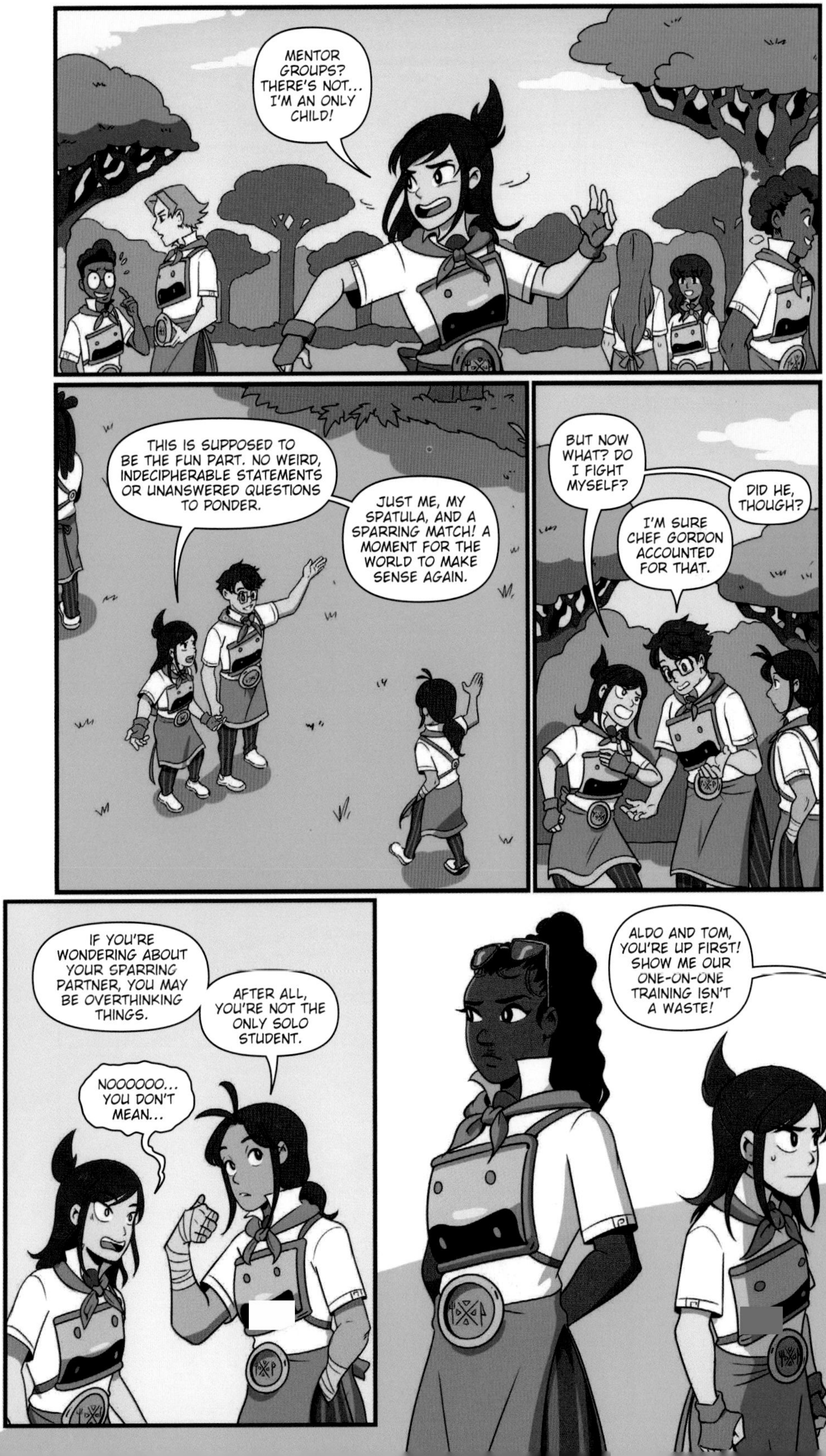

MENTOR GROUPS? THERE'S NOT... I'M AN ONLY CHILD!
THIS IS SUPPOSED TO BE THE FUN PART. NO WEIRD, INDECIPHERABLE STATEMENTS OR UNANSWERED QUESTIONS TO PONDER.
JUST ME, MY SPATULA, AND A SPARRING MATCH! A MOMENT FOR THE WORLD TO MAKE SENSE AGAIN.
BUT NOW WHAT? DO I FIGHT MYSELF?
I'M SURE CHEF GORDON ACCOUNTED FOR THAT.
DID HE, THOUGH?
IF YOU'RE WONDERING ABOUT YOUR SPARRING PARTNER, YOU MAY BE OVERTHINKING THINGS.
AFTER ALL, YOU'RE NOT THE ONLY SOLO STUDENT.
NOOOOOO... YOU DON'T MEAN...
ALDO AND TOM, YOU'RE UP FIRST! SHOW ME OUR ONE-ON-ONE TRAINING ISN'T A WASTE!

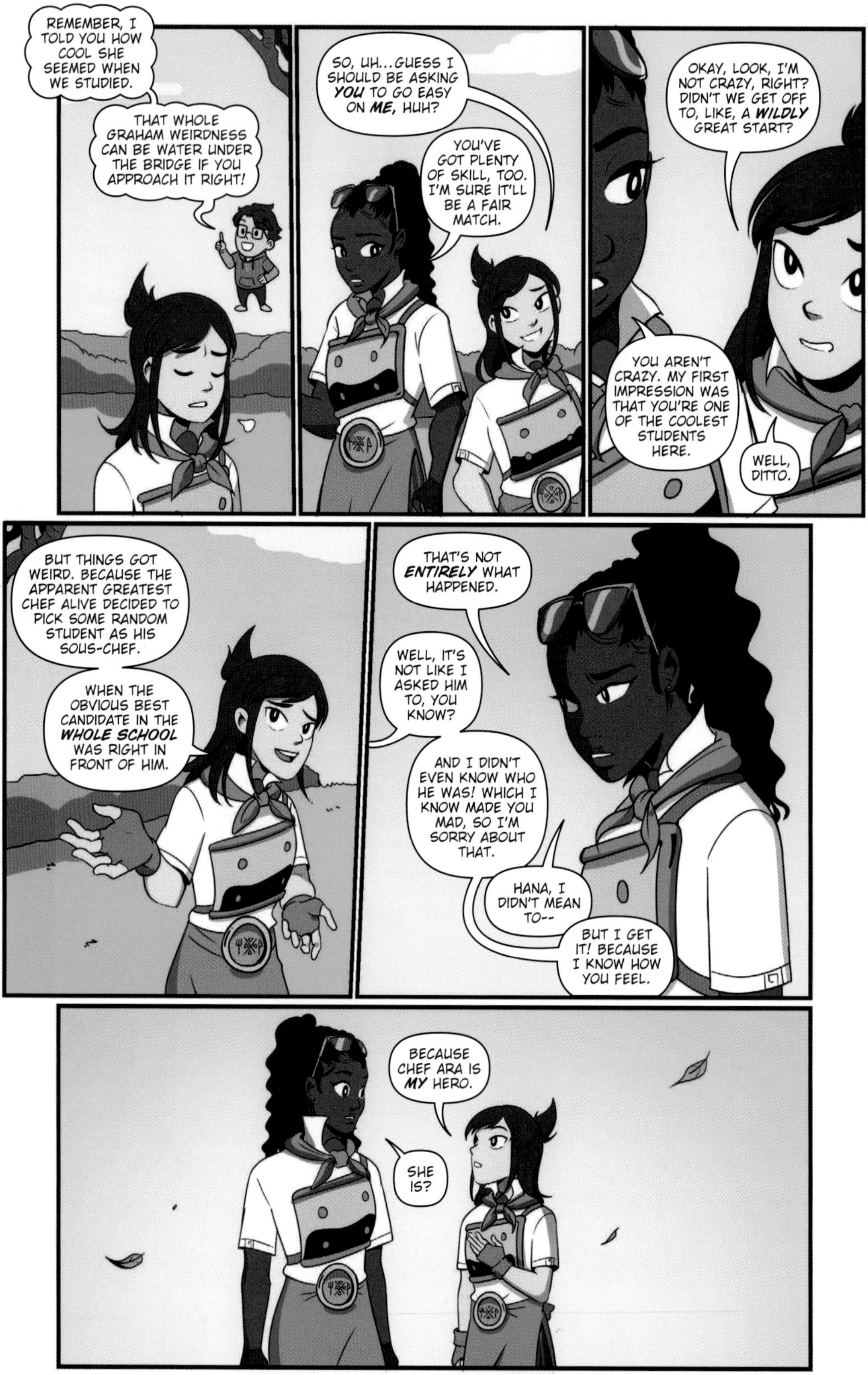
REMEMBER, I TOLD YOU HOW COOL SHE SEEMED WHEN WE STUDIED.
THAT WHOLE GRAHAM WEIRDNESS CAN BE WATER UNDER THE BRIDGE IF YOU APPROACH IT RIGHT!
SO, UH...GUESS I SHOULD BE ASKING *YOU* TO GO EASY ON *ME*, HUH?
YOU'VE GOT PLENTY OF SKILL, TOO. I'M SURE IT'LL BE A FAIR MATCH.
OKAY, LOOK, I'M NOT CRAZY, RIGHT? DIDN'T WE GET OFF TO, LIKE, A *WILDLY* GREAT START?
YOU AREN'T CRAZY. MY FIRST IMPRESSION WAS THAT YOU'RE ONE OF THE COOLEST STUDENTS HERE.
WELL, DITTO.
BUT THINGS GOT WEIRD. BECAUSE THE APPARENT GREATEST CHEF ALIVE DECIDED TO PICK SOME RANDOM STUDENT AS HIS SOUS-CHEF.
WHEN THE OBVIOUS BEST CANDIDATE IN THE *WHOLE SCHOOL* WAS RIGHT IN FRONT OF HIM.
THAT'S NOT *ENTIRELY* WHAT HAPPENED.
WELL, IT'S NOT LIKE I ASKED HIM TO, YOU KNOW?
AND I DIDN'T EVEN KNOW WHO HE WAS! WHICH I KNOW MADE YOU MAD, SO I'M SORRY ABOUT THAT.
HANA, I DIDN'T MEAN TO--
BUT I GET IT! BECAUSE I KNOW HOW YOU FEEL.
BECAUSE CHEF ARA IS *MY* HERO.
SHE IS?

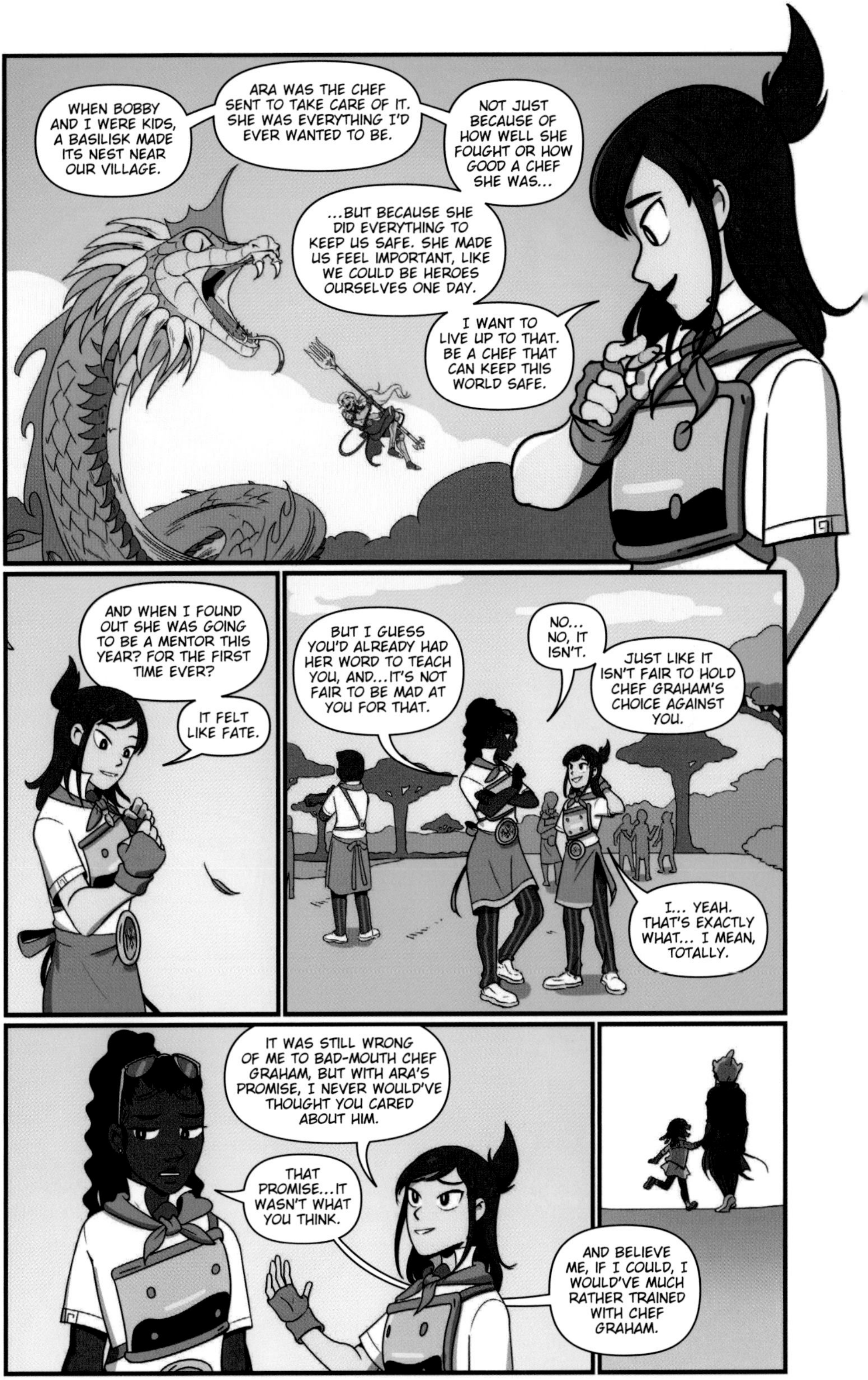
WHEN BOBBY AND I WERE KIDS, A BASILISK MADE ITS NEST NEAR OUR VILLAGE.
ARA WAS THE CHEF SENT TO TAKE CARE OF IT. SHE WAS EVERYTHING I'D EVER WANTED TO BE.
NOT JUST BECAUSE OF HOW WELL SHE FOUGHT OR HOW GOOD A CHEF SHE WAS...
...BUT BECAUSE SHE DID EVERYTHING TO KEEP US SAFE. SHE MADE US FEEL IMPORTANT, LIKE WE COULD BE HEROES OURSELVES ONE DAY.
I WANT TO LIVE UP TO THAT. BE A CHEF THAT CAN KEEP THIS WORLD SAFE.
AND WHEN I FOUND OUT SHE WAS GOING TO BE A MENTOR THIS YEAR? FOR THE FIRST TIME EVER?
IT FELT LIKE FATE.
BUT I GUESS YOU'D ALREADY HAD HER WORD TO TEACH YOU, AND...IT'S NOT FAIR TO BE MAD AT YOU FOR THAT.
NO... NO, IT ISN'T.
JUST LIKE IT ISN'T FAIR TO HOLD CHEF GRAHAM'S CHOICE AGAINST YOU.
I... YEAH. THAT'S EXACTLY WHAT... I MEAN, TOTALLY.
IT WAS STILL WRONG OF ME TO BAD-MOUTH CHEF GRAHAM, BUT WITH ARA'S PROMISE, I NEVER WOULD'VE THOUGHT YOU CARED ABOUT HIM.
THAT PROMISE...IT WASN'T WHAT YOU THINK.
AND BELIEVE ME, IF I COULD, I WOULD'VE MUCH RATHER TRAINED WITH CHEF GRAHAM.

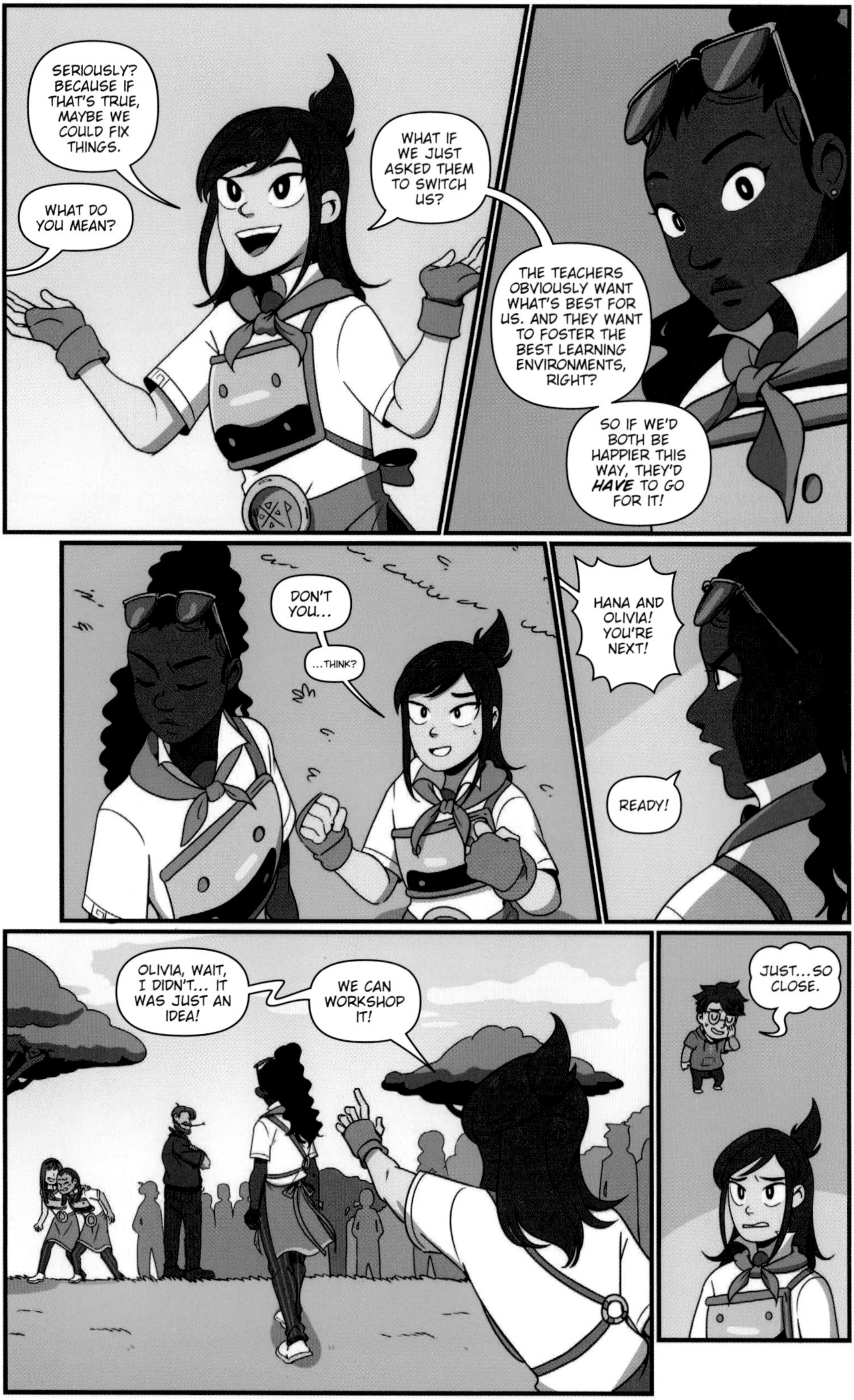
SERIOUSLY? BECAUSE IF THAT'S TRUE, MAYBE WE COULD FIX THINGS.
WHAT DO YOU MEAN?
WHAT IF WE JUST ASKED THEM TO SWITCH US?
THE TEACHERS OBVIOUSLY WANT WHAT'S BEST FOR US. AND THEY WANT TO FOSTER THE BEST LEARNING ENVIRONMENTS, RIGHT?
SO IF WE'D BOTH BE HAPPIER THIS WAY, THEY'D ***HAVE*** TO GO FOR IT!
DON'T YOU...
...THINK?
HANA AND OLIVIA! YOU'RE NEXT!
READY!
OLIVIA, WAIT, I DIDN'T... IT WAS JUST AN IDEA!
WE CAN WORKSHOP IT!
JUST...SO CLOSE.

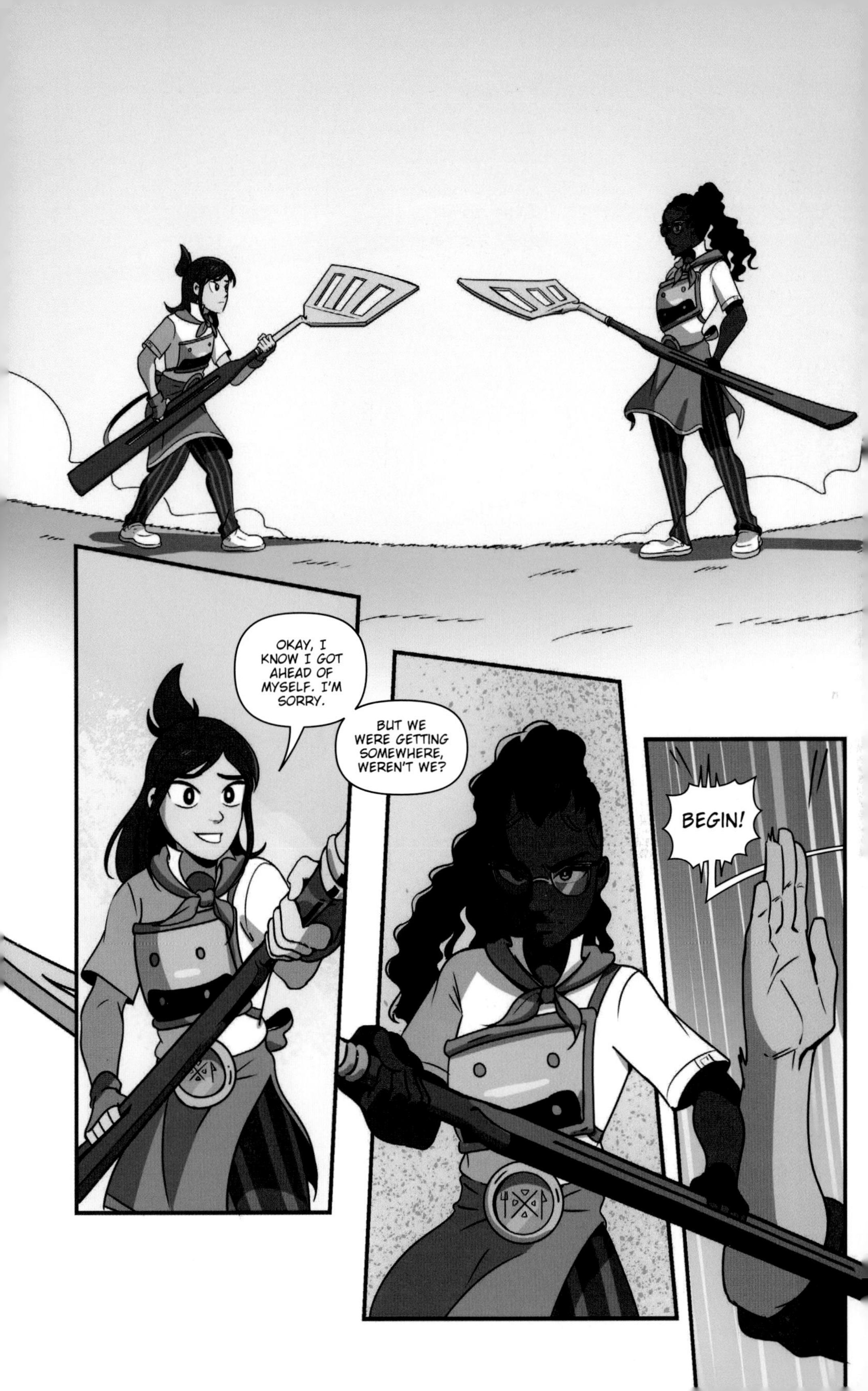
OKAY, I KNOW I GOT AHEAD OF MYSELF. I'M SORRY.
BUT WE WERE GETTING SOMEWHERE, WEREN'T WE?
BEGIN!

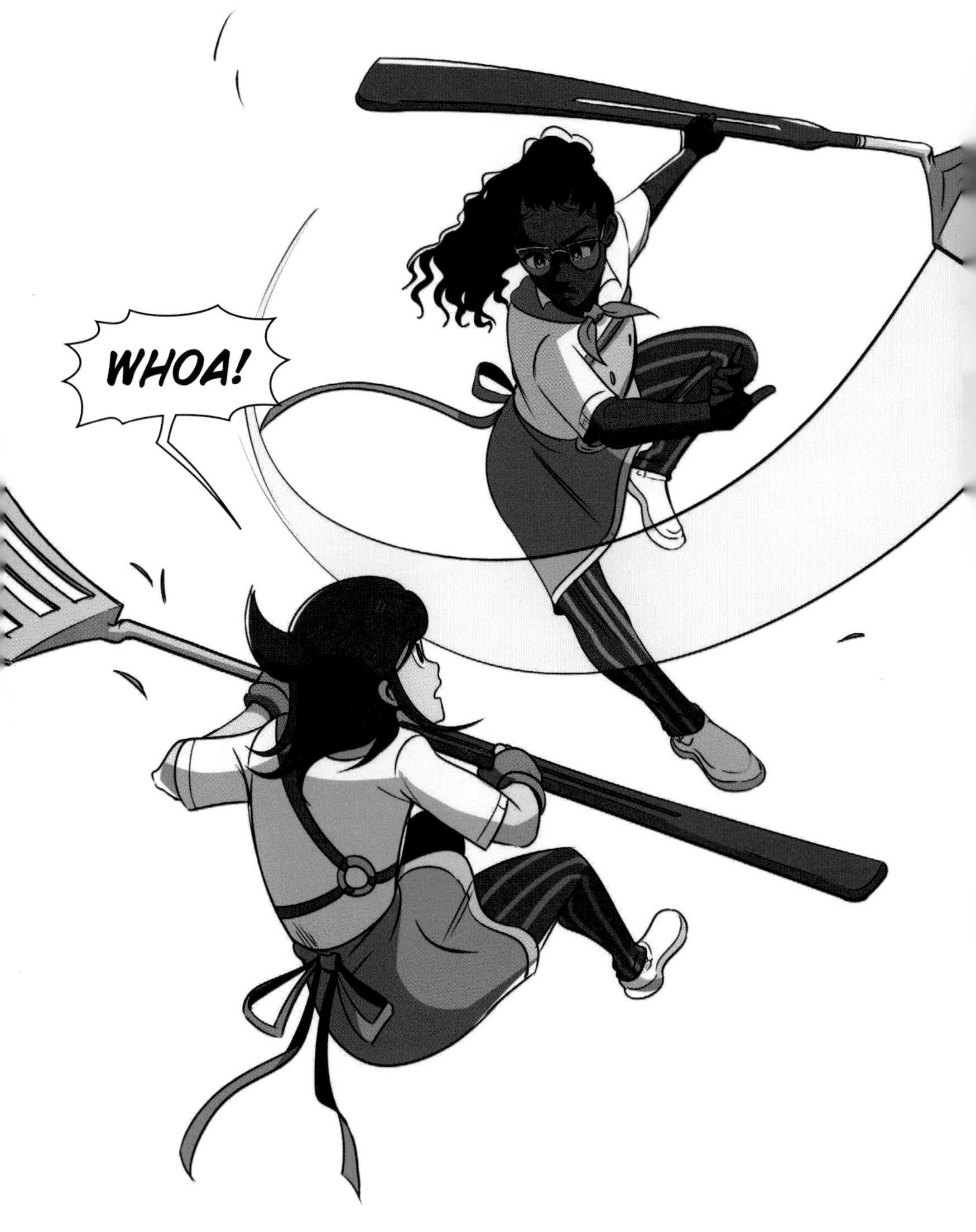
WHOA!

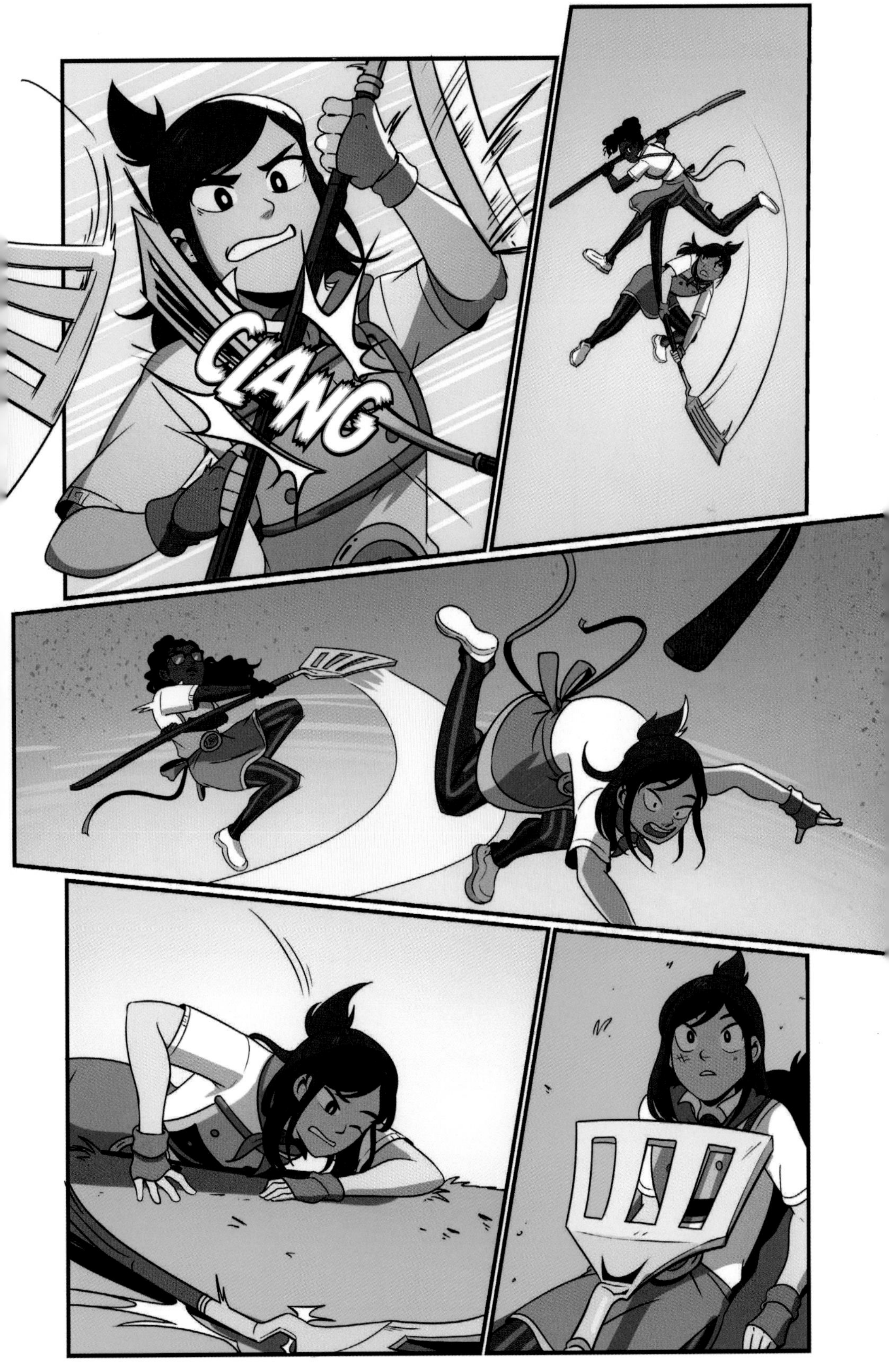
CLANG

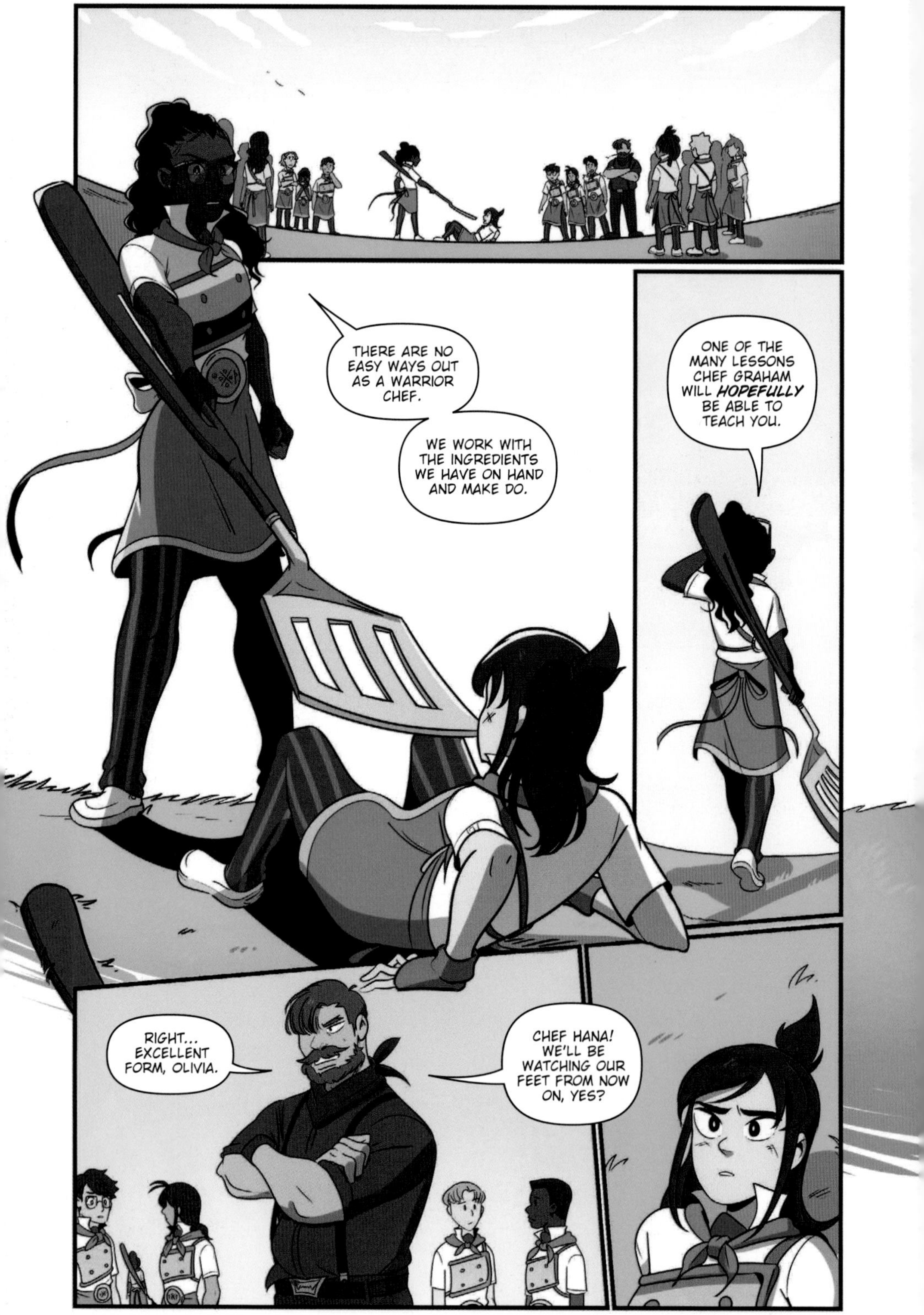

THERE ARE NO EASY WAYS OUT AS A WARRIOR CHEF.
WE WORK WITH THE INGREDIENTS WE HAVE ON HAND AND MAKE DO.
ONE OF THE MANY LESSONS CHEF GRAHAM WILL ***HOPEFULLY*** BE ABLE TO TEACH YOU.
RIGHT... EXCELLENT FORM, OLIVIA.
CHEF HANA! WE'LL BE WATCHING OUR FEET FROM NOW ON, YES?

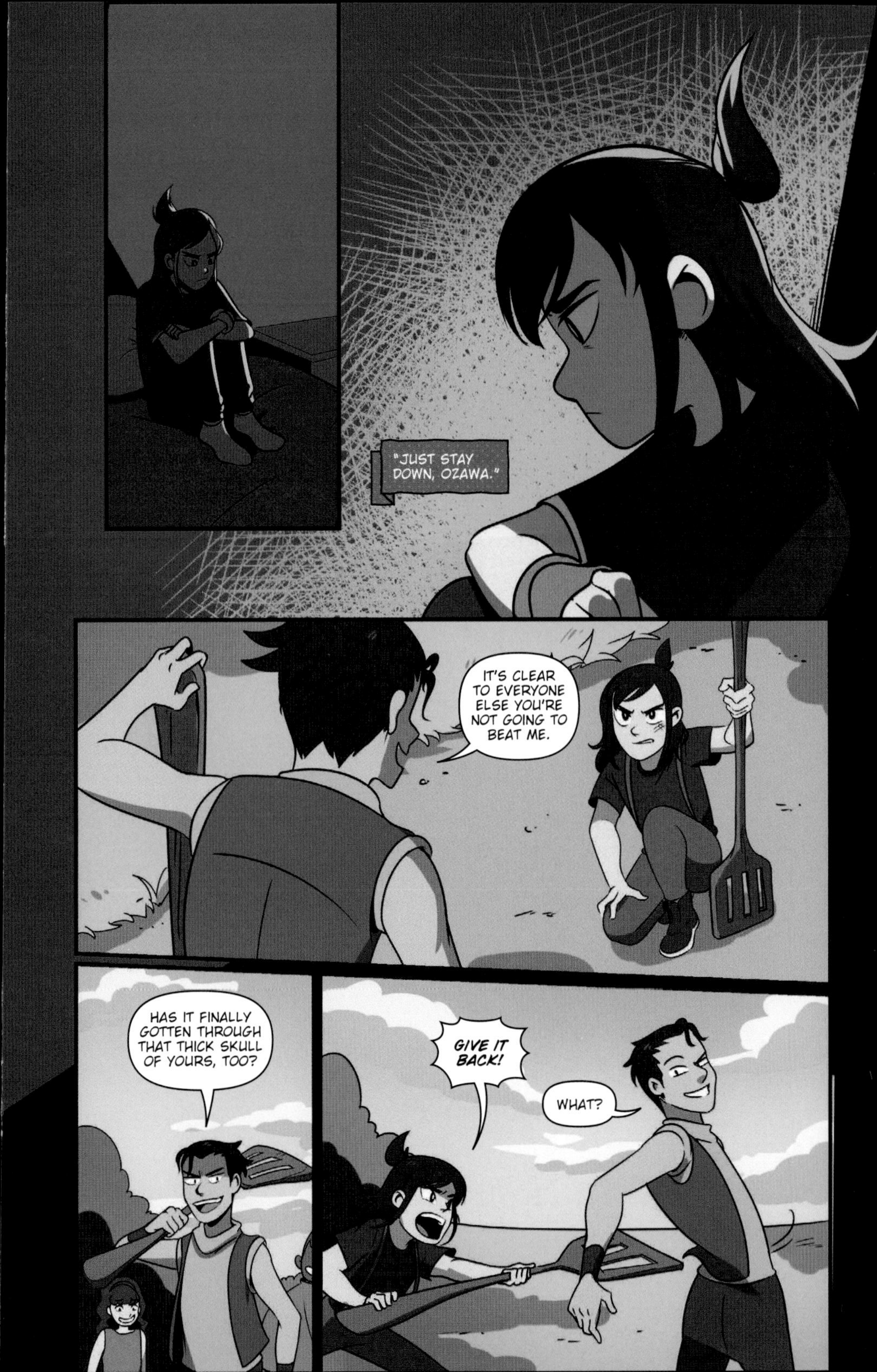
"JUST STAY DOWN, OZAWA."
IT'S CLEAR TO EVERYONE ELSE YOU'RE NOT GOING TO BEAT ME.
HAS IT FINALLY GOTTEN THROUGH THAT THICK SKULL OF YOURS, TOO?
GIVE IT BACK!
WHAT?

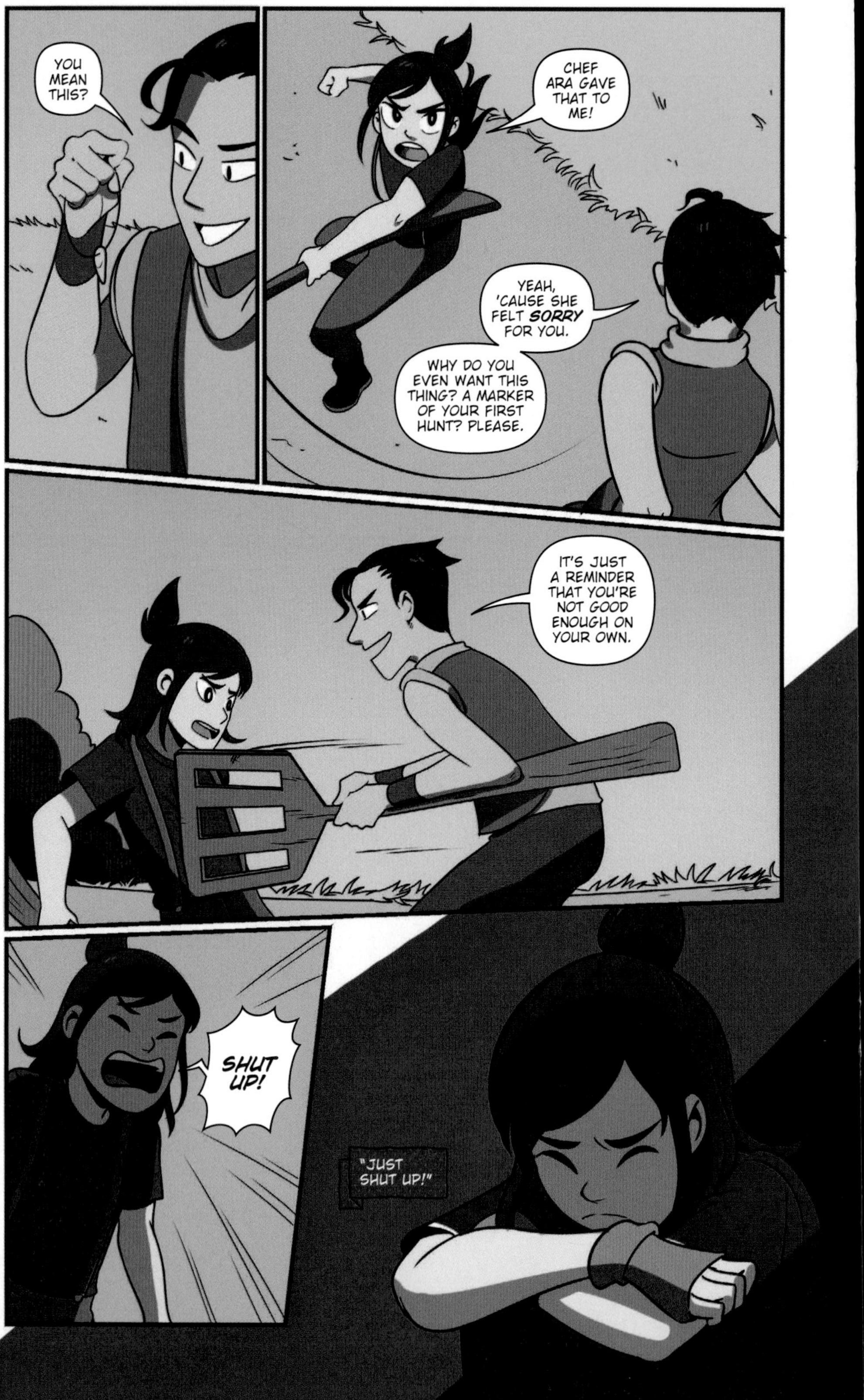
YOU MEAN THIS?
CHEF ARA GAVE THAT TO ME!
YEAH, 'CAUSE SHE FELT SORRY FOR YOU.
WHY DO YOU EVEN WANT THIS THING? A MARKER OF YOUR FIRST HUNT? PLEASE.
IT'S JUST A REMINDER THAT YOU'RE NOT GOOD ENOUGH ON YOUR OWN.
SHUT UP!
"JUST SHUT UP!"

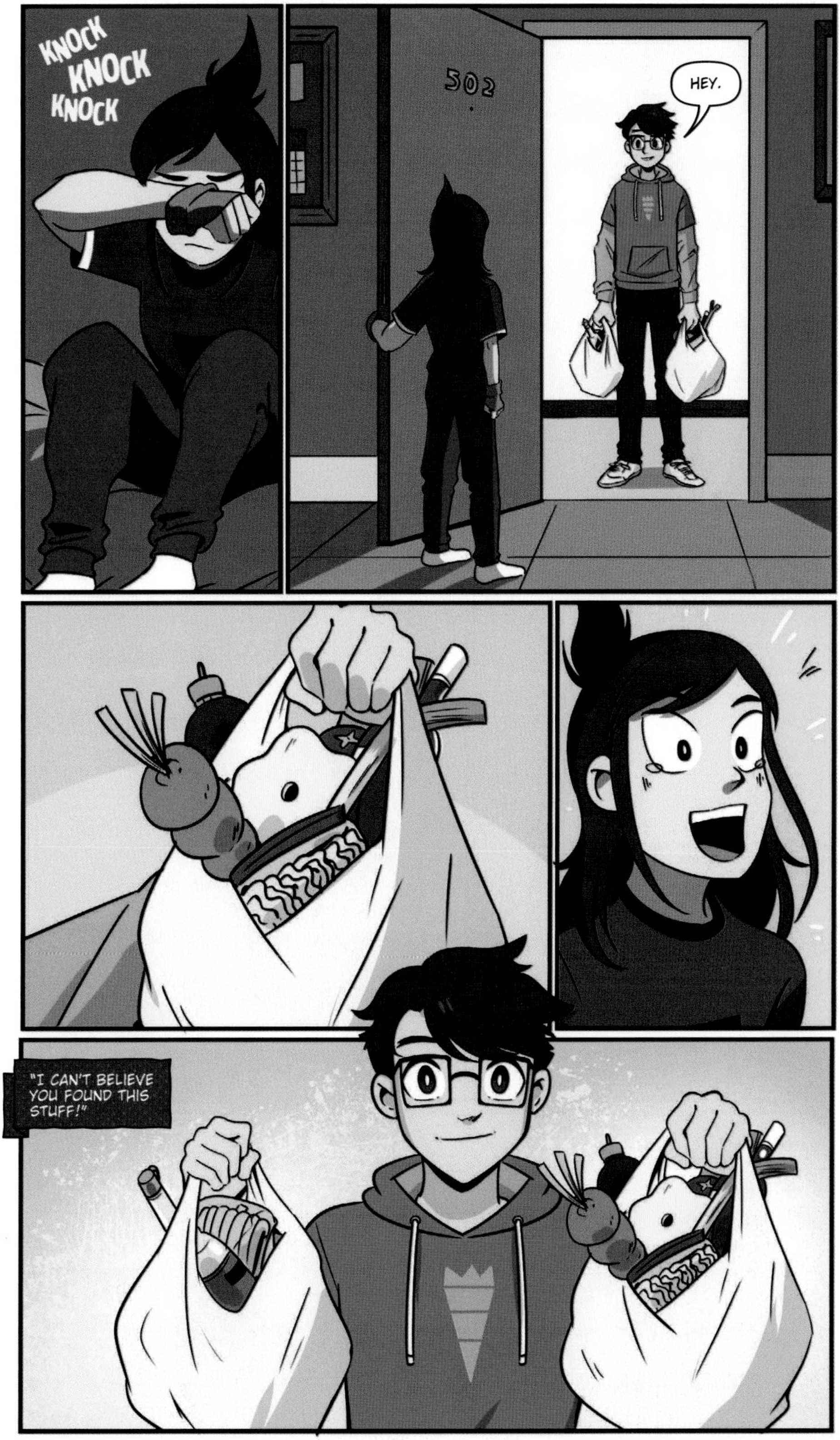
KNOCK
KNOCK
KNOCK
502
HEY.
"I CAN'T BELIEVE YOU FOUND THIS STUFF!"

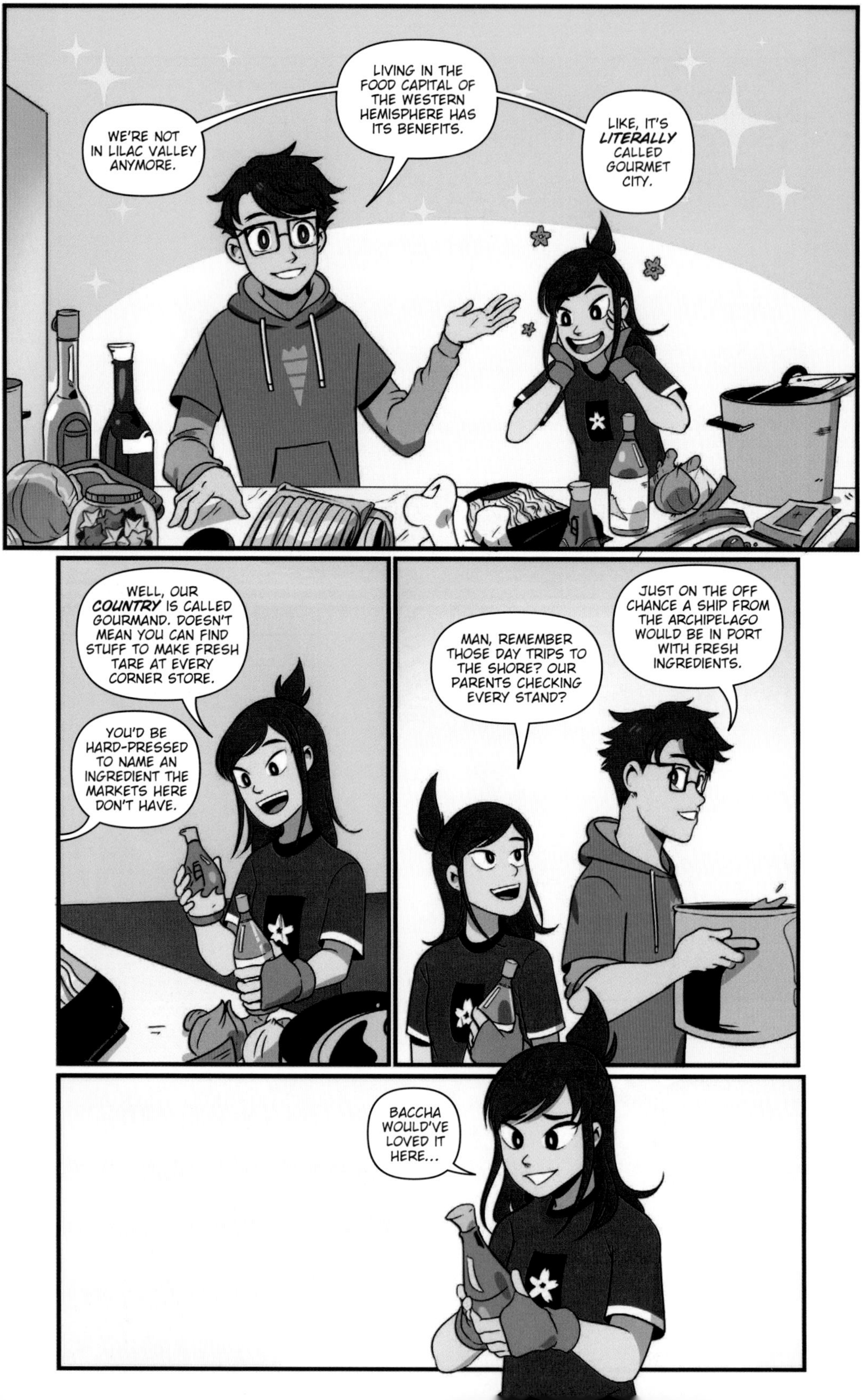
WE'RE NOT IN LILAC VALLEY ANYMORE.
LIVING IN THE FOOD CAPITAL OF THE WESTERN HEMISPHERE HAS ITS BENEFITS.
LIKE, IT'S *LITERALLY* CALLED GOURMET CITY.
WELL, OUR **COUNTRY** IS CALLED GOURMAND. DOESN'T MEAN YOU CAN FIND STUFF TO MAKE FRESH TARE AT EVERY CORNER STORE.
YOU'D BE HARD-PRESSED TO NAME AN INGREDIENT THE MARKETS HERE DON'T HAVE.
MAN, REMEMBER THOSE DAY TRIPS TO THE SHORE? OUR PARENTS CHECKING EVERY STAND?
JUST ON THE OFF CHANCE A SHIP FROM THE ARCHIPELAGO WOULD BE IN PORT WITH FRESH INGREDIENTS.
BACCHA WOULD'VE LOVED IT HERE...

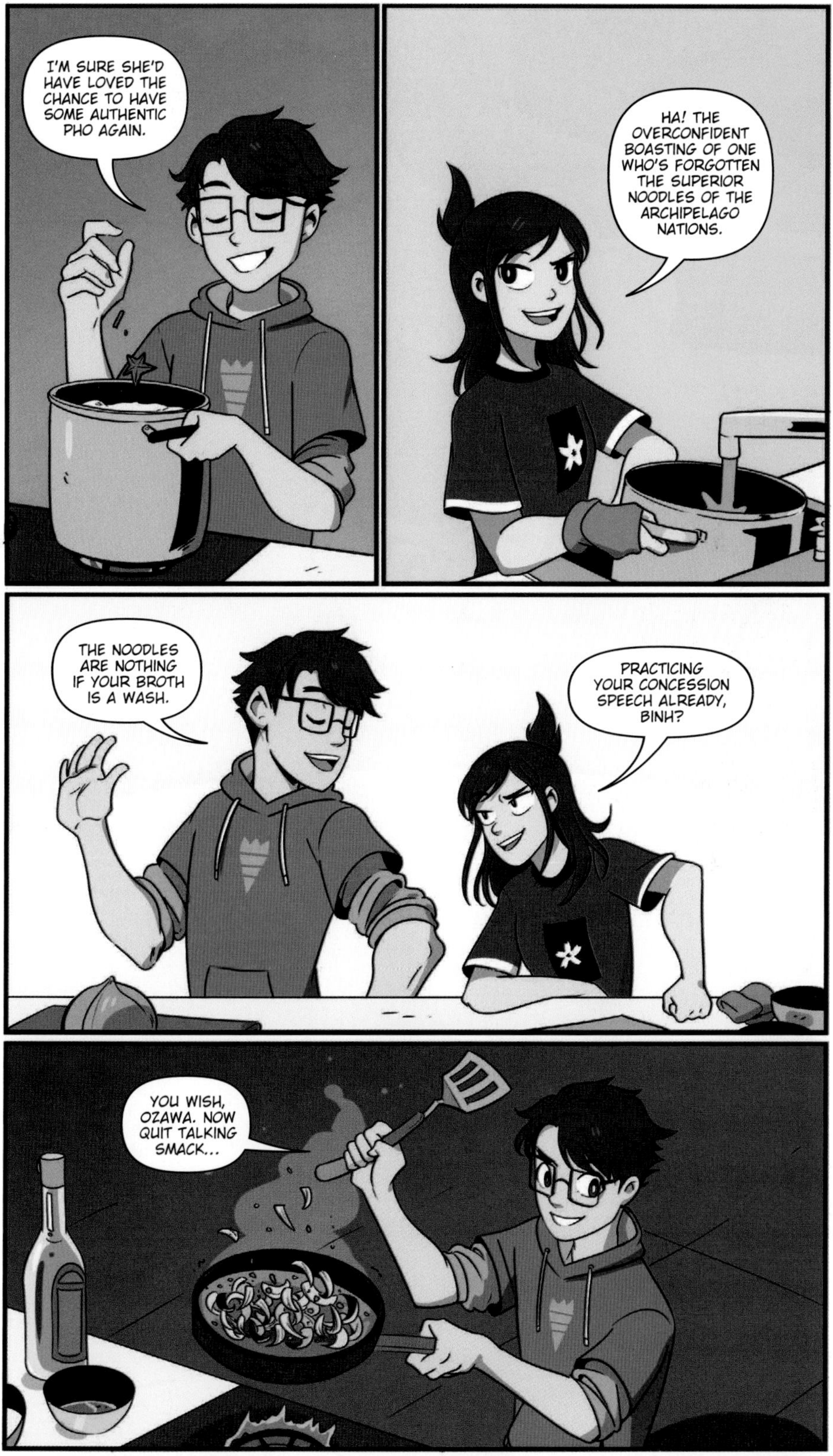
I'M SURE SHE'D HAVE LOVED THE CHANCE TO HAVE SOME AUTHENTIC PHO AGAIN.
HA! THE OVERCONFIDENT BOASTING OF ONE WHO'S FORGOTTEN THE SUPERIOR NOODLES OF THE ARCHIPELAGO NATIONS.
THE NOODLES ARE NOTHING IF YOUR BROTH IS A WASH.
PRACTICING YOUR CONCESSION SPEECH ALREADY, BINH?
YOU WISH, OZAWA. NOW QUIT TALKING SMACK...

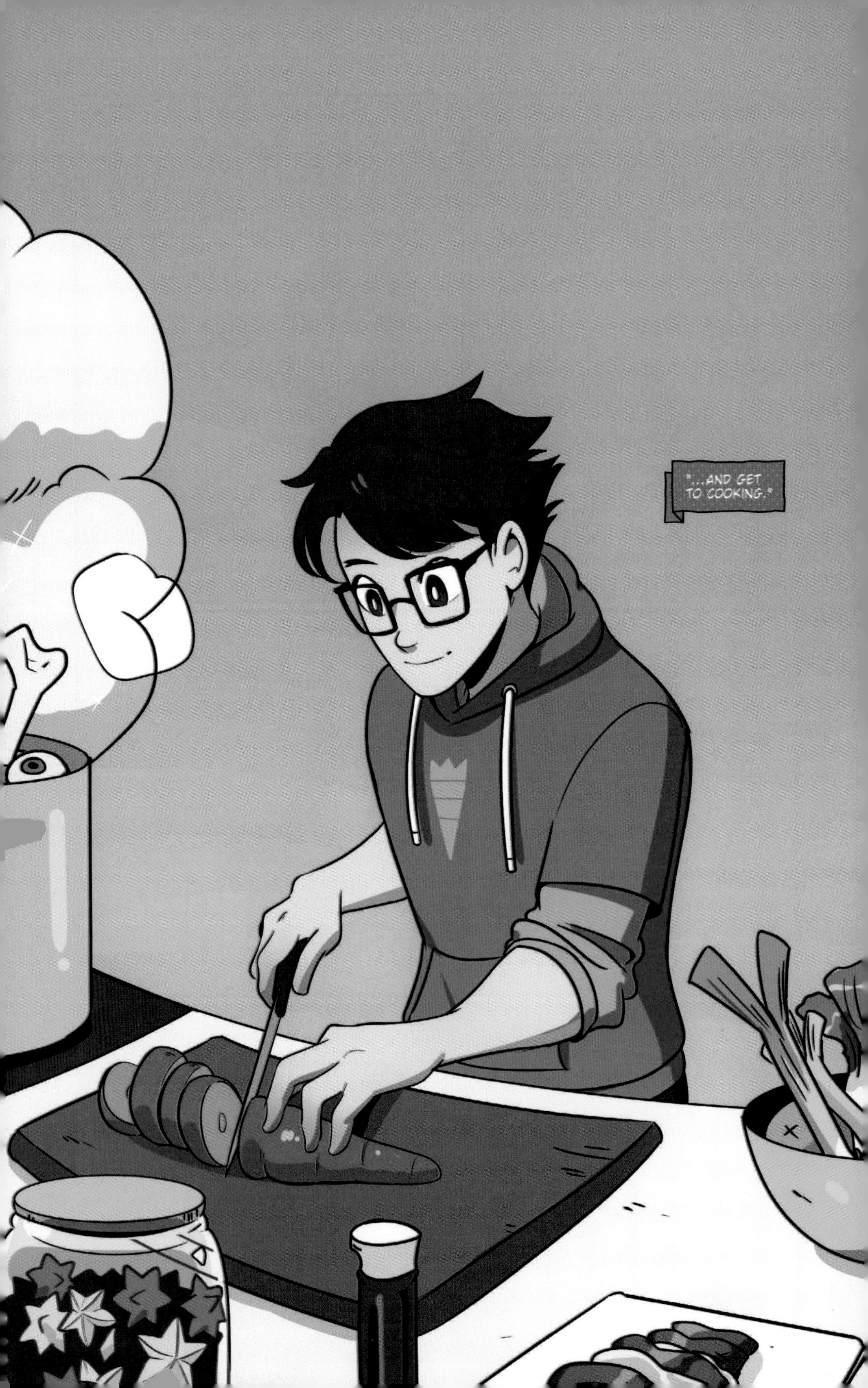
"...AND GET TO COOKING."

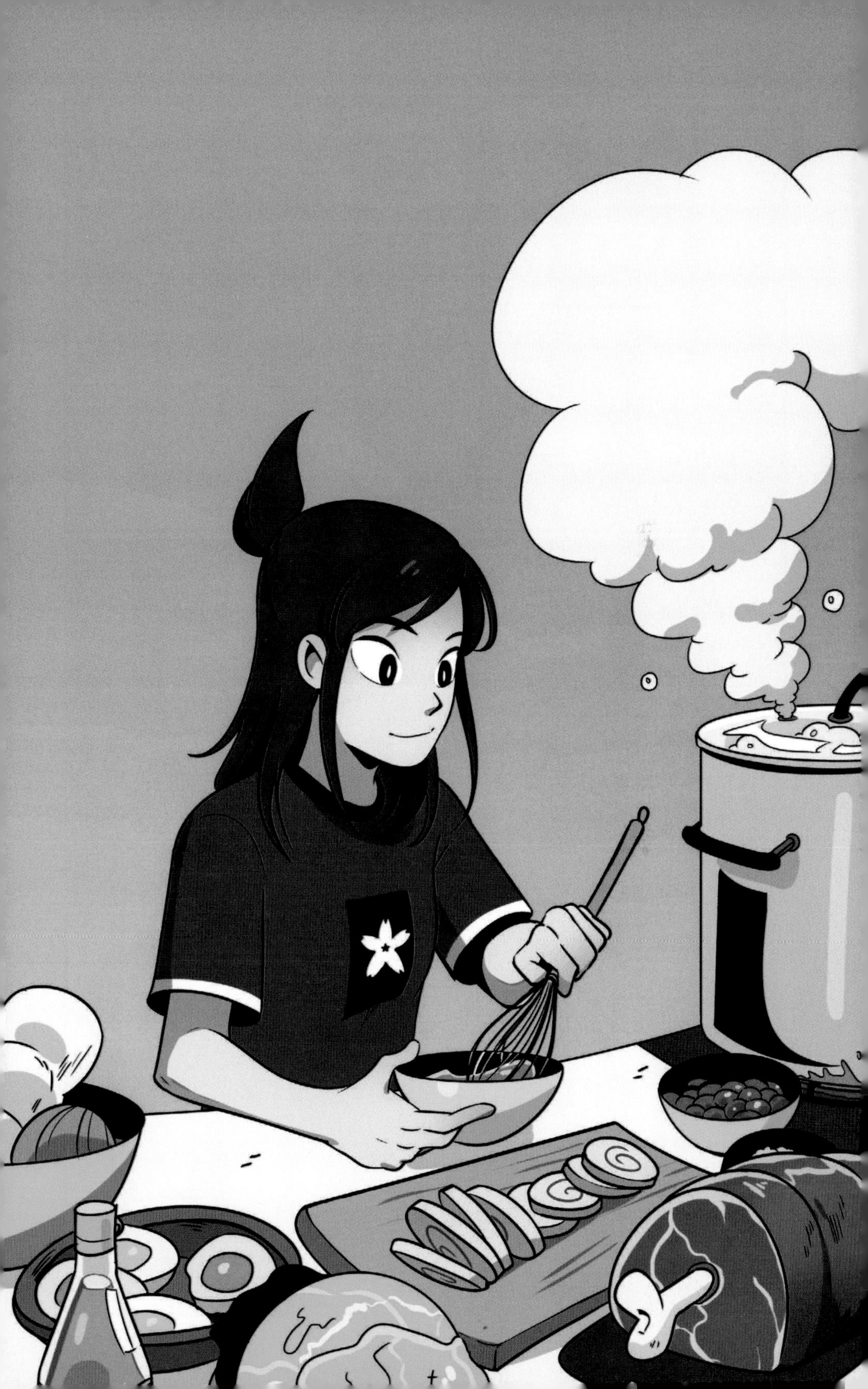

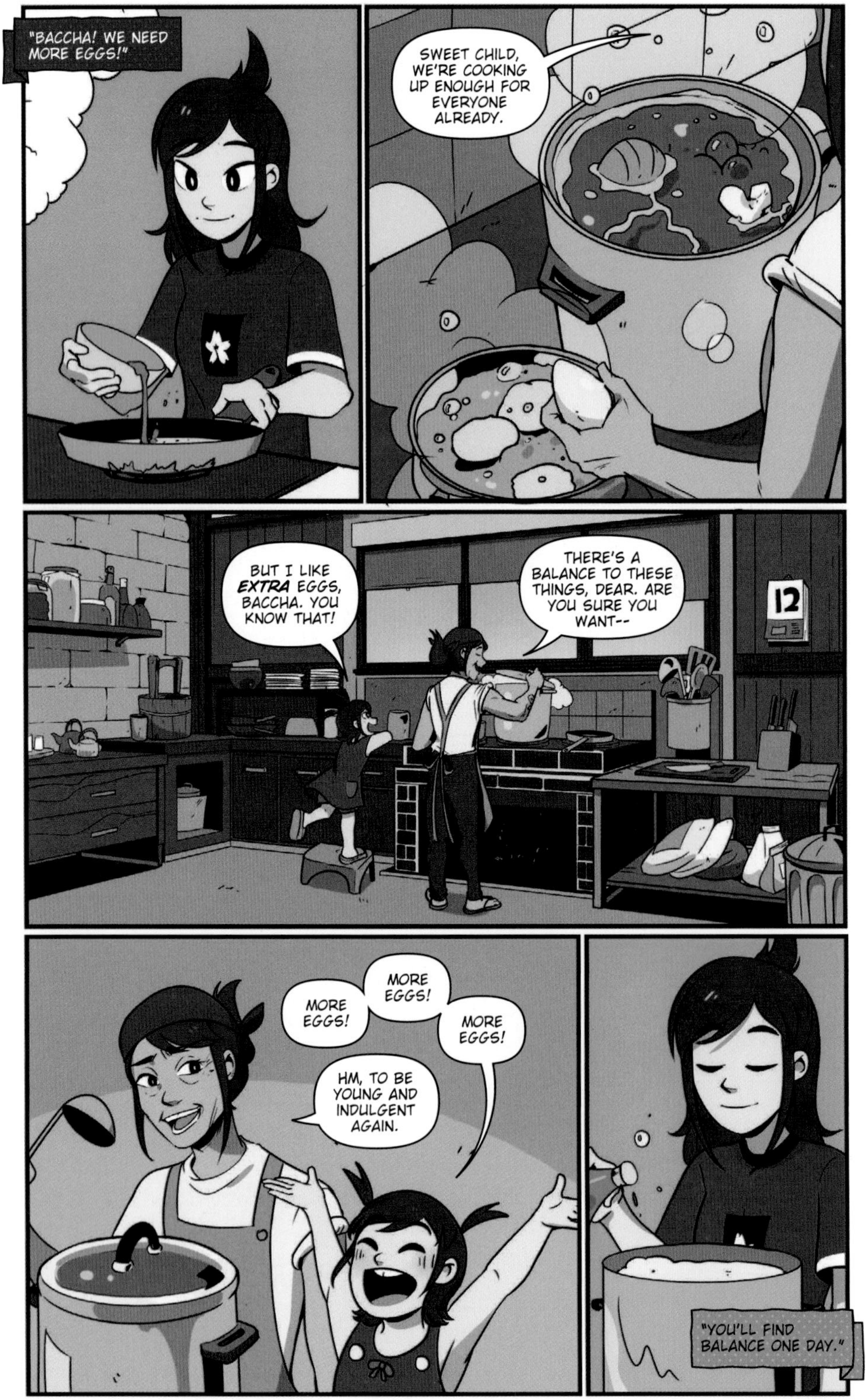
"BACCHA! WE NEED MORE EGGS!"
SWEET CHILD, WE'RE COOKING UP ENOUGH FOR EVERYONE ALREADY.
BUT I LIKE *EXTRA* EGGS, BACCHA. YOU KNOW THAT!
THERE'S A BALANCE TO THESE THINGS, DEAR. ARE YOU SURE YOU WANT--
12
MORE EGGS!
MORE EGGS!
MORE EGGS!
HM, TO BE YOUNG AND INDULGENT AGAIN.
"YOU'LL FIND BALANCE ONE DAY."

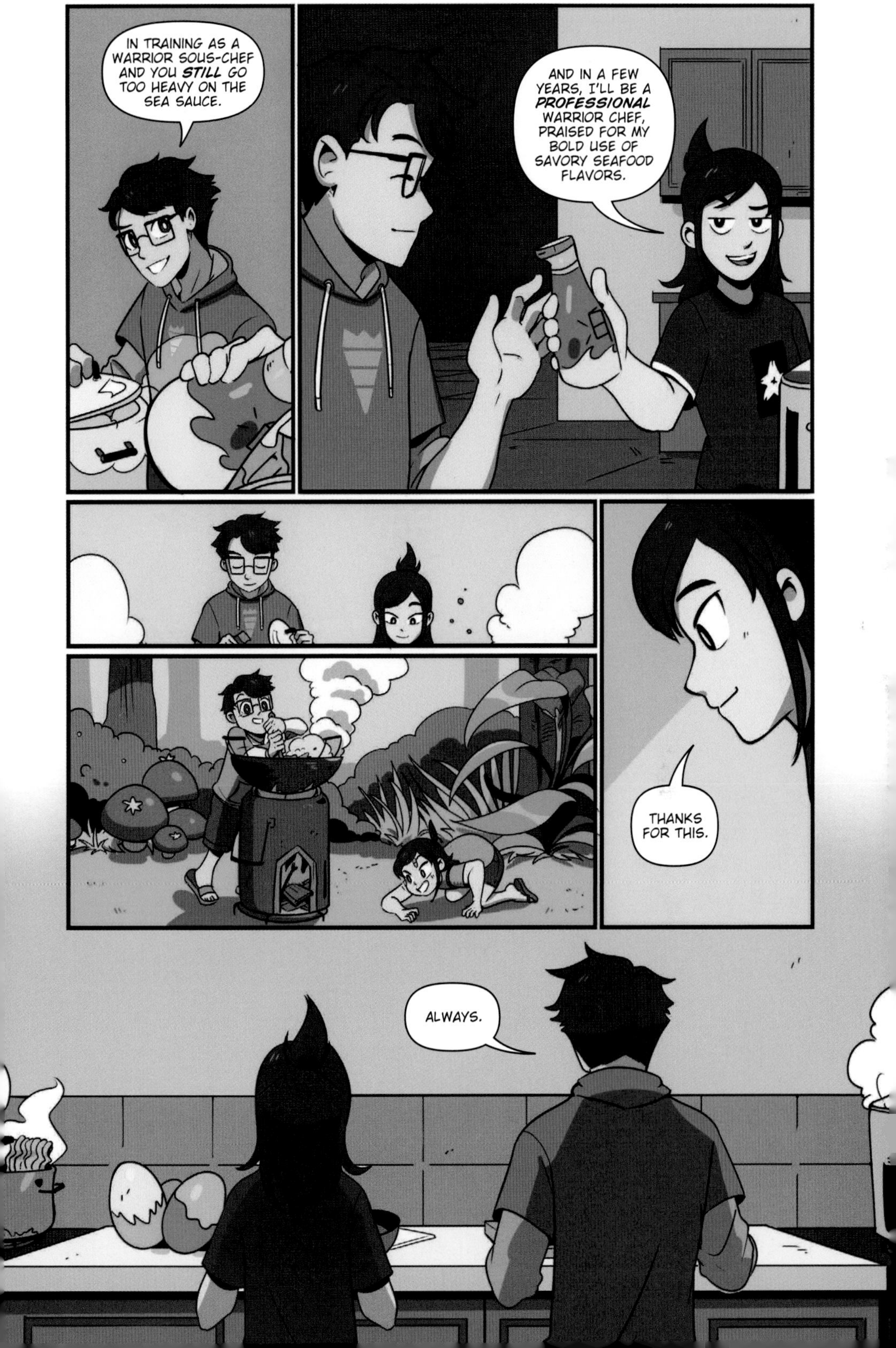
IN TRAINING AS A WARRIOR SOUS-CHEF AND YOU **STILL** GO TOO HEAVY ON THE SEA SAUCE.
AND IN A FEW YEARS, I'LL BE A ***PROFESSIONAL*** WARRIOR CHEF, PRAISED FOR MY BOLD USE OF SAVORY SEAFOOD FLAVORS.
THANKS FOR THIS.
ALWAYS.

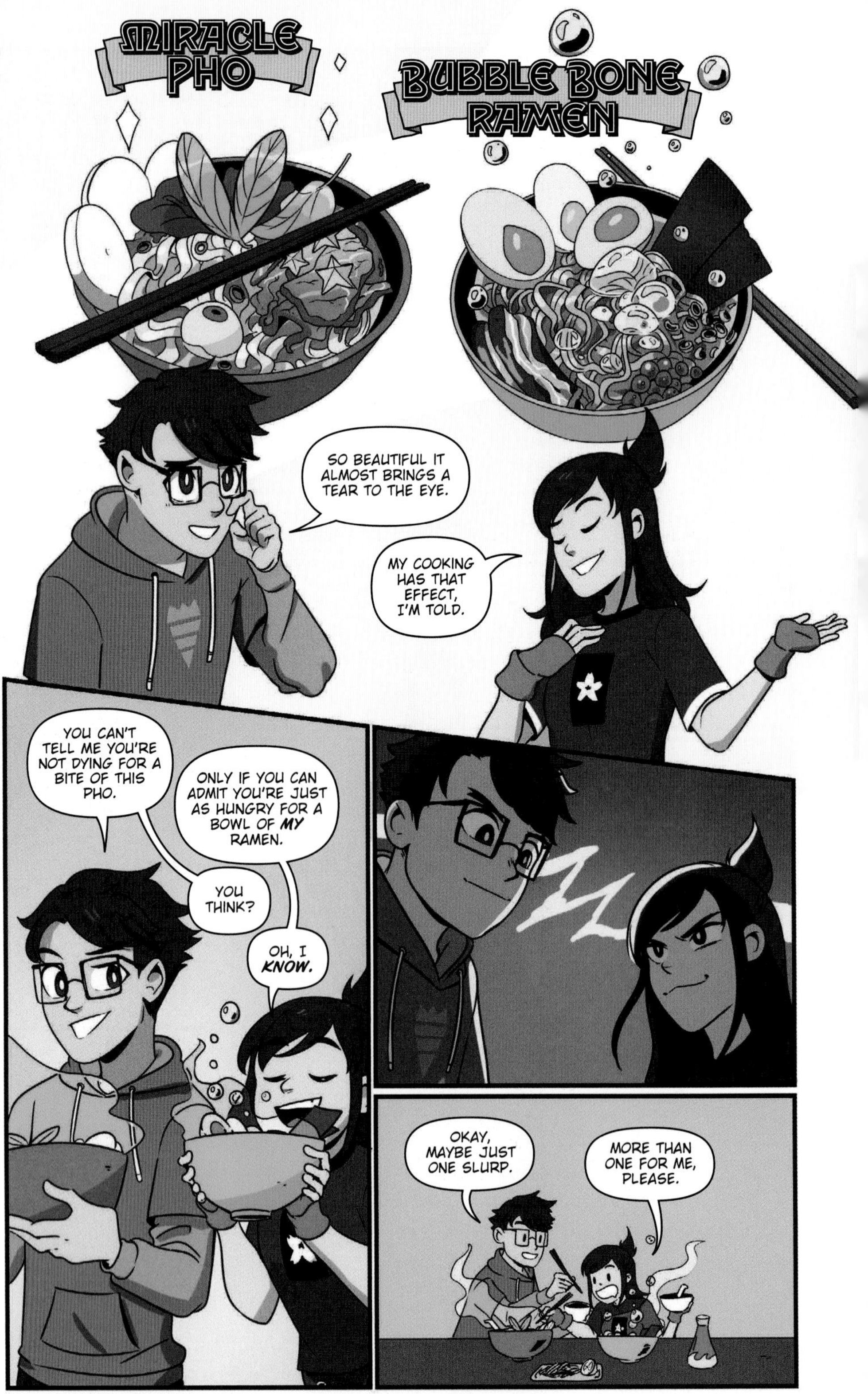

MIRACLE PHO
BUBBLE BONE RAMEN
SO BEAUTIFUL IT ALMOST BRINGS A TEAR TO THE EYE.
MY COOKING HAS THAT EFFECT, I'M TOLD.
YOU CAN'T TELL ME YOU'RE NOT DYING FOR A BITE OF THIS PHO.
ONLY IF YOU CAN ADMIT YOU'RE JUST AS HUNGRY FOR A BOWL OF *MY* RAMEN.
YOU THINK?
OH, I *KNOW.*
OKAY, MAYBE JUST ONE SLURP.
MORE THAN ONE FOR ME, PLEASE.

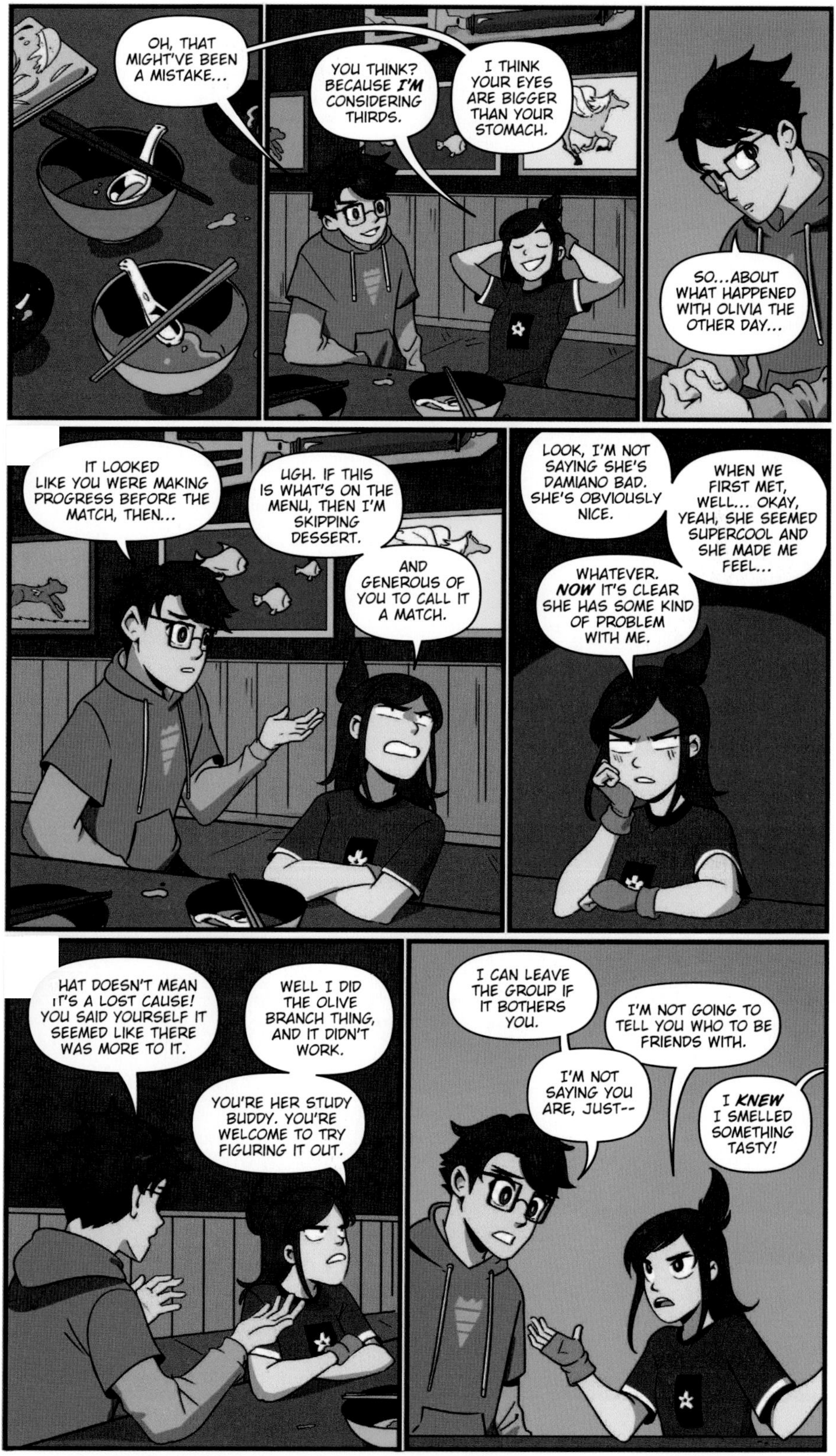
OH, THAT MIGHT'VE BEEN A MISTAKE...
YOU THINK? BECAUSE ***I'M*** CONSIDERING THIRDS.
I THINK YOUR EYES ARE BIGGER THAN YOUR STOMACH.
SO...ABOUT WHAT HAPPENED WITH OLIVIA THE OTHER DAY...
IT LOOKED LIKE YOU WERE MAKING PROGRESS BEFORE THE MATCH, THEN...
UGH. IF THIS IS WHAT'S ON THE MENU, THEN I'M SKIPPING DESSERT.
AND GENEROUS OF YOU TO CALL IT A MATCH.
LOOK, I'M NOT SAYING SHE'S DAMIANO BAD. SHE'S OBVIOUSLY NICE.
WHEN WE FIRST MET, WELL... OKAY, YEAH, SHE SEEMED SUPERCOOL AND SHE MADE ME FEEL...
WHATEVER. ***NOW*** IT'S CLEAR SHE HAS SOME KIND OF PROBLEM WITH ME.
HAT DOESN'T MEAN IT'S A LOST CAUSE! YOU SAID YOURSELF IT SEEMED LIKE THERE WAS MORE TO IT.
WELL I DID THE OLIVE BRANCH THING, AND IT DIDN'T WORK.
YOU'RE HER STUDY BUDDY. YOU'RE WELCOME TO TRY FIGURING IT OUT.
I CAN LEAVE THE GROUP IF IT BOTHERS YOU.
I'M NOT GOING TO TELL YOU WHO TO BE FRIENDS WITH.
I'M NOT SAYING YOU ARE, JUST--
I ***KNEW*** I SMELLED SOMETHING TASTY!

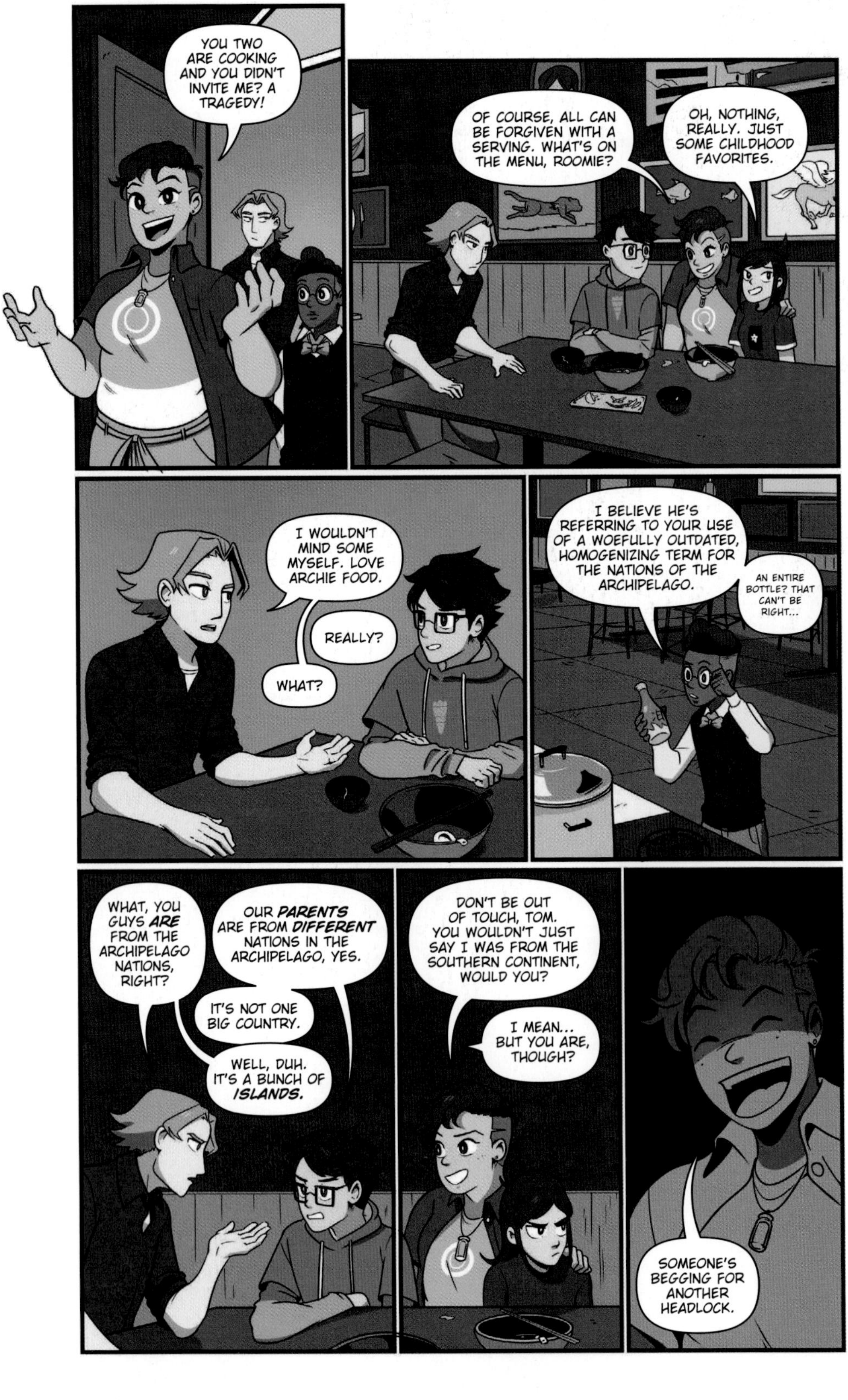
YOU TWO ARE COOKING AND YOU DIDN'T INVITE ME? A TRAGEDY!
OF COURSE, ALL CAN BE FORGIVEN WITH A SERVING. WHAT'S ON THE MENU, ROOMIE?
OH, NOTHING, REALLY. JUST SOME CHILDHOOD FAVORITES.
I WOULDN'T MIND SOME MYSELF. LOVE ARCHIE FOOD.
REALLY?
WHAT?
I BELIEVE HE'S REFERRING TO YOUR USE OF A WOEFULLY OUTDATED, HOMOGENIZING TERM FOR THE NATIONS OF THE ARCHIPELAGO.
AN ENTIRE BOTTLE? THAT CAN'T BE RIGHT...
WHAT, YOU GUYS ARE FROM THE ARCHIPELAGO NATIONS, RIGHT?
OUR PARENTS ARE FROM DIFFERENT NATIONS IN THE ARCHIPELAGO, YES.
IT'S NOT ONE BIG COUNTRY.
WELL, DUH. IT'S A BUNCH OF ISLANDS.
DON'T BE OUT OF TOUCH, TOM. YOU WOULDN'T JUST SAY I WAS FROM THE SOUTHERN CONTINENT, WOULD YOU?
I MEAN... BUT YOU ARE, THOUGH?
SOMEONE'S BEGGING FOR ANOTHER HEADLOCK.

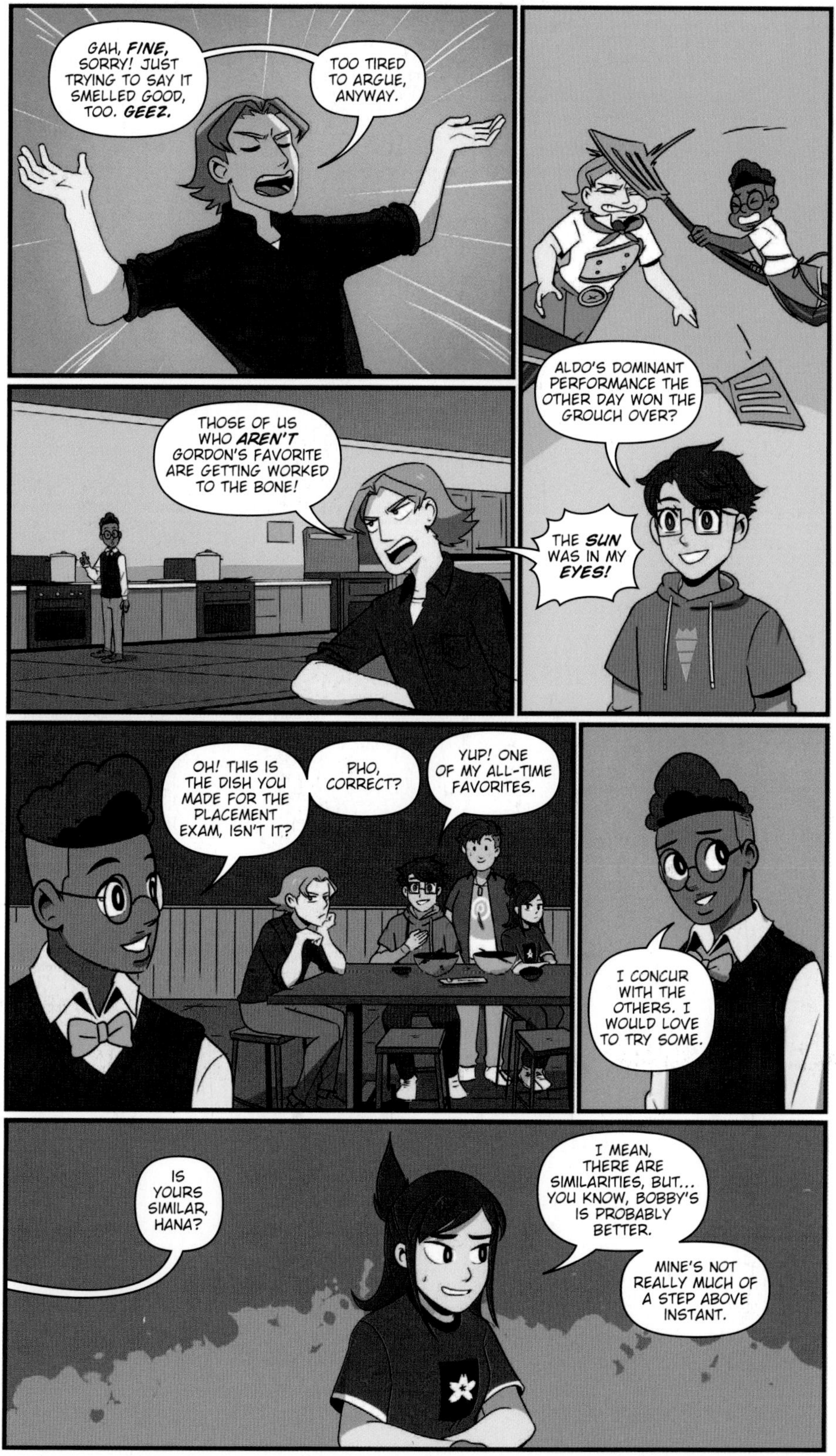
GAH, FINE, SORRY! JUST TRYING TO SAY IT SMELLED GOOD, TOO. GEEZ.
TOO TIRED TO ARGUE, ANYWAY.
THOSE OF US WHO AREN'T GORDON'S FAVORITE ARE GETTING WORKED TO THE BONE!
ALDO'S DOMINANT PERFORMANCE THE OTHER DAY WON THE GROUCH OVER?
THE SUN WAS IN MY EYES!
OH! THIS IS THE DISH YOU MADE FOR THE PLACEMENT EXAM, ISN'T IT?
PHO, CORRECT?
YUP! ONE OF MY ALL-TIME FAVORITES.
I CONCUR WITH THE OTHERS. I WOULD LOVE TO TRY SOME.
IS YOURS SIMILAR, HANA?
I MEAN, THERE ARE SIMILARITIES, BUT... YOU KNOW, BOBBY'S IS PROBABLY BETTER.
MINE'S NOT REALLY MUCH OF A STEP ABOVE INSTANT.

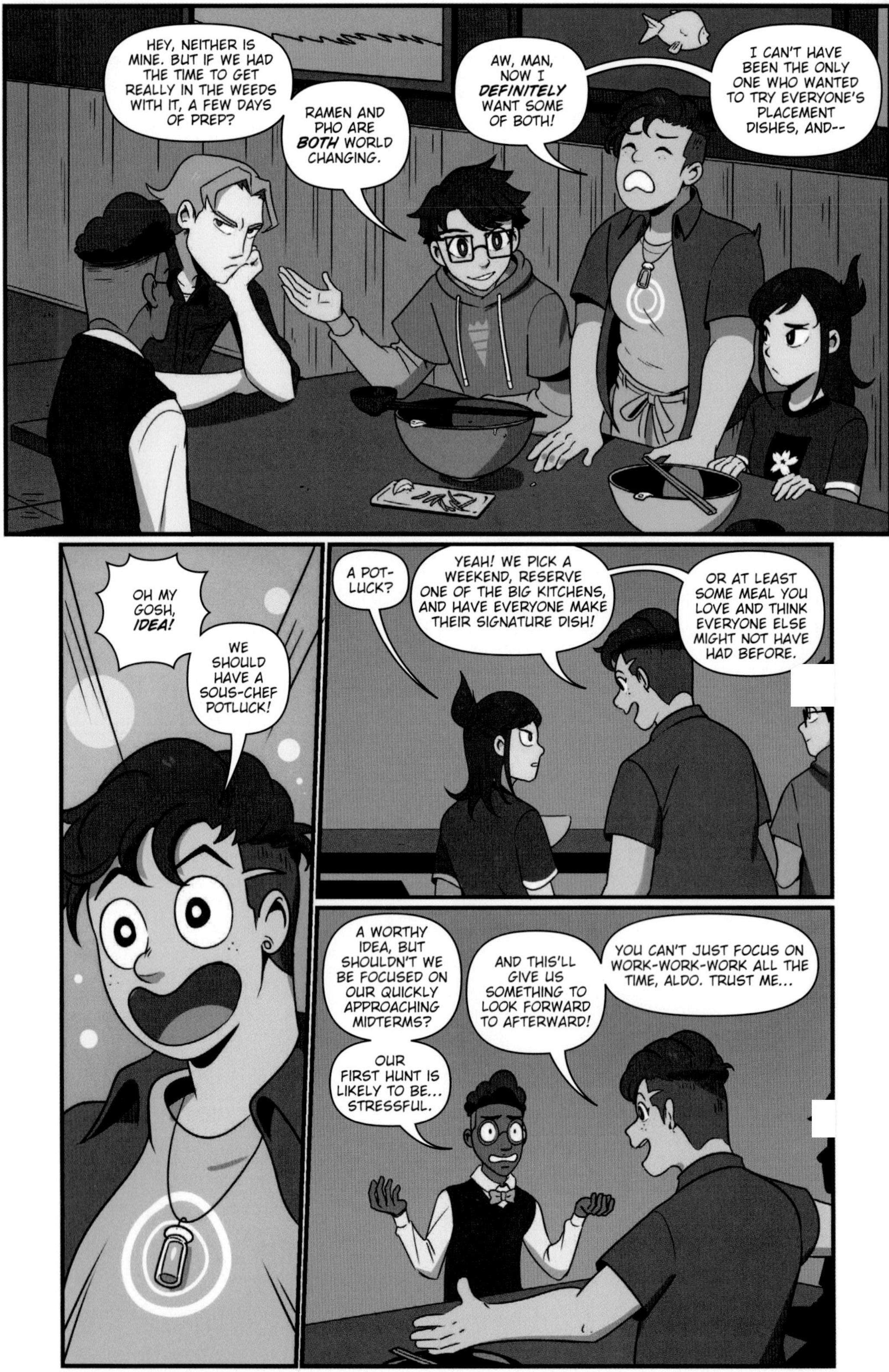
HEY, NEITHER IS MINE. BUT IF WE HAD THE TIME TO GET REALLY IN THE WEEDS WITH IT, A FEW DAYS OF PREP?
RAMEN AND PHO ARE *BOTH* WORLD CHANGING.
AW, MAN, NOW I *DEFINITELY* WANT SOME OF BOTH!
I CAN'T HAVE BEEN THE ONLY ONE WHO WANTED TO TRY EVERYONE'S PLACEMENT DISHES, AND--
OH MY GOSH, *IDEA!*
WE SHOULD HAVE A SOUS-CHEF POTLUCK!
A POT-LUCK?
YEAH! WE PICK A WEEKEND, RESERVE ONE OF THE BIG KITCHENS, AND HAVE EVERYONE MAKE THEIR SIGNATURE DISH!
OR AT LEAST SOME MEAL YOU LOVE AND THINK EVERYONE ELSE MIGHT NOT HAVE HAD BEFORE.
A WORTHY IDEA, BUT SHOULDN'T WE BE FOCUSED ON OUR QUICKLY APPROACHING MIDTERMS?
OUR FIRST HUNT IS LIKELY TO BE... STRESSFUL.
AND THIS'LL GIVE US SOMETHING TO LOOK FORWARD TO AFTERWARD!
YOU CAN'T JUST FOCUS ON WORK-WORK-WORK ALL THE TIME, ALDO. TRUST ME...

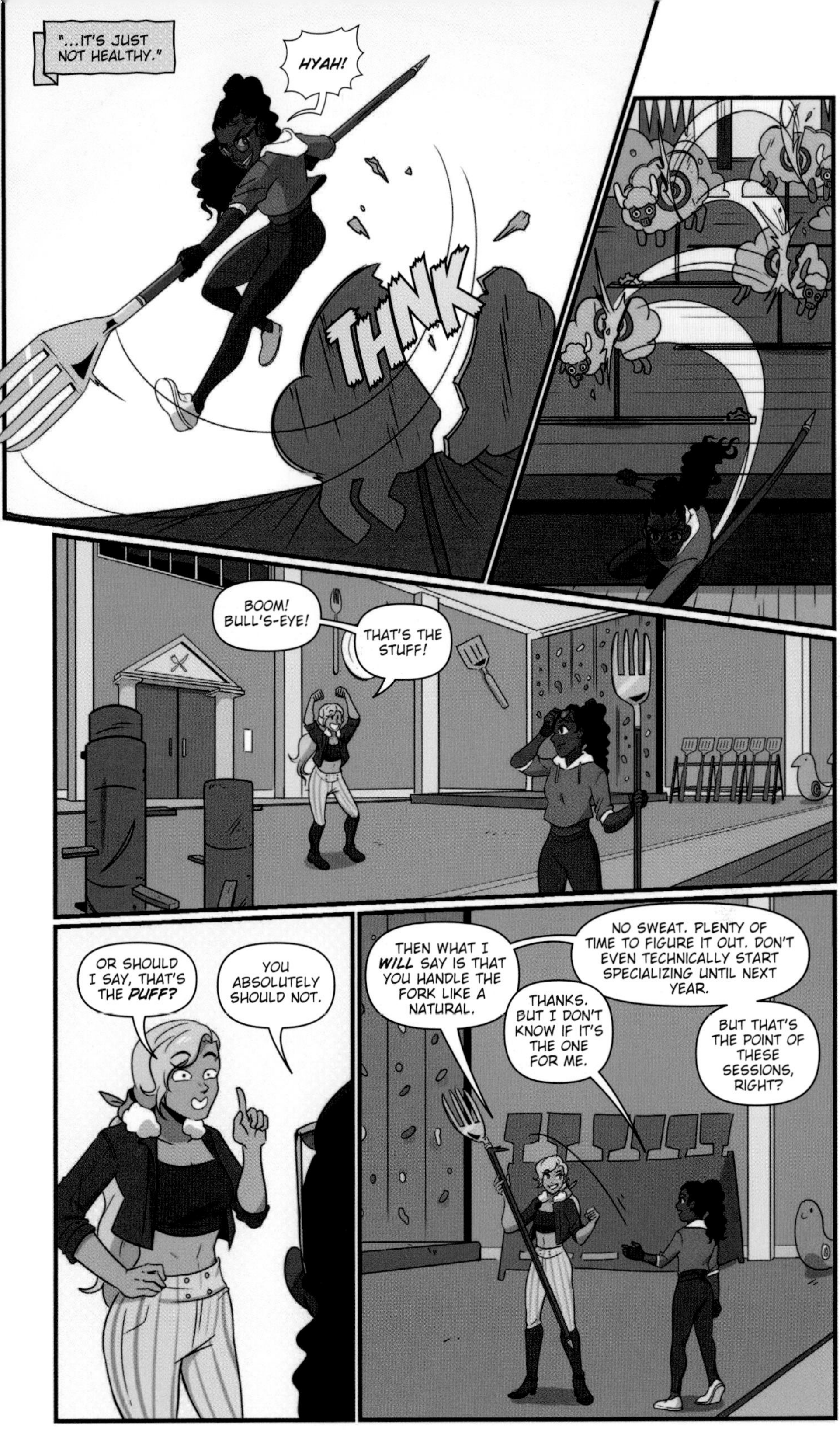
"...IT'S JUST NOT HEALTHY."
HYAH!
THNK
BOOM! BULL'S-EYE!
THAT'S THE STUFF!
OR SHOULD I SAY, THAT'S THE *PUFF?*
YOU ABSOLUTELY SHOULD NOT.
THEN WHAT I *WILL* SAY IS THAT YOU HANDLE THE FORK LIKE A NATURAL.
THANKS. BUT I DON'T KNOW IF IT'S THE ONE FOR ME.
NO SWEAT. PLENTY OF TIME TO FIGURE IT OUT. DON'T EVEN TECHNICALLY START SPECIALIZING UNTIL NEXT YEAR.
BUT THAT'S THE POINT OF THESE SESSIONS, RIGHT?

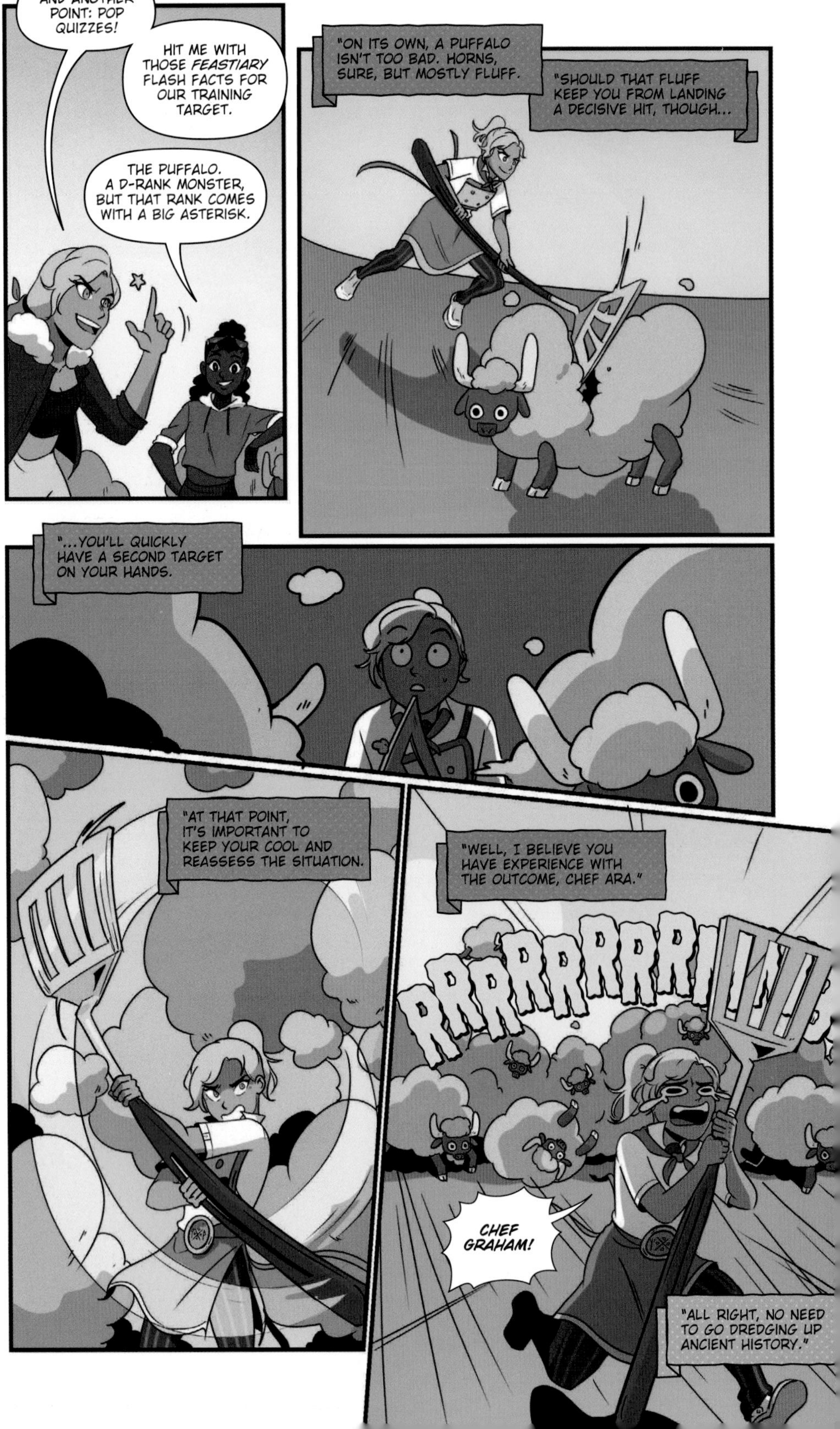
AND ANOTHER POINT: POP QUIZZES!
HIT ME WITH THOSE *FEASTIARY* FLASH FACTS FOR OUR TRAINING TARGET.
THE PUFFALO. A D-RANK MONSTER, BUT THAT RANK COMES WITH A BIG ASTERISK.
"ON ITS OWN, A PUFFALO ISN'T TOO BAD. HORNS, SURE, BUT MOSTLY FLUFF.
"SHOULD THAT FLUFF KEEP YOU FROM LANDING A DECISIVE HIT, THOUGH...
"...YOU'LL QUICKLY HAVE A SECOND TARGET ON YOUR HANDS.
"AT THAT POINT, IT'S IMPORTANT TO KEEP YOUR COOL AND REASSESS THE SITUATION.
"WELL, I BELIEVE YOU HAVE EXPERIENCE WITH THE OUTCOME, CHEF ARA."
RRRRRRRRI
CHEF GRAHAM!
"ALL RIGHT, NO NEED TO GO DREDGING UP ANCIENT HISTORY."

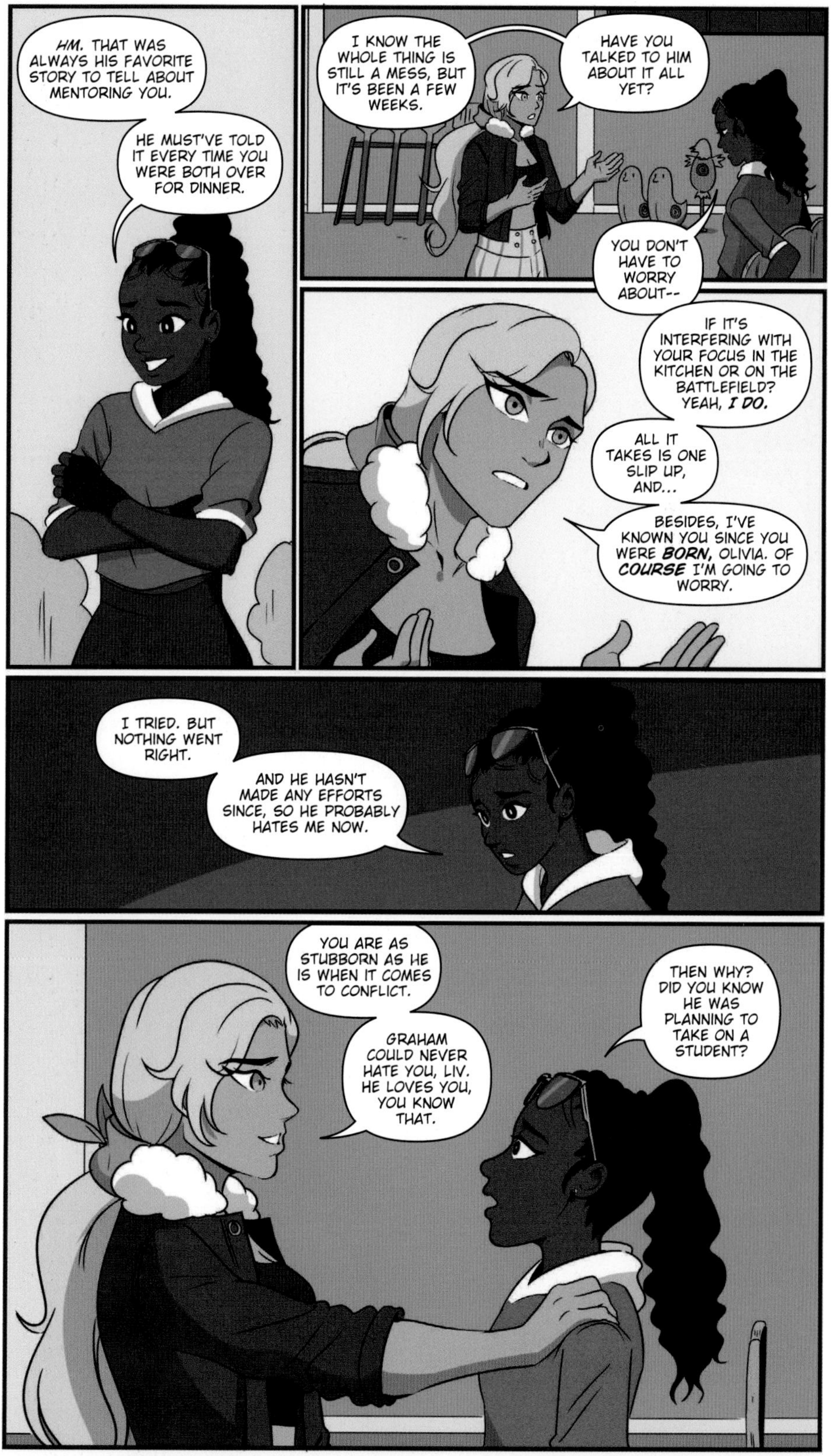
HM. THAT WAS ALWAYS HIS FAVORITE STORY TO TELL ABOUT MENTORING YOU.
HE MUST'VE TOLD IT EVERY TIME YOU WERE BOTH OVER FOR DINNER.
I KNOW THE WHOLE THING IS STILL A MESS, BUT IT'S BEEN A FEW WEEKS.
HAVE YOU TALKED TO HIM ABOUT IT ALL YET?
YOU DON'T HAVE TO WORRY ABOUT--
IF IT'S INTERFERING WITH YOUR FOCUS IN THE KITCHEN OR ON THE BATTLEFIELD? YEAH, I DO.
ALL IT TAKES IS ONE SLIP UP, AND...
BESIDES, I'VE KNOWN YOU SINCE YOU WERE BORN, OLIVIA. OF COURSE I'M GOING TO WORRY.
I TRIED. BUT NOTHING WENT RIGHT.
AND HE HASN'T MADE ANY EFFORTS SINCE, SO HE PROBABLY HATES ME NOW.
YOU ARE AS STUBBORN AS HE IS WHEN IT COMES TO CONFLICT.
GRAHAM COULD NEVER HATE YOU, LIV. HE LOVES YOU, YOU KNOW THAT.
THEN WHY? DID YOU KNOW HE WAS PLANNING TO TAKE ON A STUDENT?

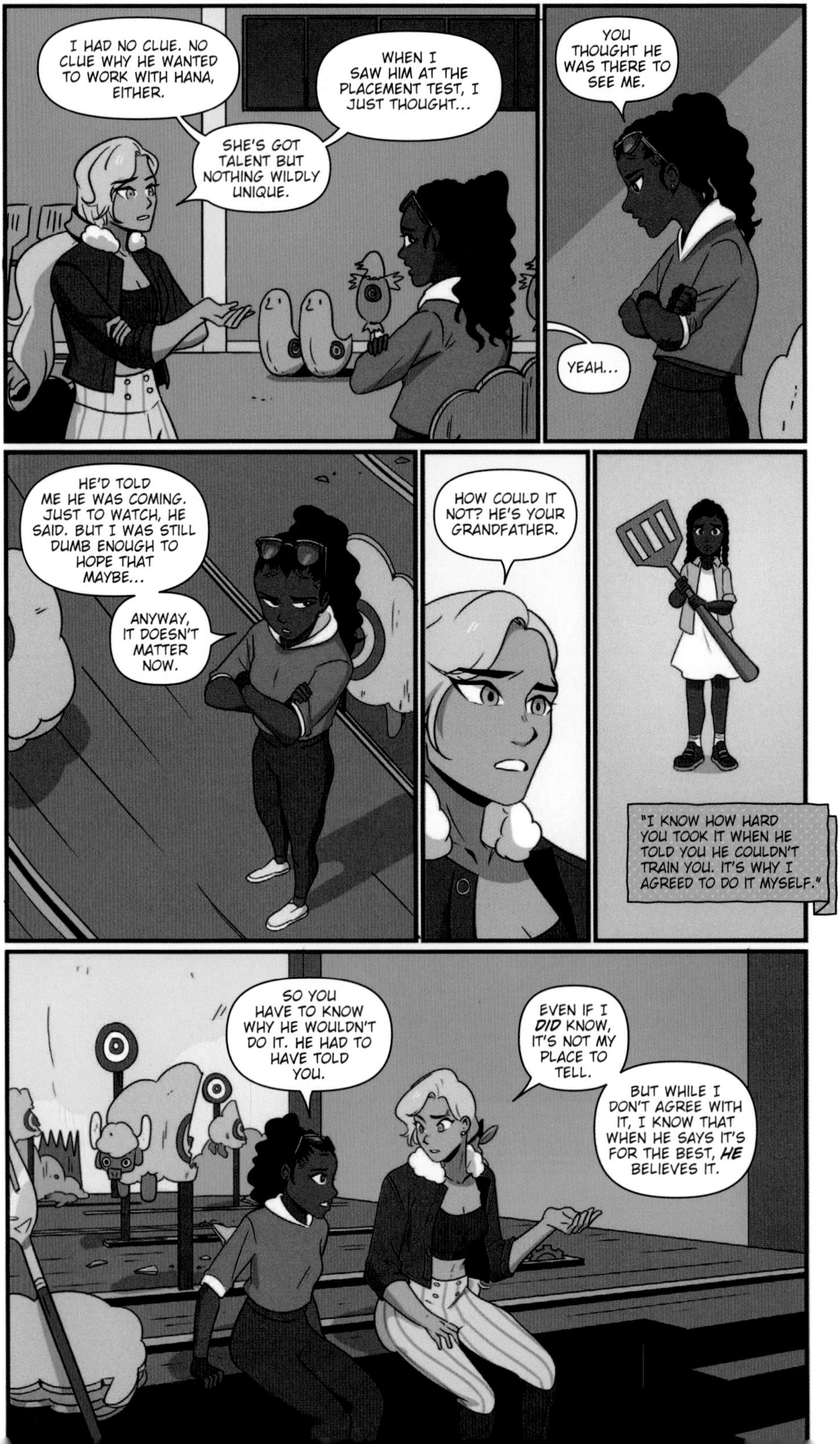

I HAD NO CLUE. NO CLUE WHY HE WANTED TO WORK WITH HANA, EITHER.
SHE'S GOT TALENT BUT NOTHING WILDLY UNIQUE.
WHEN I SAW HIM AT THE PLACEMENT TEST, I JUST THOUGHT...
YOU THOUGHT HE WAS THERE TO SEE ME.
YEAH...
HE'D TOLD ME HE WAS COMING. JUST TO WATCH, HE SAID. BUT I WAS STILL DUMB ENOUGH TO HOPE THAT MAYBE...
ANYWAY, IT DOESN'T MATTER NOW.
HOW COULD IT NOT? HE'S YOUR GRANDFATHER.
"I KNOW HOW HARD YOU TOOK IT WHEN HE TOLD YOU HE COULDN'T TRAIN YOU. IT'S WHY I AGREED TO DO IT MYSELF."
SO YOU HAVE TO KNOW WHY HE WOULDN'T DO IT. HE HAD TO HAVE TOLD YOU.
EVEN IF I *DID* KNOW, IT'S NOT MY PLACE TO TELL.
BUT WHILE I DON'T AGREE WITH IT, I KNOW THAT WHEN HE SAYS IT'S FOR THE BEST, *HE* BELIEVES IT.

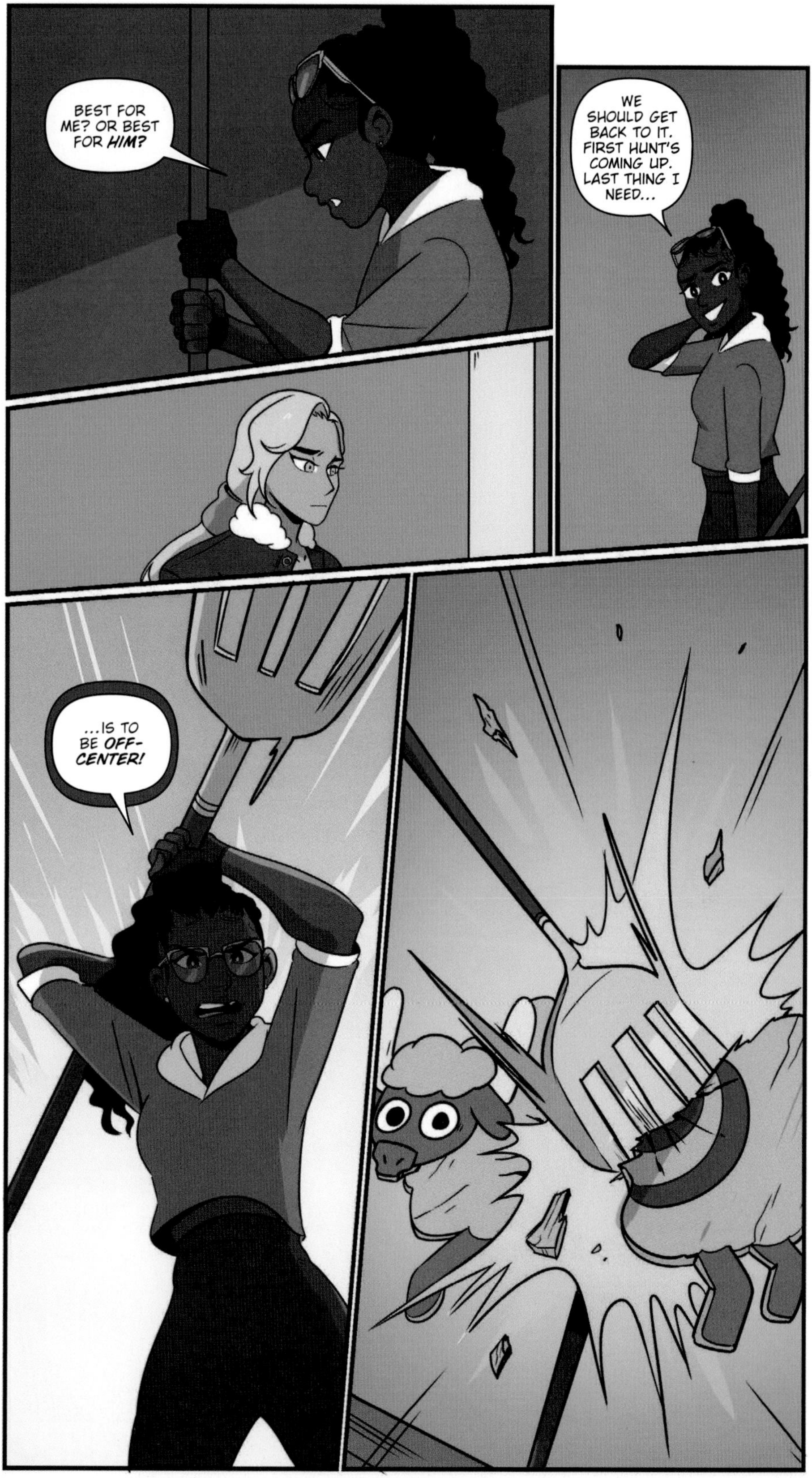
BEST FOR ME? OR BEST FOR *HIM?*
WE SHOULD GET BACK TO IT. FIRST HUNT'S COMING UP. LAST THING I NEED...
...IS TO BE *OFF-CENTER!*

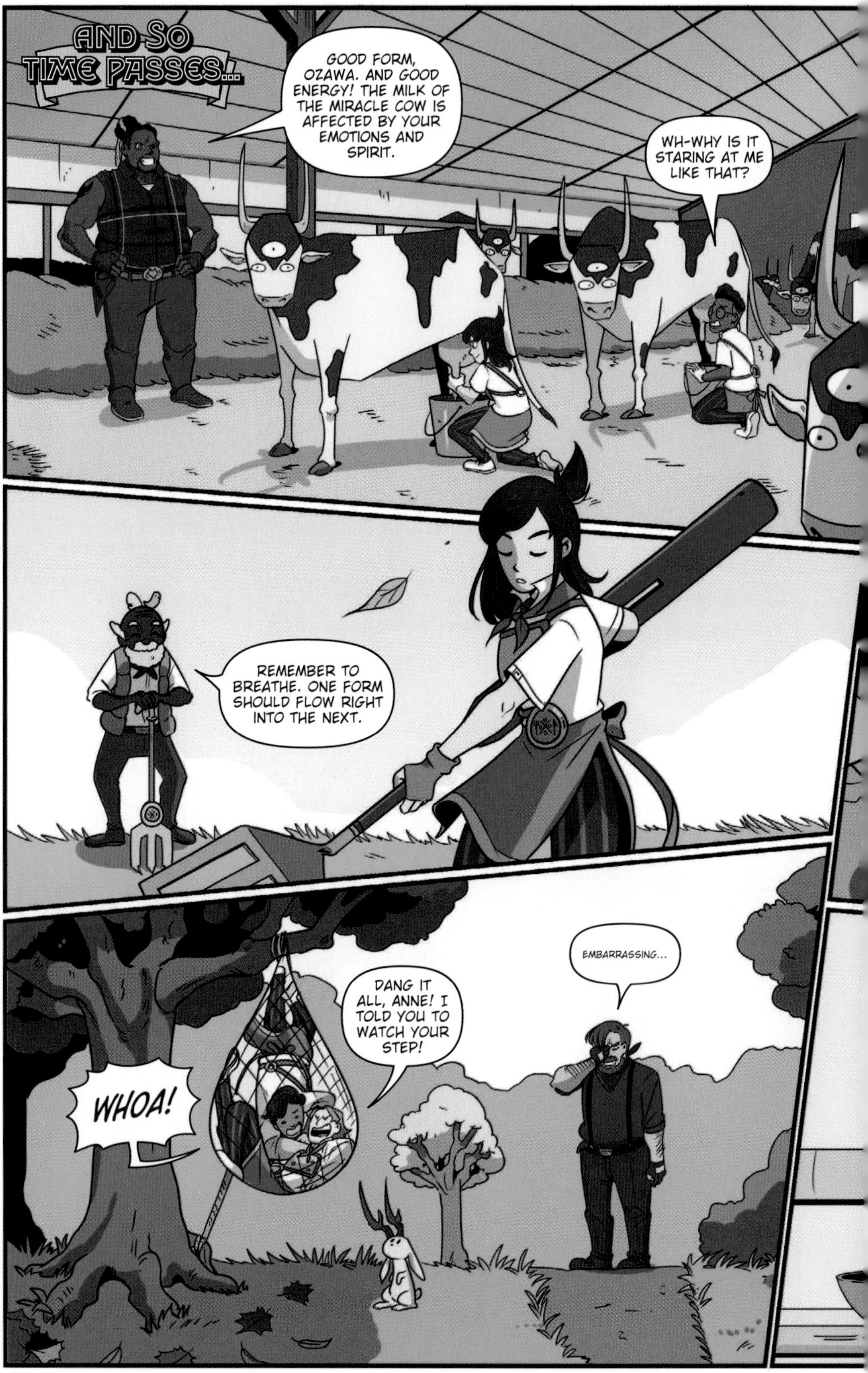
AND SO TIME PASSES...
GOOD FORM, OZAWA. AND GOOD ENERGY! THE MILK OF THE MIRACLE COW IS AFFECTED BY YOUR EMOTIONS AND SPIRIT.
WH-WHY IS IT STARING AT ME LIKE THAT?
REMEMBER TO BREATHE. ONE FORM SHOULD FLOW RIGHT INTO THE NEXT.
WHOA!
DANG IT ALL, ANNE! I TOLD YOU TO WATCH YOUR STEP!
EMBARRASSING...

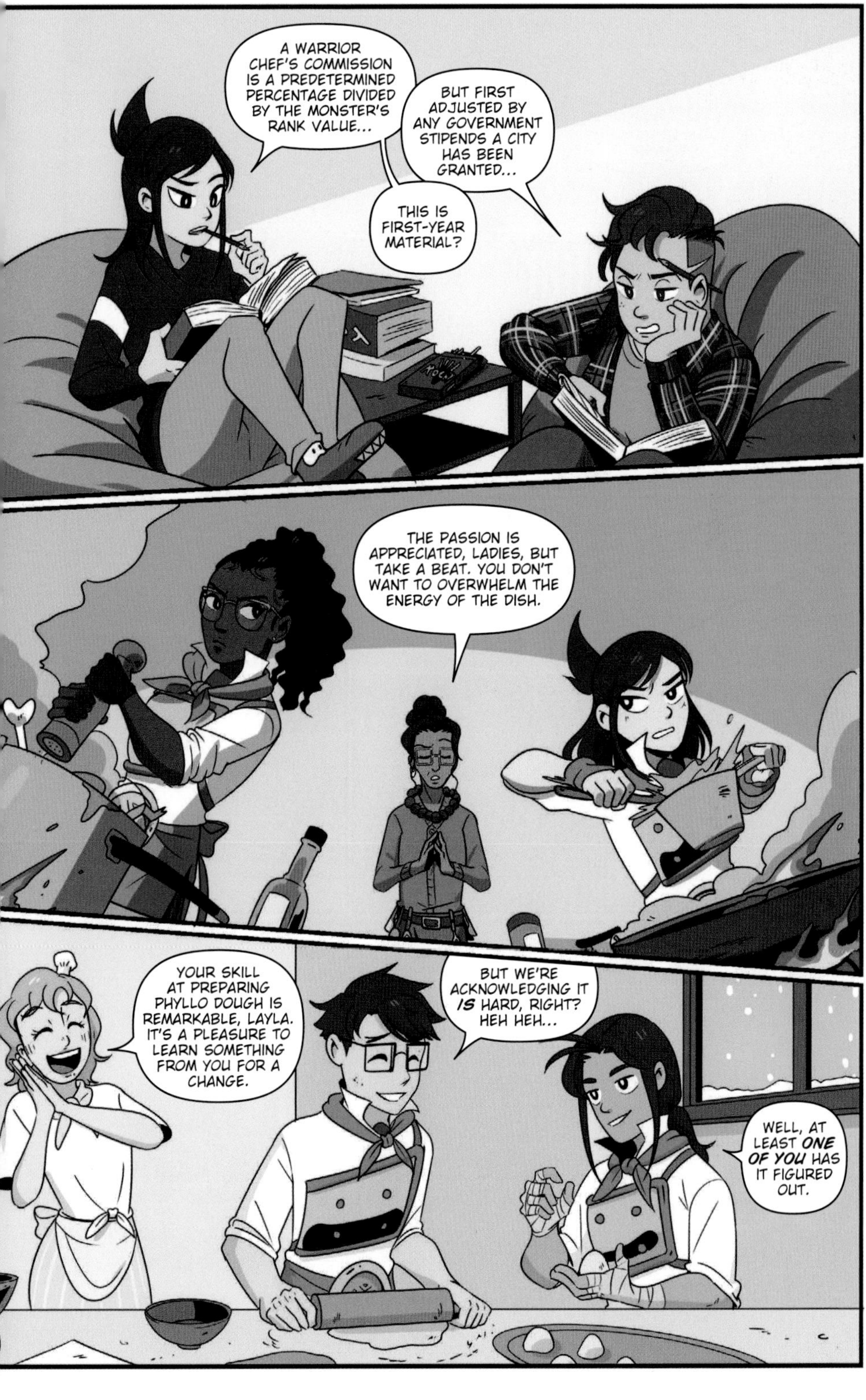
A WARRIOR CHEF'S COMMISSION IS A PREDETERMINED PERCENTAGE DIVIDED BY THE MONSTER'S RANK VALUE...
BUT FIRST ADJUSTED BY ANY GOVERNMENT STIPENDS A CITY HAS BEEN GRANTED...
THIS IS FIRST-YEAR MATERIAL?
THE PASSION IS APPRECIATED, LADIES, BUT TAKE A BEAT. YOU DON'T WANT TO OVERWHELM THE ENERGY OF THE DISH.
YOUR SKILL AT PREPARING PHYLLO DOUGH IS REMARKABLE, LAYLA. IT'S A PLEASURE TO LEARN SOMETHING FROM YOU FOR A CHANGE.
BUT WE'RE ACKNOWLEDGING IT ***IS*** HARD, RIGHT? HEH HEH...
WELL, AT LEAST ***ONE OF YOU*** HAS IT FIGURED OUT.

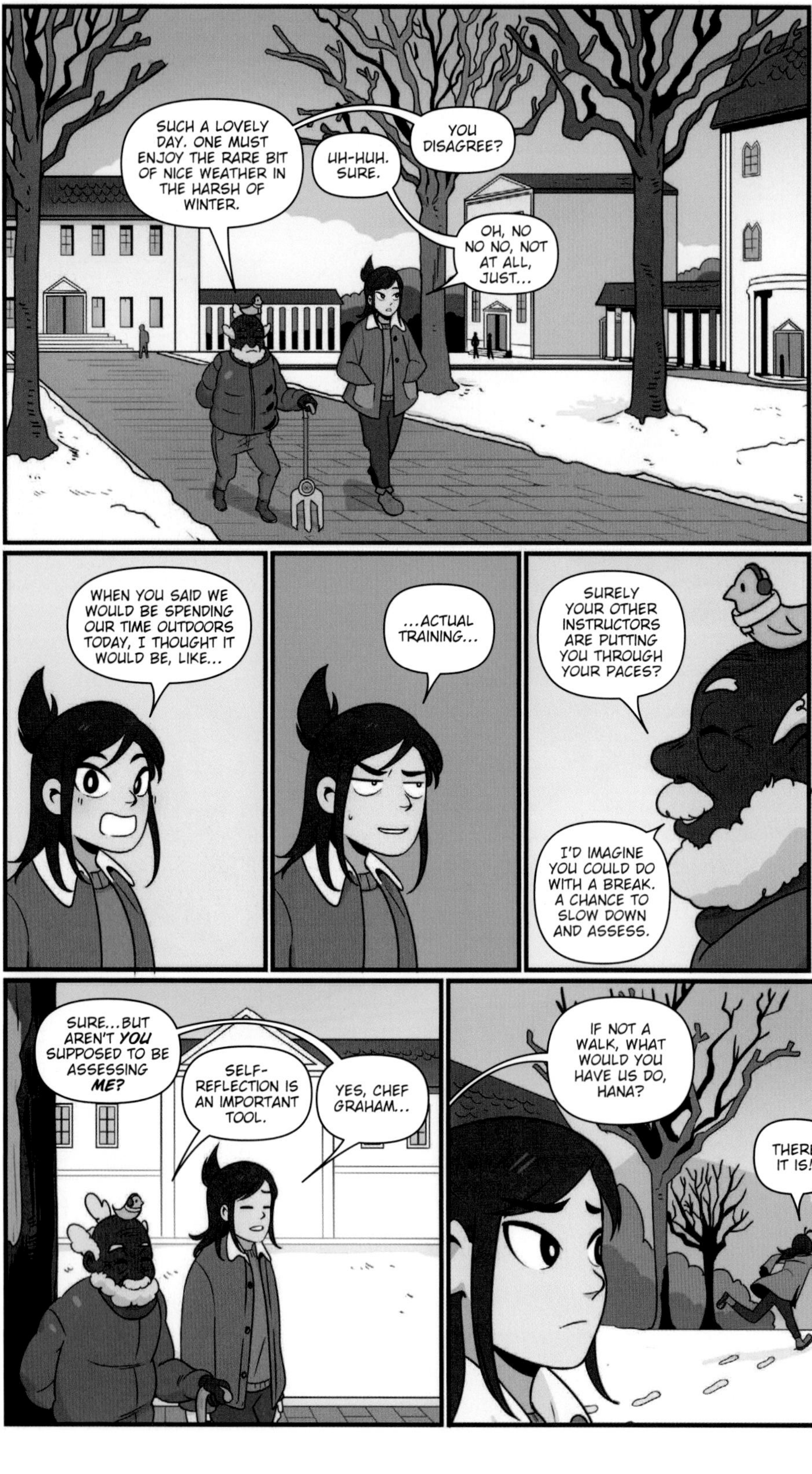
SUCH A LOVELY DAY. ONE MUST ENJOY THE RARE BIT OF NICE WEATHER IN THE HARSH OF WINTER.
UH-HUH. SURE.
YOU DISAGREE?
OH, NO NO NO, NOT AT ALL, JUST...
WHEN YOU SAID WE WOULD BE SPENDING OUR TIME OUTDOORS TODAY, I THOUGHT IT WOULD BE, LIKE...
...ACTUAL TRAINING...
SURELY YOUR OTHER INSTRUCTORS ARE PUTTING YOU THROUGH YOUR PACES?
I'D IMAGINE YOU COULD DO WITH A BREAK. A CHANCE TO SLOW DOWN AND ASSESS.
SURE...BUT AREN'T ***YOU*** SUPPOSED TO BE ASSESSING ***ME?***
SELF-REFLECTION IS AN IMPORTANT TOOL.
YES, CHEF GRAHAM...
IF NOT A WALK, WHAT WOULD YOU HAVE US DO, HANA?
THERE IT IS!

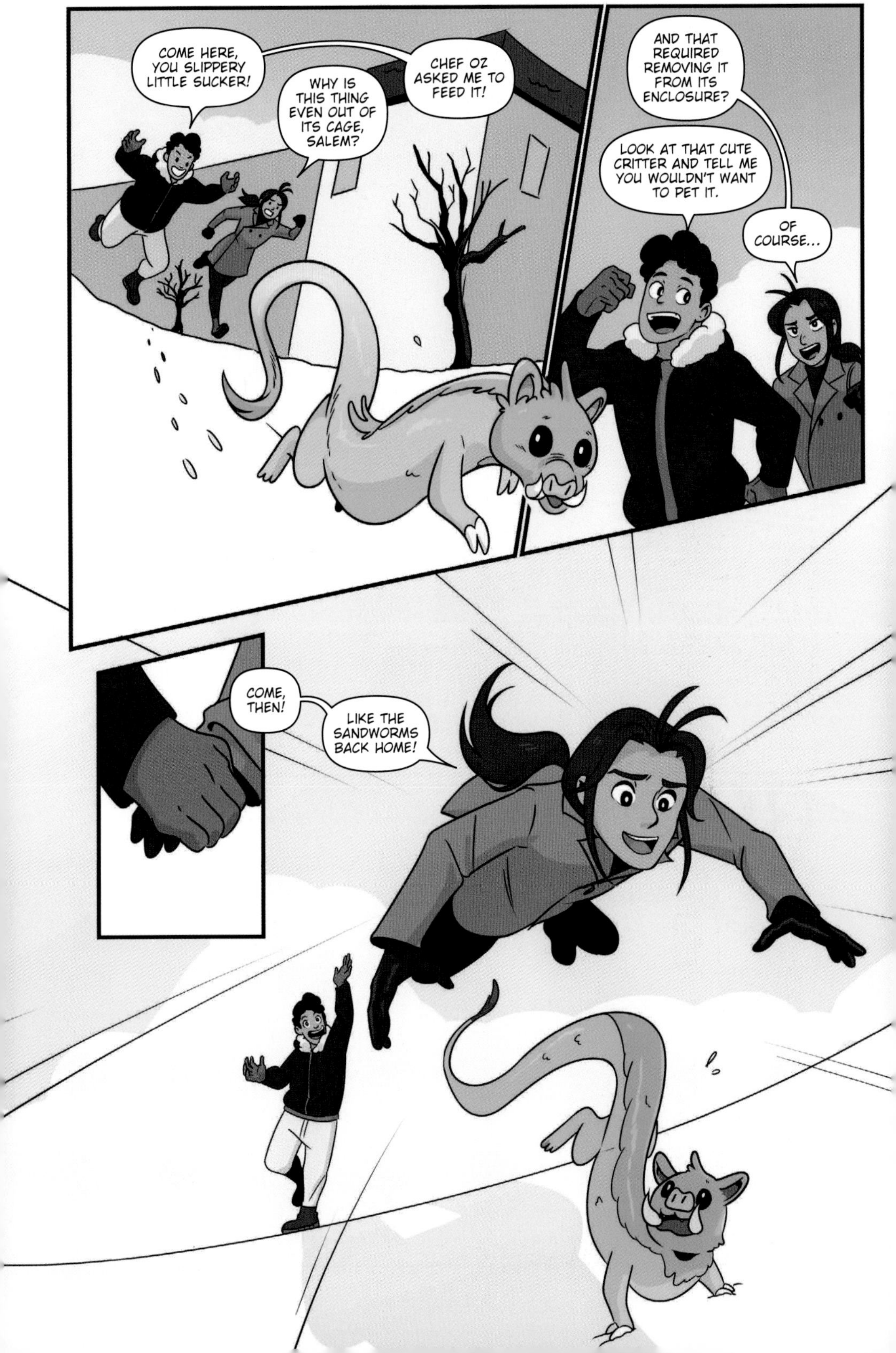
COME HERE, YOU SLIPPERY LITTLE SUCKER!
WHY IS THIS THING EVEN OUT OF ITS CAGE, SALEM?
CHEF OZ ASKED ME TO FEED IT!
AND THAT REQUIRED REMOVING IT FROM ITS ENCLOSURE?
LOOK AT THAT CUTE CRITTER AND TELL ME YOU WOULDN'T WANT TO PET IT.
OF COURSE...
COME, THEN!
LIKE THE SANDWORMS BACK HOME!

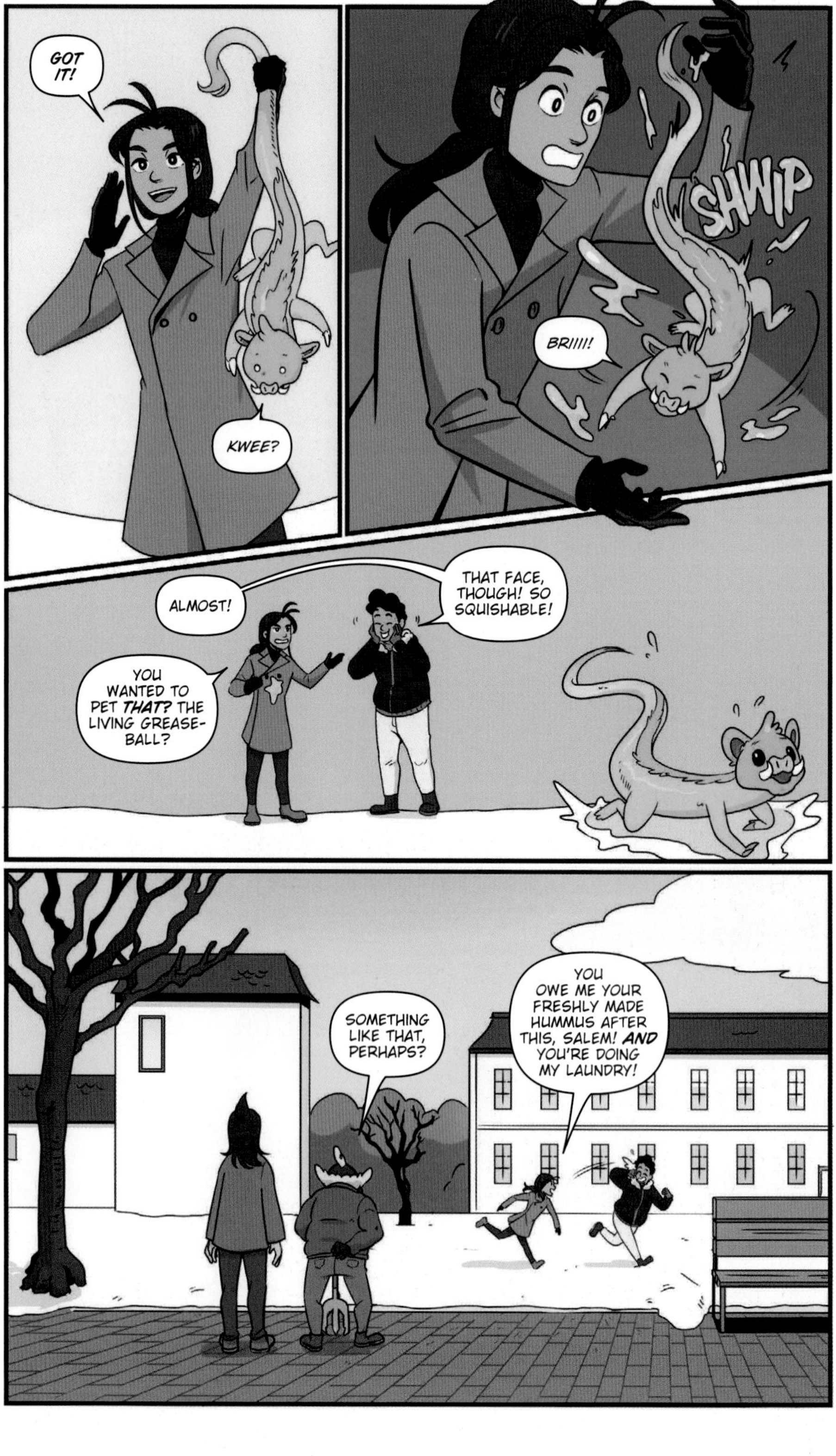
GOT IT!
KWEE?
SHWIP
BRIIII!
ALMOST!
YOU WANTED TO PET *THAT?* THE LIVING GREASE-BALL?
THAT FACE, THOUGH! SO SQUISHABLE!
SOMETHING LIKE THAT, PERHAPS?
YOU OWE ME YOUR FRESHLY MADE HUMMUS AFTER THIS, SALEM! *AND* YOU'RE DOING MY LAUNDRY!

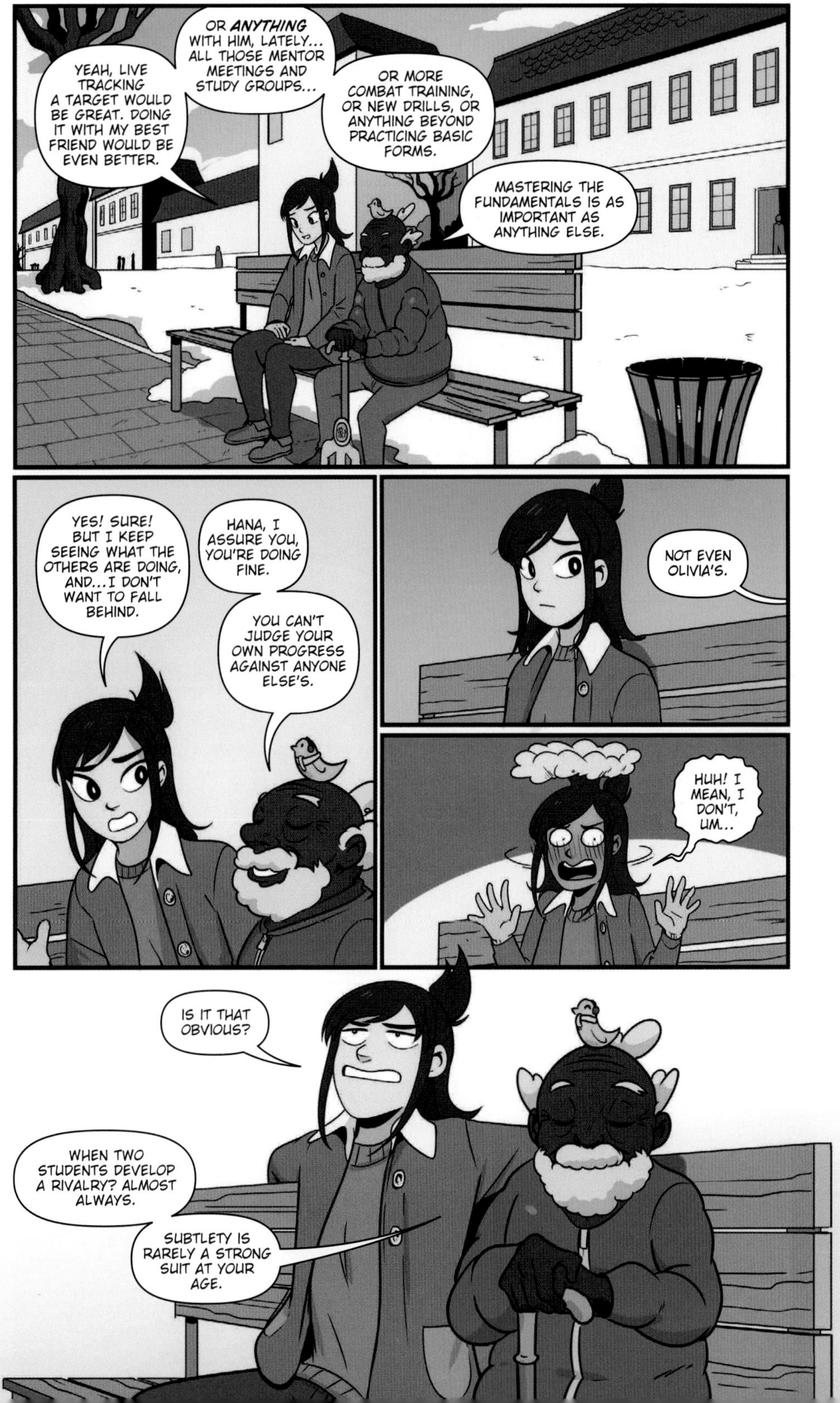
YEAH, LIVE TRACKING A TARGET WOULD BE GREAT. DOING IT WITH MY BEST FRIEND WOULD BE EVEN BETTER.
OR ANYTHING WITH HIM, LATELY... ALL THOSE MENTOR MEETINGS AND STUDY GROUPS...
OR MORE COMBAT TRAINING, OR NEW DRILLS, OR ANYTHING BEYOND PRACTICING BASIC FORMS.
MASTERING THE FUNDAMENTALS IS AS IMPORTANT AS ANYTHING ELSE.
YES! SURE! BUT I KEEP SEEING WHAT THE OTHERS ARE DOING, AND...I DON'T WANT TO FALL BEHIND.
HANA, I ASSURE YOU, YOU'RE DOING FINE.
YOU CAN'T JUDGE YOUR OWN PROGRESS AGAINST ANYONE ELSE'S.
NOT EVEN OLIVIA'S.
HUH! I MEAN, I DON'T, UM...
IS IT THAT OBVIOUS?
WHEN TWO STUDENTS DEVELOP A RIVALRY? ALMOST ALWAYS.
SUBTLETY IS RARELY A STRONG SUIT AT YOUR AGE.

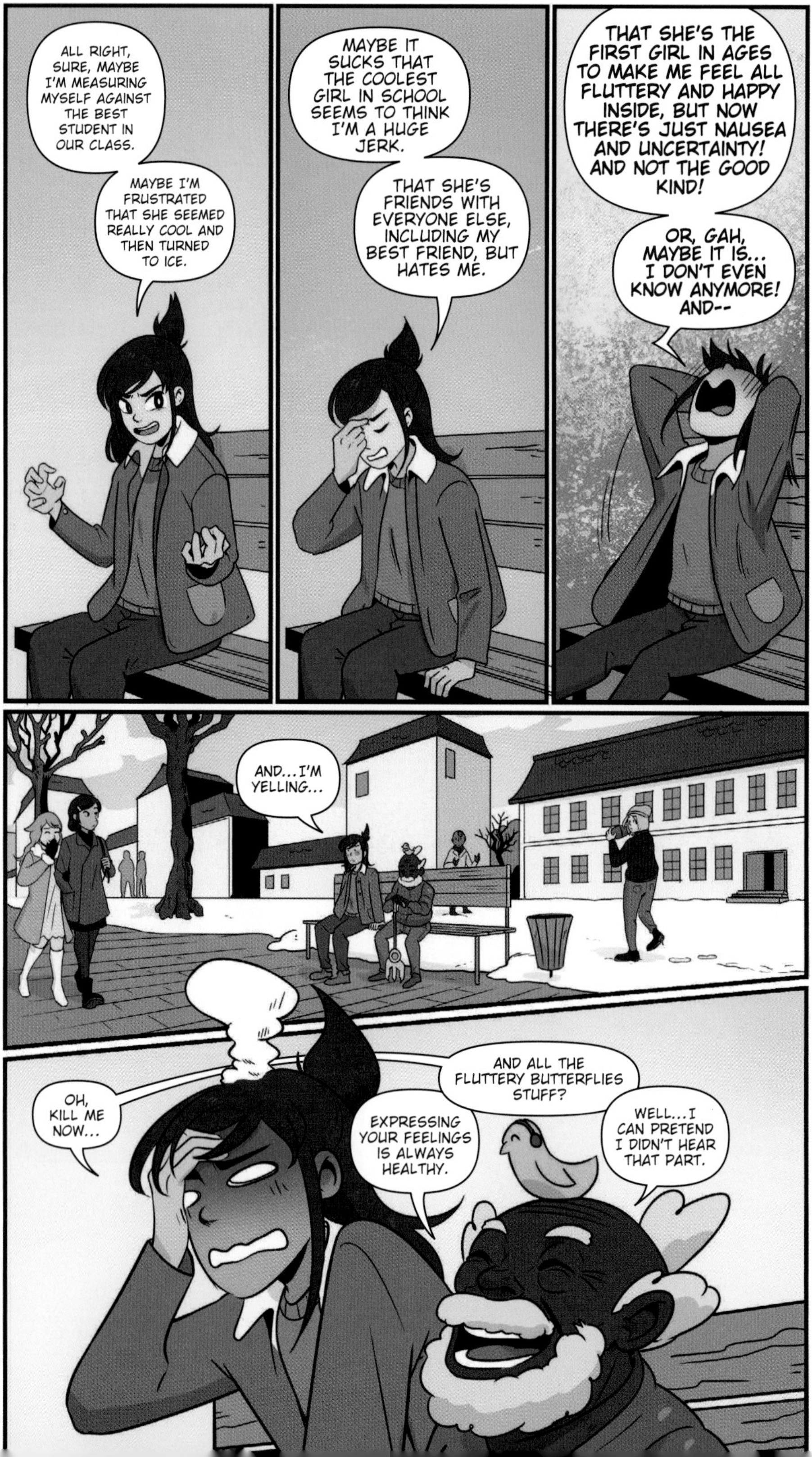
ALL RIGHT, SURE, MAYBE I'M MEASURING MYSELF AGAINST THE BEST STUDENT IN OUR CLASS.
MAYBE I'M FRUSTRATED THAT SHE SEEMED REALLY COOL AND THEN TURNED TO ICE.
MAYBE IT SUCKS THAT THE COOLEST GIRL IN SCHOOL SEEMS TO THINK I'M A HUGE JERK.
THAT SHE'S FRIENDS WITH EVERYONE ELSE, INCLUDING MY BEST FRIEND, BUT HATES ME.
THAT SHE'S THE FIRST GIRL IN AGES TO MAKE ME FEEL ALL FLUTTERY AND HAPPY INSIDE, BUT NOW THERE'S JUST NAUSEA AND UNCERTAINTY! AND NOT THE GOOD KIND!
OR, GAH, MAYBE IT IS... I DON'T EVEN KNOW ANYMORE! AND--
AND...I'M YELLING...
OH, KILL ME NOW...
AND ALL THE FLUTTERY BUTTERFLIES STUFF?
EXPRESSING YOUR FEELINGS IS ALWAYS HEALTHY.
WELL...I CAN PRETEND I DIDN'T HEAR THAT PART.

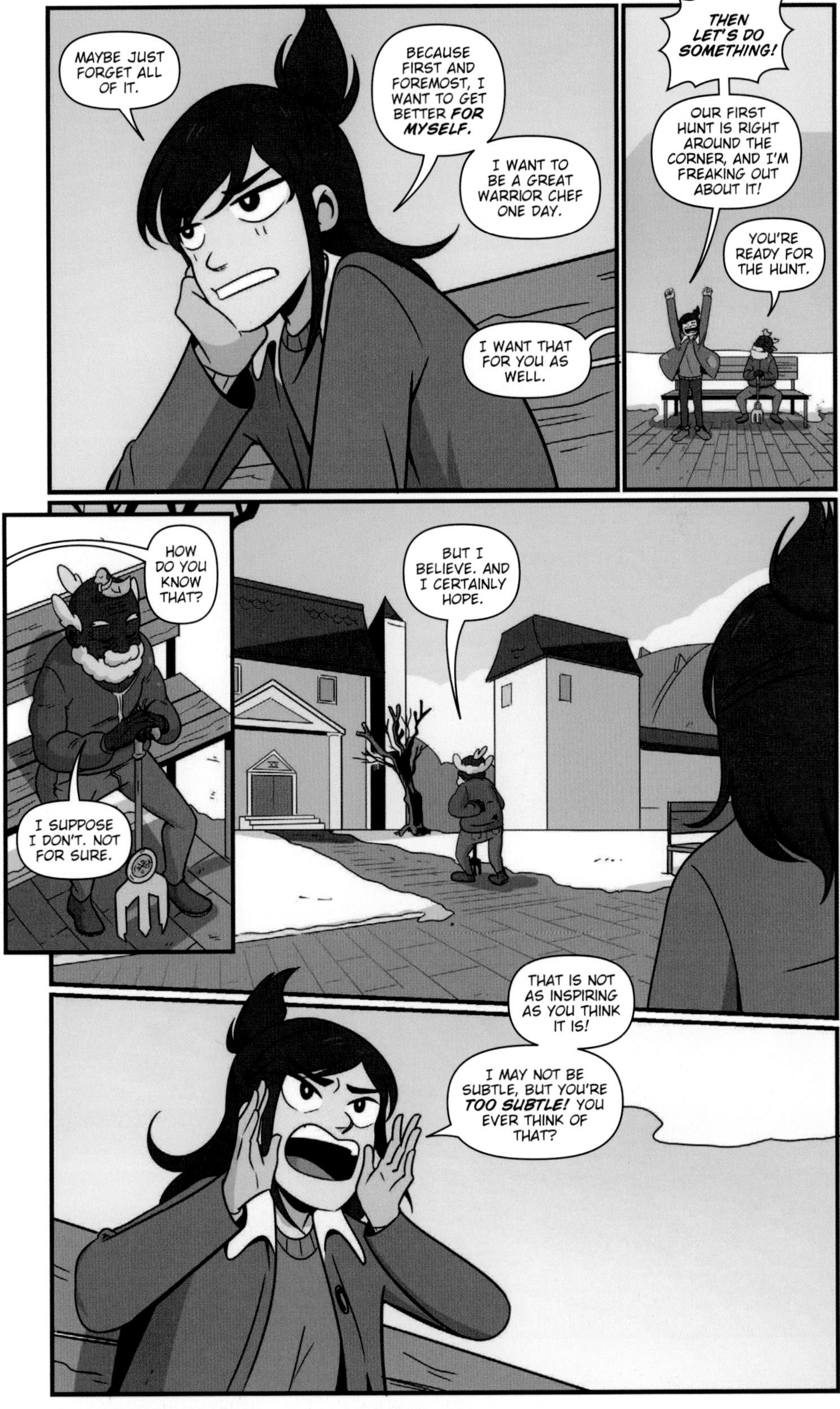
MAYBE JUST FORGET ALL OF IT.
BECAUSE FIRST AND FOREMOST, I WANT TO GET BETTER ***FOR MYSELF.***
I WANT TO BE A GREAT WARRIOR CHEF ONE DAY.
I WANT THAT FOR YOU AS WELL.
THEN LET'S DO SOMETHING!
OUR FIRST HUNT IS RIGHT AROUND THE CORNER, AND I'M FREAKING OUT ABOUT IT!
YOU'RE READY FOR THE HUNT.
HOW DO YOU KNOW THAT?
I SUPPOSE I DON'T. NOT FOR SURE.
BUT I BELIEVE. AND I CERTAINLY HOPE.
THAT IS NOT AS INSPIRING AS YOU THINK IT IS!
I MAY NOT BE SUBTLE, BUT YOU'RE ***TOO SUBTLE!*** YOU EVER THINK OF THAT?

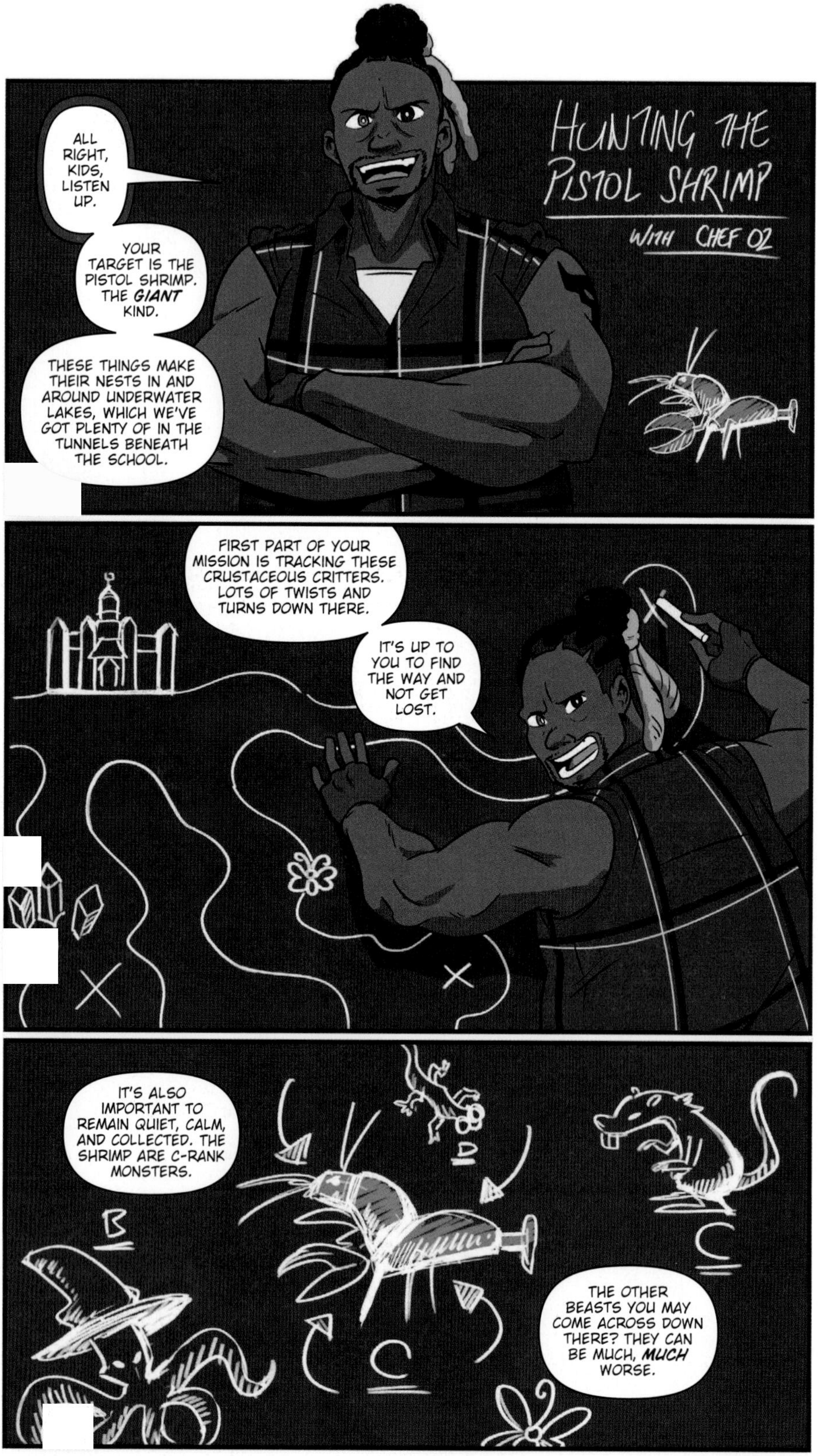
HUNTING THE PISTOL SHRIMP
WITH CHEF OZ
ALL RIGHT, KIDS, LISTEN UP.
YOUR TARGET IS THE PISTOL SHRIMP. THE GIANT KIND.
THESE THINGS MAKE THEIR NESTS IN AND AROUND UNDERWATER LAKES, WHICH WE'VE GOT PLENTY OF IN THE TUNNELS BENEATH THE SCHOOL.
FIRST PART OF YOUR MISSION IS TRACKING THESE CRUSTACEOUS CRITTERS. LOTS OF TWISTS AND TURNS DOWN THERE.
IT'S UP TO YOU TO FIND THE WAY AND NOT GET LOST.
IT'S ALSO IMPORTANT TO REMAIN QUIET, CALM, AND COLLECTED. THE SHRIMP ARE C-RANK MONSTERS.
D
C
B
C
THE OTHER BEASTS YOU MAY COME ACROSS DOWN THERE? THEY CAN BE MUCH, MUCH WORSE.

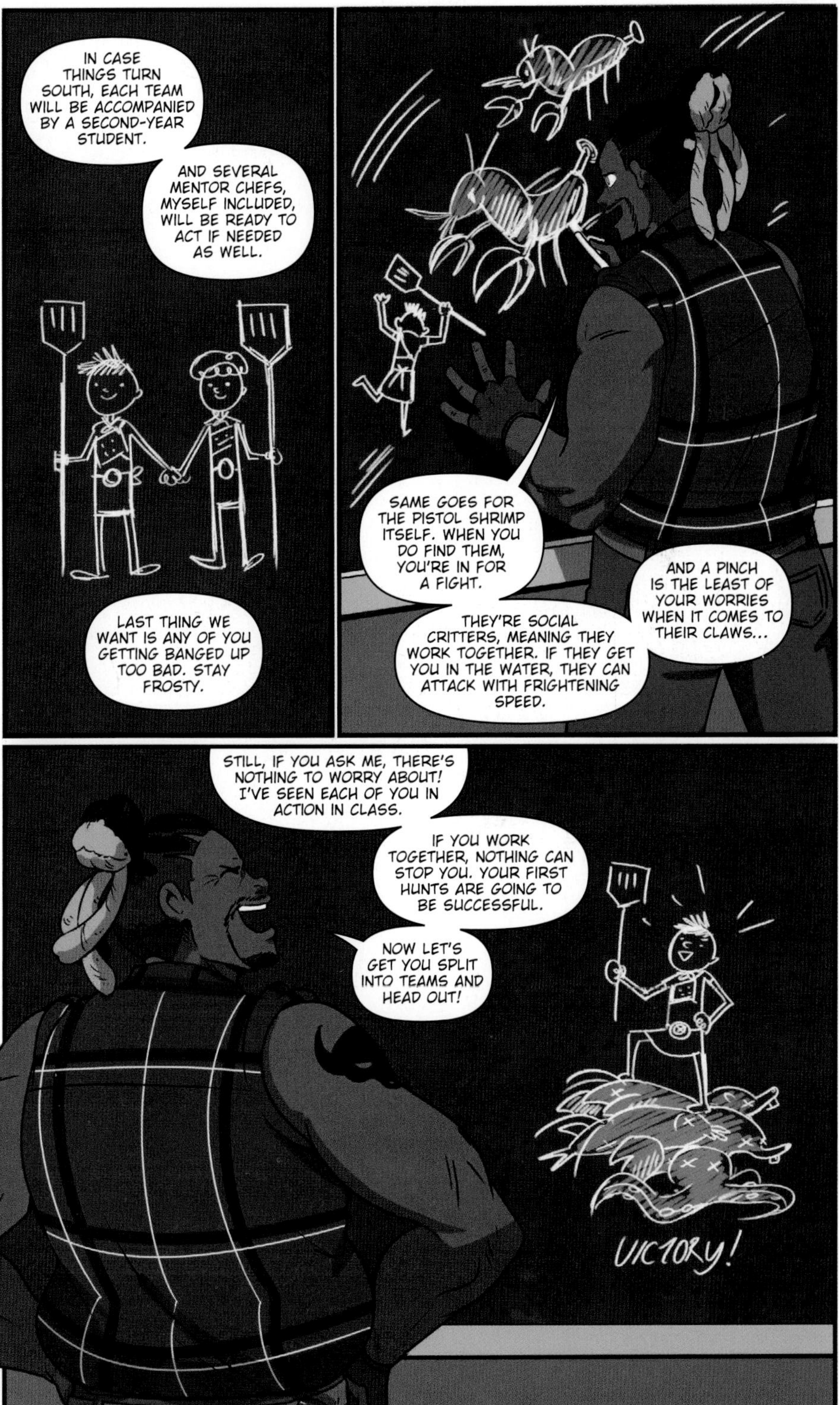
IN CASE THINGS TURN SOUTH, EACH TEAM WILL BE ACCOMPANIED BY A SECOND-YEAR STUDENT.
AND SEVERAL MENTOR CHEFS, MYSELF INCLUDED, WILL BE READY TO ACT IF NEEDED AS WELL.
LAST THING WE WANT IS ANY OF YOU GETTING BANGED UP TOO BAD. STAY FROSTY.
SAME GOES FOR THE PISTOL SHRIMP ITSELF. WHEN YOU DO FIND THEM, YOU'RE IN FOR A FIGHT.
THEY'RE SOCIAL CRITTERS, MEANING THEY WORK TOGETHER. IF THEY GET YOU IN THE WATER, THEY CAN ATTACK WITH FRIGHTENING SPEED.
AND A PINCH IS THE LEAST OF YOUR WORRIES WHEN IT COMES TO THEIR CLAWS...
STILL, IF YOU ASK ME, THERE'S NOTHING TO WORRY ABOUT! I'VE SEEN EACH OF YOU IN ACTION IN CLASS.
IF YOU WORK TOGETHER, NOTHING CAN STOP YOU. YOUR FIRST HUNTS ARE GOING TO BE SUCCESSFUL.
NOW LET'S GET YOU SPLIT INTO TEAMS AND HEAD OUT!
VICTORY!

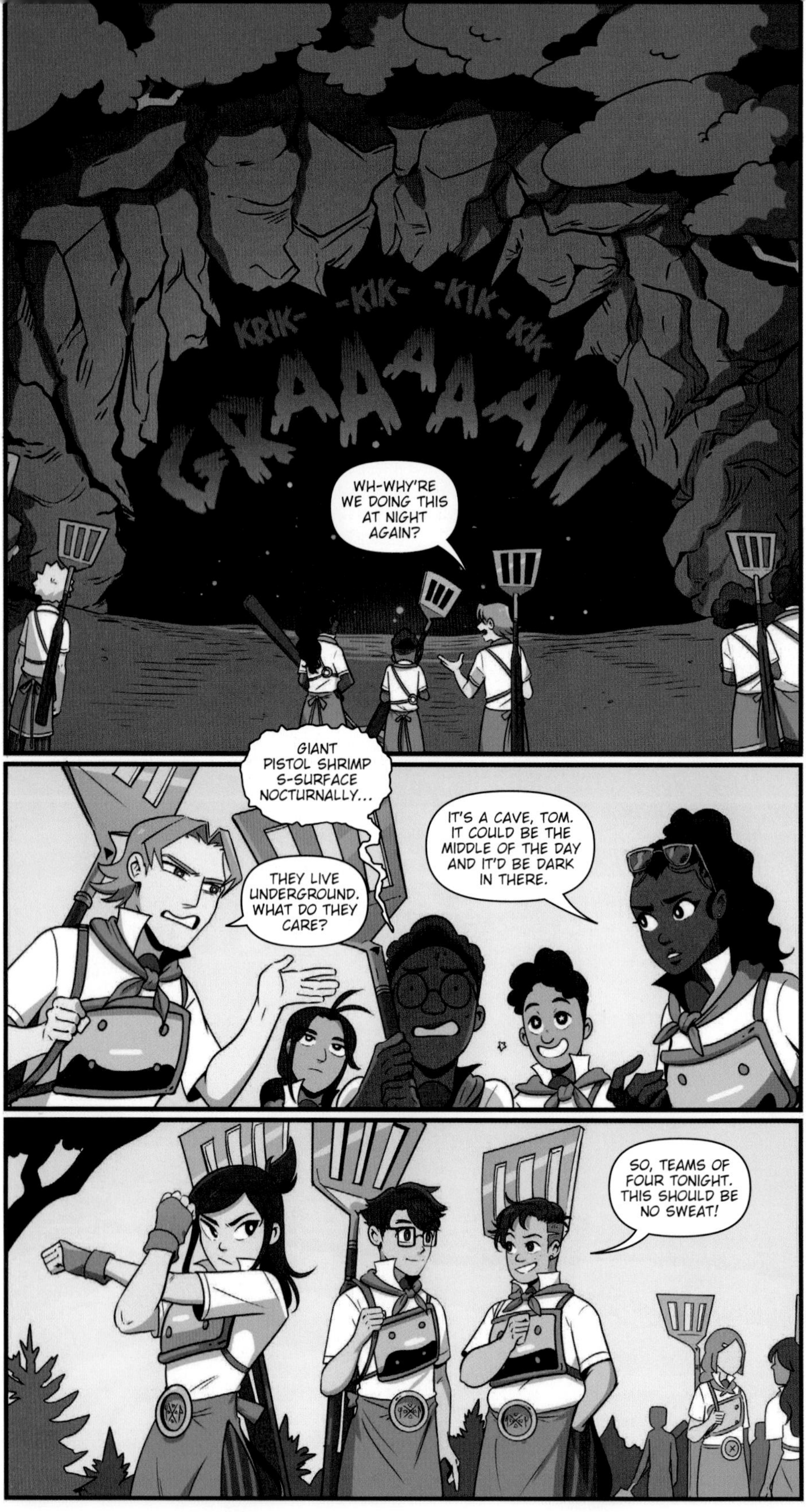
KRIK- -KIK- -KIK- KIK
GRAAAAAN
WH-WHY'RE WE DOING THIS AT NIGHT AGAIN?
GIANT PISTOL SHRIMP S-SURFACE NOCTURNALLY...
THEY LIVE UNDERGROUND. WHAT DO THEY CARE?
IT'S A CAVE, TOM. IT COULD BE THE MIDDLE OF THE DAY AND IT'D BE DARK IN THERE.
SO, TEAMS OF FOUR TONIGHT. THIS SHOULD BE NO SWEAT!

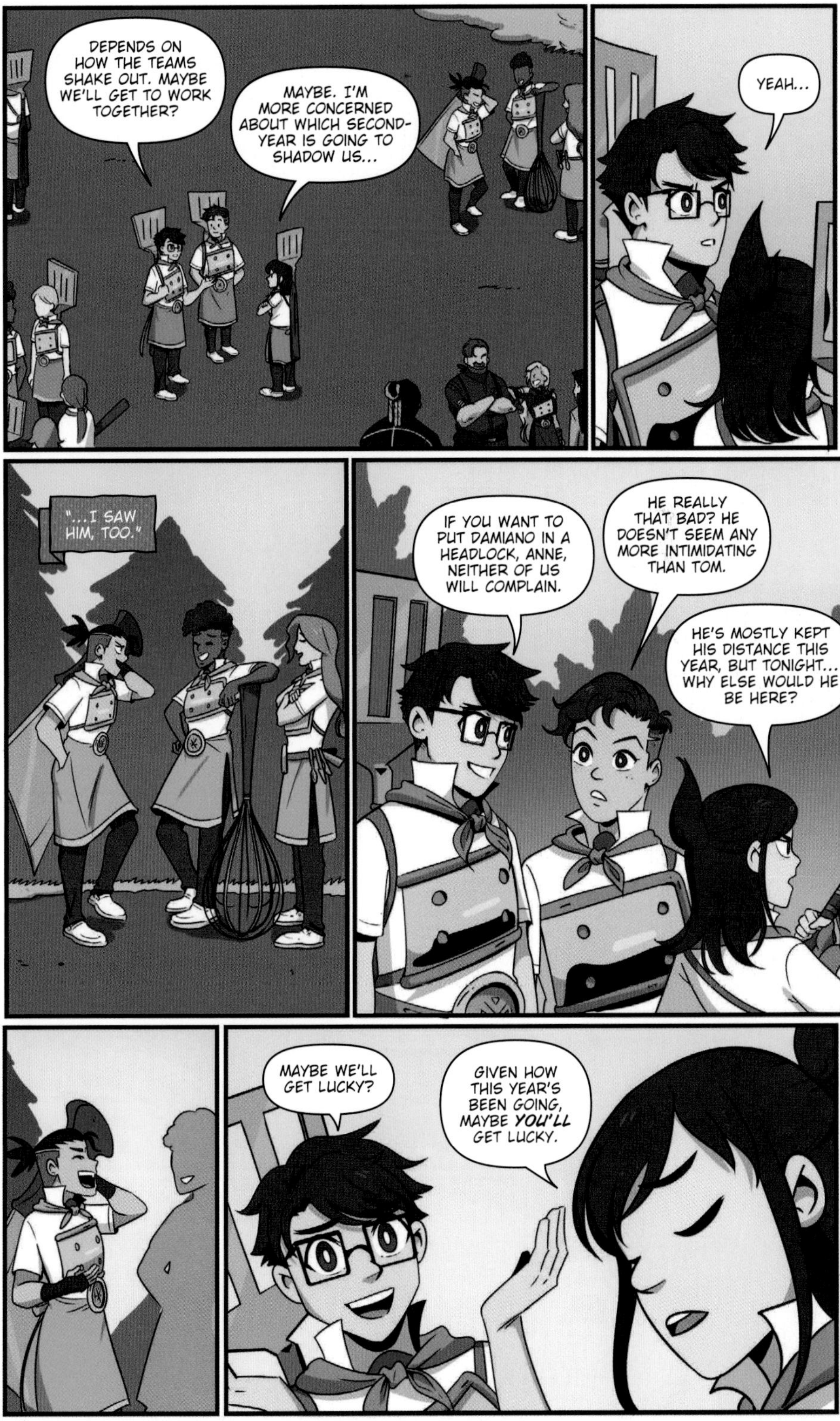
DEPENDS ON HOW THE TEAMS SHAKE OUT. MAYBE WE'LL GET TO WORK TOGETHER?
MAYBE. I'M MORE CONCERNED ABOUT WHICH SECOND-YEAR IS GOING TO SHADOW US...
YEAH...
"...I SAW HIM, TOO."
IF YOU WANT TO PUT DAMIANO IN A HEADLOCK, ANNE, NEITHER OF US WILL COMPLAIN.
HE REALLY THAT BAD? HE DOESN'T SEEM ANY MORE INTIMIDATING THAN TOM.
HE'S MOSTLY KEPT HIS DISTANCE THIS YEAR, BUT TONIGHT... WHY ELSE WOULD HE BE HERE?
MAYBE WE'LL GET LUCKY?
GIVEN HOW THIS YEAR'S BEEN GOING, MAYBE *YOU'LL* GET LUCKY.

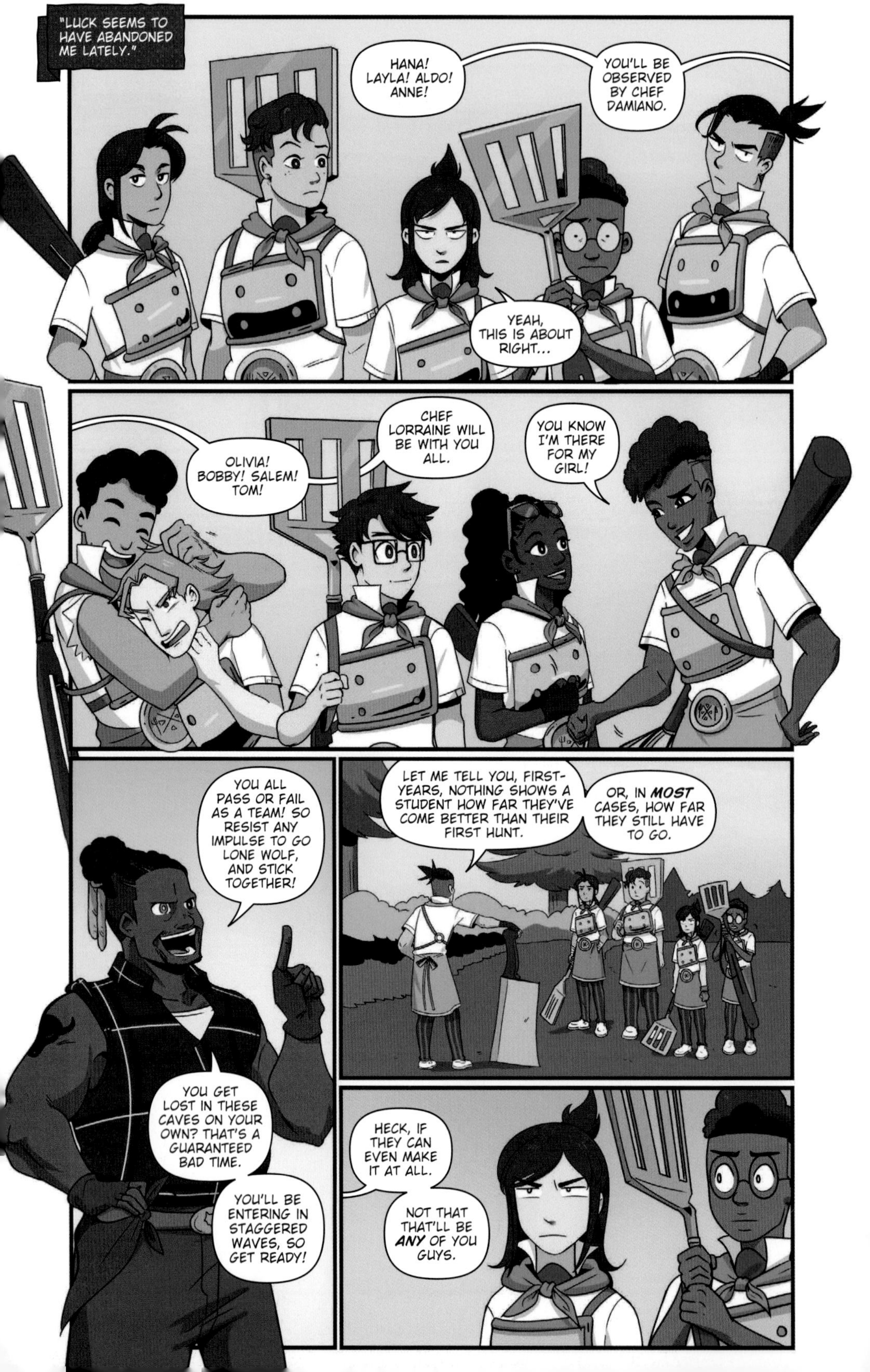
"LUCK SEEMS TO HAVE ABANDONED ME LATELY."
HANA! LAYLA! ALDO! ANNE!
YOU'LL BE OBSERVED BY CHEF DAMIANO.
YEAH, THIS IS ABOUT RIGHT...
OLIVIA! BOBBY! SALEM! TOM!
CHEF LORRAINE WILL BE WITH YOU ALL.
YOU KNOW I'M THERE FOR MY GIRL!
YOU ALL PASS OR FAIL AS A TEAM! SO RESIST ANY IMPULSE TO GO LONE WOLF, AND STICK TOGETHER!
YOU GET LOST IN THESE CAVES ON YOUR OWN? THAT'S A GUARANTEED BAD TIME.
YOU'LL BE ENTERING IN STAGGERED WAVES, SO GET READY!
LET ME TELL YOU, FIRST-YEARS, NOTHING SHOWS A STUDENT HOW FAR THEY'VE COME BETTER THAN THEIR FIRST HUNT.
OR, IN MOST CASES, HOW FAR THEY STILL HAVE TO GO.
HECK, IF THEY CAN EVEN MAKE IT AT ALL.
NOT THAT THAT'LL BE ANY OF YOU GUYS.

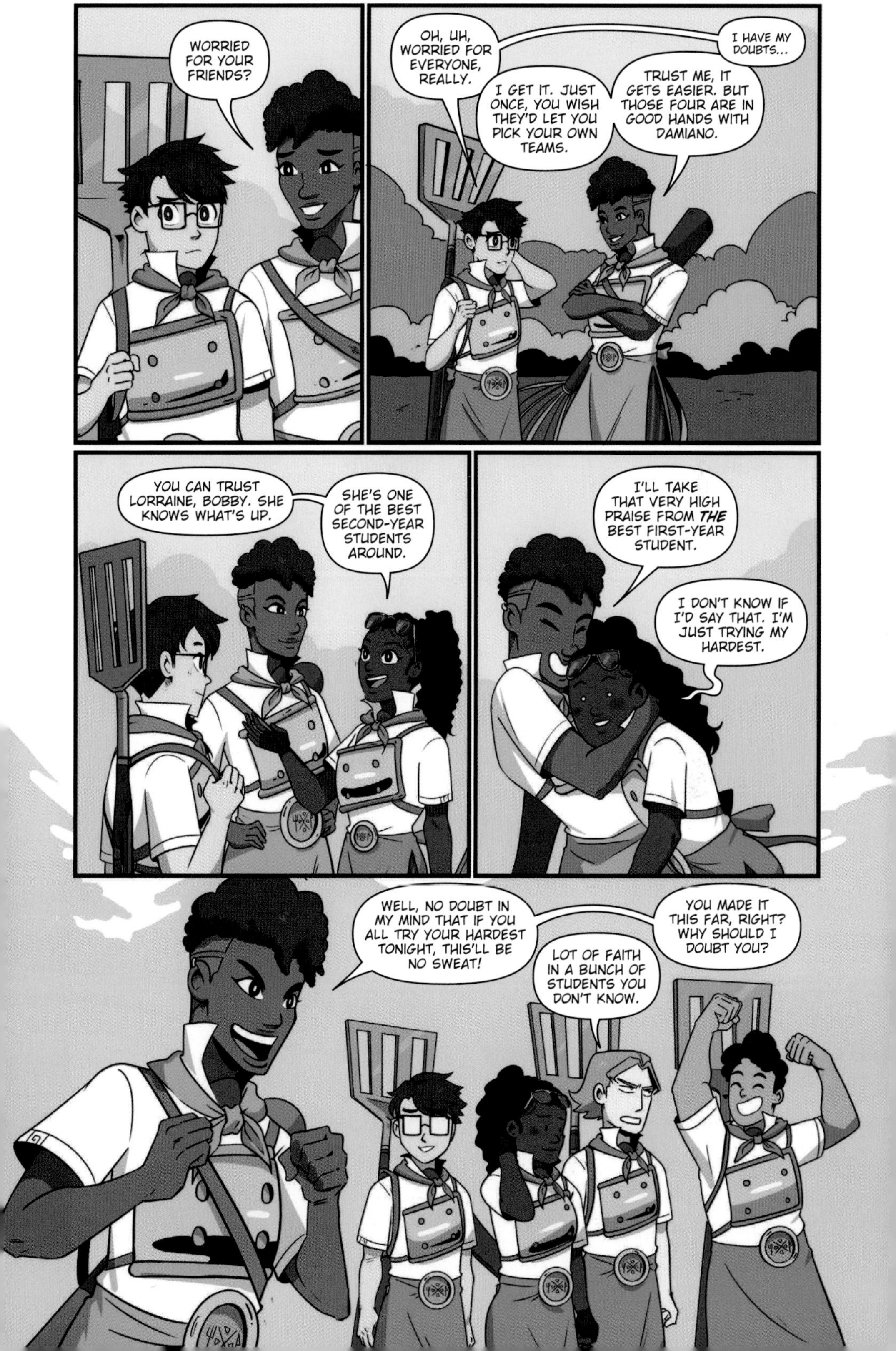
WORRIED FOR YOUR FRIENDS?
OH, UH, WORRIED FOR EVERYONE, REALLY.
I HAVE MY DOUBTS...
I GET IT. JUST ONCE, YOU WISH THEY'D LET YOU PICK YOUR OWN TEAMS.
TRUST ME, IT GETS EASIER. BUT THOSE FOUR ARE IN GOOD HANDS WITH DAMIANO.
YOU CAN TRUST LORRAINE, BOBBY. SHE KNOWS WHAT'S UP.
SHE'S ONE OF THE BEST SECOND-YEAR STUDENTS AROUND.
I'LL TAKE THAT VERY HIGH PRAISE FROM *THE* BEST FIRST-YEAR STUDENT.
I DON'T KNOW IF I'D SAY THAT. I'M JUST TRYING MY HARDEST.
WELL, NO DOUBT IN MY MIND THAT IF YOU ALL TRY YOUR HARDEST TONIGHT, THIS'LL BE NO SWEAT!
YOU MADE IT THIS FAR, RIGHT? WHY SHOULD I DOUBT YOU?
LOT OF FAITH IN A BUNCH OF STUDENTS YOU DON'T KNOW.

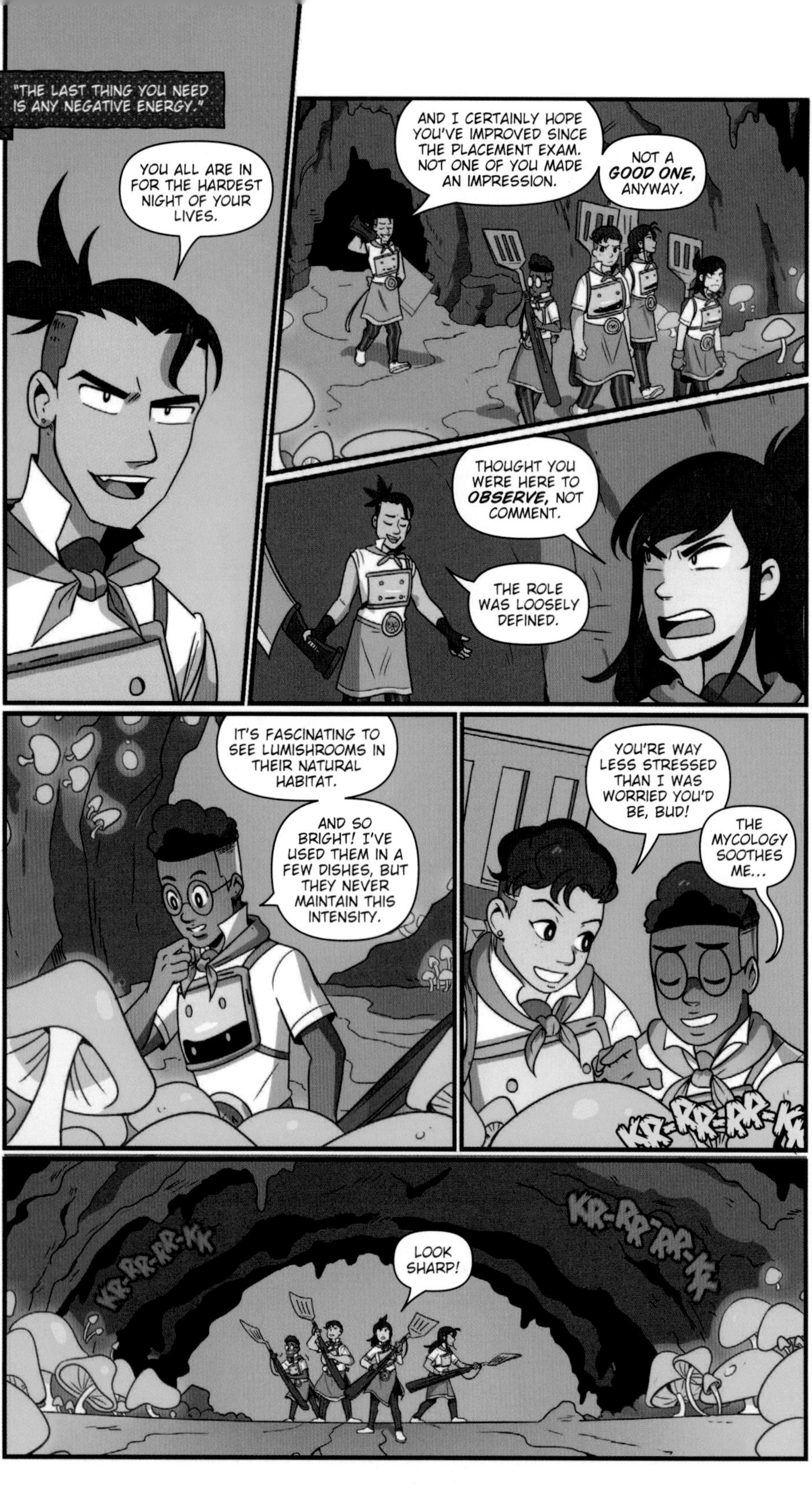
"THE LAST THING YOU NEED IS ANY NEGATIVE ENERGY."
YOU ALL ARE IN FOR THE HARDEST NIGHT OF YOUR LIVES.
AND I CERTAINLY HOPE YOU'VE IMPROVED SINCE THE PLACEMENT EXAM. NOT ONE OF YOU MADE AN IMPRESSION.
NOT A GOOD ONE, ANYWAY.
THOUGHT YOU WERE HERE TO OBSERVE, NOT COMMENT.
THE ROLE WAS LOOSELY DEFINED.
IT'S FASCINATING TO SEE LUMISHROOMS IN THEIR NATURAL HABITAT.
AND SO BRIGHT! I'VE USED THEM IN A FEW DISHES, BUT THEY NEVER MAINTAIN THIS INTENSITY.
YOU'RE WAY LESS STRESSED THAN I WAS WORRIED YOU'D BE, BUD!
THE MYCOLOGY SOOTHES ME...
KR-RR-RR-KK
KR-RR-RR-KK
KR-RR-RR-KK
LOOK SHARP!

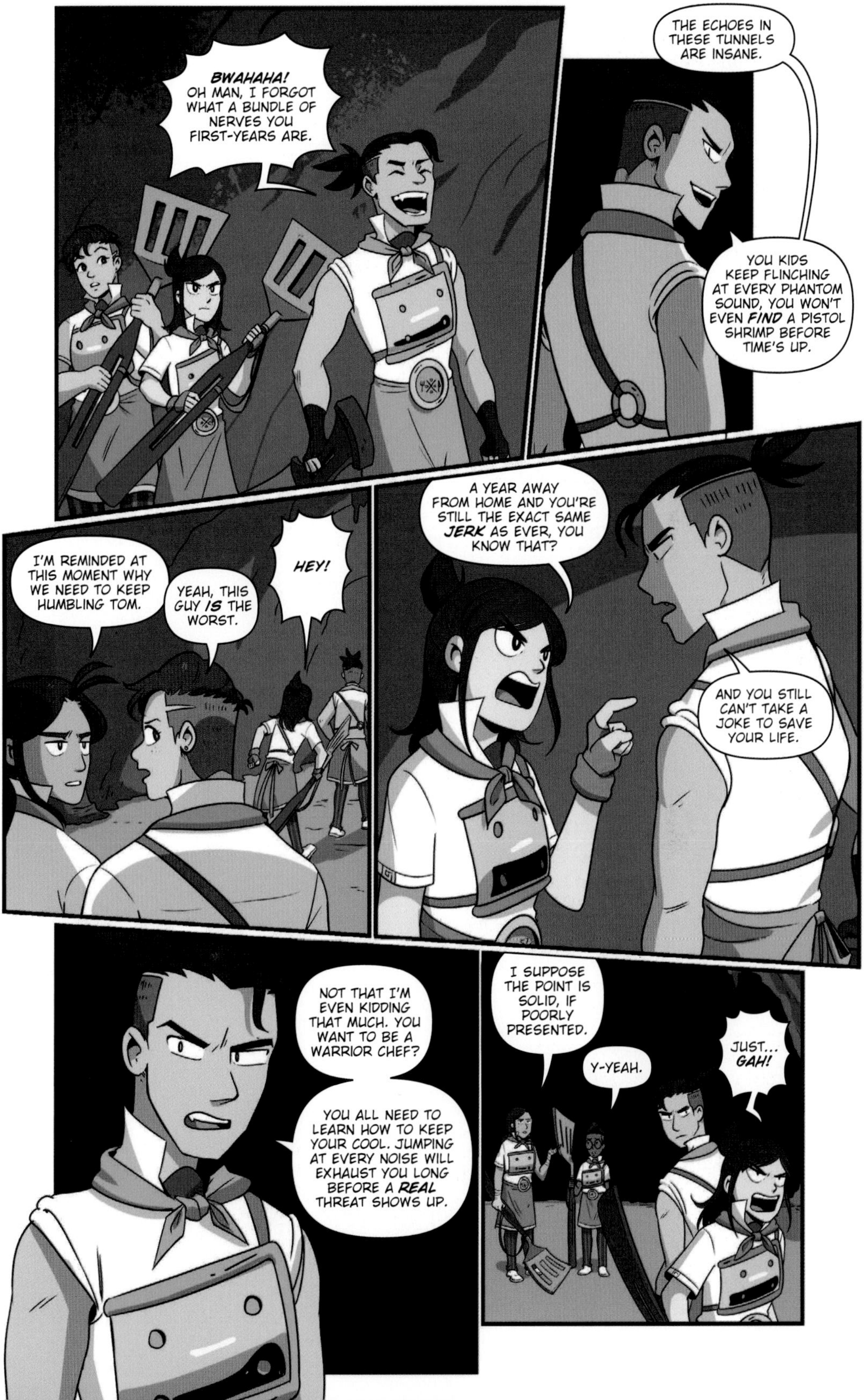
BWAHAHA! OH MAN, I FORGOT WHAT A BUNDLE OF NERVES YOU FIRST-YEARS ARE.
THE ECHOES IN THESE TUNNELS ARE INSANE.
YOU KIDS KEEP FLINCHING AT EVERY PHANTOM SOUND, YOU WON'T EVEN FIND A PISTOL SHRIMP BEFORE TIME'S UP.
I'M REMINDED AT THIS MOMENT WHY WE NEED TO KEEP HUMBLING TOM.
YEAH, THIS GUY IS THE WORST.
HEY!
A YEAR AWAY FROM HOME AND YOU'RE STILL THE EXACT SAME JERK AS EVER, YOU KNOW THAT?
AND YOU STILL CAN'T TAKE A JOKE TO SAVE YOUR LIFE.
NOT THAT I'M EVEN KIDDING THAT MUCH. YOU WANT TO BE A WARRIOR CHEF?
YOU ALL NEED TO LEARN HOW TO KEEP YOUR COOL. JUMPING AT EVERY NOISE WILL EXHAUST YOU LONG BEFORE A REAL THREAT SHOWS UP.
I SUPPOSE THE POINT IS SOLID, IF POORLY PRESENTED.
Y-YEAH.
JUST... GAH!

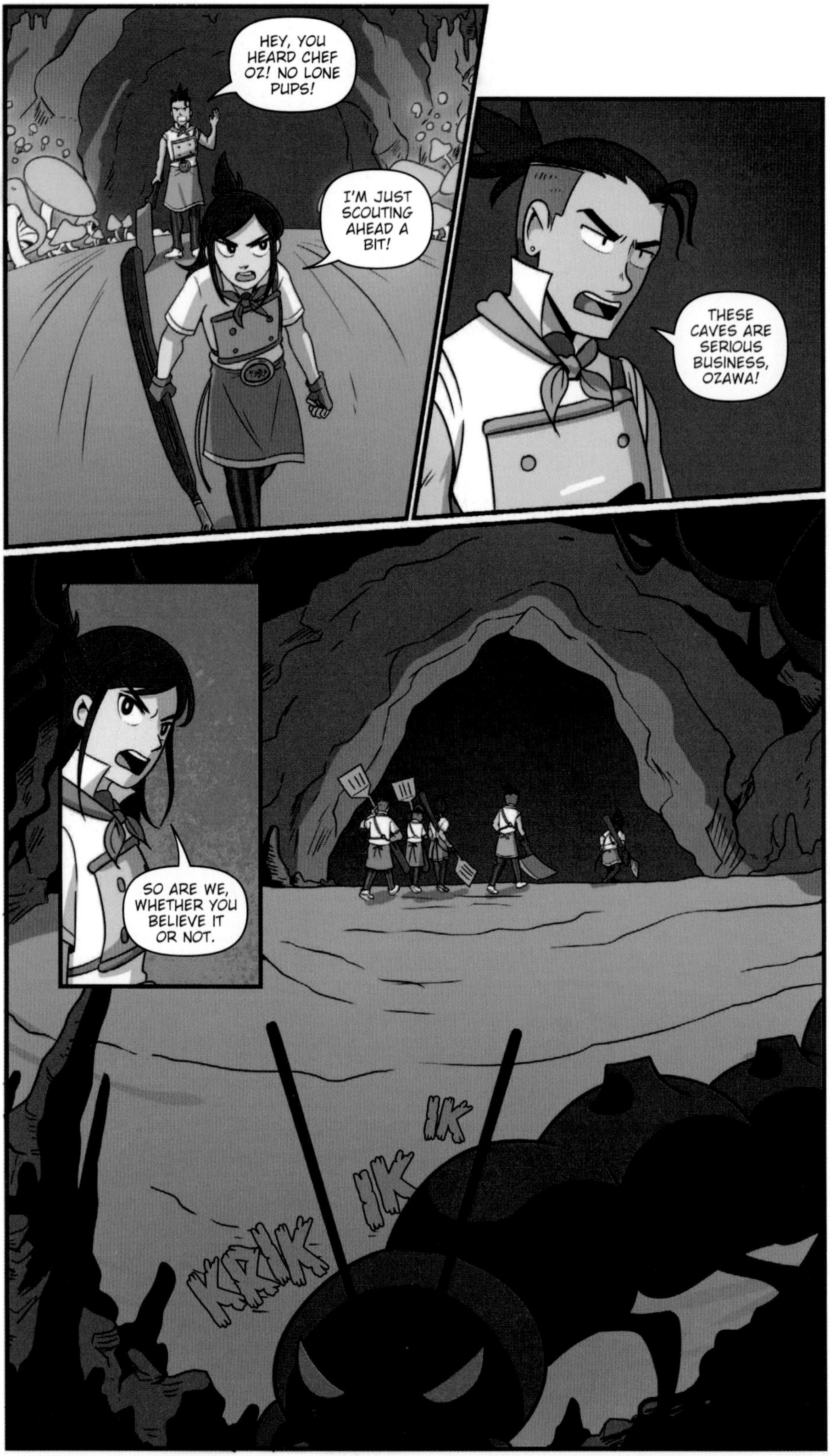

HEY, YOU HEARD CHEF OZ! NO LONE PUPS!
I'M JUST SCOUTING AHEAD A BIT!
THESE CAVES ARE SERIOUS BUSINESS, OZAWA!
SO ARE WE, WHETHER YOU BELIEVE IT OR NOT.
IK
IK
KRIK

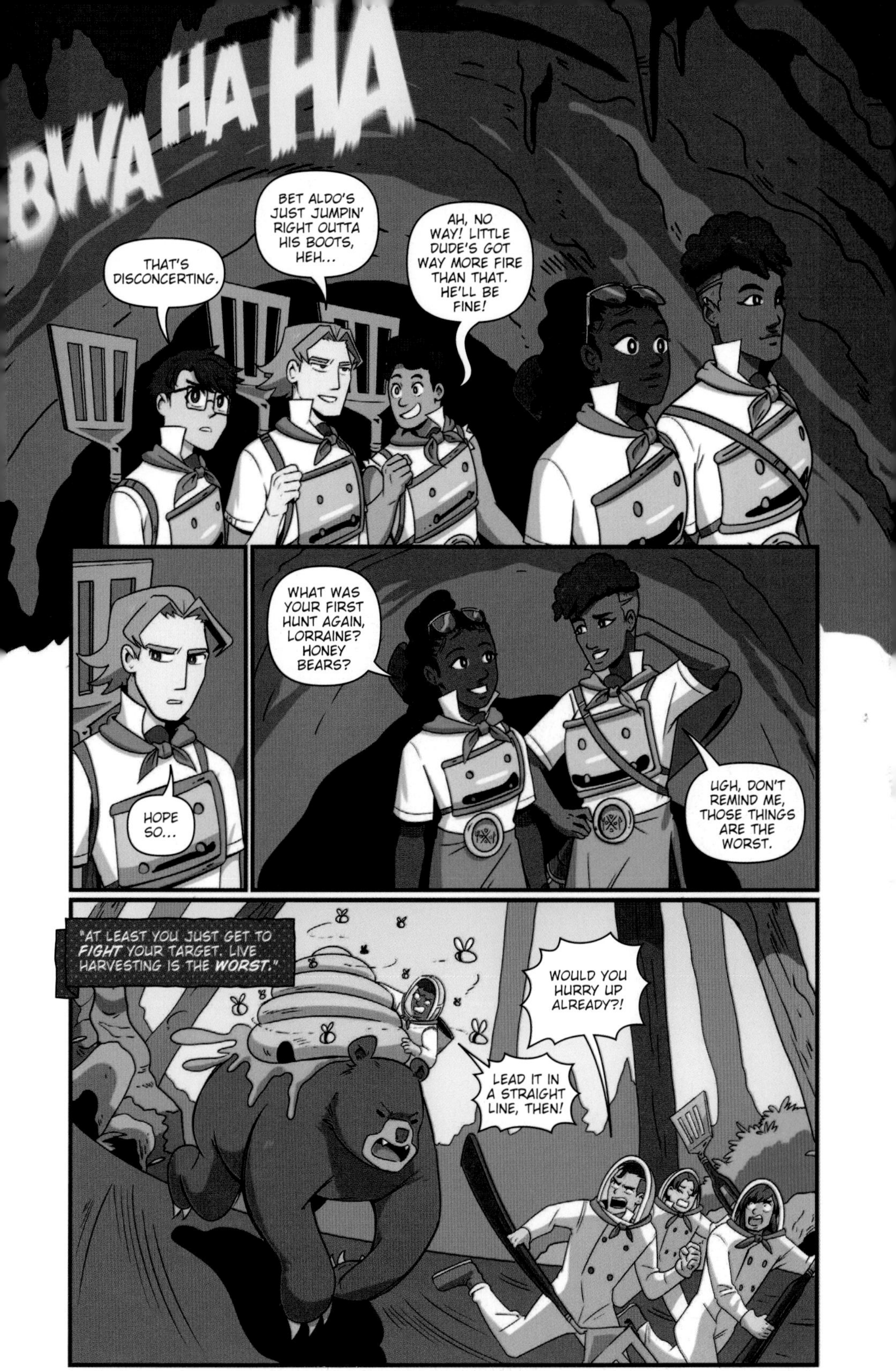
BWA HA HA HA
THAT'S DISCONCERTING.
BET ALDO'S JUST JUMPIN' RIGHT OUTTA HIS BOOTS, HEH...
AH, NO WAY! LITTLE DUDE'S GOT WAY MORE FIRE THAN THAT. HE'LL BE FINE!
HOPE SO...
WHAT WAS YOUR FIRST HUNT AGAIN, LORRAINE? HONEY BEARS?
UGH, DON'T REMIND ME, THOSE THINGS ARE THE WORST.
"AT LEAST YOU JUST GET TO FIGHT YOUR TARGET. LIVE HARVESTING IS THE WORST."
WOULD YOU HURRY UP ALREADY?!
LEAD IT IN A STRAIGHT LINE, THEN!

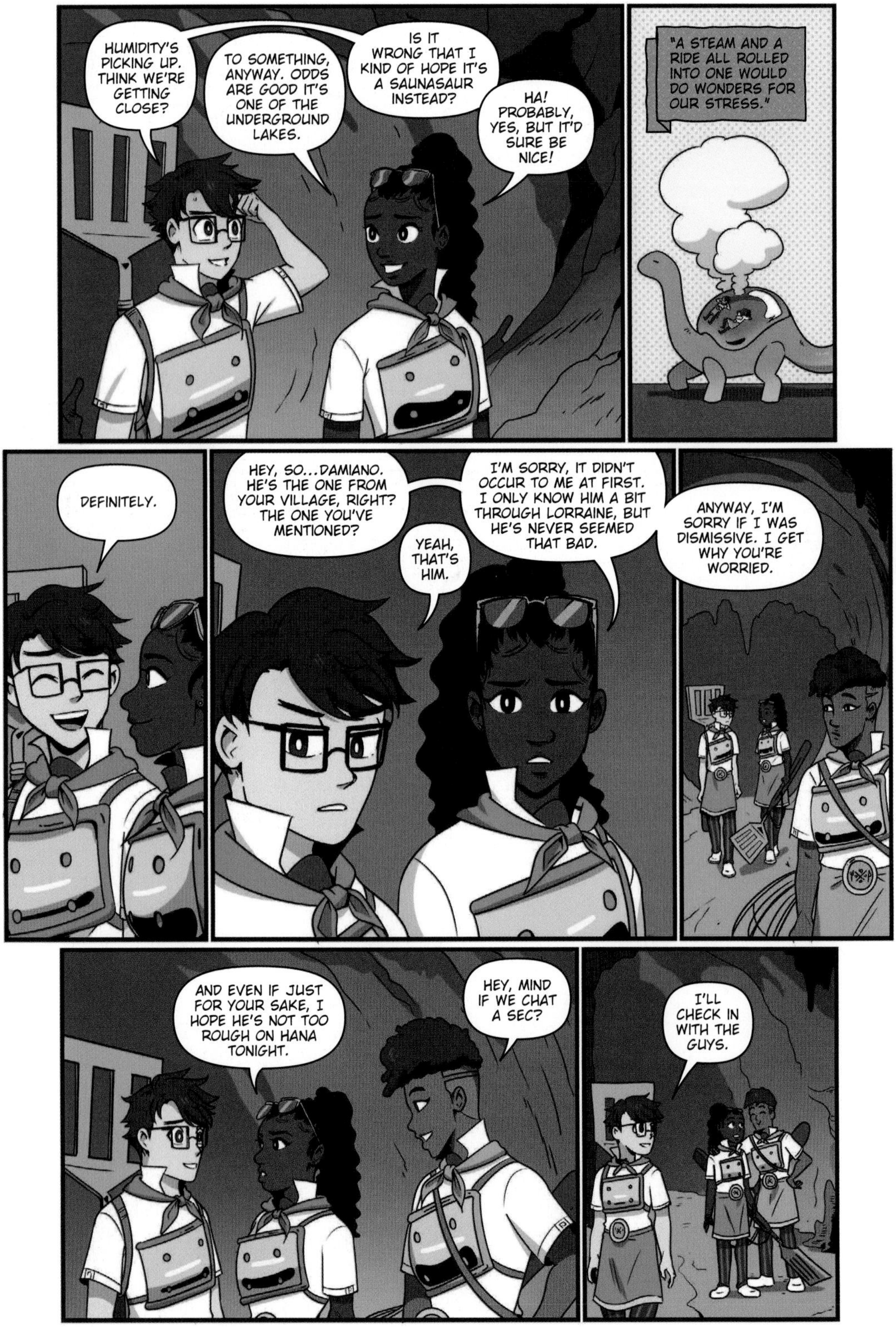
HUMIDITY'S PICKING UP. THINK WE'RE GETTING CLOSE?
TO SOMETHING, ANYWAY. ODDS ARE GOOD IT'S ONE OF THE UNDERGROUND LAKES.
IS IT WRONG THAT I KIND OF HOPE IT'S A SAUNASAUR INSTEAD?
HA! PROBABLY, YES, BUT IT'D SURE BE NICE!
"A STEAM AND A RIDE ALL ROLLED INTO ONE WOULD DO WONDERS FOR OUR STRESS."
DEFINITELY.
HEY, SO...DAMIANO. HE'S THE ONE FROM YOUR VILLAGE, RIGHT? THE ONE YOU'VE MENTIONED?
YEAH, THAT'S HIM.
I'M SORRY, IT DIDN'T OCCUR TO ME AT FIRST. I ONLY KNOW HIM A BIT THROUGH LORRAINE, BUT HE'S NEVER SEEMED THAT BAD.
ANYWAY, I'M SORRY IF I WAS DISMISSIVE. I GET WHY YOU'RE WORRIED.
AND EVEN IF JUST FOR YOUR SAKE, I HOPE HE'S NOT TOO ROUGH ON HANA TONIGHT.
HEY, MIND IF WE CHAT A SEC?
I'LL CHECK IN WITH THE GUYS.

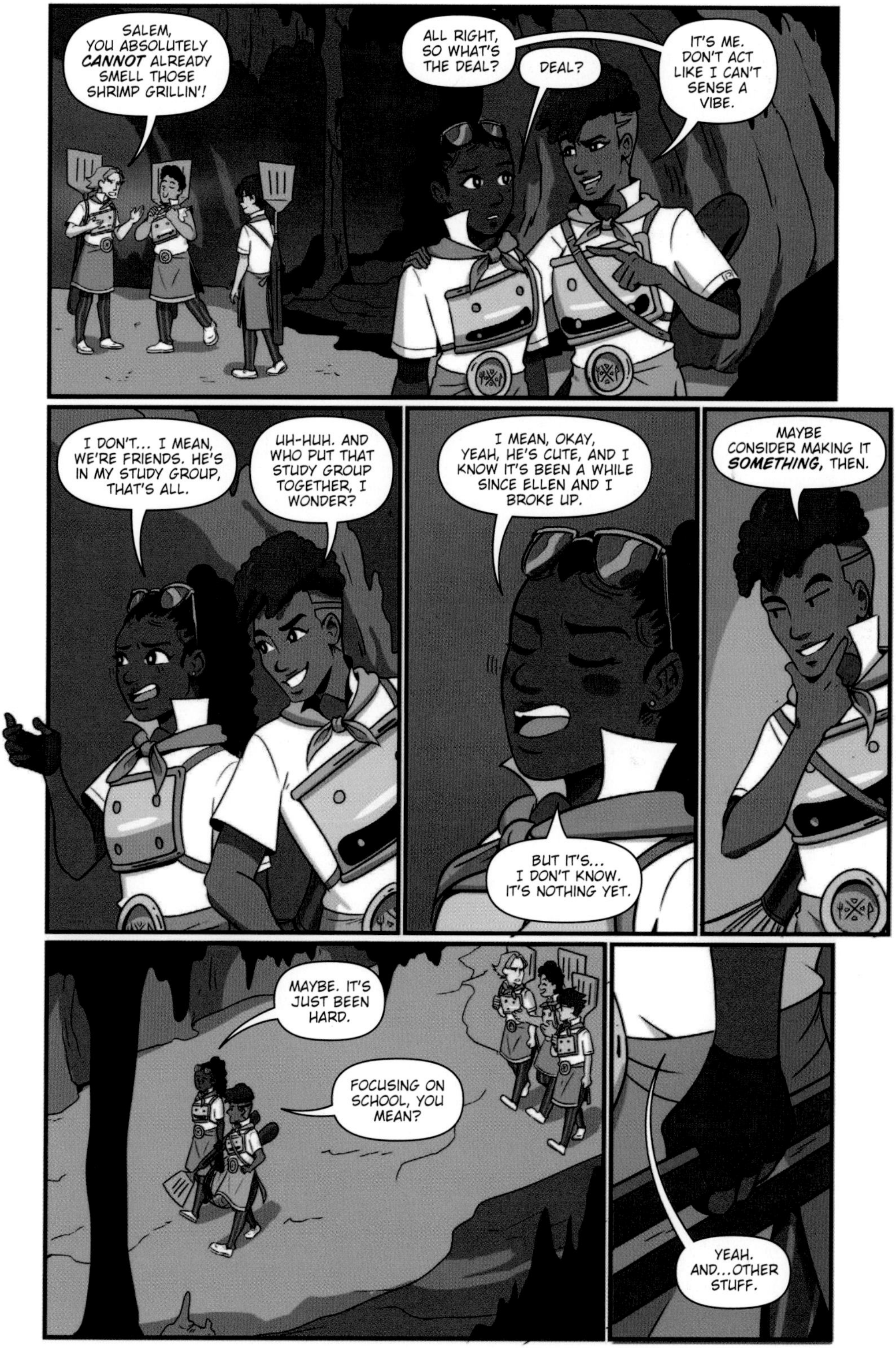
SALEM, YOU ABSOLUTELY **CANNOT** ALREADY SMELL THOSE SHRIMP GRILLIN'!
ALL RIGHT, SO WHAT'S THE DEAL?
DEAL?
IT'S ME. DON'T ACT LIKE I CAN'T SENSE A VIBE.
I DON'T... I MEAN, WE'RE FRIENDS. HE'S IN MY STUDY GROUP, THAT'S ALL.
UH-HUH. AND WHO PUT THAT STUDY GROUP TOGETHER, I WONDER?
I MEAN, OKAY, YEAH, HE'S CUTE, AND I KNOW IT'S BEEN A WHILE SINCE ELLEN AND I BROKE UP.
BUT IT'S... I DON'T KNOW. IT'S NOTHING YET.
MAYBE CONSIDER MAKING IT **SOMETHING,** THEN.
MAYBE. IT'S JUST BEEN HARD.
FOCUSING ON SCHOOL, YOU MEAN?
YEAH. AND...OTHER STUFF.

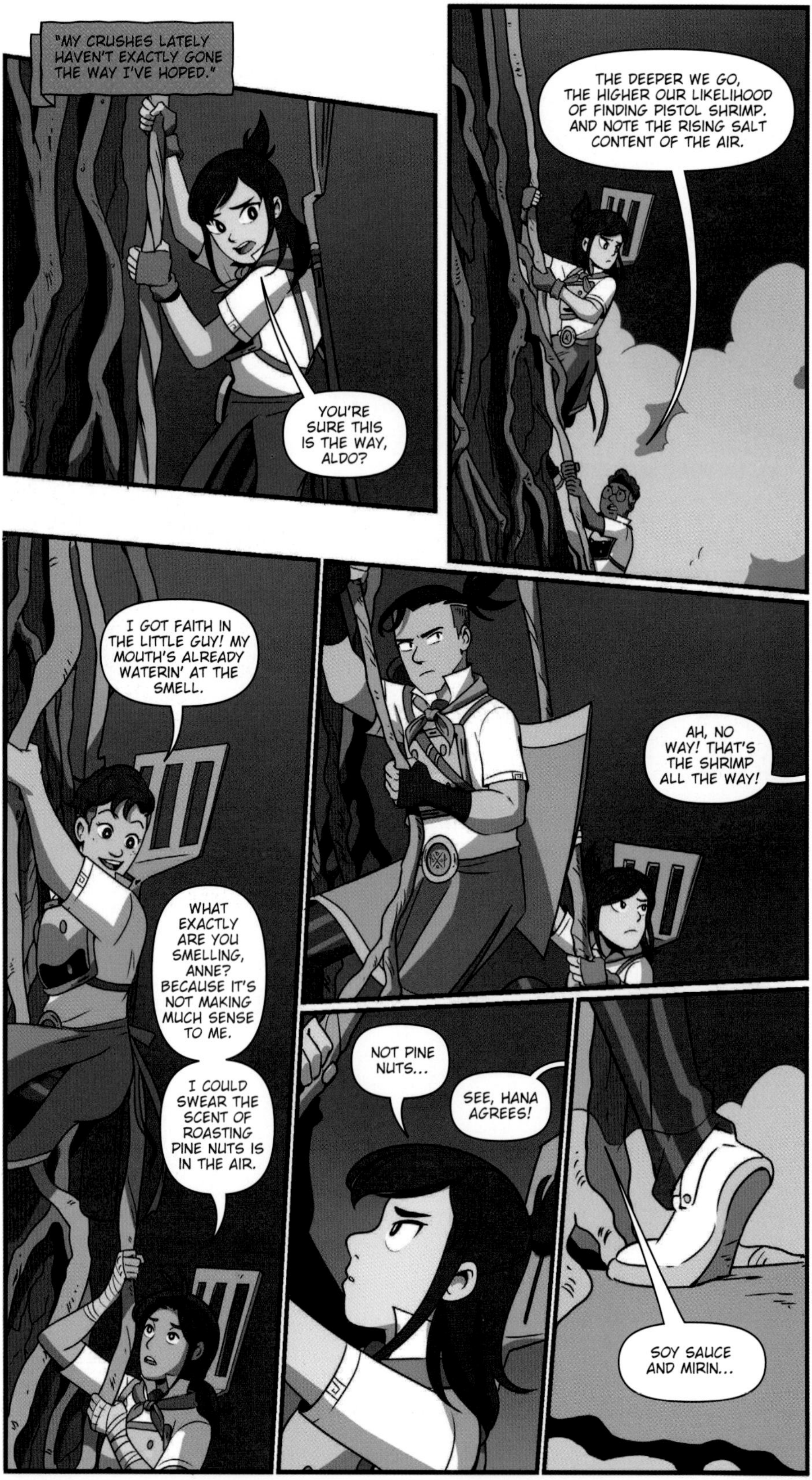
"MY CRUSHES LATELY HAVEN'T EXACTLY GONE THE WAY I'VE HOPED."
YOU'RE SURE THIS IS THE WAY, ALDO?
THE DEEPER WE GO, THE HIGHER OUR LIKELIHOOD OF FINDING PISTOL SHRIMP. AND NOTE THE RISING SALT CONTENT OF THE AIR.
I GOT FAITH IN THE LITTLE GUY! MY MOUTH'S ALREADY WATERIN' AT THE SMELL.
AH, NO WAY! THAT'S THE SHRIMP ALL THE WAY!
WHAT EXACTLY ARE YOU SMELLING, ANNE? BECAUSE IT'S NOT MAKING MUCH SENSE TO ME.
I COULD SWEAR THE SCENT OF ROASTING PINE NUTS IS IN THE AIR.
NOT PINE NUTS...
SEE, HANA AGREES!
SOY SAUCE AND MIRIN...

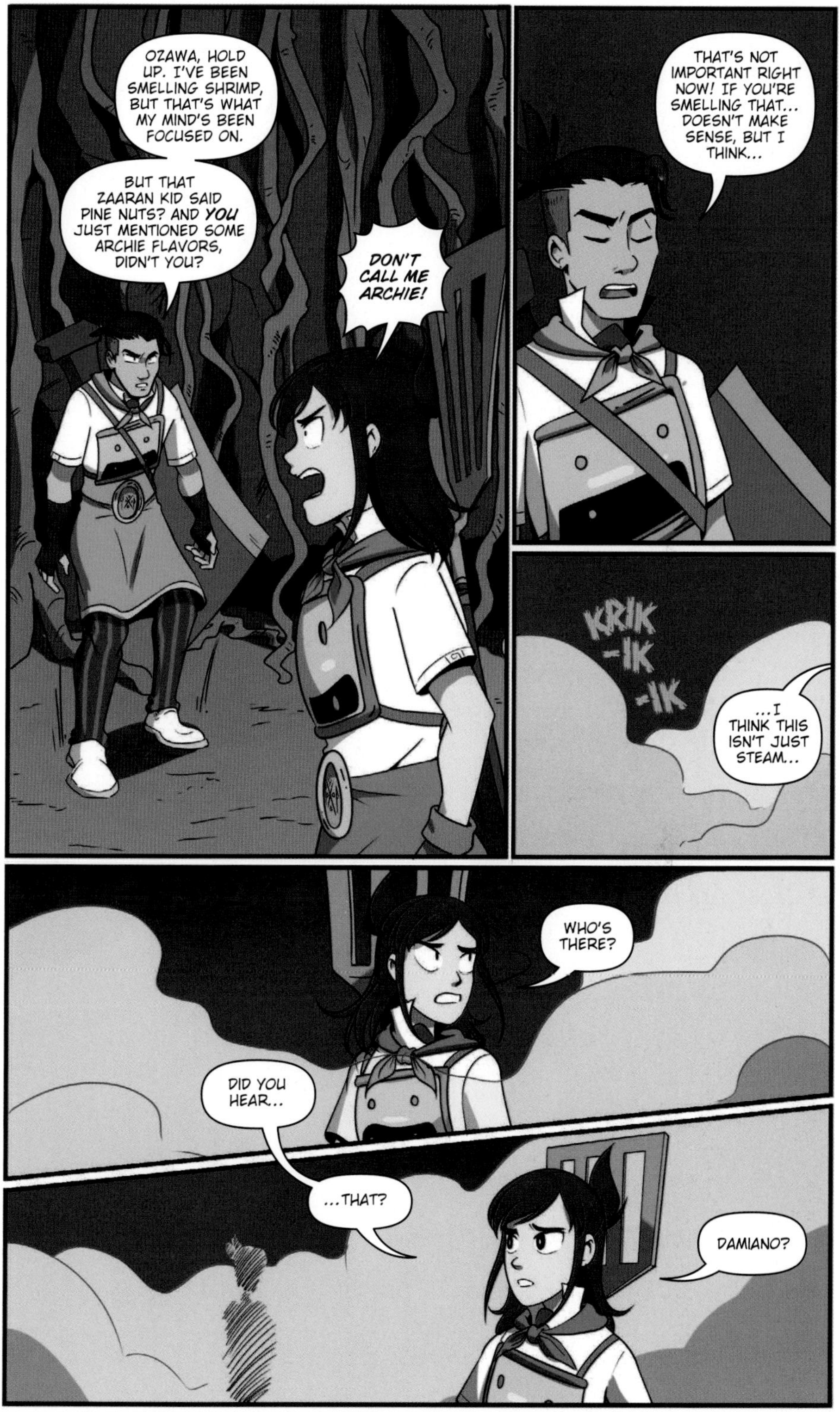
OZAWA, HOLD UP. I'VE BEEN SMELLING SHRIMP, BUT THAT'S WHAT MY MIND'S BEEN FOCUSED ON.
BUT THAT ZAARAN KID SAID PINE NUTS? AND *YOU* JUST MENTIONED SOME ARCHIE FLAVORS, DIDN'T YOU?
DON'T CALL ME ARCHIE!
THAT'S NOT IMPORTANT RIGHT NOW! IF YOU'RE SMELLING THAT... DOESN'T MAKE SENSE, BUT I THINK...
KRIK -IK -IK
...I THINK THIS ISN'T JUST STEAM...
WHO'S THERE?
DID YOU HEAR..
...THAT?
DAMIANO?

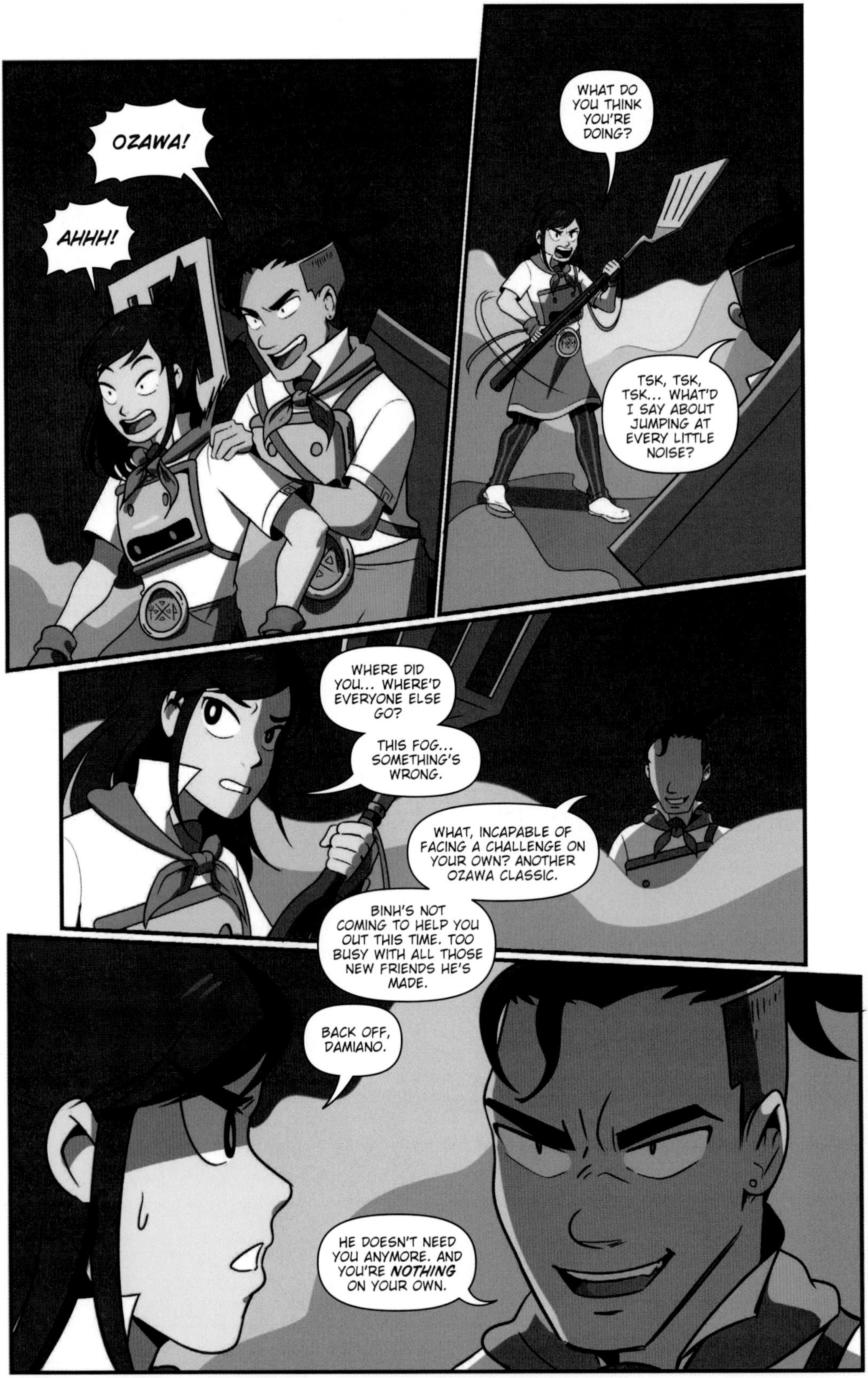
OZAWA!
AHHH!
WHAT DO YOU THINK YOU'RE DOING?
TSK, TSK, TSK... WHAT'D I SAY ABOUT JUMPING AT EVERY LITTLE NOISE?
WHERE DID YOU... WHERE'D EVERYONE ELSE GO?
THIS FOG... SOMETHING'S WRONG.
WHAT, INCAPABLE OF FACING A CHALLENGE ON YOUR OWN? ANOTHER OZAWA CLASSIC.
BINH'S NOT COMING TO HELP YOU OUT THIS TIME. TOO BUSY WITH ALL THOSE NEW FRIENDS HE'S MADE.
BACK OFF, DAMIANO.
HE DOESN'T NEED YOU ANYMORE. AND YOU'RE ***NOTHING*** ON YOUR OWN.

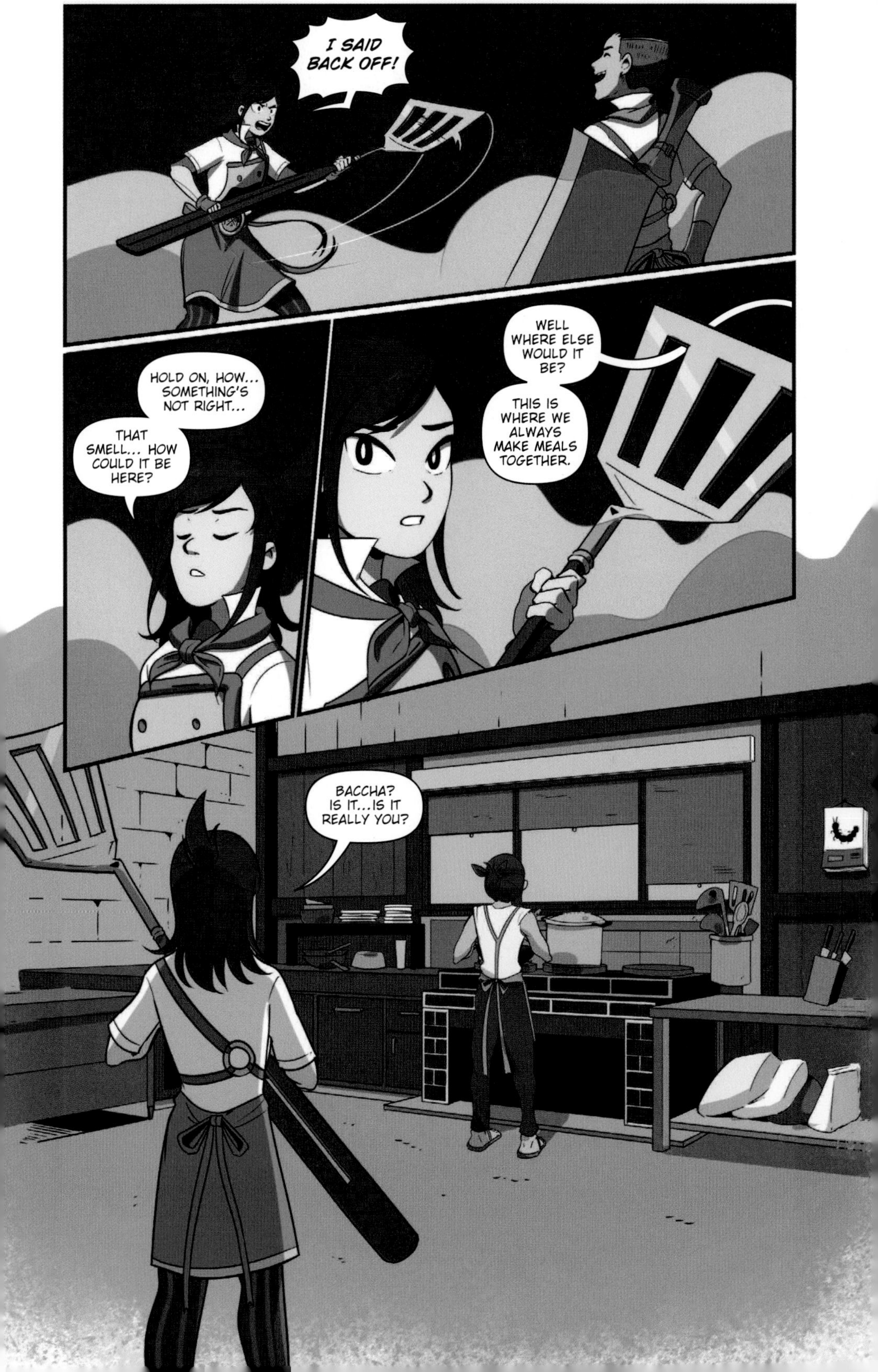
I SAID BACK OFF!
HOLD ON, HOW... SOMETHING'S NOT RIGHT...
THAT SMELL... HOW COULD IT BE HERE?
WELL WHERE ELSE WOULD IT BE?
THIS IS WHERE WE ALWAYS MAKE MEALS TOGETHER.
BACCHA? IS IT...IS IT REALLY YOU?

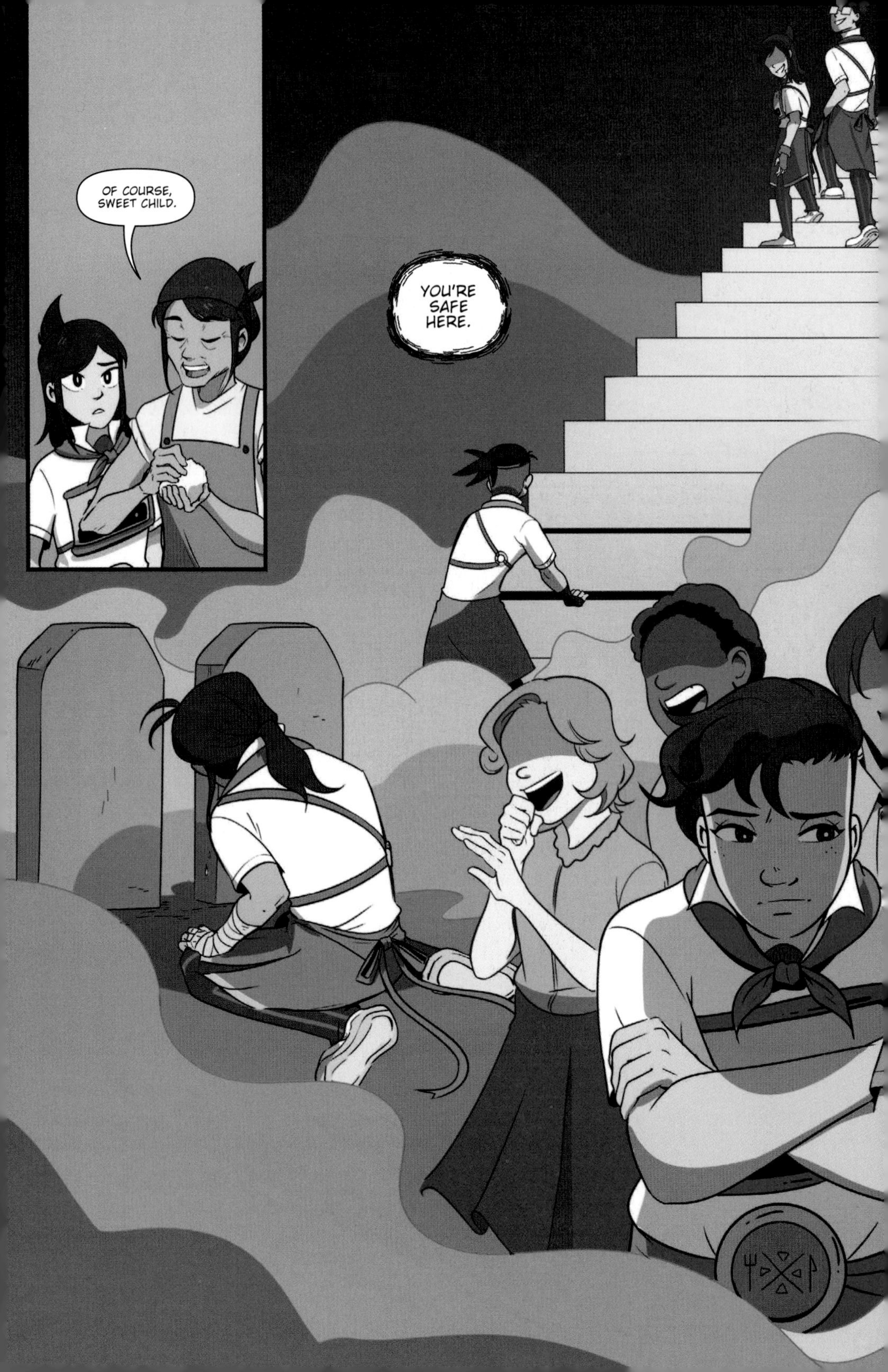
OF COURSE, SWEET CHILD.
YOU'RE SAFE HERE.

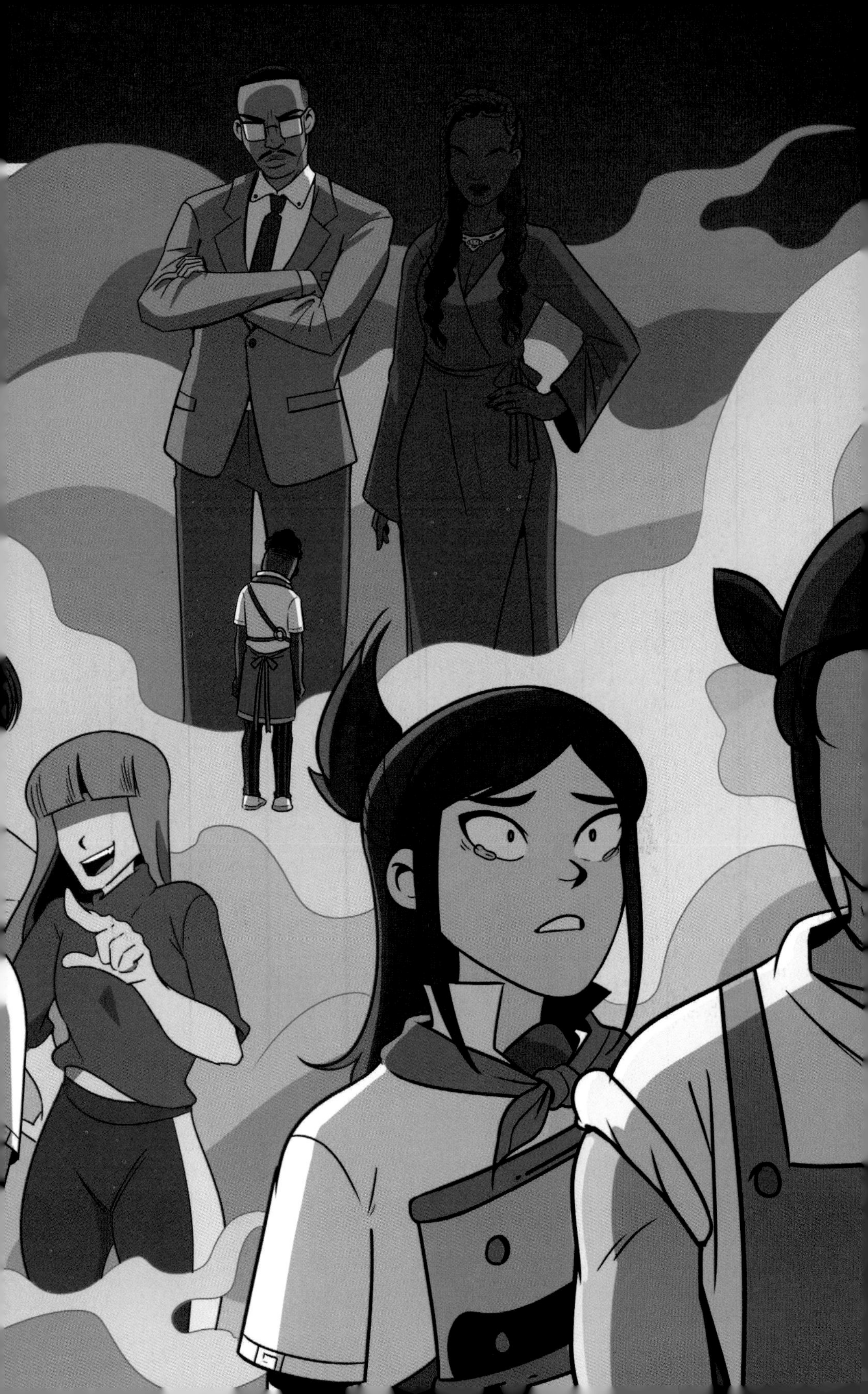

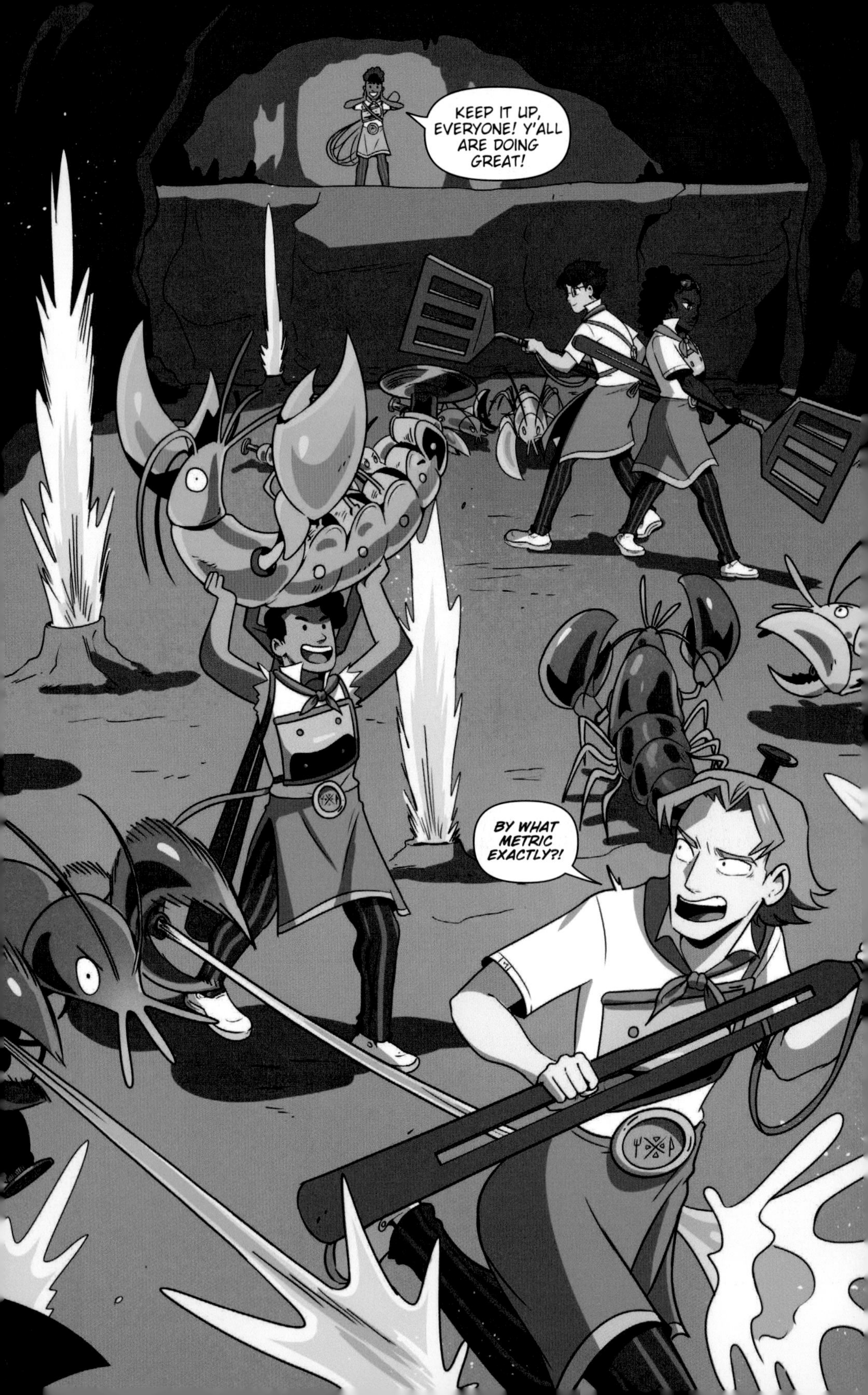
KEEP IT UP, EVERYONE! Y'ALL ARE DOING GREAT!
BY WHAT METRIC EXACTLY?!

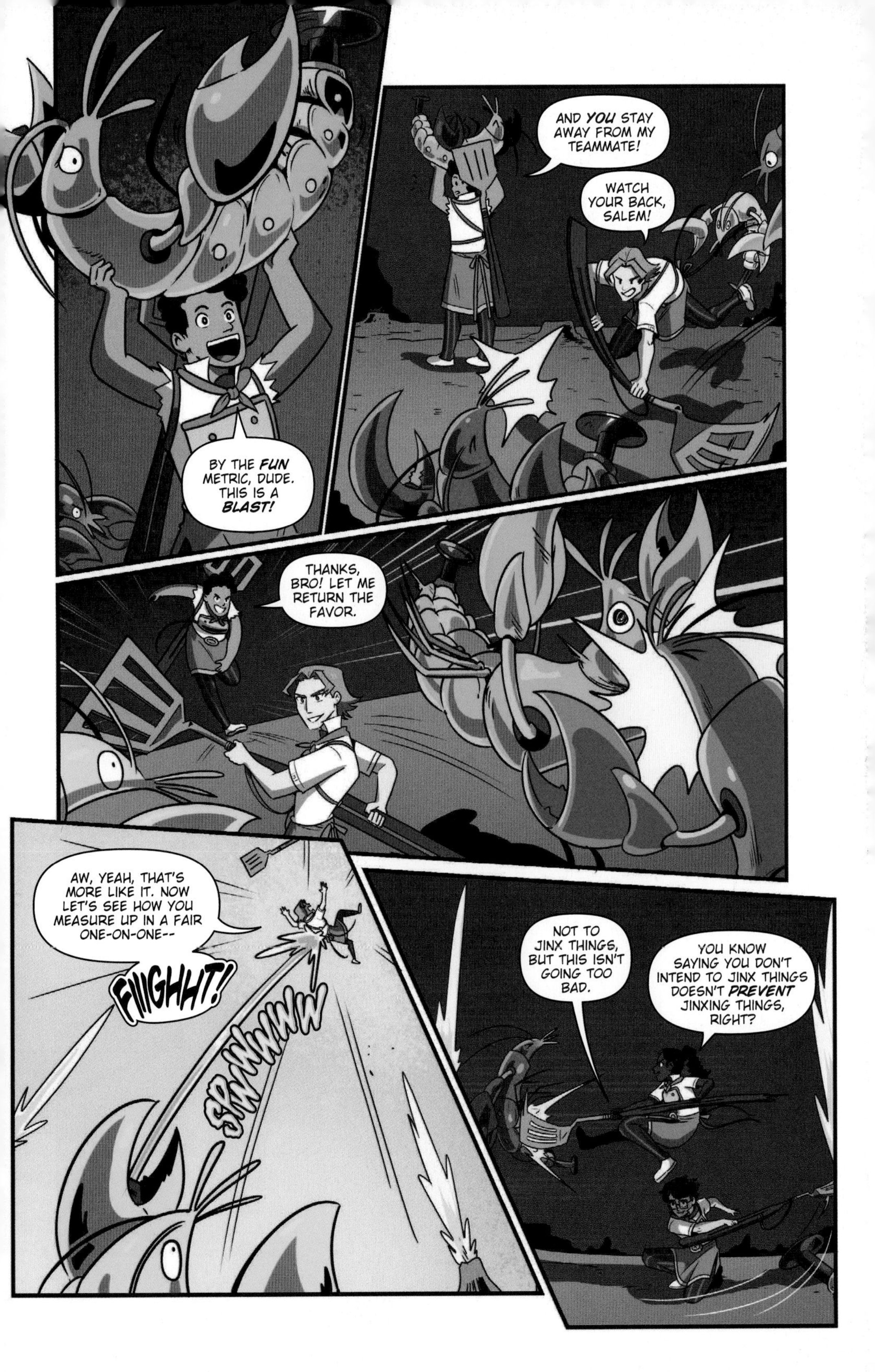
BY THE FUN METRIC, DUDE. THIS IS A BLAST!
AND YOU STAY AWAY FROM MY TEAMMATE!
WATCH YOUR BACK, SALEM!
THANKS, BRO! LET ME RETURN THE FAVOR.
AW, YEAH, THAT'S MORE LIKE IT. NOW LET'S SEE HOW YOU MEASURE UP IN A FAIR ONE-ON-ONE--
FIIIGHHT!
SRWWWWW
NOT TO JINX THINGS, BUT THIS ISN'T GOING TOO BAD.
YOU KNOW SAYING YOU DON'T INTEND TO JINX THINGS DOESN'T PREVENT JINXING THINGS, RIGHT?

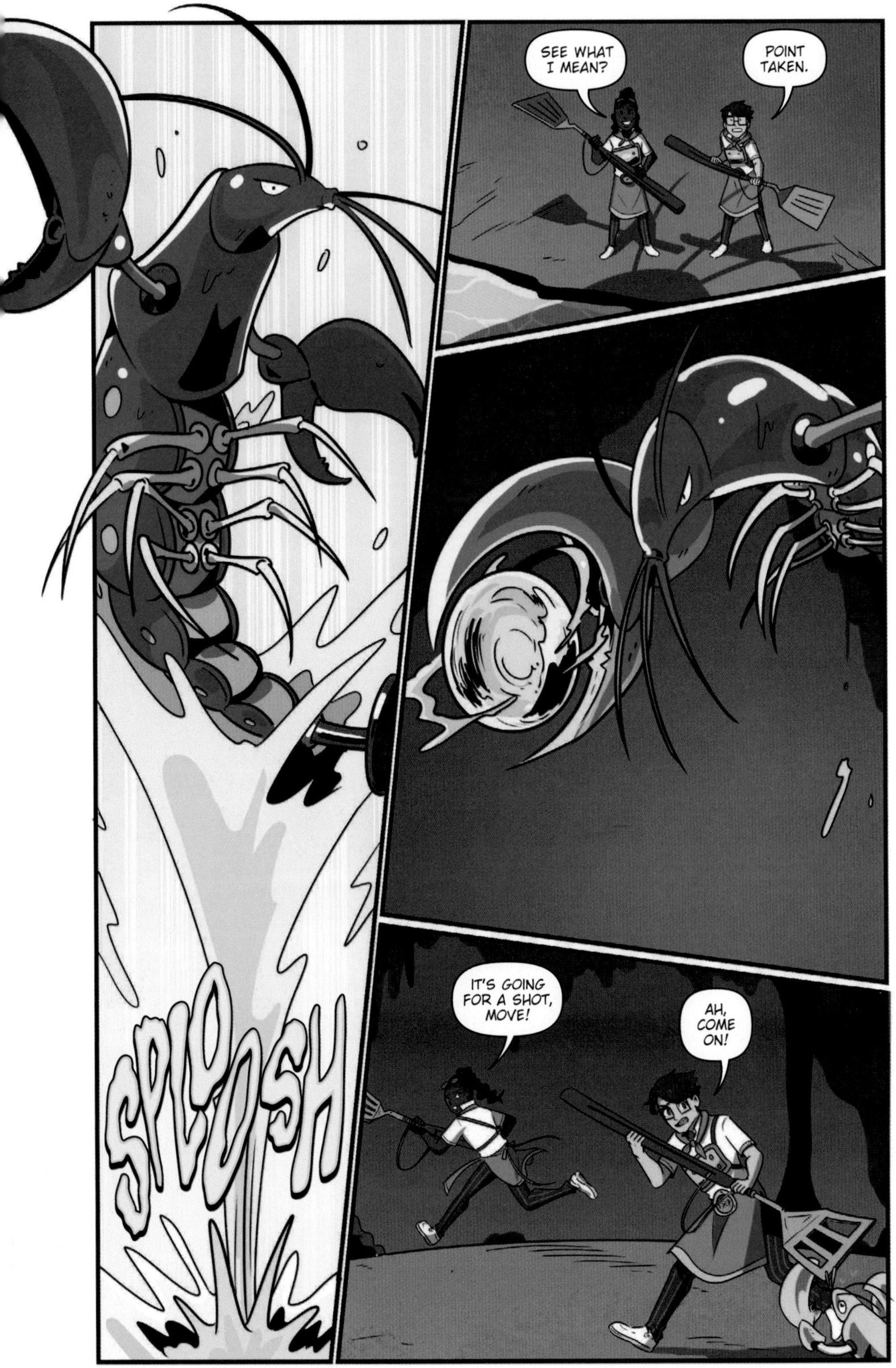
SPLOOSH
SEE WHAT I MEAN?
POINT TAKEN.
IT'S GOING FOR A SHOT, MOVE!
AH, COME ON!

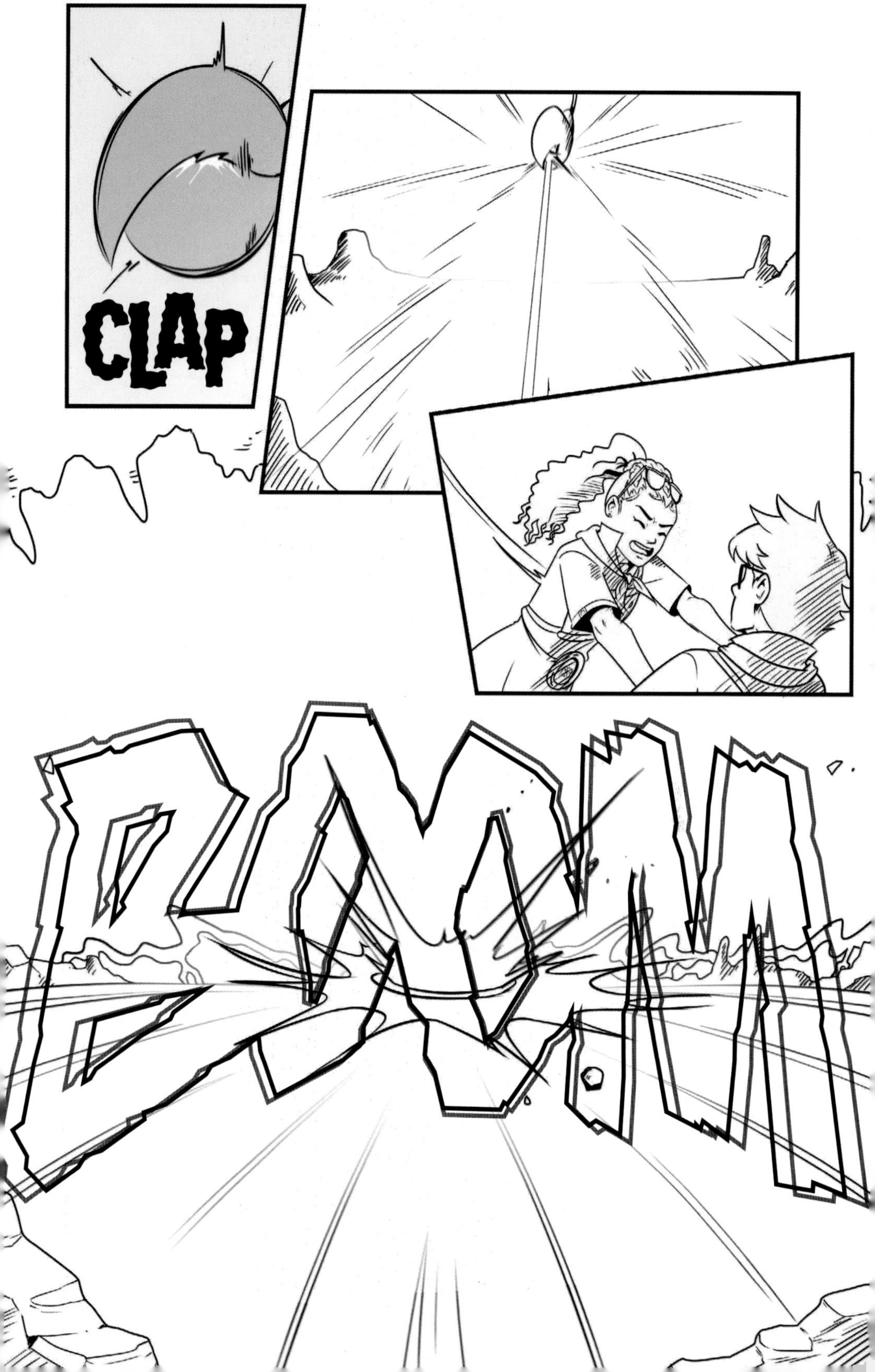
CLAP
DOOM

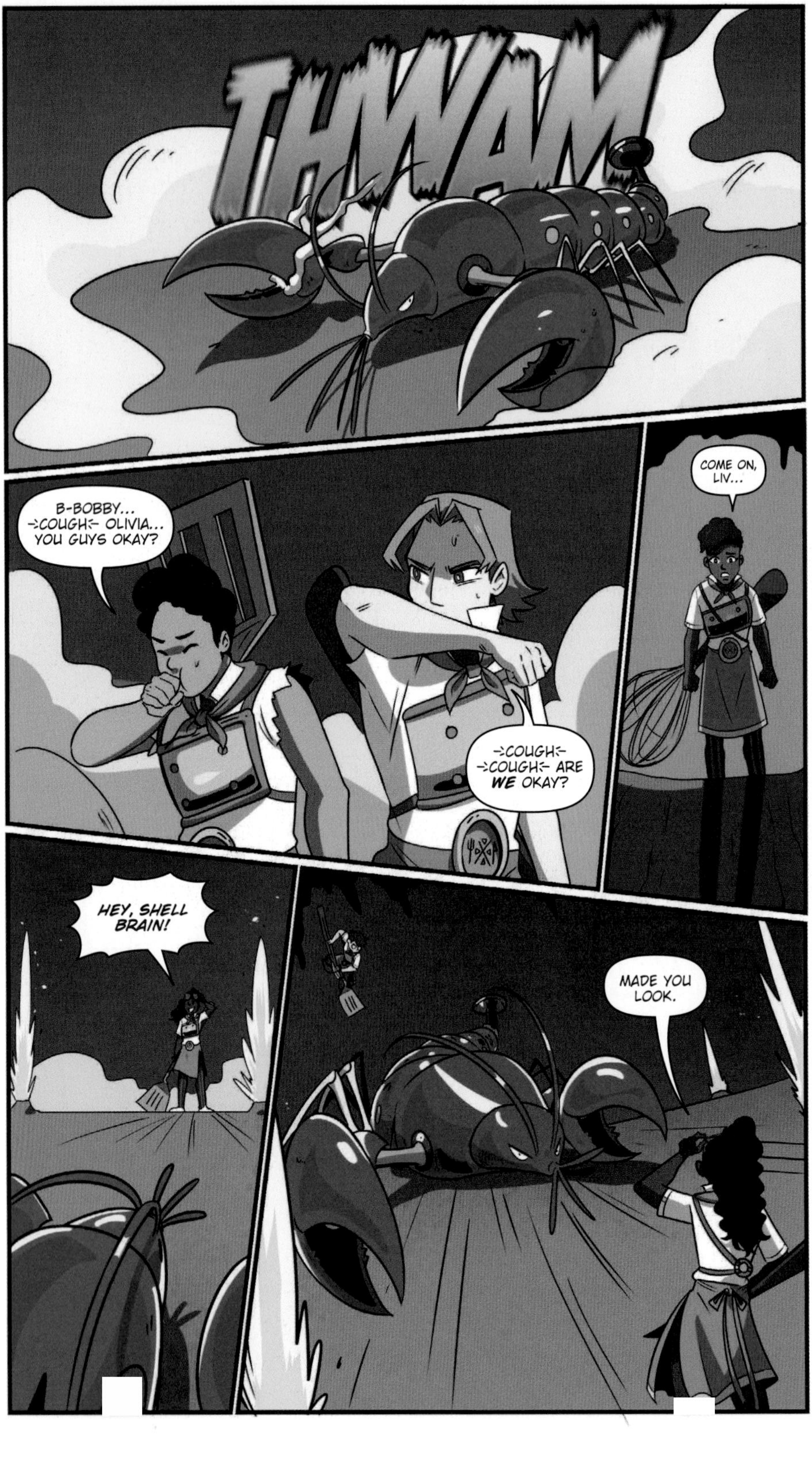
THWAM!
B-BOBBY... -COUGH- OLIVIA... YOU GUYS OKAY?
-COUGH- -COUGH- ARE WE OKAY?
COME ON, LIV...
HEY, SHELL BRAIN!
MADE YOU LOOK.

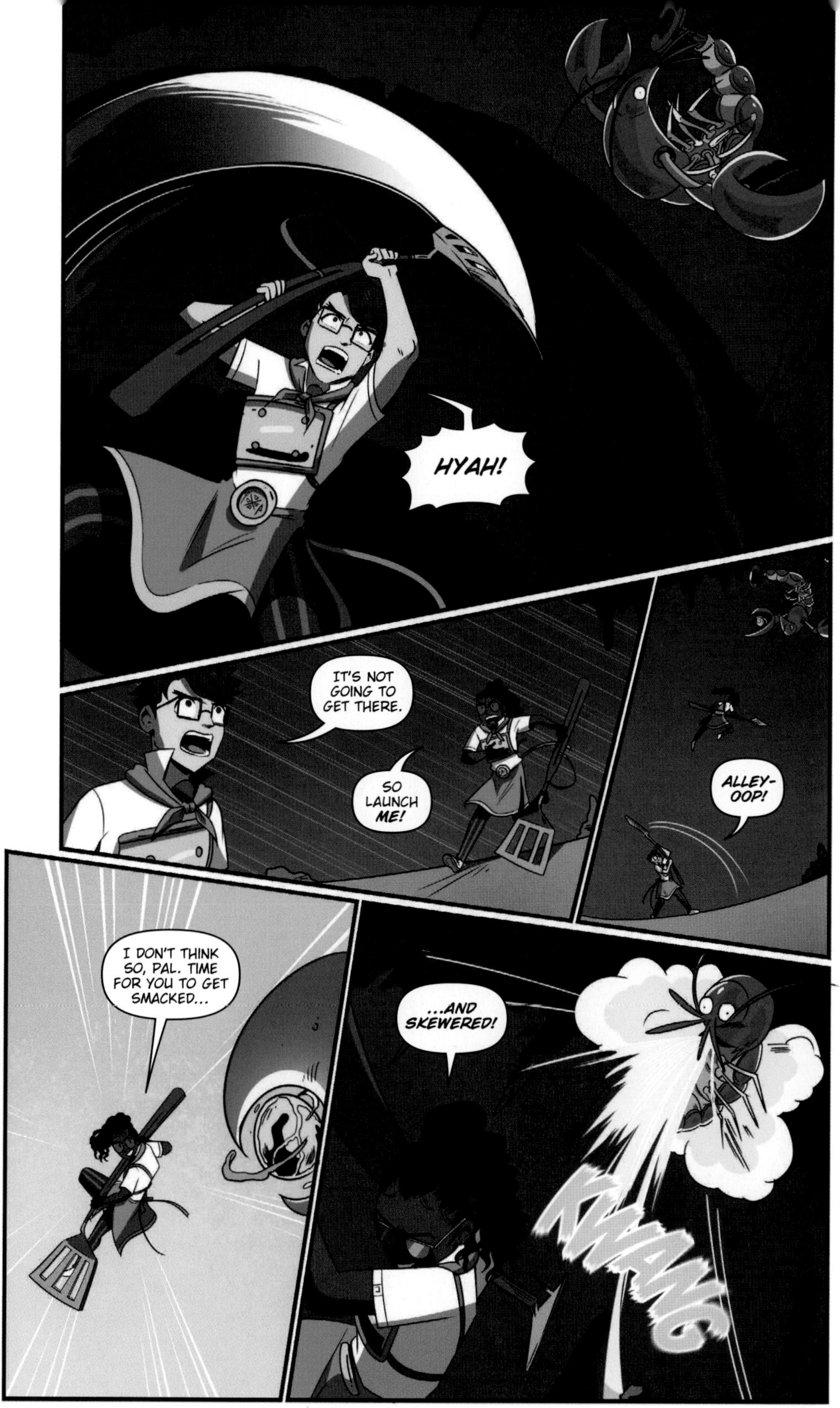
HYAH!
IT'S NOT GOING TO GET THERE.
SO LAUNCH ME!
ALLEY-OOP!
I DON'T THINK SO, PAL. TIME FOR YOU TO GET SMACKED...
...AND SKEWERED!
KWANG

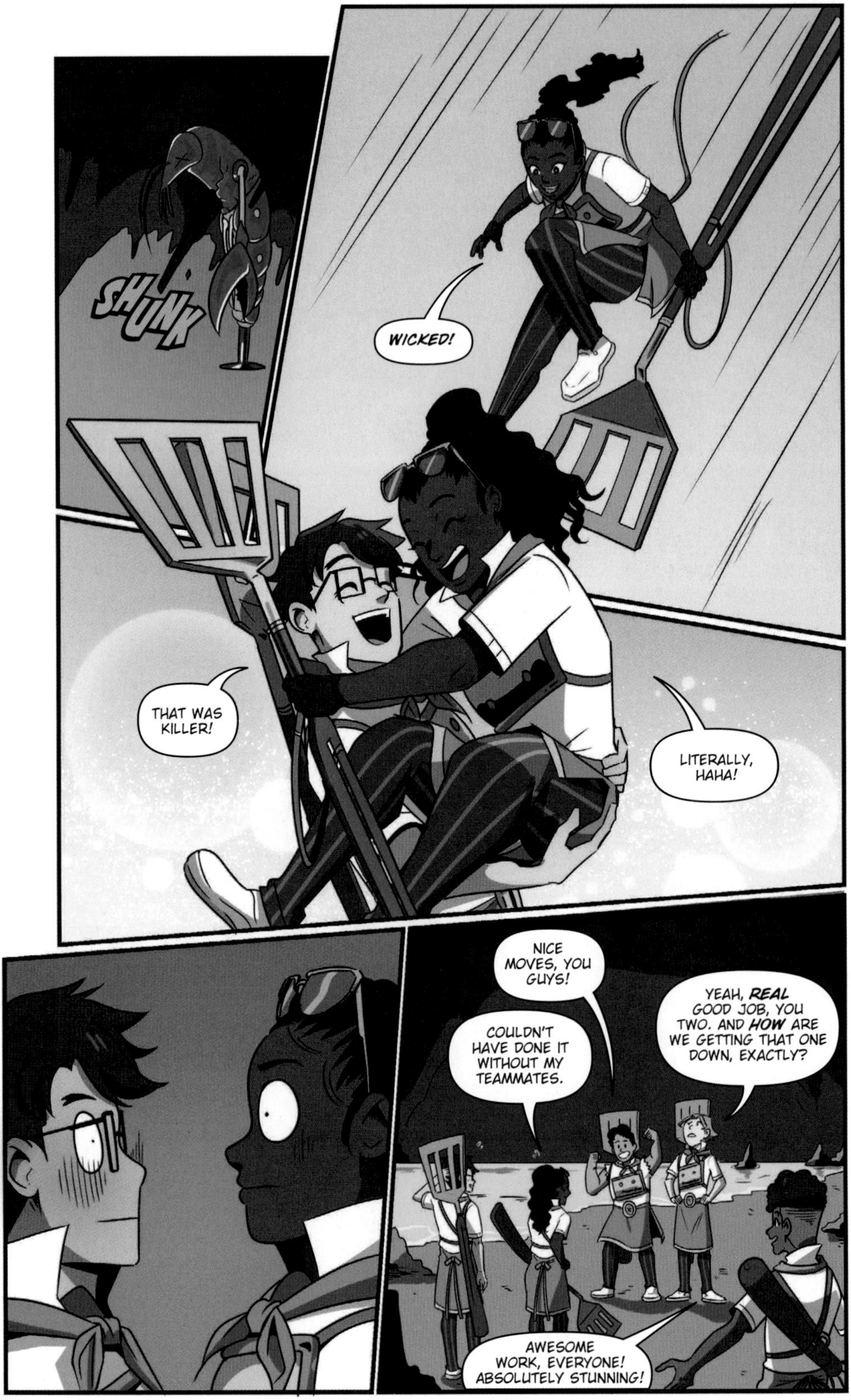
SHUNK
WICKED!
THAT WAS KILLER!
LITERALLY, HAHA!
NICE MOVES, YOU GUYS!
COULDN'T HAVE DONE IT WITHOUT MY TEAMMATES.
YEAH, REAL GOOD JOB, YOU TWO. AND HOW ARE WE GETTING THAT ONE DOWN, EXACTLY?
AWESOME WORK, EVERYONE! ABSOLUTELY STUNNING!

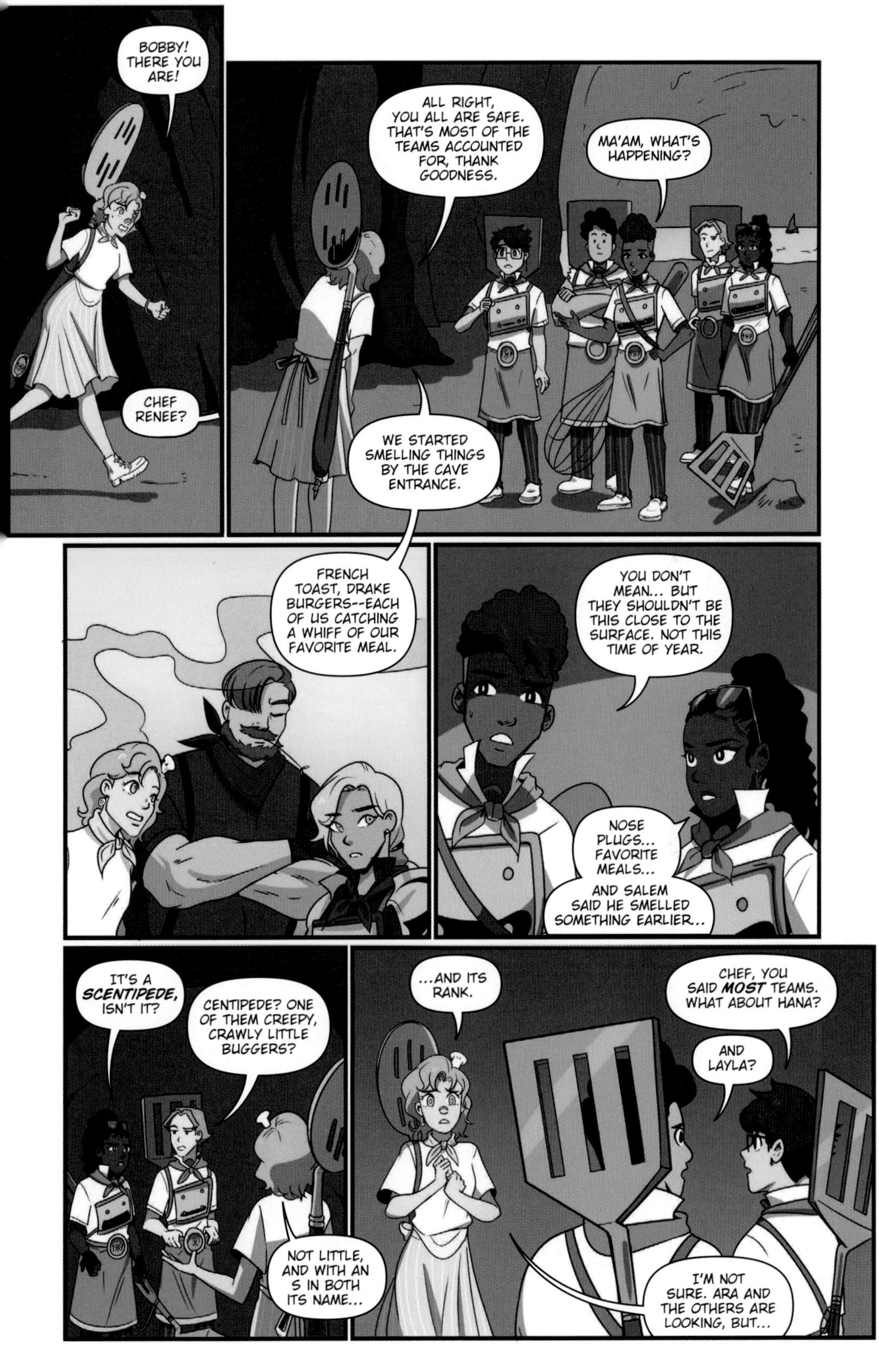
BOBBY! THERE YOU ARE!
CHEF RENEE?
ALL RIGHT, YOU ALL ARE SAFE. THAT'S MOST OF THE TEAMS ACCOUNTED FOR, THANK GOODNESS.
MA'AM, WHAT'S HAPPENING?
WE STARTED SMELLING THINGS BY THE CAVE ENTRANCE.
FRENCH TOAST, DRAKE BURGERS--EACH OF US CATCHING A WHIFF OF OUR FAVORITE MEAL.
YOU DON'T MEAN... BUT THEY SHOULDN'T BE THIS CLOSE TO THE SURFACE. NOT THIS TIME OF YEAR.
NOSE PLUGS... FAVORITE MEALS...
AND SALEM SAID HE SMELLED SOMETHING EARLIER...
IT'S A ***SCENTIPEDE,*** ISN'T IT?
CENTIPEDE? ONE OF THEM CREEPY, CRAWLY LITTLE BUGGERS?
NOT LITTLE, AND WITH AN S IN BOTH ITS NAME...
...AND ITS RANK.
CHEF, YOU SAID **MOST** TEAMS. WHAT ABOUT HANA?
AND LAYLA?
I'M NOT SURE. ARA AND THE OTHERS ARE LOOKING, BUT...

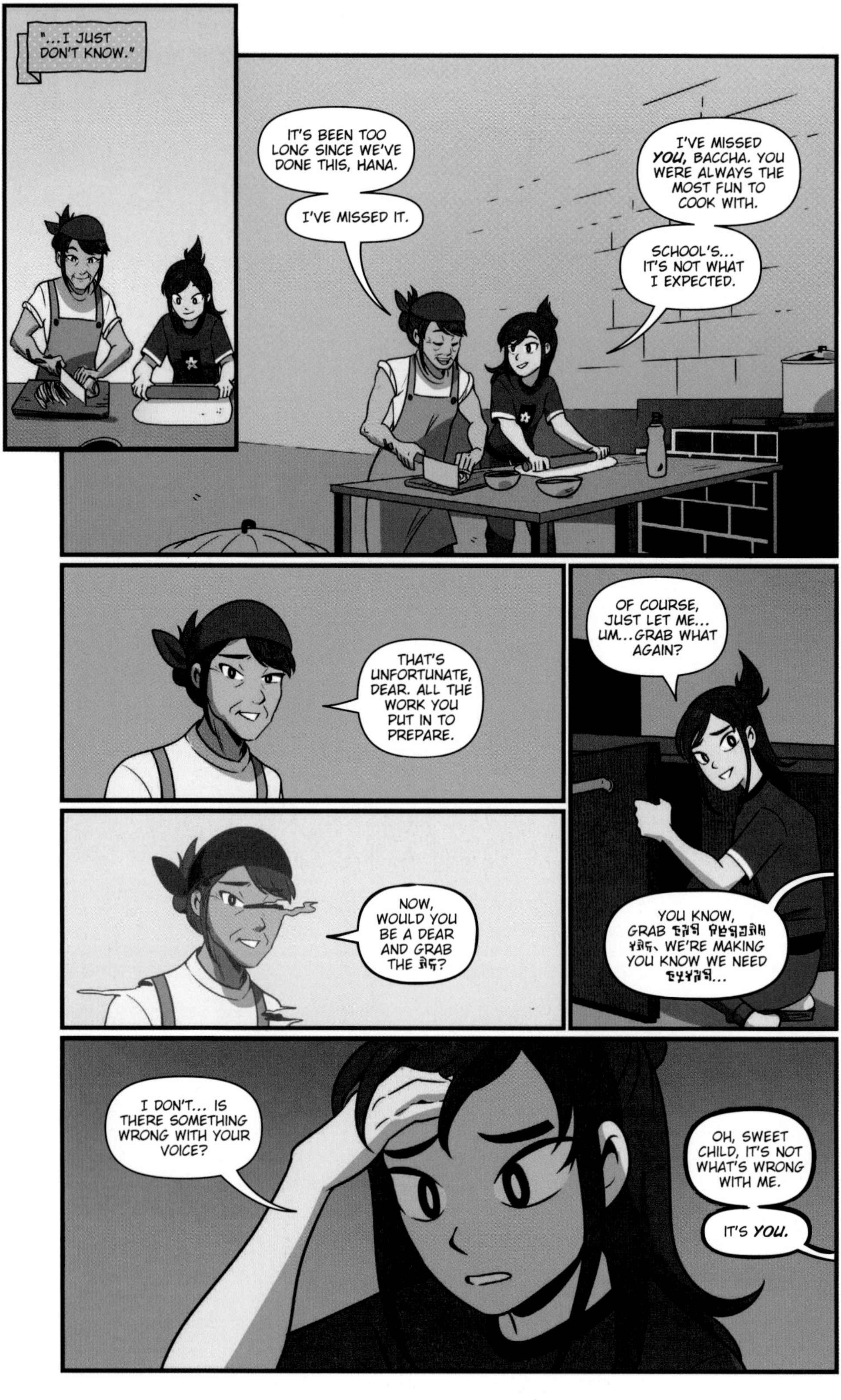
"...I JUST DON'T KNOW."
IT'S BEEN TOO LONG SINCE WE'VE DONE THIS, HANA.
I'VE MISSED IT.
I'VE MISSED *YOU*, BACCHA. YOU WERE ALWAYS THE MOST FUN TO COOK WITH.
SCHOOL'S... IT'S NOT WHAT I EXPECTED.
THAT'S UNFORTUNATE, DEAR. ALL THE WORK YOU PUT IN TO PREPARE.
NOW, WOULD YOU BE A DEAR AND GRAB THE
OF COURSE, JUST LET ME... UM...GRAB WHAT AGAIN?
YOU KNOW, GRAB
WE'RE MAKING
YOU KNOW WE NEED
I DON'T... IS THERE SOMETHING WRONG WITH YOUR VOICE?
OH, SWEET CHILD, IT'S NOT WHAT'S WRONG WITH ME.
IT'S *YOU.*

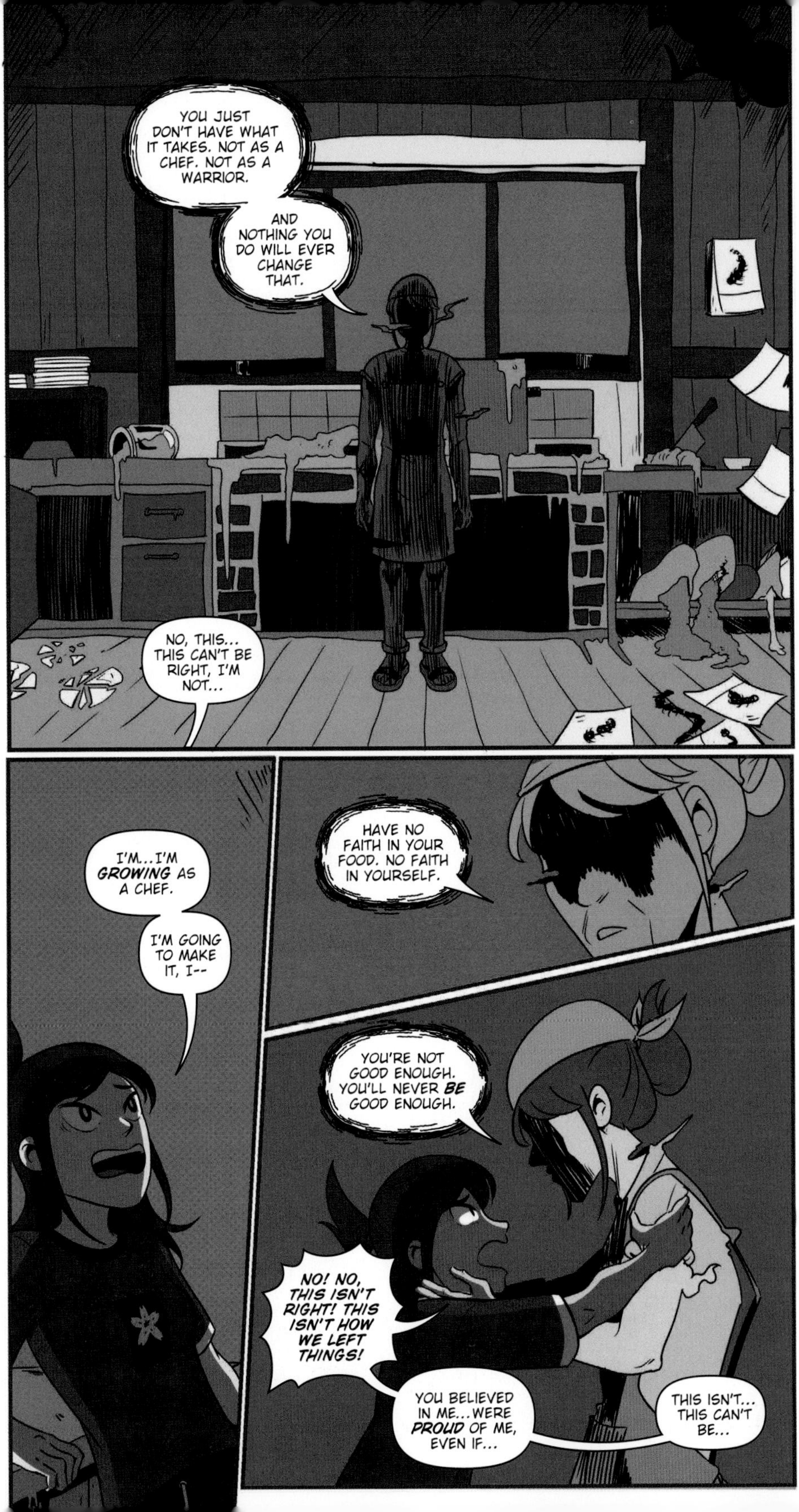
YOU JUST DON'T HAVE WHAT IT TAKES. NOT AS A CHEF. NOT AS A WARRIOR.
AND NOTHING YOU DO WILL EVER CHANGE THAT.
NO, THIS... THIS CAN'T BE RIGHT, I'M NOT...
I'M...I'M *GROWING* AS A CHEF.
I'M GOING TO MAKE IT, I--
HAVE NO FAITH IN YOUR FOOD. NO FAITH IN YOURSELF.
YOU'RE NOT GOOD ENOUGH. YOU'LL NEVER *BE* GOOD ENOUGH.
NO! NO, THIS ISN'T RIGHT! THIS ISN'T HOW WE LEFT THINGS!
YOU BELIEVED IN ME...WERE *PROUD* OF ME, EVEN IF...
THIS ISN'T... THIS CAN'T BE...

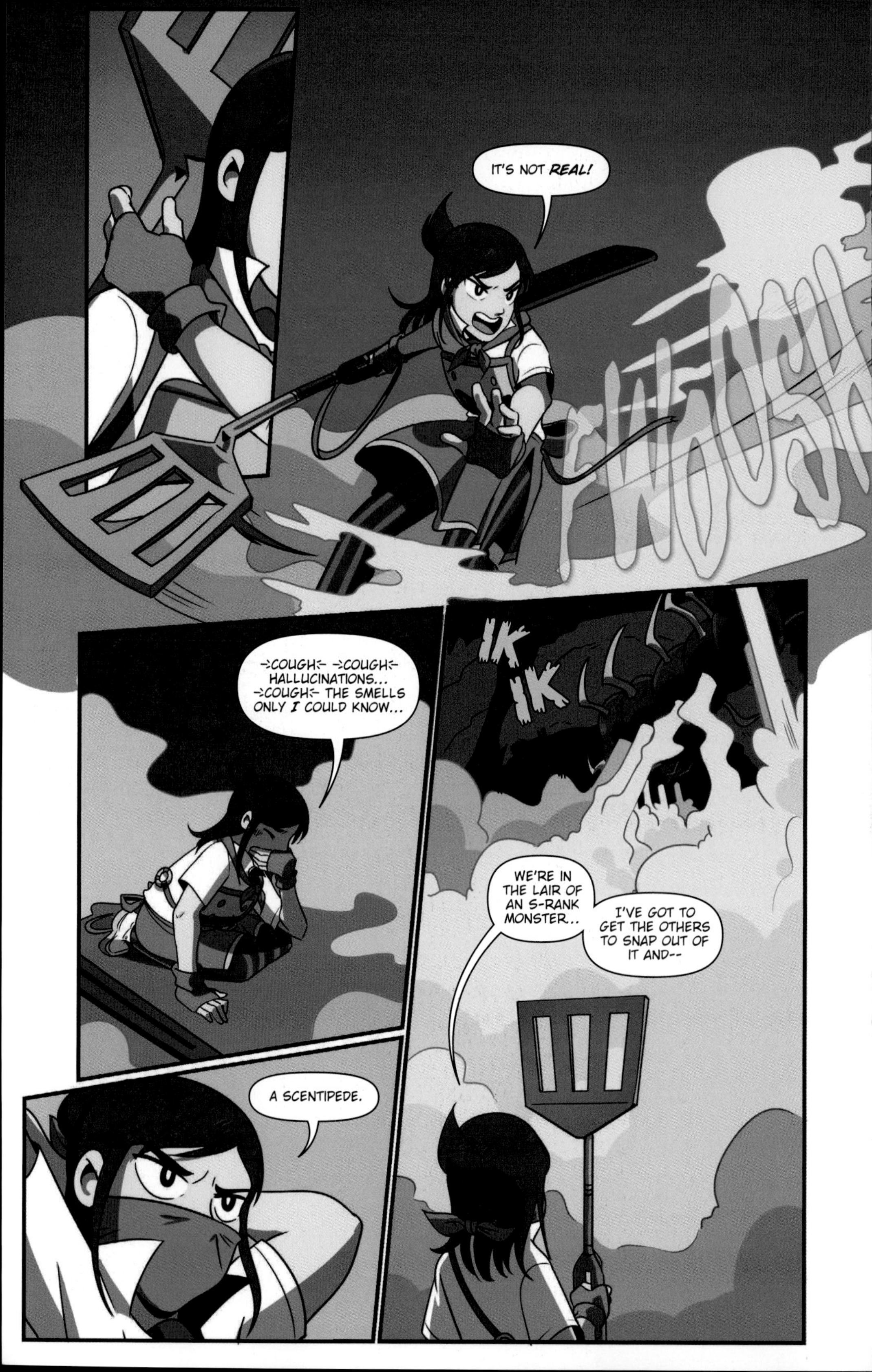
IT'S NOT REAL!
FWOOSH
-COUGH- -COUGH- HALLUCINATIONS... -COUGH- THE SMELLS ONLY I COULD KNOW...
IK IK
WE'RE IN THE LAIR OF AN S-RANK MONSTER...
I'VE GOT TO GET THE OTHERS TO SNAP OUT OF IT AND--
A SCENTIPEDE.

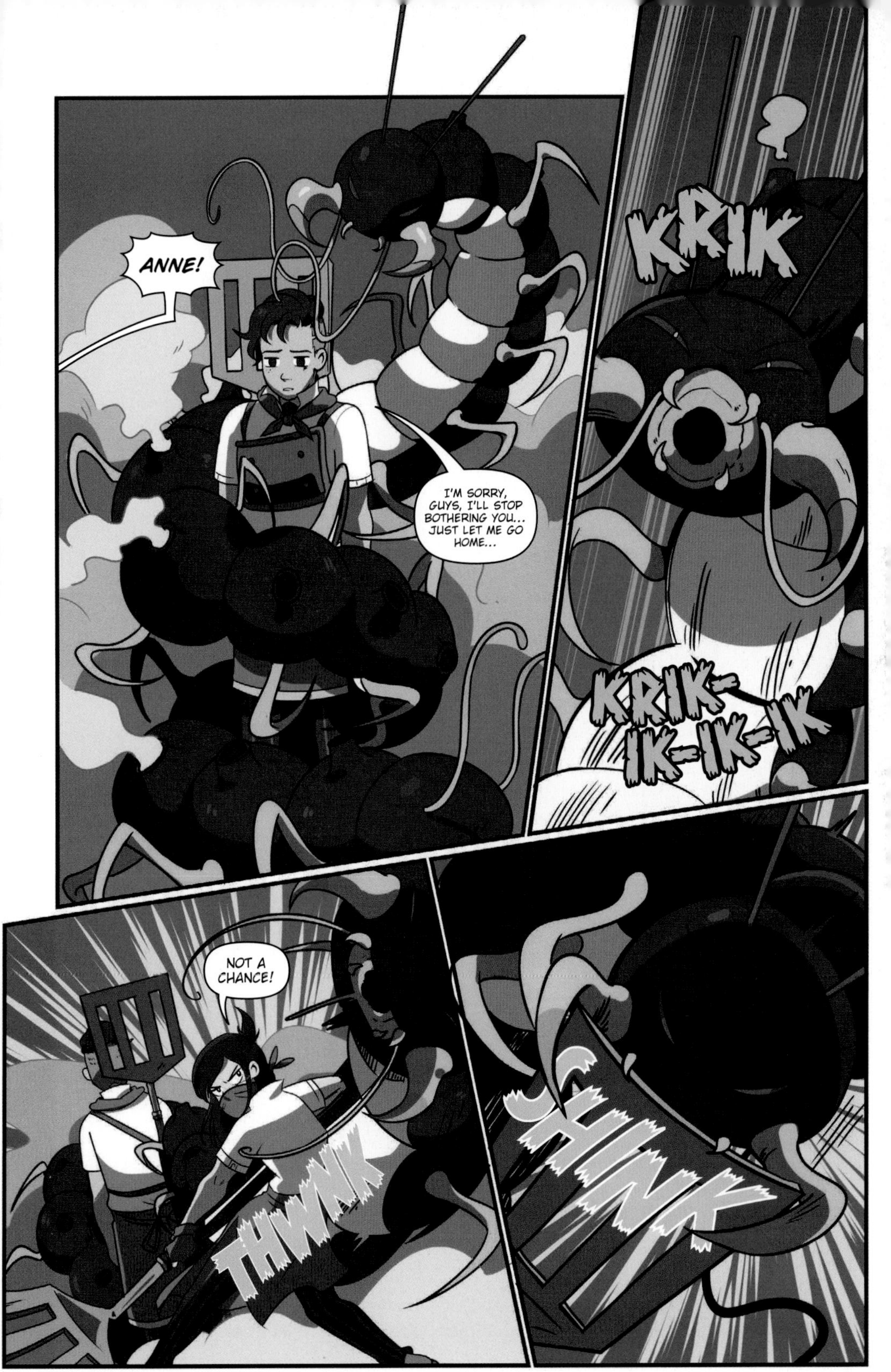
ANNE!
I'M SORRY, GUYS, I'LL STOP BOTHERING YOU... JUST LET ME GO HOME...
KRIK
KRIK-IK-IK-IK
NOT A CHANCE!
THWNK
SHINK

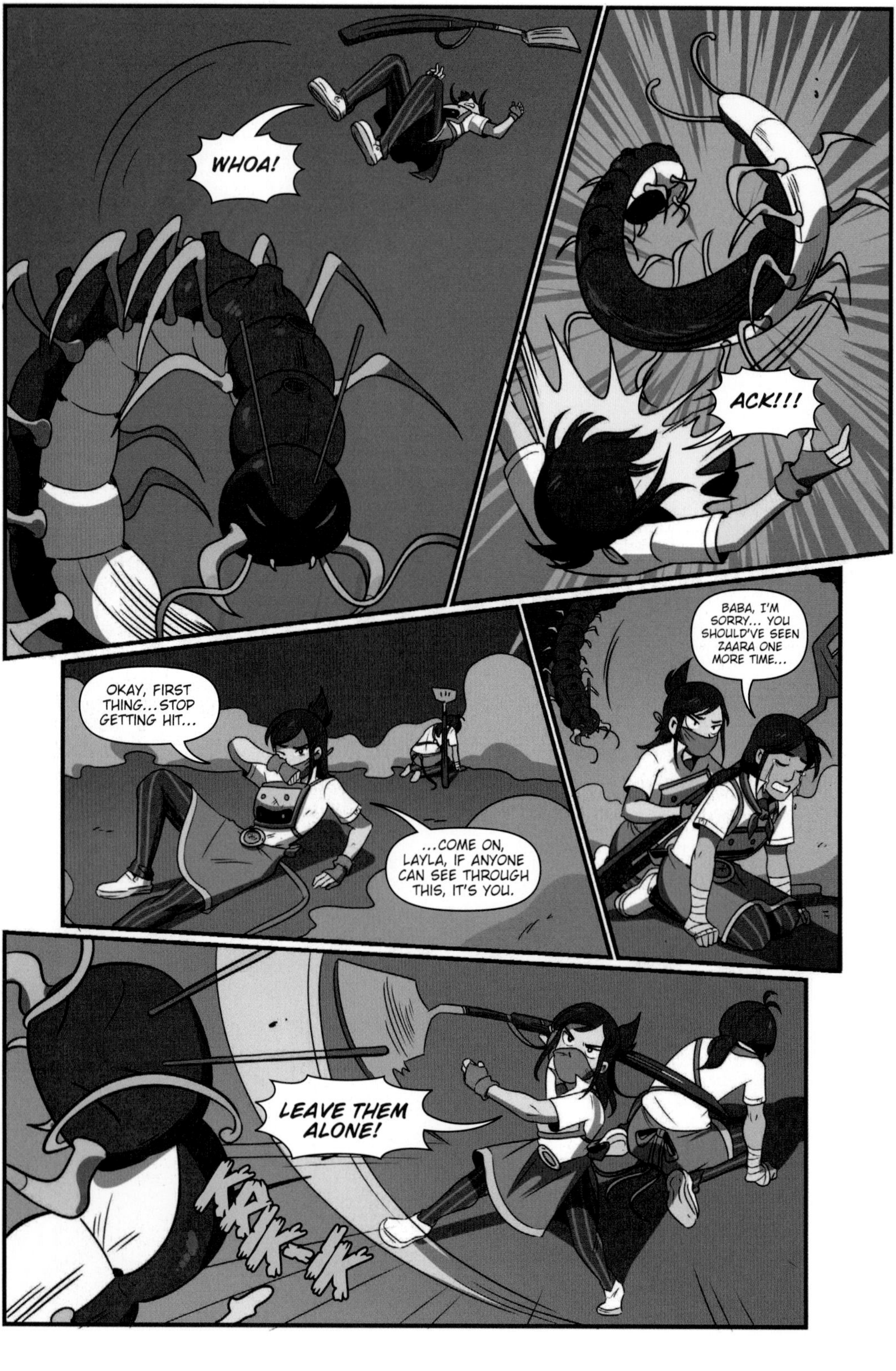
WHOA!
ACK!!!
OKAY, FIRST THING...STOP GETTING HIT...
...COME ON, LAYLA, IF ANYONE CAN SEE THROUGH THIS, IT'S YOU.
BABA, I'M SORRY... YOU SHOULD'VE SEEN ZAARA ONE MORE TIME...
LEAVE THEM ALONE!
KRIK-IK

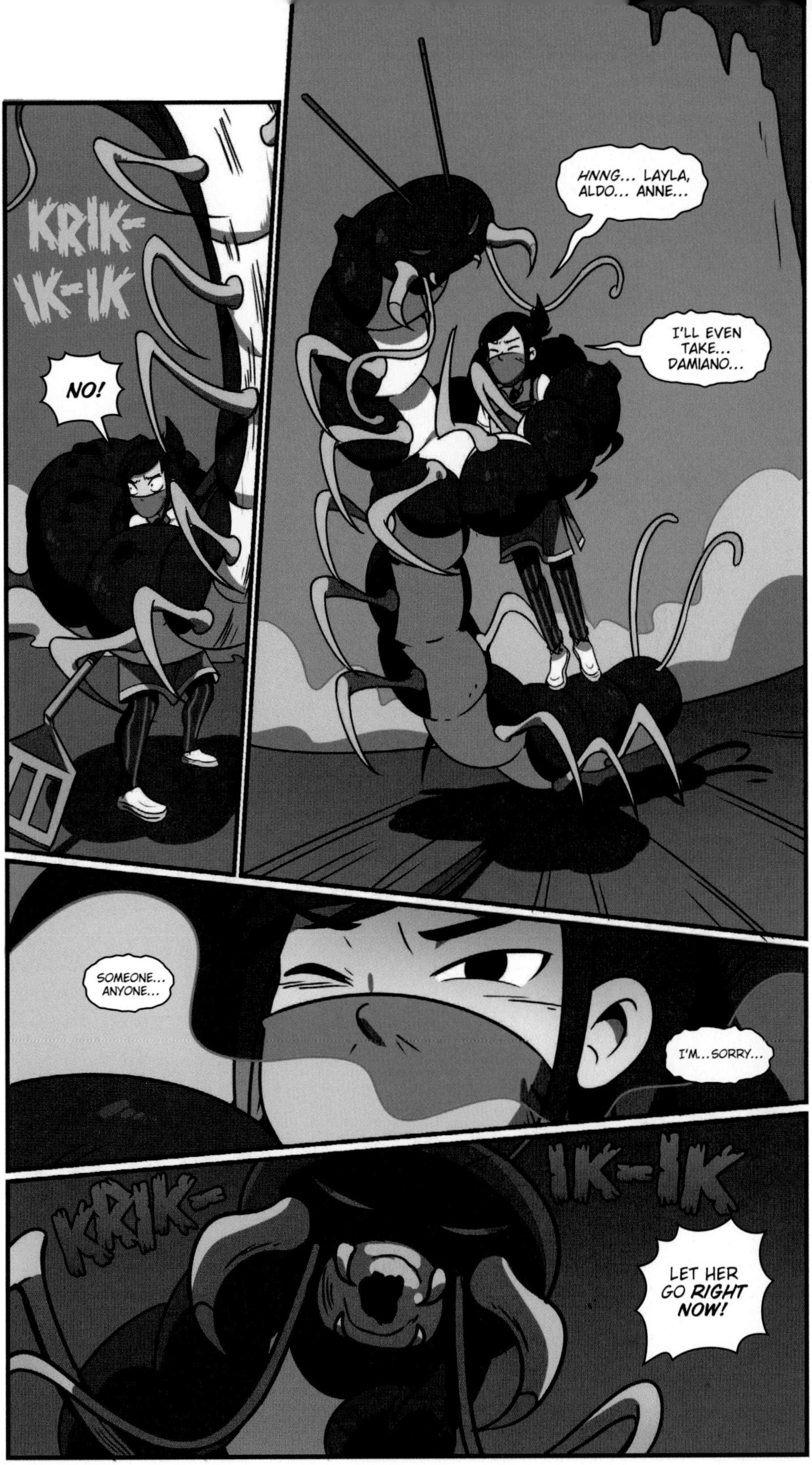
KRIK-IK-IK
NO!
HNNG... LAYLA, ALDO... ANNE...
I'LL EVEN TAKE... DAMIANO...
SOMEONE... ANYONE...
I'M...SORRY...
KRIK-IK-IK
LET HER GO RIGHT NOW!

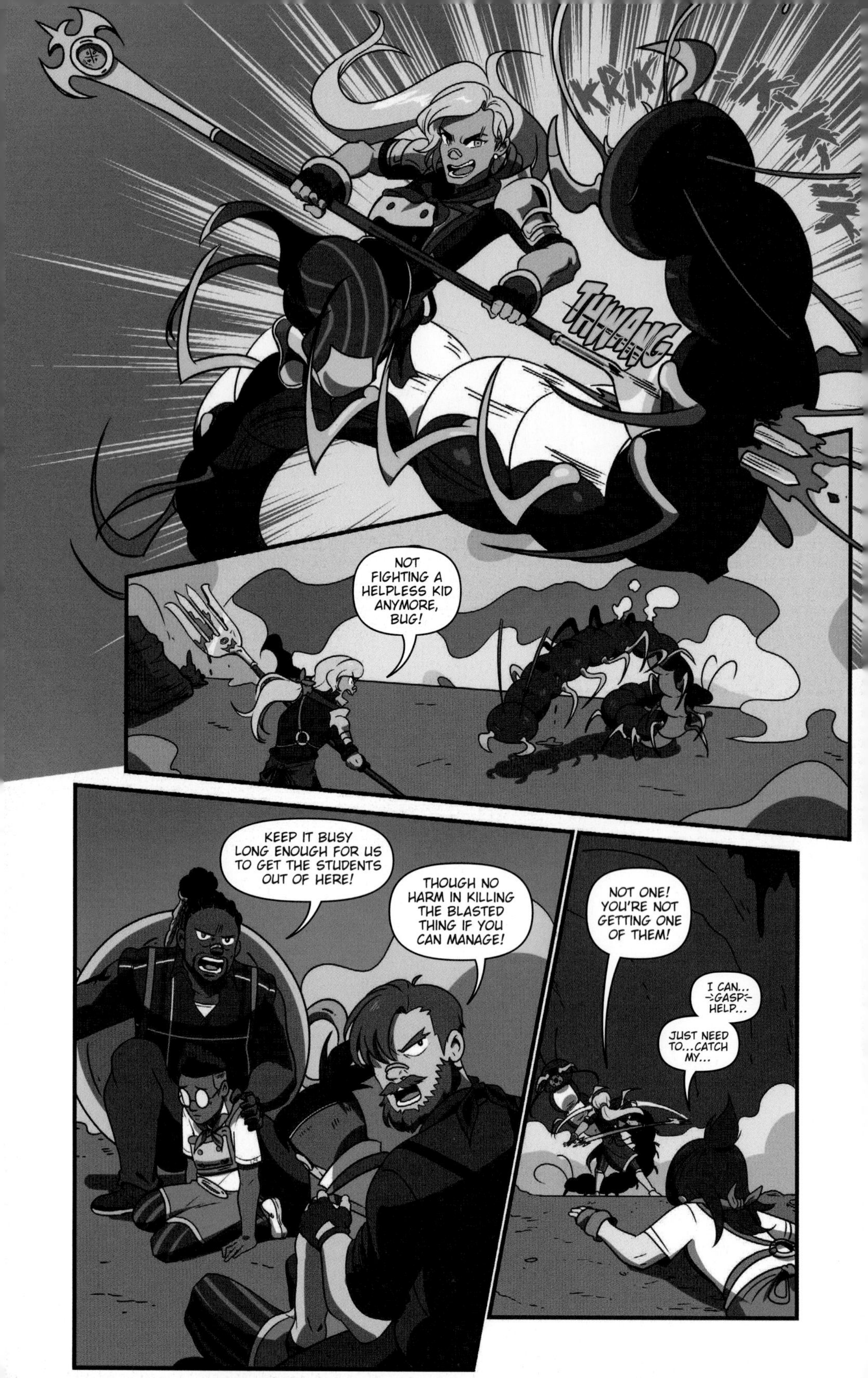
KRIK-K-K-K
THWANG
NOT FIGHTING A HELPLESS KID ANYMORE, BUG!
KEEP IT BUSY LONG ENOUGH FOR US TO GET THE STUDENTS OUT OF HERE!
THOUGH NO HARM IN KILLING THE BLASTED THING IF YOU CAN MANAGE!
NOT ONE! YOU'RE NOT GETTING ONE OF THEM!
I CAN... -GASP- HELP...
JUST NEED TO...CATCH MY...

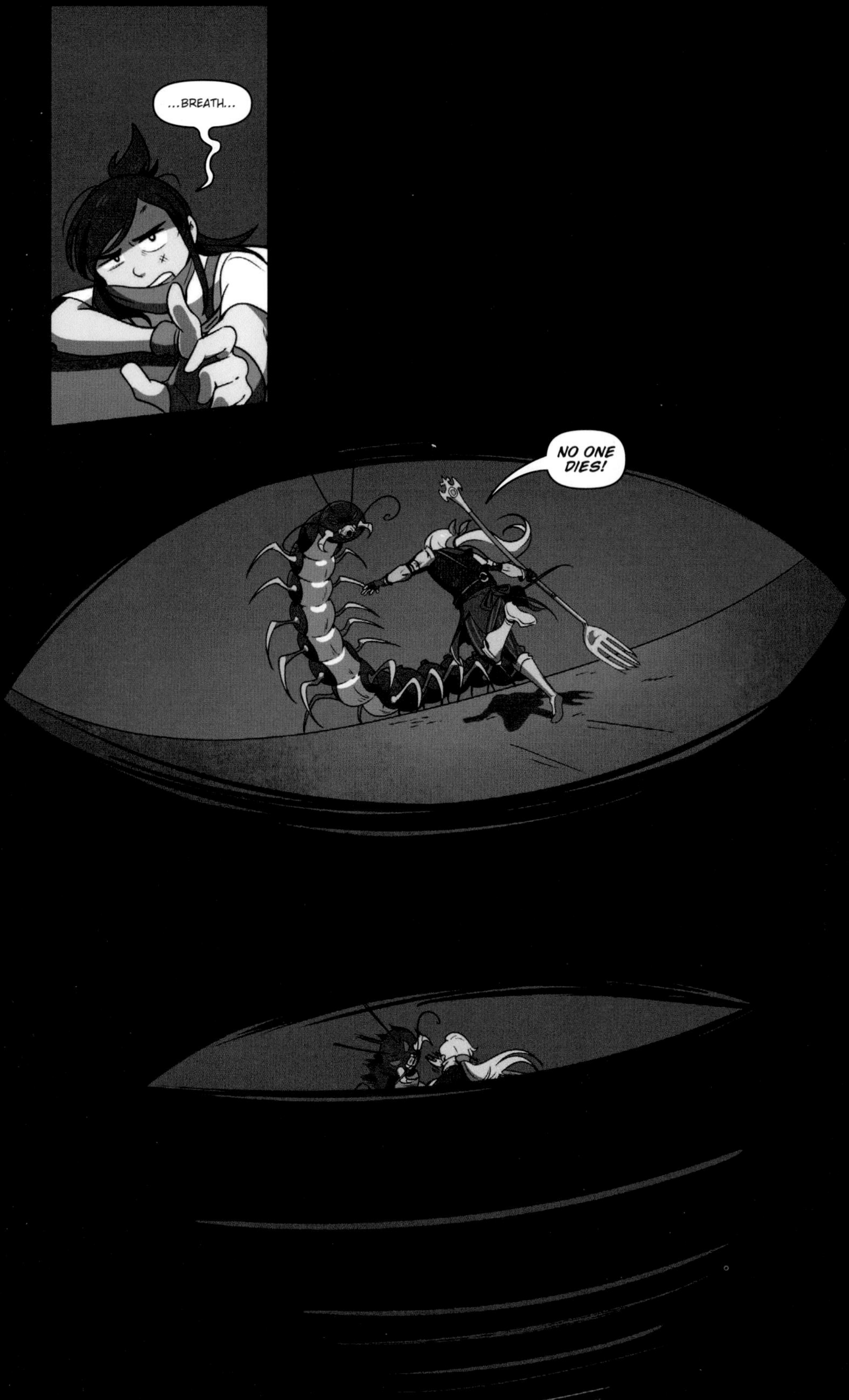
...BREATH...
NO ONE DIES!

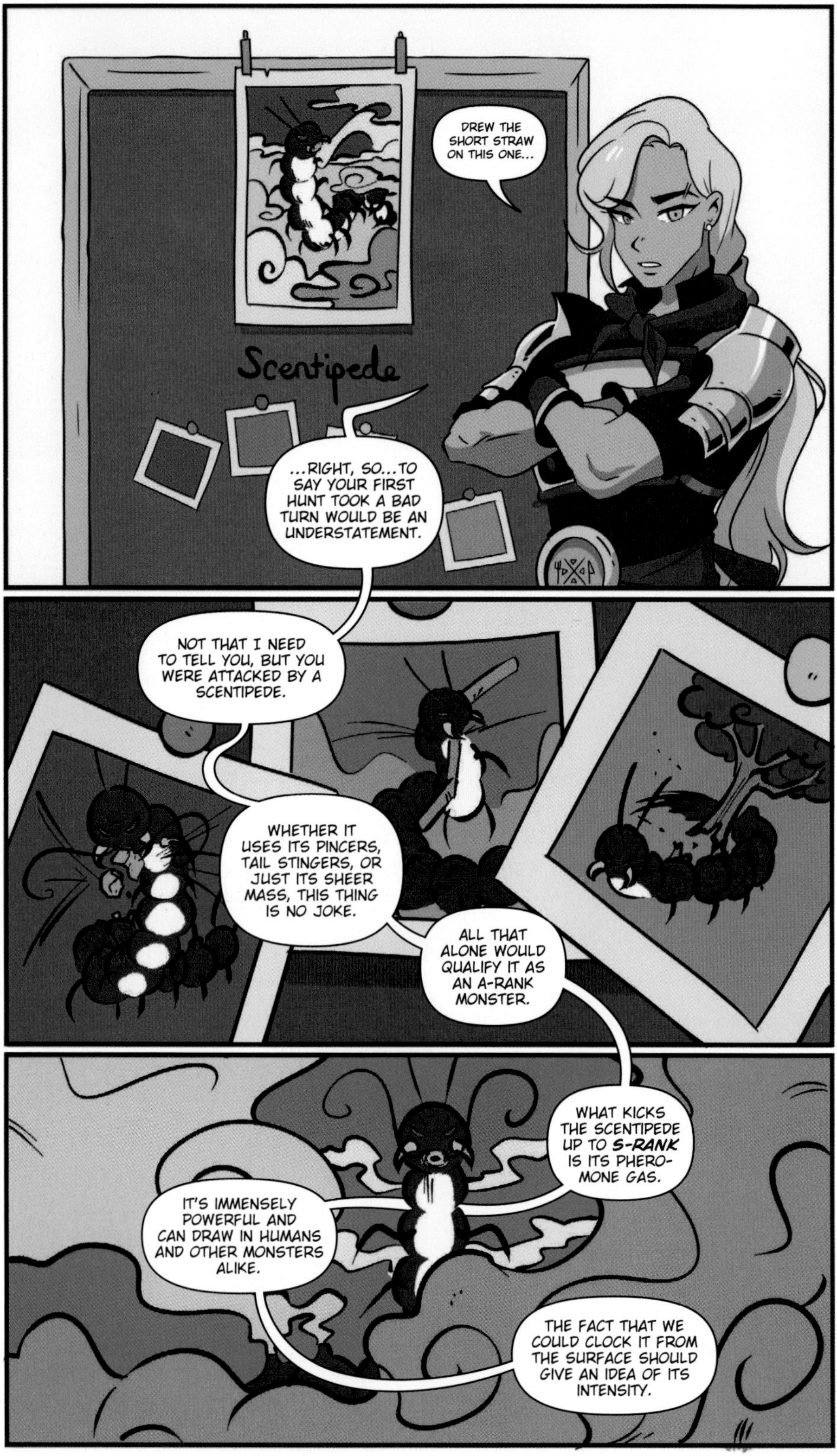
DREW THE SHORT STRAW ON THIS ONE...
Scentipede
...RIGHT, SO...TO SAY YOUR FIRST HUNT TOOK A BAD TURN WOULD BE AN UNDERSTATEMENT.
NOT THAT I NEED TO TELL YOU, BUT YOU WERE ATTACKED BY A SCENTIPEDE.
WHETHER IT USES ITS PINCERS, TAIL STINGERS, OR JUST ITS SHEER MASS, THIS THING IS NO JOKE.
ALL THAT ALONE WOULD QUALIFY IT AS AN A-RANK MONSTER.
WHAT KICKS THE SCENTIPEDE UP TO ***S-RANK*** IS ITS PHERO-MONE GAS.
IT'S IMMENSELY POWERFUL AND CAN DRAW IN HUMANS AND OTHER MONSTERS ALIKE.
THE FACT THAT WE COULD CLOCK IT FROM THE SURFACE SHOULD GIVE AN IDEA OF ITS INTENSITY.

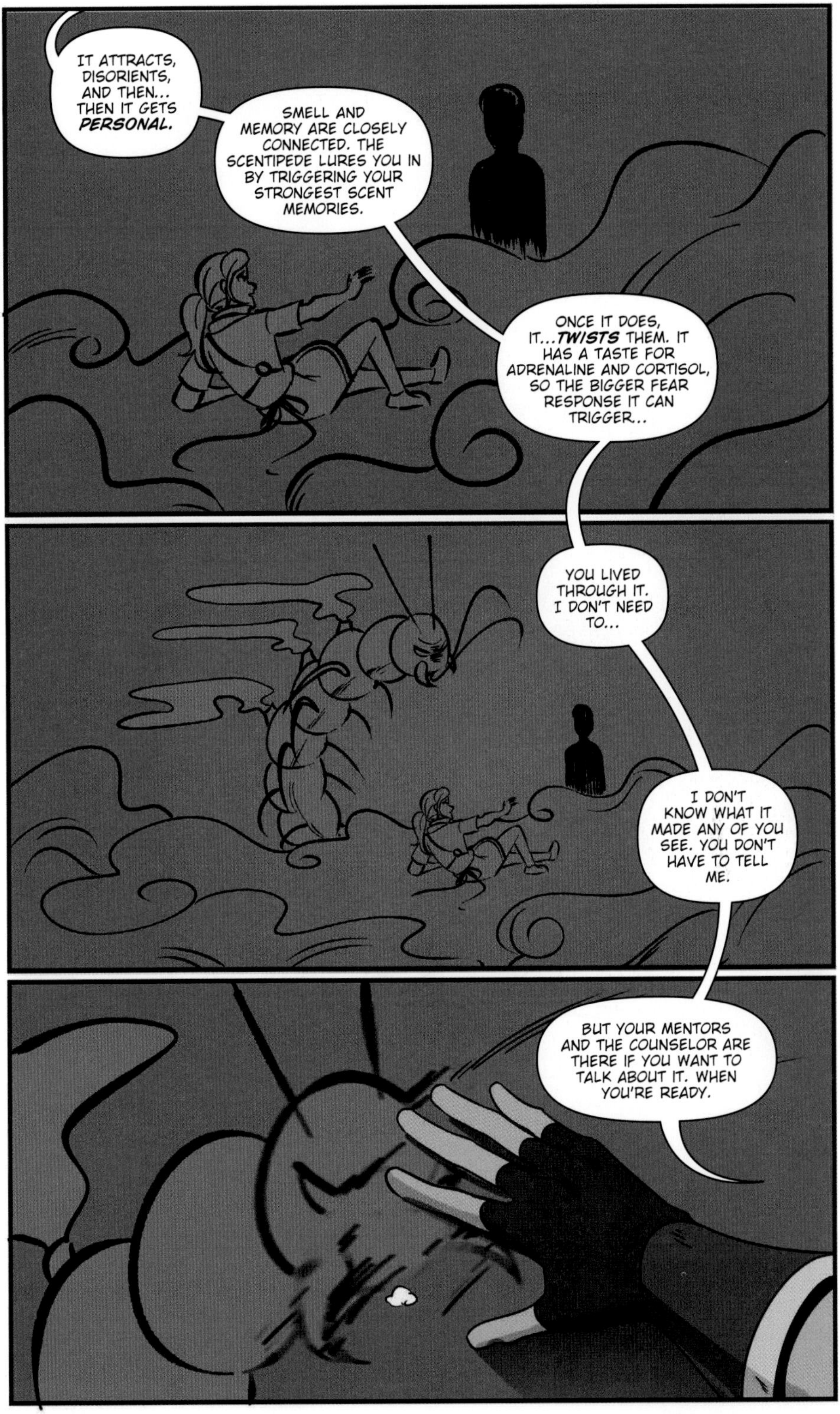
IT ATTRACTS, DISORIENTS, AND THEN... THEN IT GETS **PERSONAL.**
SMELL AND MEMORY ARE CLOSELY CONNECTED. THE SCENTIPEDE LURES YOU IN BY TRIGGERING YOUR STRONGEST SCENT MEMORIES.
ONCE IT DOES, IT...**TWISTS** THEM. IT HAS A TASTE FOR ADRENALINE AND CORTISOL, SO THE BIGGER FEAR RESPONSE IT CAN TRIGGER...
YOU LIVED THROUGH IT. I DON'T NEED TO...
I DON'T KNOW WHAT IT MADE ANY OF YOU SEE. YOU DON'T HAVE TO TELL ME.
BUT YOUR MENTORS AND THE COUNSELOR ARE THERE IF YOU WANT TO TALK ABOUT IT. WHEN YOU'RE READY.

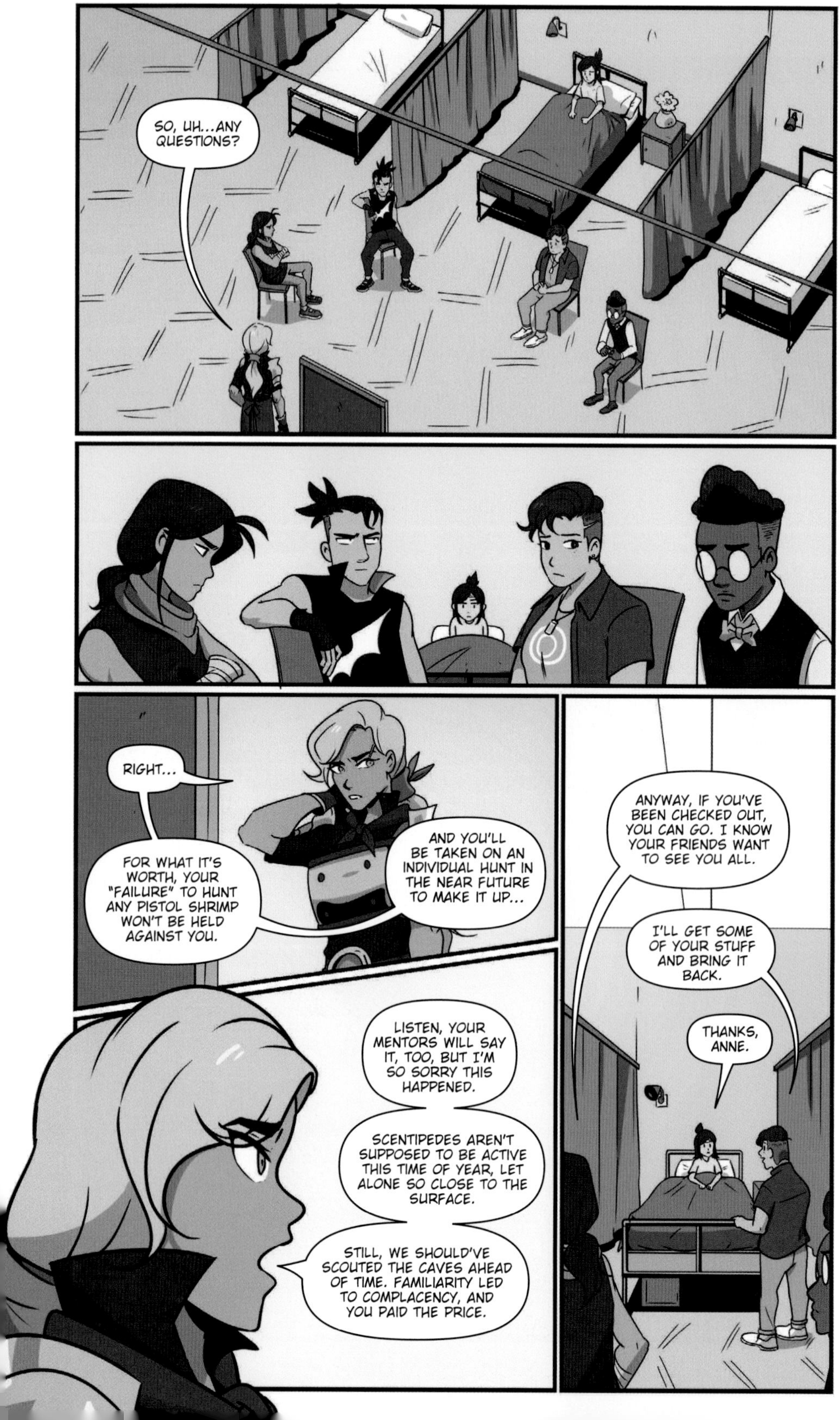
SO, UH...ANY QUESTIONS?
RIGHT...
FOR WHAT IT'S WORTH, YOUR "FAILURE" TO HUNT ANY PISTOL SHRIMP WON'T BE HELD AGAINST YOU.
AND YOU'LL BE TAKEN ON AN INDIVIDUAL HUNT IN THE NEAR FUTURE TO MAKE IT UP...
LISTEN, YOUR MENTORS WILL SAY IT, TOO, BUT I'M SO SORRY THIS HAPPENED.
SCENTIPEDES AREN'T SUPPOSED TO BE ACTIVE THIS TIME OF YEAR, LET ALONE SO CLOSE TO THE SURFACE.
STILL, WE SHOULD'VE SCOUTED THE CAVES AHEAD OF TIME. FAMILIARITY LED TO COMPLACENCY, AND YOU PAID THE PRICE.
ANYWAY, IF YOU'VE BEEN CHECKED OUT, YOU CAN GO. I KNOW YOUR FRIENDS WANT TO SEE YOU ALL.
I'LL GET SOME OF YOUR STUFF AND BRING IT BACK.
THANKS, ANNE.

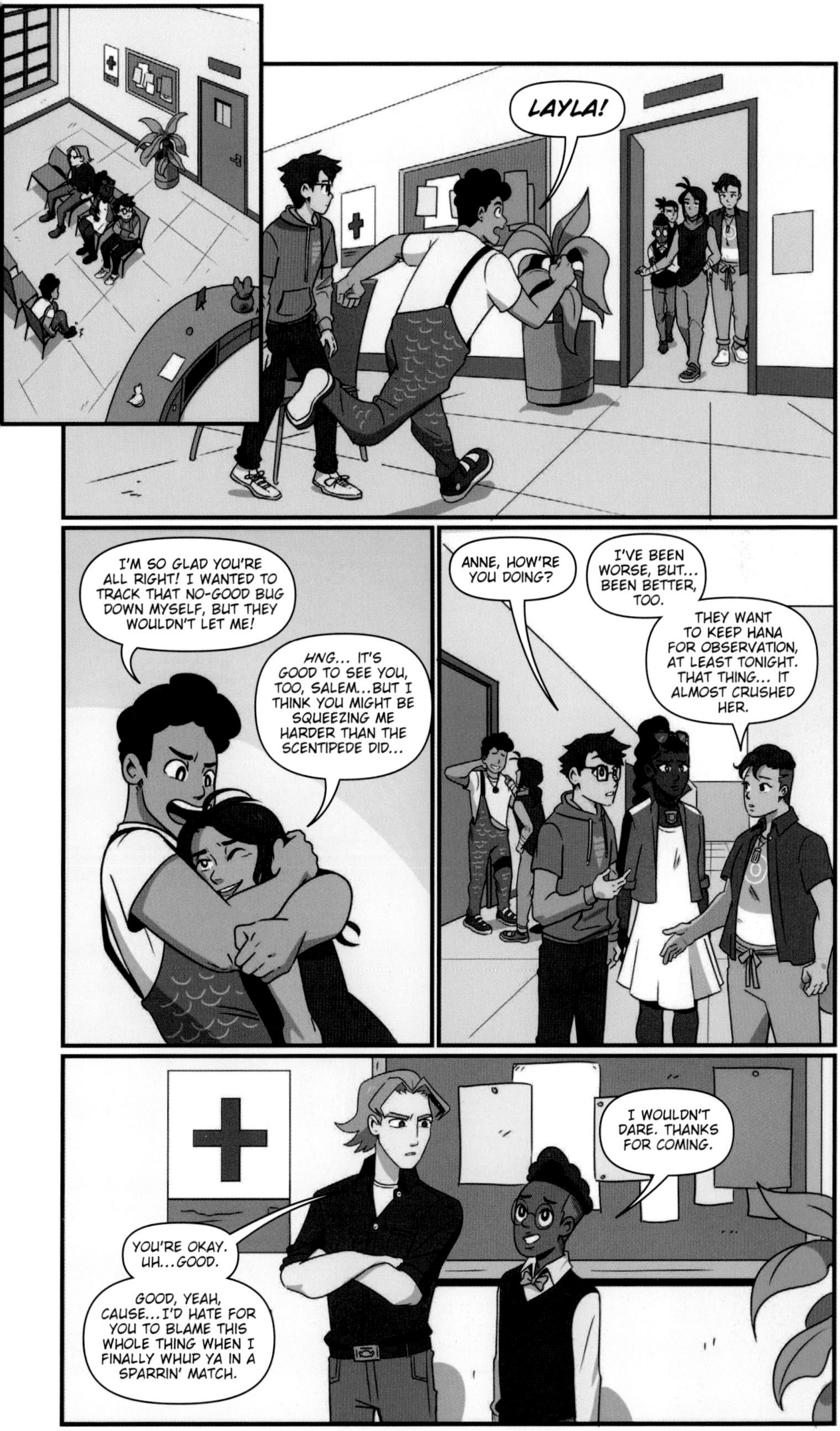
LAYLA!
I'M SO GLAD YOU'RE ALL RIGHT! I WANTED TO TRACK THAT NO-GOOD BUG DOWN MYSELF, BUT THEY WOULDN'T LET ME!
HNG... IT'S GOOD TO SEE YOU, TOO, SALEM...BUT I THINK YOU MIGHT BE SQUEEZING ME HARDER THAN THE SCENTIPEDE DID...
ANNE, HOW'RE YOU DOING?
I'VE BEEN WORSE, BUT... BEEN BETTER, TOO.
THEY WANT TO KEEP HANA FOR OBSERVATION, AT LEAST TONIGHT. THAT THING... IT ALMOST CRUSHED HER.
YOU'RE OKAY. UH...GOOD.
GOOD, YEAH, CAUSE...I'D HATE FOR YOU TO BLAME THIS WHOLE THING WHEN I FINALLY WHUP YA IN A SPARRIN' MATCH.
I WOULDN'T DARE. THANKS FOR COMING.

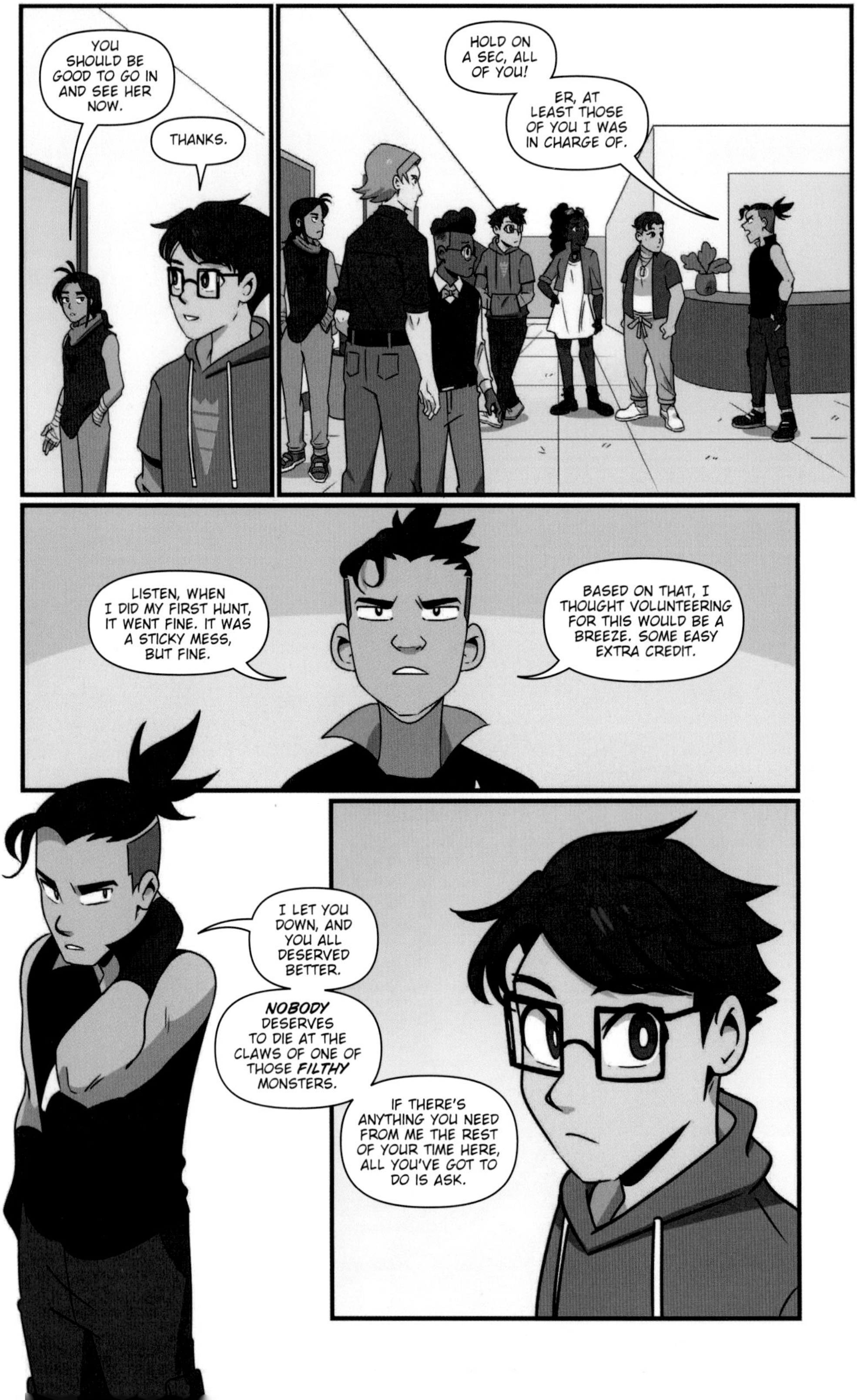
YOU SHOULD BE GOOD TO GO IN AND SEE HER NOW.
THANKS.
HOLD ON A SEC, ALL OF YOU!
ER, AT LEAST THOSE OF YOU I WAS IN CHARGE OF.
LISTEN, WHEN I DID MY FIRST HUNT, IT WENT FINE. IT WAS A STICKY MESS, BUT FINE.
BASED ON THAT, I THOUGHT VOLUNTEERING FOR THIS WOULD BE A BREEZE. SOME EASY EXTRA CREDIT.
I LET YOU DOWN, AND YOU ALL DESERVED BETTER.
NOBODY DESERVES TO DIE AT THE CLAWS OF ONE OF THOSE ***FILTHY*** MONSTERS.
IF THERE'S ANYTHING YOU NEED FROM ME THE REST OF YOUR TIME HERE, ALL YOU'VE GOT TO DO IS ASK.

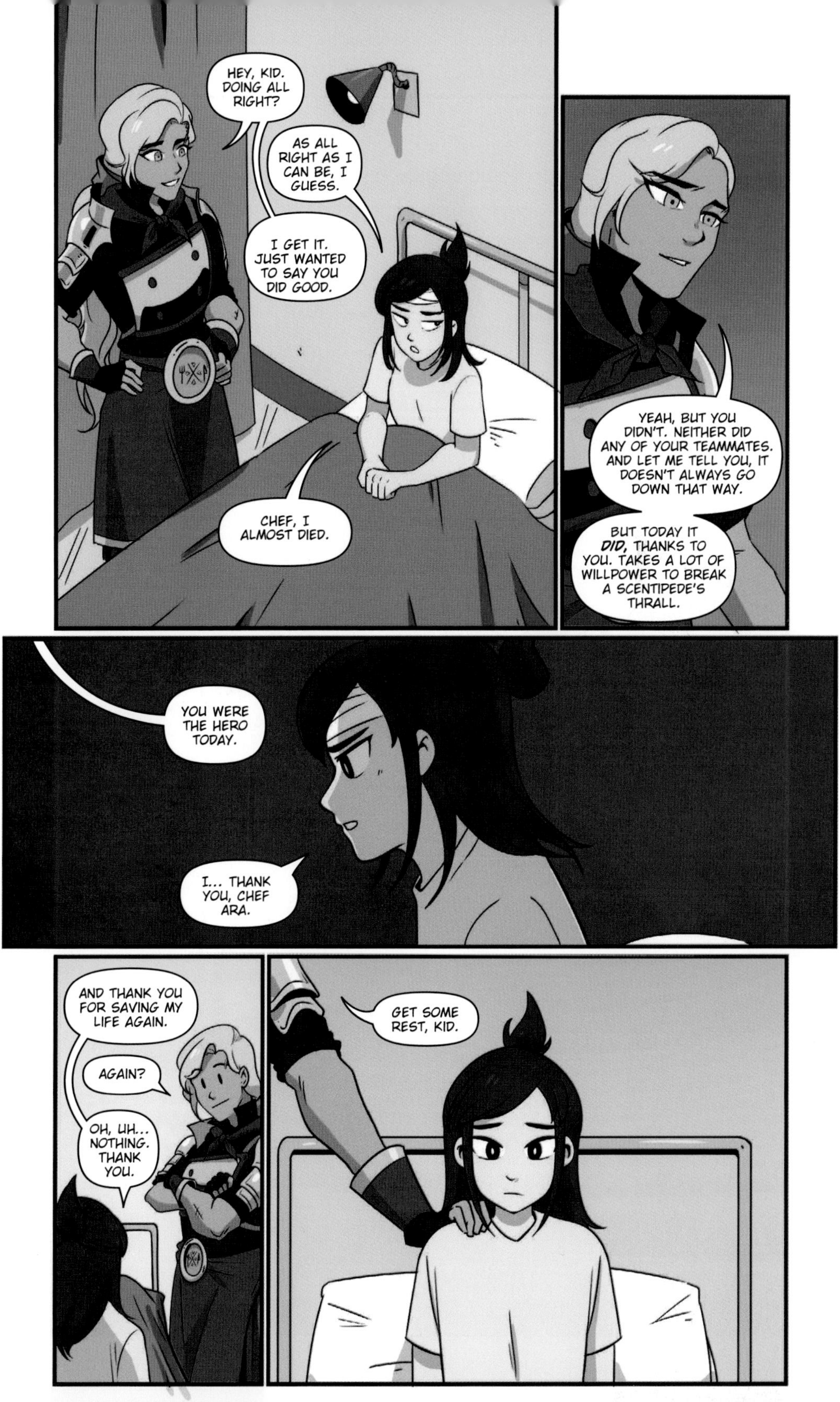
HEY, KID. DOING ALL RIGHT?
AS ALL RIGHT AS I CAN BE, I GUESS.
I GET IT. JUST WANTED TO SAY YOU DID GOOD.
CHEF, I ALMOST DIED.
YEAH, BUT YOU DIDN'T. NEITHER DID ANY OF YOUR TEAMMATES. AND LET ME TELL YOU, IT DOESN'T ALWAYS GO DOWN THAT WAY.
BUT TODAY IT *DID*, THANKS TO YOU. TAKES A LOT OF WILLPOWER TO BREAK A SCENTIPEDE'S THRALL.
YOU WERE THE HERO TODAY.
I... THANK YOU, CHEF ARA.
AND THANK YOU FOR SAVING MY LIFE AGAIN.
AGAIN?
OH, UH... NOTHING. THANK YOU.
GET SOME REST, KID.

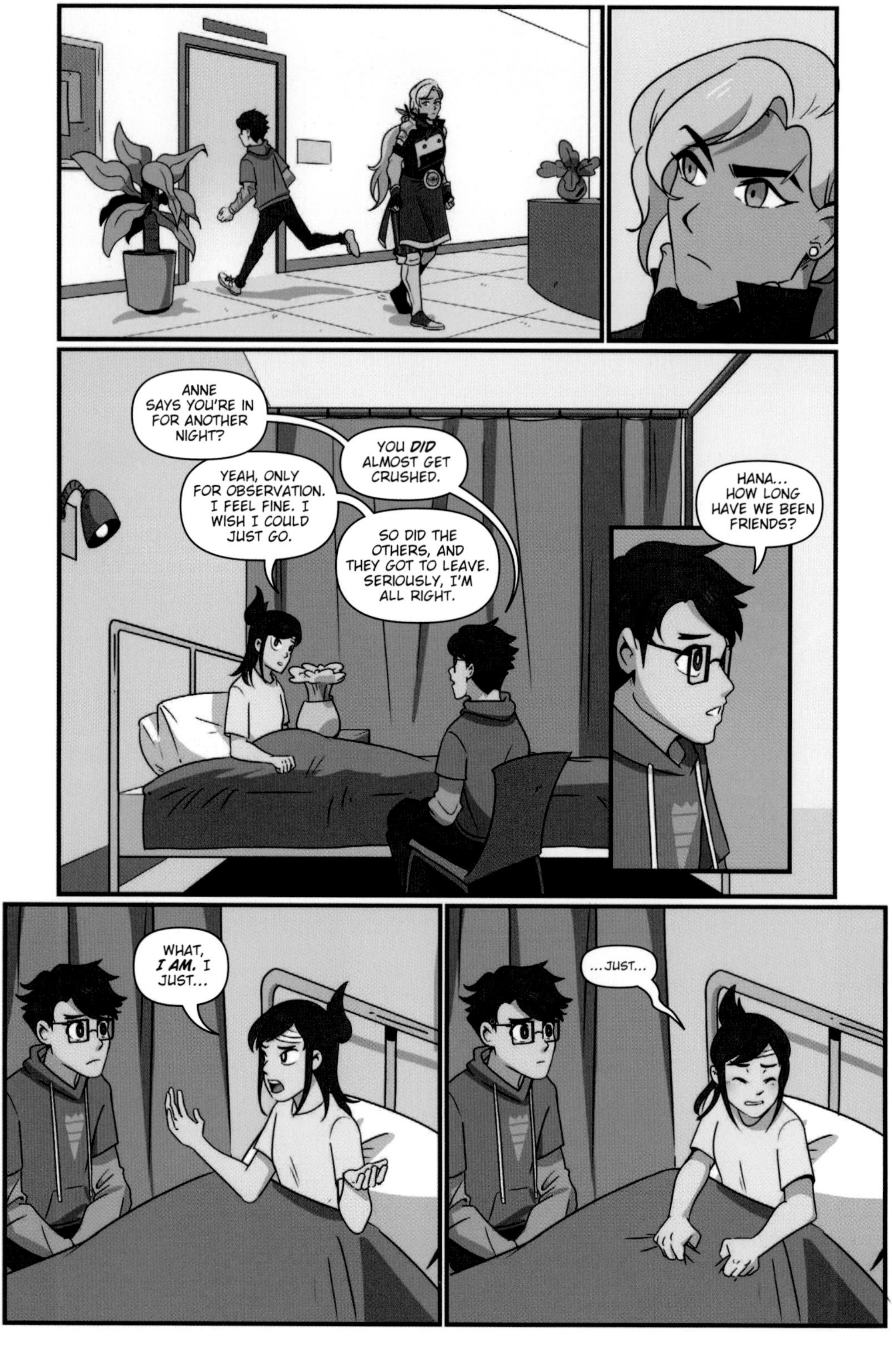
ANNE SAYS YOU'RE IN FOR ANOTHER NIGHT?
YOU ***DID*** ALMOST GET CRUSHED.
YEAH, ONLY FOR OBSERVATION. I FEEL FINE. I WISH I COULD JUST GO.
SO DID THE OTHERS, AND THEY GOT TO LEAVE. SERIOUSLY, I'M ALL RIGHT.
HANA... HOW LONG HAVE WE BEEN FRIENDS?
WHAT, ***I AM.*** I JUST...
...JUST...

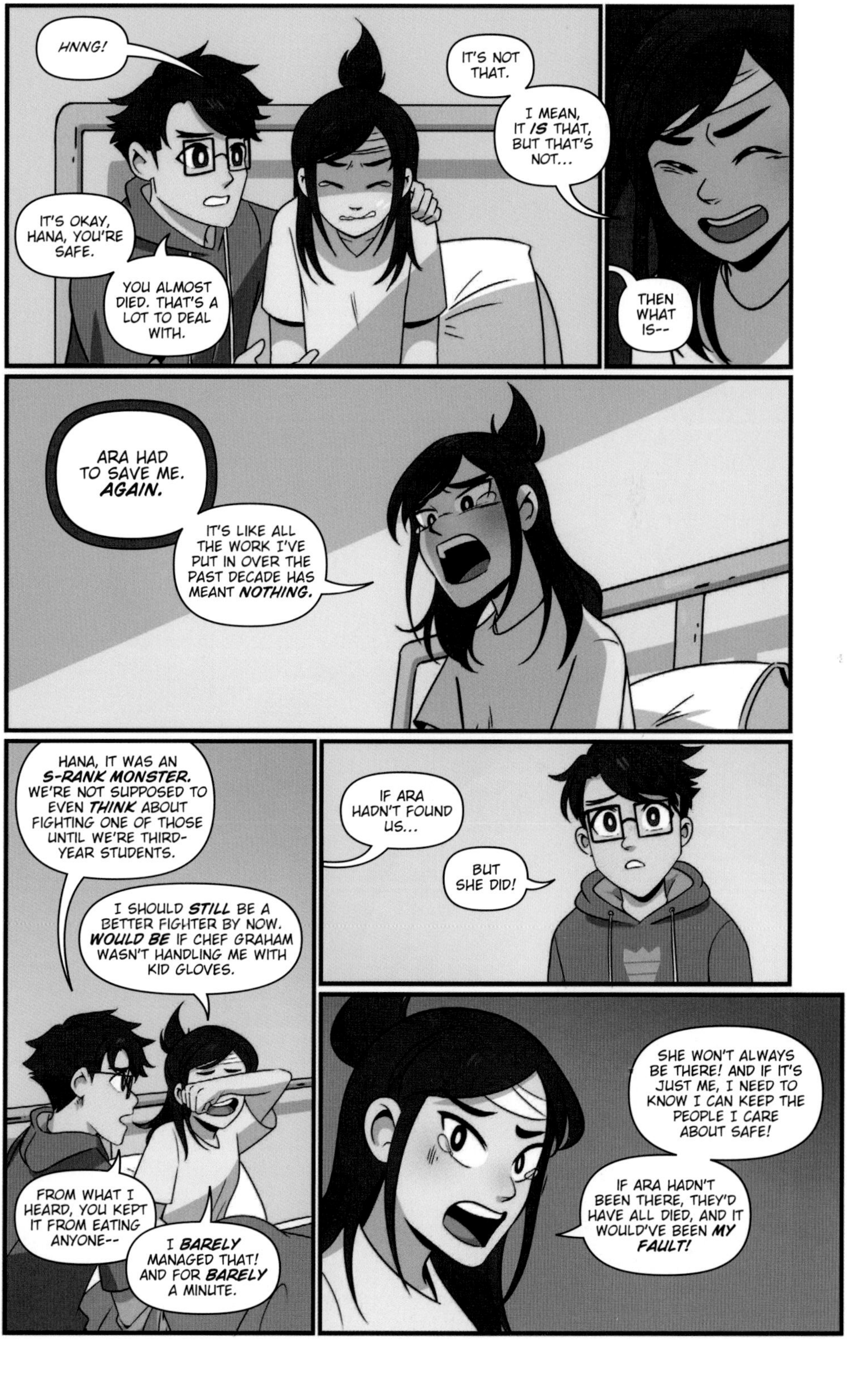
HNNG!
IT'S OKAY, HANA, YOU'RE SAFE.
YOU ALMOST DIED. THAT'S A LOT TO DEAL WITH.
IT'S NOT THAT.
I MEAN, IT *IS* THAT, BUT THAT'S NOT...
THEN WHAT IS--
ARA HAD TO SAVE ME. **AGAIN.**
IT'S LIKE ALL THE WORK I'VE PUT IN OVER THE PAST DECADE HAS MEANT **NOTHING.**
HANA, IT WAS AN **S-RANK MONSTER.** WE'RE NOT SUPPOSED TO EVEN **THINK** ABOUT FIGHTING ONE OF THOSE UNTIL WE'RE THIRD-YEAR STUDENTS.
I SHOULD **STILL** BE A BETTER FIGHTER BY NOW. **WOULD BE** IF CHEF GRAHAM WASN'T HANDLING ME WITH KID GLOVES.
FROM WHAT I HEARD, YOU KEPT IT FROM EATING ANYONE--
I **BARELY** MANAGED THAT! AND FOR **BARELY** A MINUTE.
IF ARA HADN'T FOUND US...
BUT SHE DID!
SHE WON'T ALWAYS BE THERE! AND IF IT'S JUST ME, I NEED TO KNOW I CAN KEEP THE PEOPLE I CARE ABOUT SAFE!
IF ARA HADN'T BEEN THERE, THEY'D HAVE ALL DIED, AND IT WOULD'VE BEEN **MY FAULT!**

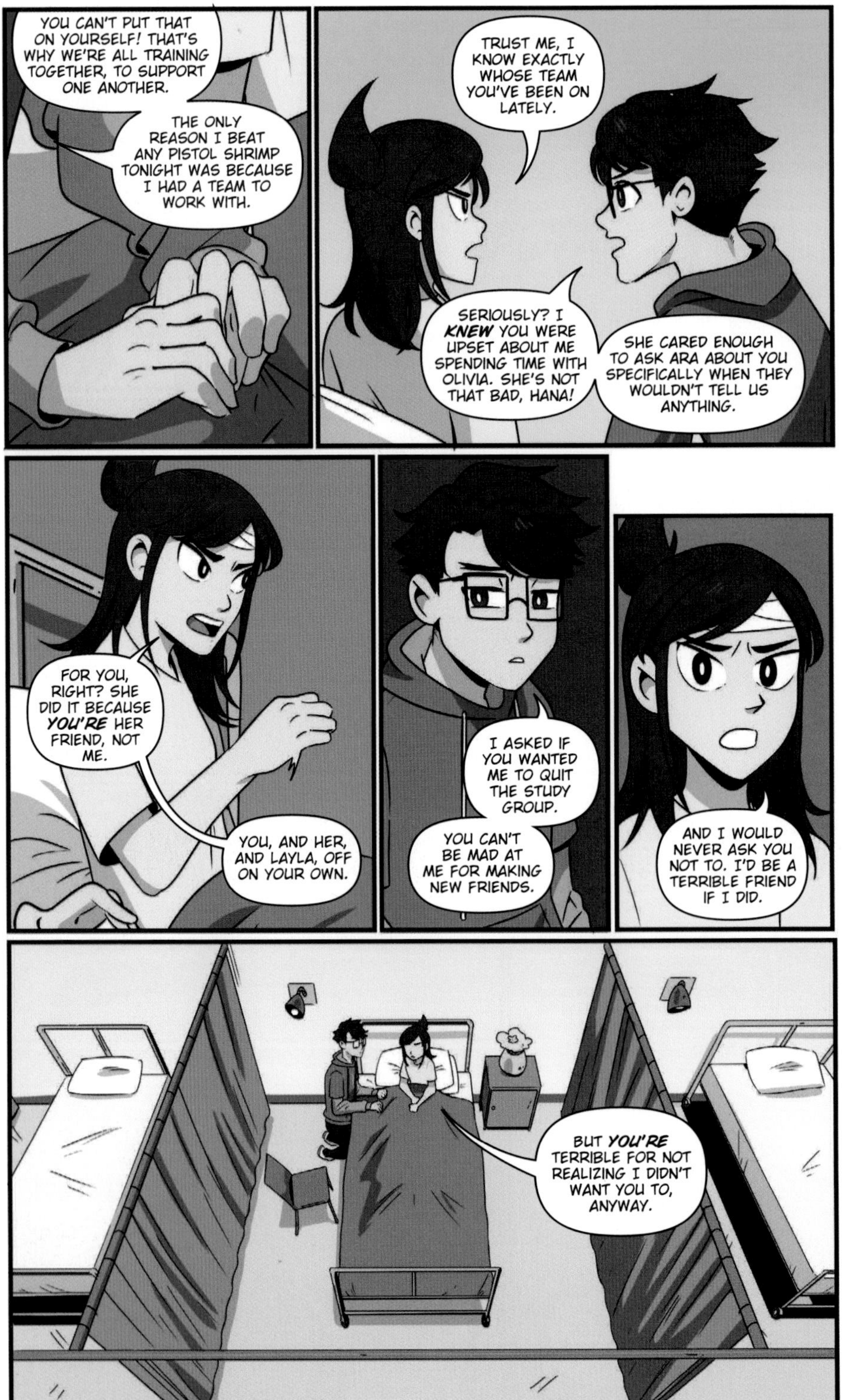
YOU CAN'T PUT THAT ON YOURSELF! THAT'S WHY WE'RE ALL TRAINING TOGETHER, TO SUPPORT ONE ANOTHER.
THE ONLY REASON I BEAT ANY PISTOL SHRIMP TONIGHT WAS BECAUSE I HAD A TEAM TO WORK WITH.
TRUST ME, I KNOW EXACTLY WHOSE TEAM YOU'VE BEEN ON LATELY.
SERIOUSLY? I ***KNEW*** YOU WERE UPSET ABOUT ME SPENDING TIME WITH OLIVIA. SHE'S NOT THAT BAD, HANA!
SHE CARED ENOUGH TO ASK ARA ABOUT YOU SPECIFICALLY WHEN THEY WOULDN'T TELL US ANYTHING.
FOR YOU, RIGHT? SHE DID IT BECAUSE ***YOU'RE*** HER FRIEND, NOT ME.
YOU, AND HER, AND LAYLA, OFF ON YOUR OWN.
I ASKED IF YOU WANTED ME TO QUIT THE STUDY GROUP.
YOU CAN'T BE MAD AT ME FOR MAKING NEW FRIENDS.
AND I WOULD NEVER ASK YOU NOT TO. I'D BE A TERRIBLE FRIEND IF I DID.
BUT ***YOU'RE*** TERRIBLE FOR NOT REALIZING I DIDN'T WANT YOU TO, ANYWAY.

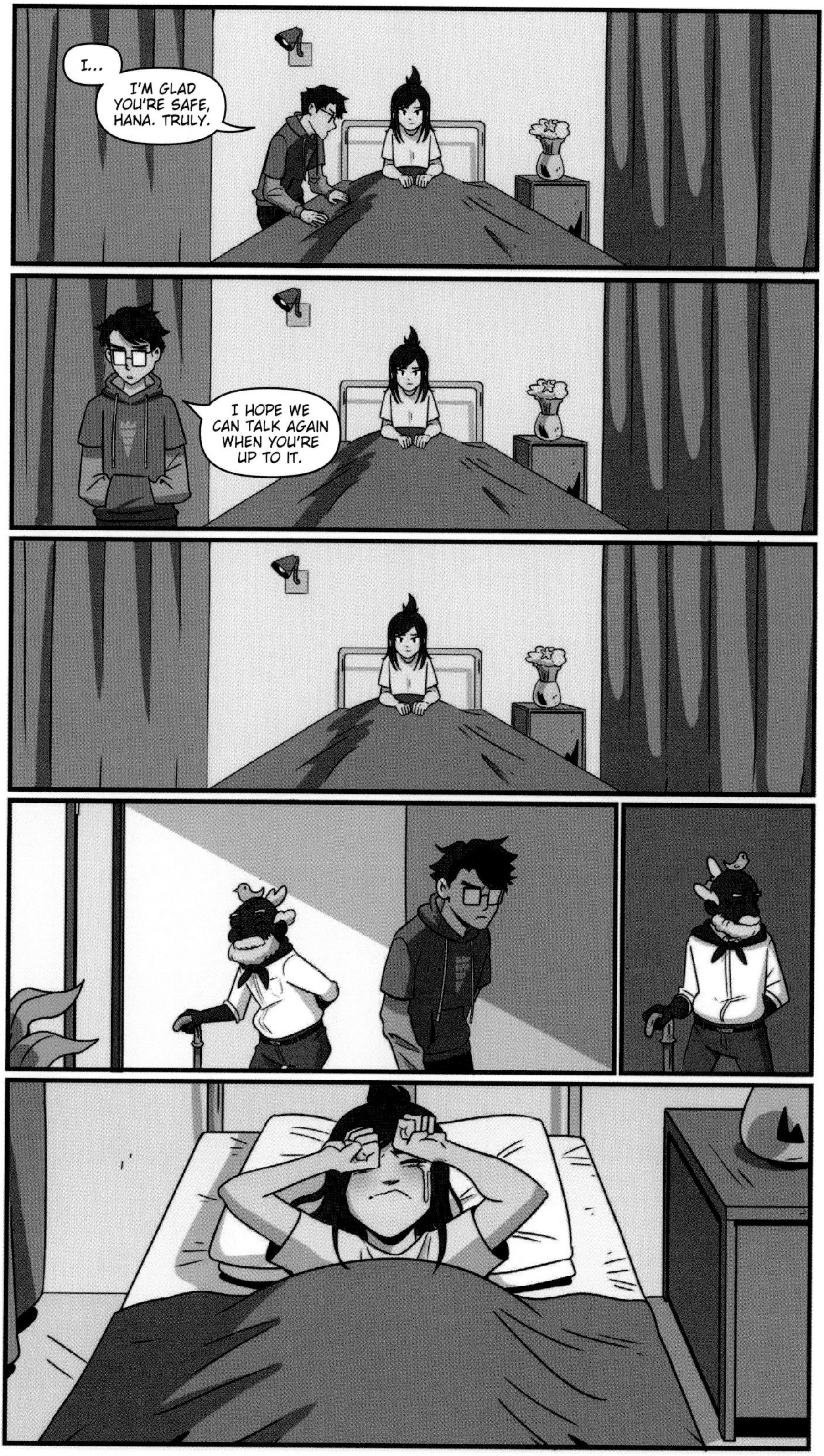
I...
I'M GLAD YOU'RE SAFE, HANA. TRULY.
I HOPE WE CAN TALK AGAIN WHEN YOU'RE UP TO IT.

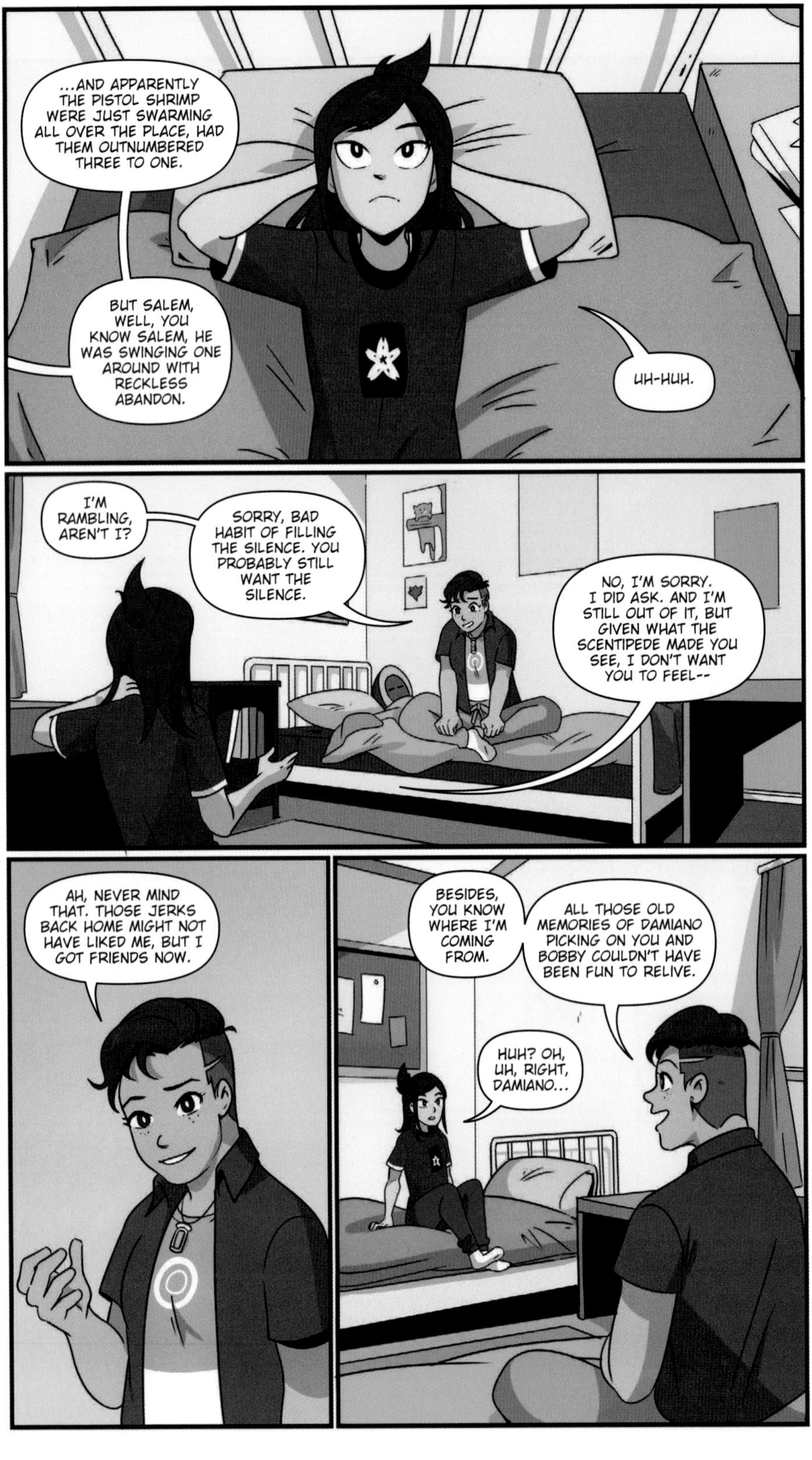
...AND APPARENTLY THE PISTOL SHRIMP WERE JUST SWARMING ALL OVER THE PLACE, HAD THEM OUTNUMBERED THREE TO ONE.
BUT SALEM, WELL, YOU KNOW SALEM, HE WAS SWINGING ONE AROUND WITH RECKLESS ABANDON.
UH-HUH.
I'M RAMBLING, AREN'T I?
SORRY, BAD HABIT OF FILLING THE SILENCE. YOU PROBABLY STILL WANT THE SILENCE.
NO, I'M SORRY. I DID ASK. AND I'M STILL OUT OF IT, BUT GIVEN WHAT THE SCENTIPEDE MADE YOU SEE, I DON'T WANT YOU TO FEEL--
AH, NEVER MIND THAT. THOSE JERKS BACK HOME MIGHT NOT HAVE LIKED ME, BUT I GOT FRIENDS NOW.
BESIDES, YOU KNOW WHERE I'M COMING FROM.
ALL THOSE OLD MEMORIES OF DAMIANO PICKING ON YOU AND BOBBY COULDN'T HAVE BEEN FUN TO RELIVE.
HUH? OH, UH, RIGHT, DAMIANO...

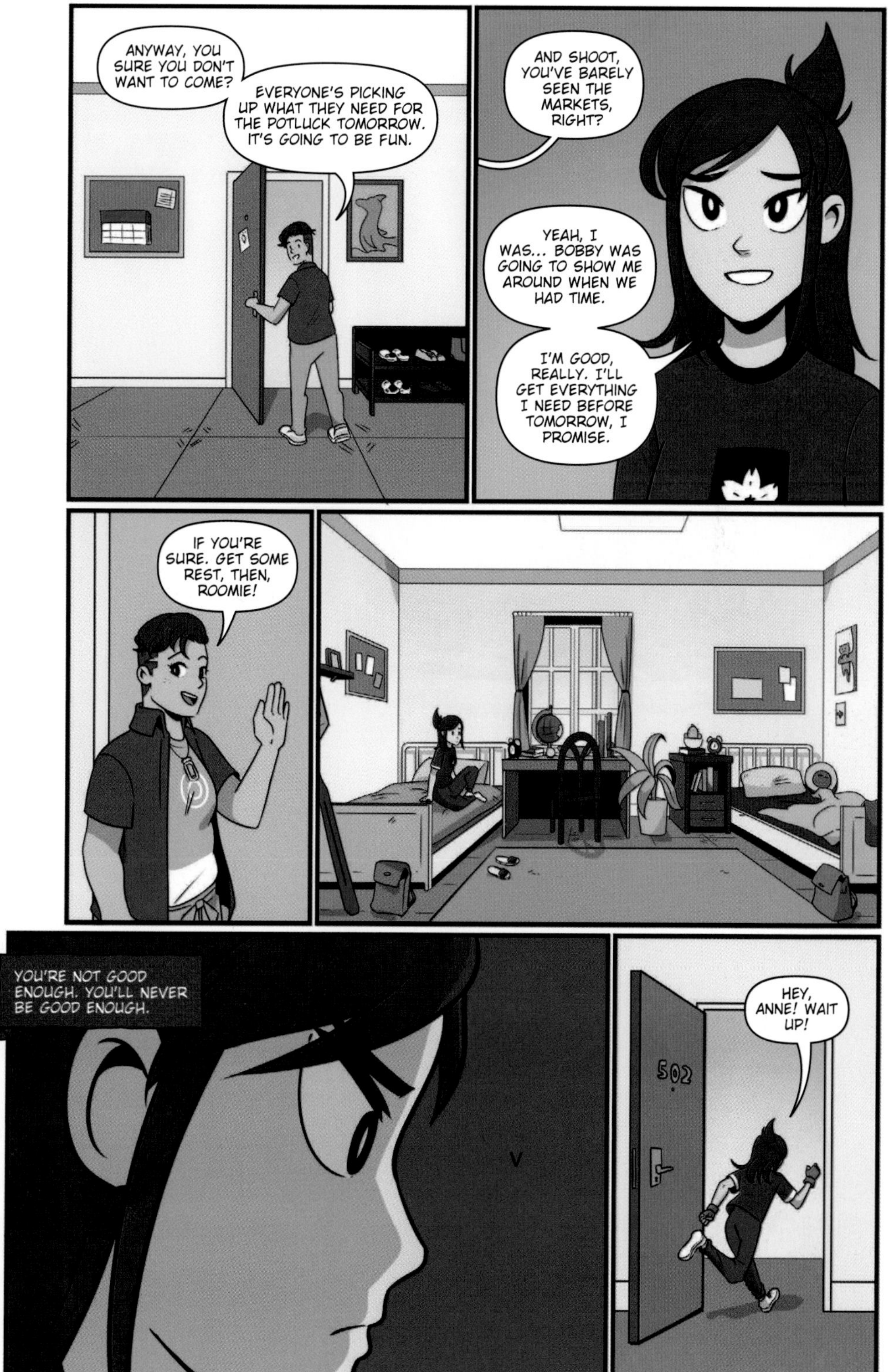
ANYWAY, YOU SURE YOU DON'T WANT TO COME?
EVERYONE'S PICKING UP WHAT THEY NEED FOR THE POTLUCK TOMORROW. IT'S GOING TO BE FUN.
AND SHOOT, YOU'VE BARELY SEEN THE MARKETS, RIGHT?
YEAH, I WAS... BOBBY WAS GOING TO SHOW ME AROUND WHEN WE HAD TIME.
I'M GOOD, REALLY. I'LL GET EVERYTHING I NEED BEFORE TOMORROW, I PROMISE.
IF YOU'RE SURE. GET SOME REST, THEN, ROOMIE!
YOU'RE NOT GOOD ENOUGH. YOU'LL NEVER BE GOOD ENOUGH.
502
HEY, ANNE! WAIT UP!

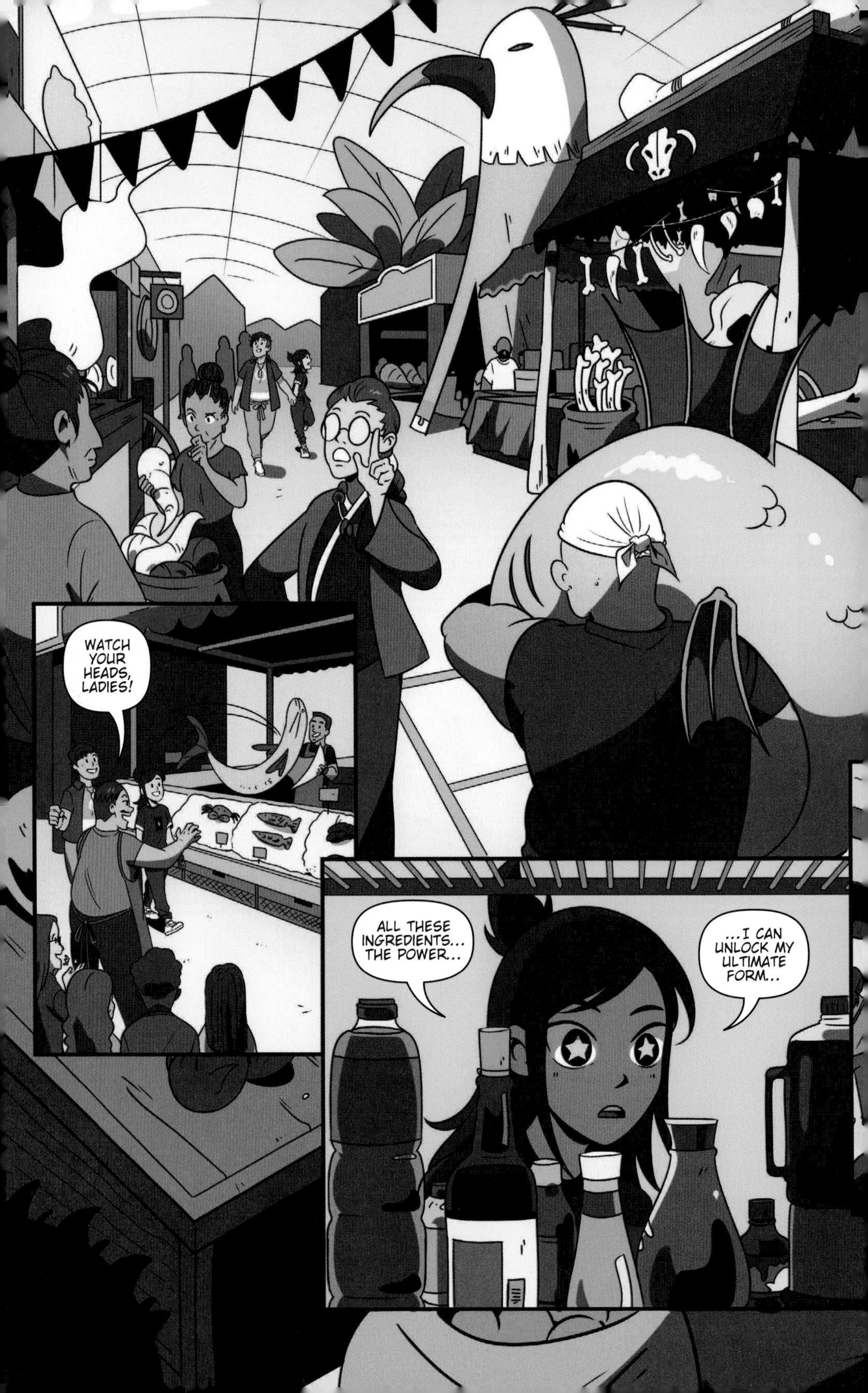
WATCH YOUR HEADS, LADIES!
ALL THESE INGREDIENTS... THE POWER...
...I CAN UNLOCK MY ULTIMATE FORM...

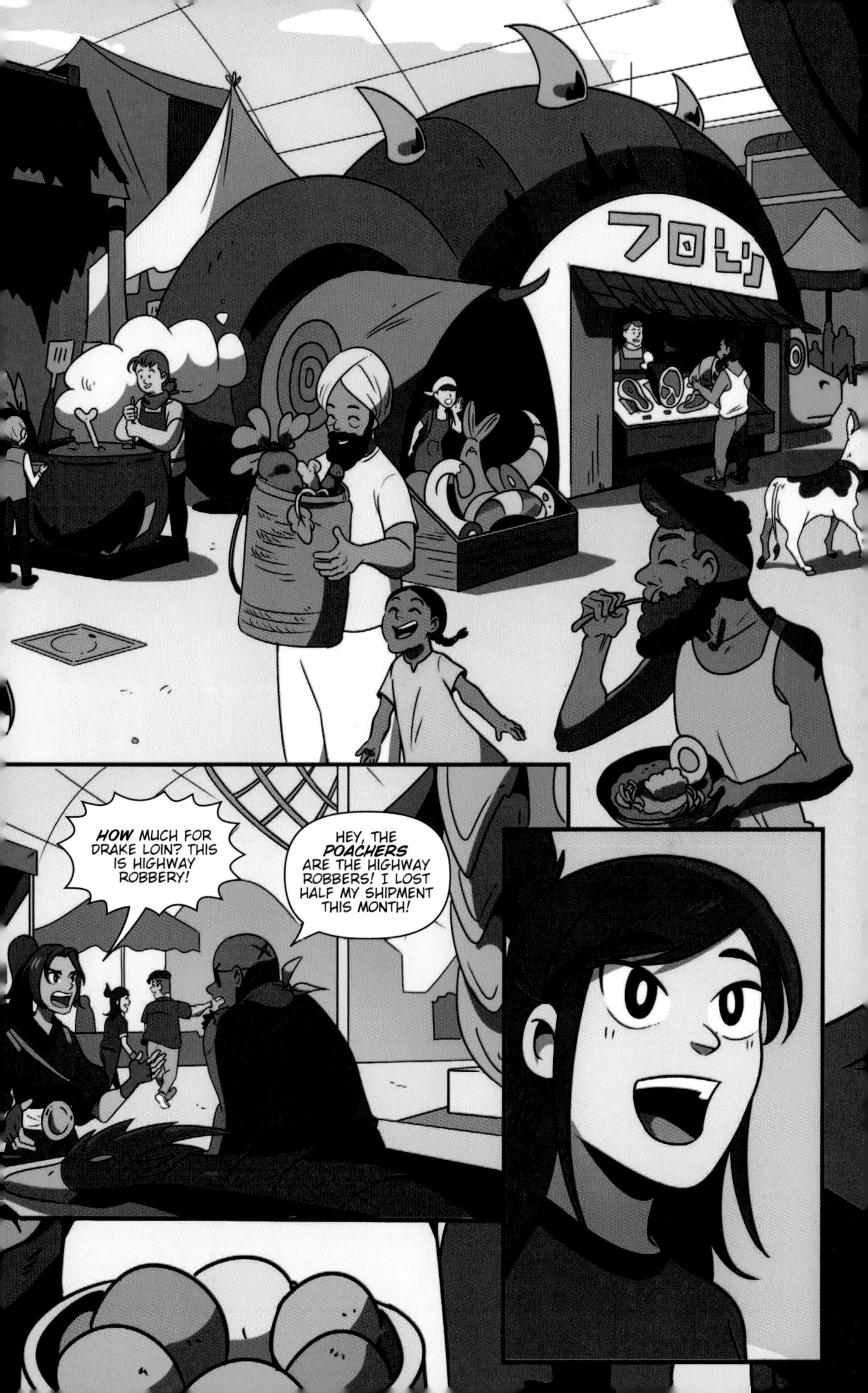

フロレリ
HOW MUCH FOR DRAKE LOIN? THIS IS HIGHWAY ROBBERY!
HEY, THE POACHERS ARE THE HIGHWAY ROBBERS! I LOST HALF MY SHIPMENT THIS MONTH!

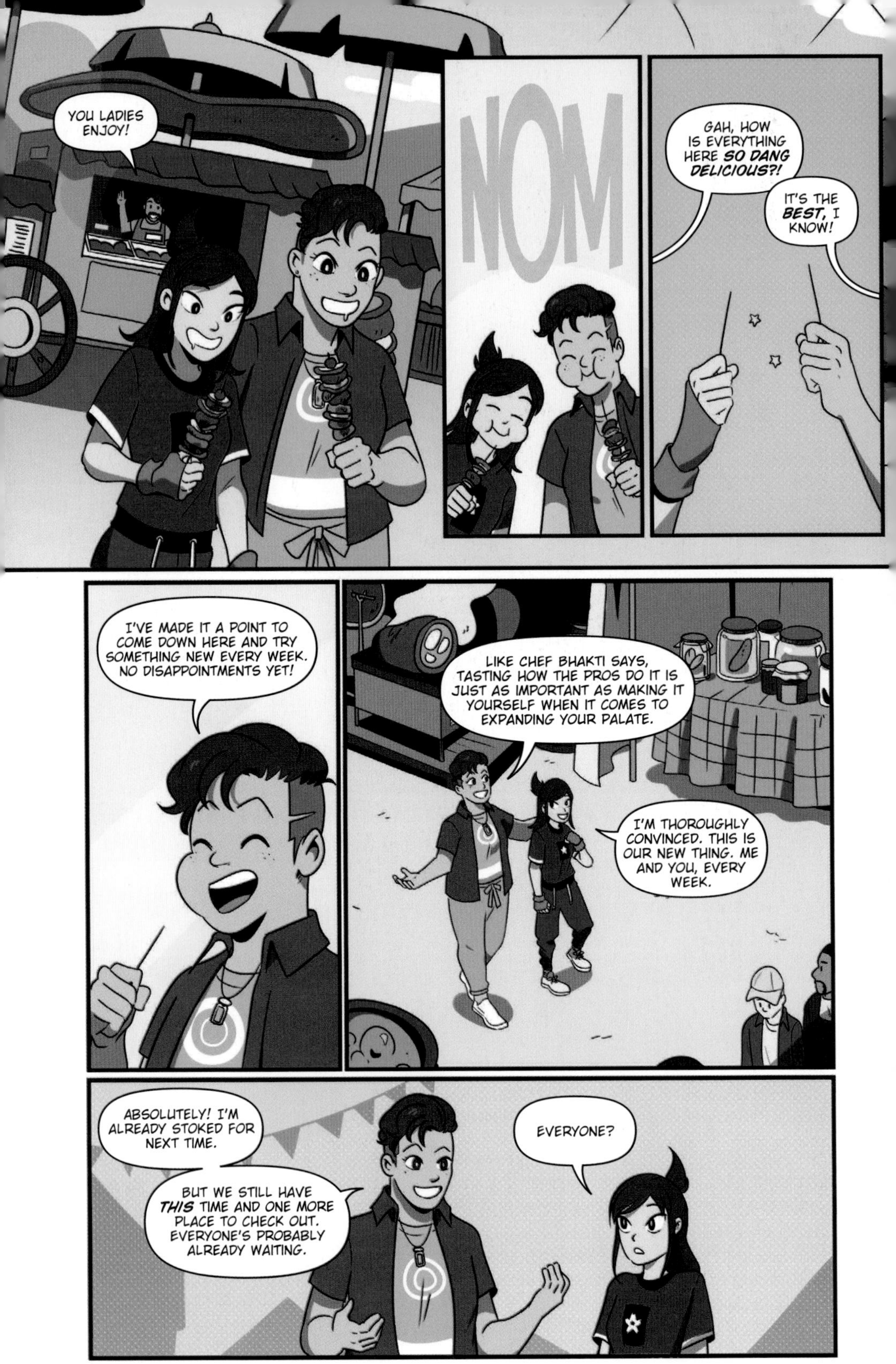
YOU LADIES ENJOY!
NOM
GAH, HOW IS EVERYTHING HERE SO DANG DELICIOUS?!
IT'S THE BEST, I KNOW!
I'VE MADE IT A POINT TO COME DOWN HERE AND TRY SOMETHING NEW EVERY WEEK. NO DISAPPOINTMENTS YET!
LIKE CHEF BHAKTI SAYS, TASTING HOW THE PROS DO IT IS JUST AS IMPORTANT AS MAKING IT YOURSELF WHEN IT COMES TO EXPANDING YOUR PALATE.
I'M THOROUGHLY CONVINCED. THIS IS OUR NEW THING. ME AND YOU, EVERY WEEK.
ABSOLUTELY! I'M ALREADY STOKED FOR NEXT TIME.
BUT WE STILL HAVE THIS TIME AND ONE MORE PLACE TO CHECK OUT. EVERYONE'S PROBABLY ALREADY WAITING.
EVERYONE?

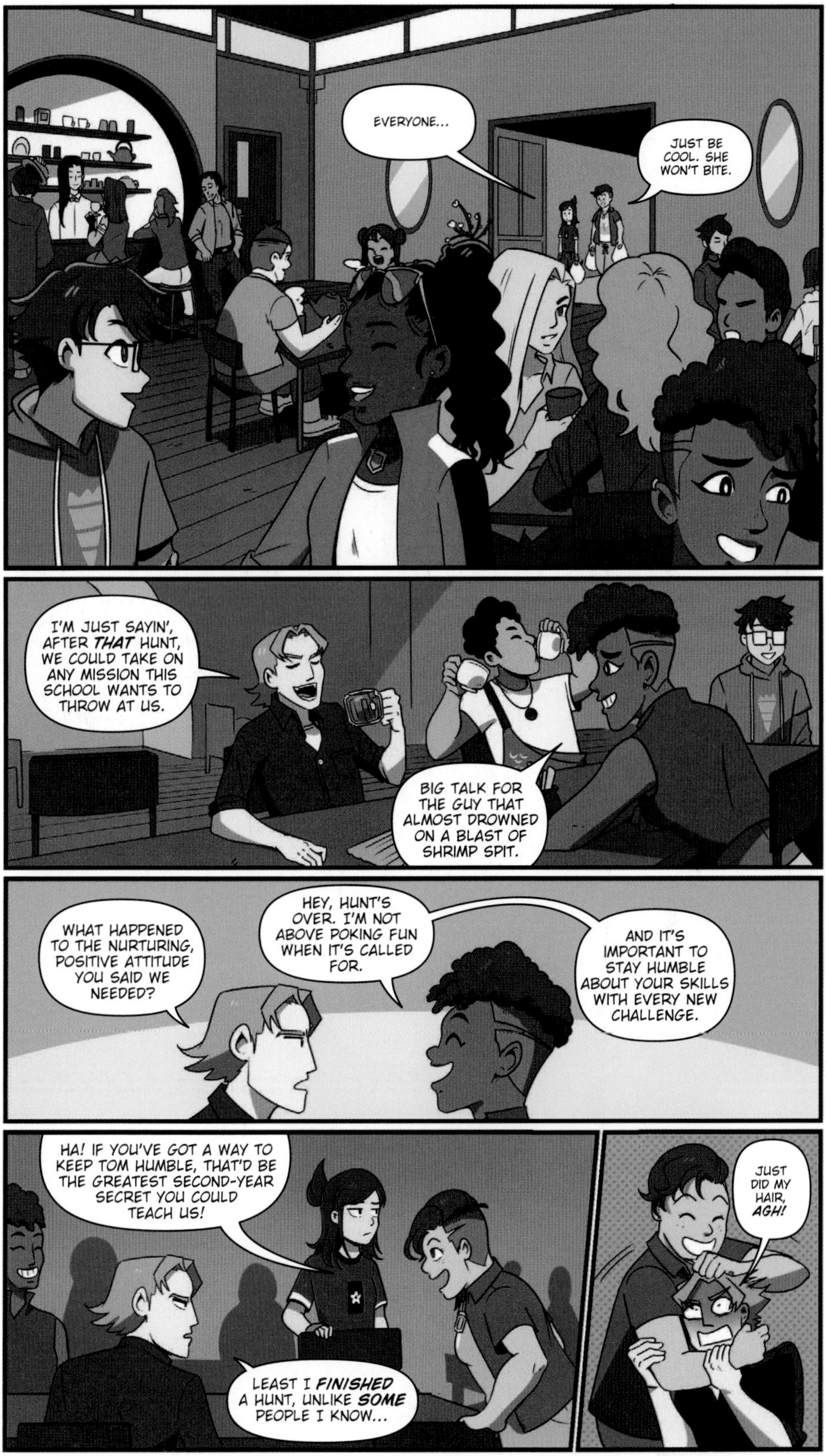
EVERYONE...
JUST BE COOL. SHE WON'T BITE.
I'M JUST SAYIN', AFTER THAT HUNT, WE COULD TAKE ON ANY MISSION THIS SCHOOL WANTS TO THROW AT US.
BIG TALK FOR THE GUY THAT ALMOST DROWNED ON A BLAST OF SHRIMP SPIT.
WHAT HAPPENED TO THE NURTURING, POSITIVE ATTITUDE YOU SAID WE NEEDED?
HEY, HUNT'S OVER. I'M NOT ABOVE POKING FUN WHEN IT'S CALLED FOR.
AND IT'S IMPORTANT TO STAY HUMBLE ABOUT YOUR SKILLS WITH EVERY NEW CHALLENGE.
HA! IF YOU'VE GOT A WAY TO KEEP TOM HUMBLE, THAT'D BE THE GREATEST SECOND-YEAR SECRET YOU COULD TEACH US!
LEAST I FINISHED A HUNT, UNLIKE SOME PEOPLE I KNOW...
JUST DID MY HAIR, AGH!

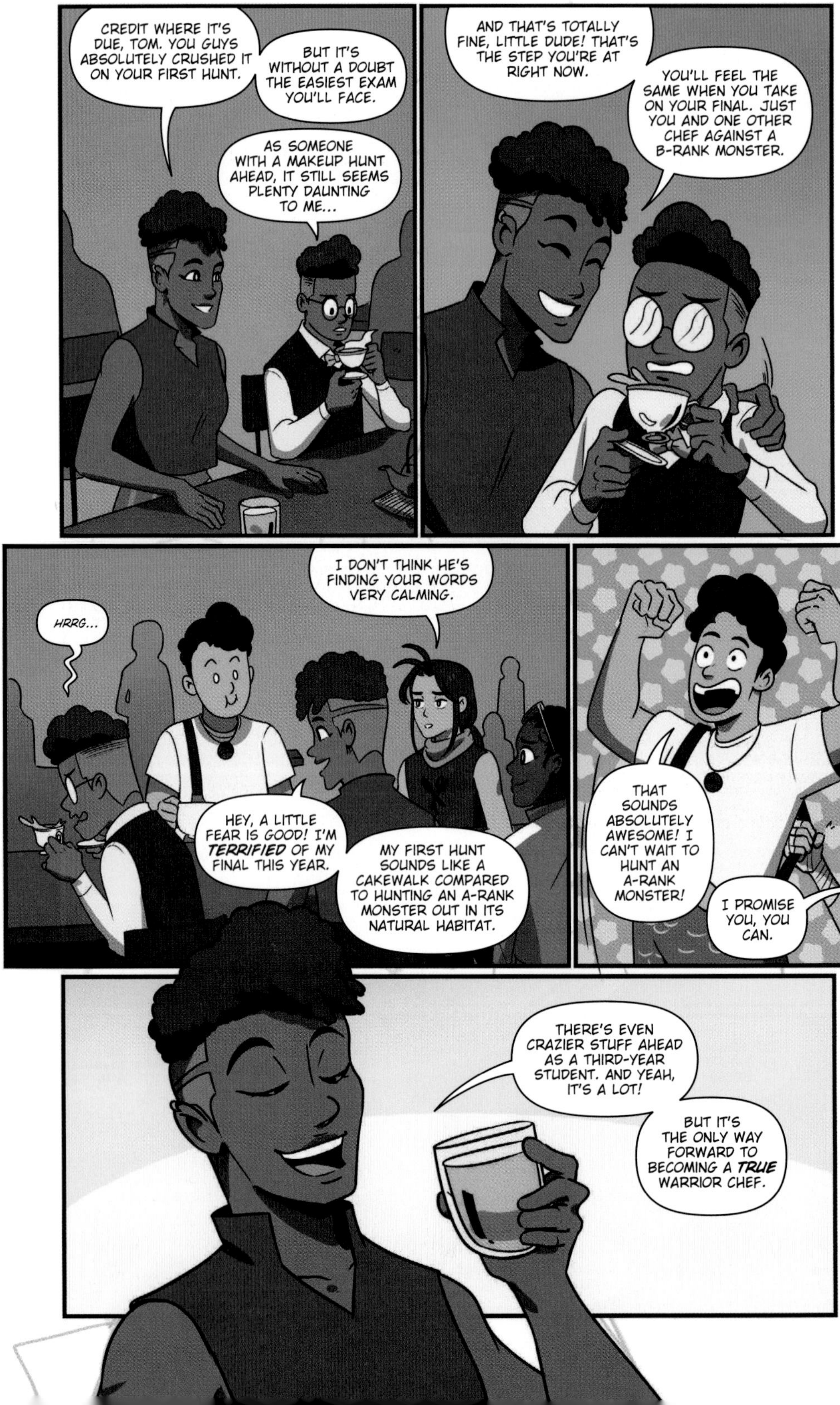
CREDIT WHERE IT'S DUE, TOM. YOU GUYS ABSOLUTELY CRUSHED IT ON YOUR FIRST HUNT.
BUT IT'S WITHOUT A DOUBT THE EASIEST EXAM YOU'LL FACE.
AS SOMEONE WITH A MAKEUP HUNT AHEAD, IT STILL SEEMS PLENTY DAUNTING TO ME...
AND THAT'S TOTALLY FINE, LITTLE DUDE! THAT'S THE STEP YOU'RE AT RIGHT NOW.
YOU'LL FEEL THE SAME WHEN YOU TAKE ON YOUR FINAL. JUST YOU AND ONE OTHER CHEF AGAINST A B-RANK MONSTER.
HRRG...
I DON'T THINK HE'S FINDING YOUR WORDS VERY CALMING.
HEY, A LITTLE FEAR IS GOOD! I'M ***TERRIFIED*** OF MY FINAL THIS YEAR.
MY FIRST HUNT SOUNDS LIKE A CAKEWALK COMPARED TO HUNTING AN A-RANK MONSTER OUT IN ITS NATURAL HABITAT.
THAT SOUNDS ABSOLUTELY AWESOME! I CAN'T WAIT TO HUNT AN A-RANK MONSTER!
I PROMISE YOU, YOU CAN.
THERE'S EVEN CRAZIER STUFF AHEAD AS A THIRD-YEAR STUDENT. AND YEAH, IT'S A LOT!
BUT IT'S THE ONLY WAY FORWARD TO BECOMING A ***TRUE*** WARRIOR CHEF.

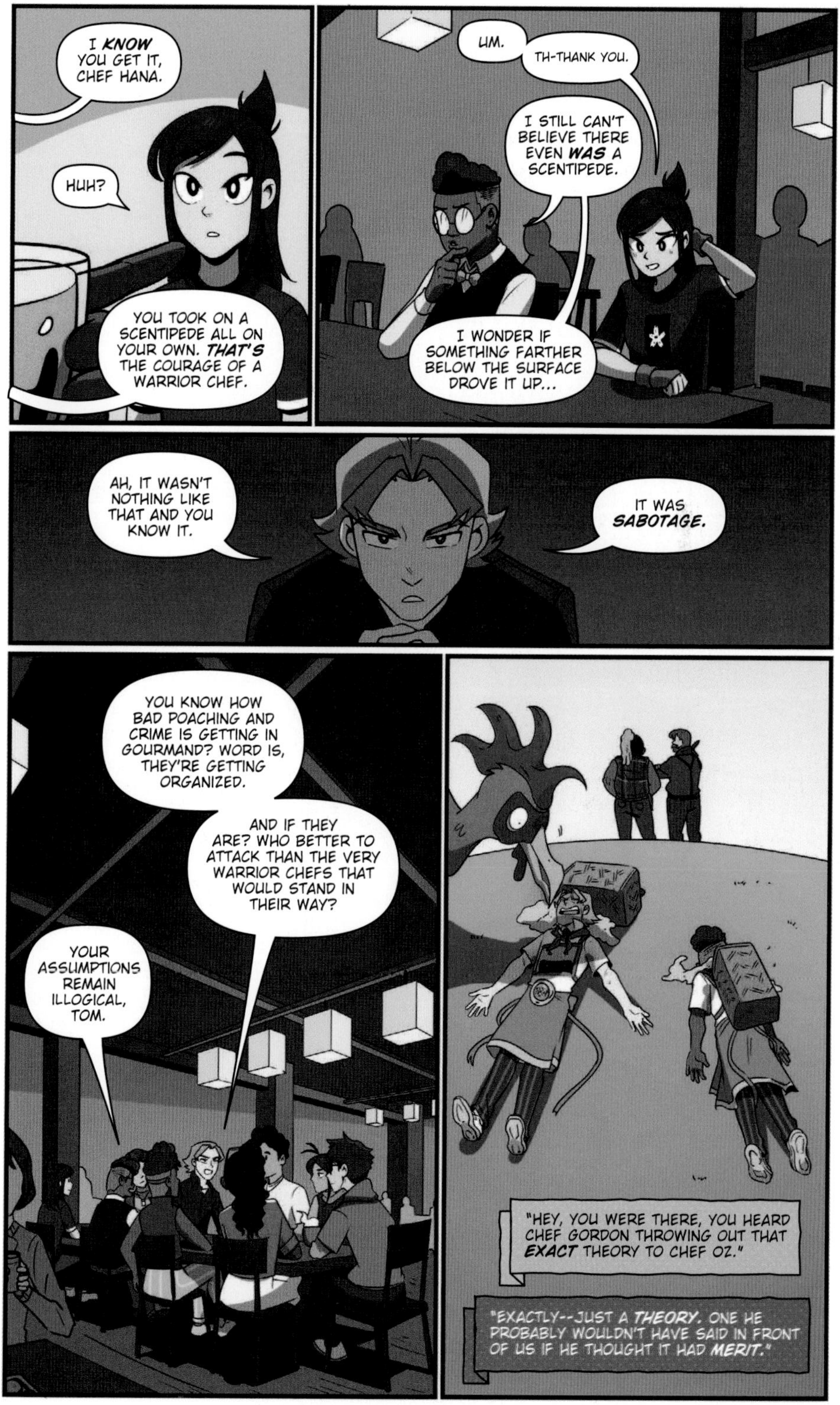
I KNOW YOU GET IT, CHEF HANA.
HUH?
YOU TOOK ON A SCENTIPEDE ALL ON YOUR OWN. THAT'S THE COURAGE OF A WARRIOR CHEF.
UM.
TH-THANK YOU.
I STILL CAN'T BELIEVE THERE EVEN WAS A SCENTIPEDE.
I WONDER IF SOMETHING FARTHER BELOW THE SURFACE DROVE IT UP...
AH, IT WASN'T NOTHING LIKE THAT AND YOU KNOW IT.
IT WAS SABOTAGE.
YOU KNOW HOW BAD POACHING AND CRIME IS GETTING IN GOURMAND? WORD IS, THEY'RE GETTING ORGANIZED.
AND IF THEY ARE? WHO BETTER TO ATTACK THAN THE VERY WARRIOR CHEFS THAT WOULD STAND IN THEIR WAY?
YOUR ASSUMPTIONS REMAIN ILLOGICAL, TOM.
"HEY, YOU WERE THERE, YOU HEARD CHEF GORDON THROWING OUT THAT EXACT THEORY TO CHEF OZ."
"EXACTLY--JUST A THEORY. ONE HE PROBABLY WOULDN'T HAVE SAID IN FRONT OF US IF HE THOUGHT IT HAD MERIT."

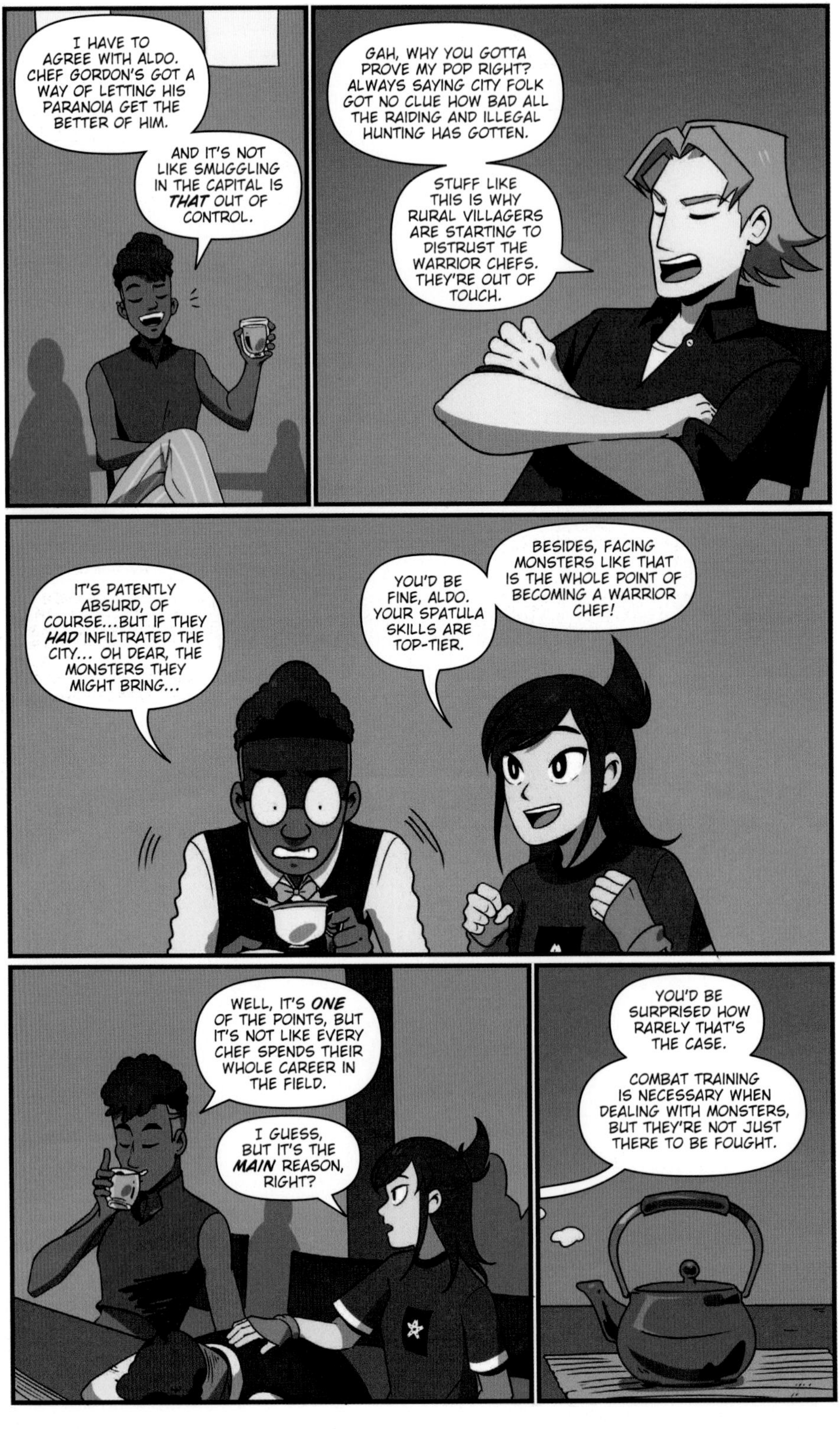
I HAVE TO AGREE WITH ALDO. CHEF GORDON'S GOT A WAY OF LETTING HIS PARANOIA GET THE BETTER OF HIM.
AND IT'S NOT LIKE SMUGGLING IN THE CAPITAL IS *THAT* OUT OF CONTROL.
GAH, WHY YOU GOTTA PROVE MY POP RIGHT? ALWAYS SAYING CITY FOLK GOT NO CLUE HOW BAD ALL THE RAIDING AND ILLEGAL HUNTING HAS GOTTEN.
STUFF LIKE THIS IS WHY RURAL VILLAGERS ARE STARTING TO DISTRUST THE WARRIOR CHEFS. THEY'RE OUT OF TOUCH.
IT'S PATENTLY ABSURD, OF COURSE...BUT IF THEY *HAD* INFILTRATED THE CITY... OH DEAR, THE MONSTERS THEY MIGHT BRING...
YOU'D BE FINE, ALDO. YOUR SPATULA SKILLS ARE TOP-TIER.
BESIDES, FACING MONSTERS LIKE THAT IS THE WHOLE POINT OF BECOMING A WARRIOR CHEF!
WELL, IT'S *ONE* OF THE POINTS, BUT IT'S NOT LIKE EVERY CHEF SPENDS THEIR WHOLE CAREER IN THE FIELD.
I GUESS, BUT IT'S THE *MAIN* REASON, RIGHT?
YOU'D BE SURPRISED HOW RARELY THAT'S THE CASE.
COMBAT TRAINING IS NECESSARY WHEN DEALING WITH MONSTERS, BUT THEY'RE NOT JUST THERE TO BE FOUGHT.

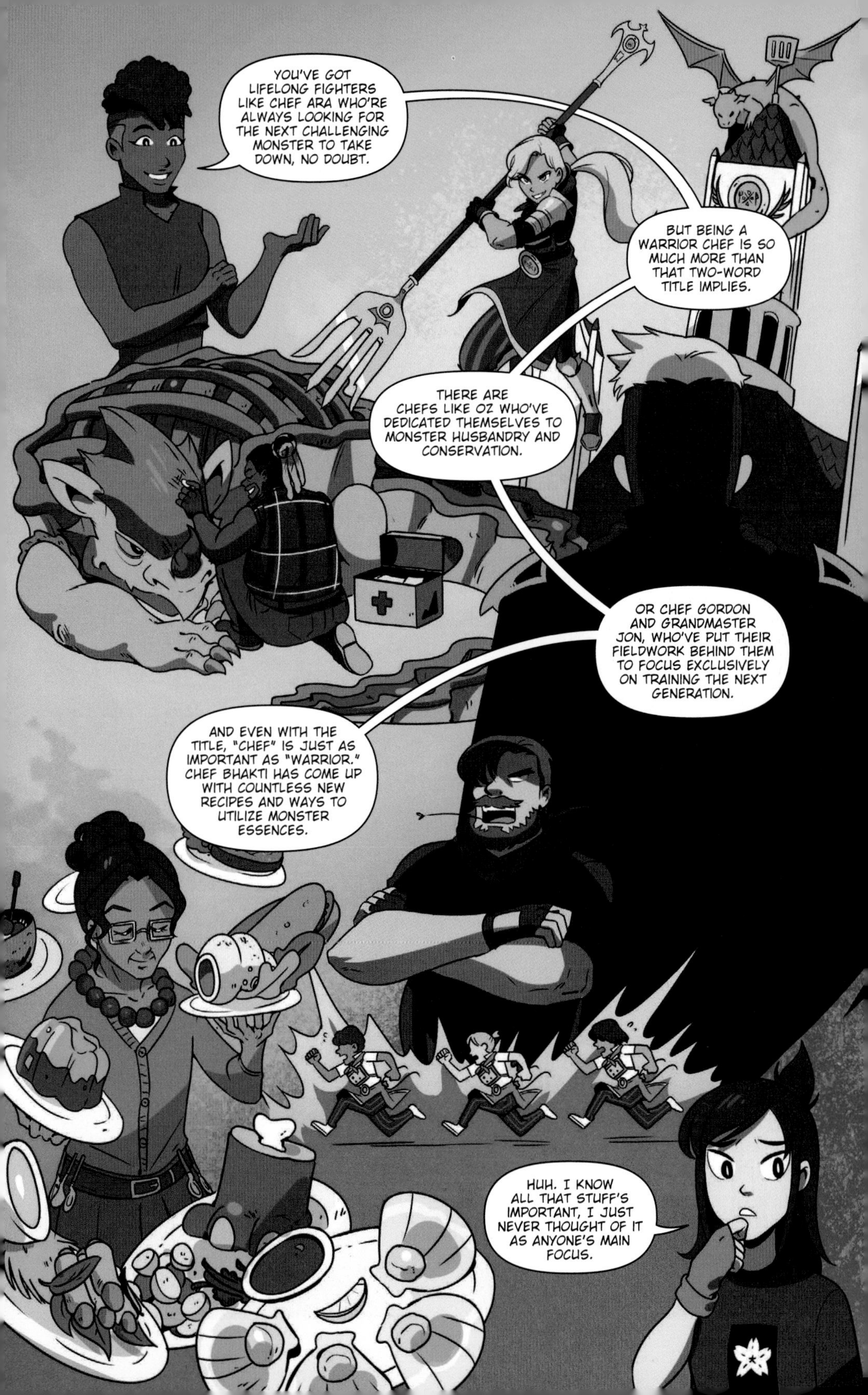
YOU'VE GOT LIFELONG FIGHTERS LIKE CHEF ARA WHO'RE ALWAYS LOOKING FOR THE NEXT CHALLENGING MONSTER TO TAKE DOWN, NO DOUBT.
BUT BEING A WARRIOR CHEF IS SO MUCH MORE THAN THAT TWO-WORD TITLE IMPLIES.
THERE ARE CHEFS LIKE OZ WHO'VE DEDICATED THEMSELVES TO MONSTER HUSBANDRY AND CONSERVATION.
OR CHEF GORDON AND GRANDMASTER JON, WHO'VE PUT THEIR FIELDWORK BEHIND THEM TO FOCUS EXCLUSIVELY ON TRAINING THE NEXT GENERATION.
AND EVEN WITH THE TITLE, "CHEF" IS JUST AS IMPORTANT AS "WARRIOR." CHEF BHAKTI HAS COME UP WITH COUNTLESS NEW RECIPES AND WAYS TO UTILIZE MONSTER ESSENCES.
HUH. I KNOW ALL THAT STUFF'S IMPORTANT, I JUST NEVER THOUGHT OF IT AS ANYONE'S MAIN FOCUS.

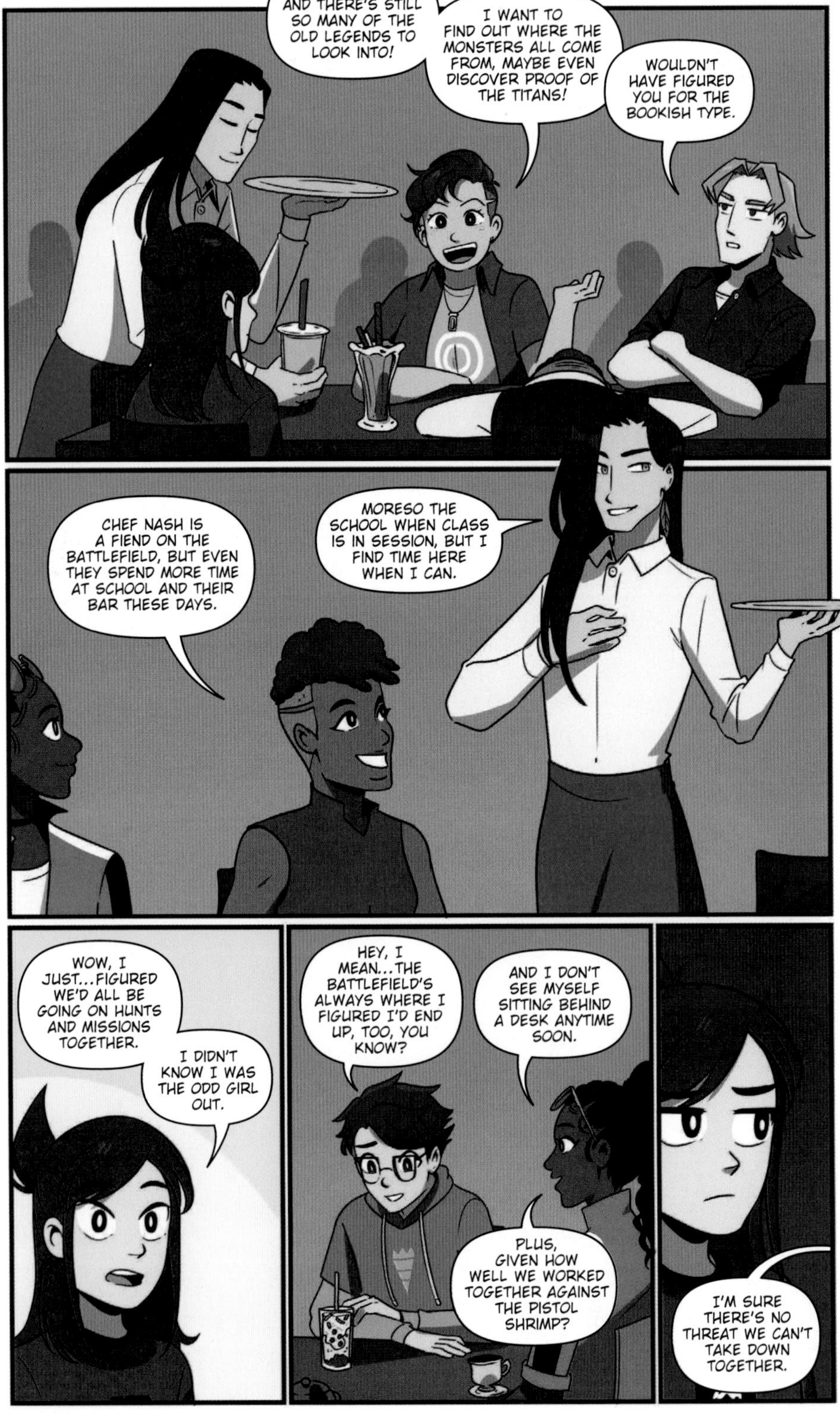
OH TOTALLY! AND THERE'S STILL SO MANY OF THE OLD LEGENDS TO LOOK INTO!
I WANT TO FIND OUT WHERE THE MONSTERS ALL COME FROM, MAYBE EVEN DISCOVER PROOF OF THE TITANS!
WOULDN'T HAVE FIGURED YOU FOR THE BOOKISH TYPE.
CHEF NASH IS A FIEND ON THE BATTLEFIELD, BUT EVEN THEY SPEND MORE TIME AT SCHOOL AND THEIR BAR THESE DAYS.
MORESO THE SCHOOL WHEN CLASS IS IN SESSION, BUT I FIND TIME HERE WHEN I CAN.
WOW, I JUST...FIGURED WE'D ALL BE GOING ON HUNTS AND MISSIONS TOGETHER.
I DIDN'T KNOW I WAS THE ODD GIRL OUT.
HEY, I MEAN...THE BATTLEFIELD'S ALWAYS WHERE I FIGURED I'D END UP, TOO, YOU KNOW?
AND I DON'T SEE MYSELF SITTING BEHIND A DESK ANYTIME SOON.
PLUS, GIVEN HOW WELL WE WORKED TOGETHER AGAINST THE PISTOL SHRIMP?
I'M SURE THERE'S NO THREAT WE CAN'T TAKE DOWN TOGETHER.

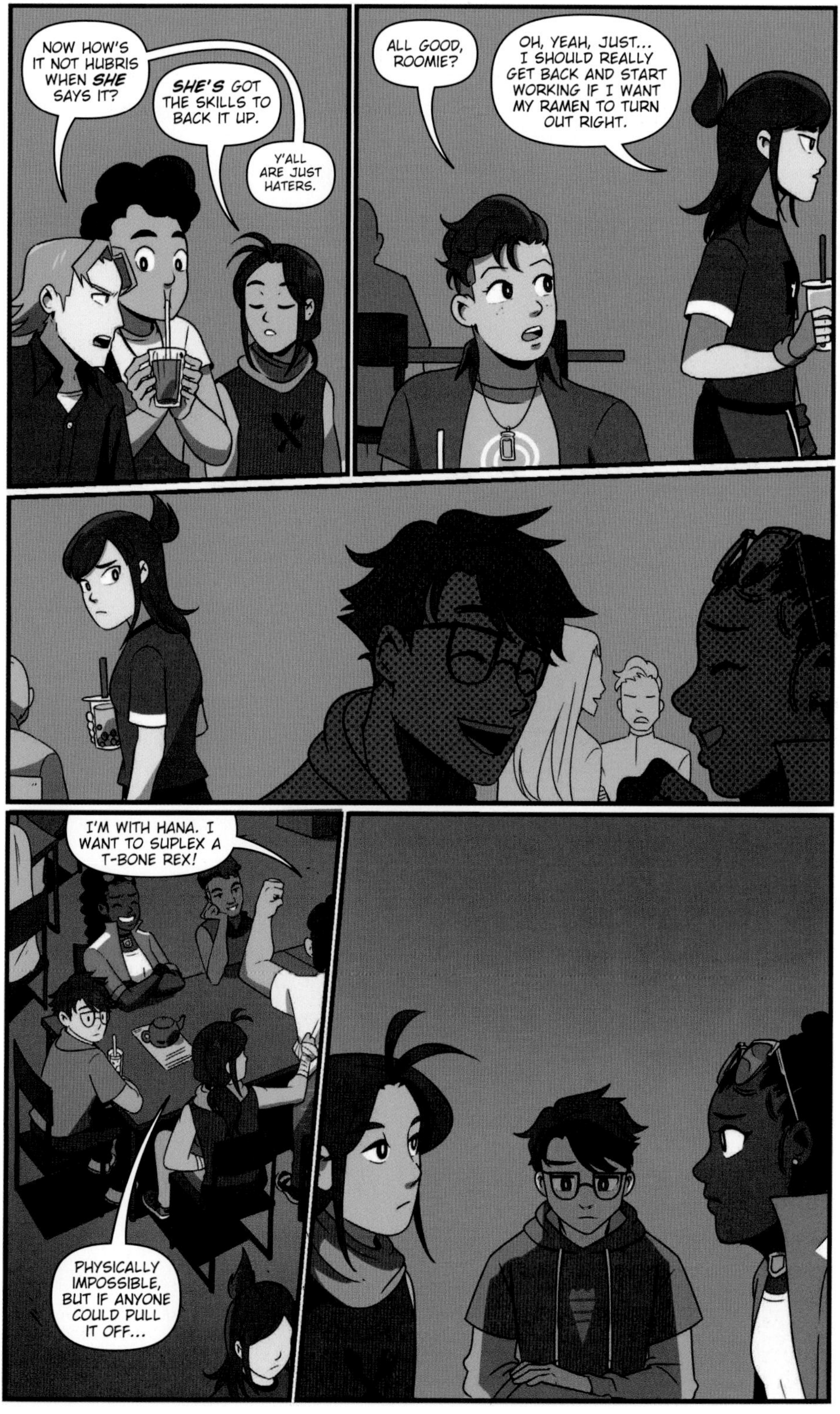
NOW HOW'S IT NOT HUBRIS WHEN *SHE* SAYS IT?
SHE'S GOT THE SKILLS TO BACK IT UP.
Y'ALL ARE JUST HATERS.
ALL GOOD, ROOMIE?
OH, YEAH, JUST... I SHOULD REALLY GET BACK AND START WORKING IF I WANT MY RAMEN TO TURN OUT RIGHT.
I'M WITH HANA. I WANT TO SUPLEX A T-BONE REX!
PHYSICALLY IMPOSSIBLE, BUT IF ANYONE COULD PULL IT OFF...

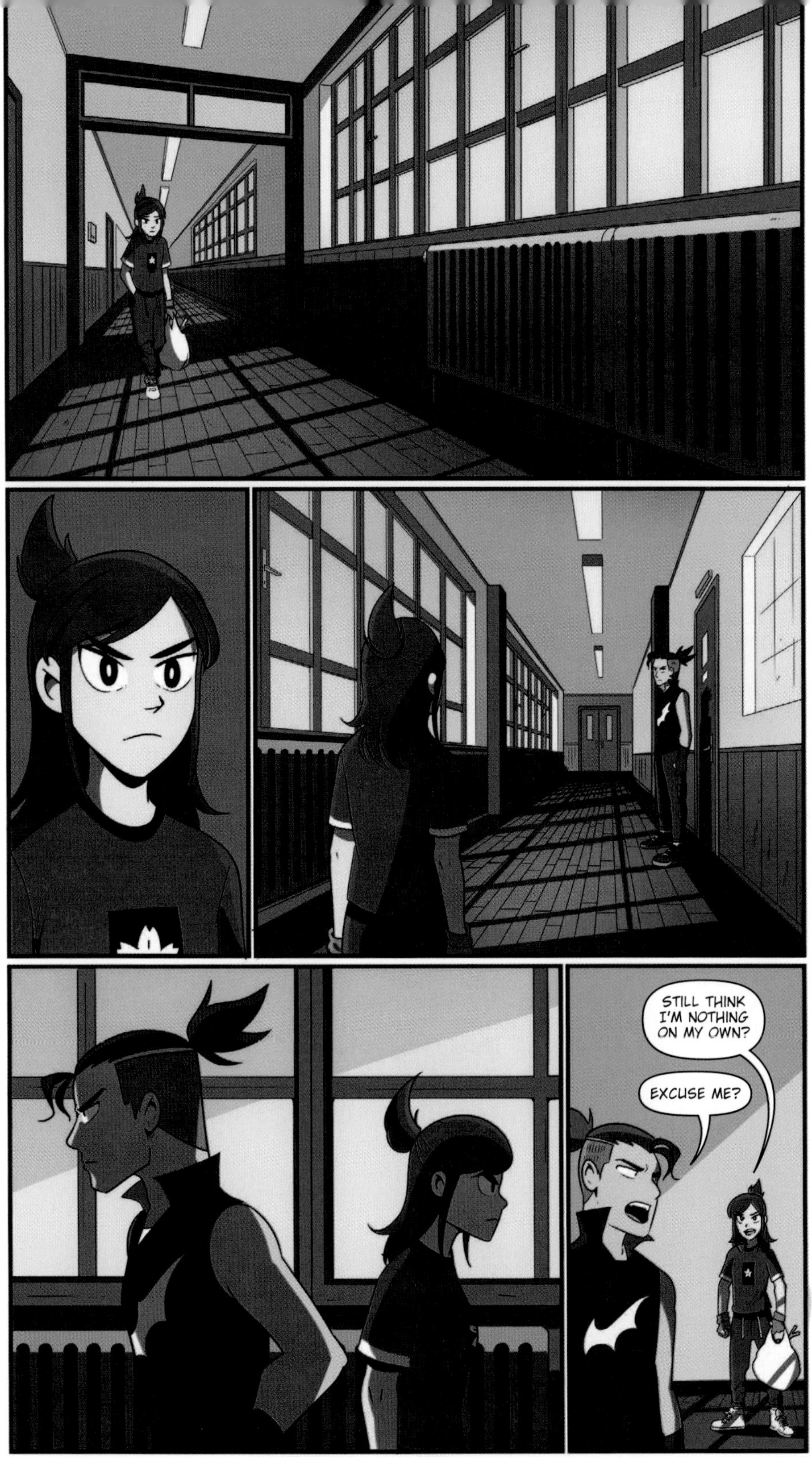
STILL THINK I'M NOTHING ON MY OWN?
EXCUSE ME?

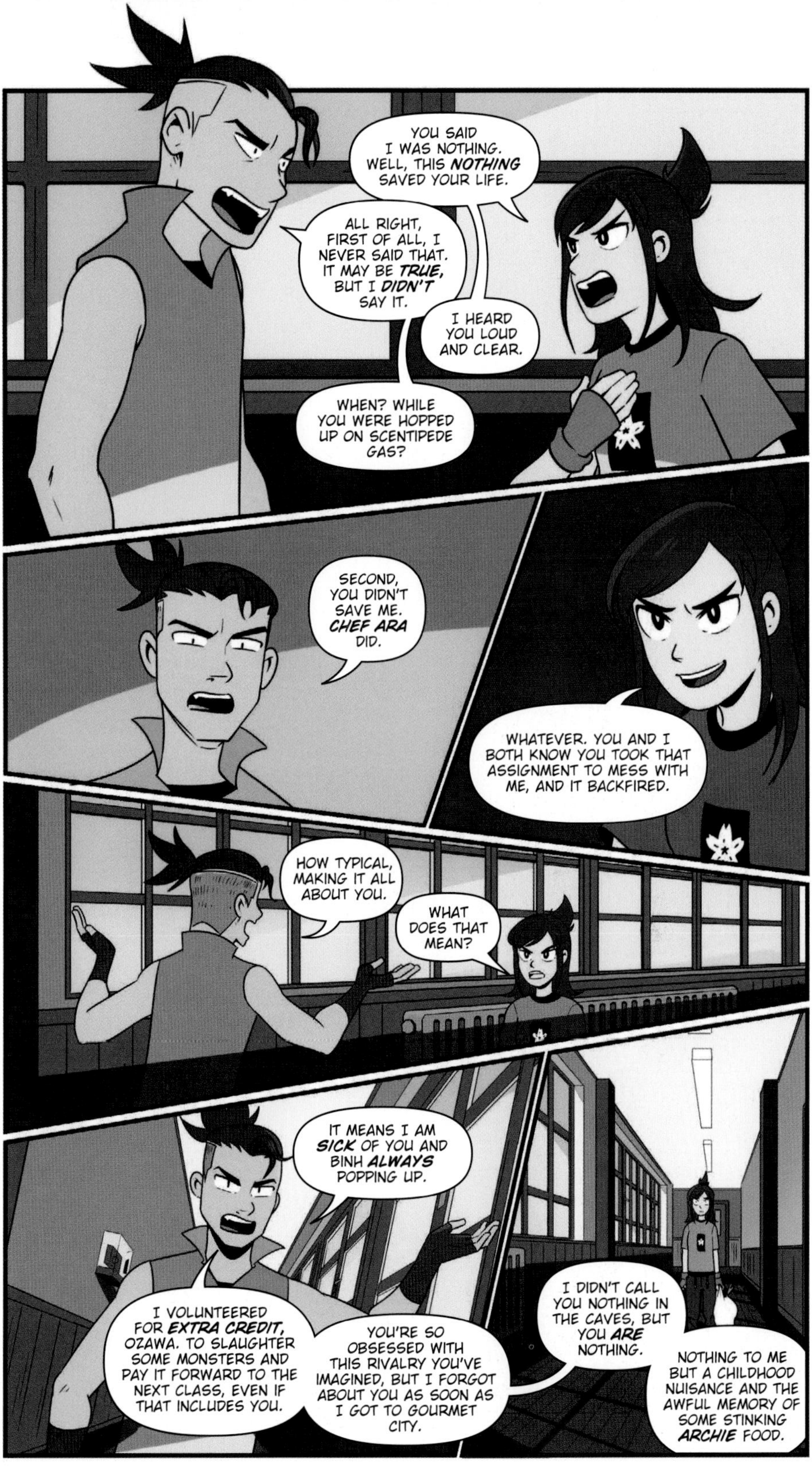
YOU SAID I WAS NOTHING. WELL, THIS *NOTHING* SAVED YOUR LIFE.
ALL RIGHT, FIRST OF ALL, I NEVER SAID THAT. IT MAY BE *TRUE,* BUT I *DIDN'T* SAY IT.
I HEARD YOU LOUD AND CLEAR.
WHEN? WHILE YOU WERE HOPPED UP ON SCENTIPEDE GAS?
SECOND, YOU DIDN'T SAVE ME. *CHEF ARA* DID.
WHATEVER. YOU AND I BOTH KNOW YOU TOOK THAT ASSIGNMENT TO MESS WITH ME, AND IT BACKFIRED.
HOW TYPICAL, MAKING IT ALL ABOUT YOU.
WHAT DOES THAT MEAN?
IT MEANS I AM *SICK* OF YOU AND BINH *ALWAYS* POPPING UP.
I VOLUNTEERED FOR *EXTRA CREDIT,* OZAWA. TO SLAUGHTER SOME MONSTERS AND PAY IT FORWARD TO THE NEXT CLASS, EVEN IF THAT INCLUDES YOU.
YOU'RE SO OBSESSED WITH THIS RIVALRY YOU'VE IMAGINED, BUT I FORGOT ABOUT YOU AS SOON AS I GOT TO GOURMET CITY.
I DIDN'T CALL YOU NOTHING IN THE CAVES, BUT YOU *ARE* NOTHING.
NOTHING TO ME BUT A CHILDHOOD NUISANCE AND THE AWFUL MEMORY OF SOME STINKING *ARCHIE* FOOD.

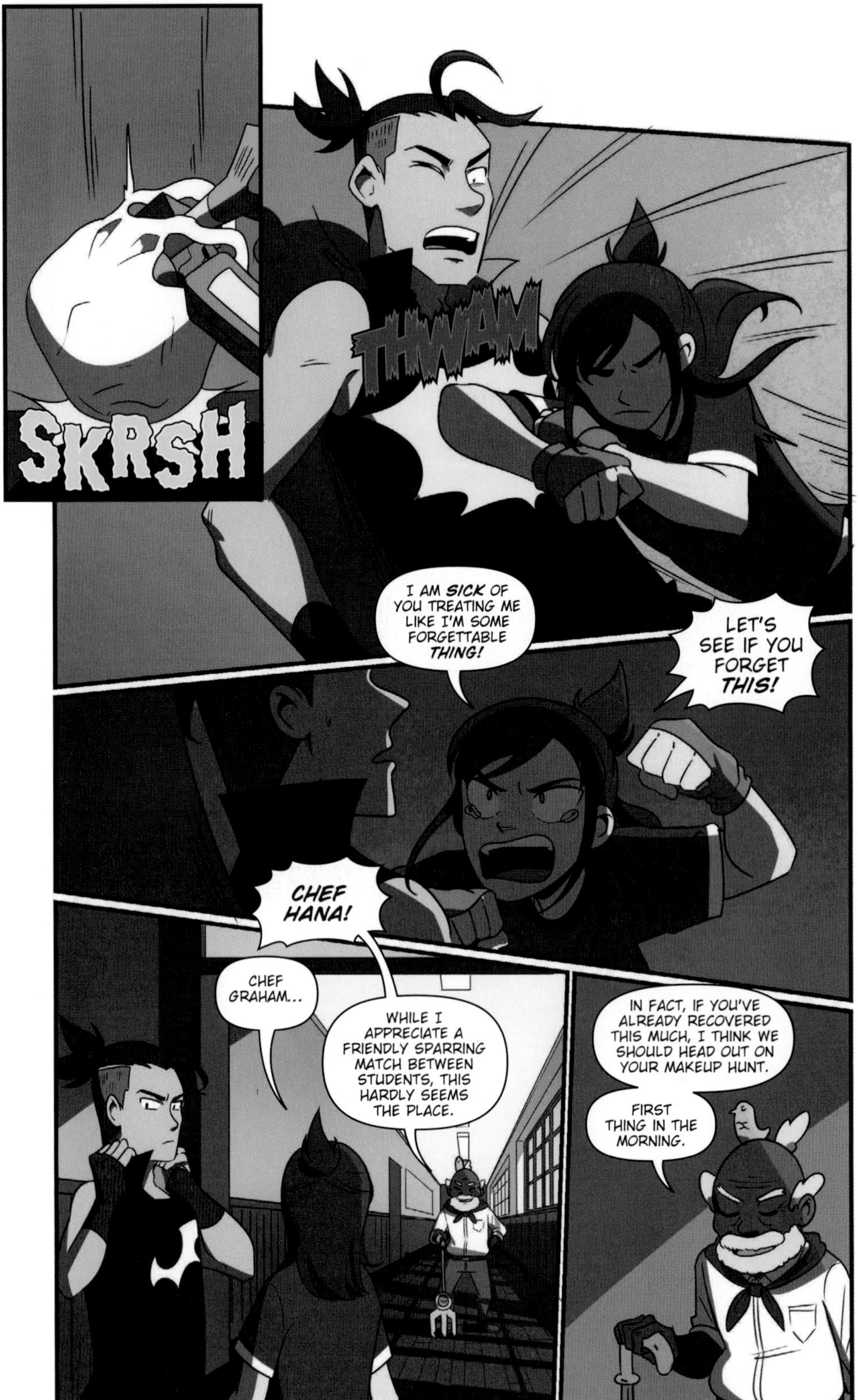
SKRSH
THWAM
I AM SICK OF YOU TREATING ME LIKE I'M SOME FORGETTABLE THING!
LET'S SEE IF YOU FORGET THIS!
CHEF HANA!
CHEF GRAHAM...
WHILE I APPRECIATE A FRIENDLY SPARRING MATCH BETWEEN STUDENTS, THIS HARDLY SEEMS THE PLACE.
IN FACT, IF YOU'VE ALREADY RECOVERED THIS MUCH, I THINK WE SHOULD HEAD OUT ON YOUR MAKEUP HUNT.
FIRST THING IN THE MORNING.

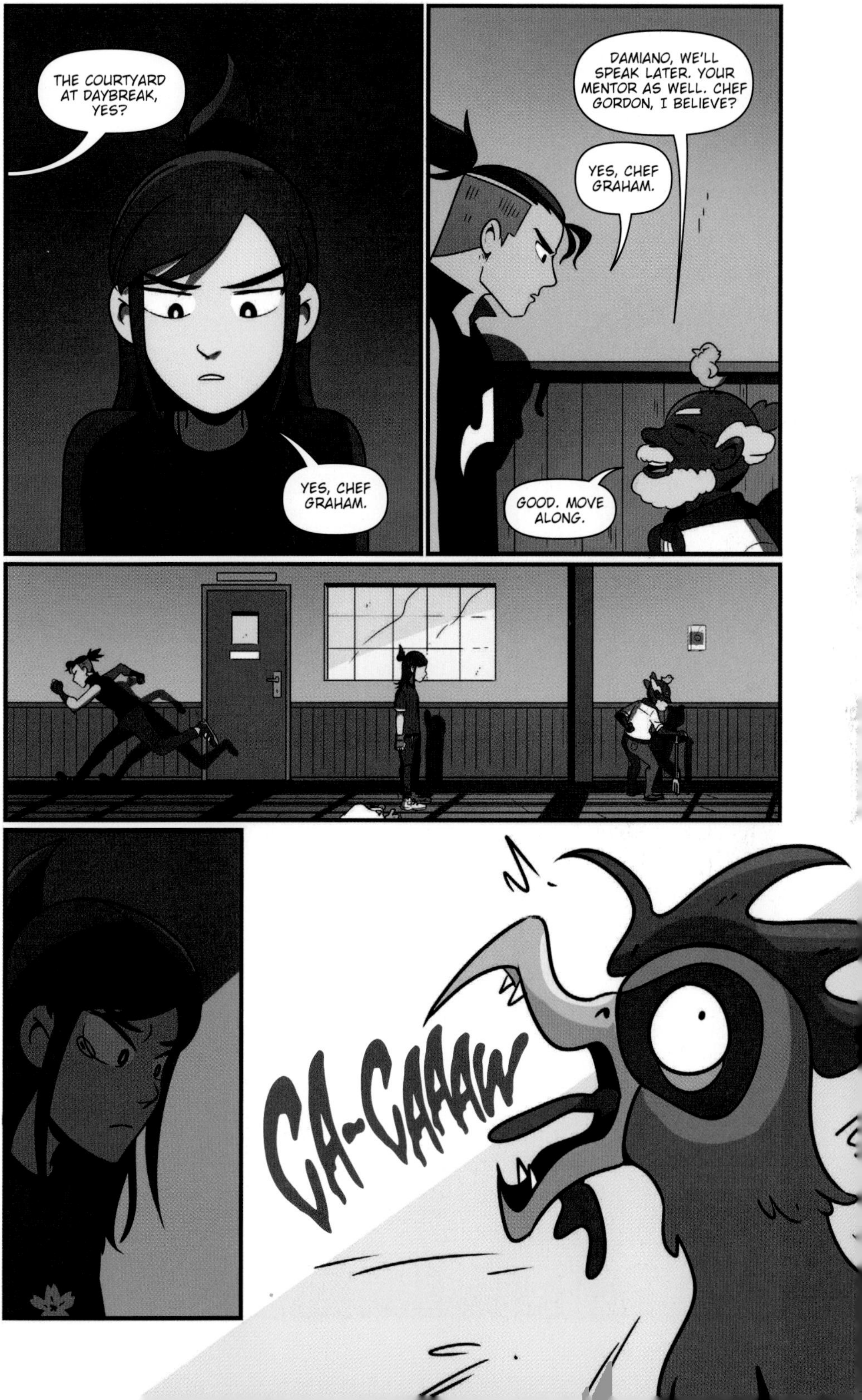
THE COURTYARD AT DAYBREAK, YES?
YES, CHEF GRAHAM.
DAMIANO, WE'LL SPEAK LATER. YOUR MENTOR AS WELL. CHEF GORDON, I BELIEVE?
YES, CHEF GRAHAM.
GOOD. MOVE ALONG.
CA-CAAAW

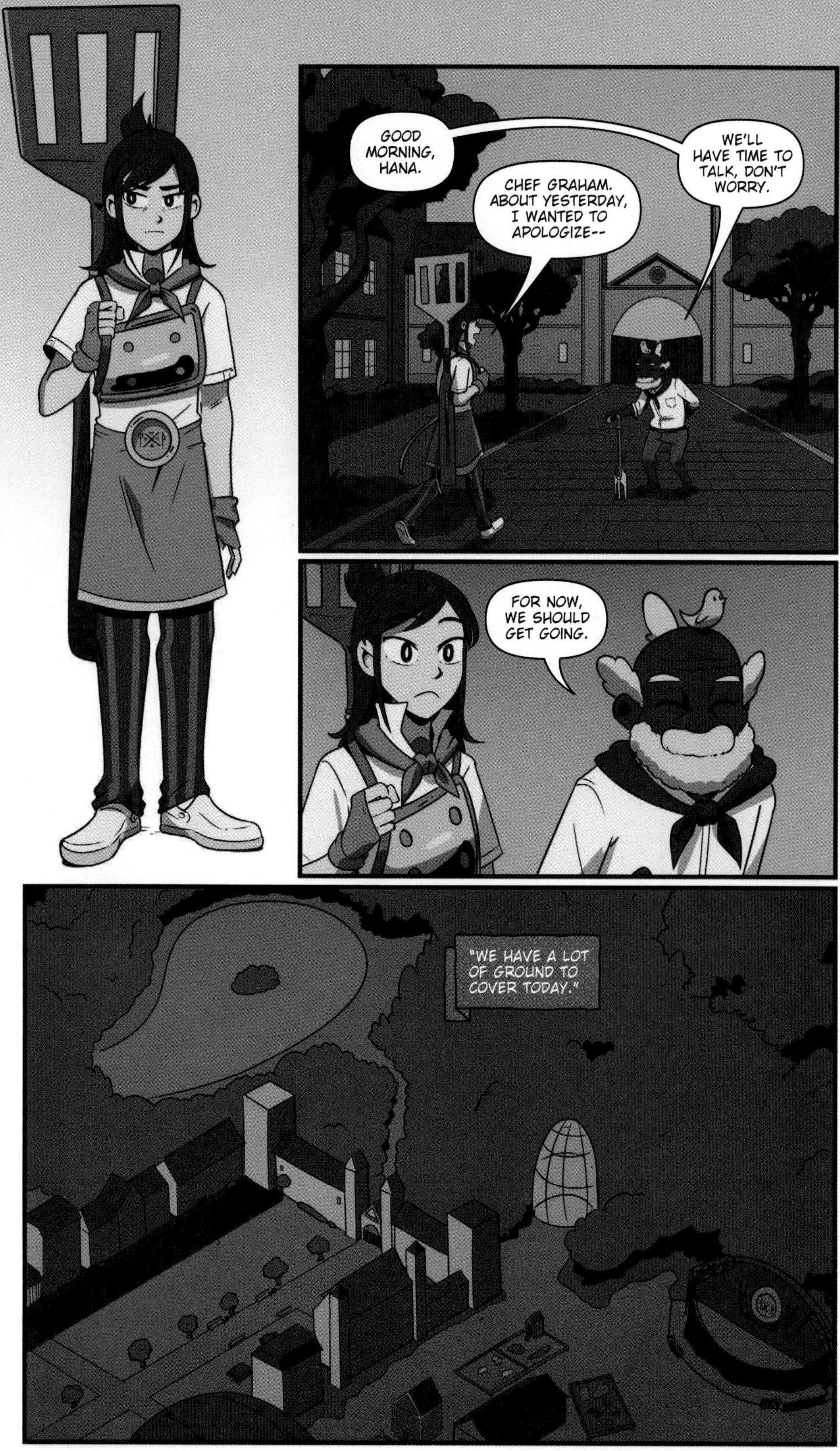
GOOD MORNING, HANA.
CHEF GRAHAM. ABOUT YESTERDAY, I WANTED TO APOLOGIZE--
WE'LL HAVE TIME TO TALK, DON'T WORRY.
FOR NOW, WE SHOULD GET GOING.
"WE HAVE A LOT OF GROUND TO COVER TODAY."

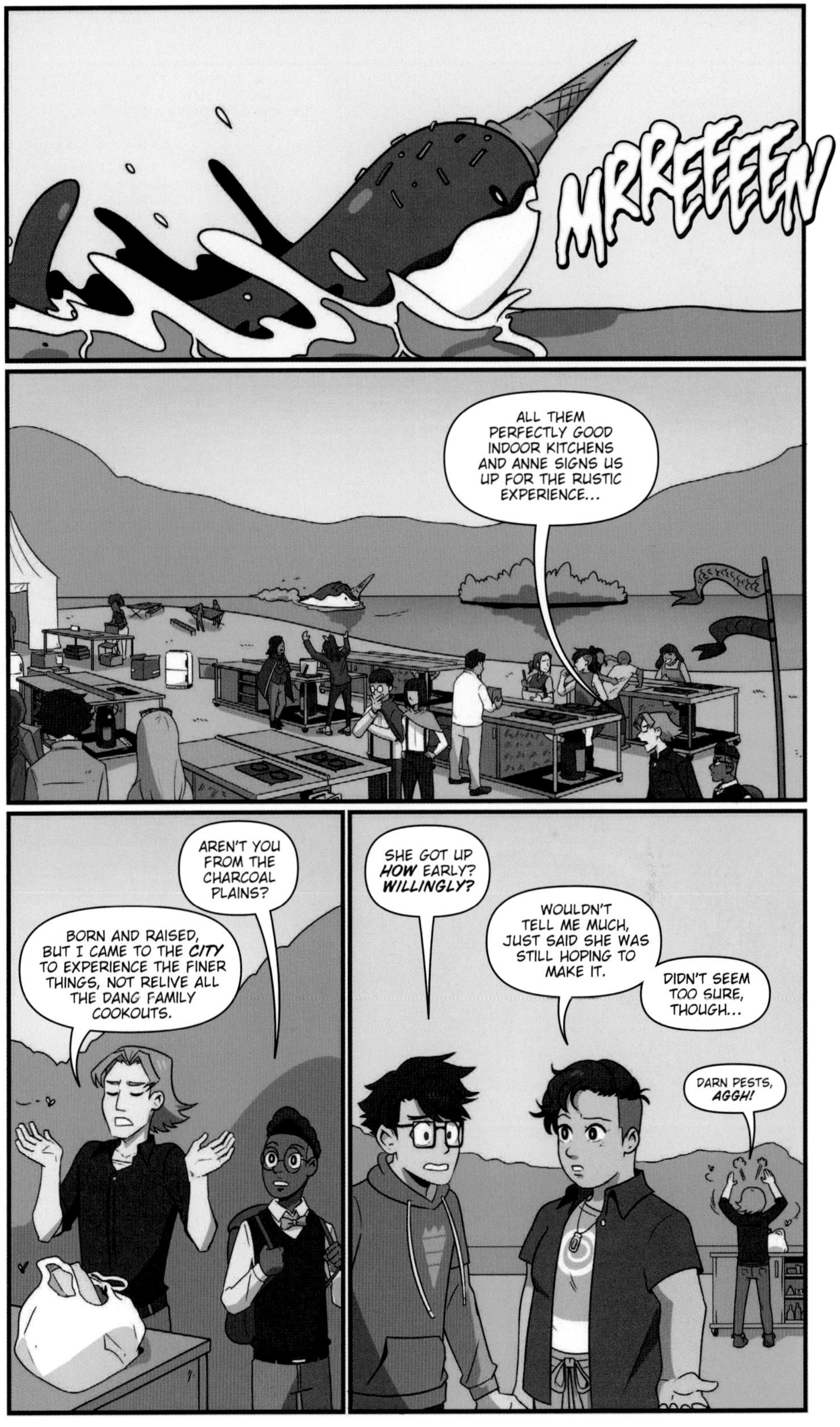
MRREEEEN
ALL THEM PERFECTLY GOOD INDOOR KITCHENS AND ANNE SIGNS US UP FOR THE RUSTIC EXPERIENCE...
AREN'T YOU FROM THE CHARCOAL PLAINS?
BORN AND RAISED, BUT I CAME TO THE *CITY* TO EXPERIENCE THE FINER THINGS, NOT RELIVE ALL THE DANG FAMILY COOKOUTS.
SHE GOT UP *HOW* EARLY? *WILLINGLY?*
WOULDN'T TELL ME MUCH, JUST SAID SHE WAS STILL HOPING TO MAKE IT.
DIDN'T SEEM TOO SURE, THOUGH...
DARN PESTS, *AGGH!*

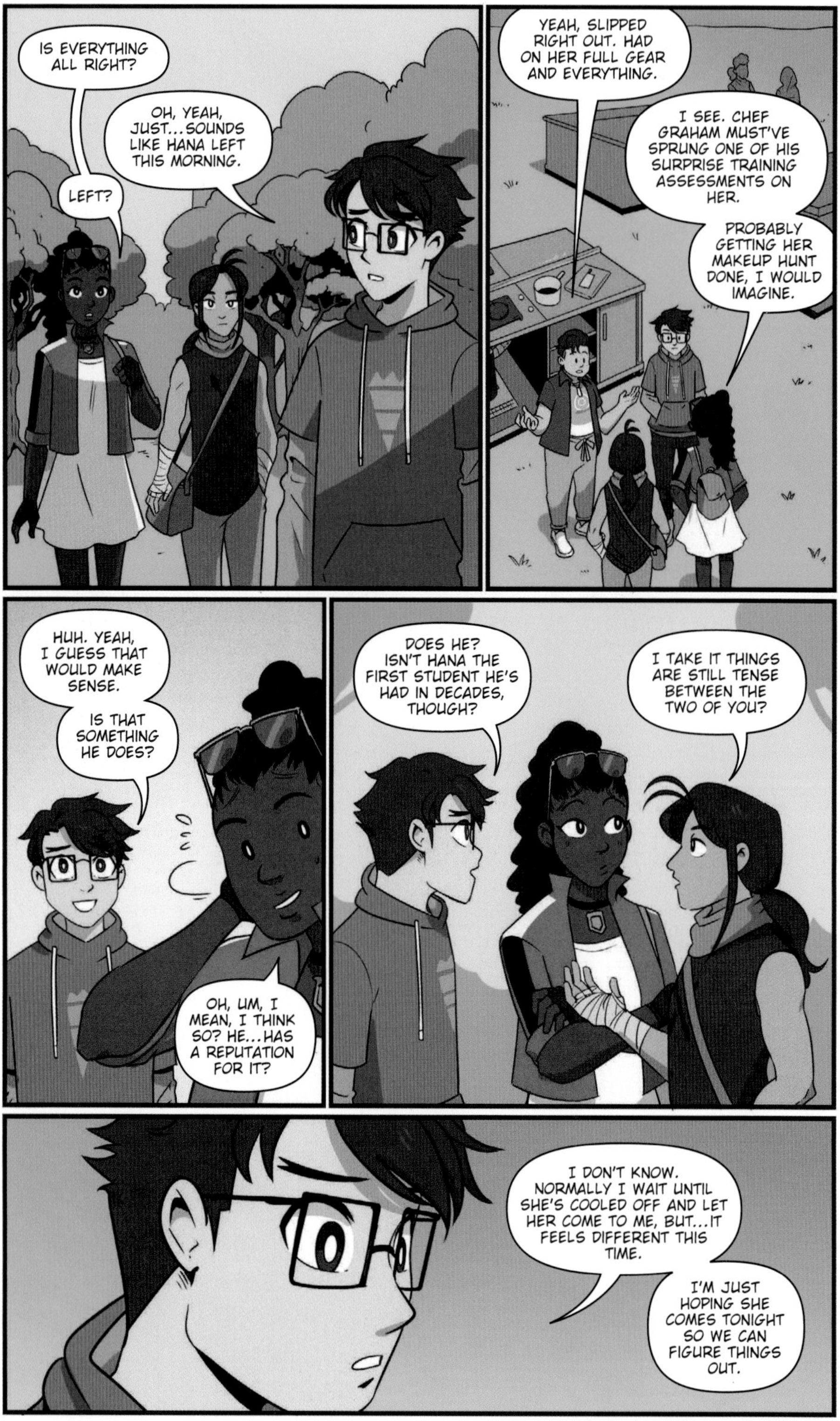
IS EVERYTHING ALL RIGHT?
OH, YEAH, JUST... SOUNDS LIKE HANA LEFT THIS MORNING.
LEFT?
YEAH, SLIPPED RIGHT OUT. HAD ON HER FULL GEAR AND EVERYTHING.
I SEE. CHEF GRAHAM MUST'VE SPRUNG ONE OF HIS SURPRISE TRAINING ASSESSMENTS ON HER.
PROBABLY GETTING HER MAKEUP HUNT DONE, I WOULD IMAGINE.
HUH. YEAH, I GUESS THAT WOULD MAKE SENSE.
IS THAT SOMETHING HE DOES?
OH, UM, I MEAN, I THINK SO? HE... HAS A REPUTATION FOR IT?
DOES HE? ISN'T HANA THE FIRST STUDENT HE'S HAD IN DECADES, THOUGH?
I TAKE IT THINGS ARE STILL TENSE BETWEEN THE TWO OF YOU?
I DON'T KNOW. NORMALLY I WAIT UNTIL SHE'S COOLED OFF AND LET HER COME TO ME, BUT... IT FEELS DIFFERENT THIS TIME.
I'M JUST HOPING SHE COMES TONIGHT SO WE CAN FIGURE THINGS OUT.

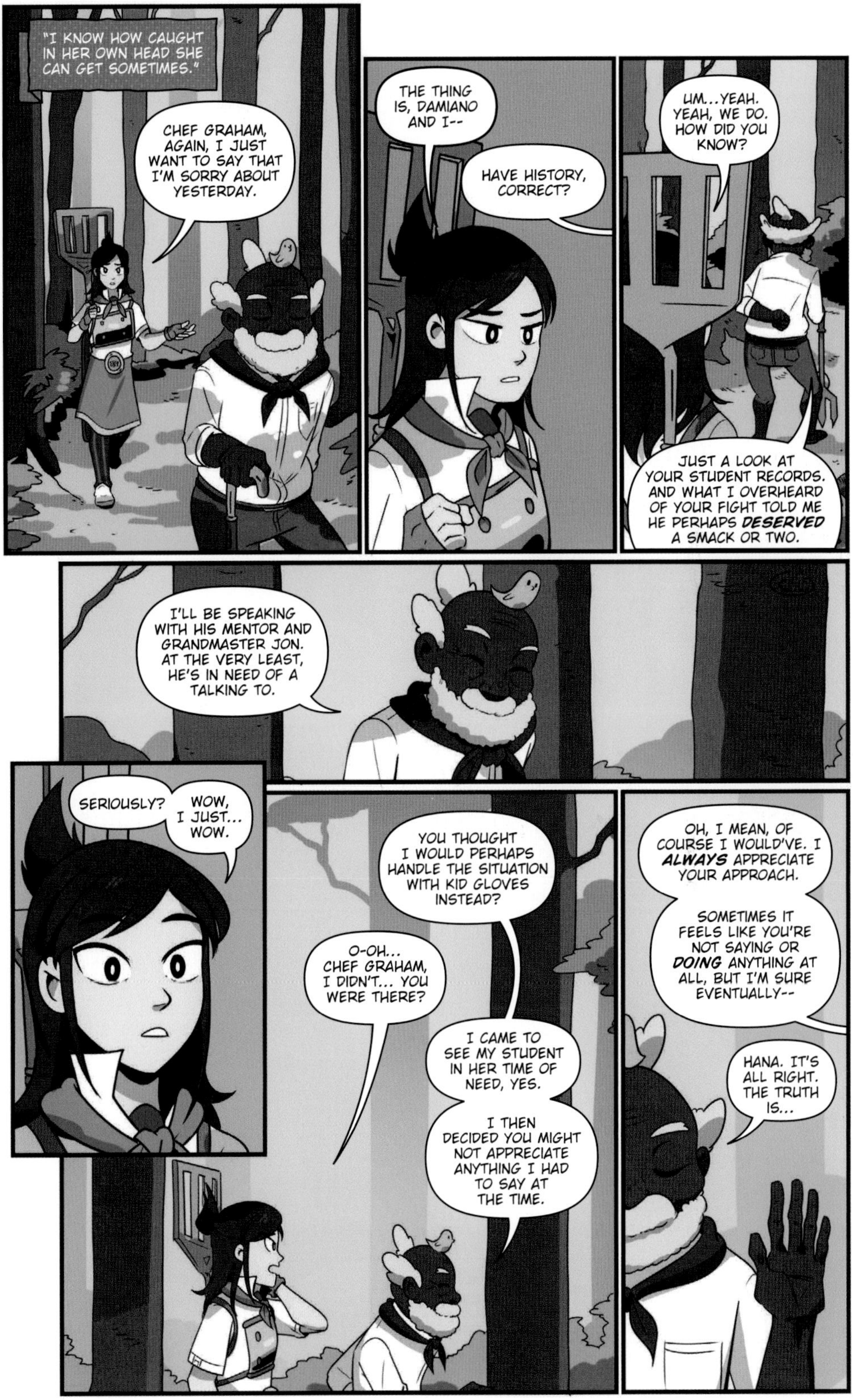
"I KNOW HOW CAUGHT IN HER OWN HEAD SHE CAN GET SOMETIMES."
CHEF GRAHAM, AGAIN, I JUST WANT TO SAY THAT I'M SORRY ABOUT YESTERDAY.
THE THING IS, DAMIANO AND I--
HAVE HISTORY, CORRECT?
UM...YEAH. YEAH, WE DO. HOW DID YOU KNOW?
JUST A LOOK AT YOUR STUDENT RECORDS. AND WHAT I OVERHEARD OF YOUR FIGHT TOLD ME HE PERHAPS ***DESERVED*** A SMACK OR TWO.
I'LL BE SPEAKING WITH HIS MENTOR AND GRANDMASTER JON. AT THE VERY LEAST, HE'S IN NEED OF A TALKING TO.
SERIOUSLY?
WOW, I JUST... WOW.
YOU THOUGHT I WOULD PERHAPS HANDLE THE SITUATION WITH KID GLOVES INSTEAD?
O-OH... CHEF GRAHAM, I DIDN'T... YOU WERE THERE?
I CAME TO SEE MY STUDENT IN HER TIME OF NEED, YES.
I THEN DECIDED YOU MIGHT NOT APPRECIATE ANYTHING I HAD TO SAY AT THE TIME.
OH, I MEAN, OF COURSE I WOULD'VE. I ***ALWAYS*** APPRECIATE YOUR APPROACH.
SOMETIMES IT FEELS LIKE YOU'RE NOT SAYING OR ***DOING*** ANYTHING AT ALL, BUT I'M SURE EVENTUALLY--
HANA. IT'S ALL RIGHT. THE TRUTH IS...

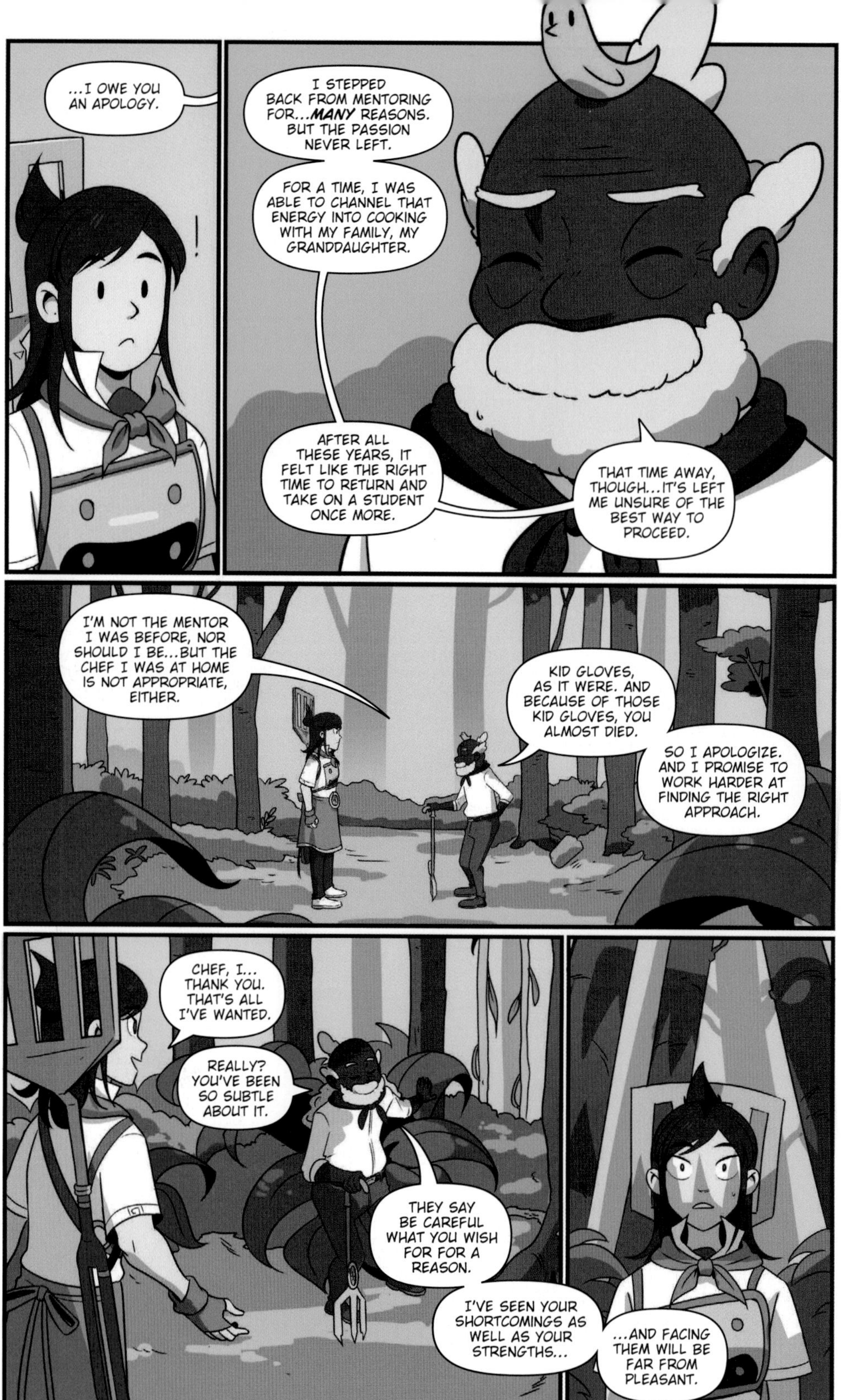
...I OWE YOU AN APOLOGY.
!
I STEPPED BACK FROM MENTORING FOR...MANY REASONS. BUT THE PASSION NEVER LEFT.
FOR A TIME, I WAS ABLE TO CHANNEL THAT ENERGY INTO COOKING WITH MY FAMILY, MY GRANDDAUGHTER.
AFTER ALL THESE YEARS, IT FELT LIKE THE RIGHT TIME TO RETURN AND TAKE ON A STUDENT ONCE MORE.
THAT TIME AWAY, THOUGH...IT'S LEFT ME UNSURE OF THE BEST WAY TO PROCEED.
I'M NOT THE MENTOR I WAS BEFORE, NOR SHOULD I BE...BUT THE CHEF I WAS AT HOME IS NOT APPROPRIATE, EITHER.
KID GLOVES, AS IT WERE. AND BECAUSE OF THOSE KID GLOVES, YOU ALMOST DIED.
SO I APOLOGIZE. AND I PROMISE TO WORK HARDER AT FINDING THE RIGHT APPROACH.
CHEF, I... THANK YOU. THAT'S ALL I'VE WANTED.
REALLY? YOU'VE BEEN SO SUBTLE ABOUT IT.
THEY SAY BE CAREFUL WHAT YOU WISH FOR FOR A REASON.
I'VE SEEN YOUR SHORTCOMINGS AS WELL AS YOUR STRENGTHS...
...AND FACING THEM WILL BE FAR FROM PLEASANT.

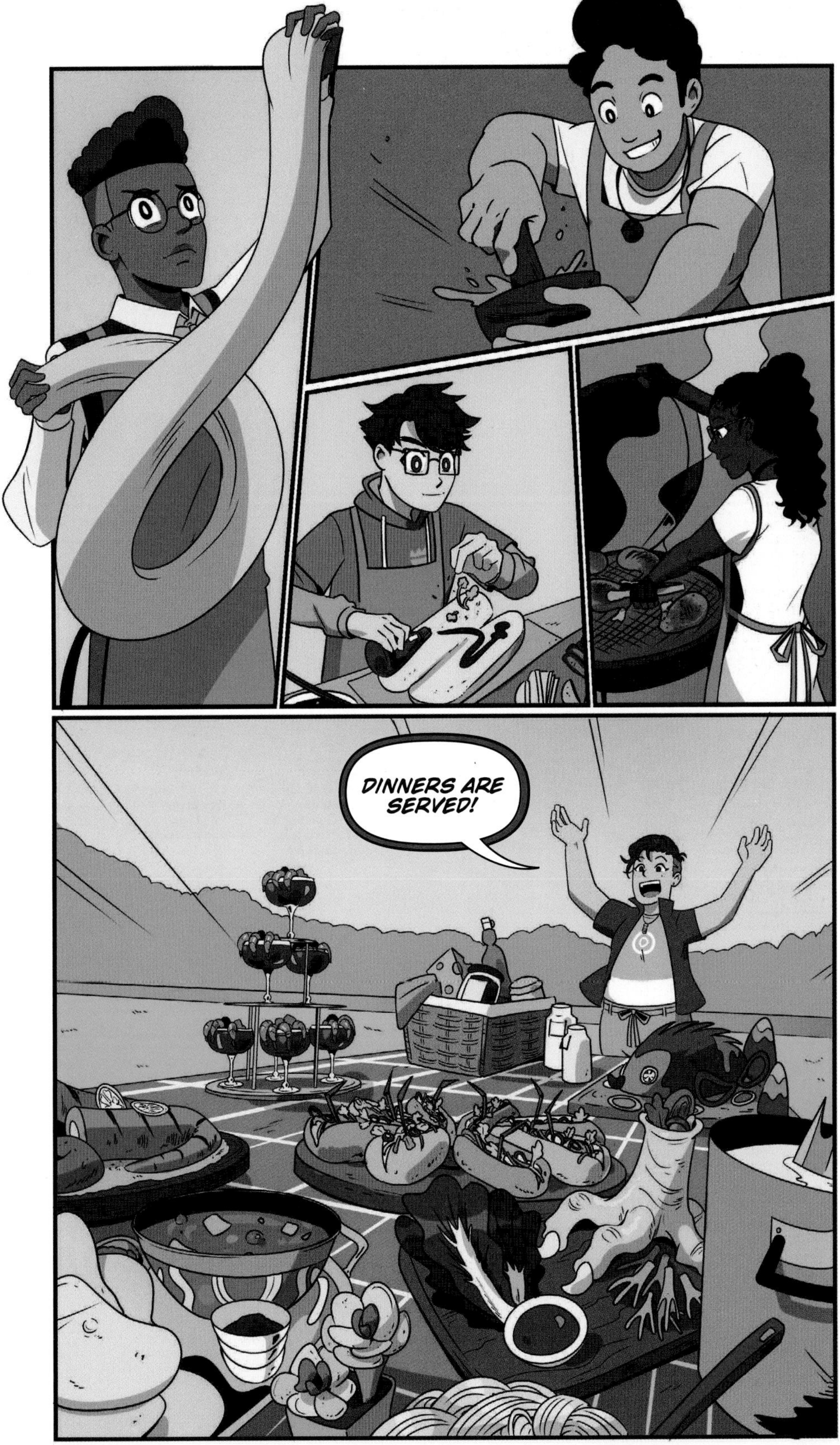
DINNERS ARE SERVED!

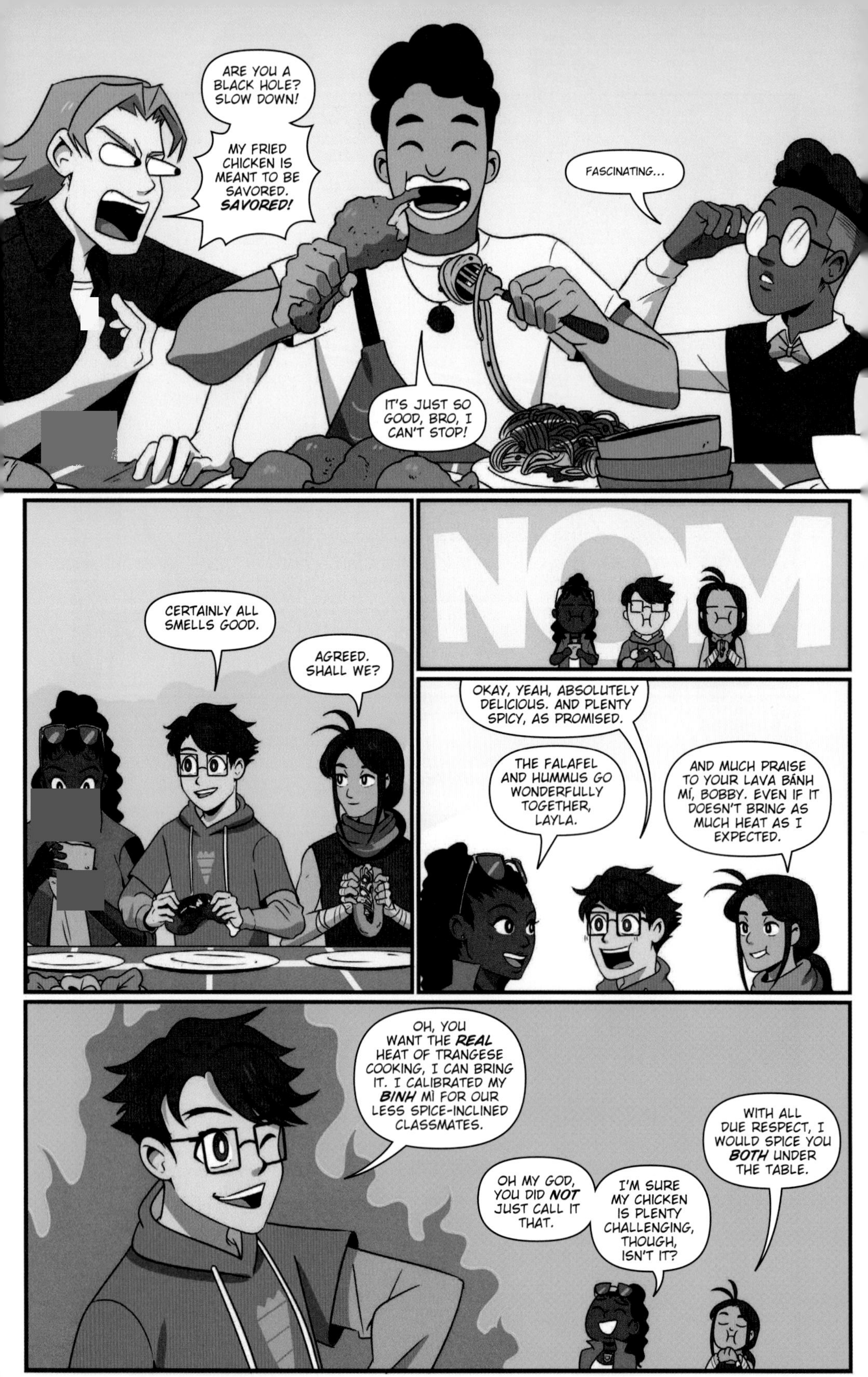
ARE YOU A BLACK HOLE? SLOW DOWN!
MY FRIED CHICKEN IS MEANT TO BE SAVORED. ***SAVORED!***
FASCINATING...
IT'S JUST SO GOOD, BRO, I CAN'T STOP!
CERTAINLY ALL SMELLS GOOD.
AGREED. SHALL WE?
NOM
OKAY, YEAH, ABSOLUTELY DELICIOUS. AND PLENTY SPICY, AS PROMISED.
THE FALAFEL AND HUMMUS GO WONDERFULLY TOGETHER, LAYLA.
AND MUCH PRAISE TO YOUR LAVA BÁNH MÍ, BOBBY. EVEN IF IT DOESN'T BRING AS MUCH HEAT AS I EXPECTED.
OH, YOU WANT THE ***REAL*** HEAT OF TRANGESE COOKING, I CAN BRING IT. I CALIBRATED MY ***BINH*** MÌ FOR OUR LESS SPICE-INCLINED CLASSMATES.
OH MY GOD, YOU DID ***NOT*** JUST CALL IT THAT.
I'M SURE MY CHICKEN IS PLENTY CHALLENGING, THOUGH, ISN'T IT?
WITH ALL DUE RESPECT, I WOULD SPICE YOU ***BOTH*** UNDER THE TABLE.

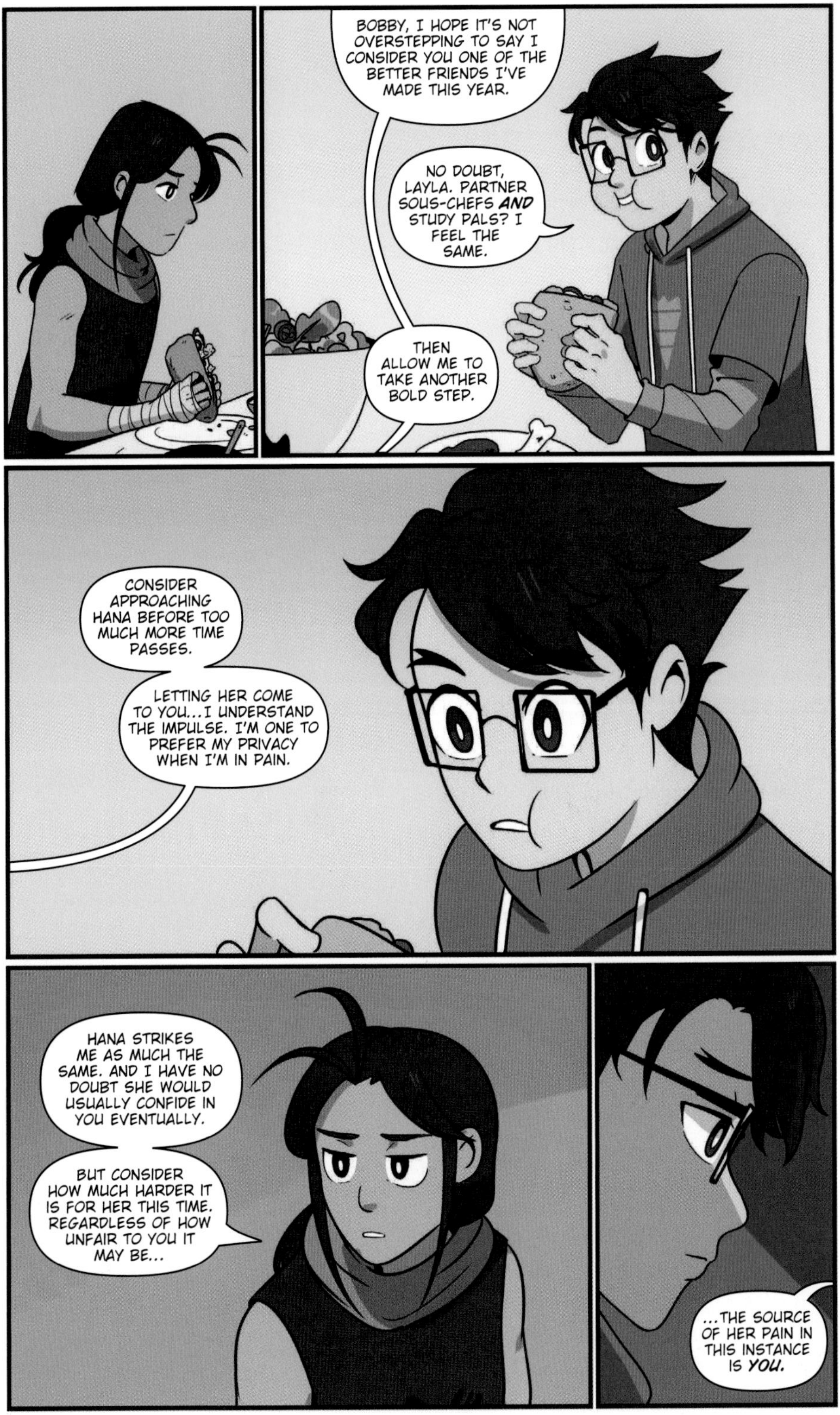
BOBBY, I HOPE IT'S NOT OVERSTEPPING TO SAY I CONSIDER YOU ONE OF THE BETTER FRIENDS I'VE MADE THIS YEAR.
NO DOUBT, LAYLA. PARTNER SOUS-CHEFS **AND** STUDY PALS? I FEEL THE SAME.
THEN ALLOW ME TO TAKE ANOTHER BOLD STEP.
CONSIDER APPROACHING HANA BEFORE TOO MUCH MORE TIME PASSES.
LETTING HER COME TO YOU...I UNDERSTAND THE IMPULSE. I'M ONE TO PREFER MY PRIVACY WHEN I'M IN PAIN.
HANA STRIKES ME AS MUCH THE SAME. AND I HAVE NO DOUBT SHE WOULD USUALLY CONFIDE IN YOU EVENTUALLY.
BUT CONSIDER HOW MUCH HARDER IT IS FOR HER THIS TIME. REGARDLESS OF HOW UNFAIR TO YOU IT MAY BE...
...THE SOURCE OF HER PAIN IN THIS INSTANCE IS ***YOU.***

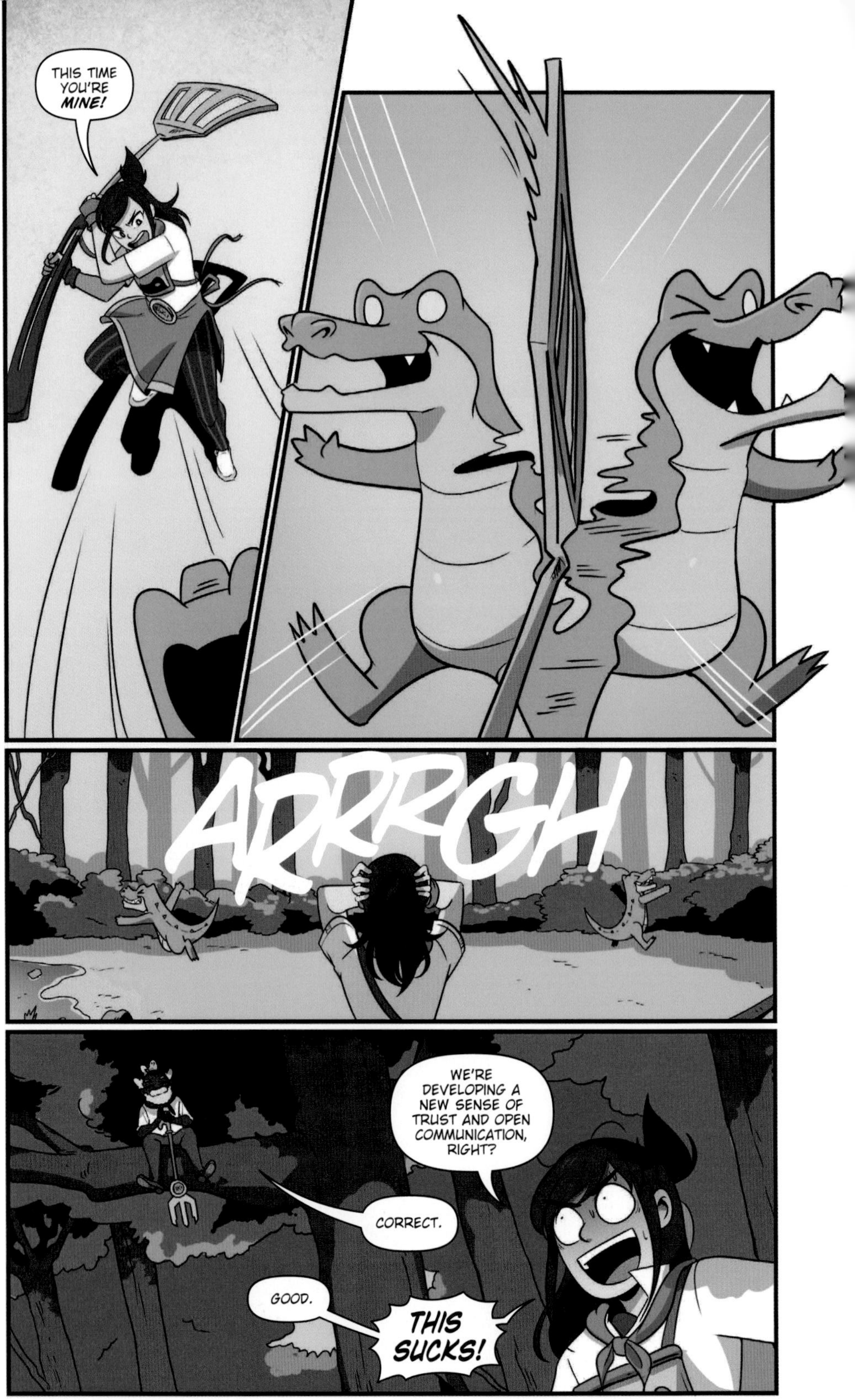
THIS TIME YOU'RE MINE!
ARRRGH
WE'RE DEVELOPING A NEW SENSE OF TRUST AND OPEN COMMUNICATION, RIGHT?
CORRECT.
GOOD.
THIS SUCKS!

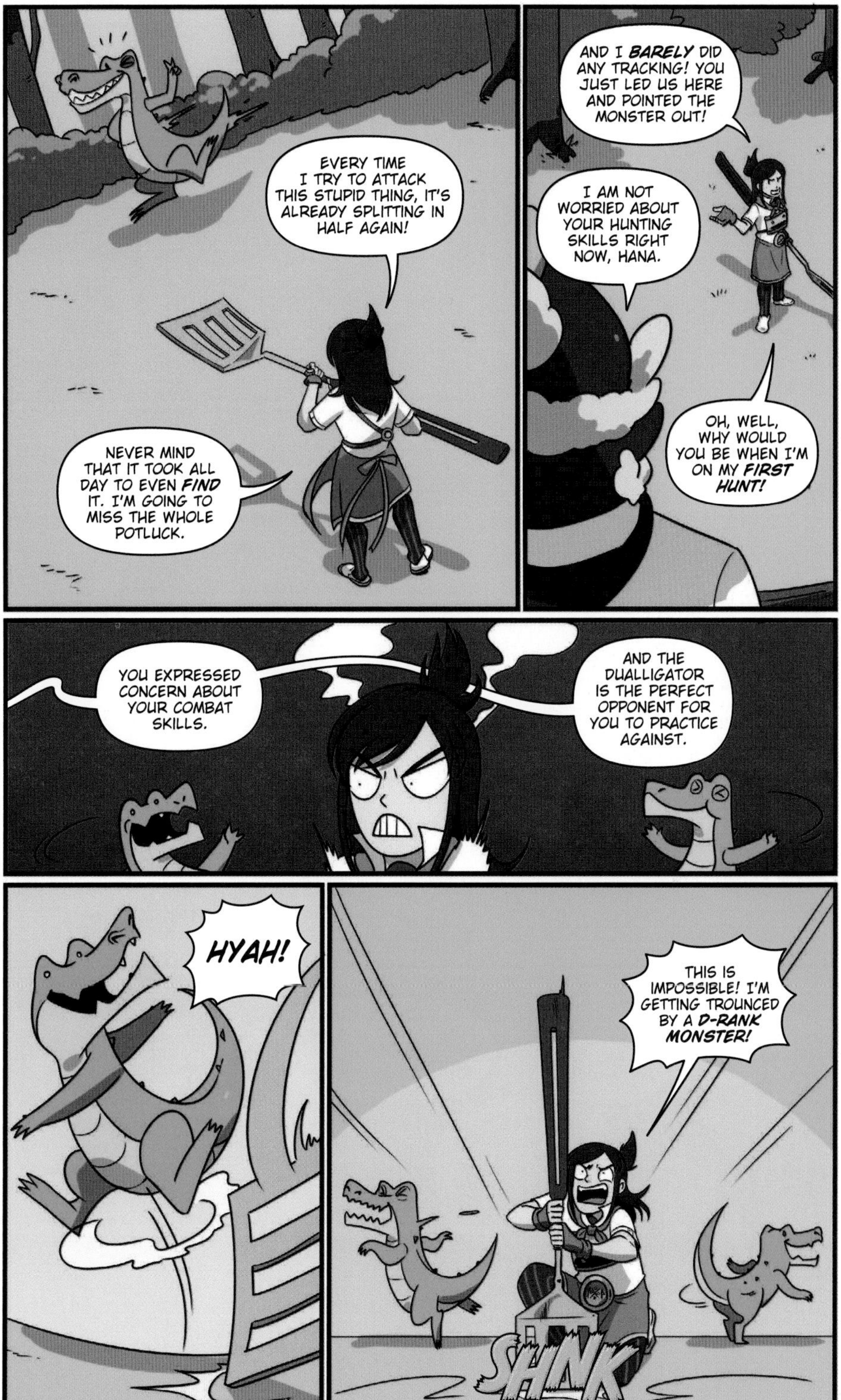
EVERY TIME I TRY TO ATTACK THIS STUPID THING, IT'S ALREADY SPLITTING IN HALF AGAIN!
NEVER MIND THAT IT TOOK ALL DAY TO EVEN FIND IT. I'M GOING TO MISS THE WHOLE POTLUCK.
AND I BARELY DID ANY TRACKING! YOU JUST LED US HERE AND POINTED THE MONSTER OUT!
I AM NOT WORRIED ABOUT YOUR HUNTING SKILLS RIGHT NOW, HANA.
OH, WELL, WHY WOULD YOU BE WHEN I'M ON MY FIRST HUNT!
YOU EXPRESSED CONCERN ABOUT YOUR COMBAT SKILLS.
AND THE DUALLIGATOR IS THE PERFECT OPPONENT FOR YOU TO PRACTICE AGAINST.
HYAH!
THIS IS IMPOSSIBLE! I'M GETTING TROUNCED BY A D-RANK MONSTER!
SHNK

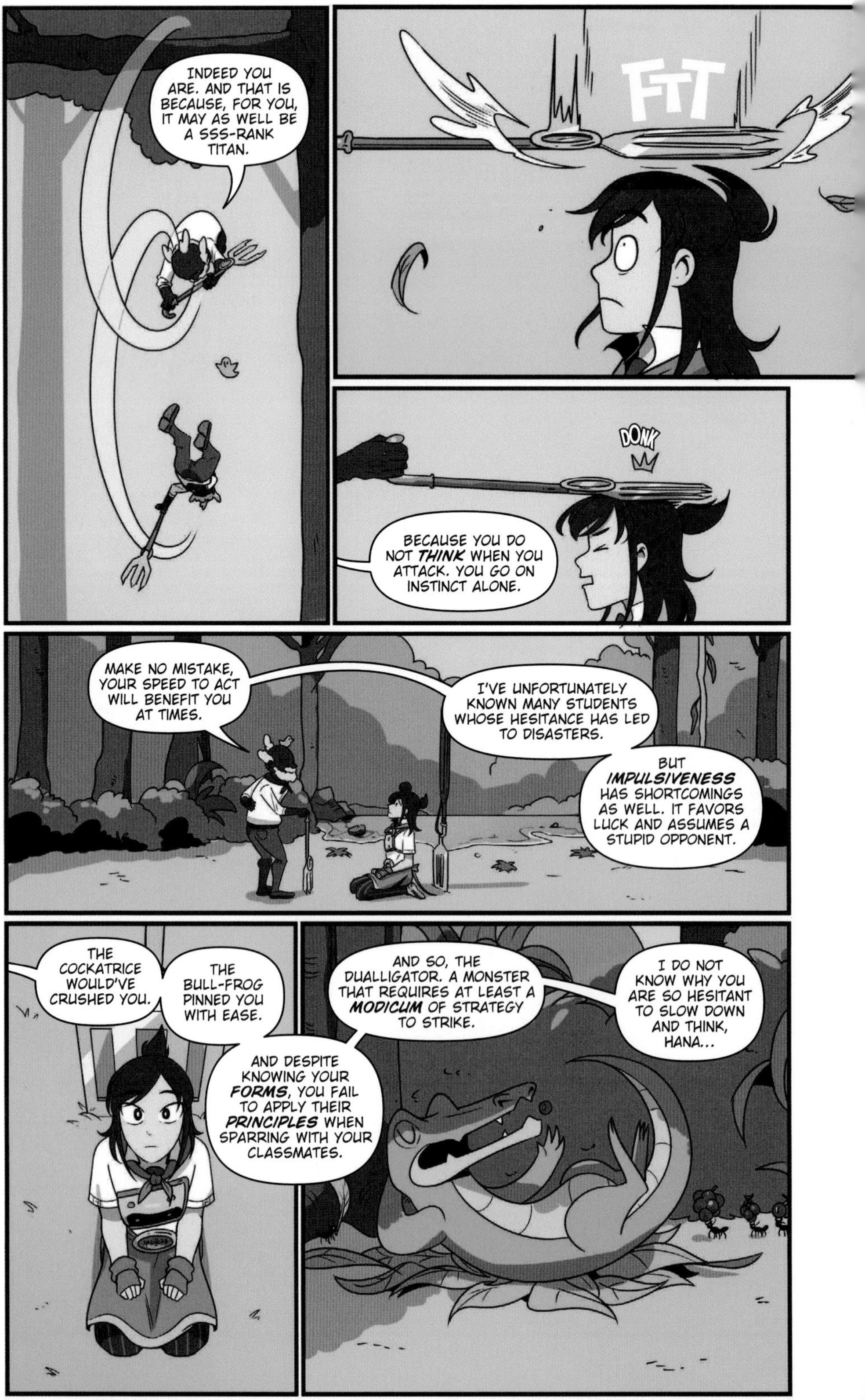
INDEED YOU ARE. AND THAT IS BECAUSE, FOR YOU, IT MAY AS WELL BE A SSS-RANK TITAN.
FTT
DONK
BECAUSE YOU DO NOT *THINK* WHEN YOU ATTACK. YOU GO ON INSTINCT ALONE.
MAKE NO MISTAKE, YOUR SPEED TO ACT WILL BENEFIT YOU AT TIMES.
I'VE UNFORTUNATELY KNOWN MANY STUDENTS WHOSE HESITANCE HAS LED TO DISASTERS.
BUT ***IMPULSIVENESS*** HAS SHORTCOMINGS AS WELL. IT FAVORS LUCK AND ASSUMES A STUPID OPPONENT.
THE COCKATRICE WOULD'VE CRUSHED YOU.
THE BULL-FROG PINNED YOU WITH EASE.
AND DESPITE KNOWING YOUR ***FORMS***, YOU FAIL TO APPLY THEIR ***PRINCIPLES*** WHEN SPARRING WITH YOUR CLASSMATES.
AND SO, THE DUALLIGATOR. A MONSTER THAT REQUIRES AT LEAST A ***MODICUM*** OF STRATEGY TO STRIKE.
I DO NOT KNOW WHY YOU ARE SO HESITANT TO SLOW DOWN AND THINK, HANA...

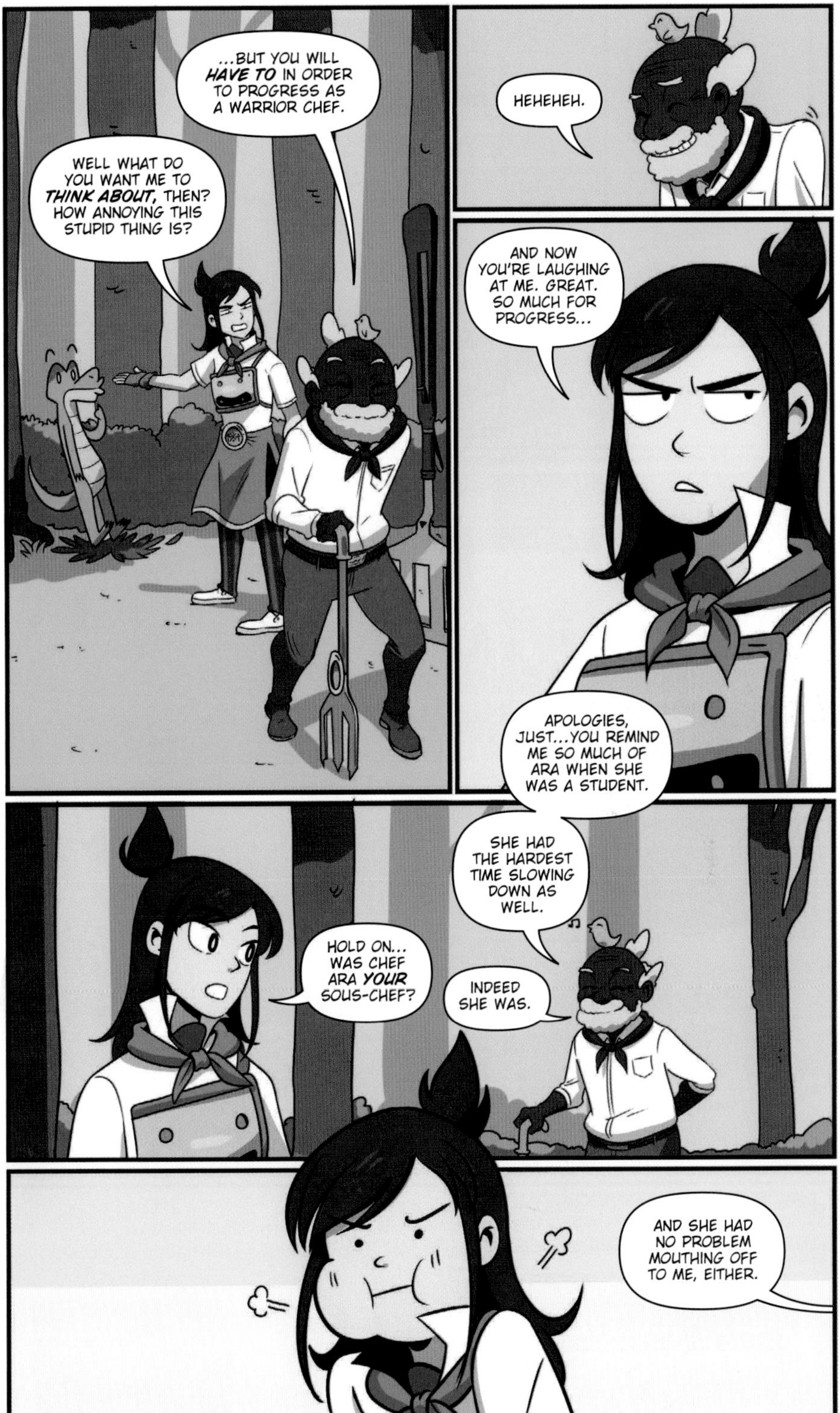
WELL WHAT DO YOU WANT ME TO THINK ABOUT, THEN? HOW ANNOYING THIS STUPID THING IS?
...BUT YOU WILL HAVE TO IN ORDER TO PROGRESS AS A WARRIOR CHEF.
HEHEHEH.
AND NOW YOU'RE LAUGHING AT ME. GREAT. SO MUCH FOR PROGRESS...
APOLOGIES, JUST...YOU REMIND ME SO MUCH OF ARA WHEN SHE WAS A STUDENT.
SHE HAD THE HARDEST TIME SLOWING DOWN AS WELL.
HOLD ON... WAS CHEF ARA YOUR SOUS-CHEF?
INDEED SHE WAS.
AND SHE HAD NO PROBLEM MOUTHING OFF TO ME, EITHER.

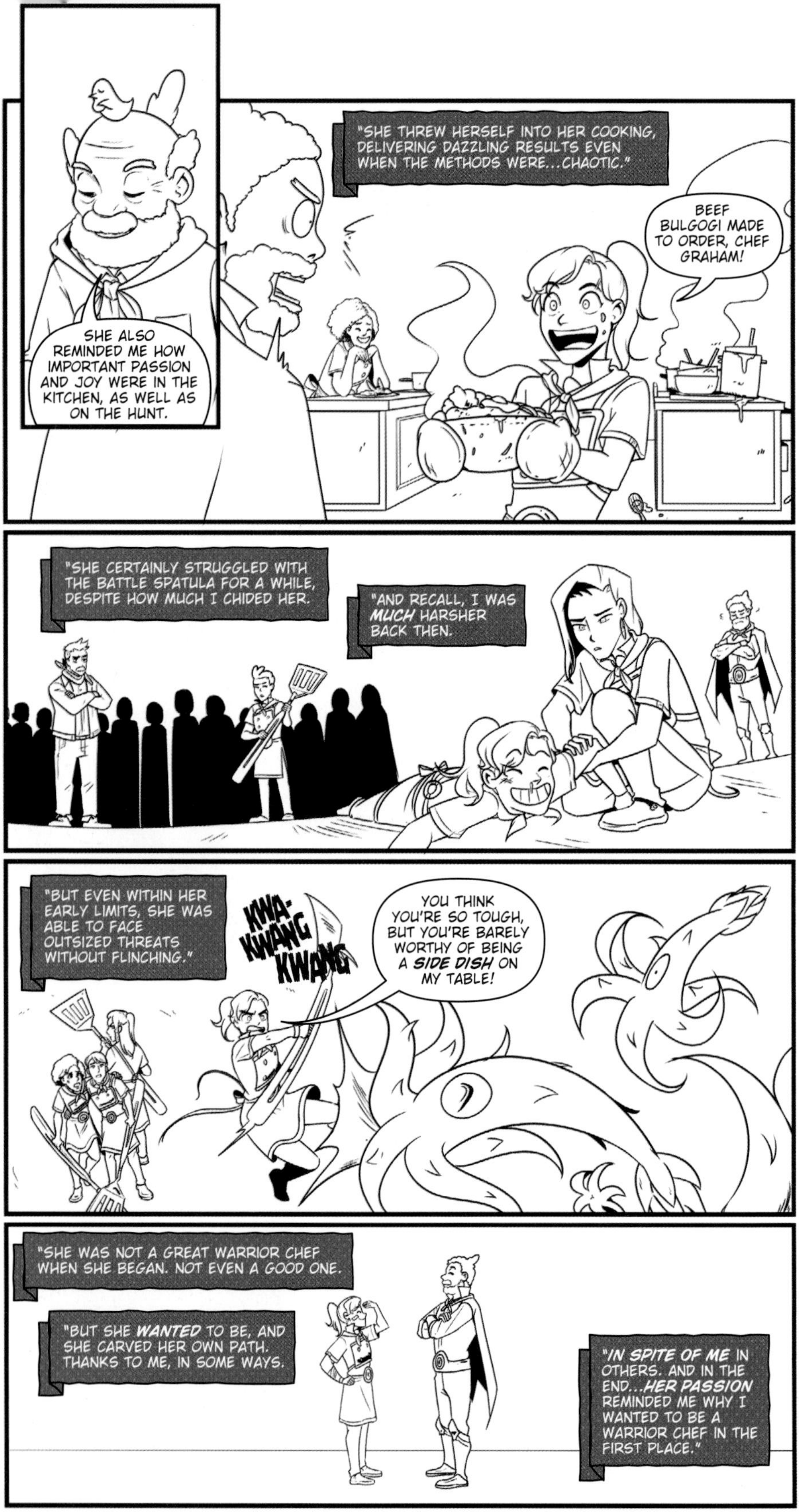

"SHE THREW HERSELF INTO HER COOKING, DELIVERING DAZZLING RESULTS EVEN WHEN THE METHODS WERE...CHAOTIC."
BEEF BULGOGI MADE TO ORDER, CHEF GRAHAM!
SHE ALSO REMINDED ME HOW IMPORTANT PASSION AND JOY WERE IN THE KITCHEN, AS WELL AS ON THE HUNT.
"SHE CERTAINLY STRUGGLED WITH THE BATTLE SPATULA FOR A WHILE, DESPITE HOW MUCH I CHIDED HER.
"AND RECALL, I WAS *MUCH* HARSHER BACK THEN.
"BUT EVEN WITHIN HER EARLY LIMITS, SHE WAS ABLE TO FACE OUTSIZED THREATS WITHOUT FLINCHING."
KWA-KWANG KWANG
YOU THINK YOU'RE SO TOUGH, BUT YOU'RE BARELY WORTHY OF BEING A *SIDE DISH* ON MY TABLE!
"SHE WAS NOT A GREAT WARRIOR CHEF WHEN SHE BEGAN. NOT EVEN A GOOD ONE.
"BUT SHE *WANTED* TO BE, AND SHE CARVED HER OWN PATH. THANKS TO ME, IN SOME WAYS.
"*IN SPITE OF ME* IN OTHERS. AND IN THE END...*HER PASSION* REMINDED ME WHY I WANTED TO BE A WARRIOR CHEF IN THE FIRST PLACE."

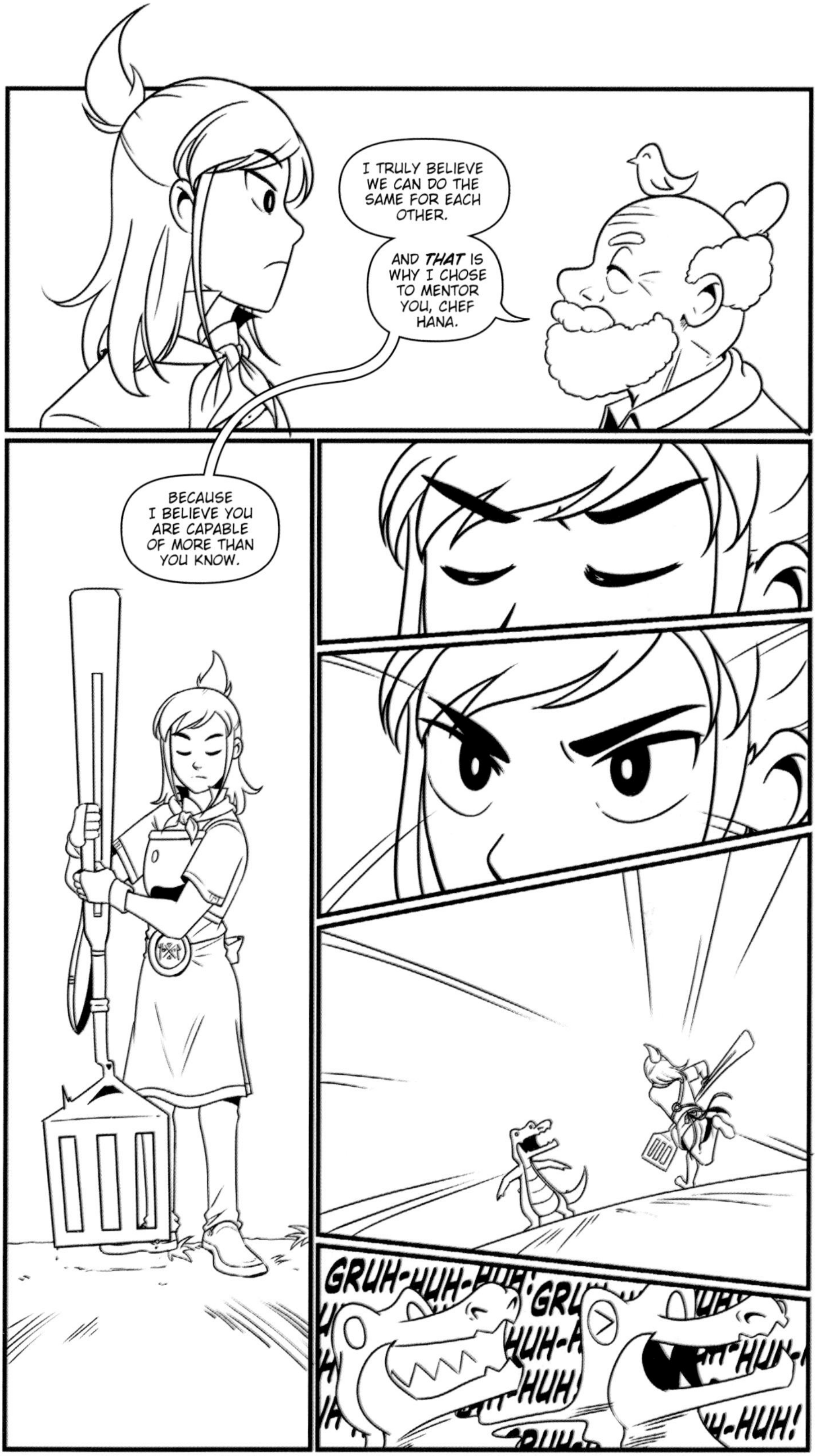
I TRULY BELIEVE WE CAN DO THE SAME FOR EACH OTHER.
AND *THAT* IS WHY I CHOSE TO MENTOR YOU, CHEF HANA.
BECAUSE I BELIEVE YOU ARE CAPABLE OF MORE THAN YOU KNOW.
GRUH-HUH-HUH! GRUH-HUH-HUH-HUH! HUH-HUH!

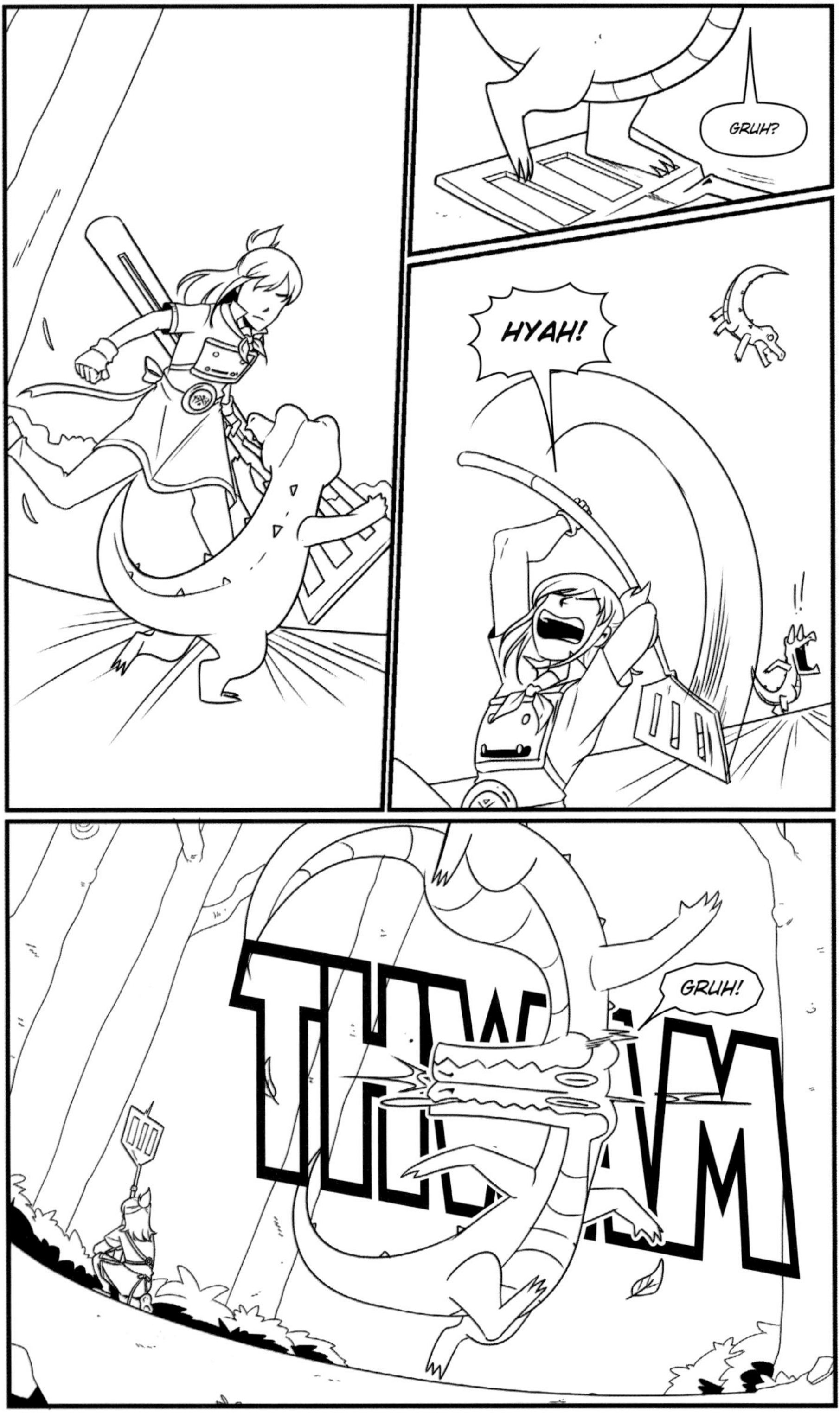
GRUH?
HYAH!
!!
THWAM
GRUH!

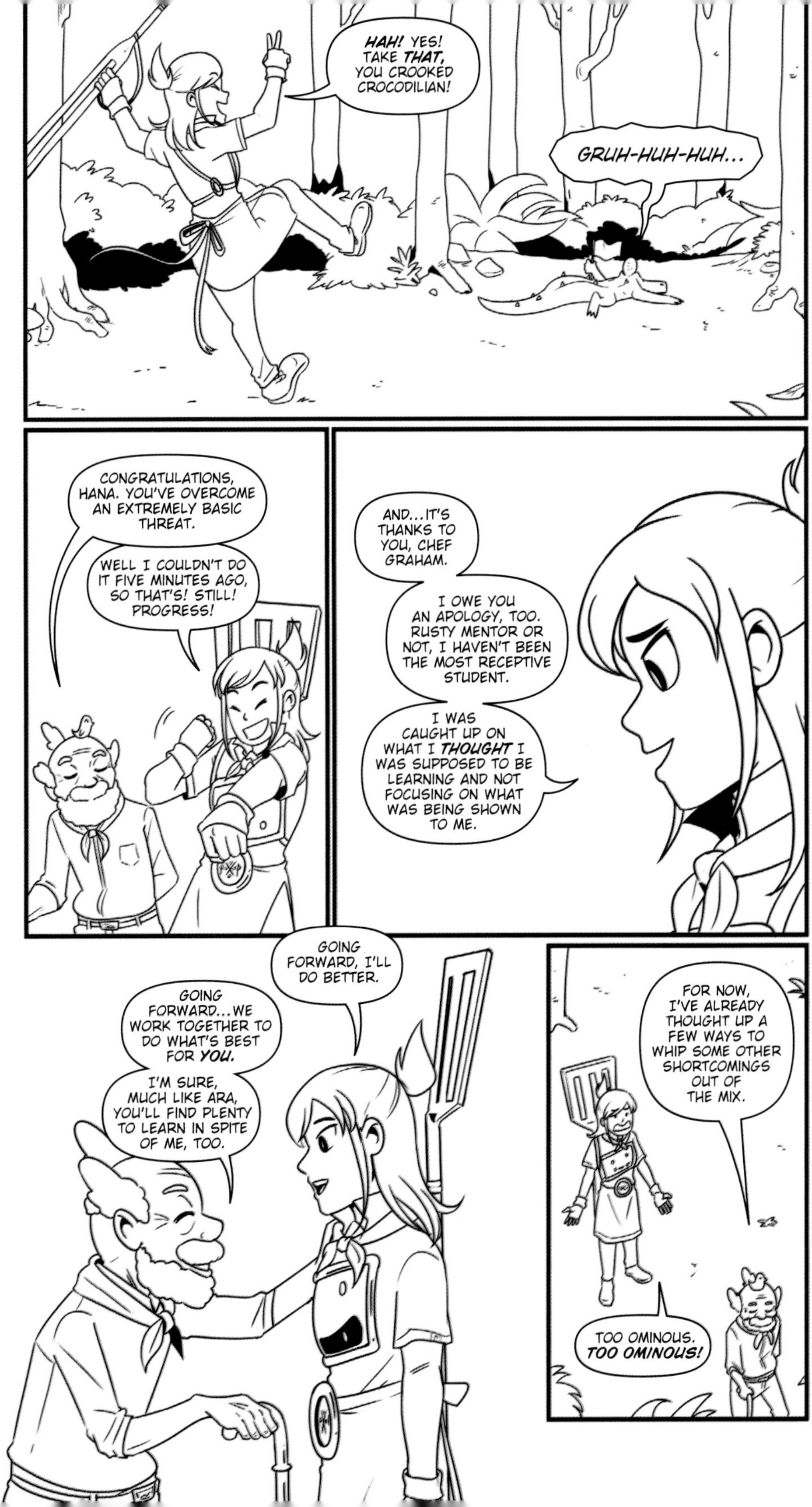
HAH! YES! TAKE THAT, YOU CROOKED CROCODILIAN!
GRUH-HUH-HUH...
CONGRATULATIONS, HANA. YOU'VE OVERCOME AN EXTREMELY BASIC THREAT.
WELL I COULDN'T DO IT FIVE MINUTES AGO, SO THAT'S! STILL! PROGRESS!
AND...IT'S THANKS TO YOU, CHEF GRAHAM.
I OWE YOU AN APOLOGY, TOO. RUSTY MENTOR OR NOT, I HAVEN'T BEEN THE MOST RECEPTIVE STUDENT.
I WAS CAUGHT UP ON WHAT I THOUGHT I WAS SUPPOSED TO BE LEARNING AND NOT FOCUSING ON WHAT WAS BEING SHOWN TO ME.
GOING FORWARD, I'LL DO BETTER.
GOING FORWARD...WE WORK TOGETHER TO DO WHAT'S BEST FOR YOU.
I'M SURE, MUCH LIKE ARA, YOU'LL FIND PLENTY TO LEARN IN SPITE OF ME, TOO.
FOR NOW, I'VE ALREADY THOUGHT UP A FEW WAYS TO WHIP SOME OTHER SHORTCOMINGS OUT OF THE MIX.
TOO OMINOUS. TOO OMINOUS!

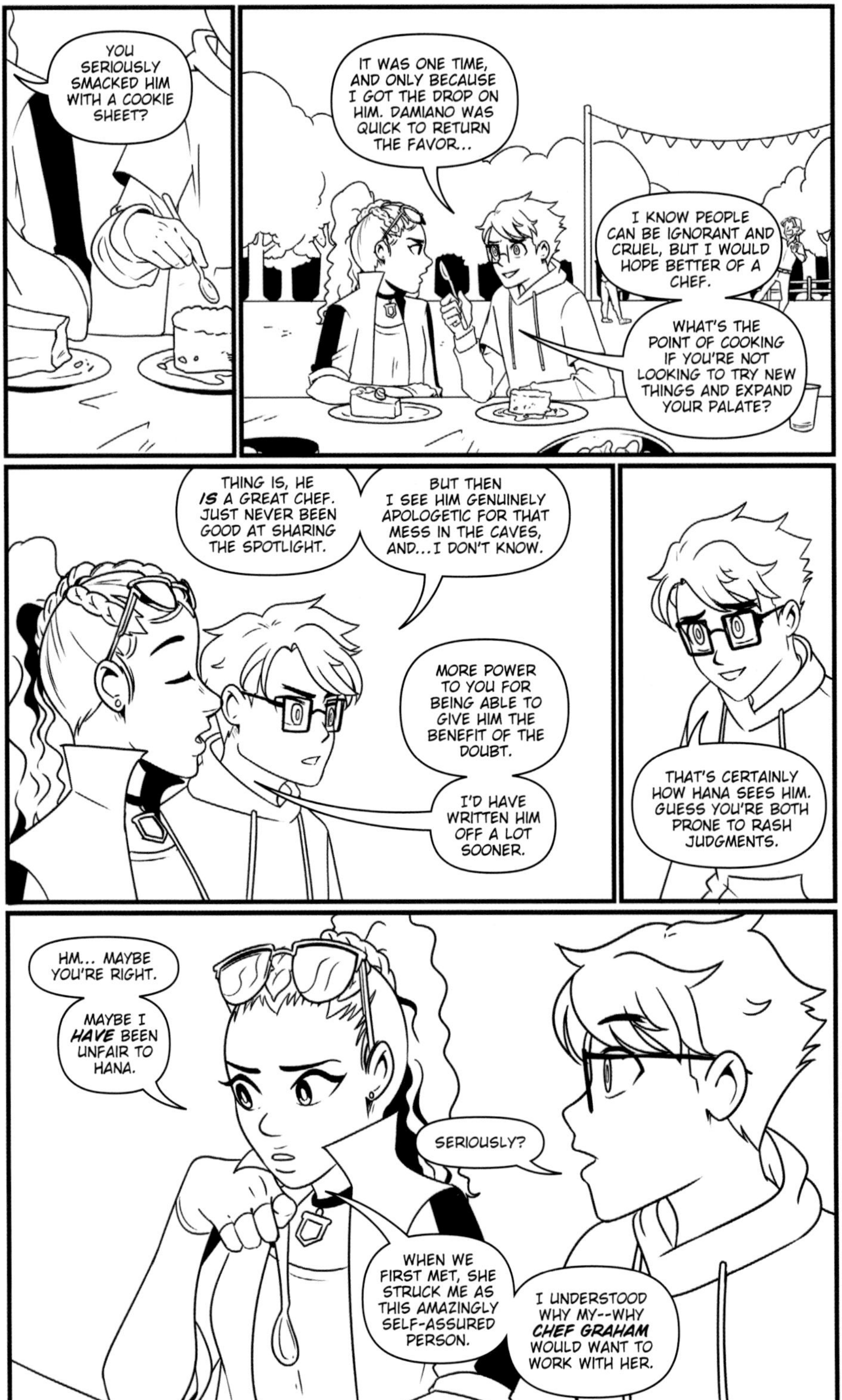
YOU SERIOUSLY SMACKED HIM WITH A COOKIE SHEET?
IT WAS ONE TIME, AND ONLY BECAUSE I GOT THE DROP ON HIM. DAMIANO WAS QUICK TO RETURN THE FAVOR...
I KNOW PEOPLE CAN BE IGNORANT AND CRUEL, BUT I WOULD HOPE BETTER OF A CHEF.
WHAT'S THE POINT OF COOKING IF YOU'RE NOT LOOKING TO TRY NEW THINGS AND EXPAND YOUR PALATE?
THING IS, HE *IS* A GREAT CHEF. JUST NEVER BEEN GOOD AT SHARING THE SPOTLIGHT.
BUT THEN I SEE HIM GENUINELY APOLOGETIC FOR THAT MESS IN THE CAVES, AND...I DON'T KNOW.
MORE POWER TO YOU FOR BEING ABLE TO GIVE HIM THE BENEFIT OF THE DOUBT.
I'D HAVE WRITTEN HIM OFF A LOT SOONER.
THAT'S CERTAINLY HOW HANA SEES HIM. GUESS YOU'RE BOTH PRONE TO RASH JUDGMENTS.
HM... MAYBE YOU'RE RIGHT.
MAYBE I ***HAVE*** BEEN UNFAIR TO HANA.
SERIOUSLY?
WHEN WE FIRST MET, SHE STRUCK ME AS THIS AMAZINGLY SELF-ASSURED PERSON.
I UNDERSTOOD WHY MY--WHY ***CHEF GRAHAM*** WOULD WANT TO WORK WITH HER.

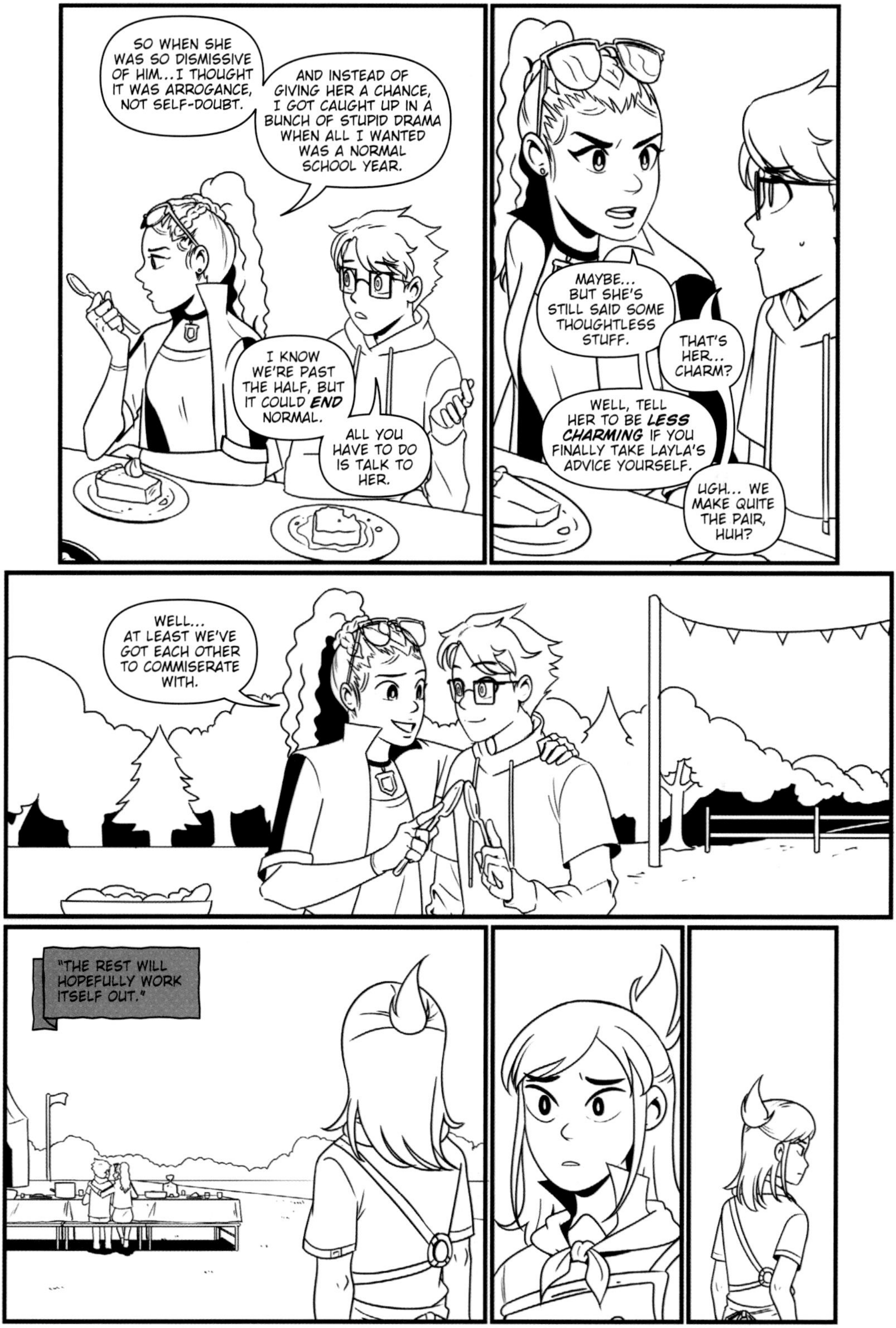
SO WHEN SHE WAS SO DISMISSIVE OF HIM...I THOUGHT IT WAS ARROGANCE, NOT SELF-DOUBT.
AND INSTEAD OF GIVING HER A CHANCE, I GOT CAUGHT UP IN A BUNCH OF STUPID DRAMA WHEN ALL I WANTED WAS A NORMAL SCHOOL YEAR.
I KNOW WE'RE PAST THE HALF, BUT IT COULD END NORMAL.
ALL YOU HAVE TO DO IS TALK TO HER.
MAYBE... BUT SHE'S STILL SAID SOME THOUGHTLESS STUFF.
THAT'S HER... CHARM?
WELL, TELL HER TO BE LESS CHARMING IF YOU FINALLY TAKE LAYLA'S ADVICE YOURSELF.
UGH... WE MAKE QUITE THE PAIR, HUH?
WELL... AT LEAST WE'VE GOT EACH OTHER TO COMMISERATE WITH.
"THE REST WILL HOPEFULLY WORK ITSELF OUT."

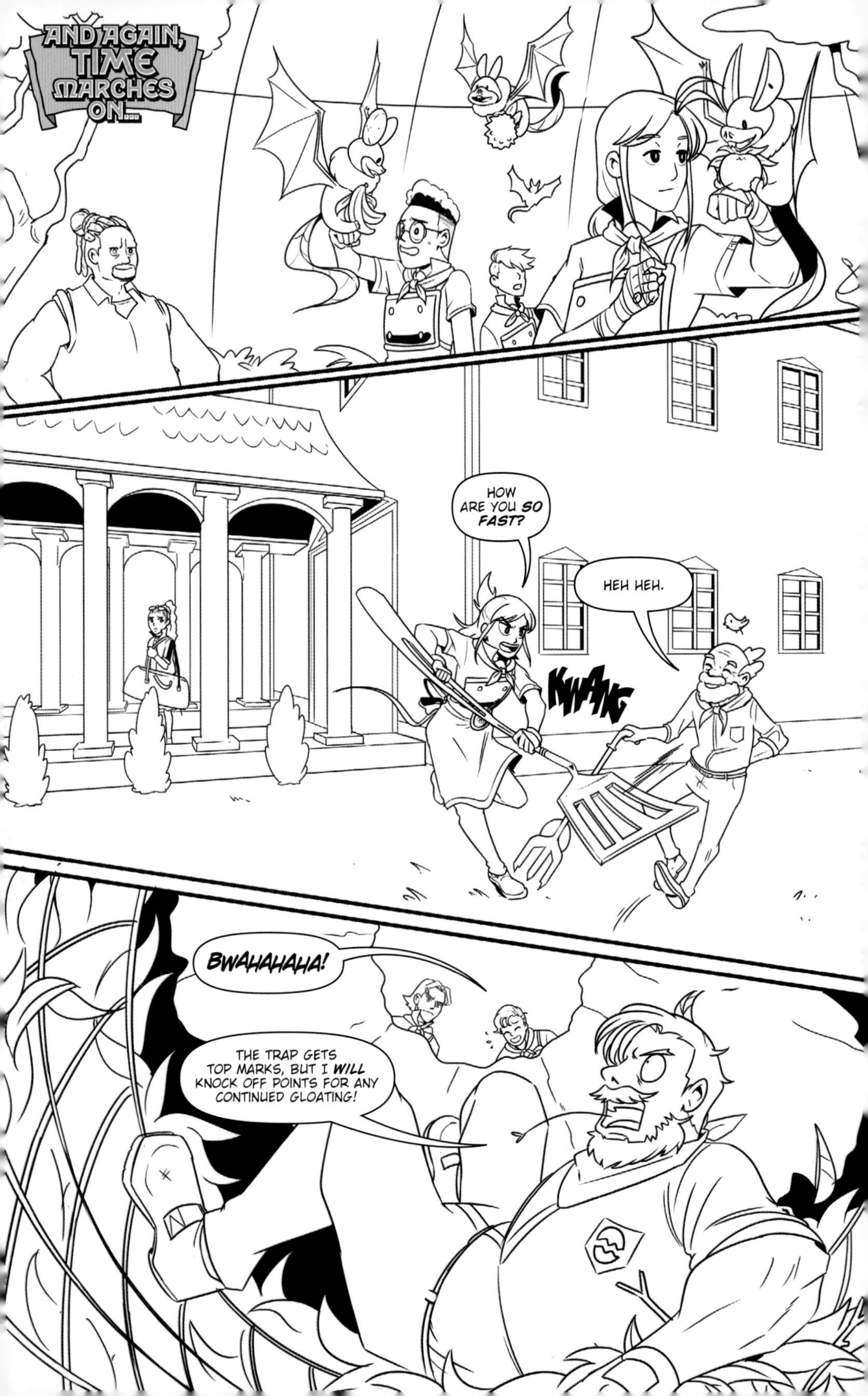
AND AGAIN, TIME MARCHES ON...
HOW ARE YOU SO FAST?
HEH HEH.
KWANG
BWAHAHAHA!
THE TRAP GETS TOP MARKS, BUT I WILL KNOCK OFF POINTS FOR ANY CONTINUED GLOATING!

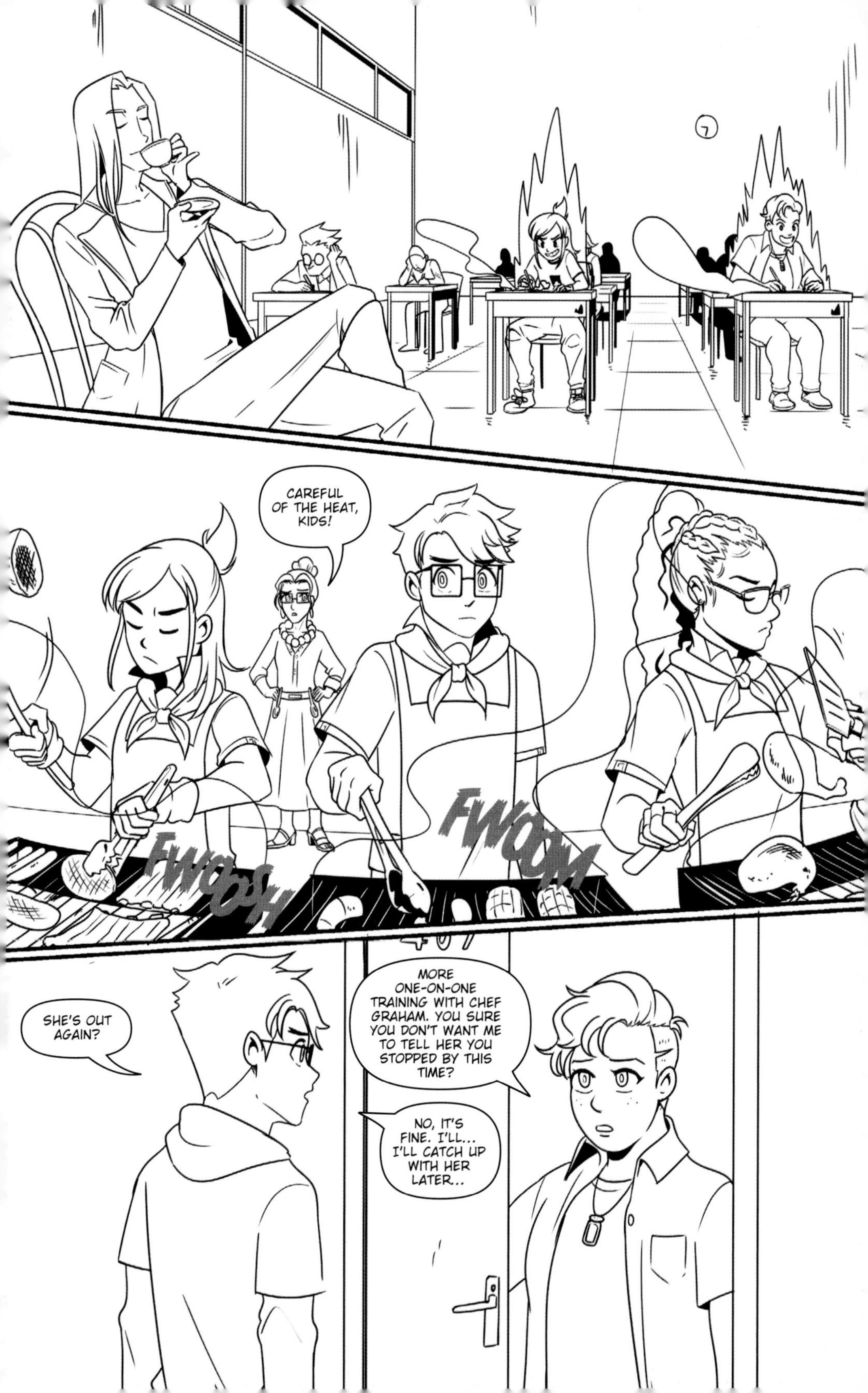
CAREFUL OF THE HEAT, KIDS!
FWOOSH
FWOOM
SHE'S OUT AGAIN?
MORE ONE-ON-ONE TRAINING WITH CHEF GRAHAM. YOU SURE YOU DON'T WANT ME TO TELL HER YOU STOPPED BY THIS TIME?
NO, IT'S FINE. I'LL... I'LL CATCH UP WITH HER LATER...

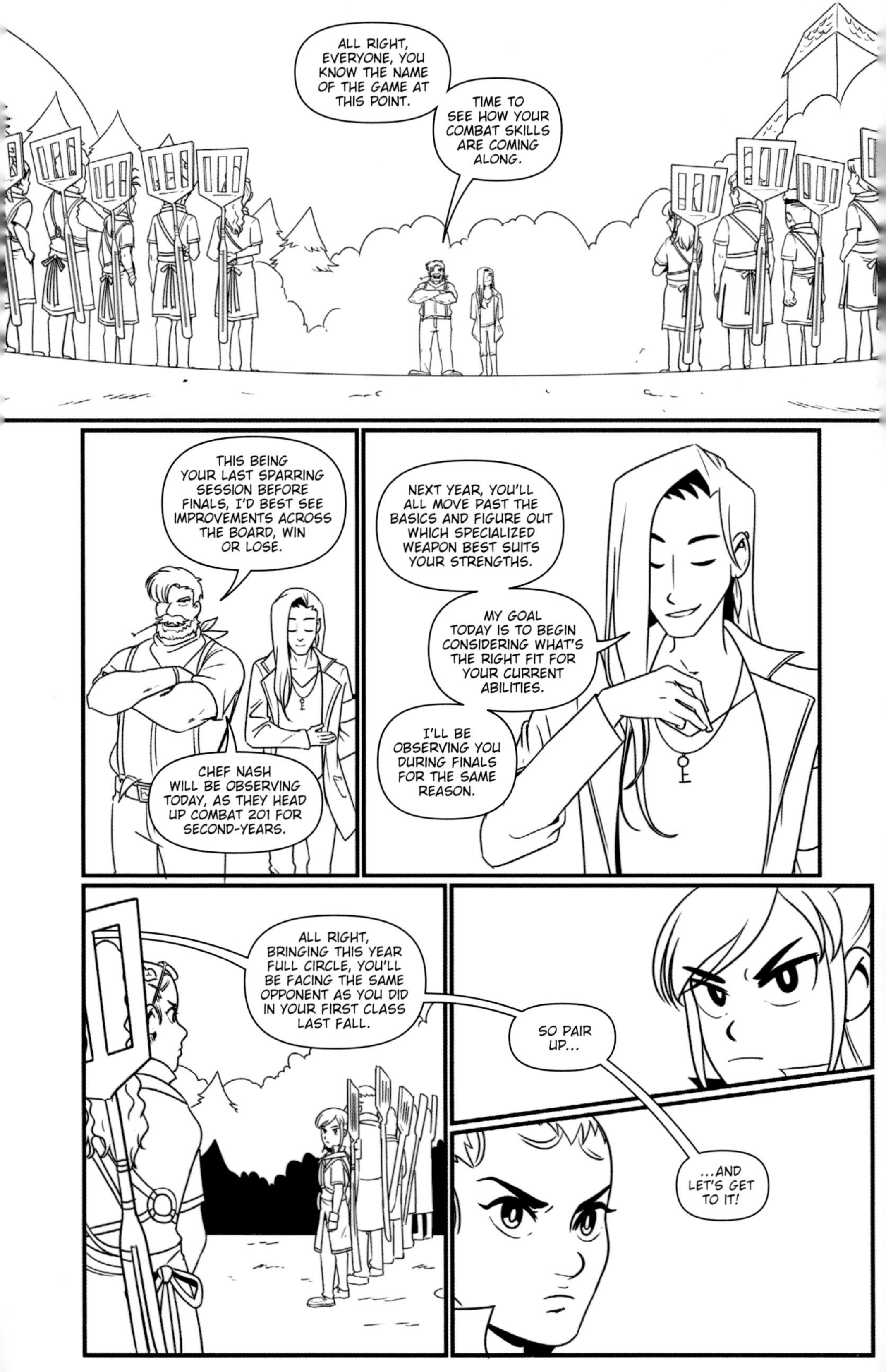
ALL RIGHT, EVERYONE, YOU KNOW THE NAME OF THE GAME AT THIS POINT.
TIME TO SEE HOW YOUR COMBAT SKILLS ARE COMING ALONG.
THIS BEING YOUR LAST SPARRING SESSION BEFORE FINALS, I'D BEST SEE IMPROVEMENTS ACROSS THE BOARD, WIN OR LOSE.
CHEF NASH WILL BE OBSERVING TODAY, AS THEY HEAD UP COMBAT 201 FOR SECOND-YEARS.
NEXT YEAR, YOU'LL ALL MOVE PAST THE BASICS AND FIGURE OUT WHICH SPECIALIZED WEAPON BEST SUITS YOUR STRENGTHS.
MY GOAL TODAY IS TO BEGIN CONSIDERING WHAT'S THE RIGHT FIT FOR YOUR CURRENT ABILITIES.
I'LL BE OBSERVING YOU DURING FINALS FOR THE SAME REASON.
ALL RIGHT, BRINGING THIS YEAR FULL CIRCLE, YOU'LL BE FACING THE SAME OPPONENT AS YOU DID IN YOUR FIRST CLASS LAST FALL.
SO PAIR UP...
...AND LET'S GET TO IT!

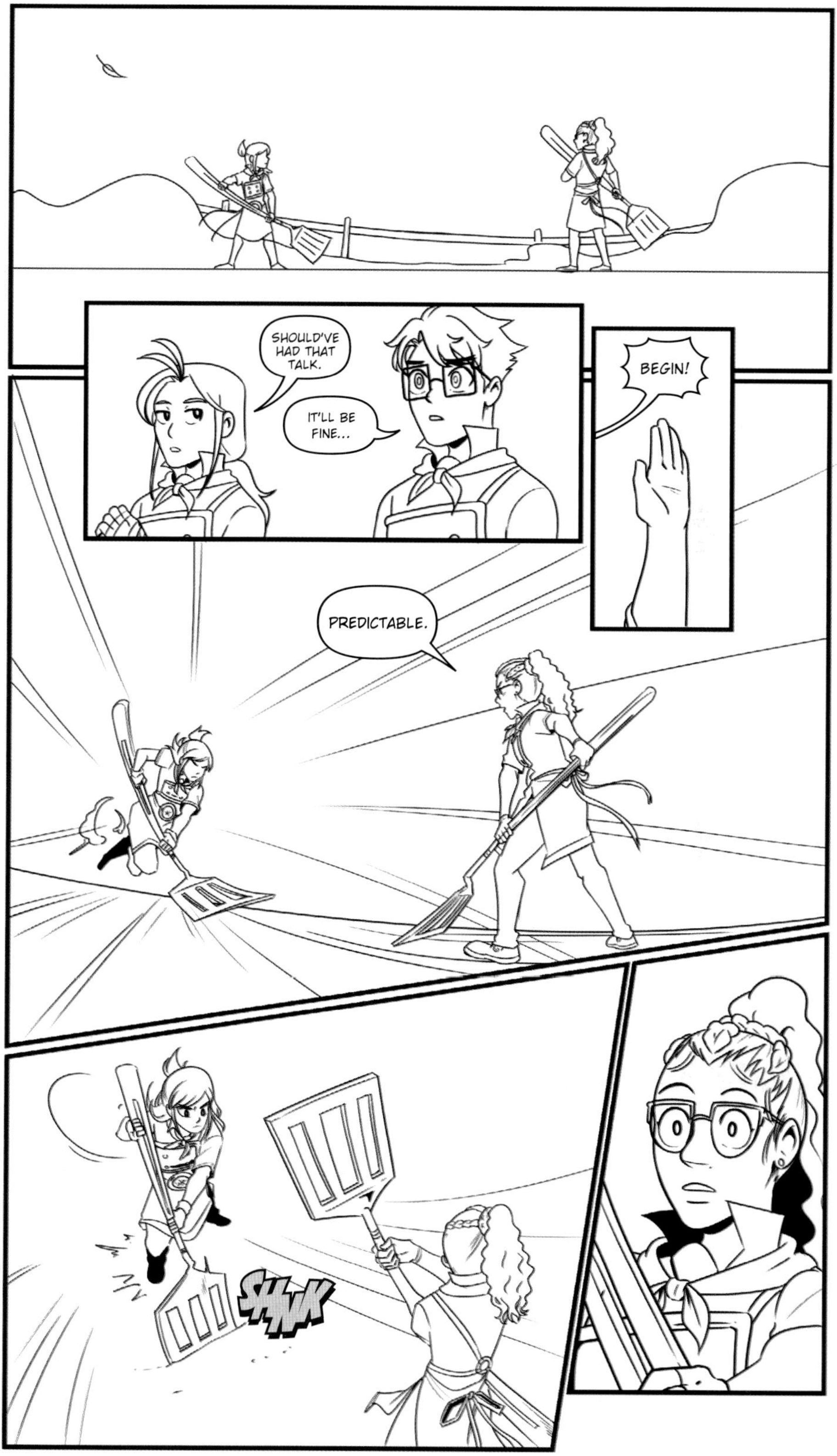
SHOULD'VE HAD THAT TALK.
IT'LL BE FINE...
BEGIN!
PREDICTABLE.
SHNK

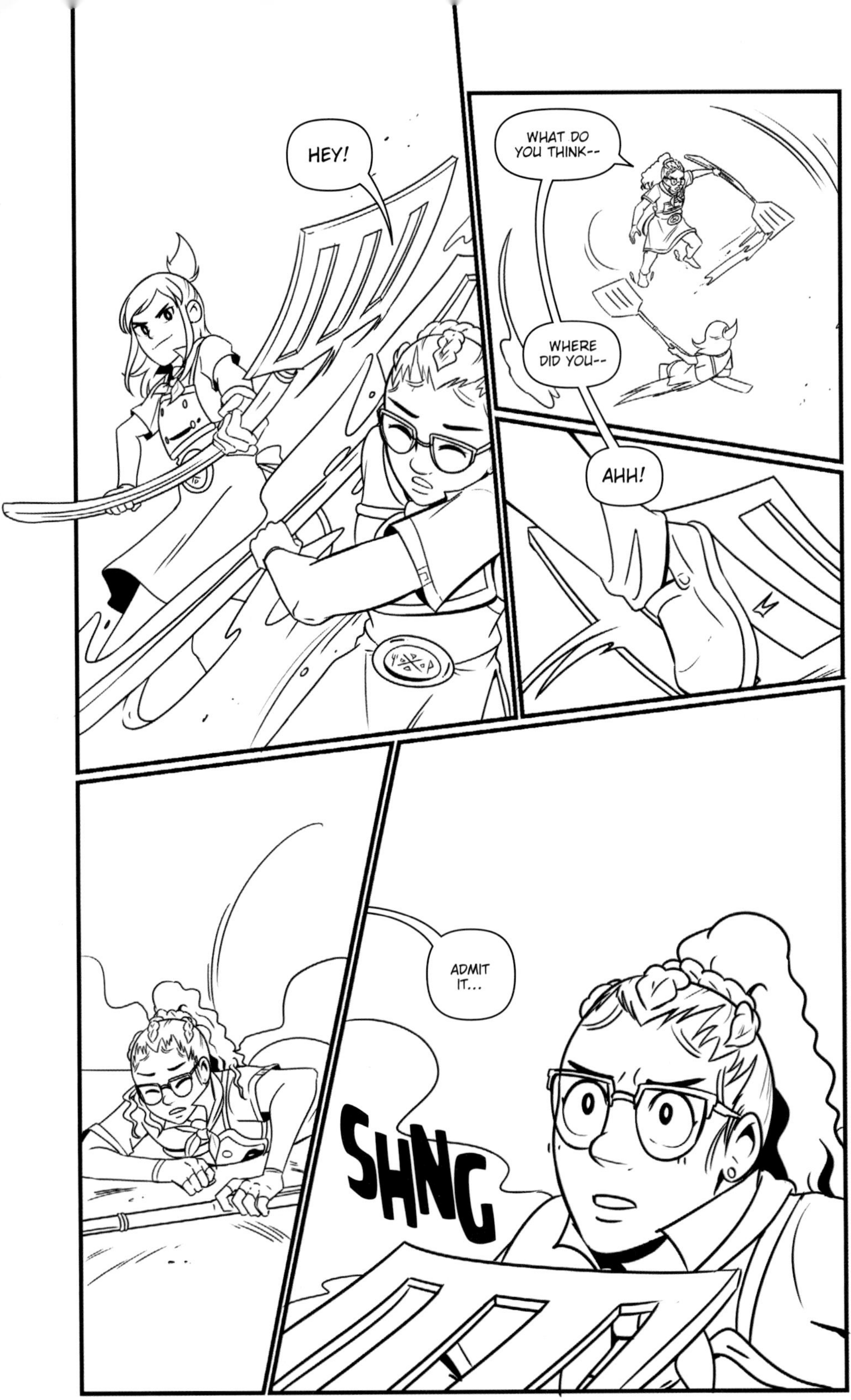
HEY!
WHAT DO YOU THINK--
WHERE DID YOU--
AHH!
ADMIT IT...
SHNG

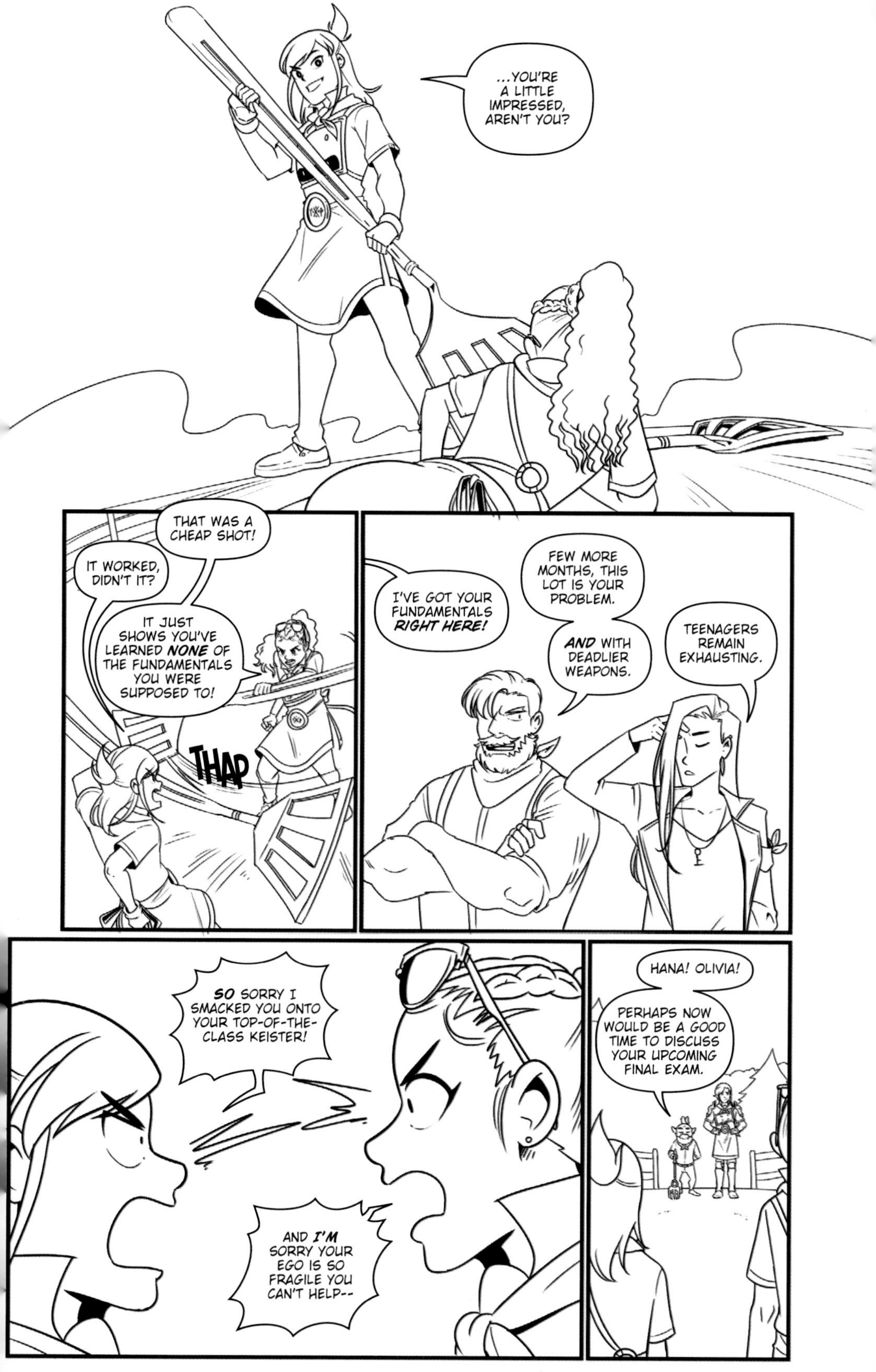
...YOU'RE A LITTLE IMPRESSED, AREN'T YOU?
THAT WAS A CHEAP SHOT!
IT WORKED, DIDN'T IT?
IT JUST SHOWS YOU'VE LEARNED NONE OF THE FUNDAMENTALS YOU WERE SUPPOSED TO!
THAP
I'VE GOT YOUR FUNDAMENTALS RIGHT HERE!
FEW MORE MONTHS, THIS LOT IS YOUR PROBLEM.
AND WITH DEADLIER WEAPONS.
TEENAGERS REMAIN EXHAUSTING.
SO SORRY I SMACKED YOU ONTO YOUR TOP-OF-THE-CLASS KEISTER!
AND I'M SORRY YOUR EGO IS SO FRAGILE YOU CAN'T HELP--
HANA! OLIVIA!
PERHAPS NOW WOULD BE A GOOD TIME TO DISCUSS YOUR UPCOMING FINAL EXAM.

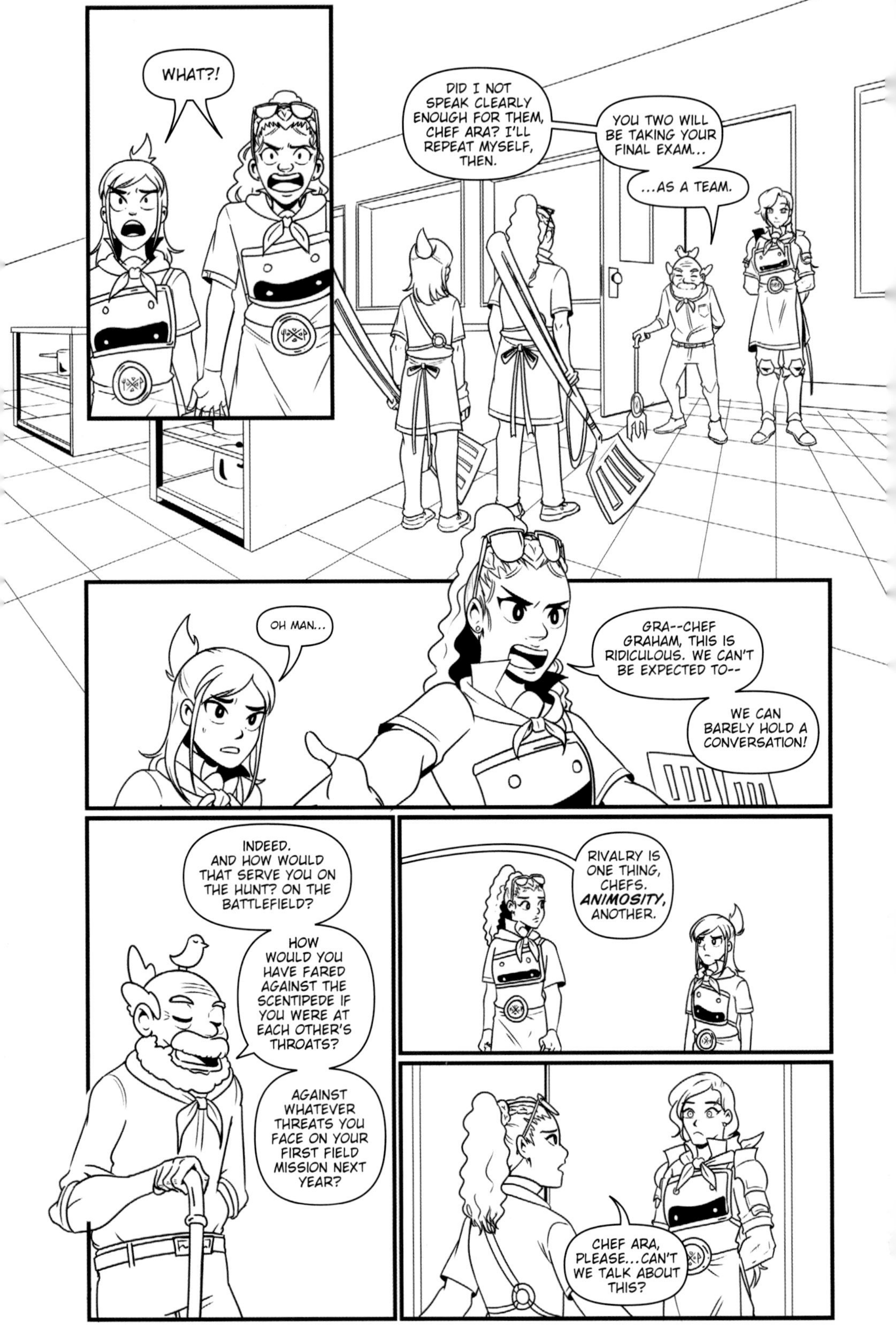
WHAT?!
DID I NOT SPEAK CLEARLY ENOUGH FOR THEM, CHEF ARA? I'LL REPEAT MYSELF, THEN.
YOU TWO WILL BE TAKING YOUR FINAL EXAM...
...AS A TEAM.
OH MAN...
GRA--CHEF GRAHAM, THIS IS RIDICULOUS. WE CAN'T BE EXPECTED TO--
WE CAN BARELY HOLD A CONVERSATION!
INDEED. AND HOW WOULD THAT SERVE YOU ON THE HUNT? ON THE BATTLEFIELD?
HOW WOULD YOU HAVE FARED AGAINST THE SCENTIPEDE IF YOU WERE AT EACH OTHER'S THROATS?
AGAINST WHATEVER THREATS YOU FACE ON YOUR FIRST FIELD MISSION NEXT YEAR?
RIVALRY IS ONE THING, CHEFS. ***ANIMOSITY,*** ANOTHER.
CHEF ARA, PLEASE...CAN'T WE TALK ABOUT THIS?

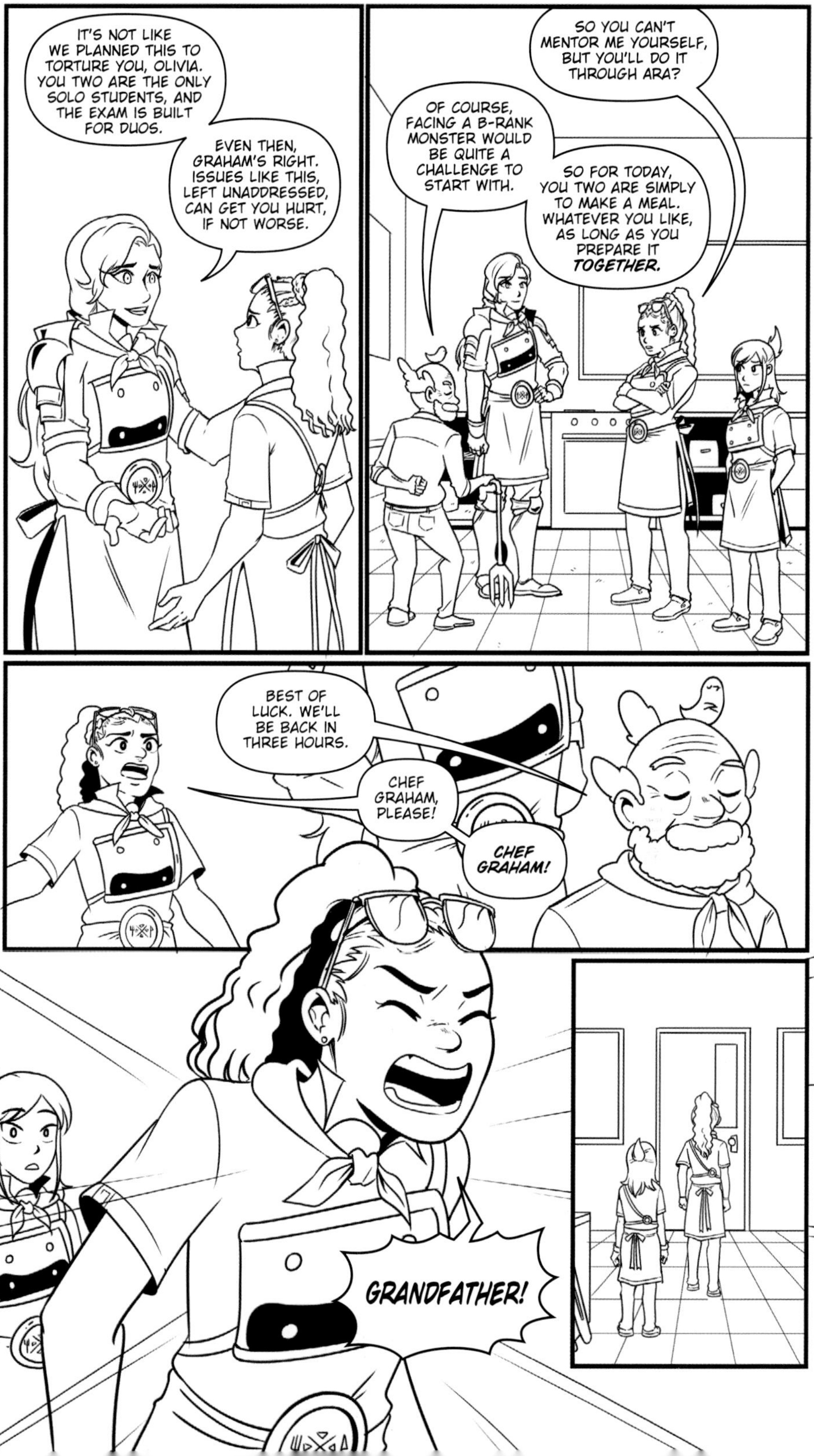
IT'S NOT LIKE WE PLANNED THIS TO TORTURE YOU, OLIVIA. YOU TWO ARE THE ONLY SOLO STUDENTS, AND THE EXAM IS BUILT FOR DUOS.
EVEN THEN, GRAHAM'S RIGHT. ISSUES LIKE THIS, LEFT UNADDRESSED, CAN GET YOU HURT, IF NOT WORSE.
OF COURSE, FACING A B-RANK MONSTER WOULD BE QUITE A CHALLENGE TO START WITH.
SO FOR TODAY, YOU TWO ARE SIMPLY TO MAKE A MEAL. WHATEVER YOU LIKE, AS LONG AS YOU PREPARE IT TOGETHER.
SO YOU CAN'T MENTOR ME YOURSELF, BUT YOU'LL DO IT THROUGH ARA?
BEST OF LUCK. WE'LL BE BACK IN THREE HOURS.
CHEF GRAHAM, PLEASE!
CHEF GRAHAM!
GRANDFATHER!

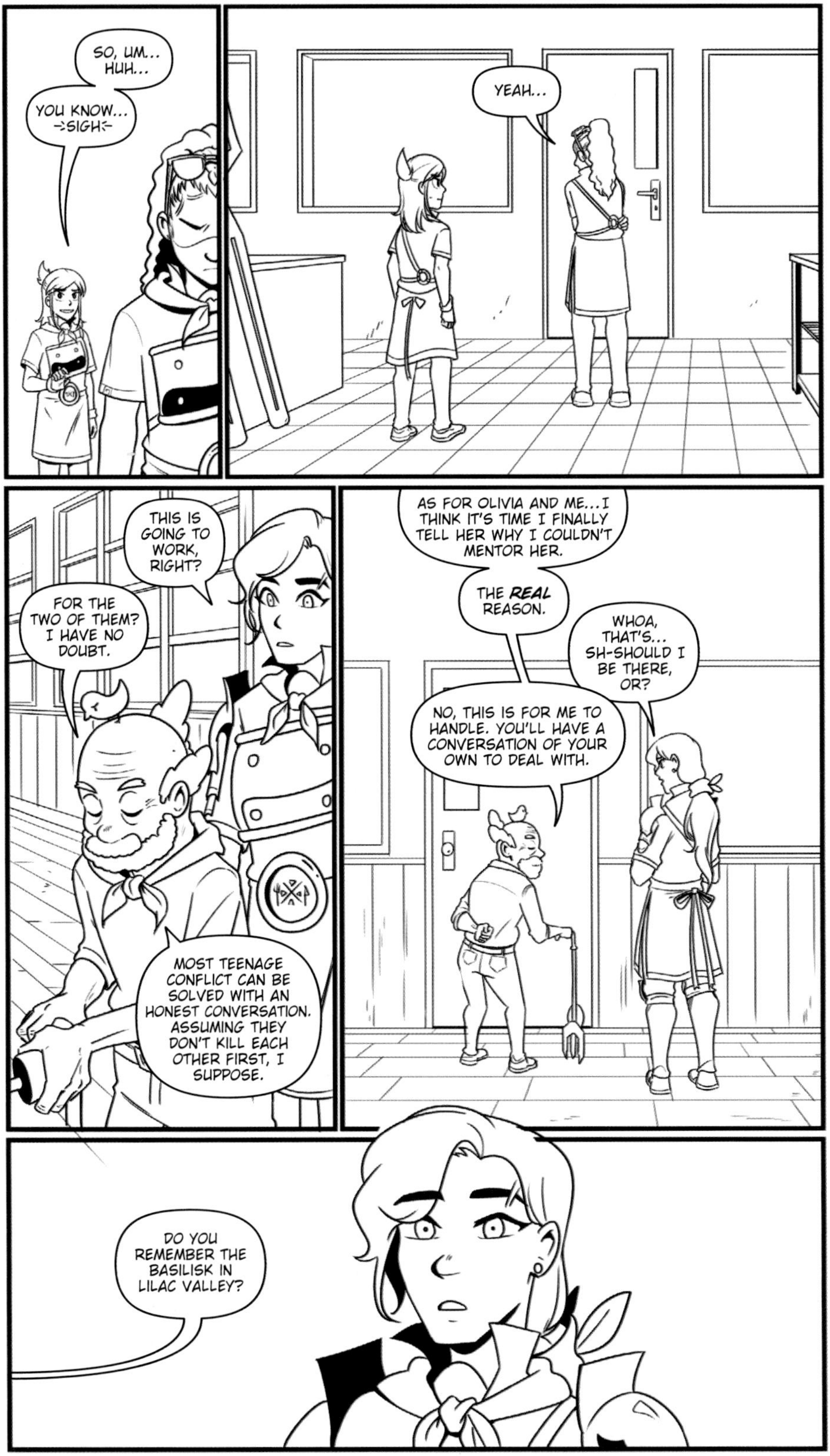

SO, UM... HUH...
YOU KNOW... -SIGH-
YEAH...
THIS IS GOING TO WORK, RIGHT?
FOR THE TWO OF THEM? I HAVE NO DOUBT.
MOST TEENAGE CONFLICT CAN BE SOLVED WITH AN HONEST CONVERSATION. ASSUMING THEY DON'T KILL EACH OTHER FIRST, I SUPPOSE.
AS FOR OLIVIA AND ME...I THINK IT'S TIME I FINALLY TELL HER WHY I COULDN'T MENTOR HER.
THE *REAL* REASON.
WHOA, THAT'S... SH-SHOULD I BE THERE, OR?
NO, THIS IS FOR ME TO HANDLE. YOU'LL HAVE A CONVERSATION OF YOUR OWN TO DEAL WITH.
DO YOU REMEMBER THE BASILISK IN LILAC VALLEY?

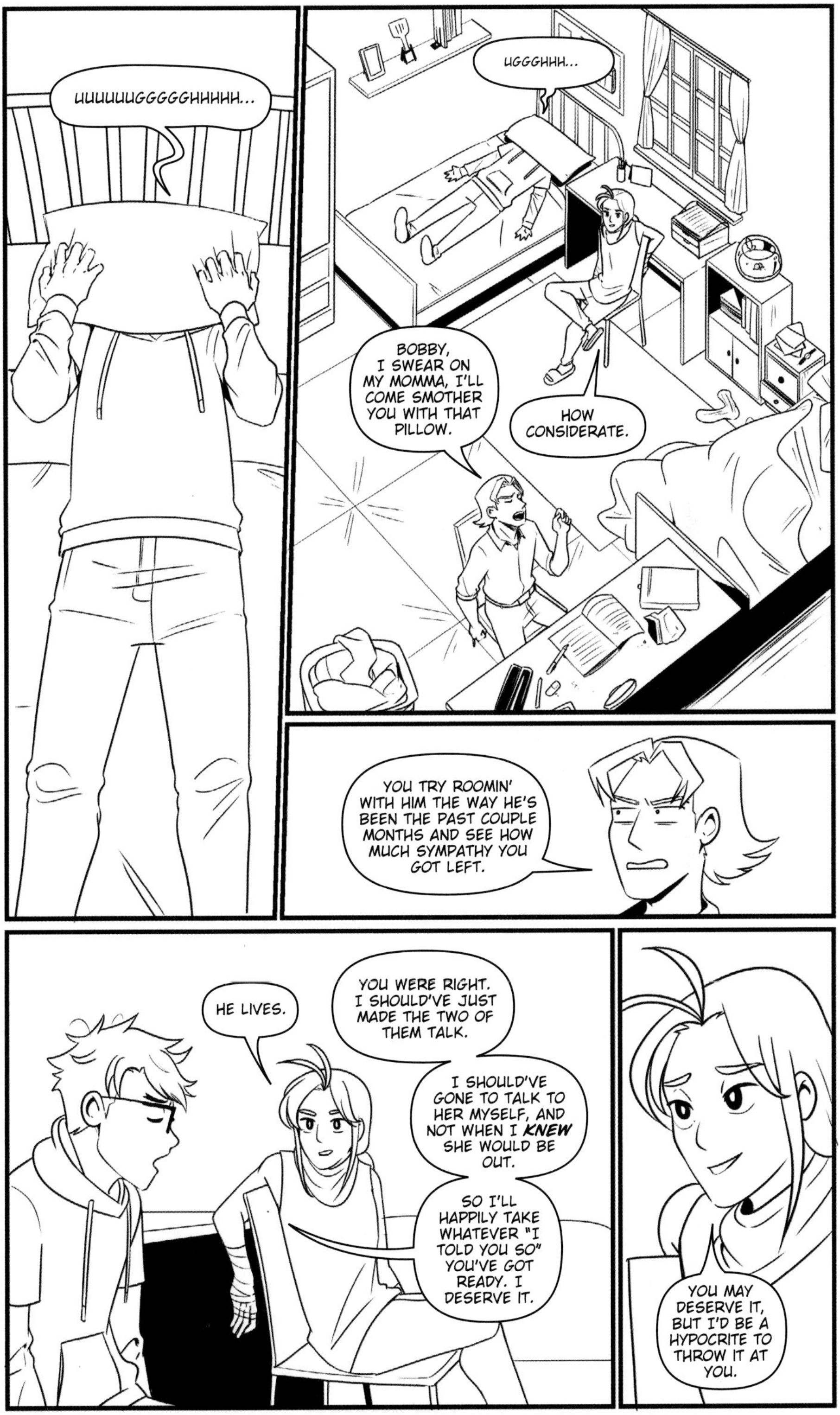
UUUUUUGGGGGHHHHH...
UGGGHHH...
BOBBY, I SWEAR ON MY MOMMA, I'LL COME SMOTHER YOU WITH THAT PILLOW.
HOW CONSIDERATE.
YOU TRY ROOMIN' WITH HIM THE WAY HE'S BEEN THE PAST COUPLE MONTHS AND SEE HOW MUCH SYMPATHY YOU GOT LEFT.
HE LIVES.
YOU WERE RIGHT. I SHOULD'VE JUST MADE THE TWO OF THEM TALK.
I SHOULD'VE GONE TO TALK TO HER MYSELF, AND NOT WHEN I *KNEW* SHE WOULD BE OUT.
SO I'LL HAPPILY TAKE WHATEVER "I TOLD YOU SO" YOU'VE GOT READY. I DESERVE IT.
YOU MAY DESERVE IT, BUT I'D BE A HYPOCRITE TO THROW IT AT YOU.

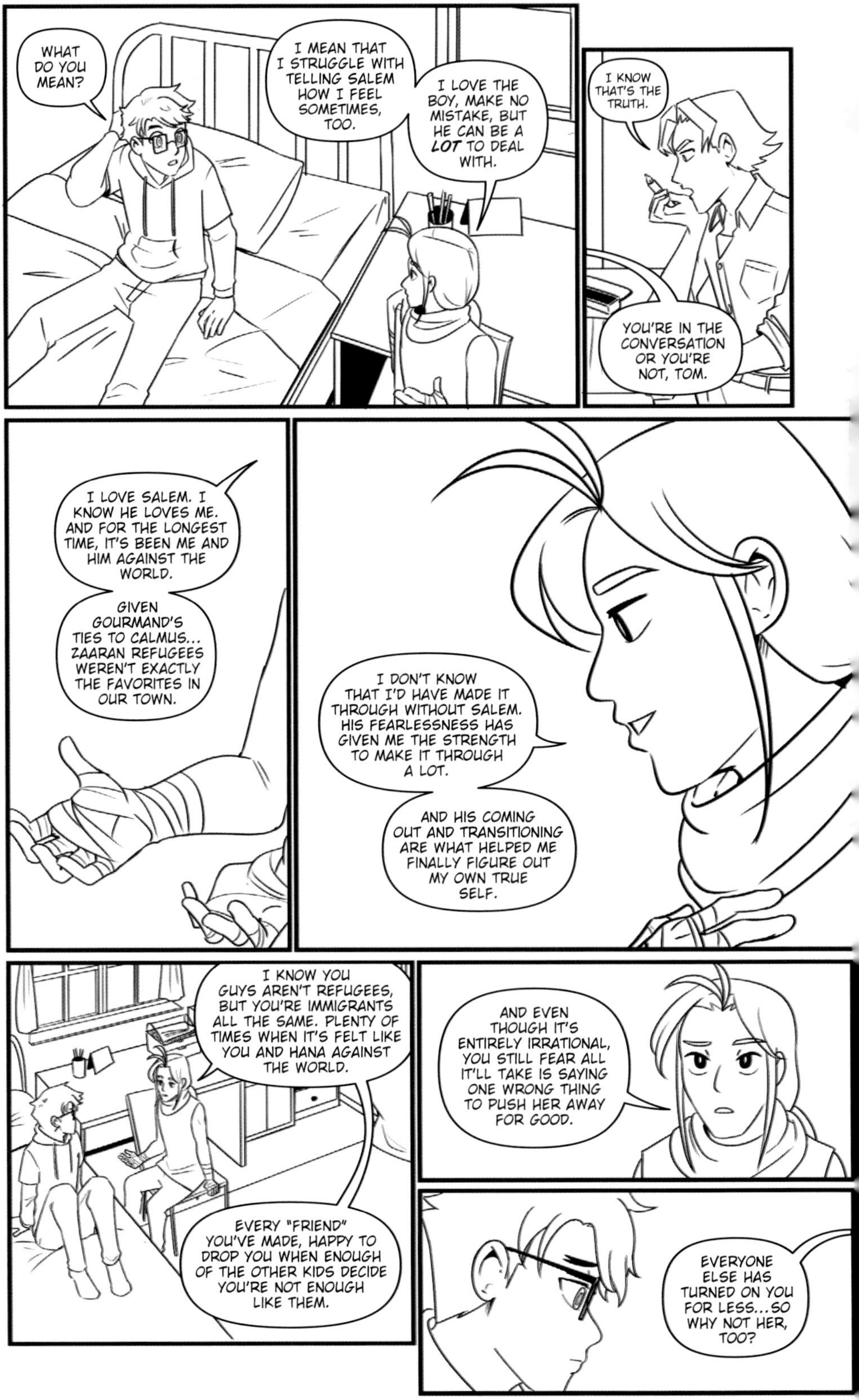

WHAT DO YOU MEAN?
I MEAN THAT I STRUGGLE WITH TELLING SALEM HOW I FEEL SOMETIMES, TOO.
I LOVE THE BOY, MAKE NO MISTAKE, BUT HE CAN BE A *LOT* TO DEAL WITH.
I KNOW THAT'S THE TRUTH.
YOU'RE IN THE CONVERSATION OR YOU'RE NOT, TOM.
I LOVE SALEM. I KNOW HE LOVES ME. AND FOR THE LONGEST TIME, IT'S BEEN ME AND HIM AGAINST THE WORLD.
GIVEN GOURMAND'S TIES TO CALMUS... ZAARAN REFUGEES WEREN'T EXACTLY THE FAVORITES IN OUR TOWN.
I DON'T KNOW THAT I'D HAVE MADE IT THROUGH WITHOUT SALEM. HIS FEARLESSNESS HAS GIVEN ME THE STRENGTH TO MAKE IT THROUGH A LOT.
AND HIS COMING OUT AND TRANSITIONING ARE WHAT HELPED ME FINALLY FIGURE OUT MY OWN TRUE SELF.
I KNOW YOU GUYS AREN'T REFUGEES, BUT YOU'RE IMMIGRANTS ALL THE SAME. PLENTY OF TIMES WHEN IT'S FELT LIKE YOU AND HANA AGAINST THE WORLD.
EVERY "FRIEND" YOU'VE MADE, HAPPY TO DROP YOU WHEN ENOUGH OF THE OTHER KIDS DECIDE YOU'RE NOT ENOUGH LIKE THEM.
AND EVEN THOUGH IT'S ENTIRELY IRRATIONAL, YOU STILL FEAR ALL IT'LL TAKE IS SAYING ONE WRONG THING TO PUSH HER AWAY FOR GOOD.
EVERYONE ELSE HAS TURNED ON YOU FOR LESS...SO WHY NOT HER, TOO?

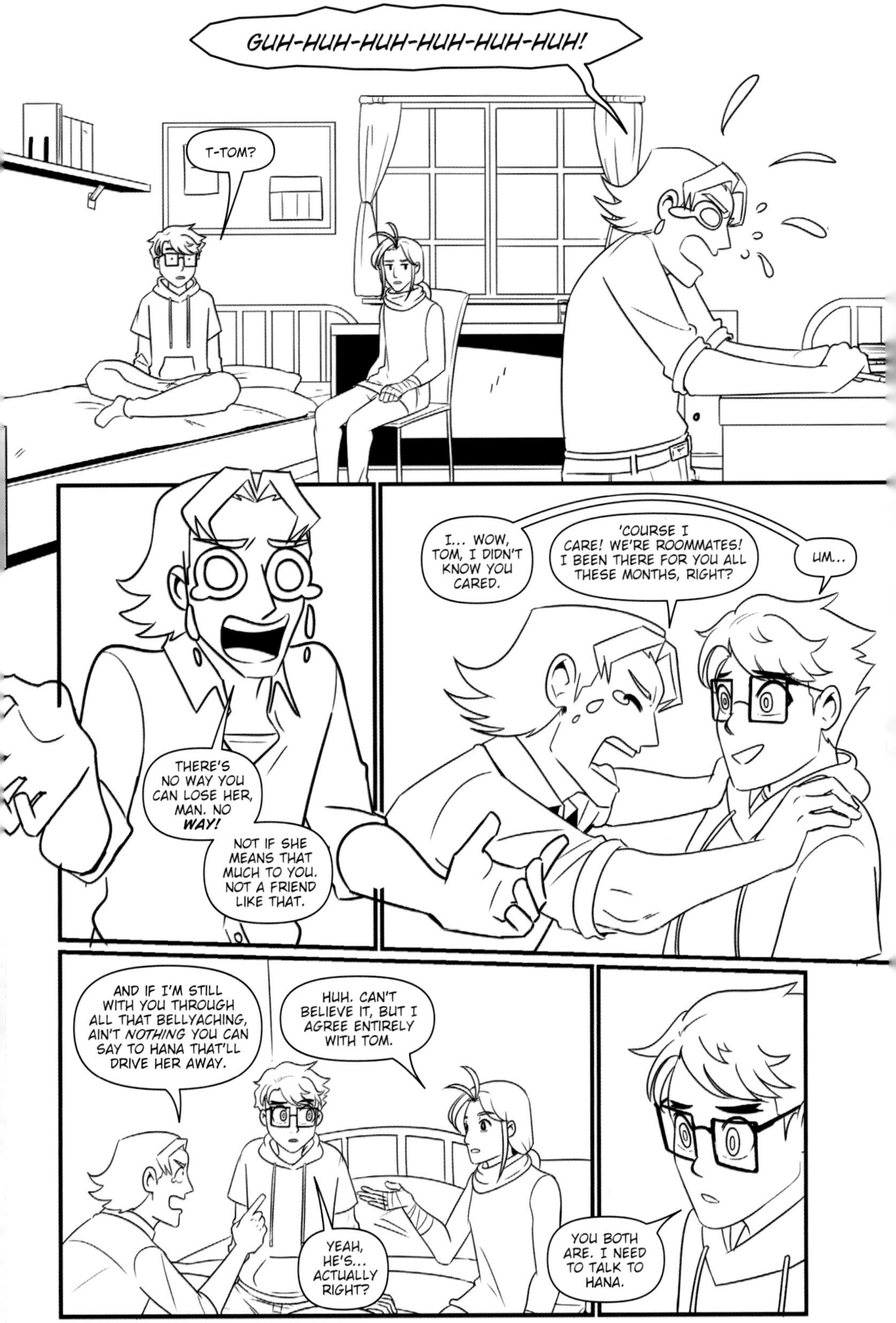
GUH-HUH-HUH-HUH-HUH-HUH!
T-TOM?
THERE'S NO WAY YOU CAN LOSE HER, MAN. NO *WAY!*
NOT IF SHE MEANS THAT MUCH TO YOU. NOT A FRIEND LIKE THAT.
I... WOW, TOM, I DIDN'T KNOW YOU CARED.
'COURSE I CARE! WE'RE ROOMMATES! I BEEN THERE FOR YOU ALL THESE MONTHS, RIGHT?
UM...
AND IF I'M STILL WITH YOU THROUGH ALL THAT BELLYACHING, AIN'T *NOTHING* YOU CAN SAY TO HANA THAT'LL DRIVE HER AWAY.
HUH. CAN'T BELIEVE IT, BUT I AGREE ENTIRELY WITH TOM.
YEAH, HE'S... ACTUALLY RIGHT?
YOU BOTH ARE. I NEED TO TALK TO HANA.

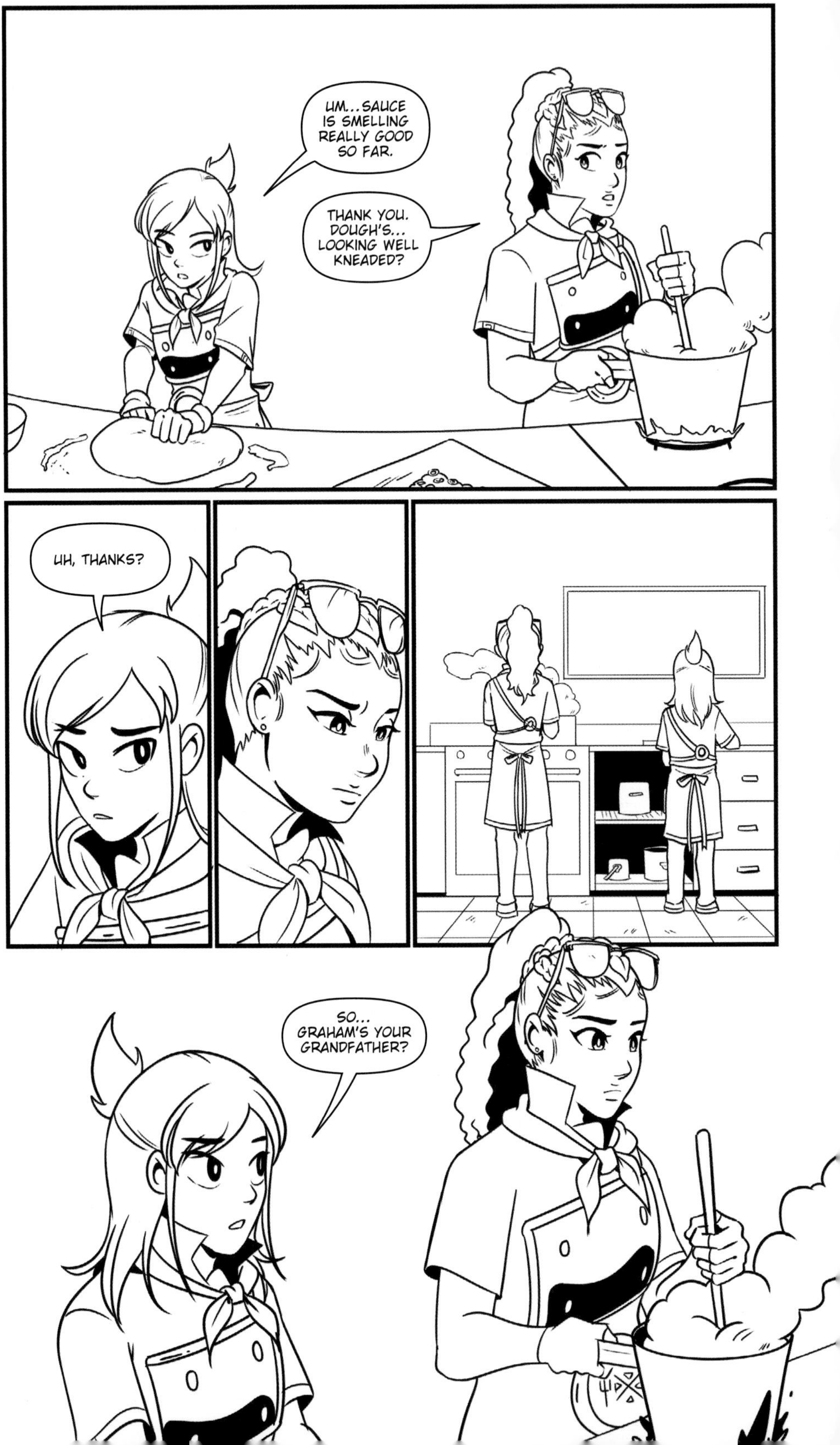
UM...SAUCE IS SMELLING REALLY GOOD SO FAR.
THANK YOU. DOUGH'S... LOOKING WELL KNEADED?
UH, THANKS?
SO... GRAHAM'S YOUR GRANDFATHER?

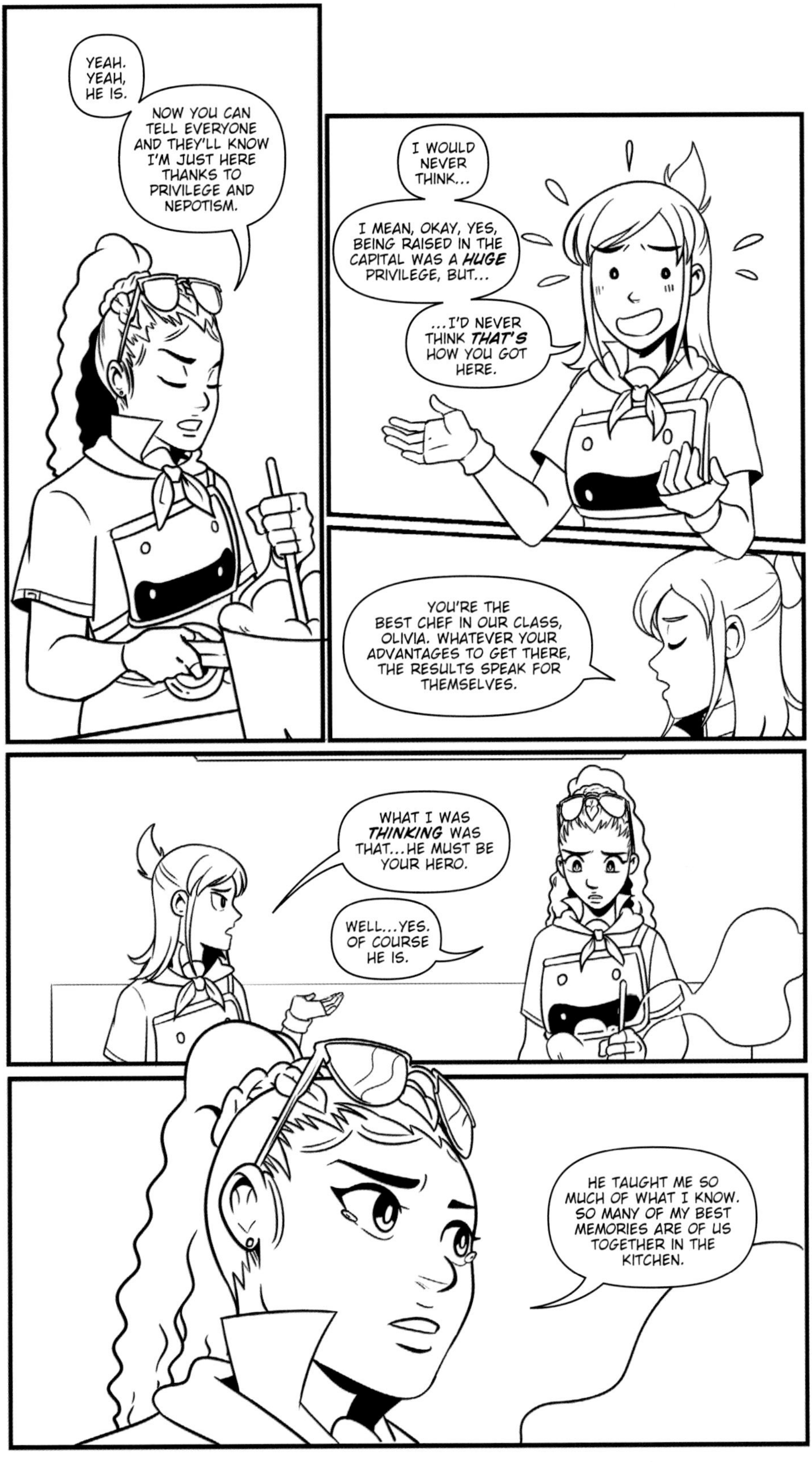
YEAH. YEAH, HE IS.
NOW YOU CAN TELL EVERYONE AND THEY'LL KNOW I'M JUST HERE THANKS TO PRIVILEGE AND NEPOTISM.
I WOULD NEVER THINK...
I MEAN, OKAY, YES, BEING RAISED IN THE CAPITAL WAS A ***HUGE*** PRIVILEGE, BUT...
...I'D NEVER THINK ***THAT'S*** HOW YOU GOT HERE.
YOU'RE THE BEST CHEF IN OUR CLASS, OLIVIA. WHATEVER YOUR ADVANTAGES TO GET THERE, THE RESULTS SPEAK FOR THEMSELVES.
WHAT I WAS ***THINKING*** WAS THAT...HE MUST BE YOUR HERO.
WELL...YES. OF COURSE HE IS.
HE TAUGHT ME SO MUCH OF WHAT I KNOW. SO MANY OF MY BEST MEMORIES ARE OF US TOGETHER IN THE KITCHEN.

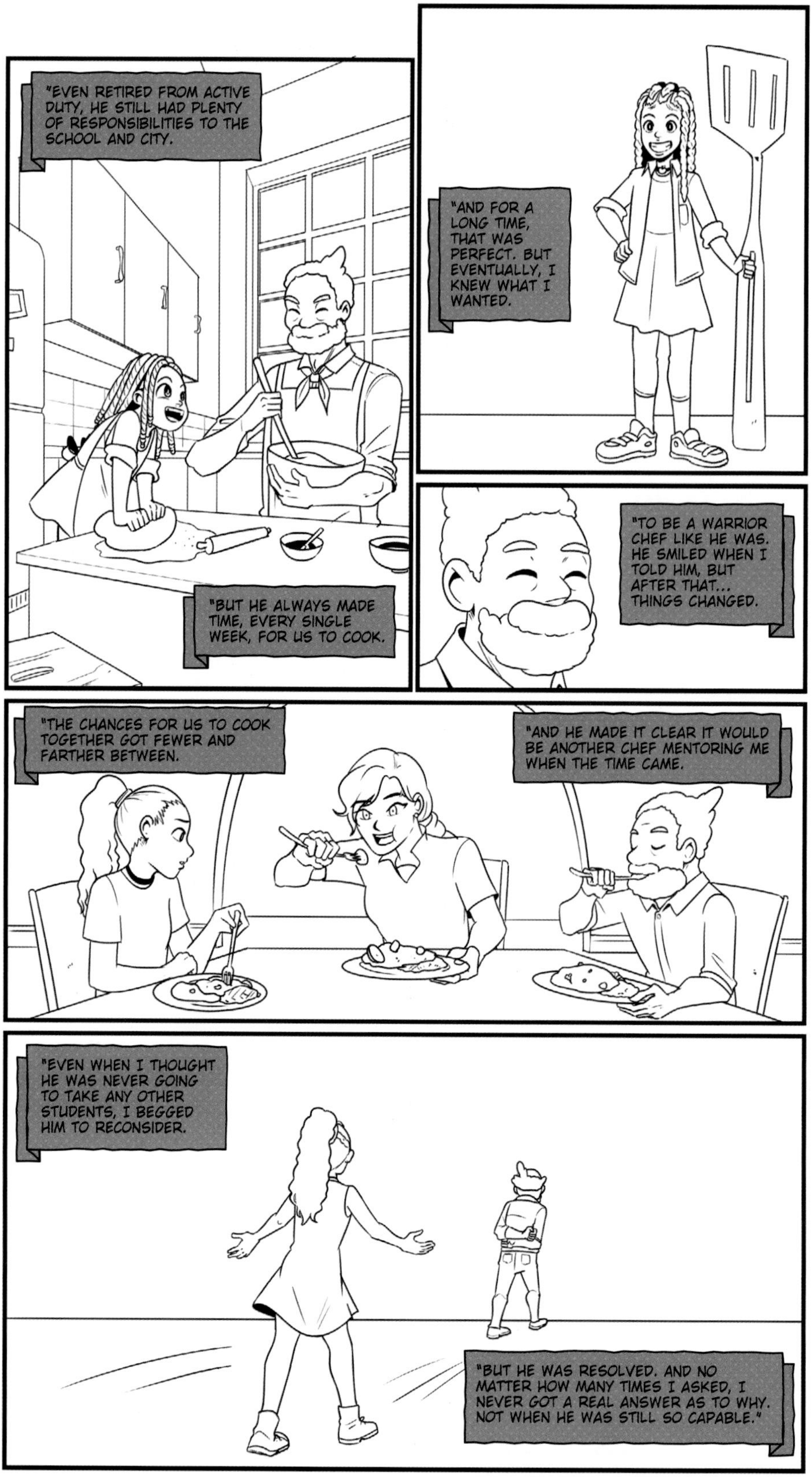
"EVEN RETIRED FROM ACTIVE DUTY, HE STILL HAD PLENTY OF RESPONSIBILITIES TO THE SCHOOL AND CITY.
"BUT HE ALWAYS MADE TIME, EVERY SINGLE WEEK, FOR US TO COOK.
"AND FOR A LONG TIME, THAT WAS PERFECT. BUT EVENTUALLY, I KNEW WHAT I WANTED.
"TO BE A WARRIOR CHEF LIKE HE WAS. HE SMILED WHEN I TOLD HIM, BUT AFTER THAT... THINGS CHANGED.
"THE CHANCES FOR US TO COOK TOGETHER GOT FEWER AND FARTHER BETWEEN.
"AND HE MADE IT CLEAR IT WOULD BE ANOTHER CHEF MENTORING ME WHEN THE TIME CAME.
"EVEN WHEN I THOUGHT HE WAS NEVER GOING TO TAKE ANY OTHER STUDENTS, I BEGGED HIM TO RECONSIDER.
"BUT HE WAS RESOLVED. AND NO MATTER HOW MANY TIMES I ASKED, I NEVER GOT A REAL ANSWER AS TO WHY. NOT WHEN HE WAS STILL SO CAPABLE."

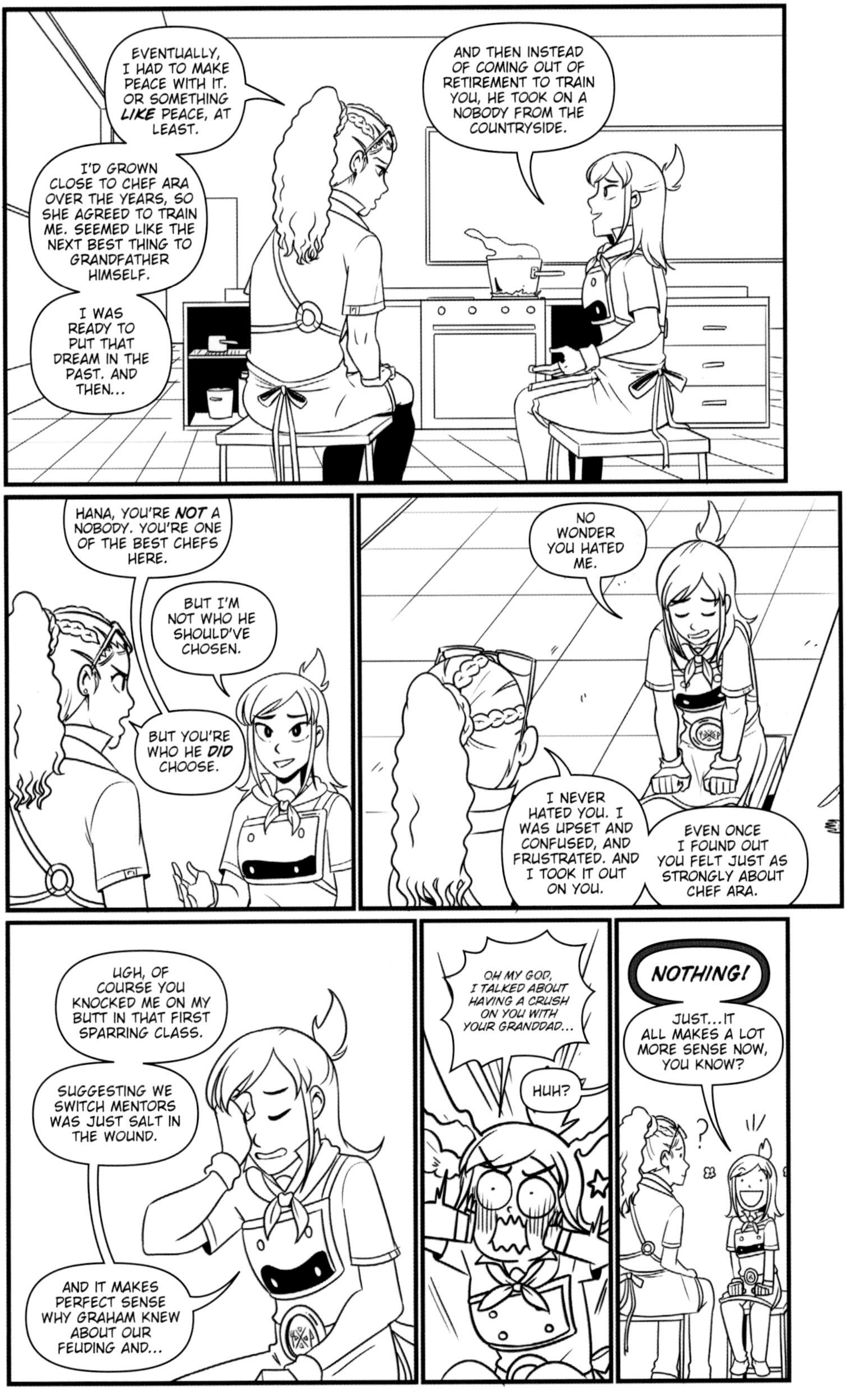
EVENTUALLY, I HAD TO MAKE PEACE WITH IT. OR SOMETHING *LIKE* PEACE, AT LEAST.
I'D GROWN CLOSE TO CHEF ARA OVER THE YEARS, SO SHE AGREED TO TRAIN ME. SEEMED LIKE THE NEXT BEST THING TO GRANDFATHER HIMSELF.
I WAS READY TO PUT THAT DREAM IN THE PAST. AND THEN...
AND THEN INSTEAD OF COMING OUT OF RETIREMENT TO TRAIN YOU, HE TOOK ON A NOBODY FROM THE COUNTRYSIDE.
HANA, YOU'RE ***NOT*** A NOBODY. YOU'RE ONE OF THE BEST CHEFS HERE.
BUT I'M NOT WHO HE SHOULD'VE CHOSEN.
BUT YOU'RE WHO HE ***DID*** CHOOSE.
NO WONDER YOU HATED ME.
I NEVER HATED YOU. I WAS UPSET AND CONFUSED, AND FRUSTRATED. AND I TOOK IT OUT ON YOU.
EVEN ONCE I FOUND OUT YOU FELT JUST AS STRONGLY ABOUT CHEF ARA.
UGH, OF COURSE YOU KNOCKED ME ON MY BUTT IN THAT FIRST SPARRING CLASS.
SUGGESTING WE SWITCH MENTORS WAS JUST SALT IN THE WOUND.
AND IT MAKES PERFECT SENSE WHY GRAHAM KNEW ABOUT OUR FEUDING AND...
OH MY GOD, I TALKED ABOUT HAVING A CRUSH ON YOU WITH YOUR GRANDDAD...
HUH?
NOTHING!
JUST...IT ALL MAKES A LOT MORE SENSE NOW, YOU KNOW?

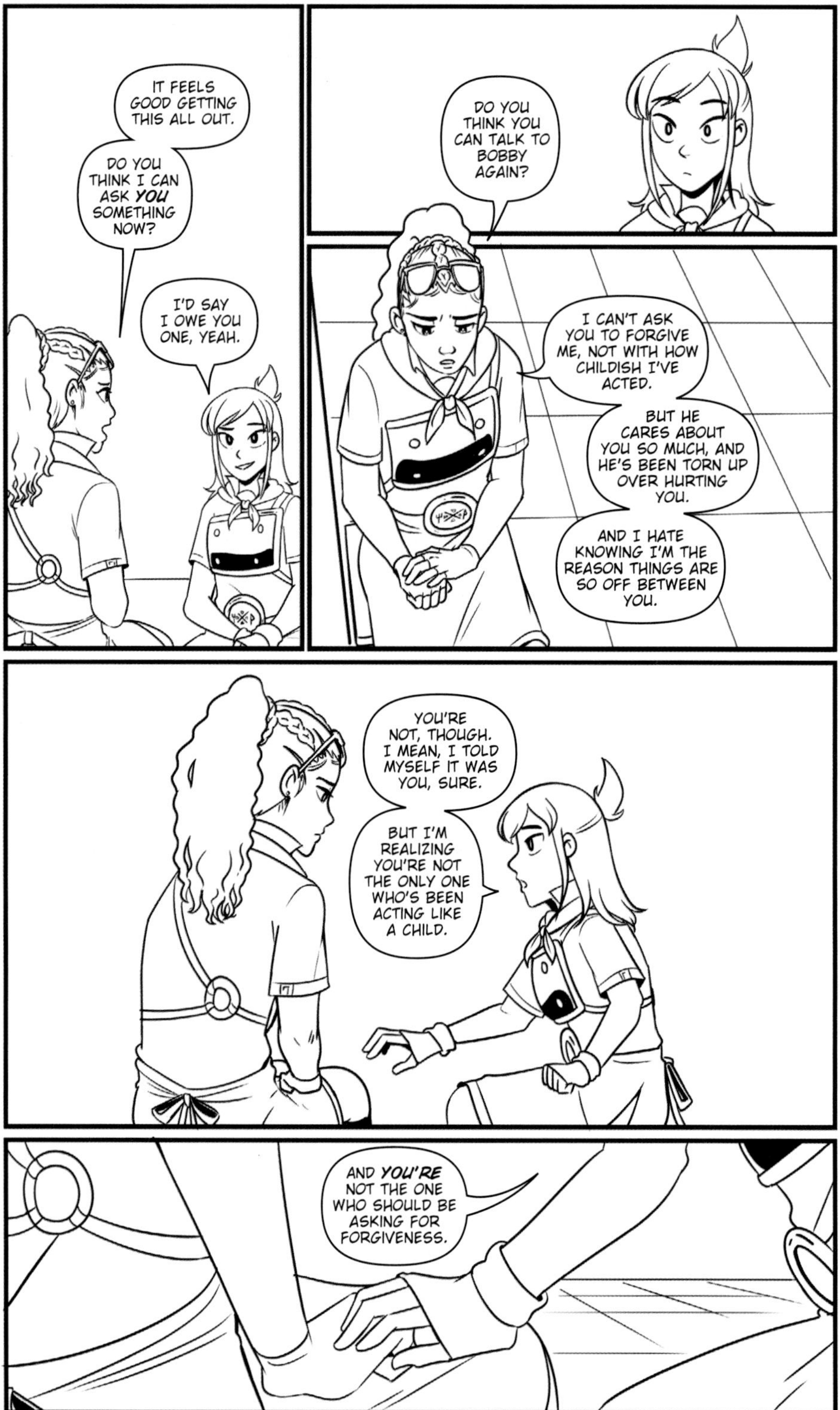
IT FEELS GOOD GETTING THIS ALL OUT.
DO YOU THINK I CAN ASK *YOU* SOMETHING NOW?
I'D SAY I OWE YOU ONE, YEAH.
DO YOU THINK YOU CAN TALK TO BOBBY AGAIN?
I CAN'T ASK YOU TO FORGIVE ME, NOT WITH HOW CHILDISH I'VE ACTED.
BUT HE CARES ABOUT YOU SO MUCH, AND HE'S BEEN TORN UP OVER HURTING YOU.
AND I HATE KNOWING I'M THE REASON THINGS ARE SO OFF BETWEEN YOU.
YOU'RE NOT, THOUGH. I MEAN, I TOLD MYSELF IT WAS YOU, SURE.
BUT I'M REALIZING YOU'RE NOT THE ONLY ONE WHO'S BEEN ACTING LIKE A CHILD.
AND *YOU'RE* NOT THE ONE WHO SHOULD BE ASKING FOR FORGIVENESS.

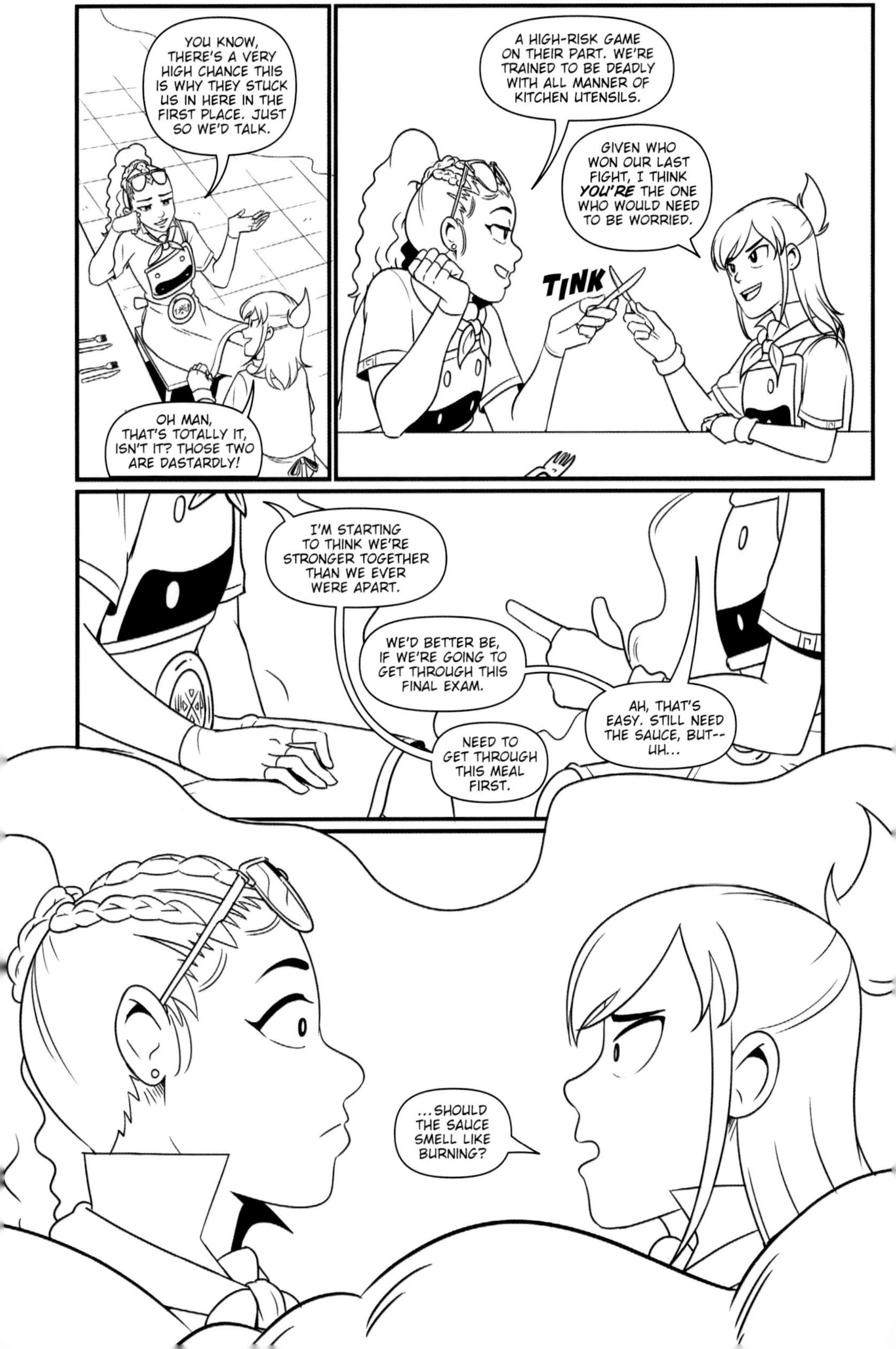
YOU KNOW, THERE'S A VERY HIGH CHANCE THIS IS WHY THEY STUCK US IN HERE IN THE FIRST PLACE. JUST SO WE'D TALK.
OH MAN, THAT'S TOTALLY IT, ISN'T IT? THOSE TWO ARE DASTARDLY!
A HIGH-RISK GAME ON THEIR PART. WE'RE TRAINED TO BE DEADLY WITH ALL MANNER OF KITCHEN UTENSILS.
GIVEN WHO WON OUR LAST FIGHT, I THINK YOU'RE THE ONE WHO WOULD NEED TO BE WORRIED.
TINK
I'M STARTING TO THINK WE'RE STRONGER TOGETHER THAN WE EVER WERE APART.
WE'D BETTER BE, IF WE'RE GOING TO GET THROUGH THIS FINAL EXAM.
NEED TO GET THROUGH THIS MEAL FIRST.
AH, THAT'S EASY. STILL NEED THE SAUCE, BUT-- UH...
...SHOULD THE SAUCE SMELL LIKE BURNING?

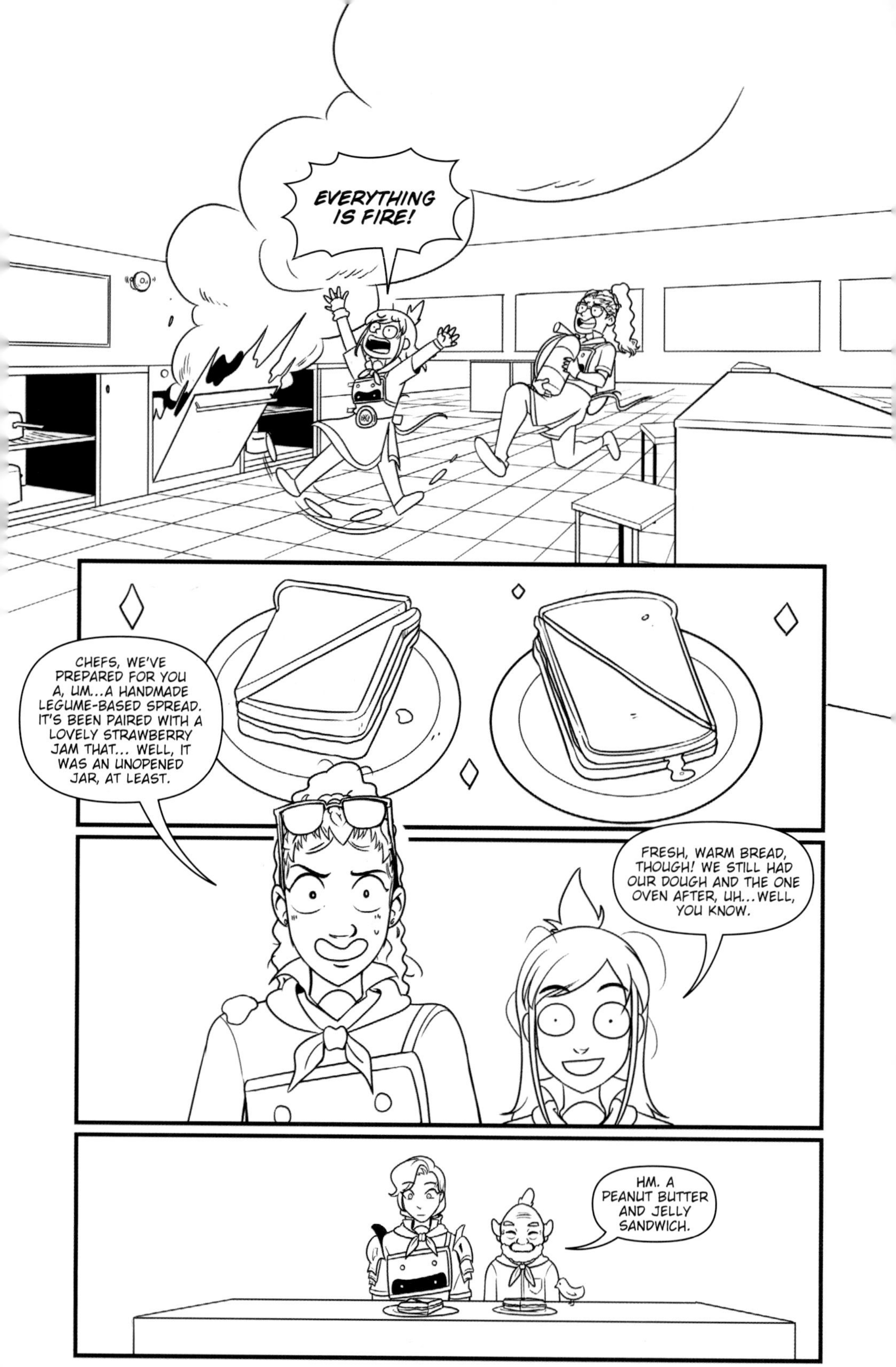
EVERYTHING IS FIRE!
CHEFS, WE'VE PREPARED FOR YOU A, UM...A HANDMADE LEGUME-BASED SPREAD. IT'S BEEN PAIRED WITH A LOVELY STRAWBERRY JAM THAT... WELL, IT WAS AN UNOPENED JAR, AT LEAST.
FRESH, WARM BREAD, THOUGH! WE STILL HAD OUR DOUGH AND THE ONE OVEN AFTER, UH...WELL, YOU KNOW.
HM. A PEANUT BUTTER AND JELLY SANDWICH.

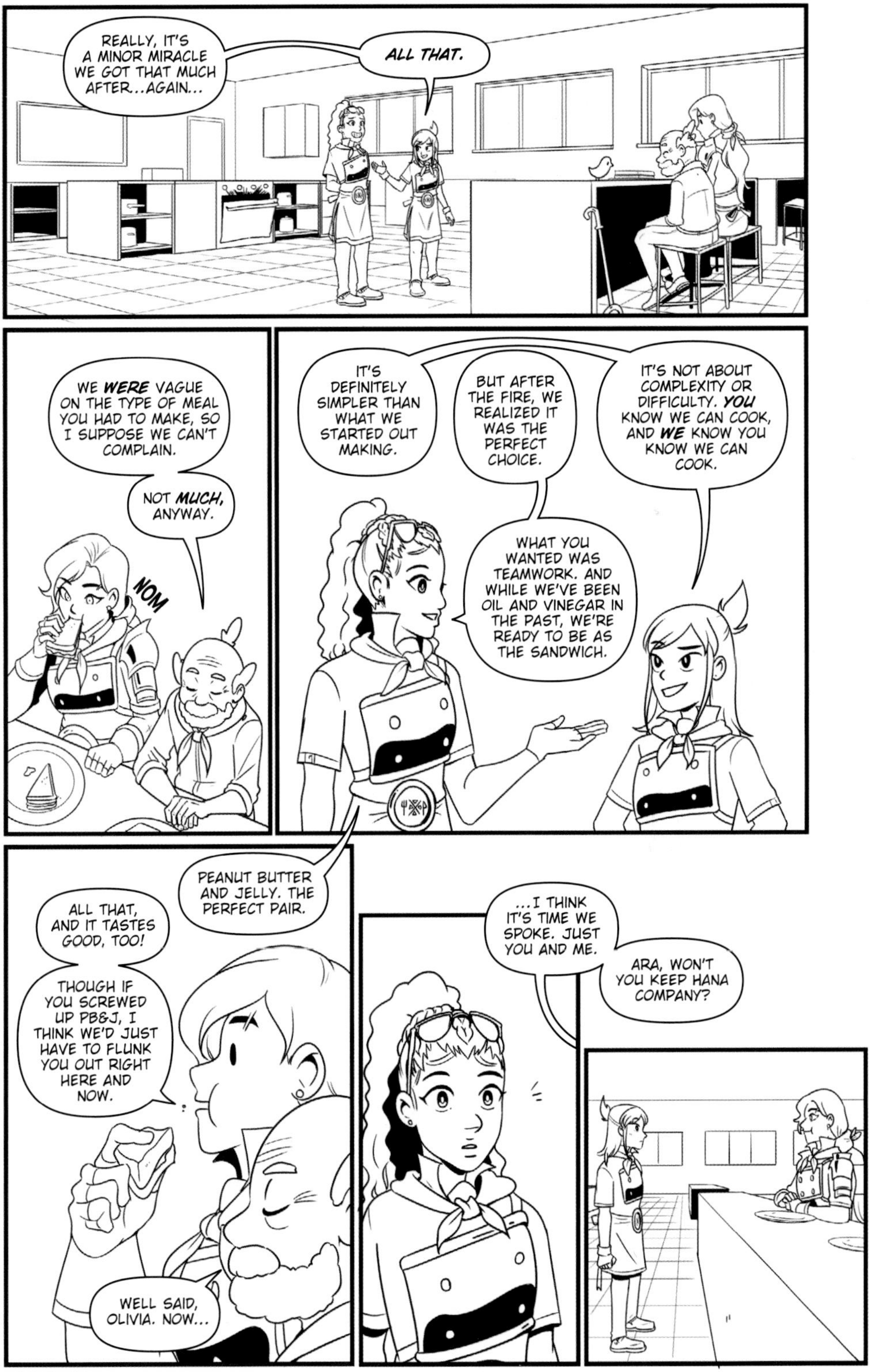
REALLY, IT'S A MINOR MIRACLE WE GOT THAT MUCH AFTER...AGAIN...
ALL THAT.
WE WERE VAGUE ON THE TYPE OF MEAL YOU HAD TO MAKE, SO I SUPPOSE WE CAN'T COMPLAIN.
NOT MUCH, ANYWAY.
NOM
IT'S DEFINITELY SIMPLER THAN WHAT WE STARTED OUT MAKING.
BUT AFTER THE FIRE, WE REALIZED IT WAS THE PERFECT CHOICE.
WHAT YOU WANTED WAS TEAMWORK. AND WHILE WE'VE BEEN OIL AND VINEGAR IN THE PAST, WE'RE READY TO BE AS THE SANDWICH.
IT'S NOT ABOUT COMPLEXITY OR DIFFICULTY. YOU KNOW WE CAN COOK, AND WE KNOW YOU KNOW WE CAN COOK.
PEANUT BUTTER AND JELLY. THE PERFECT PAIR.
ALL THAT, AND IT TASTES GOOD, TOO!
THOUGH IF YOU SCREWED UP PB&J, I THINK WE'D JUST HAVE TO FLUNK YOU OUT RIGHT HERE AND NOW.
WELL SAID, OLIVIA. NOW...
...I THINK IT'S TIME WE SPOKE. JUST YOU AND ME.
ARA, WON'T YOU KEEP HANA COMPANY?

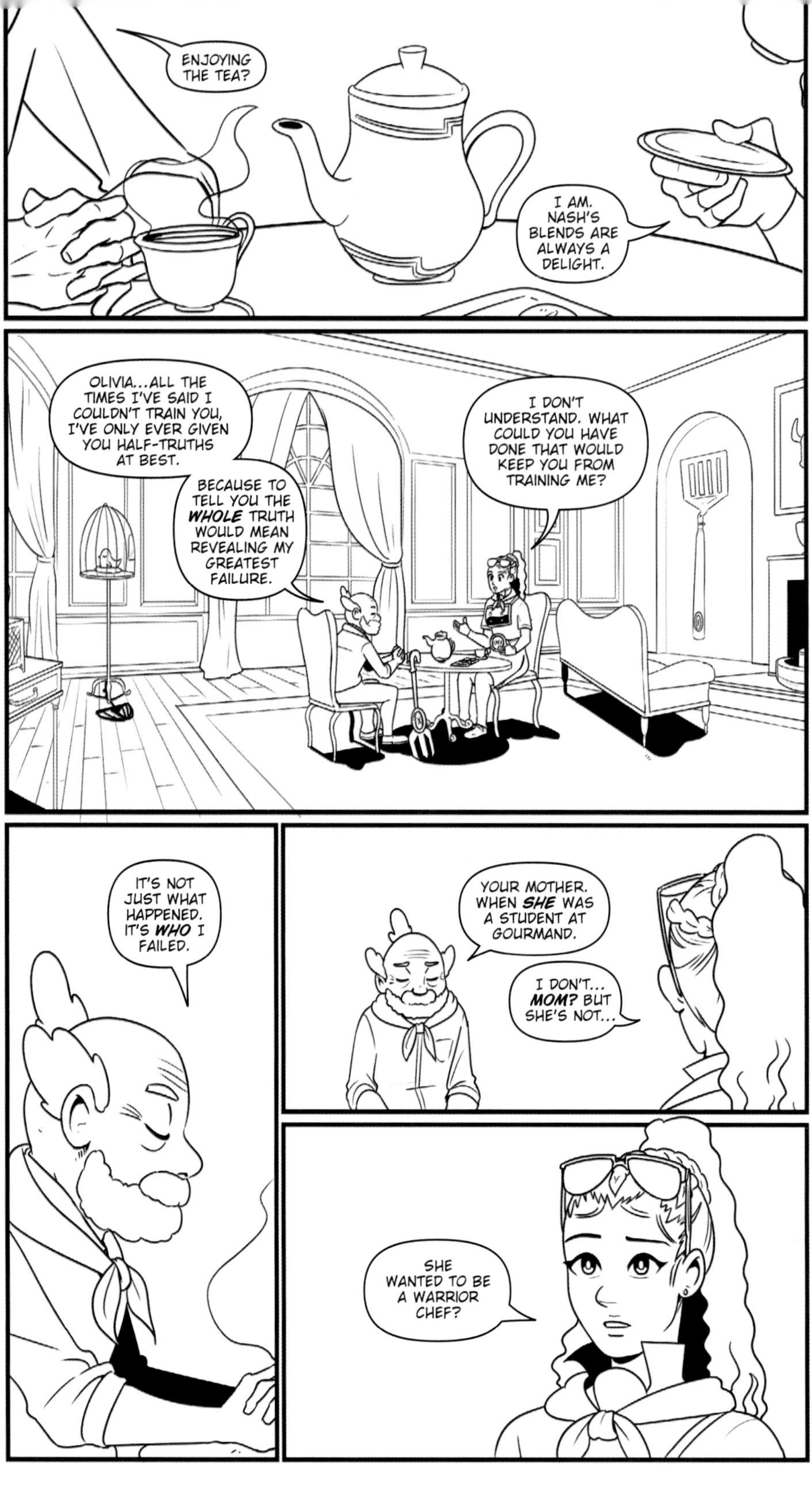

ENJOYING THE TEA?
I AM. NASH'S BLENDS ARE ALWAYS A DELIGHT.
OLIVIA...ALL THE TIMES I'VE SAID I COULDN'T TRAIN YOU, I'VE ONLY EVER GIVEN YOU HALF-TRUTHS AT BEST.
BECAUSE TO TELL YOU THE WHOLE TRUTH WOULD MEAN REVEALING MY GREATEST FAILURE.
I DON'T UNDERSTAND. WHAT COULD YOU HAVE DONE THAT WOULD KEEP YOU FROM TRAINING ME?
IT'S NOT JUST WHAT HAPPENED. IT'S WHO I FAILED.
YOUR MOTHER. WHEN SHE WAS A STUDENT AT GOURMAND.
I DON'T... MOM? BUT SHE'S NOT...
SHE WANTED TO BE A WARRIOR CHEF?

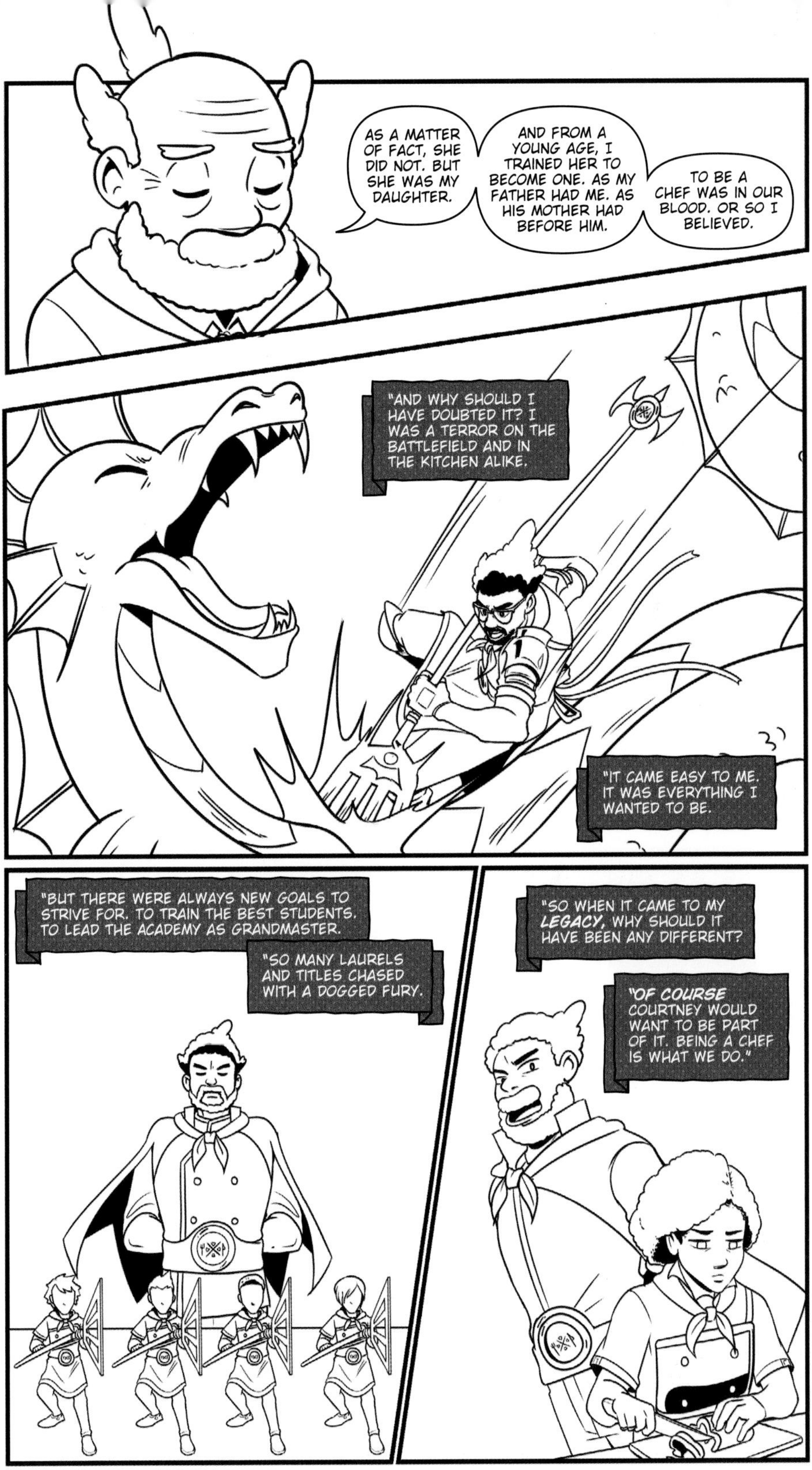
AS A MATTER OF FACT, SHE DID NOT. BUT SHE WAS MY DAUGHTER.
AND FROM A YOUNG AGE, I TRAINED HER TO BECOME ONE. AS MY FATHER HAD ME. AS HIS MOTHER HAD BEFORE HIM.
TO BE A CHEF WAS IN OUR BLOOD. OR SO I BELIEVED.
"AND WHY SHOULD I HAVE DOUBTED IT? I WAS A TERROR ON THE BATTLEFIELD AND IN THE KITCHEN ALIKE.
"IT CAME EASY TO ME. IT WAS EVERYTHING I WANTED TO BE.
"BUT THERE WERE ALWAYS NEW GOALS TO STRIVE FOR. TO TRAIN THE BEST STUDENTS. TO LEAD THE ACADEMY AS GRANDMASTER.
"SO MANY LAURELS AND TITLES CHASED WITH A DOGGED FURY.
"SO WHEN IT CAME TO MY *LEGACY,* WHY SHOULD IT HAVE BEEN ANY DIFFERENT?
"OF COURSE COURTNEY WOULD WANT TO BE PART OF IT. BEING A CHEF IS WHAT WE DO."

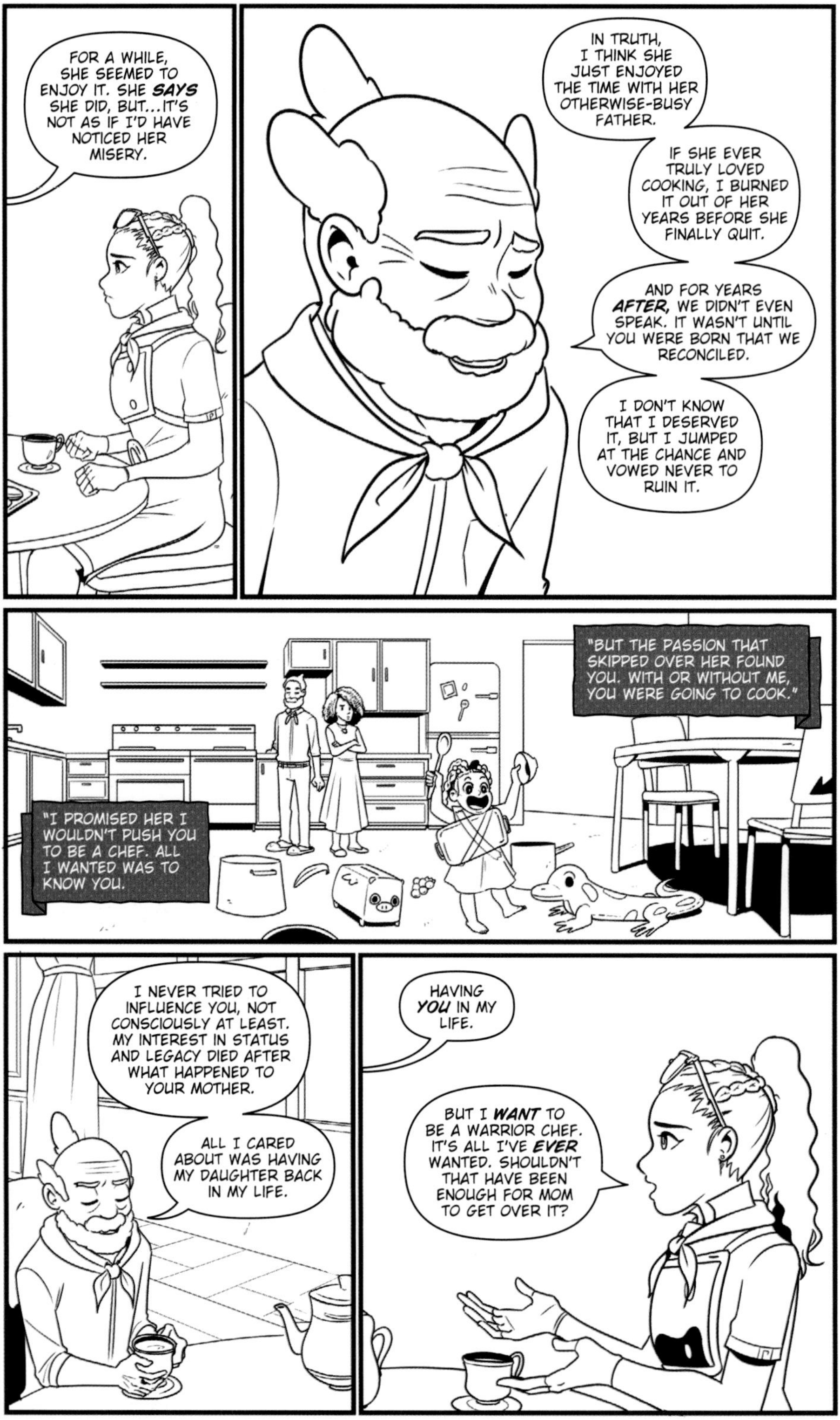
FOR A WHILE, SHE SEEMED TO ENJOY IT. SHE SAYS SHE DID, BUT...IT'S NOT AS IF I'D HAVE NOTICED HER MISERY.
IN TRUTH, I THINK SHE JUST ENJOYED THE TIME WITH HER OTHERWISE-BUSY FATHER.
IF SHE EVER TRULY LOVED COOKING, I BURNED IT OUT OF HER YEARS BEFORE SHE FINALLY QUIT.
AND FOR YEARS AFTER, WE DIDN'T EVEN SPEAK. IT WASN'T UNTIL YOU WERE BORN THAT WE RECONCILED.
I DON'T KNOW THAT I DESERVED IT, BUT I JUMPED AT THE CHANCE AND VOWED NEVER TO RUIN IT.
"I PROMISED HER I WOULDN'T PUSH YOU TO BE A CHEF. ALL I WANTED WAS TO KNOW YOU.
"BUT THE PASSION THAT SKIPPED OVER HER FOUND YOU. WITH OR WITHOUT ME, YOU WERE GOING TO COOK."
I NEVER TRIED TO INFLUENCE YOU, NOT CONSCIOUSLY AT LEAST. MY INTEREST IN STATUS AND LEGACY DIED AFTER WHAT HAPPENED TO YOUR MOTHER.
ALL I CARED ABOUT WAS HAVING MY DAUGHTER BACK IN MY LIFE.
HAVING YOU IN MY LIFE.
BUT I WANT TO BE A WARRIOR CHEF. IT'S ALL I'VE EVER WANTED. SHOULDN'T THAT HAVE BEEN ENOUGH FOR MOM TO GET OVER IT?

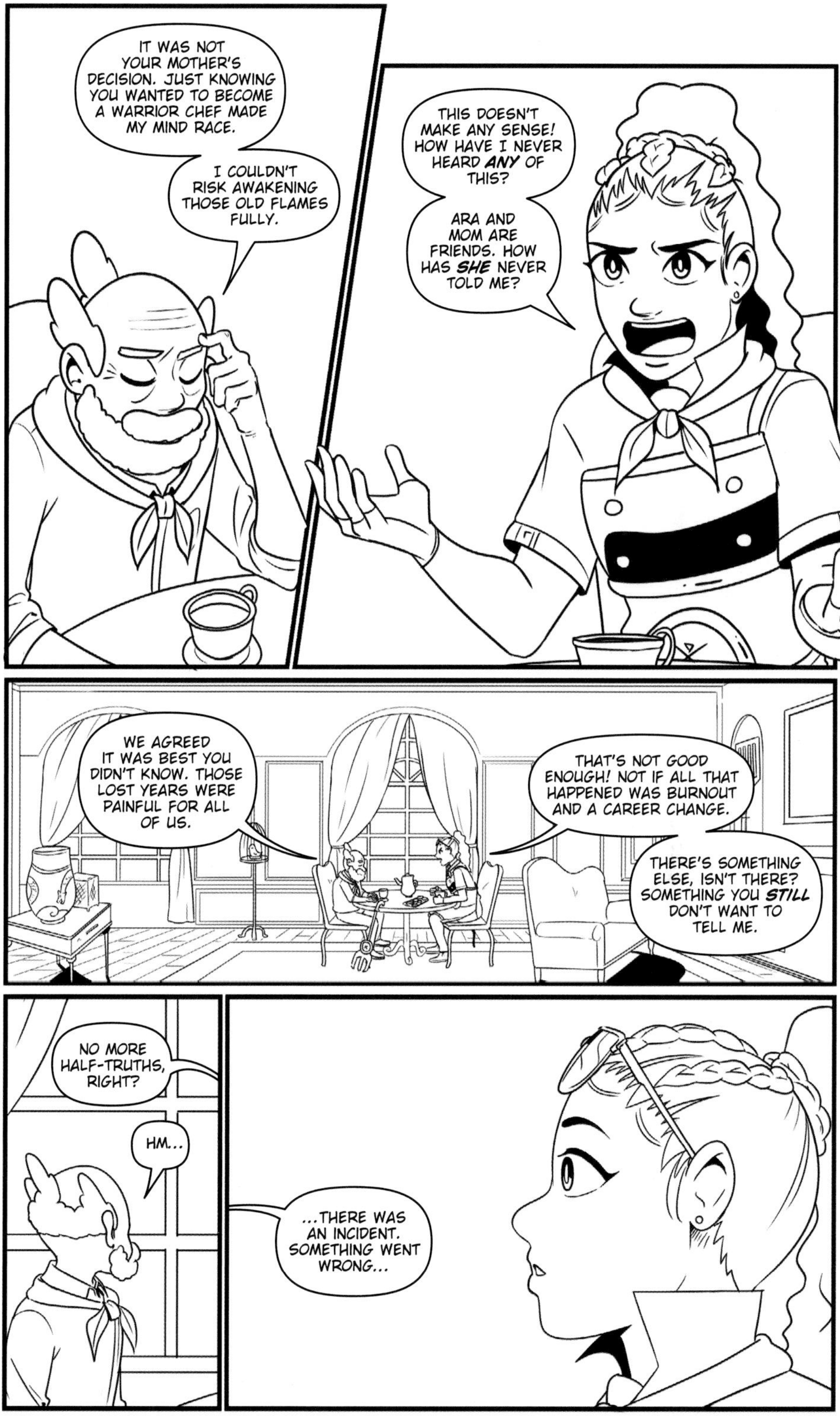
IT WAS NOT YOUR MOTHER'S DECISION. JUST KNOWING YOU WANTED TO BECOME A WARRIOR CHEF MADE MY MIND RACE.
I COULDN'T RISK AWAKENING THOSE OLD FLAMES FULLY.
THIS DOESN'T MAKE ANY SENSE! HOW HAVE I NEVER HEARD *ANY* OF THIS?
ARA AND MOM ARE FRIENDS. HOW HAS *SHE* NEVER TOLD ME?
WE AGREED IT WAS BEST YOU DIDN'T KNOW. THOSE LOST YEARS WERE PAINFUL FOR ALL OF US.
THAT'S NOT GOOD ENOUGH! NOT IF ALL THAT HAPPENED WAS BURNOUT AND A CAREER CHANGE.
THERE'S SOMETHING ELSE, ISN'T THERE? SOMETHING YOU *STILL* DON'T WANT TO TELL ME.
NO MORE HALF-TRUTHS, RIGHT?
HM...
...THERE WAS AN INCIDENT. SOMETHING WENT WRONG...

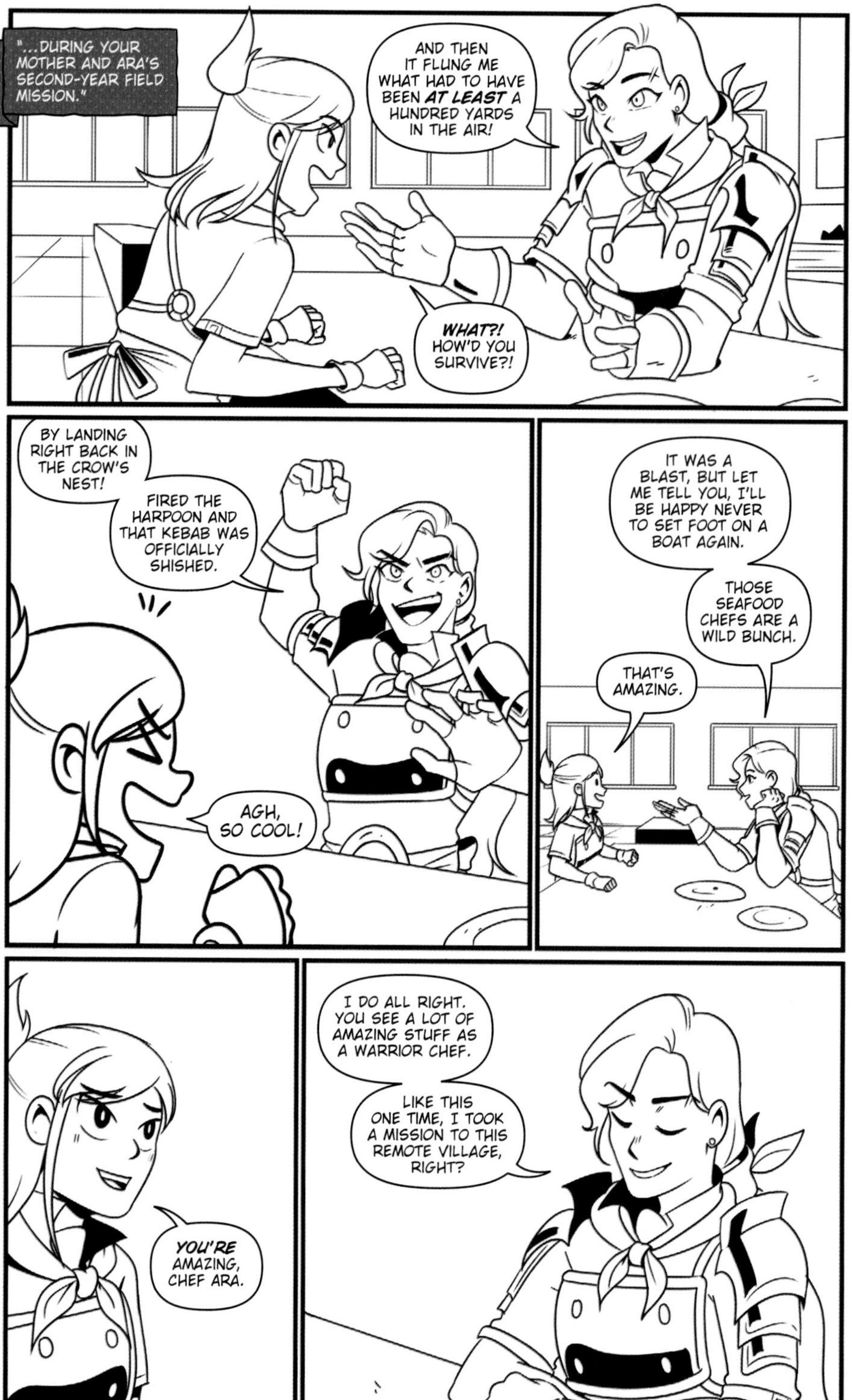
"...DURING YOUR MOTHER AND ARA'S SECOND-YEAR FIELD MISSION."
AND THEN IT FLUNG ME WHAT HAD TO HAVE BEEN AT LEAST A HUNDRED YARDS IN THE AIR!
WHAT?! HOW'D YOU SURVIVE?!
BY LANDING RIGHT BACK IN THE CROW'S NEST!
FIRED THE HARPOON AND THAT KEBAB WAS OFFICIALLY SHISHED.
AGH, SO COOL!
IT WAS A BLAST, BUT LET ME TELL YOU, I'LL BE HAPPY NEVER TO SET FOOT ON A BOAT AGAIN.
THOSE SEAFOOD CHEFS ARE A WILD BUNCH.
THAT'S AMAZING.
YOU'RE AMAZING, CHEF ARA.
I DO ALL RIGHT. YOU SEE A LOT OF AMAZING STUFF AS A WARRIOR CHEF.
LIKE THIS ONE TIME, I TOOK A MISSION TO THIS REMOTE VILLAGE, RIGHT?

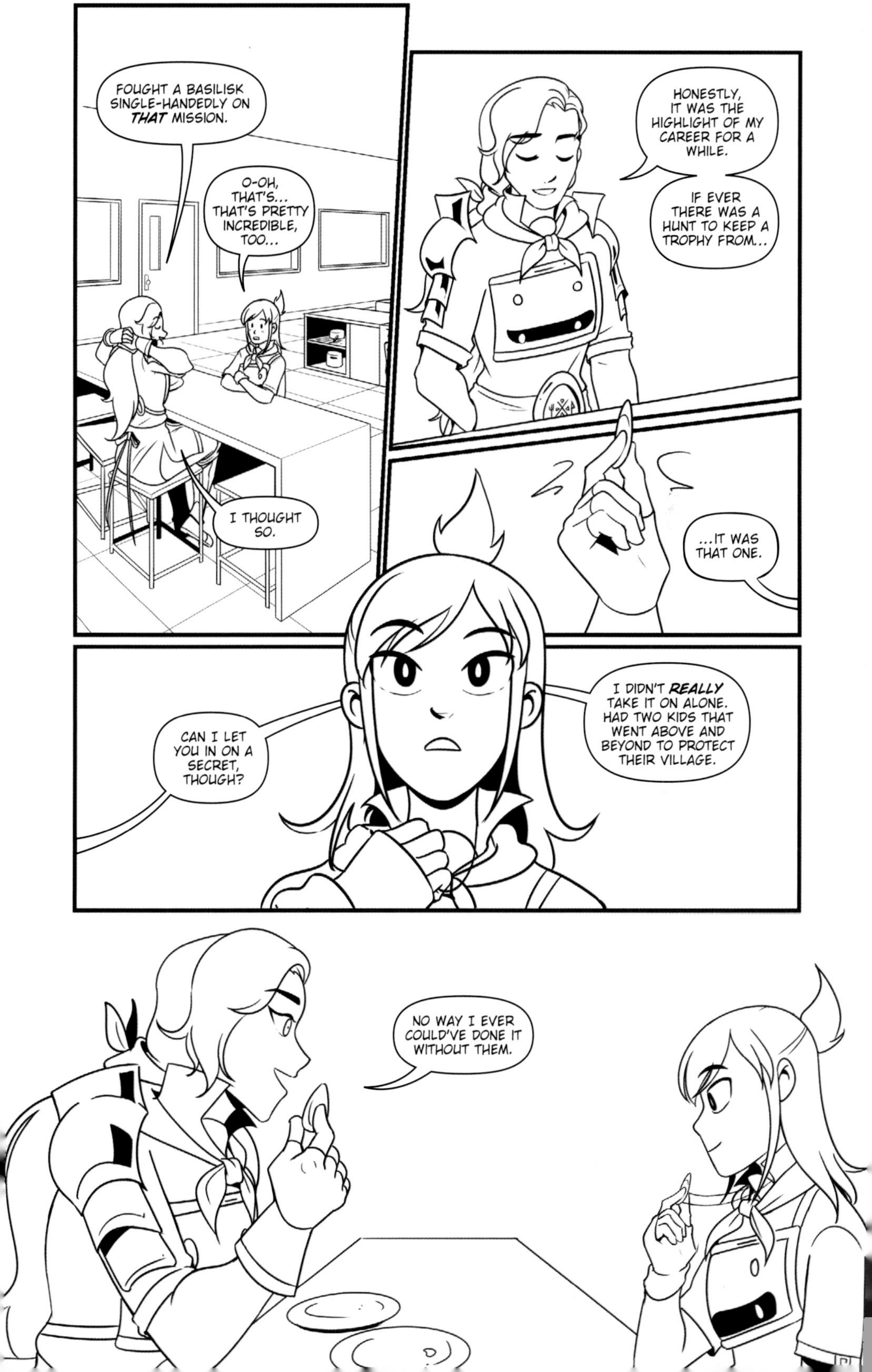
FOUGHT A BASILISK SINGLE-HANDEDLY ON *THAT* MISSION.
O-OH, THAT'S... THAT'S PRETTY INCREDIBLE, TOO...
I THOUGHT SO.
HONESTLY, IT WAS THE HIGHLIGHT OF MY CAREER FOR A WHILE.
IF EVER THERE WAS A HUNT TO KEEP A TROPHY FROM...
...IT WAS THAT ONE.
CAN I LET YOU IN ON A SECRET, THOUGH?
I DIDN'T ***REALLY*** TAKE IT ON ALONE. HAD TWO KIDS THAT WENT ABOVE AND BEYOND TO PROTECT THEIR VILLAGE.
NO WAY I EVER COULD'VE DONE IT WITHOUT THEM.

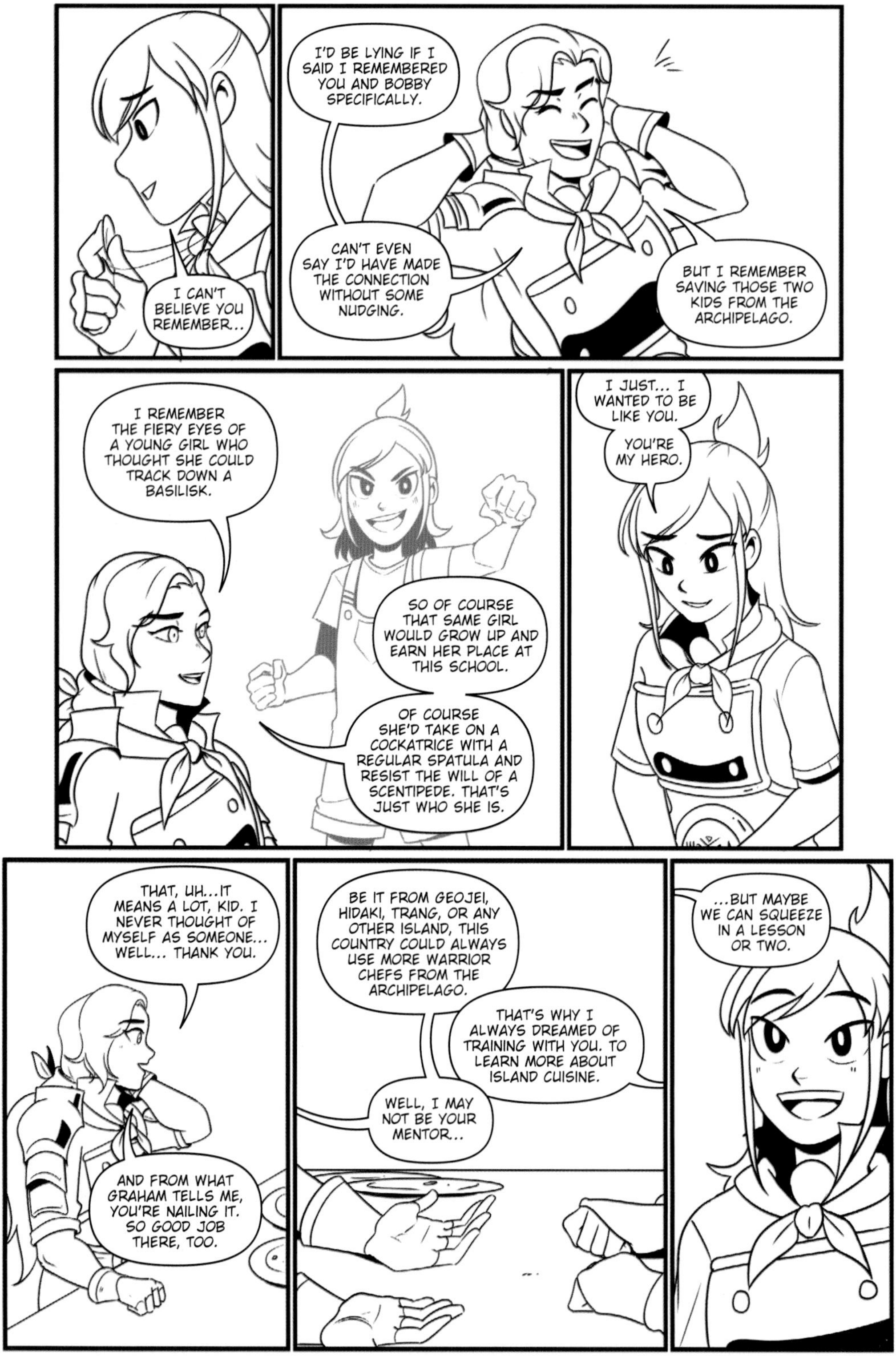
I CAN'T BELIEVE YOU REMEMBER...
I'D BE LYING IF I SAID I REMEMBERED YOU AND BOBBY SPECIFICALLY.
CAN'T EVEN SAY I'D HAVE MADE THE CONNECTION WITHOUT SOME NUDGING.
BUT I REMEMBER SAVING THOSE TWO KIDS FROM THE ARCHIPELAGO.
I REMEMBER THE FIERY EYES OF A YOUNG GIRL WHO THOUGHT SHE COULD TRACK DOWN A BASILISK.
SO OF COURSE THAT SAME GIRL WOULD GROW UP AND EARN HER PLACE AT THIS SCHOOL.
OF COURSE SHE'D TAKE ON A COCKATRICE WITH A REGULAR SPATULA AND RESIST THE WILL OF A SCENTIPEDE. THAT'S JUST WHO SHE IS.
I JUST... I WANTED TO BE LIKE YOU.
YOU'RE MY HERO.
THAT, UH...IT MEANS A LOT, KID. I NEVER THOUGHT OF MYSELF AS SOMEONE... WELL... THANK YOU.
AND FROM WHAT GRAHAM TELLS ME, YOU'RE NAILING IT. SO GOOD JOB THERE, TOO.
BE IT FROM GEOJEI, HIDAKI, TRANG, OR ANY OTHER ISLAND, THIS COUNTRY COULD ALWAYS USE MORE WARRIOR CHEFS FROM THE ARCHIPELAGO.
THAT'S WHY I ALWAYS DREAMED OF TRAINING WITH YOU. TO LEARN MORE ABOUT ISLAND CUISINE.
WELL, I MAY NOT BE YOUR MENTOR...
...BUT MAYBE WE CAN SQUEEZE IN A LESSON OR TWO.

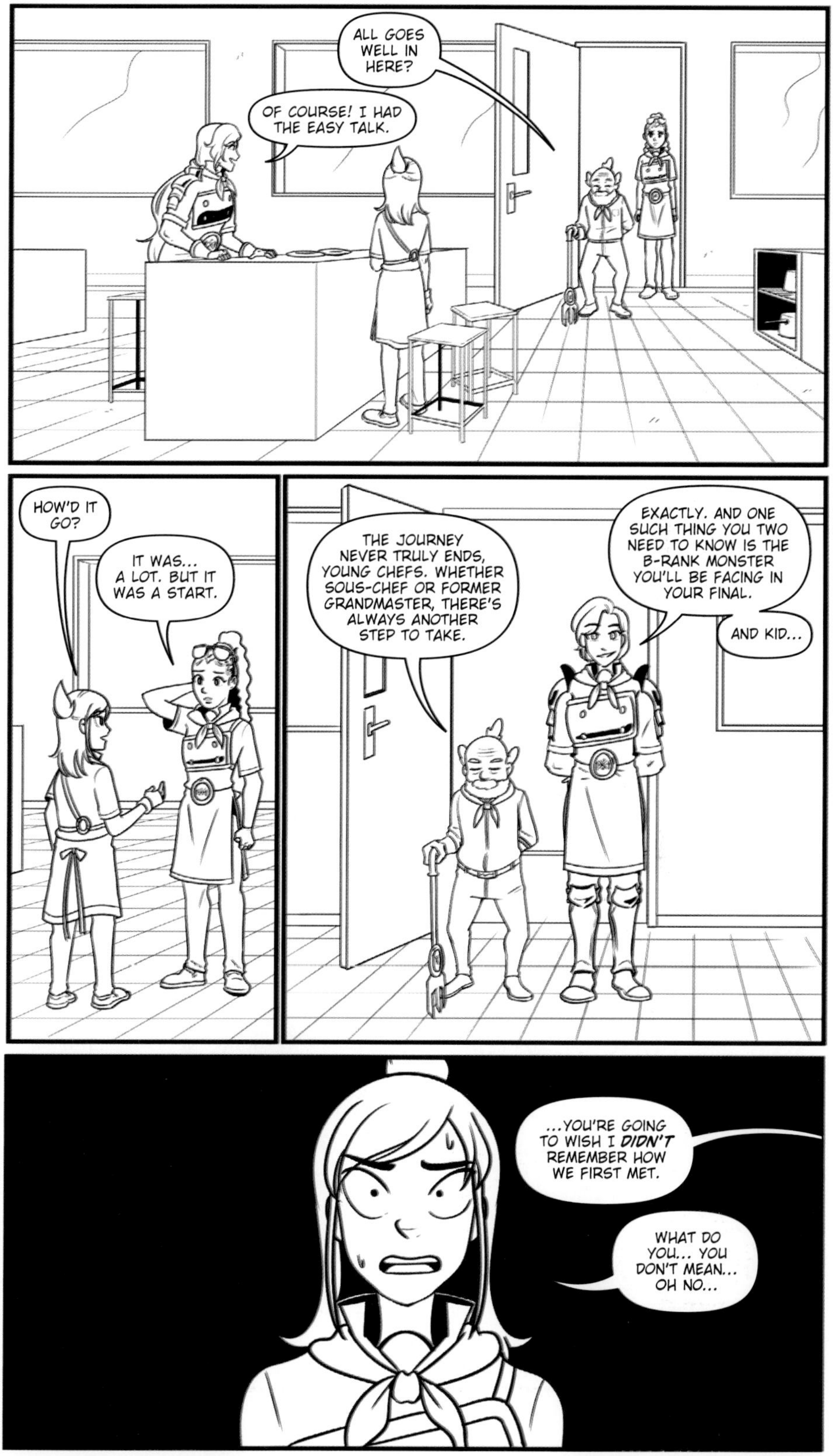
ALL GOES WELL IN HERE?
OF COURSE! I HAD THE EASY TALK.
HOW'D IT GO?
IT WAS... A LOT. BUT IT WAS A START.
THE JOURNEY NEVER TRULY ENDS, YOUNG CHEFS. WHETHER SOUS-CHEF OR FORMER GRANDMASTER, THERE'S ALWAYS ANOTHER STEP TO TAKE.
EXACTLY. AND ONE SUCH THING YOU TWO NEED TO KNOW IS THE B-RANK MONSTER YOU'LL BE FACING IN YOUR FINAL.
AND KID...
...YOU'RE GOING TO WISH I *DIDN'T* REMEMBER HOW WE FIRST MET.
WHAT DO YOU... YOU DON'T MEAN... OH NO...

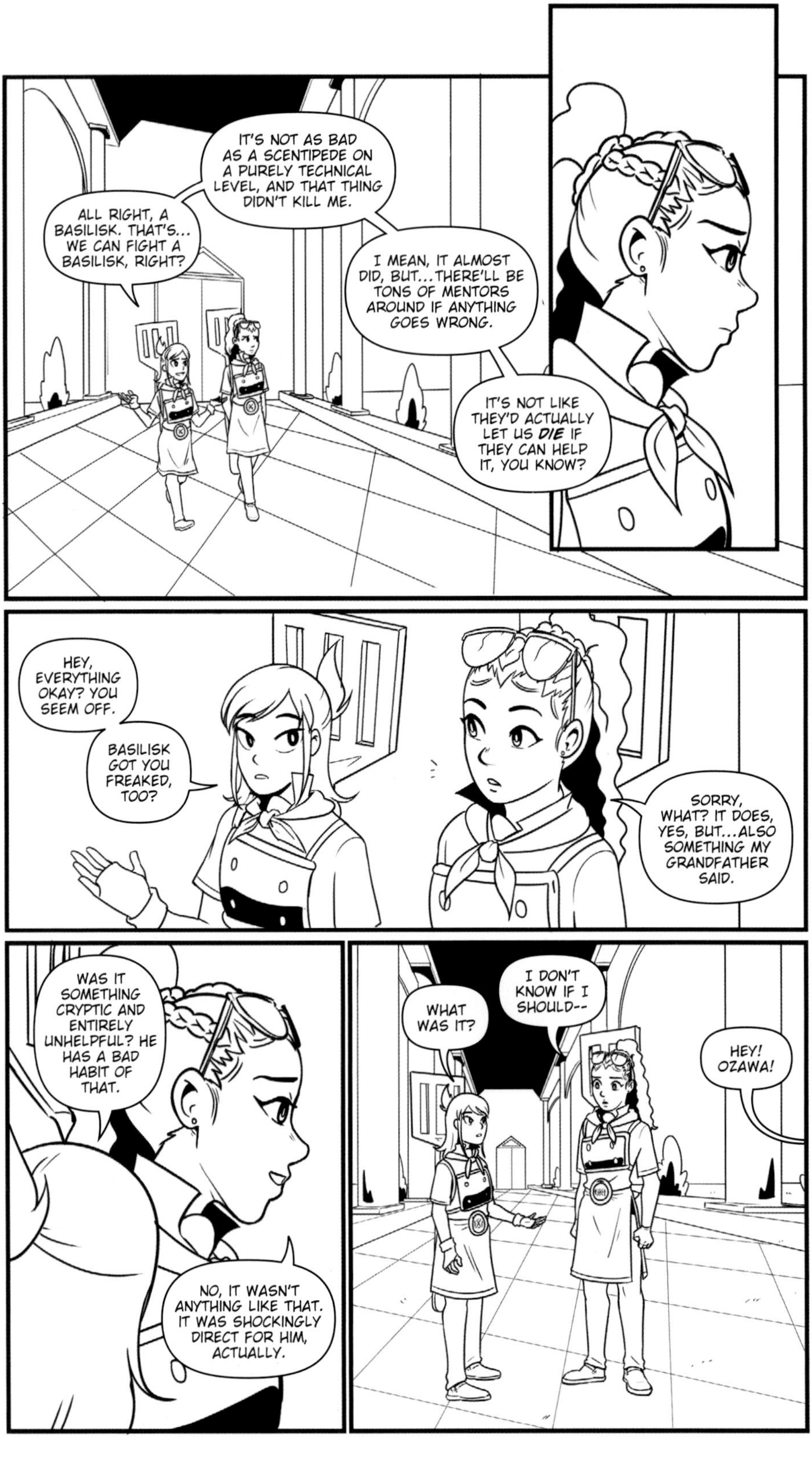
ALL RIGHT, A BASILISK. THAT'S... WE CAN FIGHT A BASILISK, RIGHT?
IT'S NOT AS BAD AS A SCENTIPEDE ON A PURELY TECHNICAL LEVEL, AND THAT THING DIDN'T KILL ME.
I MEAN, IT ALMOST DID, BUT...THERE'LL BE TONS OF MENTORS AROUND IF ANYTHING GOES WRONG.
IT'S NOT LIKE THEY'D ACTUALLY LET US *DIE* IF THEY CAN HELP IT, YOU KNOW?
HEY, EVERYTHING OKAY? YOU SEEM OFF.
BASILISK GOT YOU FREAKED, TOO?
SORRY, WHAT? IT DOES, YES, BUT...ALSO SOMETHING MY GRANDFATHER SAID.
WAS IT SOMETHING CRYPTIC AND ENTIRELY UNHELPFUL? HE HAS A BAD HABIT OF THAT.
NO, IT WASN'T ANYTHING LIKE THAT. IT WAS SHOCKINGLY DIRECT FOR HIM, ACTUALLY.
WHAT WAS IT?
I DON'T KNOW IF I SHOULD--
HEY! OZAWA!

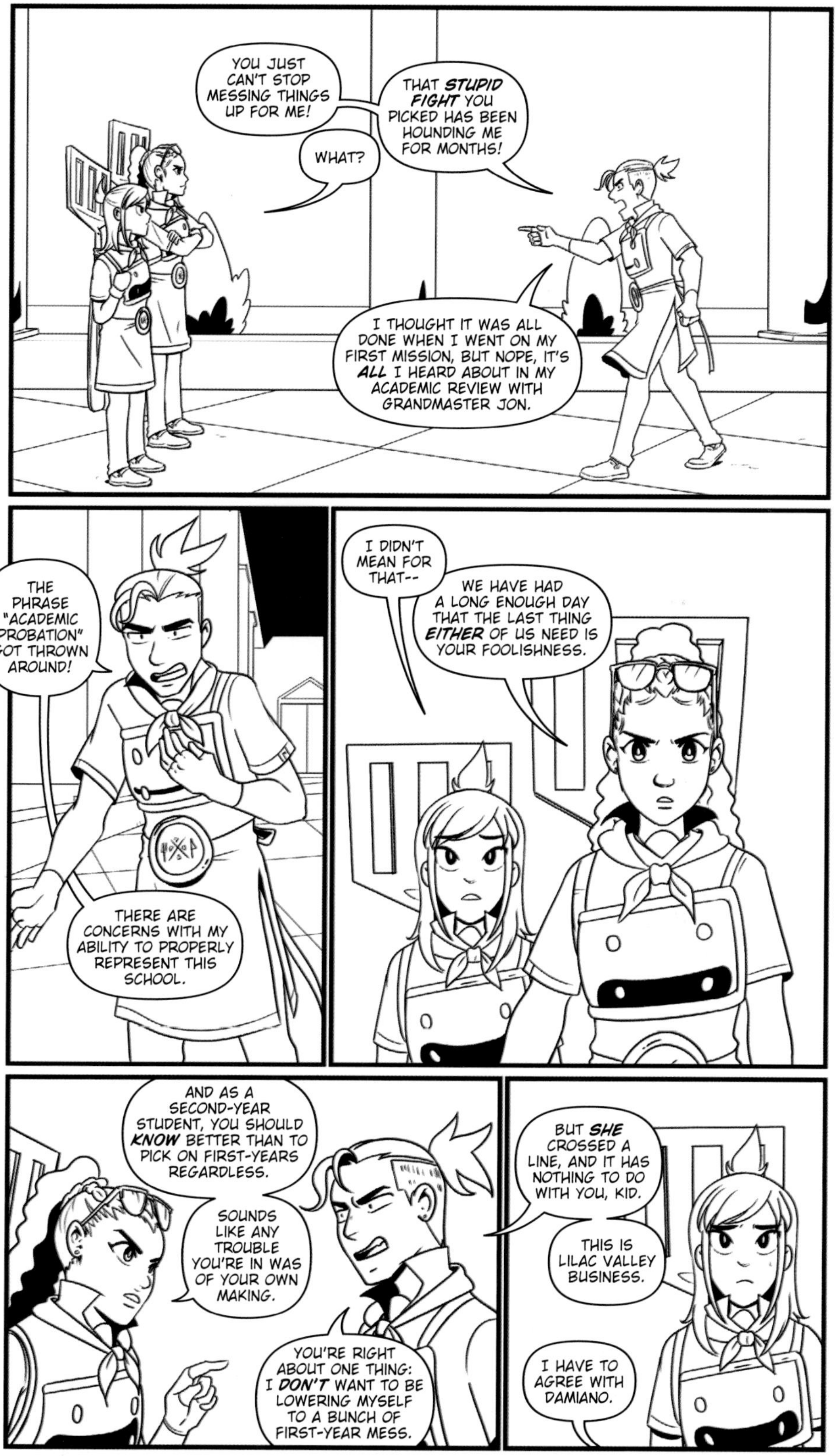
YOU JUST CAN'T STOP MESSING THINGS UP FOR ME!
THAT STUPID FIGHT YOU PICKED HAS BEEN HOUNDING ME FOR MONTHS!
WHAT?
I THOUGHT IT WAS ALL DONE WHEN I WENT ON MY FIRST MISSION, BUT NOPE, IT'S ALL I HEARD ABOUT IN MY ACADEMIC REVIEW WITH GRANDMASTER JON.
THE PHRASE "ACADEMIC PROBATION" GOT THROWN AROUND!
THERE ARE CONCERNS WITH MY ABILITY TO PROPERLY REPRESENT THIS SCHOOL.
I DIDN'T MEAN FOR THAT--
WE HAVE HAD A LONG ENOUGH DAY THAT THE LAST THING EITHER OF US NEED IS YOUR FOOLISHNESS.
AND AS A SECOND-YEAR STUDENT, YOU SHOULD KNOW BETTER THAN TO PICK ON FIRST-YEARS REGARDLESS.
SOUNDS LIKE ANY TROUBLE YOU'RE IN WAS OF YOUR OWN MAKING.
YOU'RE RIGHT ABOUT ONE THING: I DON'T WANT TO BE LOWERING MYSELF TO A BUNCH OF FIRST-YEAR MESS.
BUT SHE CROSSED A LINE, AND IT HAS NOTHING TO DO WITH YOU, KID.
THIS IS LILAC VALLEY BUSINESS.
I HAVE TO AGREE WITH DAMIANO.

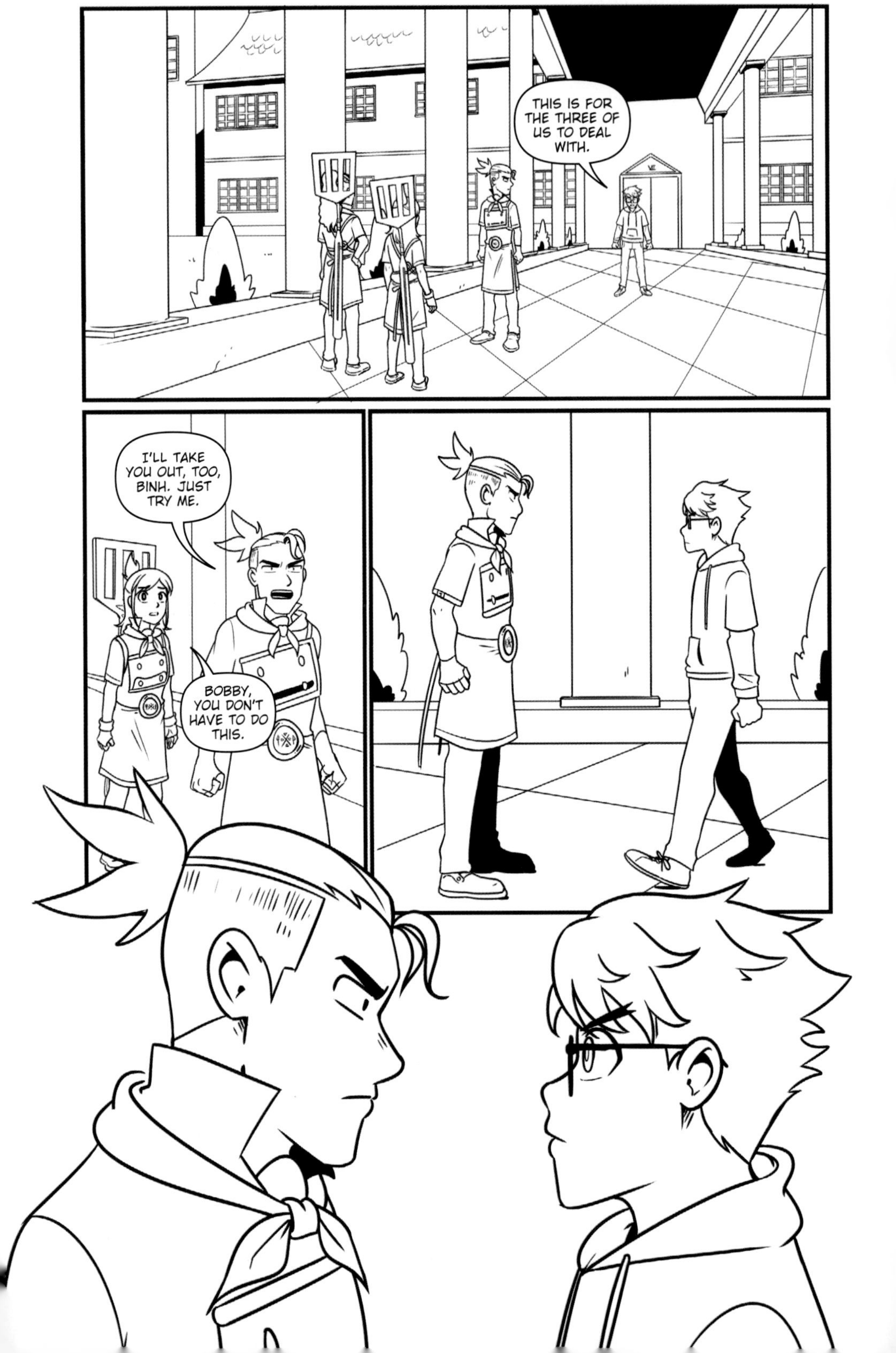
THIS IS FOR THE THREE OF US TO DEAL WITH.
I'LL TAKE YOU OUT, TOO, BINH. JUST TRY ME.
BOBBY, YOU DON'T HAVE TO DO THIS.

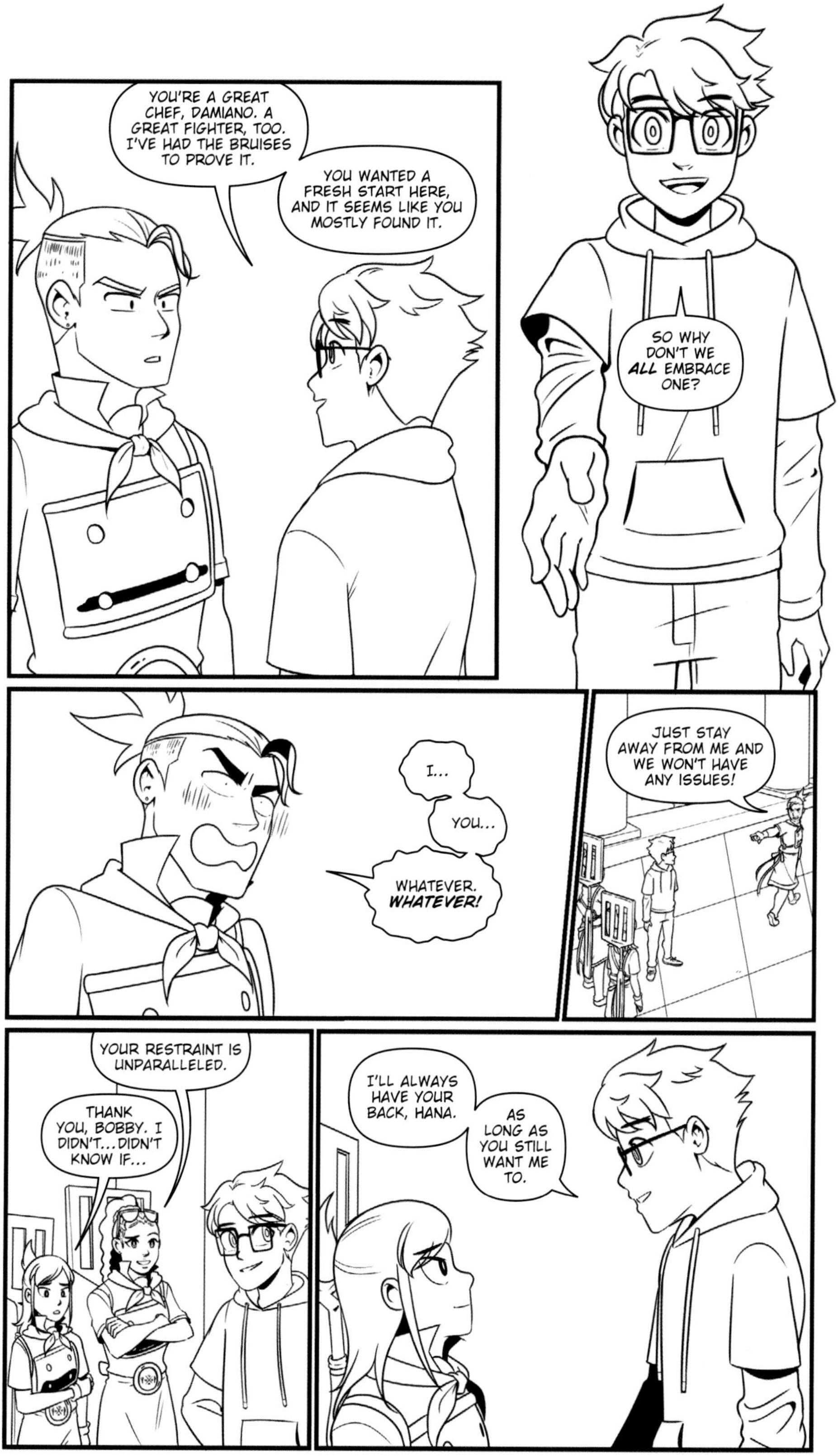
YOU'RE A GREAT CHEF, DAMIANO. A GREAT FIGHTER, TOO. I'VE HAD THE BRUISES TO PROVE IT.
YOU WANTED A FRESH START HERE, AND IT SEEMS LIKE YOU MOSTLY FOUND IT.
SO WHY DON'T WE ***ALL*** EMBRACE ONE?
I...
YOU...
WHATEVER. ***WHATEVER!***
JUST STAY AWAY FROM ME AND WE WON'T HAVE ANY ISSUES!
YOUR RESTRAINT IS UNPARALLELED.
THANK YOU, BOBBY. I DIDN'T...DIDN'T KNOW IF...
I'LL ALWAYS HAVE YOUR BACK, HANA.
AS LONG AS YOU STILL WANT ME TO.

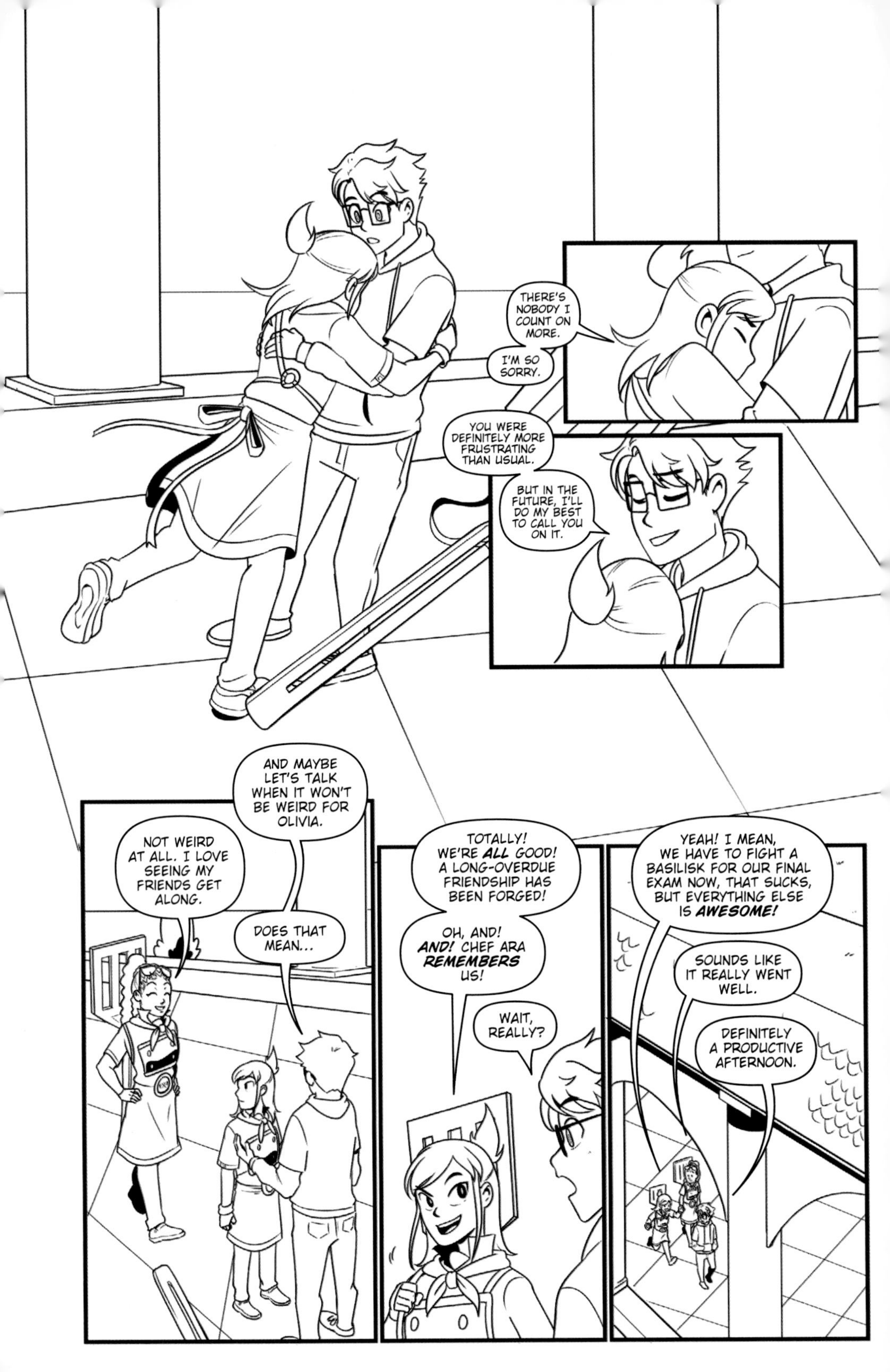
THERE'S NOBODY I COUNT ON MORE.
I'M SO SORRY.
YOU WERE DEFINITELY MORE FRUSTRATING THAN USUAL.
BUT IN THE FUTURE, I'LL DO MY BEST TO CALL YOU ON IT.
AND MAYBE LET'S TALK WHEN IT WON'T BE WEIRD FOR OLIVIA.
NOT WEIRD AT ALL. I LOVE SEEING MY FRIENDS GET ALONG.
DOES THAT MEAN...
TOTALLY! WE'RE ALL GOOD! A LONG-OVERDUE FRIENDSHIP HAS BEEN FORGED!
OH, AND! AND! CHEF ARA REMEMBERS US!
WAIT, REALLY?
YEAH! I MEAN, WE HAVE TO FIGHT A BASILISK FOR OUR FINAL EXAM NOW, THAT SUCKS, BUT EVERYTHING ELSE IS AWESOME!
SOUNDS LIKE IT REALLY WENT WELL.
DEFINITELY A PRODUCTIVE AFTERNOON.

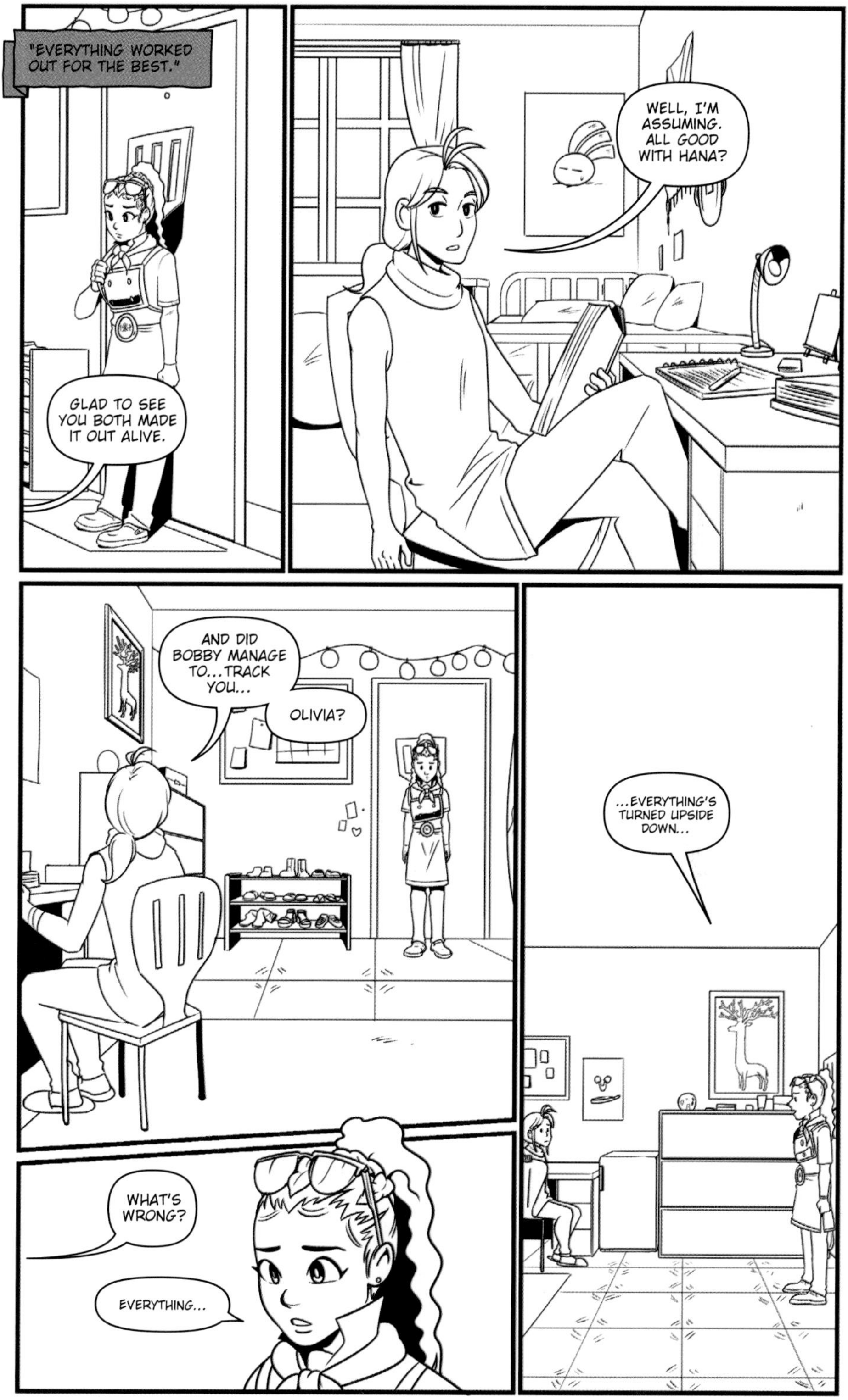
"EVERYTHING WORKED OUT FOR THE BEST."
GLAD TO SEE YOU BOTH MADE IT OUT ALIVE.
WELL, I'M ASSUMING. ALL GOOD WITH HANA?
AND DID BOBBY MANAGE TO...TRACK YOU...
OLIVIA?
...EVERYTHING'S TURNED UPSIDE DOWN...
WHAT'S WRONG?
EVERYTHING...

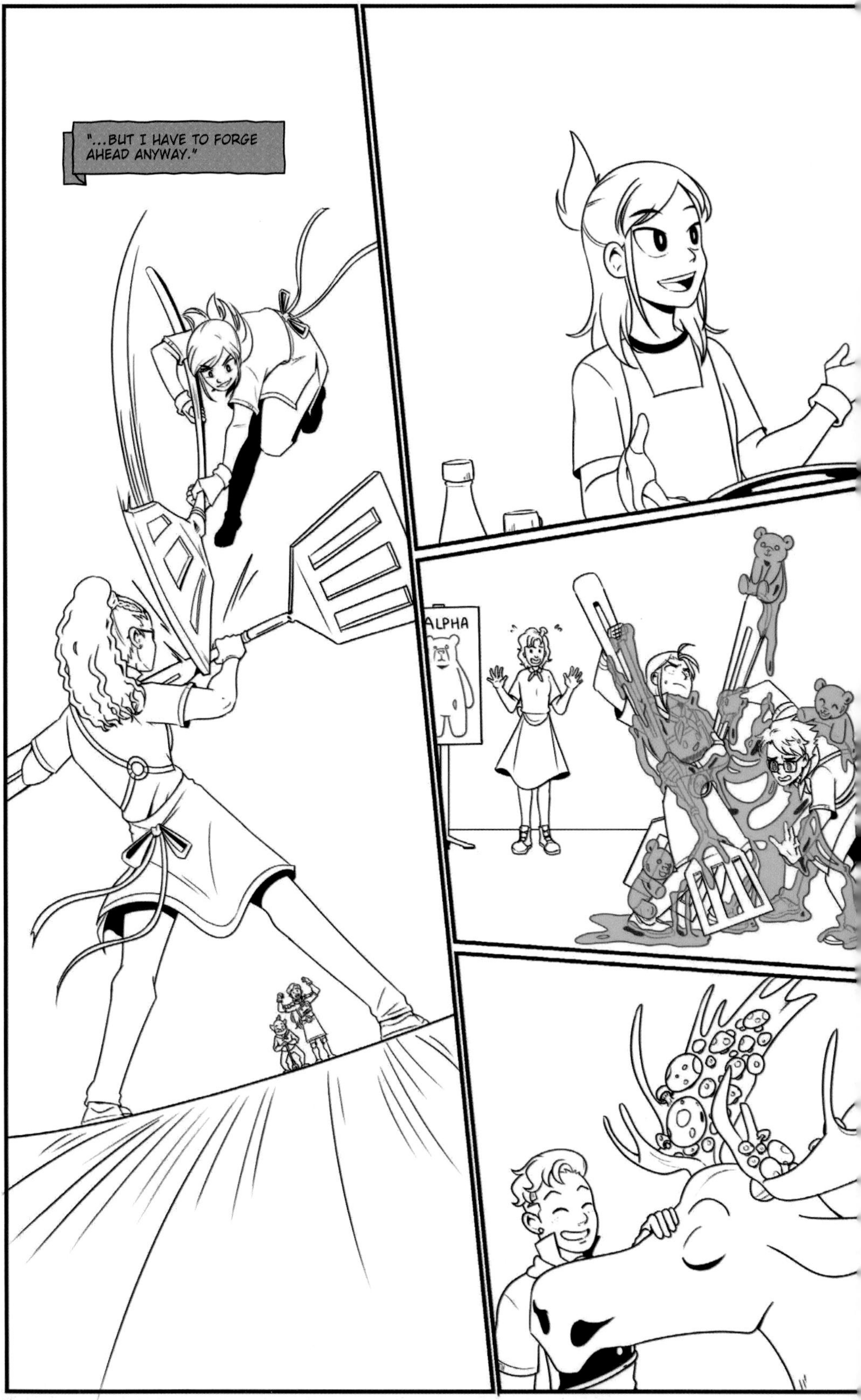
"...BUT I HAVE TO FORGE AHEAD ANYWAY."
ALPHA

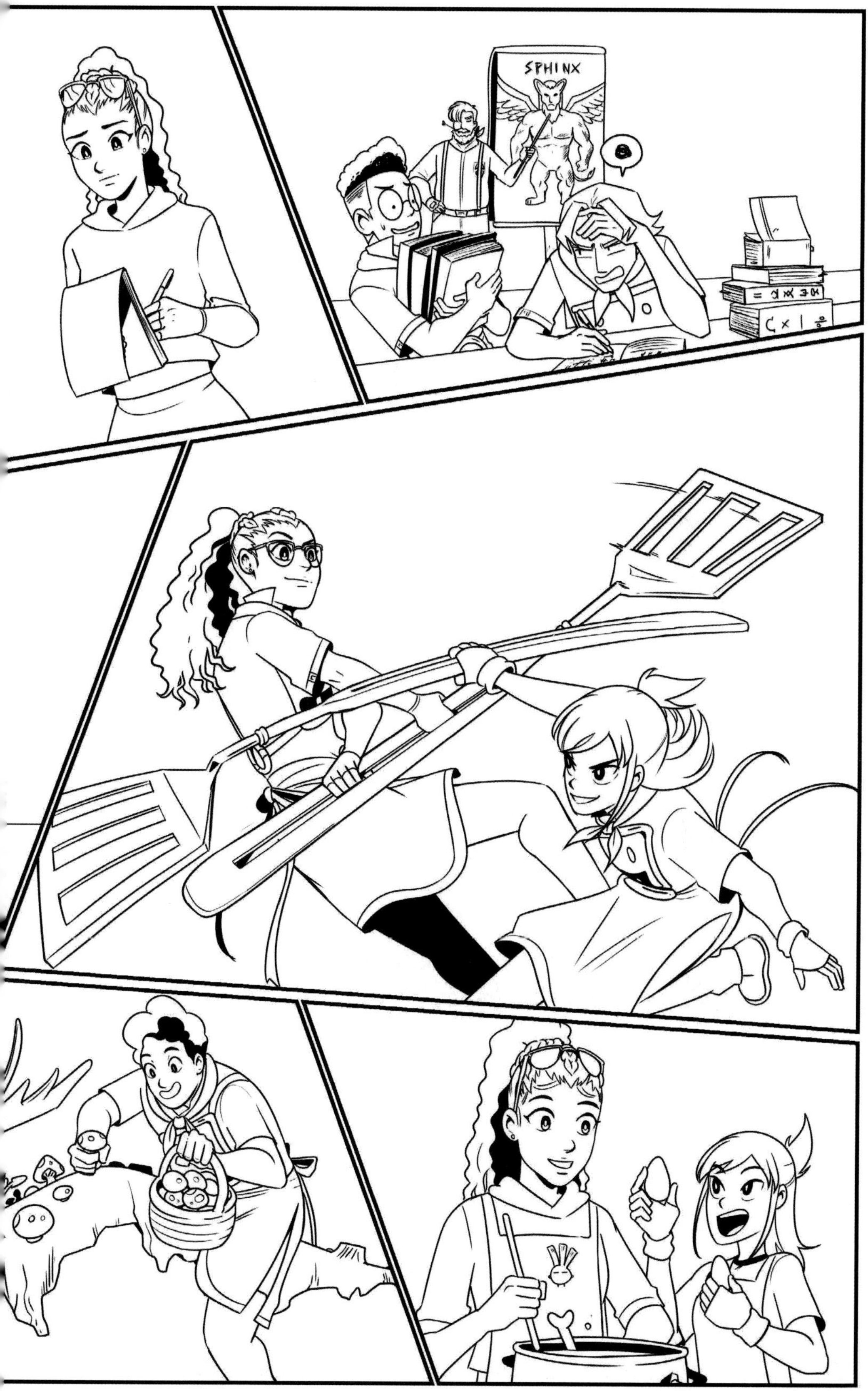
SPHINX

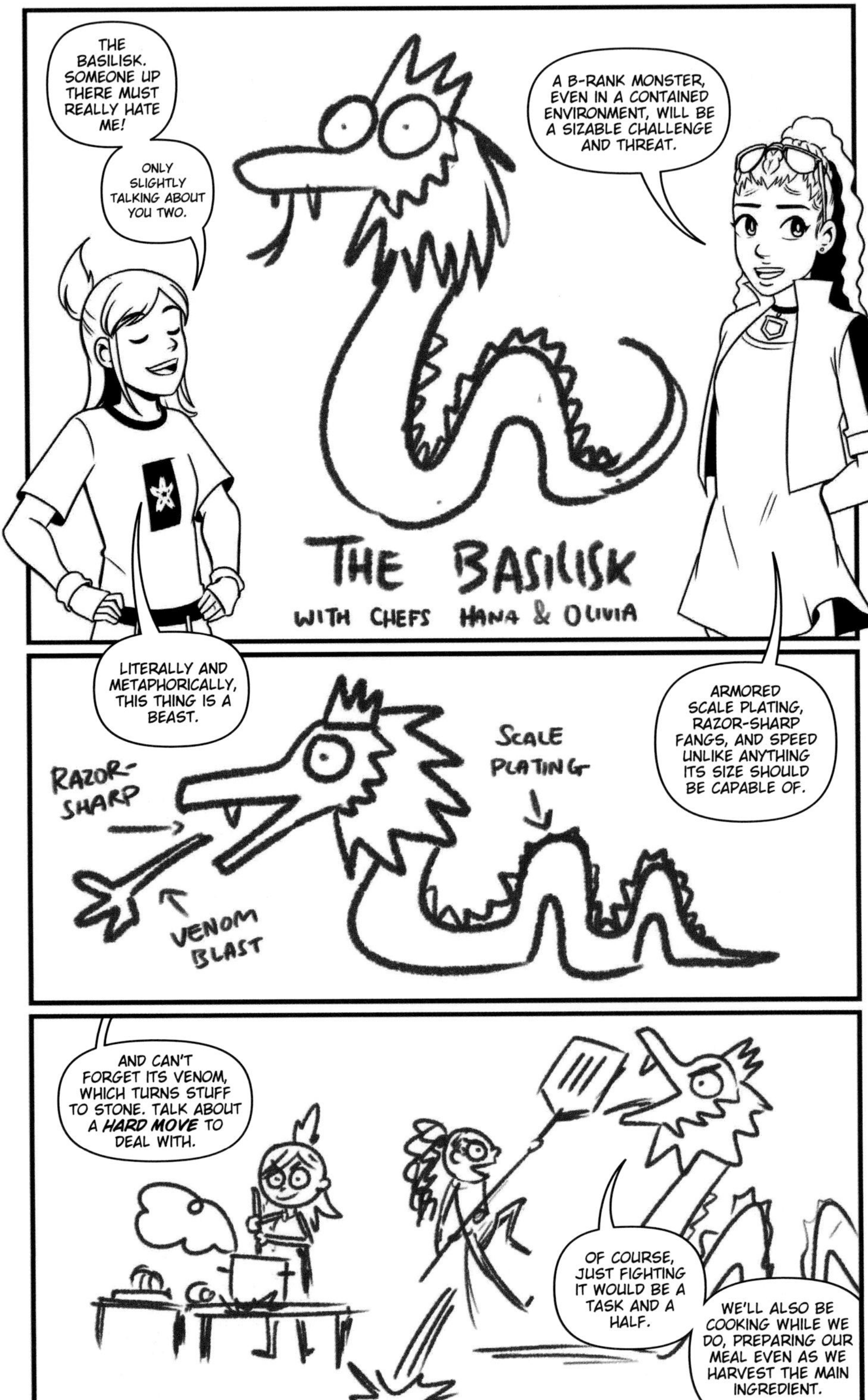
THE BASILISK. SOMEONE UP THERE MUST REALLY HATE ME!
ONLY SLIGHTLY TALKING ABOUT YOU TWO.
A B-RANK MONSTER, EVEN IN A CONTAINED ENVIRONMENT, WILL BE A SIZABLE CHALLENGE AND THREAT.
THE BASILISK
WITH CHEFS HANA & OLIVIA
LITERALLY AND METAPHORICALLY, THIS THING IS A BEAST.
ARMORED SCALE PLATING, RAZOR-SHARP FANGS, AND SPEED UNLIKE ANYTHING ITS SIZE SHOULD BE CAPABLE OF.
RAZOR-SHARP
VENOM BLAST
SCALE PLATING
AND CAN'T FORGET ITS VENOM, WHICH TURNS STUFF TO STONE. TALK ABOUT A ***HARD MOVE*** TO DEAL WITH.
OF COURSE, JUST FIGHTING IT WOULD BE A TASK AND A HALF.
WE'LL ALSO BE COOKING WHILE WE DO, PREPARING OUR MEAL EVEN AS WE HARVEST THE MAIN INGREDIENT.